I0819899

MALVINA

Chawton House Library Series: Women's Novels

Series Editors: Stephen Bending
Stephen Bygrave

Titles in this Series

1 *The Histories of Some of the Penitents in the Magdalen-House*
edited by Jennie Batchelor and Megan Hiatt

2 Stéphanie-Félicité de Genlis, *Adelaide and Theodore, or Letters on Education*
edited by Gillian Dow

3 E. M. Foster, *The Corinna of England*
edited by Sylvia Bordoni

4 Sarah Harriet Burney, *The Romance of Private Life*
edited by Lorna J. Clark

5 Alicia LeFanu, *Strathallan*
edited by Anna M. Fitzer

6 Elizabeth Sophia Tomlins, *The Victim of Fancy*
edited by Daniel Cook

7 Helen Maria Williams, *Julia*
edited by Natasha Duquette

8 Elizabeth Hervey, *The History of Ned Evans*
edited by Helena Kelly

9 Sarah Green, *Romance Readers and Romance Writers*
edited by Christopher Goulding

10 Mrs Costello, *The Soldier's Orphan*
edited by Clare Broome Saunders

11 Sarah Green, *The Private History of the Court of England*
edited by Fiona Price

12 *Translations and Continuations: Riccoboni and Brooke, Graffigny and Roberts*
edited by Marijn S. Kaplan

13 Sydney Owenson, *Florence McCarthy: An Irish Tale*
edited by Jenny McAuley

14 Frances Brooke, *The History of Lady Julia Mandeville*
edited by Enit Karafili Steiner

15 Ann Gomersall, *The Citizen*
edited by Margaret S. Yoon

16 Eliza Haywood, *The Rash Resolve and Life's Progress*
edited by Carol Stewart

17 Mary Brunton, *Self-Control*
edited by Anthony Mandal

18 Eliza Haywood, *The Invisible Spy*
edited by Carol Stewart

19 Isabelle de Montolieu, *Caroline of Lichtfield*
edited by Laura Kirkley

20 Mrs S. C. Hall, *Sketches of Irish Character*
edited by Marion Durnin

Forthcoming Titles

Charlotte Dacre, *The Confessions of the Nun of St Omer*
edited by Lucy Cogan

Marguerite Blessington, *Marmaduke Herbert; or, the Fatal Error*
edited by Susanne Schmid

Sophie Cottin, *Malvina*

Edited by

Marijn S. Kaplan

LONDON AND NEW YORK

First published 2015 by Pickering & Chatto (Publishers) Limited

Published 2016 by Routledge
2 Park Square, Milton Park, Abingdon, Oxon OX14 4RN
711 Third Avenue, New York, NY 10017, USA

Routledge is an imprint of the Taylor & Francis Group, an informa business

BRITISH LIBRARY CATALOGUING IN PUBLICATION DATA

Cottin, Madame (Sophie), 1770–1807, author.
Malvina. – (Chawton House library series. Women's novels)
I. Title II. Series III. Gunning, Elizabeth, translator.
IV. Kaplan, Marijn S., editor.
843.6-dc23

ISBN-13: 978-1-84893-460-3 (hbk)

Typeset by Pickering & Chatto (Publishers) Limited

CONTENTS

ACKNOWLEDGEMENTS

It has been a pleasure working a second time with Mark Pollard at Pickering & Chatto Publishers, and Stephen Bygrave and Stephen Bending from the University of Southampton who edit the series *Chawton House Library: Women's Novels*. Their encouragement and support have helped bring this project to fruition.

As all scholars know, librarians can prove an invaluable source of assistance during various phases of a literary project. In this case, I would like to thank Alan Brown, senior library assistant at the Bodleian Library, for providing the pages of the 1803 edition that were missing from the digitized edition online. At my home institution, the University of North Texas in Denton, Texas, United States, my appreciation goes to the staff of the Interlibrary Loan department at Willis Library and Lynne Wright in particular, who helped me get the missing pages from the 1810 edition.

Last, but certainly not least, I would like to dedicate this book to two generations of important women in my family: Truud, Liesbeth and Barbara, who showed me the importance of the female voice in the past, and Holland and Julika, who represent and confirm its impact in the future. I am the woman in the middle.

INTRODUCTION

The *Chawton House Library: Women's Novels* series includes several translations from the French. Like my *Translations and Continuations* (2011),[1] this 1803 translation of Sophie Cottin's *Malvina* (1801) by Elizabeth Gunning offers an example of an English translation by a woman of a female-authored French novel, and as such it is also 'partaking in the relatively recent trend within academia to recuperate from silence the voices of forgotten women writers and trace the networks among them' (ix). Yet, with this being the first nineteenth-century translation in the series, it speaks more broadly to issues of globalization in the Enlightenment literary marketplace, women's contributions to it, female networks within it and the role played by gender in both its process and product. Thus, while Cottin wrote *Malvina* in an effort to atone for the proto-feminist overtones of her previous novel, Gunning in fact restored such undercurrents to her translation while simultaneously striving to defend female virtue more forcefully.

Sophie Cottin (1770–1807) was born in Bordeaux into the wealthy bourgeois and Protestant Risteau family. Without any brothers and only one older sister who died in 1785 at age 17, Sophie received a sound education. At age nineteen, she married Paul Cottin, a banker seven years her senior – but did not get to enjoy for very long what appears to have been a loving marriage due to the French Revolution. In order to escape the revolutionary turmoil, the newlyweds soon fled to the Pyrenees, Spain and England, but eventually returned to Paris. Paul would have been arrested there in October 1793, but died just beforehand. Although a heart attack was blamed for his early demise, suicide has been suggested more recently.[2] Widowed Sophie abandoned the capital and moved to a family country estate in Champlan accompanied by her cousin Julie, with whom she had a very close relationship and to whose three daughters she became a substitute mother. Sophie suffered during the Revolution, lost her fortune and even appeared on the *liste des émigrés* (list of emigrants) for some time as a 'Republican traitor'. She turned down several marriage proposals, which in one case provoked a suicide on her suitor's part, but never remarried. In 1804–5 she came close to remarrying with Pierre Hyacinthe Azaïs, a pretentious philosopher, but he rejected her after she told him she could not bear children.[3] Faith always played an important role in Cottin's life. She was a talented and prolific correspondent[4] to friends, family members and Enlightenment luminaries – such as Bernardin de Saint-Pierre, Germaine de Staël and Joseph Lalande – and in 1806 she wrote some beautiful descriptions of Italy during a trip with an ailing relative.[5] Several months after her return, she died very prematurely of breast cancer at age thirty-seven.[6]

In order to assist a friend in financial need, Cottin published her first novel, *Claire d'Albe*, in 1799. Subsequently, four more novels appeared in short succession: *Malvina* (1801), *Amélie Mansfield* (1802), *Mathilde* (1805) and *Elisabeth* (1806). Additionally, the best-selling novelist wrote a Bible-inspired text entitled *La Prise de Jéricho* (*The Fall of Jericho*; 1803). *Claire d'Albe* (published anonymously) proved both the most controversial for contemporary audiences and the most feminist to modern critics, with J. H. Stewart calling the heroine's death 'an attack on the ideology of fatherhood and phallus'.[7] In short, at age twenty-two the heroine Claire has been in an arranged marriage[8] for seven years with a respectable man forty years her senior with whom she has two children. When her husband's nineteen-year-old male relative comes to stay with them, Claire and he fall in love. The husband separates them, they suffer, but eventually reunite on the tomb of Claire's father (who had arranged the marriage), where they consummate their relationship. Claire dies the following day. Although the novel was quite successful, contemporaries criticised its 'revolting immorality' and later called it 'one of Cottin's most objectionable works'.[9]

Cottin's other novels did not create as much of a stir. In *Amélie Mansfield*, a young disillusioned widow agrees to move in with an older male relative and become his heir. Her grandfather had promised his title and wealth to Amélie's cousin if he married her, but she had then eloped. However, the cousin and Amélie meet, fall in love and agree to marry despite his mother's opposition. They consummate their relationship, his mother dissuades him from marrying Amélie, Amélie dies and he follows her. *Mathilde*, the first novel not to be published anonymously, features the sixteen-year-old sister of Richard the Lionheart who travels with him to the Holy Land before becoming a nun. There she meets a Saracen warrior and they fall in love. Despite her brother's opposition, Mathilde is joined with her just-converted love, who then dies from battle wounds. Still a virgin, Mathilde enters the convent. *Elisabeth*, based on a true story, takes place in Siberia where seventeen-year-old Elisabeth lives with her parents, who are political exiles. During a long voyage undertaken to ask the tsar for their freedom, she meets a young man and they fall in love. Elisabeth succeeds in freeing her parents and Cottin hints at a happy ending with her love interest. This final novel enjoyed a very positive reception.

From the novel titles we can deduce their feminocentricity, a preference typical of the French nineteenth-century sentimental novel genre to which Cottin's work belongs[10] and which became popular among women writers after the Revolution as it allowed them to politicize their male-attributed greater capacity for feelings.[11] Jean-Jacques Rousseau, whose epistolary novel *Julie ou la nouvelle Héloïse* (1761) can be considered the earliest example of the genre in France, exerted a profound influence on Cottin. Rather than following Rousseau's ideals blindly though, Cottin rewrote them, both in her work and in her private life;[12] just like him, she is considered a pre-Romantic.[13] Whereas she continued the tradition of Richardson and earlier women writers such as Riccoboni and Graffigny, Cottin leads readers more commonly from their happy endings towards thwarted romantic love, death and tragic maternal love (like *Julie*).

Cottin's novels sold very well and were greatly beloved by many contemporaries in France and abroad, including Napoleon. Not everyone shared in this enthusiasm, however: Madame de Genlis (1746–1830), for instance, accused Cottin of having plagiarized her *Voeux téméraires* (*Rash Vows*; 1798) in *Malvina*.[14] Later in the nineteenth century, Cottin's work became gradually less popular,[15] although Victor Hugo called her 'the most accomplished novelist of her time'[16] and Marceline Desbordes-Valmore wrote an admiring poem about her.[17] Feminist scholars started to recuperate her voice from silence in the late twentieth century[18] and since then, interest in Cottin's work has soared although it still does not rival scholarly interest in her colleagues Riccoboni, Graffigny and Charrière. In 1996 Raymond Trousson published a modern French edition of *Claire d'Albe* in Europe, which facilitated easier access for modern readers; in 2002 the American Modern Language Association published the novel in both French and English. Several doctoral dissertations devoted to the author have also appeared, thus consolidating the future of Cottin scholarship on both continents.

From Cottin's correspondence published by Sykes we know that a first draft of *Malvina* was ready as early as 7 January 1799,[19] but that the author did not sell her manuscript to Maradan for 1,200 *livres* until 5 September 1800.[20] Then, in a letter from the publisher to Cottin dated 7 January 1801 he states that the novel is not ready yet but will be soon; it did indeed appear later that month.[21]

French reviews of *Malvina*, although not extremely negative, expressed some criticism. Thus the *Mercure de France* claimed that *Malvina*'s topic was not new even though Cottin had added some new elements (p. 331) and reproached the novel for having 'a little affectation and much ambition' (p. 333). Nevertheless, from Cottin's correspondence we know that *Malvina* sold so well that a mere five months later by 5 June 1801, Maradan had already prepared a second edition without changes or corrections.[22] In 1805 there followed a second revised and corrected edition published in Paris by Michaud that contained some important changes (see Volume II, note 29 of this edition). That was the last edition during Cottin's lifetime; numerous posthumous editions appeared by Michaud and other publishers. No modern edition exists.[23]

In Cottin's own words, *Malvina* is 'somewhat the correction of [*Claire d'Albe*]' because her belief that she could remain anonymous had caused her to 'paint somewhat voluptuous colours, somewhat intense passions'. Since she had been recognized as the author and already suffered a great deal because of it, she no longer wants to deprive herself of the 'most amusing activity she has found yet' and is therefore writing another novel.[24] The Notice to *Malvina*'s first edition[25] clarifies that it is not the epistolary novel she announced in *Claire* because she finds the chapter format easier; thus, *Malvina* has an omniscient narrator and several inserted letters. It also became unintentionally longer than *Claire*.

In addition to format and length – which gives *Malvina* numerous side plots with various secondary yet important characters, such as Mr Prior, a Catholic priest who is Sir Edmond's rival, and Malvina's friend Mrs St Clare and her sister Louisa – other differences set it apart from *Claire*. At its core lies the conflict between passionate love and motherly (substitute) love. The title character – widowed young after an unhappy marriage in France – moves to England to join her childhood friend Clara who has married there. When Clara dies young, Malvina promises to look after her five-year-old daughter Frances at the exclusion of all other emotional ties. Nevertheless, she breaks that vow when, having moved to Scotland to live with a female relative named Mrs Burton, she falls in love with and agrees to marry Mrs Burton's libertine nephew, Sir Edmond. His subsequent infidelity literally kills her, leaving him mourning at her tomb. The 'correction' Cottin wished to make in comparison with *Claire* likely refers to issues related to its 'revolting immorality': Malvina gives herself to Edmond after their marriage, and not while married to someone else like Claire; the chapter entitled 'Conjugal Happiness' does not divulge details of physical intimacy between the newlyweds, and Cottin purposely refuses to mention 'pleasures that my pen will not risk describing' (see Volume IV, note 27 of this edition), which contrasts sharply with the expressions of female desire and sexual pleasure present in *Claire* (2002, p. 148).

Although an entire chapter is devoted to a portrait of Malvina (Volume I, chapter II), Cottin gives not so much a physical description of her as a moral one: 'as there were few women who surpassed her in beauty, there was not one who possessed superior virtue'.[26] 'Virtue' recurs frequently in *Malvina*. For the heroine it consists in fulfilling her vow to Clara of being a substitute mother to Fanny, and avoiding the fault of choosing passionate love over maternal love. Once she commits that fault and abandons virtue, Malvina is depicted as suffering from Clara's death and the cruelty of others, such as Sir Edmond who betrays their marriage vows, Kitty Fenwick who assists him in doing so and Mrs Burton who takes away Fanny. This confirms April Alliston's argument that

> The virtue of eighteenth-century heroines ... does not consist, like manly virtue, in the performance of good deeds or serviceable actions, but rather in the avoidance of fault. Now, the avoidance of fault entails the avoidance of anything resembling a deed ... Hence the classical virtue of agency comes to be replaced by a feminine virtue of suffering, both in the current sense and in the earlier one of passivity, or 'suffering' the action of others. That suffering in turn not only justifies but demands the reader's sympathetic interest. Thus heroines are interesting when they are victims'[27]

Modern readers raised with the tenets of feminism, however, may find such heroines interesting primarily as reflecting the gender politics of their times.

Gender and its politics figure prominently in *Malvina*. Substitute motherhood and female friendship, both of which played a crucial role in Cottin's own life, lend essential meaning to Malvina's existence. Her lifelong friendship with Clara helps both women negotiate patriarchy, marriage and (substitute) motherhood.[28] Malvina subsequently experiences the power of female friendship again with Mrs St Clare – a woman bearing the same name and writing novels to earn a living in order to pay for her sister – who has been seduced and impregnated by Sir Edmond. Mrs St Clare's cautionary tale about Sir Edmond does not deter Malvina from marrying him however – an instance where female friendship does not succeed in combatting patriarchy and male prerogative. Malvina believes her love will cure Sir Edmond of his libertinism and pays for this mistake with her life. Mrs St Clare embodies additional commentary by Cottin on gender. Volume II, chapter VI, entitled 'Preface' and omitted from the second (Michaud) edition onwards, presents and then criticizes Mrs St Clare for being a female novelist. Malvina condemns novel-writing as a useless occupation for women who should not enter the public sphere once they become wives and mothers[29] whereas Mrs St Clare defends herself by saying that women 'can more particularly understand and delineate all the characteristics of sentiment, which is in some degree the history of their lives'.[30] The resulting conflict between 'femininity versus fame' represents a major paradox in Cottin's own life.[31] The author also demonstrates gender consciousness in differentiating between readers of both sexes. When Kitty Fenwick sets out to seduce Sir Edmond (again) in Volume IV, chapter VI after his marriage to Malvina, Cottin refuses to indicate whether Kitty succeeds – fearing that men would not believe her failure while women would detest her success. In order not to displease readers of either sex, Cottin leaves the question unanswered yet admits that as a woman, she is happy 'believing, that he resisted the seducing arts of Mrs Fenwick, and remained faithful to Malvina'.

Cottin enjoyed reading and music. She was a singer, composer and musician, playing the piano, harp and harmonica.[32] Not surprisingly then, *Malvina* includes numerous literary and musical references in addition to the biblical ones inspired by Cottin's Protestant faith. The novel's protagonist owes her name to Scottish poet James Macpherson's character Ossian.[33] Because of their shared interest in Ossian, Mr Prior teaches Malvina the Erse language so she might read the original text, and then falls in love with her. Additional literary references to both French and foreign poetry, and fiction from various centuries come from Dryden, Shakespeare, Rowe, Chamfort, Addison, Richardson, Sterne, Montaigne, Rousseau and Riccoboni, among others. Cottin also read her female colleagues Charrière, Staël, Ducos and Genlis. Music matters in the novel both in the love plot and in Malvina's final therapy; Cottin demonstrates her knowledge of music history as well as of various operas. Art is also discussed, particularly paintings of the Italian and French skies that Mrs Burton prefers to the real, forbidding Scottish skies.

The description of Mrs Burton's castle in Scotland[34] as having 'Gothic grandeur' that 'was increased by the lofty mountains covered with snow, which towered above it' (p. 6) links *Malvina* to the tradition of Gothic fiction – a category of Romantic literature in the vein of Horace Walpole's *Castle of Otranto* (1765) and Ann Radcliffe's oeuvre, later followed by *Frankenstein* (1818), for instance. Initially inspired by medieval buildings and ruins, the genre focuses on death, darkness and decay. Gothic fiction is usually set in old (haunted) castles that often correspond to haunted minds and its themes may include masks, isolation, madness, ghosts, the church and clergy, disease and eroticism. While Mrs Burton's castle provides the classic Gothic setting,[35] various other motifs enhance *Malvina*'s ties to the genre. Thus, Mrs St Clare's pregnant sister Louisa is imprisoned in a tower by her husband, Malvina falls victim to madness, Sir Edmond suffers from a lengthy and nearly fatal disease during which Malvina cares for him wearing the mask of a nurse, Sir Edmond's libertine impulses provoke his promiscuity, Mr Prior as a clergyman in love represents religion's decay, and the novel begins and ends with a tomb – to mention but a few.

The translator of *Malvina*, Elizabeth Gunning (1769–1823), comes from a literary family background. She was the only child of Susannah Minifie Gunning, who wrote several novels[36] – some of them in collaboration with her sister Margaret – both before her marriage and after her separation from Elizabeth's father, John Gunning, a general who distinguished himself during the Battle of Bunker Hill in 1775. On her father's side, Elizabeth also had the novelist Lady Charlotte Bury as a younger cousin. Elizabeth grew up in Edinburgh without her father while he was fighting in the war in America. Nothing is known about her education, but given that she was an only child with a novelist mother who was not writing at the time, her mother likely became involved in her education at home. Her mother belonged to the English gentry, and her father, whose sisters – the 'beautiful Gunning sisters' – married into the nobility, belonged to the Irish gentry.

In 1790–1, Elizabeth found herself at the centre of a scandal that Horace Walpole nicknamed the 'Gunninghiad' and that divided her family permanently. Exact details of the story remain elusive, but in late 1790 Elizabeth announced her engagement to the marquis of Blandford, heir to the duke of Marlborough and a brilliant prospect. When no wedding date had been set several months later, her father inquired with the duke of Marlborough. The latter's reply, as well as letters from the marquis himself, were found to be forgeries and the engagement fake. Elizabeth's father and contemporary public opinion accused her and her mother of being the forgers, but given his own financial problems, modern scholars consider him just as likely a culprit. Elizabeth and her mother became estranged from him over this, and they moved away. Later rumours implied Elizabeth actually loved the marquis of Lorn and had tried to produce a rival for her affections so he would propose to her. The matter, complete with further public accusations and defence letters, including those by Elizabeth's mother who always remained on her side and by a relative of her father's who was involved, became media fodder and Elizabeth fell victim to intense public debates, pamphlets and caricatures.[37] Her father was later sued by his mistress's husband and left the country immediately and permanently – perhaps also afraid of forgery charges. He died abroad in 1797, but did leave his wife and daughter an inheritance. While Elizabeth and her mother travelled in France, they met Irish Major James Plunkett, who had fled there in order to avoid the death sentence he had received for his role in the 1798 Irish Rebellion. Elizabeth married him in 1803 after her mother died in 1800.

A few years after the scandal, Elizabeth became a very prolific novelist and translator, producing eleven novels, five translations from the French and three books of children's stories over the course of her career. Due to her Irish family ties and her early novels also appearing in Dublin, she is occasionally considered an Irish author, but she did not live in Ireland for any extended period. Her first novel, *The Packet* (1794), refers to the scandal in both preface and plot and was well received.[38] After her mother died, Elizabeth found an unfinished novel by her, which she completed and published in 1802 as *The Heir Apparent*. Her novels have been described as 'sentimental, with heavy-footed humour, trite moralizing, a self-consciously elaborate style, and intense class-consciousness'.[39] Among her translations from the French, *Conversations on the Plurality of Worlds* stands out in that its topic comes from the domain of science. However, framed by an introduction from the male astronomer Lalande and by Fontenelle's own preface, Elizabeth's translation – in a version of the book edited by Lalande – does not make her a scientist, revealing her presence merely in 'a little learned footnoting' and qualifying her rather as a 'facilitator in scientific knowledge exchange'.[40]

The majority of Elizabeth's oeuvre appeared before her marriage, four works (three of them translations, including *Malvina*) came out in the year of her marriage (1803) and the remainder later during her marriage. A publication gap exists spanning 1804 through early 1808, which likely corresponds to the period when Elizabeth had (some of her) children being newly married and in her mid- to late-thirties. It is agreed that she had a large family, but the details remain unclear; one very detailed source suggests five children may have been born – three sons and twin daughters.[41]

After a severe illness, Elizabeth died at Melford House in Long Melford, Suffolk, on 20 July 1823, aged fifty-four.[42]In her obituary, *Gentleman's Magazine* called her 'a lady endowed with many virtues, and considerable accomplishments'.[43]

Modern scholars have been studying the international networks among Enlightenment women writers, readers and translators in order to identify and classify their contributions to the transmission of ideas and the globalization of the literary marketplace.[44] *Malvina* offers another illustration of the importance of such a transnational approach. Although Gunning visited France and Cottin visited England, no record exists of their meeting or correspondence. Nevertheless, this translation creates a link between them that highlights specifically the importance of gender in such networks – particularly in female-authored novels translated by women.

Gunning's first translation of a (male-authored) French text, *Memoirs of Madame de Barneveldt*, appeared in 1795. In its Advertisement Gunning states that she

> flatters herself that the trifling alterations she has thought it necessary to make from the original work having nothing to do with the historical, characteristical, political, or critical parts of it, will meet with indulgence, particularly from her own sex, who certainly cannot be displeased that female delicacy should be preserved in all its purity[45]

This brief declaration exposes the complex relationships at play between translator, reader, gender and text, demonstrating Gunning's awareness of, and sensitivity to, contemporary gender issues as they relate to her translations.

Superficially, Gunning's *Malvina* conforms quite closely to the French original. The translator made numerous minor changes but very few major ones, such as altering Malvina's age from twenty-one to twenty-five, implying different English standards for women living alone. She omitted some verse recitals, songs and many French footnotes ranging from Cottin defending textual choices she had made (for Malvina's portrait, Mr Prior's language) and the sources of quotations (literary, biblical) to features of Scotland more familiar to English than French readers (religion, belief in magic). Given its length, Gunning made very few mistakes (grammar, syntax, vocabulary) in the translation; she effected some minor corrections to the French (see, for instance, Volume I, chapter I and Volume II, chapter XII). However, on the surface the French and English texts resemble each other closely.

In terms of gender though, Gunning's *Malvina* includes important changes as 'female delicacy' reasserts its central role in – ironically – her first translation of a woman's text. While Cottin had wanted to scale back *Claire d'Albe*'s 'voluptuous colours' and 'intense passions' in *Malvina*, Gunning reduces them further still. She deletes passionate expressions such as '[Malvina's] breast … agitated by the same passion burning in his' (Volume II, chapter XV) and 'transported by her beauty and avid for pleasure' (Volume IV, chapter III), comments on the power of love (particularly Malvina's love for the libertine Sir Edmond), on the impossibility of resisting love and on 'conjugal happiness' (Volume IV, chapter III). Undoubtedly so that 'female delicacy should be preserved in all its purity', the extensive details of Kitty's seduction of married Sir Edmond and her being 'half nude and in a state of the most voluptuous abandon' (Volume IV, chapter VIII) are equally missing from the translation. Cottin herself seems to have become ever more sensitized to these issues, because starting with the second (Michaud) edition she omits the seduction details from the French original.

In further gender-related changes, Gunning presents women writers in a more favourable light than Cottin. In the 'Preface' chapter on women writers (Volume II, chapter VI) – also later omitted – she translates Mrs St Clare as not knowing any woman writer to have attained success in a genre other than sentimental fiction. Cottin, however, had added a lengthy footnote elaborating and claiming no woman had written 'a philosophical work, a play, or indeed one of those large productions that demand long and thoughtful reflection and that could be ranked with those of our second-rate male writers'. She attributes this to Nature equipping women's *hearts* and men's *minds* better – all of which Gunning omits. Additionally, Gunning does not extend the absence of genius to all women, like Cottin, but only to certain women, and blames women's lack of education for it, unlike Cottin. They both wonder whether women should write at all if it is merely 'to display their inadequacy' (Cottin) or 'to display their talents' (Gunning). Gunning's more positive and Cottin's conflicted opinions about women writers might be attributed in part to the former's literary family history and the latter's influence from Rousseau; once more, the translation already anticipates the second (Michaud) French edition in its revised, less harsh criticism of women writers.

Cottin and Gunning's differing opinions on women writers appear to extend to their entire sex. When Malvina attends a ball trying to forget Sir Edmond, Gunning translates that she is above trying to make Sir Edmond jealous by paying attention to another man, but omits Cottin's sexist comment that '[Malvina] is a woman and that word restores all my doubts' (Volume II, chapter VIII). They also regard motherhood differently: while Cottin, a substitute mother herself, calls Malvina Fanny's 'mother' when Mrs Burton takes her away (Volume IV, chapter X), Gunning, who had not given birth yet when she translated *Malvina*, describes her as '[Fanny's] more than mother' implying that for her, Malvina as a substitute mother had gone above and beyond the call of motherhood.

Men also receive different treatment from Cottin and Gunning. Gunning depicts men less negatively overall, perhaps in an effort to please her male readers or not frighten the female ones as much. Whereas Cottin identifies with women by saying 'our sex' when discussing how feeling sincere affection prevents women from straying unlike men, Gunning's translation states merely 'women' in general, excluding herself in the first person and thus not antagonizing male readers as directly (Volume IV, chapter VI). Also, whereas Cottin claims in the 'Preface' chapter that love does not matter as much in men's lives as in women's lives, Gunning does not concur and states that men merely have more trouble writing about the topic. And when Gunning refers to 'the inconstancy of man', she omits Cottin's elaboration on the subject and her condemnation of Sir Edmond's inconstancy in Volume IV, chapter VI, as well as her footnote listing unfaithful male protagonists in literature. This list is followed by 'etc. etc. etc. etc.' to indicate their prevalence, but all 'etc.'s are – again – deleted from the second

(Michaud) edition onwards. Instead, Gunning creates a new paragraph explaining why Sir Edmond, lacking humility, was seduced a second time by Kitty.

Cottin's *Malvina* in translation by Gunning exemplifies how French and British women contributed to the globalization of the early nineteenth-century literary marketplace, disseminating French cultural capital to Britain. Although a female-authored text, the most significant changes *Malvina* underwent in translation are in fact gender-related: Gunning portrays women, women writers and men more positively than Cottin, while simultaneously aiming to protect 'female delicacy' more vigorously by reducing or eliminating expressions and scenes of passion and (extramarital) seduction. Ironically, Cottin had set a similar goal for herself in writing *Malvina*, and she implemented several of Gunning's changes in her own later edition.

Notes

1. It contains Frances Brooke's 1760 translation of Marie Jeanne Riccoboni's *Lettres de Juliette Catesby* (*Letters from Juliette Catesby*) and Miss Roberts's 1774 *The Peruvian Letters*, a translation of Françoise de Graffigny's *Lettres d'une Péruvienne* (*Letters from a Peruvian Woman*) as well as a continuation, followed by Roberts's own continuation.
2. See C. Cazenobe, 'Une préromantique méconnue: Madame Cottin', *Travaux de littérature*, 1 (1988), pp. 175–202, on p. 177.
3. Infertility is the theme of one of the rare modern full-length critical studies of Cottin's oeuvre by M. J. Call: *Infertility and the Novels of Sophie Cottin* (2002).
4. See the 'Correspondence' section in the Bibliography. Articles by Roulston ('Gendering the Self in Eighteenth-Century Women's Letters') and Cusset ('"Ceci n'est point une lettre"': échange épistolaire et mystique de la transparence. Le cas de Sophie Cottin (1770–1807)') examine Cottin's correspondence specifically.
5. For a correspondence-based study of this journey, see my article 'Femininity, Fame, Faith and Philosophy: Sophie Cottin's 1806 Voyage to Italy'.
6. L. C. Sykes provides detailed biographical information – see: *Madame Cottin* (Oxford: Basil Blackwell, 1949). S. Spencer's 2005 article ('Sophie Cottin') presents the most recent biography and bibliography.
7. *Gynographs: French Novels by Women of the Late Eighteenth Century* (Lincoln, NE and London: University of Nebraska Press, 1993), p. 186.
8. See R. P. Thomas 'Arranged Marriages and Marriage Arrangements in Eighteenth-Century French Novels by Women' (*Women in French Studies*, 14 (2006), pp. 37–49) for an analysis of this arranged marriage.
9. Stewart, *Gynographs*, pp. 172–5.
10. See M. Cohen, *The Sentimental Education of the Novel* (Princeton, NJ: Princeton University Press, 1999), p. 47. On the genre, also see B. Louichon, *Romancières sentimentales* (Paris: Presses Universitaires de Vincennes, 2009).
11. See C. Hesse, *The Other Enlightenment: How French Women Became Modern* (Princeton, NJ: Princeton University Press, 2001), pp. 142–5.
12. See my article ('Femininity, Fame, Faith and Philosophy') and C. Cusset ('Rousseau's Legacy: Glory and Femininity at the End of the Eighteenth Century: Sophie Cottin and Elisabeth Vigée-Lebrun'). R. Trousson presents *Claire d'Albe* as a rewriting of Rousseau's *Julie* ('Sophie Cottin disciple indocile de Jean-Jacques Rousseau'); S. Spencer ascribes to

the former a 'more audacious female morality' ('"Reading in Pairs": *La Nouvelle Héloïse* and *Claire d'Albe*', *Romance Languages Annual*, 7 (1995), pp. 166–72, on p. 170).

13. By Cazenobe ('Une préromantique méconnue: Madame Cottin') and Bertrand-Jennings (*Un autre mal du siècle: le romantisme des romancières, 1800–1846*), among others.
14. Sykes, *Madame Cottin*, pp. 224–8.
15. *Elisabeth* and its reception in the United States into the twentieth century form an exception (See Spencer 'Sophie Cottin', pp. 113–14).
16. Sykes, *Madame Cottin*, p. 256.
17. Sykes, *Madame Cottin*, p. 258.
18. Cazenobe and Trousson in Europe, and Stewart and Spencer in the United States, for instance.
19. Sykes, *Madame Cottin*, p. 322.
20. Sykes, *Madame Cottin*, pp. 399–400.
21. Sykes, *Madame Cottin*, pp. 44, 401.
22. Sykes, *Madame Cottin*, p. 401.
23. H. Krief's *Vivre libre et écrire* contains some excerpts of *Malvina*, as well as a useful introduction about female novelists during the Revolution.
24. Sykes, *Madame Cottin*, p. 330.
25. Reproduced in the editorial notes (Volume I, note 3) to *Malvina*.
26. We note here that although Cottin describes Malvina twice as having 'cheveux blonds' ('blond hair'), Gunning gives her 'light brown' and 'auburn' hair, respectively.
27. A. Alliston, *Virtue's Faults: Correspondences in Eighteenth-Century British and French Women's Fiction* (Stanford, CA: Stanford University Press, 1996), p. 86.
28. See J. Todd's study on the role of women's friendship in literature: *Women's Friendship in Literature* (New York, NY: Columbia University Press, 1980).
29. This criticism includes women composers – see Volume II, note 29.
30. On the different implications of this for men and women, see Cohen, *The Sentimental Education of the Novel*, p. 47.
31. See the section by that name in my article 'Femininity, Fame, Faith and Philosophy' for a summary of various critics' analyses.
32. Sykes, *Madame Cottin*, p. 20.
33. See Volume I, note 32 for details.
34. On the role of Scotland in *Malvina*, see P. Pelckmans, 'L'Écosse des romancières'.
35. See the article by R. Craig on how Cottin uses the castle as Gothic and libertine spaces in her sentimental novel to create an early Romantic hybrid.
36. They are described as 'exceedingly harmless; an absence of plot forming their most original characteristic' (*Dictionary of National Biography*, vol. 23, p. 349).
37. See the articles by P. Perkins ('The Fictional Identities of Elizabeth Gunning') and T. Beebee ('Publicity, Privacy, and the Power of Fiction in the Gunning Letters') for more background on the scandal.
38. Perkins considers it an effort to redeem the author's image in the public eye.
39. I. Grundy, 'Gunning, Elizabeth (1769–1823)', in *Oxford Dictionary of National Biography* (Oxford: Oxford University Press, 2004), at http://www.oxforddnb.com/view/article/11745 [accessed 21 July 2014].
40. A. E. Martin '"No Tincture of Learning?" Aphra Behn as (Re)Writer and Translator', *UCL Translation in History Lectures* (24 October 2013), at http://www.ucl.ac.uk/translation-studies/translation-in-history/documents/Martin-Aphra-Behn-pdf [accessed 21 July 2014].
41. *Notes and Queries*, 6th series, vol. 4 (30 July 1881), p. 89.

42. *Orlando: Women's Writing in the British Isles from the Beginnings to the Present* offers detailed biographical and bibliographical information (eds S. Brown, P. Clements and I. Grundy (Cambridge: Cambridge University Press Online, 2006), at http://orlando.cambridge.org/ [accessed March 25 2014]).
43. *Gentleman's Magazine, and Historical Chronicle*, vol. 93, part 2 (August 1823), p. 190.
44. See for instance S. van Dijk (ed.), *WomenWriters*, at http://neww.huygens.knaw.nl/ [accessed 23 March 2015] and the volumes that G. Dow co-edited: *Women Readers in Europe: Readers, Writers, Salonnières, 1750–1900*, special issue of *Women's Writing*, 18:1 (February 2011).
45. E. Gunning Plunkett, *Memoirs of Madame de Barneveldt, Translated from the French* (London: Low; Booker, 1795).

SELECT BIBLIOGRAPHY

Primary Material

Sophie Cottin

Reviews

Critical Review, Appendix to vol. 16 (January–April 1809), pp. 502–11.

Mercure de France, Ventôse, An IX (February–March 1801), pp. 331–5.

Morning Chronicle, 24 November 1808.

Monthly Review, Appendix to vol. 57 (September–December 1808), pp. 471–3.

Published Works

Claire d'Albe (Paris: Maradan, 1799).

Malvina (Paris: Maradan, 1801).

Amélie Mansfield (Paris: Maradan, 1802).

La Prise de Jericho, Mélanges de littérature publiés par J.-B.-A. Suard (Paris: Dentu, 1803), pp. 55–113.

Mathilde (Paris: Giguet et Michaud, 1805).

Élisabeth (Paris: Giguet et Michaud, 1806).

Claire d'Albe, in *Romans de femmes du XVIIIe siècle*, ed. R. Trousson (Paris: Robert Laffont, 1996), pp. 691–772.

Claire d'Albe: *An English Translation*, trans. and ed. M. Cohen (New York, NY: Modern Language Association, 2002).

Claire d'Albe: The Original French Text, ed. M. Cohen (New York, NY: Modern Language Association, 2002)

Claire d'Albe (Paris: Indigo & Côté-femmes, 2004).

'Malvina', in H. Krief (ed.), *Vivre libre et écrire: Anthologie des romancières de la période révolutionnaire (1789–1800)* (Oxford: Voltaire Foundation; Paris: Presses de l'Université Paris-Sorbonne, 2005), pp. 254–83.

Correspondence

Arnelle [Madame de Clauzade], *Une oubliée: Madame Cottin d'après sa correspondance* (Paris: Librairie Plon, 1914).

Correspondance, Nouvelles acquisitions françaises (NAF) 15970–15986, Département des manuscrits, Bibliothèque Nationale, Paris.

Sykes, L. C., *Madame Cottin* (Oxford: Basil Blackwell, 1949).

Elizabeth Gunning Plunkett

Reviews

Morning Chronicle, 24 December 1803.

Published Works

Lord Fitzhenry (London: Bell, 1794).

The Packet (London: Bell, 1794).

Memoirs of Madame de Barneveldt, Translated from the French (London: Low; Booker, 1795).

The Foresters (London: Sampson Low, 1796).

The Orphans of Snowdon (London: Lowndes, 1797).

The Gipsy Countess (London: Longman and Rees, 1799).

A Sequel to Family Stories; or Evenings at my Grandmother's. Intended for Young Persons, of Eight Years Old (London: Tabart, 1802).

Family Stories; or Evenings at my Grandmother's. Intended for Young Persons, of Eight Years Old (London: Tabart, 1802).

The Farmer's Boy (London: Crosby, 1802).

The Heir Apparent (London: Ridgway and Symonds, 1802).

The Village Library. Intended for the Use of Young Persons (London: Crosby, 1802).

Conversations on the Plurality of Worlds, Translated from a Late Paris Edition (London: Cundee, 1803).

Malvina, Translated from the French (London: Hurst, Chapple and Dutton, 1803).

The War Office (London: n.p., 1803).

The Wife with Two Husbands, a tragi-comedy, in three acts, translated from the French (London: Symonds, 1803).

The Exile of Erin (London: Crosby, 1808).

Dangers Through Life; Or the Victim of Seduction (London: Ebers, 1810).

Sentimental Anecdotes, Translated from the French (London: Chapple, 1811).

The Victims of Seduction, or, Memoirs of a Man of Fashion: A Tale of Modern Times (London: Jones, 1815).

Secondary Material

Alliston, A., *Virtue's Faults: Correspondences in Eighteenth-Century British and French Women's Fiction* (Stanford, CA: Stanford University Press, 1996).

Beebee, T. O., 'Publicity, Privacy, and the Power of Fiction in the Gunning Letters', *Eighteenth-Century Fiction*, 20:1 (Autumn 2007), pp. 61–88.

Bertrand-Jennings, C., *Un autre mal du siècle: le romantisme des romancières, 1800–1846* (Toulouse: Presses Universitaires du Mirail, 2005).

Call, M. J., *Infertility and the Novels of Sophie Cottin* (Newark, DE: University of Delaware Press, 2002).

Cazenobe, C., 'Une préromantique méconnue: Madame Cottin', *Travaux de littérature*, 1 (1988), pp. 175–202.

Clements, P., I. Grundy and S. Brown (eds), *Orlando: Women's Writing in the British Isles from the Beginnings to the Present* (Cambridge: Cambridge University Press Online, 2006), at http://orlando. cambridge.org/ [accessed March 25 2014].

Cohen, M., *The Sentimental Education of the Novel* (Princeton, NJ: Princeton University Press, 1999).

Craig, R., 'Imaginaire des lieux dans *Malvina*', *Arborescences: Revue d'Études Françaises*, 3 (July 2013), at http://www.erudit.org/revue/arbo/2013/v/n3/1017366ar.html [accessed 22 July 2014].

Cuillé, T. B., 'Cottin, Krüdener, and Musical Mesmerism', in *Narrative Interludes: Musical Tableaux in Eighteenth-Century French Texts* (Toronto: University of Toronto Press, 2006), pp. 144–72.

Cusset, C., '"Ceci n'est point une lettre"': échange épistolaire et mystique de la transparence. Le cas de Sophie Cottin (1770–1807)', in M. Bossis (ed.), *La lettre à la croisée de l'individuel et du social* (Paris: Editions Kimé, 1994), pp. 48–53.

—, 'Rousseau's Legacy: Glory and Femininity at the End of the Eighteenth Century: Sophie Cottin and Elisabeth Vigée-Lebrun', in R. Bonnel and C. Rubinger (eds), *Femmes savantes et femmes d'esprit: Women Intellectuals of the French Eighteenth Century* (New York, NY: Peter Lang, 1994), pp. 401–18.

Dow, G. and K. Astbury (eds), *Women Readers in Europe: Readers, Writers, Salonnières, 1750–1900*, special issue of *Women's Writing*, 18:1 (February 2011).

Dow, G. and H. Brown (eds), *Readers, Writers, Salonnières: Female Networks in Europe, 1700–1900* (Bern: Peter Lang, 2011).

Gaskill, H. (ed.), *The Reception of Ossian in Europe* (London and New York, NY: Thoemmes Continuum, 2004).

Gentleman's Magazine, and Historical Chronicle, vol. 93, part 2 (August 1823).

Grundy, I., 'Gunning, Elizabeth (1769–1823)', in *Oxford Dictionary of National Biography* (Oxford: Oxford University Press, 2004), at http://www.oxforddnb.com/view/article/11745 [accessed 21 July 2014].

Hesse, C., *The Other Enlightenment: How French Women Became Modern* (Princeton, NJ: Princeton University Press, 2001).

Journal des débats, 6 July 1803, p. 4.

Kaplan, M. S (ed.), *Translations and Continuations: Riccoboni and Brooke, Graffigny and Roberts* (London: Pickering & Chatto, 2011).

—, 'Femininity, Fame, Faith and Philosophy: Sophie Cottin's 1806 Voyage to Italy', *Women In French Studies*, 22 (2014), pp. 9–19.

Letzter, J. and R. Adelson, 'French Women Opera Composers and the Aesthetics of Rousseau', *Feminist Studies*, 26:1 (Spring 2000), pp. 69–100.

—, *Women Writing Opera: Creativity and Controversy in the Age of the French Revolution* (Berkeley, CA: University of California Press, 2001).

Louichon, B., *Romancières sentimentales* (Paris: Presses Universitaires de Vincennes, 2009).

Martin, A. E., '"No Tincture of Learning?" Aphra Behn as (Re)Writer and Translator', *UCL Translation in History Lectures* (24 October 2013), at http://www.ucl.ac.uk/translation-studies/translation-in-history/documents/Martin-Aphra-Behn-pdf. [accessed 21 July 2014].

Notes and Queries, 6th series, vol. 4 (July–December 1881).

Pelckmans, P., 'L'Écosse des romancières', in N. Ferrand (ed.), *Locus in Fabula. La topique de l'espace dans les fictions françaises d'Ancien Régime* (Louvain: Peeters, 2004), pp. 249–59.

Perkins, P., 'The Fictional Identities of Elizabeth Gunning', *Tulsa Studies in Women's Literature*, 15:1 (Spring 1996), pp. 83–98.

Riskin, J., 'The Mesmerism Investigation and the Crisis of Sensibilist Science', in *Science in the Age of Sensibility: The Sentimental Empiricists of the French Enlightenment* (Chicago, IL: University of Chicago Press, 2002), pp. 189–225.

Roulston, C., 'Gendering the Self in Eighteenth-Century Women's Letters', in A. Strugnell (ed.), *Correspondence and Epistolary Fiction; La Fête; Science and Medicine; Voltaire* (Oxford: Voltaire Foundation, 2002), pp. 93–103.

Smiles, S., *A Publisher and His Friends: Memoir and Correspondence of the Late John Murray, with an Account of the Origin and Progress of the House, 1768–1843*, 2nd edn, 2 vols (London: John Murray Albemarle Street, 1891), vol. 1.

Spencer, S. I., '"Reading in Pairs": *La Nouvelle Héloïse* and *Claire d'Albe*', *Romance Languages Annual*, 7 (1995), pp. 166–72.

—, 'Sophie Cottin', in S. I. Spencer (ed.), *Writers of the French Enlightenment, Dictionary of Literary Biography*, 375 vols (New York, NY: Thomson Gale, 2005), vol. 313, pp. 113–20.

Stephen, L. and S. Lee, *Dictionary of National Biography*, 63 vols (London: Smith, Elder & Co., 1890), vol. 23.

Stewart, J. H., *Gynographs: French Novels by Women of the Late Eighteenth Century* (Lincoln, NE and London: University of Nebraska Press, 1993).

Thomas, R. P., 'Arranged Marriages and Marriage Arrangements in Eighteenth-Century French Novels by Women', *Women in French Studies*, 14 (2006), pp. 37–49.

Todd, J., *Women's Friendship in Literature* (New York, NY: Columbia University Press, 1980).

Trousson, R., 'Sophie Cottin disciple indocile de Jean-Jacques Rousseau', in *Rêver Rousseau, Études Jean-Jacques Rousseau*, 8 (Montmorency: Musée Jean-Jacques Rousseau, 1996), pp. 72–87.

van Dijk, S., *WomenWriters*, at http://neww.huygens.knaw.nl/ [accessed 23 March 2015].

NOTE ON THE TEXT

Although Sophie Cottin's *Malvina* carries 'An IX–1800' ('Year IX–1800') as its publication date, it actually appeared in 1801 with Maradan in Paris. Elizabeth Gunning's 1803 translation of *Malvina* is the first and only one into English. Before this, the novel had already been translated into German in 1802–3. During the first half of the nineteenth century alone, it was also translated into Dutch in 1816–17, Russian in 1816–18,[1] Danish in 1821, Swedish in 1827–8, Spanish in 1833, Romanian in 1841 and Greek in 1842.[2]

The text reproduced here is the first English edition from 1803 published by Hurst, Chapple and Dutton, held in the Chawton House Library and the Bodleian Library,[3] among a very small collection of libraries worldwide. An advertisement in the *Morning Chronicle* announced its publication in four volumes on Saturday 24 December 1803. It is advertised as 'An Interesting Novel' and listed with a price of 16 shillings.

An 1804 reprint exists which is carried by a larger group of libraries. It has title page details identical to the 1803 edition, with the exception of the date listed on each title page and the printer information listed on the title page to Volume IV: 'H. Reynell, Printer, 21, Piccadilly'. This information appears on the title pages of the first three volumes in the 1803 edition, but reads 'Stower, Printer, Charles-Street, Hatton-Garden' on the title page to its Volume IV. The 1803 and 1804 books possess identical text and pagination, but their table of contents pages differ: in 1803, it is missing in Volume I and present at the end of Volume II, while appearing after the title pages of Volumes III and IV, as is the case for all volumes in 1804.

A second and final edition of Gunning's translation appeared in 1810 with Chapple (only) in London and it is to this edition that the 1803 edition is compared here. The printer information given is 'London, Printed, by John Dean, 57, Wardour-street, Soho'. The second edition contains relatively few and only minor changes compared to the first edition.

It appears that contemporary British periodicals did not review the translation upon publication, perhaps because anti-French sentiment reigned again after the Peace of Amiens had ended in May 1803 and hostilities between the two nations had resumed. However, British opinion of the novel became public in 1808–9 when two periodicals printed reviews of the French novel published posthumously in London by Colburn in 1809.[4] Elizabeth Inchbald was asked on 31 December 1808 to review it, but declined because she did not have enough confidence in her knowledge of French.[5] The *Monthly Review* in 1808 is most interested in the biography preceding the novel but says about *Malvina*: 'we experience some tediousness in the progress of its events, and the termination is effected by means the most improbable' and 'the productions of her (Cottin's) pen cannot fail to be highly interesting, though in a moral view they may be intitled only to a very mixed and qualified approbation'.[6] The *Critical Review* in 1809 expresses a much harsher opinion about Cottin's oeuvre and graver concern about its morality:

> amidst all the language of exalted and virtuous sentiment, with which these works abound, there is in the avowed principle which inspired and pervades them, an insidious sophistry most dangerous to the heart, and most pernicious to the understanding of young and susceptible females[7]

Malvina specifically is considered 'greatly and dangerously immoral'[8] and one of France's 'pernicious romances' the importation of which Napoleon's edicts do not prevent very efficiently.[9] In spite of these negative reviews, the translation's second edition appeared the following year in 1810.

I have changed Gunning's translation as little as possible and have included in the editorial notes only significant deviations from the French original (changes, omissions, additions). All translations in the editorial material are mine unless otherwise indicated. Gunning did not preserve all of Cottin's footnotes. When she did, I have kept them as footnotes; when she did not, I have mentioned this in the editorial notes and provided the original footnote text with a translation. A list of silent corrections that were made is provided, as is a list of textual variants between the 1803 and 1810 editions.

Notes

1. I thank Elena Gretchanaia for this information.
2. I thank Eirini Rizaki for this information.
3. I have used the text at the Bodleian Library since the one at the Chawton House Library is not in a fit condition for extensive consultation.
4. According to the *Morning Chronicle*, the book appeared on Thursday 24 November 1808.
5. See S. Smiles, *A Publisher and His Friends: Memoir and Correspondence of the Late John Murray, with an Account of the Origin and Progress of the House, 1768–1843*, 2nd edn, 2 vols (London: John Murray Albemarle Street, 1891), vol. 1, pp. 121–2.
6. *Monthly Review*, Appendix to vol. 57 (September–December 1808), pp. 471–3, on p. 473.
7. *Critical Review*, Appendix to vol. 16 (January–April 1809), pp. 502–11, on p. 505.
8. *Critical Review*, Appendix to vol. 16, p. 510.
9. *Critical Review*, Appendix to vol. 16, p. 511.

MALVINA,[1]
by Madame C****,

Authoress of Claire d'Albe, and Amelia Mansfield.[2]

Translated from the French,

by Miss Gunning,

in four volumes.

VOL. I.

London:

printed for T. Hurst, Paternoster-Row;

C. Chapple, Pall-Mall, and Southampton-

Row, Russell-Square; and R. Dutton,

Gracechurch-Street.

H. Reynell, Printer, 21, Piccadilly.

1803.

MALVINA.[3]

CHAP. 1.[4]

Adieu, beloved Earth! sacred asylum which contains all that is dearest to my heart! Adieu, precious remains of my friend, my companion, my sister! Thus said the sorrowing Malvina de Sorcy, as her tears fell on the tomb of her beloved friend, whom she had recently lost. – Adieu, dear shade! whom I shall never cease to regret; the destiny which pursues me, now tears me from the melancholy and soothing consolation of daily weeping over thy ashes. – I am going far from this spot, and ah how soon will the briar extend its rude branches over the stone which covers thee, and in a little time will even conceal it from the eye of friendship. I am going! and the dear remembrance of thee will accompany me for ever,[5] while the frivolous admirers of thy youth will no longer remember thy existence. – Though Heaven, by continuing my life, prevents me from joining the dearest part of myself; that cruel moment which separated us, will never be effaced. – Ah! I shall continually behold that sweet smile, with which you endeavoured to console me; – and that last expressive look, which penetrated my soul as it was arrested by the seal of death. – Madam, the carriage is ready, said a little girl who came running, and interrupted Malvina's melancholy soliloquy. She was followed by an attendant,[6] who, observing Malvina on her knees in the snow, and her bosom touching the icy stone, hastily exclaimed,[7] Good God, madam! are you determined to die on the tomb of my lady? It is a mercy from Heaven that you are obliged to leave this place! for though the season is so severe, you cannot resist visiting this tomb, morning and evening. – Malvina arose in silence, without attending to what had been said, for grief in such a mind as she possessed, withdraws it from the world. The situation of such beings is as little known as understood, and but few, very few, will even take the trouble to develope them. Ah, how few are there which can even comprehend the silent language which explains the sorrows, on which sensibility banquets, or ever mark its liquid essence, that falls involuntarily from the eye, while its deep source is enshrined in the heart.[8]

Malvina de Sorcy was a French woman, who was left a widow at five-and-twenty,[9] of a man she had never loved. – As soon as she became independent, she eagerly embraced the first moment of her liberty to unite herself once more to the friend of her infancy;[10] who had been married some years to a gentleman in England. – She hastened to her,[11] and for three years they lived together, and enjoyed the charms of disinterested friendship: whose sweet and soothing influence mitigated the sorrow, which the depraved conduct of Lady Sheridan's husband occasioned: and softened to Malvina the impossibility of returning to her native country, after her so long residing in England.[12] – Some friends, however, intimated to her, that she must resolve to give up her friend, or resign her fortune in France.[13] – She instantly decided in favor of her friend; and this sacrifice was the spontaneous determination of her heart; which Lady Sheridan observing, thought it her duty to point out how very injurious this disinterested conduct would prove to herself, but without effect, and Malvina alone never could be persuaded to think so: and from that time she possessed no other fortune, but the sum she had brought with her, and placed with a banker; and which produced a very slender income. She resigned every superfluity in dress, and deprived herself of every amusement suitable to her age, and only existed in the pleasure of seeing and loving her friend.

On losing that friend, she felt indifferent where she resided, without relations or friends, in a strange land: her misfortunes appeared too great for any outward circumstance to aggravate or relieve. – Lady Sheridan, when dying, had obtained leave from her husband, that their daughter, who was five years old, should be resigned up to the care of Malvina, who was to undertake the sole direction of her education. – This promise was not given from the regard he entertained for his lady, but rather to relieve himself from a duty which might in the slightest degree, restrain him from his ungovernable love of play, and dissipation. – Though the presence of Malvina and[14] his daughter could not prevent the speedy re-union of his riotous and debauched companions, yet, at times, it might have been rather an obstacle to their frequent meetings, as Malvina was regarded by him in the light of a censor. – For that reason, he immediately informed her she must provide herself with another abode. – Malvina, perfectly satisfied with the delightful privilege of taking with her the child of her beloved friend, was rejoiced to have it in her power, to quit a house, where her feelings were shocked, on beholding the indecent mirth of such unthinking beings, take place of mourning, and which she considered, and deeply felt as an insult to her grief, and the memory of her valued friend. – While she was considering what course to take, conscious that she was too young to live alone, and likewise that her fortune would not permit her to take a house;[15] at the same time she was perfectly assured, from her knowledge of the character of Lord Sheridan, that she could not expect much from him, towards the education of his daughter;[16] she enjoyed a secret satisfaction in the idea, that she alone, would have the pleasure of supporting and educating[17] the child of her Clara.

In this uncertainty, she resolved to write to a relation of her mother's, who resided in the north of Scotland; informing her of her situation, her taste for retirement, and her desire of her residing with her, on the stipend she mentioned. Mrs. Burton,[18] returned her an answer, wherein she accepted her proposal with pleasure, and on her own terms: that having long been neglected by her family, she should rejoice to punish their neglect; and though she had frequently been the dupe of such complaisance, it should never prevent her from considering it as one of her first pleasures; if she could be serviceable to her fellow creatures, or protect, or assist[19] her relations.

At another time, Malvina would have thought very different of the manner in which Mrs. Burton had accepted her request; but in the present state of her mind, the grief by which she was absorbed, did not permit her time to reflect on it. She was anxious to leave a house where she had enjoyed the only happy hours of her life; she must no longer shed tears over the cold clay which covered the remains of her Clara. She must bid an eternal adieu to that tomb, which was the only memento that remained to tell she had once existed.

It was there, she was renewing the vows she made of devoting her life to the care and education of her Fanny, and never to divide her affection with any other object. – A vow, though rash, dictated by the fervor of an exalted friendship, and which maternal affection received with transport; and the heartfelt satisfaction of having sweetened the last moments of her friend, occasioned Malvina to renew it with the most pious enthusiasm. – She was repeating it, when Tomkins,[20] her maid, came to fetch her from the tomb. She permitted herself to be conducted in silence to the carriage which was waiting for them, which as soon as she had entered, her tears ceased to flow. – There are sorrows that sink so deep into the heart, that they are neither to be expressed by tears or complaints; but whose deep source silently corrodes life's vital current.[21]

It was the latter end of the month of November. The trees were despoiled of their decorations, and the uniform mantle of snow which covered the earth, presented to the eye a monotonous and inanimate picture of desolation. The extreme cold, kept every person under their own roof, the roads appeared deserted, and the villages as they passed, seemed uninhabited. – The birds were silent, and the waters at rest in their icy prisons. – The howlings of the north winds alone interrupted the universal silence. They alone informed the world, that the repose of nature was not that of death. But such scenes were pleasing to Malvina, they were in sympathy with her grief¾though they were less gloomy than her mourning, and less melancholy than her soul. – Absorbed by a train of the deepest reflections, her eye wandered over every successive scene without fixing on any object. – Every thing became to her a source of afflicting reflections.

Alas, said Malvina, mentally, yet a few months,[22] and all nature will be renovated; the trees will recover their verdure, the flowers their perfume; a secret fire still circulates in the sap, and they all retain life – though apparently dead. Ah, how different is the grief-worn mind! which neither the winter's frost, or the roses bloom can alter; Nature can effect no change in me, all seems immutable in my soul.

Tomkins, Peter[23] an old French domestic, and the little Frances,[24] were the companions of Malvina's journey. She insisted on Peter's getting into the carriage, chusing rather to retard her journey in the day,[25] than permit him to be exposed to the severe cold. Both her attendants were sensible of the kindness and situation of their mistress: neither he or Tomkins offered to interrupt the silence, and they respected her too much, to attempt consoling her. – It was at last interrupted by little Frances, who, when not asleep, asked a thousand artless questions of Malvina and the good old servant.[26] Malvina listened with attention to the sound of her voice, which already resembled her mothers, and caused every fibre of Malvina's heart to thrill, with painful recollections, and yet produced the only pleasure she was capable of feeling.

After a journey of ten days, Malvina arrived at the place of her destination, in the county of—,[27] which separates the north of Scotland from the south. – The castle of Mrs. Burton was situated a few miles from—,[28] whose Gothic grandeur[29] was increased by the lofty mountains covered with snow, which towered above it; the immense lake of Tay[30] which bathed its walls, rendered its situation wildly sublime.

Malvina felt a secret pleasure as she surveyed the country of her favorite bard,[31] Ossian,[32] where his name was yet remembered with a wild enthusiasm. – Partial to those writings, she fancied she beheld the form of her loved friend in the mists which surrounded her. The wind murmured on the heath, it seemed as if the shade was advancing; she listened to the distant rushing of the torrent, and imagined she could distinguish the groans of her friend. Her sickly imagination was filled with the phantoms which had once been; and of the inhabitants of the country which she had travelled through.

Her name, which was the same as that of the daughter-in-law of Ossian, seemed to sanction the interest which she felt, as she revolved in her mind the picture of other times in this country, though faded by the touch of time. – It was not however to be imputed as a fault to Malvina, feeling in this manner, for possessing one of those ardent and exalted minds which always are attracted by the sublime and wonderful; and who are ever seeking it, and too often lose themselves in the pursuit. – Tender and melancholy grief alone seemed to withdraw her mind, and usurp it entirely. – In her happier days, her imagination was lively and brilliant; but even then it did not appear in words – it was the heart alone that spake.

'Twas near nine o'clock in the evening when she arrived at Mrs. Burton's; all nature was wrapped in silent darkness. The postillion advanced near the margin of the wide ditch which surrounded the castle, and they perceived the drawbridge was already drawn up. Peter, uneasy that his mistress should be kept so late in these dangerous roads, hastily alighted, to endeavour to find a passage to the walls. After groping some time in the dark, he found a narrow foot path which lead to the walls, and was terminated by a small gate, barricadoed with iron. He knocked violently, without effect, though the noise which was echoed back, reverberated from mountain to mountain; and for a moment disturbed the profound silence which reigned around, and as it died away, universal stillness again resumed its empire. He exerted all his strength to mount the bars of the gate, and catching hold of some branches of ivy which covered it, he found a rope, which he pulled with violence. The deep and heavy sound of a bell to which it belonged, resounded in the castle, and seemed to put all within in motion: they soon heard voices calling, and answering, and could distinguish lights from different quarters, whose brightness gleamed on the surrounding darkness. The weight of the heavy gates groaned on their hinges – the bridge was let down, and Malvina's carriage rolled into the court. Mrs. Burton waited in the vestibule; on seeing Malvina, she appeared much surprised; but quickly recovering herself, she said, with much politeness and affability, that a long journey, undertaken at such a severe time of the season, required much rest, and that she would take the liberty of conducting her to her apartment, before she introduced her to the company who were at present in the castle.

As this was exactly what Malvina most desired, she followed her cousin to the chamber which was appropriated for her. Mrs. Burton would not enter into conversation with her, fearful she might encrease her fatigue, and after having made her take some refreshment, she insisted on her retiring to rest, telling her, though she earnestly wished to be better acquainted, and enjoy the pleasure of her society, yet she should deprive herself of that satisfaction, that Malvina[33] might devote a few days to recover from her fatigue.

She accompanied those words by fixing on Malvina a look, which expressed much uneasiness; which Malvina, being overpowered by her own melancholy reflections, did not observe, and returned her acknowledgments to Mrs. Burton for the liberty she so kindly gave her, conscious, that for some time, general conversation would be very irksome, and would be a punishment she could not support. As soon as she had put her little Frances to bed,[34] she wished her cousin a good night,[35] when, perhaps, from the fatigue of her journey, and the continual agitation she had experienced for some months, acted as a soporific to her harrassed mind, and produced a few hours quiet repose.

CHAP. II.

Portrait.[36]

Unhappy Malvina! Thou for some hours may'st cease to suffer; sleep has spread his balmy covering over thy deep wound, and for some moments at least thou may'st forget thou art alone in the world. But if it is true that dreams are influenced by the thoughts of the day, then, you yet are miserable! However, during this apparent moment of peace, I will endeavour to give a sketch of that admirable woman, whose mind, qualities, and figure, formed a tout ensemble that can only belong to herself, two of whom are seldom, if ever, found in the world.

But can I do her justice by description? There are terms for beauty, grace, and wit; but for that undefinable charm which penetrates, subdues, and captivates, that dwells only in the soul, and yet gains the love and attention of all, even to overlook her foibles; how can I delineate such? It is not by saying what it is, but what inspired Malvina, that would pourtray her. It is not the eulogiums which attend the mention of her name, but the emotion with which it was pronounced, that could give the idea. Those who were admitted to her confidence, who could see and hear her, can alone feel it, and must think of her with very different sentiments from every other: though the captivating charm is nameless, for that which pleased above every other in her, is not to be delineated.

With great wit, she possessed something so superior to it, that it passed unregarded, and while most women are so vain of the praise which is lavished on them, on that account, Malvina would have lost much, if hers had been noticed.[i] I do not pretend to assert, that the pensive[37] Malvina was faultless, but, in her, it appeared to encrease her attractions.[38] It was no particular charm or quality that was remarkable in her, for, except that uniform goodness, where so many virtues were blended and united, not one appeared prominent in her character, because all were in harmony.

Malvina possessed that innate complaisance which politeness in vain endeavours to imitate. It was neither from effort or design, but because the pleasure of others was always dearer to her than her own. She was as obliging to a stranger as a friend; it was only in the recesses of the heart, that she cherished and retained her affection for those she valued. Those alone, who were beloved by Malvina, knew this, and the extent to which her ideas of friendship were raised. Those whom she favoured with that secret title, might truly say they were beloved; she felt and inspired those genuine sentiments which are not either known or understood, and are perfectly unfashionable in the present world; but such were Malvina's, that she would sacrifice both life and fortune without reserve. In short, to finish the picture of Malvina, I shall not enlarge on her benevolence, and kindness, for the subject would be inexhaustible; nor on the delight she experienced in being the secret author of happiness and prosperity to others.[39] If it is a truth that we were endowed with virtues by the Supreme Being, to serve as a light to direct us to know, and approach nearer to him; who then could have more confidence, and feel so deeply, the existence of a God and a Saviour, as Malvina? It was her sincere piety alone which made her regard this life only, as it gave the promise of a better.

Though from nature endowed with a tender, and even a passionate heart, Malvina had never loved. Habituated from her infancy to live with her friend, in the enjoyment of that friendship, she placed all her felicity, and never felt the existence of any other affection. Perhaps[40] a serious passion might have convinced her of her error, but the man to whom she had been united, was not calculated to inspire such a one; not so much from the disproportion of their ages, as uncongeniality of character. Malvina derived no advantage from the ill-suited union, yet it evinced the sweetness and gentleness of her disposition, by her uniform manner of sustaining it.[41] She was gratified, by having obtained the entire confidence of her husband; for though her beauty had attracted his senses, her modesty and gentleness rivetted his affection. Timid, modest, even when noticed, her chaste eyes often cast down, left her unconscious that she was the object of universal attention: as there were few women who surpassed her in beauty, there was not one who possessed superior virtue.[42]

Those who had secretly loved her during her marriage, as soon as she was at liberty, declared themselves, and made her very advantageous proposals; but her mind, fatigued by so long a tyranny, rather sought repose than agitation. She neither wished or desired any other felicity than what friendship afforded;[43] and Lady Sheridan was the selected of her heart.[44] The moment she was emancipated, she flew to this beloved friend, and her being unhappy, served to augment her tenderness. – Ah, who that has beheld those whom they love, miserable, or suffer in the slightest degree, but what must have felt their affection increase? Thus had Malvina attained her twenty-fifth year without having felt the power of love: not that she was incapable of feeling it, for she was the soul of sensibility; but being so long a stranger to that passion, she imagined herself invincible. – Alas! why was it not permitted, that she should ever remain ignorant of its undermining power? She fancied that sentiment could have no effect on her, and had resolved to resist its influence. For she had promised to be a mother to her little Frances, and her whole life she thought should be devoted to the performance of this duty; consequently, every thing that in the least interfered with it, she considered as a crime! With this disposition, nothing could have been more eligible to her than the retreat she had chosen; the idea of living remote from the world, where she might freely indulge her sorrows, and attend to her darling charge, had spread a soothing calm over her agitated soul.

CHAP. III.

A more perfect acquaintance with the characters.

It was late the next morning when Malvina arose: as soon as she was dressed, she looked round her apartment, then looking from the casements, she was enchanted with the different views which they presented of nature's scenery.[45ii] The blue lake, obscured by the mists which were slowly rising from its bosom, which prevented the eye from tracing its extent. On one side, mountains covered with forests of black firs, whose towering heads bid defiance to the fury of the storm; interspersed by deep glens, in the bosom of which rushed an impetuous torrent,[iii] whose incessant roar was contrasted by the silence which reigned at the foot of the mountains, which bordered the lake, whose base was laden by enormous masses of granite, piled on each other, without the smallest vestige of vegetation, afforded the pensive eye the image of chaos and desolation[46] only.

While Malvina was gazing attentively at this scene, she was interrupted by a voice which seemed interested in her welfare. On turning from the window, she perceived Mrs. Burton in the most elegant undress, who smilingly said, ah, my fair cousin, you must not expect to find in this rude clime, the ever smiling scenery of France. It is there only, that nature displays all her beneficence; here, we behold only her severity and rigour. But while we wait for the season which will give a gayer appearance to our mountains, I have taken care to provide you with views by the best masters of the Italian and Flemish schools. In my opinion, it is more pleasing to contemplate the skies of Italy and France, in painting, than those of Scotland, in reality. Malvina raised her eyes, and beheld many beautiful pieces, disposed with much taste, on the green paper which adorned her cabinet. Much affected by this attention, and attributing it to Mrs. B's[47] goodness of heart, she took her hand, at the same time, expressing to her cousin, her grateful sense of her kindness. These attentions inform me what you are, for the being who can be so delicately attentive to a stranger, must constitute the happiness of all around her.

That at least is what I aspire to do, replied Mrs. Burton, and has been the principal inducement which prompted me to live in this seclusion. This estate being a lordship, has therefore a number of vassals; I protect and comfort them, and they regard me as the arbiter of their destiny.[48] Malvina, though she approved this arrangement, which Mrs. B. described and pronounced with no small share of self complaisance; yet she did not feel the least affected by it, and secretly reproached herself for not being more sensible of Mrs. B's merit. Perhaps an observer less indulgent, or more enlightened, might have thought, that when goodness was made a boast, instead of being seen by actions, it may be honored it is true, but it never can be properly felt.

As you have so kindly permitted me (said Malvina) to pass some days in my apartment, I shall profit by your obliging indulgence, and continue alone, far from a world, which I have long since quitted. You are free, perfectly at liberty, cousin, interrupted Mrs. B. – I always wish my friends to feel themselves at home when with me, and the more at their ease I observe them, the more agreeable it will be; and I certainly shall not make you an exception to this general rule. I will not ask you to accompany me into the saloon, as I shall have for some days a society which would only fatigue and distress you, as they are young people who are all very gay and noisy. – But when we are en-famille, I must insist on your going down.

Malvina bowed, and her cousin left her: during several days she saw very little of her, nor did she regret the loss. – Misfortune had elevated and increased her habitual devotion, and this disposition so inherent to virtuous and sensible souls, made her cherish solitude with enthusiasm – Solitude has ever been the sacred retreat of religion in all ages:[49] but the good Tomkins did not like to see her mistress perpetually confined to her apartment. – It appeared to her that a little dissipation would be the only relief for sorrow; and she thought it very unkind in Mrs. B to permit her cousin to sit weeping alone, when there was so much gaiety in the saloon. – She determined to speak to Malvina when she took in her breakfast. – Will you not go down stairs to day, madam? All the company depart to morrow, and if I might presume to offer my advice, I think you would be amused below? – Ah! my good Tomkins, you too well know that I am not disposed for amusement. But, dear madam, if you would only try, besides every one wishes so much to see you. – But I am not acquainted with any of the persons who are there. That is of little consequence; they have heard you mentioned, and are impatient to see you. – They have all questioned me, why does not your lady appear – Is it because she is ill? Why does she conceal herself – Is it because she is ugly? And, when I answered this question with disdain,[50] it redoubled their curiosity. – And do you imagine I shall quit my retirement to please such beings? – Ah, said little Frances, do tell mama who that pretty gentleman is, who wishes more than any body to see her; who played with me, and gave me sweetmeats. That is Sir Edmond Burton, replied Tomkins, the nephew of Mrs. B. He is as handsome as an angel,[iv] and so affable and obliging to every person: it is true they say he is a very great libertine, but I know nothing of the matter, as I pay no attention to the idle tittle tattle of servants. You are perfectly right, replied her mistress, avoid those conversations as much as possible, if you wish to live in tranquillity. – My cousin appears to be an excellent woman, and as to that, madam, replied Tomkins, it is not what every one here says; for I have already heard such things, but Heaven preserve me from speaking ill of my neighbours. I only wish that you, madam, would consent to amuse yourself a little; when I observe you so often weeping, I feel as if I was ten years older. My good Tomkins, gently replied Malvina, leave me the choice of my amusements I desire, and rest assured, that I experience more delight in my solitude, than I should any where else. Tomkins shook her head without conviction, but not daring to urge her request farther, she retired in silence.

Two days after this conversation,[v] Mrs B. sent to inform her cousin that she should expect the pleasure of her company to take breakfast. Though this invitation was rather a restraint to Malvina, she could not refuse it, and on her going down, she found Mrs. B in the saloon, and breakfast ready. At last, my dear Malvina said she, all my visitors are departed, and I can now enjoy the pleasure of your company. I fear, answered Malvina, it will not suit you, and you will complain, not without reason, if you have no other society than mine.[51] Why do you think so, cousin? you appear very amiable! I am never entirely alone, and I will introduce you at dinner to those who constantly reside with me: but this morning I have reserved you for myself. Malvina felt more constrained than gratified by this attention. She wished to reply, but not having any thing to entertain her cousin with, she was shocked at the idea of a conversation of so many hours to support, and this idea augmented the difficulty. In this disposition, she was seated with a look of sorrow near the fire, before a table, on which was served a profusion of delicacies. – Mrs. B. did not affectedly press her to eat, but only recommended what she thought most agreeable, and endeavoured, by her gaity, to enliven Malvina;[52] who politely acknowledged her kindness, though fatigued by so much attention. She would have preferred neglect to those officious services which did not permit her a moment's respite.[vi] Mrs. B. wished to be thought very polite and affectionate, yet her natural disposition could not be concealed, and her attentions wanted that interesting cordiality which immediately places every one at their ease.[53]

Breakfast over, and the conversation exhausted, Mrs. B. proposed shewing Malvina the castle, which being accepted, she first accompanied her to a saloon appropriated for music, where she observed a variety of instruments of the most elegant kind. From thence, they proceeded to a spacious and well furnished library, which led into a long gallery of pictures: this was kept perfectly dry and warm from flues, which were branched in several directions, and united in one large stove near Mrs. B's. apartment, over which she had constructed a green-house, where every exotic plant and flower,[54vii] were cultivated in the greatest profusion. – Where the rose, orange, and hyacinth, exhaled their perfumes into her dressing room. – This little spot had the walls painted in fresco, representing a grove, intermixed with tufts of flowers, so well represented, that you might imagine you were in the fields.[55] In the lower part of this gay assemblage, was an Ottoman, placed under an alcove, which was half concealed by a crape curtain, and seemed formed for the repose of voluptuousness.

Though Malvina had always been accustomed to affluence in her own country, and also at Lady Sheridan's, yet, never had the reality of such refined luxury struck her sight. It would have seemed incredible even at Paris, or London: what then must it have appeared when she beheld such luxury in the north of Scotland? What, thought Malvina, must such a multiplicity of ornaments, and the whole of what I have seen, have cost, besides the continual care and attention they require? Malvina thought less than half of what had been expended here, would have founded a seminary or hospital; as in so rude a place it would have been an unexpected blessing to the poor. This luxurious retreat, formed a contrast which rather shocked than delighted a reflective mind. – Malvina was absorbed by these ideas, when Mrs. B. as if she had penetrated them, said, my fair cousin, you appear surprised I observe, at what you have seen, not expecting so much luxury in this part of the world, and perhaps condemn me for having bestowed so much of my attention on such things: but, believe me, when I assure you I did not construct this little paradise, till I had founded the most useful establishments: I have in one of the wings of this castle, a school for children; an infirmary for the sick; and a forge, where utensils of every kind are made, which I distribute gratis to the poor inhabitants of my estate. Ah! dear cousin, said

Malvina, much affected, this indeed compensates for the too great elegance of your artificial paradise. We deserve to possess pleasures when we have first considered the welfare of others. But, may I hope to be gratified by beholding these admirable institutions; here I may undoubtedly praise your taste; but it is there only that we can appreciate it to your heart.

Though I wish to oblige you, replied Mrs. B. yet it is a rule which I never trespass on, (and which I have made) never to visit those more frequently than twice in a month; I should be fearful those who superintend them, might arrogate a licence to themselves from my example, when they observed I did not abide by the rules which I had described;[a] therefore, we will wait the appointed day. As you please, replied Malvina, surprized; but may I not be allowed to go there alone? No, my dear, I must not be deprived of the gratification of attending you, as it is a pleasure I promise myself, and you will oblige me, not to go without me.

Malvina was silent, and pressed it no farther, though she could make no particular objection to the manners and conversation of Mrs. B. yet she felt a secret dislike to her, which she could not resist. For though her heart was so ready to excuse the failings of others, yet her mind was endowed with an intuitive power, and rapidity of ideas, that could penetrate in an instant into the secret motives of those who conversed with her, before thought or reflection could arise. So instantaneous is the impression received, that she often condemned herself for these involuntary feelings, yet could not resist their influence, or subdue them. In vain, by the force of reason, did she persuade herself of the injustice she might be guilty of; but the feelings of a heart would not yield to her reason: and if it is easy to deceive our judgment, it is not possible to overcome instinct.

As she was leaving Mrs. Burton, the latter said, my dear Malvina, I sincerely wish that you would consider yourself at home, and candidly inform me if you prefer dining in your own apartment; for though it may appear rather singular, that shall not be considered; as my only wish is to conform to whatever may contribute to your ease and satisfaction. Malvina was almost tempted to accept this agreeable proposal, but a moment's reflection convinced her,[viii] that, as she would be obliged to give a portion of her time to gratify her cousin, she determined to chuse the hour of dinner, as the most convenient; and acknowledging the polite attention of Mrs. Burton, said, she was only fearful her company would be too melancholy, and affect the natural gaity of her party. If it is perfectly agreeable to you, my dear Malvina, I am satisfied; but let it be without the least constraint, or else it will embitter all the pleasure I enjoy in your society? Besides, why should your sorrows be thought disagreeable to me? I am no stranger to grief; do not then, my fair cousin, be fearful of reposing yours in my bosom;[ix] I have suffered sufficient, to feel from experience, what sorrows sensibility is the source of; therefore; you may believe, I can most sincerely sympathise with yours.[x] Malvina believed, and was concerned to hear her cousin had experienced sorrow; but she felt (at the same time) that it was not to such a character as Mrs. Burton's, she would impart hers.[xi]

CHAP. IV.

Some new acquaintances.

This was the first time since Malvina had lost her friend, that she had supported a long conversation; fatigued by the exertion, she was hurrying to her apartment, when, in turning into the gallery, she was saluted by a man who appeared to be about thirty years of age, whose noble figure and appearance pourtrayed the gentleman; she slightly returned his bow, and proceeded. This person, whose name was Prior, was the only one in the castle who had not expressed the least curiosity to see Malvina.[56] He could not, however, but be surprized at the sight of her: the uncommon expression of her pensive countenance,[57] which no one ever beheld, without being interested in her favor. When she had passed, Mr. Prior looked after her till she turned out of the gallery which led to her own apartment;[xii] he stopt for an instant, and could not help dwelling on the idea she inspired, and experienced a sensation of pleasure, in being under the same roof with so apparently amiable and interesting a being.

Mr. Prior was descended from a noble family in Scotland; his parents having many children, and only a slender fortune, had educated him for the profession of a clergyman, which perfectly coincided with his wishes; being passionately fond of study and polite literature; and this allowed him to devote himself to his favourite pursuit. But this was not the best road to gain preferment in the world: selfishness and dissimulation gain far infinitely more than either fine abilities or rectitude:[58] and Mr. Prior, with the most correct principles – a mind highly cultivated, and a heart and morals, the most pure, could not gain a situation which was sufficient to afford him a maintenance. Chance, however, procured him the acquaintance of Mrs. Burton, in a journey she made to Edinburgh. She had sense sufficient to appreciate the merit of such a being as Mr. Prior; and flattered with the idea of gaining a man of noble family to reside with her, she made him the offer of being chaplain to her family, at the castle, with a salary of one hundred guineas per annum. Prejudiced in favour of Mrs. Burton, from her affability and politeness, accompanied by the delightful hope of dedicating all his leisure to study, he accepted her offer with rapture. – Charmed with the solitary and retired situation of his new asylum; his astonishment on beholding the luxuries of its interior, exceeded Malvina's; and the elegance and grandeur of this castle created suspicions in him, which experience soon proved were not without foundation. But he never divulged his opinion of Mrs. Burton to any person: Malvina alone may have the power of gaining his unlimited confidence.

When Malvina went down to dinner, she found in the saloon, Mr. Prior, and two ladies; and who, on entering, regarded her with scrutinizing curiosity. Mrs. B. arose, and met her, then said, permit me, my dear cousin,[59] to introduce you to the friends of my retirement, who will be delighted by the acquisition of your company?[b] First, I will present Mr. Prior, the chaplain of my castle, whose noble birth is his least merit; the duties he so kindly performs here, are infinitely beneath his abilities, and I am thankful his ill fortune allowed him to favour me, by accepting this trifling office. This, continued Mrs. B. turning to an elderly lady about fifty, is Mrs. Melmor, an old friend of my mother's, the widow of a man of quality, who was ruined by a law-suit; she has consented to partake of my solitude, with her daughter, whom you observe with her; this young lady, though only seventeen, is very accomplished, and her talents may be serviceable to your little orphan. Malvina replied with much sweetness, that she should be delighted to enjoy the pleasure the young lady's accomplishments would afford, for her own amusement; but would be extremely sorry to employ one moment of her time in the painful task of instructing an infant, as such a duty ought to devolve entirely on the mother. But, if I am not deceived, Madam, interrupted Mrs. Melmor, this young lady is not your daughter? No madam, replied Malvina, suppressing her tears; but her misfortunes have rendered her dearer to me than a daughter. Ah! I understand – her mother was your friend, and you have adopted this lovely child at her death. I entreat you not to interrogate my cousin on this delicate subject, said Mrs. B. I have never yet dared to mention it; I am but too sensible of the pain it would inflict, was I to touch on the source of those wounds, which time alone can ameliorate. There are such also, said Malvina, which are so deep, that even the wing of time can have no influence over them; they are incurable. Do not despair of any thing, my dear, said Mrs. B. gently kissing her cheek,[60] we shall see some day what my zealous friendship for you can accomplish.

During this conversation, Mr. Prior remained silent, and had been engaged in observing Malvina. Her pale and dejected countenance appeared to him the most interesting in the world, each sentence that she uttered, vibrated to his heart; and he wondered how it was possible any one could wish to interrupt the sweet, soft tone of her voice. He recalled in idea, the most interesting women he had seen, but not one could be compared to Malvina. Miss Melmor was the first who perceived, or at least who noticed, the abstraction of his mind. I am much deceived, said she, if the melancholy of Malvina de Sourcy has not already attached Mr. Prior; and I believe he could at this moment weep with her, at the sombre idea of his future misfortunes. What then will he feel when she relates her sorrows to him? – And why! do you apprehend that I am ignorant of them, replied Mr. Prior, with quickness? Her expression, her air, her physiognomy; are not all these the most eloquent interpreters of grief? Ah! if the unfortunate had only words to express the language of their sorrow, they would never be understood.

Malvina, who had overheard this short conversation, raised her eyes to Mr. Prior, with an expression of approbation: she had not noticed him before, and on observing him, she was prepossessed in his favour. His physiognomy, though grave and severe, at once expressed goodness, and an uncommon share of sensibility, which could not escape the penetrating eye of Malvina. To discover his peculiar character, she must have judged from her own. But this, Miss Melmor could never have discerned, even if she had passed her life with Mr. Prior. During dinner, she questioned Malvina concerning the various amusements of London: I am almost a stranger to them, she replied, as Lady Sheridan never frequented any public amusement, except to please her Lord, which he seldom required; and I never went without her. Ah, my God! replied Miss Melmor, how was it possible she could make so melancholy a use of her liberty, as to deprive herself of balls, public places, and every other amusement? I acknowledge freely, it is all the felicity I desire. Believe me, interrupted Mrs. Burton, it is possible to relinquish them very early; I have enjoyed them in the most unlimited degrees, in my youth: I have been surrounded with all that the most unbounded self-love could wish, or exult in; but I withdrew from these illusions as soon as I experienced their emptiness. I left the world before I was left by it. In vain did its alluring scenes endeavour to recall me to its fleeting pleasures; I resolutely resisted every temptation and persuasion, and determined to consecrate my future days to the real enjoyment of benevolence and friendship: and I find my happiness augmented, since I have persevered in seeking only real pleasures, which my present life can only produce.[61]

Mrs. Melmor was profuse in her eulogiums on the superior wisdom of her friend. Malvina thought them so extravagant, that she was at a loss in what manner to reply, and continued silent particularly when she observed by the expression of Mr. Prior's countenance that he with difficulty suppressed a smile which surprised her, as she had inwardly applauded her cousin. But all these floating images of the mind were soon obliterated by the quick return of the melancholy recollections which corroded her heart; and when the repast was concluded,[62] she obtained permission to retire.

CHAP. V.

The library.

Malvina, not having brought any books with her, went one morning to request her cousin's permission to take one from the library. My dear, said Mrs. B. as I never purchase any, but the best editions, I have made it a rule, never to lend them to my own sex, for in general they are so careless of them: but I shall make an exception in your favor, and you have the liberty to select those that are the most agreeable to you. Malvina thanked her, without being gratified, on receiving a favor so ungraciously conferred; which was only to enhance the obligation, which is sometimes more mortifying than a refusal.

She determined to benefit by this very *great condescension*[63] as seldom as possible. She went to the library on returning to her chamber, and observing that part which contained all the French authors, she looked at them as the friends of her youth. It was with Lady Sheridan,[64] that she had spent the sweetest moments of her life. She wept at the sight of her favorite Montague, her imagination immediately transported her to France[65] under the paternal roof, where she first read his Essay on Friendship.[66] She and her beloved Clara, attentively listened as her father read;[67] at each sentiment that spoke to the heart, their eyes met, and seemed to express, it is there that we shall prove its truth: but their timid lips had not yet uttered this in language. A secret delicacy, the natural attendant of the first sensations of the soul, reserved its ardour in the recesses of their hearts. Astonished and delighted, as their reason expanded, nature all beautiful, nature[c] appeared more so to them, when they together admired her various and wonderful productions. The flowers appeared more brilliant and lovely, when they gathered them for each other. Happy in their affections, they gave themselves up without controul, to the delightful sensations which it inspired, without investigating the source of the felicity they enjoyed. They experienced without interruption, all the innocent delight of that happy age. Friendship, pure and ingenuous, possesses all that delicate reserve, and all the charms that attend the most refined love.[68] These recollections succeeded each other with such rapidity in the mind of Malvina, that each, as it crossed the path of memory, increased her melancholy, and touched every chord of her sensible heart. She mournfully ejaculated, as her tears fell in profusion, Oh! thou first moments of my existence,[d] transporting moments, though so quickly vanished, ever to be regretted, though so transient; yet, how very deep are the traces in the region of memory, and never to be obliterated! While she was yet speaking, the door opened, and Mr. Prior appeared with some books, which he brought to replace. On seeing Malvina, he bowed respectfully, and drew back, with an intention to retire. But Malvina quickly recollecting herself,[69] made a motion with her hand, her heart being too full for utterance; she only said in a low voice, do not let my being here prevent your entrance, I am going. Mr. Prior, observing her as she passed him, with her face averted; joined his hands, and raising them, exclaimed, O Heaven, are these the creatures whom thou chastisest, while the wicked are permitted to prosper,[xiii] and possess every luxury, and even more than their hearts can desire? Affected by this involuntary exclamation, Malvina turned to Mr. Prior, as she was just quitting the library, and her eyes still bathed in tears, Yes, answered she, I have been, and am chastised;[70] yet I flattered myself I had lived innocent, and did not know I deserved so severe a punishment.

Do not murmur, replied he, against that Being, who only knows what is best for us.[71] Supplicate his mercy, and he will listen to, and comfort you; for He resides with the humble and contrite heart. He never conceals his face from the severe trials of the afflicted, and He alone can heal their wounds.[72] I feel and observe, said Malvina, that you are both good and compassionate, and that your habit has not deceived me, when I imagined, you were destined to be the support and comfort of the distressed, and a father to the unhappy. Ah! replied Mr. Prior, if I could flatter myself with so pleasing a hope as that of contributing in the least, to soothe and console your care worn mind, that day alone, would be one of the happiest of my life. I shall seem in your eyes, perhaps, one of the weakest of those confided to your care, replied Malvina, but I accept with gratitude your pious endeavours; they may probably[73] teach me, to support this living death, which seems to have left me alone in the world. It is not in me that you will find it, said Mr. Prior, but in the sublime recollection, which has been the only consolation of all Christians,[74] which is the hope of immortality; the anchor of the soul in this tabernacle of dust,[75] where we are incessantly endangered, and buffetted by the storms of passion.[e] Death is only changing our earthly dwelling; endeavour to detach your regards as much as possible from this vale of misery, and elevate them to that resting place, which was not constructed by the hands of men: but which will continue to all eternity: and there continued he, (his voice faultering from sympathy and feeling)[76] you will again meet, and be re-united to your much-loved friend.

Ah! replied Malvina, I feelingly acknowledge your conversation is a consolation to me! I certainly never had a doubt, that if we had been created for this life only, God would never have made us to be unhappy. When I reflect on the sublime state to which we are destined, (if deserving) my heart ceases to murmur; and I am overpowered with the deepest gratitude. This sentiment, which you have awakened, I shall reflect on with pleasure; and am sincerely grateful for the satisfaction your conversation has afforded me.

Malvina, delighted in having found a friend who could understand her, promised herself much pleasure in the society of Mr. Prior, and went to dinner with more satisfaction. She found Mrs. Melmor in the saloon, seated at an embroidering frame, and her daughter, reading a pamphlet, who, as Malvina came up to her, hastily closed it. Well Kitty, said her mother, shall you be ready to give Mrs. Burton an account of what she gave you to read? Certainly mama, and if she does not require more from others, than she does from herself, I think I shall deserve some praise. – But those who wish all for themselves, never have any to bestow on others. What is that you say, Kitty? – You forget whom you are speaking before?[77] Indeed mama, I do not know how you bear continual contradiction, but as to myself, the life one leads here, and the lectures I am constrained to hear, renders it so tiresome, that I cannot any longer disguise it.

And why should you, said Malvina? pleasure and gaity are the concomitants of your age, and Mrs. B. is too just to be offended at your little murmurings. If she must be astonished, cried Miss Melmor, speaking very quick, it is not in my power to lessen her surprise, but, can she ever forgive the unpardonable fault of my being displeased in her house? She is already but too willing to render me the object of her caprice, and more so, since Sir Edmond Burton was last here, because he particularly noticed me. Not that I value the preference of Sir Edmond, as I well know what an inconstant he is; he is not capable of loving any woman, as he pays the same attention, and the same compliments to all, that he does to me. But was he even to become otherwise, which I do not think possible,[78] am I not perfectly certain, that Mrs. Burton would never permit her nephew to make any other choice than the person whom she has selected; and you will see, mama, that the fortune[79] she has promised me, will be given on no other condition, than my marrying the man whom she may think most proper for me. Her mother seized the first moment she stopped to breathe, by desiring her to be silent, in a tone at once emphatic and commanding. Be silent, Kitty, and learn to respect the generous friend who has given us an asylum. Ah! my good mama, how wonderfully scrupulous you are just now, replied her giddy daughter, have I not heard you say, a thousand times more? That may be, said Mrs. Melmor, colouring with anger, but you will allow I knew to whom I was speaking.

I hope, madam, said Malvina, gravely, you do not suspect that I shall make an improper use of what I have heard? I may be astonished, but that is all. I believe, I undoubtedly believe you, replied Mrs. Melmor, much softened: a person who possesses so many virtues, cannot want discretion. – Yet, I wish to break my daughter of speaking so freely before persons whom she does not know; for you must be sensible how guarded we ought to be, when we complain of those to whom we owe every thing. No, madam, I never have felt that sensation, replied Malvina, cooly, for I think we should never even wish to receive any thing from those we do not esteem. Mrs. Melmor was just going to answer, when Mrs. Burton entered.

Good day, my dear friends, said she, I am charmed to find you together, and regret that I have lost so many pleasing moments of your company; but I hope at least, I was present in your remembrance. Did you think of me? Can you doubt it, replied Mrs. Melmor, in the softest tone possible? Are you not the soul of us all? These flattering words obtained a gracious smile from Mrs. B. and a look of contempt from Malvina. At this instant, Mr. Prior entered with a roll of papers in his hand. What have you brought us, enquired Mrs. Burton? All the gallic poetry I could collect, madam. Oh! dear, interrupted Miss Melmor, how can you have the patience to read[80] all those dull rhodomantades?[81] And how can you bestow such an epithet on the sublime works, which have immortalised the name of Ossian,[xiv] cried Mr. Prior? Is there such an instance in memory, of any one, who, in the midst of such wild mountains, has rendered his genius so known: for when the hand of desolating time, shall have destroyed every other vestige, they will remain to tell the tale of other times. He surely may be termed the Sun of ancient Caledonia,[82] since no one can extinguish those rays of glory which beam from the illustrious son of Fingal?[83] Are you not afraid? What, that the spirit of the hills, mounted on a courser of vapour, should transfix me with his meteor lance, interrupted Miss Melmor, with a satirical laugh. No really, not I indeed; when the evening draws in, and the winds howl through the dark forest, the meteors rise from the bosom of the lake; the dogs bark in the lower court; all these, I suppose, denote the anger of Ossian, which I am to be frightened at.[84]

Miss Kitty, said Mrs. B. with some hauteur, in speaking of such works, it requires a mind capable of feeling their beauties; you likewise should have read much more of it than you have, before you attempt to criticise. In that case, said Miss Melmor, in a whisper, leaning towards Malvina, she had much better not say any thing. Without having heard this, Mrs. Burton was shocked at the action; and Mrs. Melmor, who observed the displeasure of her friend, endeavoured to soften it, by accusing her daughter first. I have frequently told you, my dear Mrs. Burton, that your uncommon indulgence to Kitty, would produce a bad effect; but you would never believe me, and between ourselves, if your complexion and beauty, could permit us to suppose it, you would be the most likely to be taken for her mother, as the affections of your heart are so lively and generous. It is indeed your own fault,[85] my dear Mrs. Burton, allow me to say so, with that frankness which is so natural to my character. We are not always capable of controuling our feelings, my dear, replied her friend, it is only those who possess exquisite sensations, that do not wish to check them, and who are ever the victims of their sensibility.

Does Madame de Sorcy know the work we are speaking of, enquired Mr. Prior? at the same time presenting her the collection he had brought. I have read the French translation. You do not then know Ossian? You would not know him, even after you had read that of Macpherson,[86] nor that I have here: if difficulties are not repulsing to you, permit me the pleasure of instructing you in the Erse language,[87] that you may, when the fine weather commences, hear the descendants of Morven,[88] sing the exploits of their fathers, in all the purity of their native language. Malvina accepted this proposal with infinite pleasure; Mrs. Burton also said, she should be very happy to take some lessons, and would therefore the next morning, meet her cousin and Mr. Prior, in the library.

In the evening, Mrs. Burton received a letter, which apparently interested her very much; she read it several times, and often looked at Miss Melmor with displeasure. Malvina being near her, heard her in a low voice, say, what can be the reason of his coming here again? At last, after a long pause, she folded the letter, and said Edmond informs me, that he will be here in a few days. Really, cried Miss Melmor, in a tone of transport; Mrs. Burton looking at her with severity, added, I imagine that he comes on purpose to consult me relative to some particulars concerning his marriage with Lady Summerhill; as I hope he will at last submit to my pleasure, as he must be sensible of the advantages which he will derive from such an establishment: I do not suppose any person here will have the temerity to endeavour to persuade him otherwise. Miss Melmor blushed, and her mother looked at her with apprehension: Mr. Prior was absorbed; and Mrs. B. appeared much agitated: Malvina remained the only indifferent person in the company.

Punctual to the appointment of the next morning, in the library, Malvina found Mr. Prior. They conversed while waiting for Mrs. B. with so much earnestness, that it did not appear late; she soon after sent, to beg she might be excused for a few days, as she had not time this morning, and the two following[89] were appropriated to visit the public establishments in the castle. Malvina sent to inform her she would attend her, and was preparing to retire, when Mr. Prior detained her, by saying, why are you going so soon? I think I have been here a long time (cried she) perhaps you may think so, but the moments that I have passed with you, are so sweet, that they are as fleeting as the morning vapours, and fade like the rose, before the orb of day.[90] I assure you, Mr. Prior, that I enjoy great pleasure in your society; and if it is true that confidence can afford some consolation to sorrow, I believe it is from you only, that I shall receive it, during my residence here. As to the other persons who are in the castle, said Mr. Prior, I do not even value their good opinion; but, if it is from a congeniality of mind, and not only from a comparison with others, then I shall esteem it as one of the greatest blessings Heaven can bestow on me.

Malvina was surprised at what she heard. The expression of humility and modesty, which Mr. Prior possessed, did not appear to coincide with that opinion of superiority, which he seemed to have; and while she was reflecting what reply she should make, and endeavouring to develop this seeming paradox; the expression of her countenance informed Mr. Prior of the purport of her soliloquy. He hastily replied to her thoughts – you are astonished, I observe, at the idea I appear to entertain of myself, and you are tempted to accuse me of vanity; but it will not be long before you acknowledge your mistake, and you will be sensible that I have a right to assert, that wit alone can never understand your character; and that your soul ought not to open itself, unless it met a congenial one. Malvina, more and more astonished at a conversation, which seemed to accuse Mrs. Burton of insensibility, particularly from a man who ought to consider her as his benefactress, could not solve this seeming inconsistency in the character of Mr. Prior: and was on the point of withdrawing her esteem from him; when reading in her eyes the various emotions which agitated her, he said with quickness, in the name of Heaven, madam, suspend your opinion, and do not abuse the uncommon ascendency you have gained over me; and judge me not with such undeserved severity. I do not know how it has happened, that I have involuntarily betrayed a secret, which my most intimate friends, with repeated inquiries, have never been able to draw from me: and it has escaped me, before you, who never asked it. But this fault if it is one, must not be attributed to me; it is only from the confidence you have inspired; and it is only to you, that I should be guilty of such an indiscretion, as there is no other but yourself in the world, who can reproach me with such a fault.

Bad as your extenuation is, sir, replied she, perhaps I am the last that ought to think it so? And the confidence you repose in me, though premature, and perhaps imprudent, does not permit me the right of blaming her, who is the object of it: and if I do not censure you, how can you clear yourself from being unjust? Is it the generous Mrs. Burton, the benefactress of all who surround her, that we ought to accuse with wanting a soul; of being void of sensibility. She who has despised and relinquished the vain pleasures of the world, that she might, by her affluence, spread comfort, and mitigate the severe destiny of the miserable inhabitants of this wild retreat. Does not this evince a noble and exalted principle of humanity and benevolence? If I cannot yield her my confidence, believe me, I rather attribute it to the difference there is between us, (a difference entirely to her advantage) than to the cause to which you seem to allude.

Amiable woman, exclaimed Mr. Prior, his eyes suffused with tears, I should have been deceived in you, if you had not thought thus, at the same time, I shall be extremely deceived, if Mrs. Burton does not think the grief you feel and express, is merely the desire of being thought interesting: – for can we doubt the general ruling principle, that every one judges of another by their own heart.

If that is sufficient, replied Malvina, rising, I am still ignorant perhaps, of the motive of your unjust prejudice; but I shall be fearful, that I may imbibe a little, if I listen to you any longer. Permit me to say, that while I witness the excellent actions of Mrs. B. to all who surround her, even to those who condemn her,[91] I must be unjustly prejudiced, to be blind to her merit. I am not ungrateful, madam, replied Mr. Prior, in a serious accent, I am not even severe; when you have observed more minutely, perhaps I may gain a place in your favor, and you may perhaps regret the severe invective which you have conferred on me. On saying this, he immediately retired; Malvina remained confounded. Whatever proofs there were of Mr. Prior's being unjust, the pain she was conscious of having inflicted, which was not natural to her character voluntarily to do, created a sensation of sorrow to her heart, which oppressed it – by the idea only. In the course of the evening, she attempted to apologize to him, for the severity of which she had been guilty in the morning; but he only answered with distant politeness: appeared thoughtful, absorbed, and retired early to his own apartment.

CHAP. VI.

The hospital.

The next day Malvina, her cousin, and Mr. Prior,[xv] visited the infirmary, the school, and the forge. She took little Frances with her, that she might at that early age, imbibe in her heart, the sweet and gentle sensations of pity and benevolence. She was delighted with the order and regularity which she observed in the different establishments which she surveyed. But she marked with peculiar surprise, that the presence of Mrs. Burton, instead of creating the pleasure which she expected, appeared to inspire only the sensations of fear. She was saluted with respect, instead of the warm effusions of gratitude; and the countenances of the unhappy beings who surrounded her, had more expression of terror, than the look of satisfaction, which expecting a favor, or receiving one, (if graciously conferred)[92] generally produces.

Mrs. B. on her part, appeared more as if she was performing a task, than giving or receiving pleasure. She passed with the utmost indifference through the wards of the sick; and if she passed any one a question, it seemed rather with a design to make them remember who she was, than to evince any interest in their welfare. She questioned them, without waiting for their answers. Every person appeared under a restraint; no one daring to complain, or relate their sufferings to a person, who evinced so little inclination to listen to them.

In this manner they soon made a tour through all the apartments. They were going out, when on stepping back to speak to her cousin, she observed a poor woman, who by her gestures, endeavoured to make herself understood.[93] Malvina being perfectly ignorant of the dialect; they observed the expression of her countenance, which pourtrayed goodness and feeling, while her soft voice, and the gentleness of her look, made each person feel encouraged, when she was near them, because she appeared willing to listen to their sorrows; for the language of the heart, has but little occasion for words, to be comprehended, when it is written on the index of the countenance. Mrs. Burton quickly came up to her, and observing Malvina give some money to the poor woman, who thanked her for the gentle manner with which she presented it, infinitely more than the gift itself, said with visible displeasure, cousin, all the unfortunate persons whom I receive here, are perfectly well taken care of, and have no occasion to receive alms from a stranger. Besides, if we give to one or two,[94] all will expect it: and it is impossible by chance, to select the most deserving. I should not have supposed, madam, replied Malvina, there was any necessity for reflecting on so simple an action. This poor creature appeared to suffer more than the others, she seemed endeavouring to make me understand her afflictions; and I wished to soften them if possible.[95]

But do you know, replied Mrs. Burton, with some haughtiness, that this is the first time any stranger whom I have conducted here, thought it proper to follow their inclinations in that point, or to swerve from the rules I have established, without first obtaining my permission. I should have supposed madam, said Malvina, that I was only following your example, and therefore did not wait for the permission to perform a good action. During this dialogue, the poor woman understood that Mrs. Burton was displeased with her cousin, for having given her money; and offered to return it; when Malvina, with quickness replied, no, I will never take it again, and should have hoped, that in an asylum, dedicated to benevolence, I should not for the first time in my life have been forbidden to assist the unfortunate. Mrs. B. felt the force of this reproof, and without answering her cousin, she drew her purse, and gave the poor woman double the sum she had received from Malvina. But the gifts of vanity, as well as those of virtue, have each their price; and the poor woman would have relinquished what Mrs. Burton had given her, for one simple mark of compassion from Malvina.

During the remainder of this visit, Malvina was sensibly hurt by the air of constraint she observed on every countenance. On entering the school, she left Mrs. Burton to converse with the master; and went into the garden, where she observed several little girls seated in a circle. The eldest stood up in the center of her companions, and was singing them a song. Malvina approached this little group, making a sign for them to continue their amusement. They at first appeared intimidated, but her looks soon encouraged them, and the little songstress even ventured to take her hand, requesting her to be seated.

Malvina consented, and taking the child on her knee, she enquired how she came to speak such good English, while her companions were scarcely to be understood?[96] It is my Godfather who teaches me, madam, when he is here, and when he is not, he pays my master for speaking to me sometimes. And who is your Godfather, my dear? Sir Edmond Burton,[97] madam, it is he who has given us such nice Sunday clothes: he never comes here without bringing me something. But if he bestows every thing on you, does it not make your companions jealous? Oh no, madam, he never forgets any of us. He gave that handkerchief to Peggy, which she has on, that petticoat to Molly, those scissars to Suky; it is he who buys us all our nice things. If your Godfather is so good, you ought to love him very much? And so I do madam, dearly, I am only happy when I see him, he takes me on his lap as you do madam, every body is so happy when he is here.

They have reason,[98] added Mr. Prior, who had just placed himself behind Malvina. Sir Edmond has very great vices; but he is truly benevolent, and were it not for the gifts, which he so kindly bestows here, these poor establishments would want for almost every thing.

I have been waiting for you this hour, said Mrs. Burton, joining her cousin. At the sight of her, the children immediately disappeared, with the swiftness of a flight of birds; except the little girl whom Malvina retained: and who seemed to experience less fear on the sight of Mrs. B. from being near Malvina. Who surprised at her confidence, rudely disengaged her from Malvina, saying, that her master wanted her. The little girl, taking Malvina's hand, kissed it with fervour; and flew to join her companions. Frances, who had been much delighted with her, ran to prevent her going, and the little girl, as if dubious whether to return, stopped. When Mrs. B. who could no longer conceal her impatience, said to Malvina; cousin, desire Miss Sheridan to return, and be advised in future not to permit her to set such an example, as it will prevent the children from performing their duty.

When it interferes with the interest of others, Malvina could repress injustice by a pertinent and severe reply; but when it only regarded herself, the uncommon goodness of her heart, prevented her answering in that manner; and she only said to Mrs. Burton, do not be fearful, madam, of my giving a bad example to Frances; I think on the contrary, that by encouraging her to join in the innocent recreations of these children, I shall teach her on some future day, to excite them by her example, to prefer study to play.

From the school, they went to the forge, and Mrs. Burton there also found reason to blame Malvina, as she examined every thing with attention, and assisted by Mr. Prior, questioned all the workmen; and shewed she was interested in all she saw. Her peculiar beauty, and the dignity of her manners, lent a fascinating charm to the gentleness of her questions. She enquired the name of each, informed herself of the number of their children, and their means of providing for them. In the midst of this burning furnace, surrounded by the poor workmen, covered with tatters, scorched and blackened by the smoke and fire, she appeared in their eyes, like an angel from Heaven. They all surrounded her, surprised and delighted at her condescension, in listening to their family details. For though the inhabitants of wild mountains, they were not the less sensible of the pleasure of being noticed with kindness: and Malvina by shewing she was interested in their concerns, raised them to their proper sphere, as fellow-beings, and gave them a sensation of happiness, which all the gold Mrs. Burton possessed, could not afford.

It is thus, thought Mr. Prior, self-love may bestow a benefit, but virtue only knows, in what manner to confer them, with that undefinable sweetness, which only flows from the heart of real benevolence. Self-love acts only by the aid of fortune, but virtue will derive all resources from itself. The one may benefit by gifts; but the other cherishes and administers more happiness, from feeling and sympathy. Thus, while the donations of one demand a gratitude, which is felt as the heaviest and most galling chain, those of virtue receive it from others, as the spontaneous gift of the heart. As Mr. Prior reflected in this manner, he contemplated Malvina with the most respectful sensations – and as her head was turned from him, he melted into tears.[99]

Nothing could escape the watchful jealousy of Mrs. Burton, who imagined she was less esteemed, from the powerful effect Malvina had on every one, and though she was not near her, she perceived this action of Mr. Prior's, and this was sufficient to render her hateful. Come, come, my fair cousin, said she, with an ironical smile, it is time we should be gone, the hours of these workmen are not their own, and while we trespass on them, they are losers; during the time we are conversing with them, and amusing ourselves, they are obliged to suspend their work; and all these idle and useless questions, will not assist them to live. She immediately quitted the place, without waiting for a reply. Malvina followed, but as her cousin walked uncommonly fast, it was some time before she reached her. Mr. Prior being near her, said in a whisper, does Madame de Sorcy still think me guilty, does she not suspect that I might have been capable of judging? Malvina looked at him in silence. Mr. Prior required no other answer, and honored that respectful indulgence, which yet doubted, and that delicacy which feared to censure.

During dinner, Mrs. Burton threw out several sarcasms, against those who had assumed the veil of gentleness, in order to render themselves interesting, and by an affectation of misplaced goodness, succeeded in gaining admiration. Malvina, conscious of not meriting such reproaches, had not an idea of applying them to herself.

But Mr. Prior, who understood her intention, could not resist replying with quickness. – There are sorrows, madam, which are so unaffected, and goodness which is so interesting, that every one must perceive it; and if you attentively examine the world, you will find that such emotions so natural to the heart of man, are never supposed erroneous, but by those alone, who are capable of feigning them. Mrs. Burton was petrified by this reply, it was the first time Mr. Prior had answered her in this manner: the effect this produced, will not be seen here, but in the developement of her character it will be imagined. Malvina surprised at Mr. Prior's conversation, without the least idea of the secret motives which induced it; said with a serious voice, it appears to me, Mr. Prior, that this moment of all others, was the least calculated to establish this opinion; and when so many examples have confirmed, one alone is sufficient to destroy it. On concluding these words, she looked at her cousin, to find if possible, to whom she alluded, with an expression of tenderness, as if she wished to sooth her, for the injustice of which Mr. Prior had been guilty. But he, though afflicted at the opinion she entertained of him, continued to think of her in the most exalted light. Mrs. Burton felt that it was more impossible to pardon the reply of Malvina – than that of Mr. Prior. The one had offended her, but the other she considered as humiliating her in telling so severe a truth. Mr. Prior had satisfied his revenge, in vindicating Malvina; but she had forced her to blush.[100] When goodness has not the power to affect, it irritates. Hatred is augmented by the good it endeavours to use for us, and, of all the sufferings of self-love, the most corroding that it can experience, is, that it never forgives. When compelled to be grateful, by the person with whom it feels this constraint, it is a secret acknowledgment of its inferiority. A long silence ensued after Malvina's reply. – By prolonging it, each person felt more embarrassed, and appeared fearful of interrupting it.

Miss Melmor had scarcely heard what had been said,[101] and her mother endeavoured in vain, to guess from the eyes of Mrs. Burton, what she should attempt to alleviate her anger; though she was conscious she was not the object of her displeasure, she nevertheless felt intimidated, and was fearful of addressing her, though she wished to turn her thoughts from the cause of her chagrin.[102] At that instant the bell rung at the gate, Mrs. Burton listened with uneasiness, and soon heard the noise of horses and a carriage. It is certainly Sir Edmond, exclaimed Miss Melmor, blushing, and rising to go to the window. And suppose it is, said Mrs. B. with severity, is it proper for you to go and meet him? Keep your seat, child, said Mrs. Melmor, delighted at having said what she thought would please Mrs. B. A servant entered, and announced Sir Edmond's arrival. Dinner being concluded, Malvina arose, and requested permission to retire; which Mrs. B. granted in so gracious a manner, that from the preceding conversation, Malvina was surprised at the look of complaisance which accompanied her consent.

CHAP. VII.

An explanation.

Towards evening, Malvina was preparing to go down, when Mrs. B. entered her apartment. My dear cousin,[103] said she, in a voice of kindness, the eagerness which you evinced to leave us, on the arrival of Sir Edmond, convinces me of the repugnance which you have to worldly company. Do not imagine that I blame you; no, on the contrary, it appears to me so natural in your situation, that I will do every thing in my power to indulge you in it; consequently you are perfectly at liberty to remain alone all the time Sir Edmond continues here, and I have already given orders that you may be attended in your own apartment. You are very good, madam, replied Malvina, a little surprised, but I had much rather go down, than encrease the trouble which this will occasion. No, no, my dear,[104] you know that it is one of my first pleasures to gratify the tastes of all my friends, and I had rather deprive myself the pleasure of your society, during the short stay of Sir Edmond, than constrain your liberty. Thus then the affair is settled. No compliments, added she, interrupting Malvina, (who was attempting to speak) I am perfectly convinced of its being agreeable to you, and not any thing in the world shall prevent me from sacrificing my wishes or pleasure to the gratification of my friends. Saying this, she departed, without waiting for Malvina's reply, who could not help thinking her cousin's behaviour rather singular. But as the proposal was really agreeable to her, she acquiesced with pleasure, and never troubled herself to investigate the cause.

Consequently she arranged every thing, that she might not leave her retreat, and spent all her time, between her little charge, and her books. She enjoyed with one, a satisfaction which gratified her heart; from the other, nourishment for her mind: and in this seclusion, she experienced the sweetest moments she had tasted since her arrival at the castle.

Two days had elapsed with rapidity; on the third, in the evening, she heard a gentle rap at her door, which Tomkins having opened, Mr. Prior appeared, he approached Malvina with apparent embarrassment. Will Madame de Sorcy pardon me, for thus intruding on her solitude? as you manifested a desire of taking some lessons in the Erse language,[105] I imagined, it perhaps might be more agreeable when you are thus secluded. I have brought a clear and concise abridgment of the different grammars, which I have digested, in order to lessen the trouble of the first difficulties. If you will allow me the pleasure of attending you every day, I shall esteem myself happy in affording you all the instruction in my power? On the conclusion of this request, he hesitated, as if he had expressed a desire, which might not meet her approbation.

Malvina, truly grateful for the pains he had taken, replied (with vivacity) I am sensible of your kindness, Mr. Prior, and I anticipate, much pleasure from the instruction you promise me, provided Mrs. Burton is not offended at our not waiting for her attendance. Mrs. B., madam,[xvi] in a moment of caprice, imagined she had a desire to learn, but I who know her so well, can assure you, that if you only begin when she does, you will never get farther than the first lesson. I hope, returned Malvina, for my cousin's sake, the assurance you give me of knowing her so well, is a little exaggerated? But I will relinquish this subject, for I have had many reasons to see on this point, we shall never agree, or understand each other.

Pardon me, madam, replied Mr. Prior, seating himself near her; but your esteem is so necessary to me, that it is impossible not to defend myself against the accusation you retain of me in your heart: and Mrs. Burton is too great a stranger to you for me to imagine, I shall wound you in describing her as she really is. Stop, Mr. Prior, interrupted Malvina, when it is to abuse the confidence, to unveil the errors of those we see every day, and may I not add, a want of delicacy, when it regards those we live with? I grant it would be so, he answered, Ah! if I had not been chained here, can you suppose, that from the moment I had known Mrs. B. I would have continued in this place a day longer? But who has forged chains for you here? asked Malvina with eagerness. I will inform you, madam. I have been anxious to communicate all my thoughts to you, which I hope you will impute to the real motive, which is, that your physiognomy arrests my confidence, and the interest you have created in me, has been so lively and peculiar, that I hope you will not determine to refuse to hear me.

He pronounced these words with so much emotion, that they awakened a tender recollection in the soul of Malvina; she thought she once again heard the voice of friendship, she felt the full force of this sweet remembrance: and it occasioned her tears to fall in profusion. Mr. Prior, replied Malvina, in an affecting tone, it is exactly thus that Lady Sheridan would have expressed herself. Ah! is it possible, cried he, what, can I recall her to your imagination; ah, if I could gain the felicity of inspiring in your mind, only the smallest portion of the interest she created, then would the hand of friendship endeavour to mitigate the poignancy of your sorrow; and if those eyes, which are so often raised to Heaven, could sometimes bend their looks towards the Earth, and condescend to mingle their tears with mine, for the friend of your youth. – Ah! what an unexpected blessing would this bestow on my existence. Perhaps you might also find a trifling benefit from this participation, for the confidence is soothing at all times: and that of a friend, will sometimes supply the place of a brother.[106] That place which Clara possessed in my heart, can never be filled, replied Malvina; but believe me, 'till now you are the only being with whom I could weep: this preference I cannot account for, as I know so little of you. And that little, appears to merit so small a share of your esteem, interrupted he, smiling: – but perhaps you may form a different opinion when I resume the discourse, which the agitation of my heart obliged me to suspend.

It is now three years since I arrived here, prepossessed in favor of Mrs. Burton I thought her exactly what she appears to you; that is good, generous, and much superior to her sex in virtue, and elevation of mind: and I had flattered myself with the pleasing prospect, which residing near her afforded. The sumptuous elegance of this retreat, first occasioned my opinion to faulter, but did not entirely destroy the enthusiasm I entertained of her character. At this juncture, one of my brothers, whose affairs were very much deranged, was arrested for debt; my father and mother would have parted with most of their property to extricate him, but that not being sufficient, I addressed myself to Mrs. B. and informed her of his situation; and she consented to advance three years of my salary:[f] delighted with her generosity, I joyfully signed the agreement of remaining three years with her, and never imagined I should have reason to repent it, but I was soon undeceived. As soon as she was assured I could not leave her, from that moment her behaviour was totally altered: I no longer experienced that gracious affability which had won my respect: in its stead, she assumed a capricious despotism. I could not stoop to this galling yoke; and therefore, the first opportunity, I desired her permission to leave the castle, giving her a promise of payment for what she had advanced, and all I could save from my labour: – both which she rejected with haughtiness, shewing me the paper, the contents of which she had dictated, and in the effusion of my gratitude, I had signed without reading. I now found by this, that she had a right to detain me, and that I should forfeit my honor and good name, if I left this castle without her consent. I therefore reluctantly resigned myself to my destiny; but from that moment my eyes were opened, and I saw Mrs. Burton's real character. As I had the happiness of liberating my brother, I endeavoured to be content; and I declare to you, in the name of that friendship, which united you to Lady Sheridan, that you are the only person who has even suspected the judgment I had formed of her, and I certainly estimate the blessing granted me for my prudence, and the tedious pains I have endured, that I have at last found a heart which can sympathise with mine.

Your destiny affects and interests me, sir, replied Malvina, and I acknowledge my cousin has given you reason to complain of her. How can you explain her want of generosity with respect to you, when it is contrasted by that benevolent profusion, of which she is so prodigal to all who surround her?[107] – The good which she performs is infinitely less than it appears; the establishments which you have seen are in want of every thing. – She knows it, and will not relieve them: provided it is known and said, that she supports and comforts the unhappy, it is of little consequence to her whether it is so in reality.

But, interrupted Malvina with quickness, if benevolence did not instigate her, what motive could she have for fixing her residence in these rude mountains? – Self-love I fear has been the only motive and sole mover of that action. She hoped, that by forming asylums of benevolence, near a fairy palace, in the barren mountains of the Highlands,[108] her name would be celebrated. It was the design of an enlightened selfishness that occasioned her to erect hospitals, though they are in want of necessaries. It was this which ornamented these apartments with such profusion; it is thus that the ostentatious monuments of self-love always retain their peculiar impression, and the more they endeavour to resemble virtue, the more they are convinced,[109] that it is impossible to equal the lovely original.

Gracious Heaven, exclaimed Malvina, how very severe you are in your observations! Add also, said Mr. Prior, that they are just, madam, and allow that your own instinct is the occasion of your feeling an interest in the character of Mrs. Burton? I do not deny that my partiality for her is not equal to the esteem I think she deserves; but you must acknowledge, sir, that notwithstanding the vanity with which you have accused her, in other respects, it is impossible for any one to have less, on account of her person: for to listen to her you would imagine that she was much older, and less handsome than she appears.

When we cannot any longer hope to receive praises on the part of beauty, we endeavour to obtain it, by feigning ourselves above it, replied Mr. Prior; but rest assured this uncommon humility is only exhibited, in order to be contradicted: we are seldom the dupes of those who depreciate themselves more than usual; and candour is the last qualification we should believe she possessed. I have observed, and am certain, that when the habit of adulation is once excited, that we had rather find fault, than allow self to be forgotten. Thus you observe, she has transported all the vices of society into this retreat, and though we may call it living alone, she still lives in the world. For does not ambition govern her even here; is she not agitated and distressed for fear the union between Sir Edmond and Lady Summerhill should not take place? and her hatred toward Miss Melmor, because this young man has paid her a great deal of attention? In short, may we not apply this passage in scripture to her;* that riches have been her inheritance, but she has forgot the hand which bestowed them, and has sacrificed only to the world: it is for this reason, that when occupied by mirth and gaiety, her heart is gloomy, and all her joys end in satiety and ennui.[110]

Mr. Prior, replied Malvina (smiling) the scripture which you quote, also desires us to acquire that charity which thinks no evil, which disposes the mind to indulgence, without degenerating into credulity: and if we observe an error, not to consider it as a crime.[111] Mr. Prior blushed, and Malvina convinced him, that one of the first precepts of his station was to spare his neighbours, as in

* First of Proverbs

that case he was more guilty than any other, of judging without lenity. But the impression was received, and the injustice of which he had been the victim, had soured his temper, and given a rigid severity to his disposition, which he could not now correct. While they were discussing this point, the supper bell rung, and they were astonished to find with what rapidity time had winged his flight, while they were conversing.

Mr. Prior had never known moments of felicity equal to these enjoyed in her society since his existence, and begged permission to visit her the next day, that they might renew the conversation, or begin the first lesson. Malvina, who had felt when with him a confidence, which had some affinity to that she experienced for Lady Sheridan, consented with pleasure.

The following days, Mr. Prior was admitted, and passed some hours with her, which appeared to him only as moments which vanished with the rapidity of lightning. In contemplating and hoping to possess the friendship of Malvina, and conversing on that subject,[112] he felt a happiness he never experienced even an idea of, as it appeared to him as a foretaste of and resembled those celestial joys, which are reserved for the virtuous in an immortal state.[113] As to Malvina, it is not to be wondered at, if she was perfectly ignorant of the consequences which might result from such an intimacy. For it is age less than character, which gives this experience, and such a character may at the age of twenty-five[114] know less than any other at eighteen. A woman endowed with a tender heart and a lively and pure imagination may live long in the world without knowing this. For it exists entirely in the difference of character, and that instinctive difference which prompts each to judge of others by themselves, and it is this which forces them from error to error, drives them from misfortune to misfortune, and makes them live half their lives in a world of chimeras, of their own forming, without perceiving them.

It is difficult to be convinced, and very painful when forced to be so! What then must it be with such a character as Malvina's, who had passed her youth with a being similar to herself, both possessing the same sentiments. This union of their hearts, when confirmed by the judgment of the mind, so entirely absorbed them, and they were so happy in their affection for each other, that they lived in the world without observing those around them, or troubling themselves to investigate their actions.

Who could be astonished at their inexperience, without feeling a sensation of pity, on beholding them the dupes of their own hearts? Malvina, in the innocence of hers, had not an idea that there was reason to blame the visits of Mr. Prior. Being a stranger to love, she had not a thought that she could inspire such a sentiment; besides, his being a priest, and a Roman Catholic,[115] like herself, would have been sufficient to banish any doubts of that kind, had it been in her nature to conceive them.

CHAP. VIII.

An interview.

Eight days had elapsed with unusual swiftness, since Malvina had remained in her own apartment, during which time, she had never once seen Mrs. Burton. She was fearful she might give offence, if she any longer secluded herself, and determined to make her a visit before breakfast. – She went to her chamber, and knocking at her door, the maid informed her that Mrs. Burton was then dressing, but would see her in half an hour. Malvina requested they would acquaint her when Mrs. B. was to be visible, and on her return, she passed through the music-room, and seeing some French songs lying near a harp, she stopped to look at them. – The contemplation of these songs in her native language – that language, in which she had expressed her first sentiments, had so powerful an attraction over her, that she could not resist the impulse of reading them; and that she might understand them better, she seated herself before the harp, and accompanied it with her voice: suddenly she heard the soft notes of a German flute, which attended her. – Astonished, she turned her head, and perceived behind her chair, a young man whom she had never seen. She blushed, and would have retired, but he intreated she would not deprive him of the pleasure of hearing her sing. She raised her eyes to him who thus intreated, and cast them down immediately, blushing a deeper shade. It was one of those countenances where the fire of wit was tempered, and united with sensibility, and which could not be looked at twice with impunity.

The innocent Malvina was unconscious of the danger; and the cause which should have tempted her to retire, was the very reason which prompted her to stay. But, if the looks of Sir Edmond had so agreeably surprised her, how shall I describe what he felt on beholding her? He had heard Malvina at a distance, he drew near, listened to that voice which vibrated through his heart, and first taught him that she had one.[116] She turned, and the charm was fixed. Her beautiful light brown hair,[117] flowing in soft ringlets over her shoulders; her pure white skin, resembled the white rose, blended with a slight tinge of the carnation bloom of youth, but so faintly, that it left the eye uncertain of the real colour; her lovely white neck appeared more white, when contrasted by her dark robes; her mild dark eyes were shaded with long silken lashes, which veiled those chaste and expressive looks,[118] which ever interested the heart. Her timid modesty, astonished and enchanted him. – A new world appeared to open to him, and he indulged, without reserve, the delightful idea it occasioned, provided Malvina would enjoy it with him.

These moments so enchanting,[119] were too confused to be analysed: an impression of this kind produces sensations so extremely fascinating, that by an invisible instinct we are fearful of imbibing any thing which can alter or destroy them and we wish to remain inconscious of its existence, that its duration may be lasting. – From its birth, the other powers of the soul retire, as if from respect, fearful of intruding on the sovereign who unites with, yet reigns over them all. Malvina was near her chair, but appeared undetermined whether to reseat herself, when at that instant, Mrs. Burton entered the room.

She betrayed much surprise on perceiving Sir Edmond. Then addressing Malvina in an ironical manner; she said, I hurried, my dear cousin,[120] to prevent you the irksomeness of waiting for me; but I mark with pleasure, that you have found means to prevent it. On hearing this, Malvina acquainted Mrs. Burton with all the particulars of this chance meeting.[121] – Oh, it was all chance, retorted Mrs. Burton, with quickness! Yes, undoubtedly it was, cried Sir Edmond, and I never thought it so peculiarly so, as at this time. You are perhaps the only one then,[122] added Mrs. Burton, with visible ill-humour. Malvina guessed, and felt her meaning, and wounded by the suspicion, was retiring, without being prevented by her cousin. When Sir Edmond, alarmed at her intention, approached her, saying with eagerness; what, madam, are we going to lose you, and have you only appeared for a moment, that we may suffer from the loss your absence will occasion? Why do you keep thus cruelly secluded and invisible – do you fear, that in affording us that satisfaction, you may be too much adored?

Mrs. Burton coloured with vexation: Malvina blushed also, but not from the same motive; a sentiment sweet, but unknown to her, banished for a moment the gloomy shades of sorrow which had enveloped her, and perhaps, she would have yielded to the persuasions of Sir Edmond, had she not thought it most advisable to decline them, particularly as she perceived it was not agreeable to Mrs. Burton, who continued silent. She therefore withdrew.

Mr. Prior went to visit her early in the afternoon. Do you know, madam, said he, smiling, that your rencontre this morning has had a very powerful effect on Sir Edmond, for he could not speak on any other subject but yourself during dinner? Really, replied she, blushing. It is certainly true; but why should it astonish you? – Whoever sees you but for a moment, must feel themselves interested in all that concerns you. But Mr. Prior, said Malvina, with an air of timidity, how could I possibly be the subject of conversation, what could be said of me, who am a stranger to every one?[123] I am very glad to observe this slight emotion of curiosity, my charming friend, it gives me a hope, that this fatal grief, which threw the veil of indifference over every object, begins to withdraw a little. These words created a deeper blush on the cheek of Malvina, yet, had anyone enquired the cause of it, she would have been at a loss to have explained its origin; for she was unconscious that any motive, except curiosity, had dictated the question. That a secret intimation had occasioned her to blush, she felt as a truth.

Know then, that Sir Edmond asked a thousand questions concerning you, continued Mr. Prior, he wished to know what motive had conducted you here, and why secluded in your apartment, you appeared to shun all the world. Mrs. Burton replied, that many and continued sorrows had undermined the health of Madame de Sorcy, increased her natural timidity, and rendered the world disagreeable to her; and for this reason, she fears and shuns it. I am astonished, exclaimed Sir Edmond, that she should fear to embellish it; there is not any circle which Madame de Sorcy would not ornament! As to myself, I acknowledge I never beheld any one who could be compared with her. Malvina appeared agitated, which Mr. Prior attributed to surprise; you are astonished I perceive, at the freedom of Sir Edmond, to a woman as vain as Mrs. Burton; but I must do him the justice to allow, that notwithstanding the inconstancy of, flightiness of his gossemer[124] taste, his love of pleasure, and all the faults with which he is reproached, yet he has ever preserved his sincerity; and even to Mrs. Burton, whose character he is perfectly acquainted with, and on whom part of his fortune depends, he never condescends to disguise the truth. It is an eulogium on them both, replied Malvina, for it is perhaps, as rare to know and hear it, as to dare to assert it. But he is the only one here who possesses that privilege. It is perhaps the fault of others, interrupted Malvina, that sometimes we are unjust:[125] and when we accuse those of a fault, to whom we are so, we must not be astonished if we are repulsed with ill humour. No, replied Mr. Prior, be assured Mrs. Burton will not permit such liberties from any one, as she does from Sir Edmond, but she acquiesces, because he is the sole object of her ambition; and its accomplishment depends entirely on him. You perhaps know that she has promised to leave him all her fortune, on condition, that he will marry Lady Mary Summerhill, not that she has the least idea that it may contribute to augment his happiness; no, she does not regard so trifling a concern.

But the family of Summerhill is one of the most ancient in Scotland, and likewise possesses the most interest, and is the most favored at St James's.[126] Lord Stafford is the friend to Sir Edmond,[127] and has promised, if the marriage takes place, that he will procure a seat in parliament for him; and will also use his interest[128] to procure a peerage for Mrs. Burton.

These, madam, are the motives which have determined this affair; yet, Sir Edmond appears to comply with great reluctance, though he enjoys but a limited fortune; and very justly prefers his independence to riches and dignities. Without absolutely rejecting the alliance, he postpones it from time to time. The fear that he may relinquish it entirely, by which means she will lose the title, which has been so long the principal object of her desire, forces Mrs. Burton to coincide with, and attend to all he says. This circumstance gives him great power over her, and while he continues here, he performs many excellent actions – particularly compelling his aunt to bestow those gifts[g] on the poor establishments, which she would otherwise spend on herself.[129] I should suppose, Mr. Prior, that a character, who makes so excellent an advantage of his power, ought to be both noble and generous; and I cannot comprehend how so many estimable qualities can be united with the vices which you attribute to him?

Sir Edmond, returned Mr. Prior, had the misfortune, madam, to be his own master too early in life. – Thrown on the world without a guide, he never once endeavoured to restrain his first dissolute inclinations, and they became the source of his future corruption. His soul is certainly great and noble; I have remarked in more than one occasion, that he has carried his love of benevolence to an enthusiastic degree. His word is sacred and inviolable; courageous to temerity, his honor is dearer to him than life, and no power on earth could force him to forfeit his. He is also so disinterested, that he would have sacrificed his small fortune for the satisfaction of enabling his sister to contract a marriage which would have rendered her happy, and to satisfy the scruples of the parties who objected to the marriage on that account.[130]

Well, Mr. Prior, said Malvina, apparently delighted with the description of this character;[131] – Well, madam, and to contrast so many virtues, I must inform you, there resides in him such an inordinate passion for women, joined to such depravity of principles, that though he is just and true to all the world, he seduces and deceives them without remorse. It is not alone an irresistible inclination which forces him to act in this manner; but it is both art and design which he employs – sex is the only attraction. Not the selection of the heart; he is a stranger to every thing but intrigue, which commenced accidentally, pleasure completed, and disgust destroyed! Love – real and refined love, will ever be a stranger to him, its pure and genuine flame can never be felt, or arise in a heart prophaned by debauchery.

During the conclusion of this discourse, Malvina had fallen into a deep reverie, she appeared not to hear Mr. Prior, who, following her example, became absent and thoughtful; when Tomkins hastily opened the door, and enquired if Miss Sheridan was there? I thought she had been with you, replied Malvina, with quickness, and alarmed. I have not seen her since dinner, and I have searched in vain for her, as she is not with Mrs. Burton. Ah, my God, said Malvina, rushing out of the room, and flying from one apartment to another, without finding her. Mr. Prior, who was extremely distressed on the occasion,[132] searched the grounds for her. Malvina continuing under the greatest anxiety, repeatedly called on little Frances, as loud as possible; she heard at last a voice answer, which she recognized was her darling's.[133] She opened several doors, and in the last room, which she had not observed before, she beheld Sir Edmond, with Frances seated on his knee. The pleasure of finding her and the anxiety she had experienced united,[134] created such sensations, that her strength was nearly exhausted; when pale and trembling, she sunk into the first chair which was near the door, and held out her arms to the child, who flew into them, and Malvina pressing her to her bosom, tenderly caressed her.

Sir Edmond approached her with astonishment;[135] saying, am I so unfortunate as to have been the cause of the uneasiness you have experienced – permit me to request your pardon for this involuntary offence? I have found her, replied Malvina, shewing Frances, and I am too happy to complain of any one. Sir Edmond contemplated her in silence, his eyes suffused with tears. This is nature, added he, with vivacity, and it is only in the character where nature and simplicity resides, we can prove its effect:[136] today, he continued, you have taught me, how much she surpasses the unnatural beings who I thought possessed her traits![137] There is no good without truth. – And that truth will bring conviction, replied Malvina; if you go beyond it, we may be led astray. Certainly, replied he, others have said that before you; but no one has ever said it like you. The surprise you have created, can only be equalled by the pleasure of seeing you.[138] But, ah! I hope I have not offended you, madam, added he, on Malvina's rising to retire, as you are going to punish me for being too sincere?

I am too little accustomed to the world to understand such language, and I should have been equally pleased, had I been exempted from receiving these marks of your distinction. As she was going out, Sir Edmond followed her with an agitated air, saying, really do you think it possible to converse with you, with such a disposition as mine, and not be lost? This confession reminded Malvina of what she had heard from Mr. Prior, and she smiled involuntarily; Sir Edmond marked it, adding, I respect your silence too much, to dare to question the cause of that smile, but I imagine some one has given you an odious opinion of me? You may rest assured, returned Malvina, if they have said any evil, they have not concealed any of your good qualities, which far exceeds the bad.

Sir Edmond, who was near her, took her hand,[139] saying, perhaps you wished to believe the one more than the other? Quite the contrary, said Malvina, for when I am speaking of a stranger, I assure you I am ever inclined to dwell on the good, and believe it, in preference to the bad. Certainly I am a stranger to you, replied Sir Edmond, smiling, as she opened the door, when she perceived another door that led to the gallery was also open, which a woman appeared to close, as she uttered a shriek. The voice Malvina thought was Miss Melmor's,[140] but she immediately rejected this idea, on perceiving her enter the room at this instant. Sir Edmond pretended that he had not heard or observed any person, and respectfully bowed to Malvina as she departed.

She went down to Mrs. Burton, where she found Mr. Prior, and related to them, her finding her little darling with Sir Edmond.[141] The latter soon joined them – Malvina felt no inclination to retire, and Mrs. Burton did not think it adviseable to admonish her, though her uneasiness was not the least diminished on seeing her nephew near so charming a woman. For, ever since Malvina's arrival, she had severely repented having received her.[142] It was not the inclination which he possessed for women in general, of which she was fearful; she was conscious also, that

Malvina was endowed with something infinitely superior to that which can attract the senses only: and consequently, made her tremble for the projected union with Lady Summerhill. Notwithstanding this painful idea, she felt it was both necessary and polite in her, not to hurt the independent spirit of this haughty young man, by letting him perceive, that she wished Malvina to be kept secluded. She was perfectly sensible that such a proceeding would be the greatest inducement for him to wish to counteract it, as he would never submit to the will of others.

The most trifling opposition to his wishes, was the surest method of exciting them. It was this which had induced her to artfully persuade him that she had used every endeavour to persuade Madame de Sorcy to join their society, but all in vain, as the peculiar character of her cousin bordered on misanthropic rudeness, which never yielded to kindness or civility. On finding them together in the morning, the fear of having her ambitious views destroyed, had deprived her of the power of suppressing the first emotions of her vexation. On reflection, she recollected, in order to deceive Sir Edmond, it would be necessary to feign an appearance of satisfaction, when it happened that she could not avoid having Malvina with them.

Thus, by suppressing the anxiety she felt, she behaved with uncommon attention and kindness to her cousin, and took infinite pains to render herself amiable, which she was perfectly capable of, when she pleased; but this evening she was particularly agreeable; every one perceived it, and Malvina in particular. Thus, as her self-love was gratified, it rendered her in some degree less fearful, that her schemes might be abortive, and placed her so much at her ease, from her mind being a little relieved, that it gave a grace to all her actions. The spirited and sensible conversation of Sir Edmond, and the instructive and sententious discourse of Mr. Prior, would have rendered it rather too serious, if Malvina had not tempered its effect, by giving it an affecting and interesting turn, proceeding from the pensive tendency of her disposition.[143] As to Mrs. Melmor, she was only the echo of Mrs. Burton, by exclaiming, at the conclusion of every sentence, delightful! charming! and looking round, as much as to say, how will you answer to that? If it had not been for this, her presence would have had no more effect on the company, than if she had been a part of the furniture. Her daughter possessed no other charm for conversation, than what gaiety, with short sentences, afforded, powerful auxiliaries, with those who possess only a superficial mind. She was not the least calculated to join in a serious and continued conversation. She was also extremely fond of ridiculing all those whom she observed were partial to such rational amusement; and for some time, Mr. Prior and Madame de Sorcy, were the objects of her raillery. She hoped to have gained Sir Edmond to join her, as she well knew his talent for satire, which is rarely united with stability and goodness.

But his knowledge was extensive, and he was in possession of so great a share of good sense, as well as wit, that he could adapt his humour to the company, and be as serious in the world, as in solitude. She perceived this with vexation, and was also irritated by the pleasure he appeared to enjoy in conversing with Malvina, as it obliged her to remain silent. She sat pouting in a corner, and though Malvina frequently addressed her in discourse, she scarcely returned her an answer, and the tone and manner of her reply determined Malvina not to address her again.

At last Miss Melmor, tired of performing a part so unnatural to her character, arose with visible ill humour, and seated herself before the piano, which was at the other end of the room, and performed several pieces. Malvina was the first who went to hear, commending her taste and brilliant execution in the highest terms. Miss Melmor looked at Malvina with an expression which informed her, that her praises were totally indifferent to her; and calling to Sir Edmond, proposed to him, their singing an Italian duet together. No, no, said Mrs. Burton, as we are all together, try some of those French operas! Oh, said Malvina, looking over the books, I see you have here Armides,[144] Alcestes,[145] and Oedipe,[146] those chef d'œuvres of our nation; ah, my dear Mrs. Burton, I perceive your heart still retains a taste for the productions of France.

For my part, cried Miss Melmor, disdainfully, I do not think any thing so cold and dull as that language, and I think it impossible that any one can say what is either sweet or agreeable, who use it. Intreat Madame de Sorcy to speak a few words, replied Sir Edmond, for I am certain she will convince you of your error.[147] Perhaps not, retorted she, with increased contempt, and speaking low – my opinion is not so easily changed, my head is not so soon elevated, that a word will turn it. Ah, it is not the head that is in danger with her, said Sir Edmond! The heart you mean, replied she, ironically: but happily for some people, they have nothing to risque from that party. But, if they are believed when they say they have, like so many others, they will be deceived.[148]

During this conversation, which Malvina appearded not to notice, but of which she heard every syllable; while Mrs. Burton was gone into the next room to look for the second part of Oedipe, with which she returned, before Sir Edmond had time to reply, which disappointed him not a little; though much less so than Malvina. Let us see, Kitty, said Mrs. Burton, placing the music on the desk before her, if we cannot accompany you in this beautiful trio? Miss Melmor tried it, but she had only execution without taste. She played like a master, yet she did not distinguish better than a scholar,[149] and therefore it was impossible for them to accompany her.

I am certain said Sir Edmond, Madame de Sorcy will succeed better. If I should, returned Malvina, I shall deserve not the least merit, as I have been accustomed to this music from my infancy. Ah, then, I am not the least surprised that you have such a languishing air, said Miss Melmor, for it must be a most insipid amusement, quite sufficient to damp the spirits.

If the Italian music pleases you better, let us leave this, replied Malvina, with the utmost sweetness. No, no, cousin, said Mrs. Burton, take her place, and let this divine harmony, make us for a while forget the howling winds which seem to live only in these mountains; and fancy ourselves in our own country.

Miss Melmor abruptly rising, rudely pushed aside her chair, and seated herself at a distance, as if determined not to hear. By the aid of a light finger, and an excellent ear, Malvina executed the most difficult parts, with taste and ease. It was very possible to have a more brilliant execution, but Malvina possessed the power when she played, of speaking to the heart.

Mrs. Burton was soon tired, though she was anxious to have it believed that she was passionately fond of music, and by always asserting this, she had persuaded herself that it was really the case. But one hour devoted to harmony, was as much as she could support. Besides the presence of Malvina was a punishment to her; her talents chagrined her, and to relieve herself from so painful a situation she feigned a slight indisposition,[150] and under that pretext, obliged all the company to retire.

CHAP. IX.

The nurse.

Without knowing to what particularly to attribute it, Malvina felt that evening had passed more pleasant than usual to her. She fancied it had also been observed, and she thought she might be constrained by these engagements, if she continued to go down every day.[151] With this idea, she waited till the next day, with a curiosity mingled with inquietude, to hear if her cousin had mentioned it. But nothing transpired, her dinner was served as usual; in the evening, though tempted to join the party, yet she was fearful of going down, she secretly wished to join them, and she attributed this desire only to the hope of amusing her griefs: but, if she had only this motive, it would not have required so much reflection and solicitude: she hesitated, because she had another, and which, without endeavouring to develope it herself, she intuitively felt that others might. She remained solitary and alone. The days passed: Mrs. Burton went frequently to see her, with a view to prevent her going down, she even avoided speaking on the subject to Malvina, who dared not propose it; and always pretended to her nephew, that she had used the most pressing entreaties, to induce her to join them, but all in vain.

Things were in this train, when one morning,[152] Frances came running to her mother's chamber out of breath, saying, Anzoletta is below, mama, as the school is shut to day, she has come to play with me; will you let us go and make snow balls in court? And who is Anzoletta, my dear? Oh, it is that little girl who sung so pretty, and who speaks like us. Sir Edmond's god- daughter, said Malvina, blushing a little. Yes, mama, but that does not prevent her from being good. No, my love, quite the contrary, Sir Edmond I believe is very good himself. Indeed, mama! would you believe that our Tomkins is always telling me that he is not; that he is a storyteller, and only makes believe to be good, that he may deceive people; and a great many other things which I have quite forgot. You are quite right to forget all the ill you hear said of others; but go my love, and join your companion.[153h] The little creature kissed her, and joyfully went to enjoy this permission.

Malvina turning to Tomkins, said, why do you repeat such things to the child, tales which you ought not to pay any attention to? I am very certain, madam, that they are not tales, and I am sure I have not uttered half of what I hear daily. But I hope you will not make Frances the confidant of all the reports the servants amuse you with. Certainly not, madam, for when Mrs. Tasse comes to my room, we always take care to converse in whispers. Ah, madam, if you did but know how Sir Edmond behaves when here. You may dispense with letting me hear it, Tomkins, replied Malvina, for I have not the least curiosity to be acquainted with it.

She then left the room, not without feeling a slight wish to know in what manner Sir Edmond behaved himself, but had it been even more powerful, she would have been hurt to satisfy herself, by listening to the chit chat of a chambermaid. Without precisely knowing what were the crimes of which Sir Edmond was accused, she guessed what they possibly might be, and notwithstanding her usual lenity, she did not feel inclined to grant any in his favor.

With these ideas, she went down to the court – Anzoletta came to her in an affectionate manner, and Frances was profuse in the praises of the little companion. Malvina amused herself by running with the children, in order to keep herself warm. She saw Sir Edmond at a little distance, walking very quick. On observing her, he bowed, but passed on without stopping. Malvina paid no attention to him, and in her present disposition, she had not the slightest wish to know any thing concerning him. She was, however, rather surprised at the cool attention he paid her, and was looking which way he went, when Anzoletta came, and whispering to her, saying, I think I can guess where my god-father is going. – Perhaps he may not wish you to know, Anzoletta. No, that he does not, for he never will tell any body, when he is going to serve any one; but if you will go with me, I will shew you, and then you will see I was not deceived.

The little girl set off a running, Frances and Malvina following, not that she wished to surprise Sir Edmond, but only to prevent the children of being guilty of any indiscretion, and keep them away. She called after them, but could not make them hear, as they kept running. When they had reached the door of a small low dwelling, in one of the most retired parts of the park, Anzoletta stopped, and laying her fingers on her lips, hush, said she to Malvina, or he will hear us; and gently pushing open the door, she stept in on tiptoe, and taking Malvina's hand, she pointed to a glass door, where she observed at one end of a decent chamber, Sir Edmond, leaning on the back of an easy chair which supported an elderly woman, who appeared pale and languishing. That is good Mrs. Norton, my god-father's nurse, whispered Anzoletta; she was taken very ill this morning; and I suppose they have heard of it at the castle: it was for that reason Sir Edmond went so hastily, for he is so good, and she loves him very much.

Affected by this pleasing picture, on beholding a young man who was represented so frivolous, fulfilling the most pious duties by a sick and suffering woman, Malvina could not help reproaching herself for the disadvantageous opinion she had entertained of him a moment before. How freely did she forgive him for not attending more particularly to her, with such an excellent motive in view! She would have been miserable to have detained him an instant. Malvina was not one of those women who wished to arrest the attention; it is vanity alone which expects such unlimited sway: real love, however violent it may be, in a pure and virtuous mind, would blush at the idea of usurping one moment that could be dictated to humanity. Not that Malvina was in love with Sir Edmond; I only assert, that had she loved him or any other, it was in her character to think thus.[154] The influence of a good action on such a mind as hers,[xvii] was much more dangerous than all the passionate expressions or actions which reason can resist.

Thus, while her attention was occupied by the affecting picture before her; little Frances, who was extremely cold, and tired of waiting so long, pulled her mother's robe, and intreated her to go. Malvina did not immediately attend to her, which occasioned the child to raise her voice; on this, Sir Edmond turned his head, and coming towards the door, to see from whence the noise proceeded, perceived them. Malvina, alarmed at being surprised by him in such a situation, as if she was prying into his conduct, wished to escape unperceived, but that was impossible. She thought that her endeavouring to conceal herself, would have a worse appearance; than his finding her there and whatever it might cost her, she was determined to stay where she was.

Sir Edmond, on observing her, uttered an exclamation of surprise, and Malvina, with her eyes cast down, while a deep blush dyed her countenance, replied timidly; you must attribute my indiscretion to the affection of your god-daughter, for it was she who conducted me here, purposely that she might present you in the most amiable point of view. Come in, madam, come in, I beg of you, replied Sir Edmond, rather confounded: this sight, though so afflicting, will not terrify you. Come and contribute your kind assistance, to soothe and fortify the mind of my good nurse, against the terrors of death. She is imploring the divine mercy, and your timely entrance will enable her to perform it with greater advantage, as she may safely imagine she beholds an angel near her. Is she then so extremely ill, enquired Malvina, as she advanced, perhaps it would be proper to send for Mr. Prior?

The good woman heard her, and raising her feeble voice with apparent difficulty – No, no, said she, there is no occasion, his fine words would not afford me so much comfort as the kindness and friendship of my dear son. How much did this eulogium raise him in the eyes of Malvina, and her good opinion, allowed her to spread the mantle of benevolence over his other vices, and veil them from her view![155] Tears fell from her eyes, as she took the parched hand of the patient sufferer. You seem very ill, my good mother, said she? Malvina's accents were so extremely gentle and sweet, that it roused her attention, when looking at her,[156] said, I believe you are the Lady that Mrs. Burton brought to see the sick persons, a little while since? They all spoke of you, you relieved them, and each received a benefit from you.[157] – I thank God that He has not taken me before I saw you again. Do not speak so much, my good mother, interrupted Sir Edmond, who appeared entirely occupied with the situation of his nurse; you will exhaust your strength; take some of this cordial, and inform us if you wish for the presence of Mr. Prior. Anzoletta has been to fetch him, said Frances, who had hid herself in Malvina's robe, fearful of looking at Mrs. Norton, lest she should see her expire.

I am astonished that when any one is ill, Mr. Prior is not immediately informed of it, said Malvina, to a person who appeared to be a relation of the good woman's? Oh, madam, she replied, he is so much engaged, that one is fearful of disturbing him, he is always writing in his closet fine discourses certainly; but this employment does not leave him time to come and see us; not that he has ever refused any one when sent for, no, I do not go so far as to say that, and I know also that he can say very fine things.

The entrance of Mr. Prior put an end to the good woman's discourse. The first object which arrested his attention (even before the sick woman) was Malvina, whom he approached, saying to her; you are come here to witness this terrible moment – this moment, when the trembling and restless soul is on the borders of an unknown world. Mr. Prior, said Sir Edmond, in a whisper, pointing to his nurse, will you endeavour to speak a few words of comfort[158] which may inspire her with fortitude, and tranquilise her heart? Malvina arose, and resigning her place to Mr. Prior, she assisted Sir Edmond to support the nurse in her chair.[159] Well, my good Mrs. Norton, said Mr. Prior, your strength undoubtedly fails, and your trembling heart may fail also; but an all powerful God will be your defence; rely entirely on his mercy, and he will support you for ever; even now, though the vale of death opens before you, he will comfort and be near you.[160]

Ah, sir, His will be done and not mine – I submit without murmuring; hoping our Lord and Saviour will intercede for me. Confide in the clemency of the most holy Father and Son, my good Norton. – He is good and merciful, and when he calls us to himself when we are dust, He, with infinite goodness, will pardon us, that we may know he ought to be loved much more than he is feared.[161] He can witness I never did evil to any person, and why should I doubt his mercy? But, if I regret life, it is only on the account of my poor family who will remain in misery; and, continued she, while I lived, I gave part of all the benefits I received from my son Edmond; but on losing me, what will become of them? I will take care of them, my good mother, said Sir Edmond, with energy:

be assured they shall not want for any thing, while I have it to bestow. I know that my dear Sir Edmond has an excellent heart, said his nurse, while the last drops of nature's feeling fell from her eyes; I trust to your promises, but you are not always here. But I shall, interrupted Malvina, and I will endeavour to supply his place. Yes, my mother, added Sir Edmond, gratified at having it in his power to enter into an engagement in concert with Malvina, we will both give you our promise, that we will ever remember the welfare and interests of your children; Malvina held out her hand as a testimony of her part of the agreement, which Sir Edmond eagerly seized, and placed it between his own on the knees of the dying woman, who, affected by their actions, and perfectly easy with regard to her family, faintly articulated these words: 'Let me now, O Lord, depart in peace'?[162] – and expired in a few moments after.

On their return to the castle, the countenance of Mr. Prior was more grave; that of Malvina more thoughtful; even Sir Edmnd was serious; but soon regaining his usual vivacity, as he removed from the melancholy spectacle, he said, Churchmen, I think, have not much to do; they may be very good, and are useful by their writings, but they can never persuade me that they are so useful to the general order, as a good and honest creature who has passed her life in continual labour, and without having enjoyed her existence, terminated it in misery. And who has informed you that she did not enjoy it, replied Mr. Prior? Does not happiness belong as much to the children of virtue as to the favorites of fortune? and with this title, has not Mrs. Norton lived more satisfied than – than perhaps yourself?

Faith, that is very likely, replied Sir Edmond; in the manner in which things are arranged here below, I am convinced that the most brilliant situations are not almost the most happy. In the course of a life which we may regard in every respect, as fortunate, yet I have experienced many more hours of ennui than pleasure; and I have often had occasion to doubt the goodness of that power who has ordained that we should receive so little good, with so much evil.

These words irritated Mr. Prior, and regarding Sir Edmond with indignation, he said, in a tone the most emphatic; What art thou, son of man, thou who but yesterday was raised from the dust, that thou should dare to arraign thy Creator? Where is your title to criticise the order of the universe; thou, whose lot is so far above what thy virtues give thee a right to expect? I assure you, Mr. Prior, said Sir Edmond, smiling, that I am very sensible of my faults, and, in consequence, have a very mean opinion of my merit. But, if God wished me without faults, why did he not create me perfect, why permit the Devil to send me so many temptations, if he intends to punish me afterwards for having yielded to them? Why does he render those sins so lovely, which he prohibits me from loving, and how can I be so guilty, when I only use what he has given me? Perhaps, it is all your own fault, replied Malvina; for if you are warned by your conscience at the time that you are tempted by the passions; if you are sensible of the good, while committing the evil; then, in falling, your reason must inform you that you might have resisted.

Sir Edmond blushed, and turning to Mr. Prior, remember, said he, the purport of what has been said, and how much might be made of it; it may be of use when in the pulpit; when you wish to awaken the conscience of sinners; and open their eyes: but, continued he, there would be wanting that particular look and gesture, and those charming lips, where the graces repose near wisdom.[163] They had now reached the castle – Mr. Prior left them, and Malvina was retiring to her room, when Sir Edmond preventing her, said, ah! why madam, do you always fly from us, always impenetrable to the wishes and intreaties of Mrs. Burton? What intreaties, she replied, a little surprised? But I suppose you are ignorant that your cousin is offended at the obstinacy (pardon me the word – for it was she that said it) with which you refused her in making one of the society? Malvina smiled, you are in jest, Sir Edmond; certainly my cousin could not alledge such complaints against me.

I positively assure you, madam, that not one day has elapsed without my enquiring why we are not to see you? and each time I was informed that your cousin had repeatedly used every effort for that purpose, but they were always ineffectual. Malvina could not but perceive this was premeditated by Mrs. Burton, yet she could not develope the motive which induced it; and replied with some embarrassment: – but if I had resisted the entreaties of my cousin, why should you suppose? That you would yield to mine, interrupted Sir Edmond, with quickness. – No, madam, I have not the presumption; but as you did not live so secluded before my arrival, it is a sufficient proof that my presence is disagreeable to you; and in consequence, you must wish my absence.

You interpret my conduct in a very unfavorable light, sir, said Malvina, rather vexed, it is not you who are the occasion, but it proceeds from many beloved recollections which alone causes me to prefer solitude; and if I had imagined that my seclusion would have given Mr. Burton the least discontent, I had rather have, – My aunt, my aunt, exclaimed Sir Edmond, taking the hand of Malvina, and leading her to Mrs. Burton's apartment. Here madam, is Madame de Sorcy, who says that I am in raillery, when I assure her you have been unhappy in being deprived of her society: join your intreaties with mine, my dear aunt, and let us see if we cannot prevail.

Mrs. Burton blushed, but immediately taking his part – my cousin knows, said she, how dear her presence is to me; and if I was unwilling to restrain her love of retirement, she will appreciate my being so disinterested as to prefer her tranquillity to my pleasure. But since she is less anxious with regard to it, I shall congratulate her on the change with pleasure. This equivocal reply of Mrs. Burton's left Malvina in an uncertainty; when Sir Edmond, impatient to gain one more positive, said, I perceive, aunt, that it is decided, and I must leave you; for while I am with you, Madame de Sorcy will not willingly come among us.

I agree to your determination, Edmond, hastily interrupted Mrs. Burton; you are losing your time here, both duties and engagements call you to Edinburgh. Return there, and then my fair cousin will be at liberty.

It will not be that gentleman who restrains my liberty, said Malvina, gravely; whether he goes or stays, my inclination will not make me remain less alone, nor his presence prevent me from yielding to your desire; if it is true, madam, that you really value my company. Mrs. Burton had no alternative; she could not refuse this proposal, and she recollected, that as she could not avoid Sir Edmond's seeing Malvina, it would be much better that it should be in her presence; and it was therefore agreed, that Malvina should for the future make one of their society, as she had done before the arrival of Sir Edmond.

CHAP. X

Conversation.

During dinner, Mrs. Burton was acquainted with the death of the good Mrs. Norton, which had been the occasion of the interview between Sir Edmond and Malvina. She had not even heard that the poor woman was ill; for as she never interested herself concerning any one, she never was informed of their misfortunes. The peasants, of whom she boasted so much of protecting, were afflicted, and died without her being acquainted with it. Absorbed by ambition, she maintained a constant correspondence with Lord Stafford, that they[164] might remain faithful to their engagements, and earnestly pressed her nephew to go and fulfill them. But each returning day, Sir Edmond found a fresh excuse to evade his departure; never had he yet made so long a stay at the castle.

Miss Melmor claimed all the honor to herself; but Mrs. Burton foresaw the true reason, and it gave her great anxiety: she was continually devising means which she thought the most likely to withdraw her nephew, or render him at variance with Malvina. But, with such a character as Sir Edmond, haughty and independent, it was necessary to use persuasion instead of authority. Mrs. Burton, selfish and ambitious, had not an ingredient of gentleness in her composition. On the contrary, Malvina was mild and unassuming; how then could she create a difference with her, without giving a just cause of complaint; which, perhaps, would only render her still more interesting to Sir Edmond, and what would she gain by it? Malvina was at liberty to reside wherever she thought proper. Could she prevent her nephew from seeing her with less liberty[165] than at Burton Hall; and he might become acquainted with the means she had employed to get rid of her.

Under this perplexity, she determined to inform her cousin of the projected alliance which her sanguine hopes encouraged. She, in consequence of this, represented Sir Edmond as a very dissipated young man, without principle, fond of intrigue, and who only declined the honorable marriage which was proposed to him, because it would be a preventative to his profligacy. You may imagine the continual anxiety I labour under, my dear, she continued (with a feigned confidence) and notwithstanding the vices of my nephew, I love him tenderly, and I will obtain him an establishment which might raise him to the highest rank, and would draw him from these low intrigues. I have given him the promise of all my fortune, of which I shall deprive myself to benefit him. – Truly grateful to me, for my intentions, he has acceeded to my wishes with alacrity: and, certain of his consent, I have engaged my word to answer for him; and every thing is far advanced, with Lady Mary Summerhill, who, on his account, has refused the first offers in the kingdom;[166] but what gives me inconceivable uneasiness, is, the fear of his neglecting a promise, the performance of which, I have pledged my word for the validity of. Dear girl, grant me your assistance, and point out to him the impropriety of his conduct, and endeavour to persuade him of the necessity of his returning to Edinburgh.

Dear madam, said Malvina, what influence can I have over the will and opinions of Sir Edmond? Very little, I believe, said her cousin, for I have remarked, that he has paid less attention to you than to any other woman he has ever known, perhaps, because you are not one of those lively and showy girls who amuse him, and are similar to himself. Yet, if you do not suit his taste, he certainly esteems you, and I shall be astonished if he does not make a little sacrifice to gain yours;[xviii] and though your reflections should not have all the effect I could wish, they may produce some impression.

I assure you, replied Malvina, that I should be much embarrassed at the idea; as I am fearful it will appear very singular to Sir Edmond, that I should interfere in an affair to which he may suppose me an absolute stranger – and that I should intrude my advice on one who never asked it of me. But, my dear, said Mrs. Burton, it is only general remarks that I would mention before him; only to observe, that when a man has given a woman the hopes of his marrying her, that it is unpardonable to neglect or disappoint her the fulfilling of such engagement: and that no union can be happy, but by the opulence and dignity which it may confer. Thus, you can throw out some hints; and if he should pretend not to understand it,[167] you can make a few additions to support what I say; at least, added she, (perceiving that Malvina appeared rather dubious) and fixing on her a steady and scrutinising look, if there is not some particular reason which deters you.

The suspicions which this last sentence included, did not escape Malvina. Of what service could either her silence or advice be to either party concerned in this union: as the whole of it appeared to her more calculated to gratify the ambition of Mrs. Burton, than to promote the happiness of Sir Edmond. In this uncertainty, she determined not to reply, but wait to hear if the conclusion of this conversation might not furnish her with something more to the purpose, which she could answer with greater satisfaction to herself.

But Mrs. Burton had said only a few words, when Miss Melmor entered the room with the newspaper in her hand. Ah! my dear madam, cried she, only see, here is the account of a grand gala my Lord Stanhope is about to give at Edinburgh. What, is the brother of Lady Mary Summerhill grown so gay,[168] enquired Mrs. Burton, of her nephew, who had followed Miss Melmor?

Yes, replied he, with the utmost indifference. Oh, what infinite joy it would give me, if I could but be there, said Miss Melmor. I dare say it would; but you, Edmond, will undoubtedly make a point of hastening to Edinburgh for that purpose, said Mrs. Burton, in a tone of severity. For what reason, madam, do you imagine that I should wish to leave the present society, and at this inclement season, seek to participate of an amusement, which the love of idleness may render pleasing,[169] but which from habit, to me, has become dull and insipid. I do not mean for the sake of the amusement, Edmond, but the company: to make one of such a select and brilliant party, is what ought to induce you to be there.

Ah, madam, if you did but know the fastidious monotony which at present reigns in the great world! But the ladies, Edmond, can you have forgot that fascinating part of the world? The ladies do not now take any pains, or wish to be at the trouble of adorning it; they have become so insipidly tiresome and frivolous, that their society is uniformly fatiguing:[170] for if one utters only one word of sincerity, they will immediately reproach you with having forgot the ton[171] of good company; a phrase at present synonimous with dullness and insipidity. You are become extremely difficult, replied Mrs. Burton, suppressing her vexation; and I am really curious to know what can have produced such an unexpected change.

At these words, Miss Melmor drew up with an air of self complaisance, as much as to say, it is I who am the cause. Malvina, who had not the slightest idea that she had the least concern in any thing that had been said, continued her work, without paying any attention to them: Sir Edmond made no reply to his aunt, who added, after a moment's reflection –[xix] Well sir, if it is really true, that pleasure is fatigue, and that women are tiresome, I shall begin to draw a happy omen, and flatter myself with your reformation; as from the moment that the world begins to displease, and retirement becomes agreeable, we seek to embellish it, by bringing a companion to participate it with us: at least, you are not very distant from entering into a serious union, and are going to realize a promise which you have given. Say rather that you have advised me to give, madam. You then are guilty of a little artful chicanery, Edmond, for without your positive consent, you well know, that the lady and her family would not have looked on the marriage as a settled affair; and I desire to know, if you do not imagine that this young lady will expect you at her brother's entertainment; and if you have given her reason to expect you, are you not very blameable in disappointing her hopes?

Faith, madam, replied he, with quickness, I have never spoken to her in any manner than I have used to every other woman; a few compliments scattered by chance among them; which is a kind of traffic I am surfeited with from use, and which experience makes one neglect; a sort of false coin with which we are deceived, though the fault originates with those who receive it, more than those who give.

Malvina raised her head, and looked at him steadily. He appeared embarrassed and agitated as he sat. Mrs. Burton replied, perhaps you may accuse Lady Mary Summerhill of having too easily believed the protestations you made her; but I think it will be without reason, when you recollect the manner in which they were offered; but since you are so profound in the art of deceiving women, it neither evinces a good heart, or generosity, in blaming them, if they are the victims of your dangerous artifices. Really, madam, interrupted Sir Edmond, mortified at receiving these reproaches in the presence of Malvina, I was never either false or perfidious. – I acknowledge I have employed artifice in my intercourses with women, but the reason was, because I could not please by any other means.[172]

In the world, their coquettry keeps us in continual warfare with them, therefore it is necessary to defend oneself; and consequently, we are not blameable, if we make use of their own weapons. Besides, do we not see that they glory in the artifice they employ; then why should we be condemned, and that imputed to us as a vice of the heart, when they consider it as an additional advantage?

I believe, said Malvina, seriously, that if art is looked upon with indulgence in women, it is only to be attributed to those disagreeable moments of dependence which they are unavoidably obliged to undergo: and for this reason, perhaps, nature has kindly given this means, in order to alleviate such depressing sensations. But are not men debased, when they take advantage, and make use of such weapons against the weaker beings? They, who have the power of independence;[173] ought they not also to be sincere? When there is no occasion to make use of artifice, yet men employ it to deceive, and not only to deceive, but injure others.

Madame de Sorcy has said what is very true, added Mrs. Burton; and is it not to win the heart of Lady Mary, that you have endeavoured to make her believe that you have loved her?[174] Gracious Heaven, aunt, have a little mercy on me, replied Sir Edmond; women of the present day do not possess such tender hearts; for how is it possible they should break, when they are never touched? Their vanity perpetually guards them; it is that impregnable rampart which alone prevents the entrance of every other sentiment. And is it you, Edmond, who dare to reproach them with it? You, who have seduced her ladyship's affection, from no other cause but vanity? You, who remain here for no other reason but to afflict that interesting young creature; to encrease her love, by exciting her anxiety; which, allow me to say, is a most detestable degree of vanity. What is your opinion, my dear cousin, addressing herself to Malvina; do you think I am too severe?

Not in your judgment, madam, but in your suppositions; for you ought not to have a doubt, but that Sir Edmond, the benevolent benefactor of the distressed,[175] and foster-son of the worthy Mrs. Norton, will hasten to put an end to the torments of the woman he loves. At these words, Miss Melmor, casting a look of anger and reproach at Malvina, started up, and immediately left the room, not being able any longer to command her patience. The distinction, madam, is very pointed, replied Sir Edmond, in a voice which denoted he was rather piqued; and I certainly should have gone, had I not known that as it was to be given in three days, it consequently would be too late for me to set out.

Really, is that true, said Mrs. Burton,[xx] searching the paper with an uneasy air? But at least, Edmond, if you cannot go in time to partake of the entertainment at Edinburgh, you ought to return on account of the lady, as she will be astonished at not seeing you at her brother's; who also will condemn your neglect of her;[176] and you certainly should end her sufferings as soon as possible. Do not you think so, my dear? As I am unacquainted, madam, returned Malvina, how far the affections of the young lady may be engaged, I cannot so well determine; yet, if they are only in a slight degree, and Sir Edmond has acknowledged that he has voluntarily contributed to make her imagine that he is attached to her, I have too good an opinion of him to suppose, he will ridicule what she feels, and consequently he will realize her expectations.[177]

At this moment, Miss Melmor, who had soon returned, interrupted Malvina, by saying, Ah! do you not hear little Frances crying, she has certainly hurt herself. I do not hear any thing, said Malvina, rising, and listening attentively. Oh! I am certain it was her, and I will go and see – Malvina, alarmed, went out with Miss Melmor. No sooner had they quitted the saloon, than the latter stopped, saying, I only feigned having heard Frances cry, that I might interrupt a conversation which was insupportable to me; and to enquire of you, dear madam, why you wish Sir Edmond's absence? If it is that you may pay your court to Mrs. Burton, I must inform you, that she is very different from the idea you have drawn of her character, as she neither possesses benevolence or generosity[178] – of which virtues, Mr. Prior is continually tiring us.

For your own interest, said Malvina, with a smile bordering on contempt, I beg you will not endeavour to insinuate any of those injurious suspicions, as they will rather prove detrimental to those who assert them, than to those who are alluded to; and as to what relates to Sir Edmond, it appeared to me, that what I said, was only natural, from the subject in discourse, that produced the spontaneous and simple replys which it required; and I am astonished at the implication you have given it.

I assert, replied Miss Melmor, I have very great reason to think so, when Sir Edmond only stays here on my account. – He loves me passionately, it is his intention to marry me, and he has promised to break off his engagement with

Lady Mary Summerhill on that account. – But this is a secret, and I would not have divulged it, had I not thought, that by confiding it to you, it would convince you how much your advice must have affected us both: – but, if this affair is so far advanced, returned Malvina, cooly, what have you to fear? Do you suppose that a woman, who is such a stranger as I am to Sir Edmond, can have the least influence over the passion which he possesses for you? Not exactly that, replied the artful Kitty, but perhaps he might in some measure be influenced by those high-flown sentiments, and airs of superior judgment, which you make use of: or else it is possible you may wish to make an impression on him on your own account? I shall therefore be much obliged if you will decline in future troubling yourself with his concerns. On concluding these words, she returned immediately to the saloon, without waiting for a reply.

Malvina, made the unwilling confidant, both of Mrs. Burton and Miss Melmor,[179] would have found herself in a very perplexing predicament, if the rectitude of her intentions, and the purity of her heart, had not occasioned her to look above the difficulties of her situation. Not being sufficiently acquainted with the truth of what she had heard, she was at a loss which side to take, and absolutely determined to remain neuter, amidst all the different interests of those around her. But this part, the only one which was proper to her character, would equally disoblige Mrs. Burton and Miss Melmor; and if she did not find them enemies at present, they might probably become so.

Since Miss Melmor's confidence, Malvina had perhaps evinced more distance in her behaviour to Sir Edmond: she never went down but when they were all assembled together, and when there, paid not the least attention to the flattering compliments with which he constantly addressed her. She never felt at her ease but with Mr. Prior, whom she saw every morning, as he went to give her a lesson in the Erse[180] language. – Friendship, and its delightful confidence, often prolonged the lesson till the dinner hour.

The custom of the house was, that after breakfast, which was taken all together in the saloon, every person retired to their own apartments for the rest of the morning; and Malvina was more particular in this respect than any other. It happened one morning, after these transactions, that missing Frances at the hour she usually accustomed her to come and receive her lessons, she went down to seek for her, and found her in the saloon, playing with Sir Edmond: on observing him, she drew back, and calling the child to follow, she was retiring, when Sir Edmond came up to her, and said, since chance has favored me with the happiness of being one moment alone with you, madam, permit me to hope, that I may have the felicity to prevail on you to grant me an audience of a few minutes. Malvina blushed, and slightly bowed. Sir Edmond required no other answer; but shutting the door, and leading her to a seat, he placed himself in one near her, and thus began.

The hope that you would have taken an interest in my situation, madam, is not the motive which has prompted me to intrude on your patience: I know but too well, that you think me unworthy of inspiring you with the slightest; but as you appeared to coincide with, and support Mrs. Burton, the other day, in her desire of my returning to Edinburgh, I wish to know (if it is not an improper liberty) how far my aunt has informed you of the affairs which she says recalls me there. I know very little more of them, sir, replied Malvina, than what she repeated before you: that you had promised your hand to a charming young lady whom you loved;[181] that you had left her merely because she returned your affection; and a thousand other trifling things, which are not worth repeating.[182] That is all, said Sir Edmond, looking at her with a mixture of tenderness and anxiety; and that, I suppose, has been sufficient to determine your opinion concerning me? Since you interrogate me so minutely, sir, returned Malvina, I acknowledge that I have been astonished, that the benefactor of so many unfortunate beings, the Godfather of Anzoletta, and the humane protector of the worthy Norton, should be reproached with shading all his glory, by the want of probity,[183] the high sense of which, in my opinion, constitutes the real man of honor.

I do not pretend to exculpate myself from any of the vices which are attributed to me, madam, replied Sir Edmond – without doubt I have many, and I confess, on my coming here this time, I was far from considering them in the same point of view which I do at present. But, without particularising the motives which induced this change; and which, perhaps, she who has been the cause of it, may refuse to hear: I will for the present content myself with rectifying several mistakes, which the recital Mrs. Burton gave you must have occasioned in your mind. I have never made any engagement with Lady Mary Summerhill, madam – neither have I ever loved her; though perfectly beautiful, it is not of that kind which pleases me. Never, as one of our poets has said, can we account for the origin of love; it is never in the features of the countenance, but in the heart of the lover.[184] I have ever been silent when with her;[185] and, as she possesses a frivolity and insipidity of character, without the least sensibility, I leave you to imagine, if that kind of preference, which she has granted me, can, in the slightest degree, disturb her repose.

Then, sir, replied Malvina, perhaps Mrs. Burton will condemn you for not having informed her sooner of the disposition of the lady; that you might not have made such advances, without you had been certain of fulfilling them.[186] If I had not declared from the first moment, that I should refuse to be united to Lady Mary, replied Sir Edmond, it was only because I had not any fixed ideas of conjugal felicity. I fancied that like most others, I must resolve to take a companion, as we take a walk;[187] and in this light, her ladyship, I supposed, might do well enough: but since, an unexpected event has changed both my ideas and principles, and the union of marriage, which I looked upon with the utmost indifference, now appears to me so desirable, that all my future happiness in life depends on it: I ought to resign Lady Mary, as my heart has already done, and without the least scruple, because, as I before informed you, I have never pledged my promise either to herself or her family. If my aunt has given hers,[xxi] that must be her own fault, and she must take the consequence; I have no business with it, and I do not consider myself obliged to be answerable for her engagements, by the sacrifice of my happiness for life. Are you not of the same opinion?

Yes, sir, replied Malvina, convinced that all he had been telling her related to Miss Melmor; and I should suppose your new choice would not meet with any objections from Mrs. Burton, if she knows that your happiness depends on it. – Certainly you have only to inform her, to have it confirmed; and as to myself, sir, affected by the confidence you have favored me with, be assured of the sincerity of my wishes for the accomplishment of all that can render you happy. This compliment was sufficient to convince Sir Edmond how distant she was from comprehending his meaning; but the excessive coolness with which it was pronounced gave him hope, as such behaviour was not natural to her; he imagined she must have very particular reasons for it; or that she was affected by some peculiar sensations. As he did not wish to explain himself farther, until he could by some means ascertain whether he was mistaken, they separated.

CHAP. XI

Some slight incidents.

Sir Edmond neglected no opportunity, whenever he could convey[xxii] any thing tender or agreeable to Malvina, though in a manner rather disguised; and which she considered as an indirect method of addressing Miss Melmor. With this idea, of which she was assured, she listened to him, found him more amiable,[188] and took the most lively interest in all the praises and little concerns which related to Anzoletta:[189] yet, while this increased, would she have the force to get the better of it, when the chimera of Miss Melmor vanished, and when we shall distinctly see[190] that it was Malvina herself who was the object.

One evening after tea, the conversation turned on the morals and general corruption of the times, when it was interrupted by the arrival of some letters, which were brought to Mrs. Burton, with which she retired to her closet. Mr. Prior, whose mind was occupied with comparisons and maxims, continued the subject, which had been interrupted by the arrival of the post. It is thus, that the voluptuous person resembles a frothy torrent. For Heaven's sake, cried Miss Melmor, with quickness, I hope you are not going to preach – spare us, I entreat you, and let us enjoy the absence of Mrs. Burton, by conversing on subjects that are not so uniformly tiresome. She immediately asked a trifling question of Sir Edmond, who answered in the same manner.

Mr. Prior shrugged up his shoulders, and retired. Malvina took a book, and placed herself by the fire; and Miss Melmor[191] remained silent for a minute.[192] Then, addressing Sir Edmond, she enquired how long he had been constant to the woman he most loved?[193] I should be much puzzled to tell you, he replied, turning over the leaves of a book which he held in his hand, for at present, I think

I have never been in love. At these words, though Malvina kept her eyes fixed on the book, she ceased to read it. What! of all those women you told me of,[194] said Miss Melmor, has not one of them been capable of inspiring a serious and ardent passion? Perhaps their vanity may have led them to imagine so, replied Sir Edmond, and I may have so expressed myself in a figurative sense;[195] but how dare any one give the name of love to such *eternal passions*, whose transient flame scarcely exists a month.[196] But I cannot believe, that amidst all the beauties of London and Edinburgh, which embellished the entertainments of those cities, that not one of them should appear worthy of attaching you? Not one, at least that ever inspired me, or I should rather say, that ever interested my heart.[197]

Why, who then is there that can ever please you? (said she, scarcely able to conceal her delight) as if certain that he would whisper, 'it is you alone.' Instead of which, he opened the book which he held in his hand, and read the following paragraph, with unusual animation.

'Among the many women which attracted my eyes, and interested my heart, more than once the melody of a voice has captivated my attentive ear. – Many beauties may please me; one by the possession of one virtue, and another by a different one; but one perfect in every thing, I have never found; there has always been either a blemish, or a want of grace, which destroyed the full effect of their charms. But she alone is accomplished in every thing – Heaven has formed her the most perfect of all his creatures.'[198]

As he read the last sentence, he cast such a look of tenderness and expression on Malvina, that she felt it penetrate to her soul, and from that moment, she thought that if he had really loved Miss Melmor, he would have fixed his looks on her. Miss Melmor certainly made a similar reflection, for she appeared gloomy and ill humoured to every one during the remainder of the evening; but particularly so to Malvina.

Soon after Mrs. Burton's return into the saloon, every one was preparing to retire, when she said, apropos, Edmond, it will not be long before your new apartment will be ready for you; and at your return, you shall take possession of it. No, no, thank you, replied Sir Edmond, in a tone of animation. You may reserve it[xxiii] for some one else, I do not wish to quit my present one – it is from henceforth sacred, added he, in a low voice, and fixing his eyes on Malvina. This sentence petrified her to her seat, till recollecting herself, she immediately rose to retire.[199]

Mrs. Burton did not hear this speech, and went out, saying, he was at liberty to do just as he pleased. But, Malvina had but too well understood it: instantaneously, a secret emotion invaded her heart; confused, and agitated, she had again forgot it was time to retire, when Miss Melmor,[200] on observing her so near Sir Edmond, abruptly exclaimed, if it is being near Sir Edmond, that detains Madame de Sorcy, I think he ought to be very proud of it; for it is the first time since she has been here, that she has forgot herself. This reflection, which was but the truth, had its influence on all who heard it, except Mrs. Melmor.

Malvina arose in confusion; and going to take her work bag, which lay on the table, she inadvertently touched the hand of Sir Edmond, and drawing it away suddenly, she was retiring with precipitation, when she perceived, as she passed, in an opposite glass,[201] that Sir Edmond pressed his lips to the place she had touched. This trivial action, which no one perceived but herself, increased her emotion;[202] and surprised at what she felt, she was endeavouring to investigate it, when Sir Edmond, paying his respects, retired.[203] As soon as he was gone, Miss Melmor said, I cannot think what unaccountable caprice can attach Sir Edmond to his apartment, unless he finds it more commodious for him to receive visitants in? What is your opinion, my dear, added she, looking archly at Malvina?

Mr. Prior, incensed that any one should recall this trivial incident, with the intention of hurting the feelings of his friend, replied, with more frankness than he otherwise would – Yes, Miss Melmor, he ought to find it so, and I think that you should not have made the remark. These words disconcerted Kitty so much, that Mr. Prior was almost sorry he had uttered them: she blushed, stammered, and taking her mother's arm (who heard, but did not understand their purport) they both went up stairs.

Malvina, surprised and pensive, followed them slowly, without hearing Mr. Prior wish her good night. She retired to rest, but could not sleep; a thousand different ideas obtruded and confused her thoughts. Mrs. Burton had mentioned Sir Edmond's return. He was then going. What could the singular answer which Mr. Prior made to Miss Melmor, signify? Did it not intimate, that she sometimes went to visit Sir Edmond alone, it certainly must have been her who opened the door on the evening Malvina went to seek her Frances.[204] Besides, Mr. Prior's answer was very pointed and though he was severe in his judgments, she could not reproach him with being unjust.[205] But it cannot be possible thought Malvina, that under the eyes of a mother, Sir Edmond would be capable of seducing a simple and innocent girl? He could not so far forget the respect due to her, who received him, without restraint, as to dare to violate the sacred laws of hospitality; and the still more sacred duties of religion[206] and honor? But was not this exactly what he had been described to her? That he was a man which no consideration would prevent from gratifying his vicious inclinations.

What then could he mean by those looks, so tender and sincere; were they the effect of artifice? The voice which seemed to speak from the heart,[207] was that studied? Ah! If all these appearances were false, what could be believed? Whilst Malvina[208] was the prey of these distressing reflections – Sir Edmond, during the silence of the night, was writing the following letter to his friend:[209]

Sir Edmond Burton to Sir Charles Weymard.

If you wish to put an end to your astonishment, at my prolonged stay at this place, come thyself; and when you have beheld the reason, if your wonder continues, it will be then only at the idea that I should ever quit it. Malvina, that name, whose very sound softens and enchants, enflames and captivates my heart. – Malvina! that angelic woman,[210] in whom is united every beauty, and every virtue! – Oh, Malvina, thou surely would be too perfect, were thou but susceptible of love; for it is in the power of love alone to adorn that which appears to want not any embellishment. I returned you know, Charles, from the mere curiosity of wishing to behold that mysterious beauty, which we could not get a glimpse of the last time you was here.

From what had been said of her, my imagination was so raised, that I resolved not to leave Burton Hall again till I was certain whether the conquest was worthy the pains of attempting it. But, as the time began to appear so tedious before I had any hopes of being gratified, I amused myself with the rising attractions of Miss Melmor, by way of gaining patience, which, as she attributed, the quickness of my return to herself, I thought proper to deceive her by that idea. Kitty, you know, is handsome, and I have more reason to know it than you. I will also inform you, that I was obliged to pay her my attention above a month, which taught me, that had she been less easily won, she might have been a very alluring creature; and I believe I shall have the charity to tell her as much, as a recompense for those favours to which I no longer attach any value.

But, what are all the pleasures which either she or any other woman can bestow, compared with one look from Malvina – not worth a thought. Malvina has wrought a wonder, she has changed me, my friend; she has awakened in me, sensations to which I have ever, 'till now, been a stranger. She has touched those chords in my heart which 'till now have been mute; and I never approach even the room she is in, but I feel them vibrate![211] In her presence, I am another being, I suppress every thought, every sentiment, which is unworthy of her. Her pure breath seems to refine all who approach her; for when I am under the shade of her looks, I feel as if I was out of the reach of vice. Oh! Charles, this interesting beauty speaks much more to the heart than the senses; and I would rather aspire to her love, than ever wish to possess her; for though the attractions of her person are certainly enchanting, yet those of her mind are infinitely more so; and I never behold her expressive countenance, without saying with Dryden, 'contemplate that majestic temple, it was built by celestial hands, her soul is the divinity which inhabits it, and the edifice is not unworthy of its God'.[212]

I am as yet even uncertain if I am in the least agreeable to Malvina, but I hope; yes, I will hope, daring as it is, to gain her heart. I well know that it will take a long time to accomplish this; and that she will be still longer before she will ever confess as much;[213] but this you know will please me above all, and make me continue to love and prefer her to every other: for in this respect, she has not the least resemblance to any I have known.[214]

I rather suspect Mrs. Burton had secretly formed the design of preventing my seeing her cousin, fearing, not without reason, that such an assemblage of charms and perfections would make me disgusted with her favorite Lady Mary Summerhill: though I really never took the trouble to make the comparison, and did not even appreciate the little worth she possesses, as I cannot bear to think of a union with her. Besides, the unlimited gratitude which my aunt seems as if she would ever expect, by chaining me with the promise of her fortune, which she thinks will give her a command over all my actions; and the obligations which she thinks she has conferred, by this intended marriage, are such a burden to me, that I wish to be freed from them all. I possess a haughty spirit, my friend; and all the treasures of Solomon,[215] provided the women[216] were not included, should not tempt me to part with the smallest portion of my independence.

But I must inform you, between ourselves, that Kitty gives me no small uneasiness. The little simpleton looks upon the mere promise of marriage as an indispensible obligation, and imperiously demands the performance of it.

This is a presumption I have not been accustomed to, in these kind of reckonings, and I am really tormented by her. My chief fear is, that she will, by some means, make Malvina acquainted with it; and I am but too sure, that if that amiable woman was informed of my connection with Miss Melmor, her ideas of rectitude are so strict and delicate, that if she even loved me herself, she would take the part of her rival, and renounce me for ever. It is therefore of the greatest consequence to me that she should be kept entirely ignorant of all that has passed. My first care, therefore is, to send Kitty from this place as soon as possible. – I had the idea, in a case of such necessity, of requiring the assistance of one of you? But I have hit upon a more decent way, and one that, I think, will succeed much better, which is this: I always pretend, in the presence of Mrs. Burton, though not when Malvina is present, such a particular attachment to Miss Melmor, that my restless aunt is really alarmed at it; and in order to preserve me pure for Lady Mary, she is very busy in her endeavours to find out a suitable match for her pupil; which, when she has determined, I know she will inform me of, and I shall then have the appearance of humbly submitting to her will, and in concert with her; I shall make a point of going from hence[217] when she has given her orders to her stupid friend for the marriage of her petulant daughter, who, after my departure, will not have any other resource, when pressed by the threats of Mrs. Burton, and a husband, but to submit to the alternative; at least she will not, I hope, think of following me, though she is very capable of such a scheme; but in order to prevent so idle a fancy, I shall hint as much to Mrs. Burton, that she may keep a strict watch over her; and as I wish that not the least circumstance may be known to Malvina, I shall insinuate to my aunt, that for the sake of Lady Mary Summerhill's tranquillity, it will be necessary to keep the history of my amours a profound secret. Seduced by such a motive, she will recommend this silence to Miss Melmor, in a tone of authority which generally makes such weak characters obey her; and as my pretty Kate[218] will be thus terrified at the anger of Mrs. Burton, when I am not there to comfort her, she will be obliged to take the husband and hide her shame. Then! oh my celestial Malvina, I shall return to you, and by the persevering attentions of love, obtain that blessing, which, if I gain, will raise me above all the monarchs on earth. Ah! Charles, when I contemplate her amiable innocence, that beauty which is without a blemish, the pure emblem of nature in the first creation of the world,[219] I certainly feel that I am unworthy of her; yet, at the same time, I swear from my soul, that not any other shall ever gain her.

EDMOND B—.[220]

CHAP. XII.

Suspicions confirmed – a walk.

It was really true, that before Sir Edmond had seen Malvina, in a moment of caprice, he had attempted to gain Miss Melmor, and that he had succeeded much sooner than he had expected; for that young lady had deluded herself with the hopes of marrying him, and of becoming by that means, independent of Mrs. Burton; she was therefore easily won, and fearing that she might be surprised, if she admitted him into her own apartment, she had consented[221] to go to his, under the pretence of settling some arrangements for their approaching union. But these frequent interviews, from the thoughtlessness of Sir Edmond, and the imprudence of Miss Melmor, were not sufficiently guarded, had been suspected by Mr. Prior, who nevertheless, 'till he was confirmed in these suspicions, thought it would be reprehensible in him to permit his doubts to appear, and fearing that Malvina, may also blame him, he waited impatiently for the hour of her rising, in order to wait on her.

He found her at breakfast with her little Frances. Surprised, though not offended, at seeing him at such an early hour, she begged he would take his tea with her, and never was there so cool an invitation accepted with such avidity. He was no sooner seated by his friend, than he began the subject which was the nearest his heart, and which had induced such an early visit. Though Malvina had determined not to make any enquiries relative to that affair, yet, he had no sooner mentioned the subject, than she forgot her resolution.[222] Mr. Prior found it impossible[223] to conceal any of his thoughts from her, freely told her his opinion, and his suspicions. On hearing which, a lively blush overspread her face, and she cried, is it possible that the severe Mr. Prior, can be guilty of so much weakness, as not to have warned and reprimanded this young person, or spoken to her mother and Mrs. Burton, on the danger she is in, and above all, why has he not shewn his indignation to that base man, who under the roof of virtue, blushes not at the corruption of innocence? – Ah! it is of little, I may say no use, replied he, either to warn or reprimand, except good could accrue from it. But, when my words make not the least impression, it is best to leave it to Divine wisdom and justice, who endows the wicked with malice as a self-punishment; and intemperate pleasures, as a chastisement; I am perfectly certain, that was I to speak to Sir Edmond, he would only smile at my remonstrances, and perhaps be more indefatigable in his pursuits. Mrs. Melmor is a very weak woman, who only views things as her daughter pleases, and who, if she was to scold her would soon finish, by asking her pardon.

Mrs. Burton, from the extreme coolness of her disposition, entirely devoid of sensibility, has ever been incapable of such a weakness; and for that reason, imagines that this superior virtue (which is in reality only negative, and so very easy) is the highest excellence in her character, therefore that all women suspected of wanting chastity, she regards as a scandal to humanity. For this reason was she informed of the conduct of Miss Melmor; she would not only turn her out of the house with contempt, but would publicly expose her. As to Miss Melmor, herself, she is merely a pretty puppet, without principles or delicacy, though she does not want for cunning and address, who unites a cold heart and a weak head; and perhaps might go off with Sir Edmond if she thought that she was suspected. What then would become of her? Abandoned in a little time by her seducer, another might soon replace him; and there is no knowing were such a one would stop, as those who have dared to take the first steps in such a career, would soon give her up to another;[224] and in the end, she perhaps might be tempted to prostitute herself; and thus increase the number of those shameless and wretched women, who have once blushed at the name of virtue, but soon cease to blush at all! Why said Malvina, timidly, will not Sir Edmond marry Miss Melmor? Because she would not suit him by any means; for notwithstanding the many vices of Sir Edmond, his character and prospects are brilliant, and he possesses a nobility of soul, and an energy of mind that is not very common; on the contrary, Miss Melmor is truly incapable of the least elevation of mind. I have already delineated to you all the vices which weakness entails upon itself; and there is not one quality which it can redeem; as beauty and wit therefore, are her only advantages, I am much deceived if they will not one day render her one of the most deceitful and dangerous of coquettes. Yet do you not imagine that Sir Edmond loves her? He pretends as much, and though every person here may endeavour to prove this to me as a truth, I cannot be convinced. For the human heart is such an abyss, that although I have been this fifteen years, endeavouring, its recesses are not to be fathomed.

For my own part, said Malvina, I cannot believe but that he has a passion for her. Undeceive yourself then, my good friend, for Sir Edmond is incapable of any thing serious. A habit for debauchery has tainted his heart, but was he even susceptible of experiencing such a deep attachment as a real passion, it must be a very different woman indeed, from Miss Melmor, who could produce such a reformation. I know but one, added he, looking stedfastly at Malvina, who unites all that could be wished for such a purpose. But as the distance which separates them is unmeasurable, he will never dare to raise his hopes to her, because he must be truly sensible, that she will never deign to look down upon him.

Malvina blushed, Mr. Prior's last sentence had occasioned an uneasy sensation, and in order to conceal it, and avoid answering, she arose and went to the window – returned – opened some books – then closed them as quickly – and again walked to the window – Mr. Prior, said Malvina, notwithstanding the excessive cold, the sun is so brilliant, that it must be rather pleasant on the borders of the lake; I have never been there, and have a great inclination to take a walk that way; you must not go alone, said Mr. Prior, will you permit me the pleasure to accompany you? Certainly, and I am going to ask Mrs. Burton to walk with me. She went into her dressing- room with Frances, and they quickly returned equipped in their double furred robes. They all went down, and on entering the saloon, she perceived Miss Melmor, seated before a harp, and Sir Edmond close at her side, whispering to her with great animation. Mrs. Burton was sitting by the fire with a book which she pretended to be reading, but was intirely occupied with looking in a glass[225] which was opposite, and which gave her an opportunity of seeing all that was acting behind her, and her mind absorbed in planning the future destiny of Miss Melmor.

The entrance of Malvina, changed the disposition of all their thoughts as well as their employments. Sir Edmond, fearful that his particular attentions to Miss Melmor had given Malvina some suspicions, felt rather uneasy. He approached her, and murmured a few expressions of astonishment and pleasure at this unexpected visit. Miss Melmor cruelly disappointed by an incident which interrupted a conversation that was to her of infinite importance, saluted Malvina with an expression of anger, without condescending to look at her. Mrs. Burton who had remarked her behaviour, was secretly rejoiced that she was thus mortified, and received Malvina with unusual kindness.

The walk was proposed, which Mrs. Burton accepted with that affected complaisance which plainly evinced that she wished it to be considered as a favour, for which she demanded an adequate return by Sir Edmond,[226] with that eagerness which the love of novelty and the pleasure of being near Malvina must inspire in such a mind. Miss Melmor accepted the invitation with a careless discontent, that was conscious of the irksome situation it would place her in, yet she could not devise any probable excuse to avoid going. The leafless trees, and the rocks covered with ice, glittered with the rays of the sun, and reflected all the brilliant colours of the rainbow. The snow which cloaked all the mountains, shone with such splendor, that the eyes were almost blinded by the light, though monotonous aspect of the country.[227] While contemplating the beautiful and sublime effect of the enlightening orb of day, Mr. Prior, as his eye wandered over the snow-clad earth, particularly admired its effect on the mountains; and said, who will not think with me, on that sublime invocation which Ossian made in the time of old. 'O thou that rollest above, round as the shield of my fathers! whence are thy beams, O sun? – thy everlasting light! – thou comest forth in thy awful beauty – the stars hide themselves in the sky: the moon cold and pale sinks in the western wave, but thou thyself movest alone: who can be a companion of thy course? The oaks of the mountains fall, the mountains themselves decay with years; the ocean shrinks, and grows again; the moon herself is lost in heaven; but thou art for ever the same, rejoicing in the brightness of thy course. When the world is dark with tempests; when the thunder rolls and the lightning flies; thou lookest in thy beauty from the clouds, and laughest at the storm'.*[228]

While Mr. Prior repeated this with enthusiasm, Malvina was plunged into a reverie, on recollecting the embarrassment Sir Edmond appeared in, on her entrance into the saloon. She certainly was not offended at his attention to Miss Melmor, but why was he so fearful of letting it appear before her. Did he wish to conceal it, or to deceive her? Her haughty soul revolted at the idea of being the object of such a plan, and she determined by the coolness of her behaviour to Sir Edmond, to convince him it would be impossible to succeed with her. She remembered every thing she had heard, and all served to depreciate him in her opinion. She drew a comparison between him and Mr. Prior, much to the advantage of the latter. If the persons who were the objects of these reflections, could have guessed what was passing in her mind, Mr. Prior would have been gratified, and Sir Edmond chagrined;[229] while she listened to their conversation, and remarked their different opinions, it confirmed the idea she had recently formed. Why, said Sir Edmond, do you require that we should let the men in power observe the contempt they inspire? When by their credit they may perhaps,[230] be of infinite service in obliging others. That bluntness and candour, of which you boast so much, does it not occasion their being left entirely to the flatterers who surround them, and keep them at a distance from all who possess discernment and rectitude, and who might perhaps be of service to them; in speaking their real sentiments?[231]

What, interrupted Mr. Prior, (with quickness) when a rascal in power, because he is so, and is rich, shall he, a despicable wretch, see himself received by the man of integrity, can they observe this, without having reason to believe that every thing is sacrificed to fortune?[232] If they disguised the contempt[233] which they really inspire, would it not undoubtedly plunge them deeper in vice, when they were carressed, and consequently encourage others, who but for that would have hesitated in imitating them. – No, no, those who have felt the dignity of which a virtuous man is capable of, will never prophane the character, and those who dare to compound with virtue, gives me a sanction to think, they have never known it. What a terrible condemnation, exclaimed Sir Edmond, smiling. Do

* Ossian's Poem of Carthon.

you know that if I was to judge of men by the severity of your maxims, I doubt, I should find few of the elect, and we should run the risque of being gloriously tired[234] in Paradise? I acknowledge, said Malvina, that Mr. Prior's principles are a little severe, but he bears the similitude with those Sterne mentions in his Sermons: 'Such are the hussars who strike a blow to the right and to the left, with great adroitness, and always serve as auxiliaries to virtue'.[235] At this instance the conversation was interrupted by the appearance of a man on one of the heights of the mountain. He seemed to be in years, and stept so cautiously, that they imagined that he must be blind. Mr. Prior who regarded him with great attention said, that venerable gait, that time-silvered beard, the cautious uncertain step, and that staff which appears to serve him instead of his eyes, indeed the tout ensemble of this old man,[i] recalls to my mind the image of Ossian, such as he was in the days of old; perhaps also, he might have stood on that very spot! Oh why have I not my pencils here that I might just take that fine old head. The unfortunate creature is surrounded by precipices, said Sir Edmond, and I think it will be of more utility to assist him, than to take his portrait. The rocks are so slippery and he cannot see. On saying these words he flew to the mountain, and climbing lightly, though not without difficulty on account of the ice, and in a short time,[236] he got up to the old man, took him by the arm, and leading him with care, he wound round the turnings of the mountain, which appeared to lead to an opposite direction, where from the great distance, they soon were out of sight. Mrs. Burton, after waiting some time, and finding they did not appear, took the road to the castle. This scene had not been lost upon Malvina. The generous behaviour of Sir Edmond had pleased her, and as they returned home, she reflected upon the theory and the practice of virtue, and imagined that perhaps they were not always united, and that those who spoke the most eloquently of it, were not the persons who practiced it the best.

CHAP. XIII.

Anxieties. The return.

They had waited 'till the hour of supper in vain, for Sir Edmond, but he had not appeared, every one was astonished at his absence, and for the first time Malvina did not return to her apartment after rising from table. She was uneasy, and soon became seriously so, as she found night had advanced, and the hours succeeded each other, and they saw no signs of his return. Malvina, could scarcely suppress her fears. The season being remarkably severe, the ways very dangerous, perhaps he might have fallen,[237] have lost himself, and not able to find an asylum. Why then not send some of the servants with flambeaux, to seek, call, and assist him.

It snows extremely hard, said Mr. Prior, how then can we think of sending the men out at such a late hour? Why have we then let Sir Edmond be exposed to all the rigour of such a severe night? cried Malvina; perhaps he may have had a long way to conduct the old man, and on his returning, the darkness may have overtaken him, the cold may stupify him; perhaps, at this moment, he has not even found a rock to shelter his head.[238] The snow also will prevent him, if he could, from seeing his way. It is a pity that so generous a being should be the victim of his benevolence. While Malvina thus expressed her feelings spontaneously, she was agitated and distressed, the tears glittered in her eyes, Mr. Prior much affected by her anxiety went to her, and said, I am ready to obey you in any thing you shall direct for the best. Would you wish that I should assemble the servants, and myself lead them to seek Sir Edmond? condescend to give me your commands.

Ah, Mr. Prior, said she, has not your heart any to dictate: I am much deceived if Sir Edmond would not have found some means[239] of assisting you in such a predicament. Mr. Prior was not cruelly hurt[240] by this last reply, though it did not render him the less solicitous to fulfil any of her wishes, and was just going out for that purpose, when Mrs. Burton prevented him, by saying, had it not been for the extraordinary anxiety of my cousin, I should perhaps have been more astonished to hear both of you giving orders concerning my servants, without my leave. But, on the account I mentioned, I shall excuse it, only permit me to object to such a step, which will be giving the men so much trouble, besides the hardships they must suffer such a night as this, and all, perhaps, without being of any service to Sir Edmond, as we may very naturally conclude he will not be so imprudent as to offer to return so late as this, and that he is determined to pass the night in the cabin of the mountaineer.[241]

It is really a pity, madam, that you did not mention all this in the morning, and also have persuaded Sir Edmond that he might be sure that the old man would find his way alone. Thanks to your prudent suggestions, madam, your nephew cannot be in any danger.[242] My dear, said Mrs. Burton, in a tone of raillery, after looking at her a moment in silence: of what service is this extreme display of sensibility? Have you not sufficiently shewn that you possess it, and that we have not any occasion for farther proofs. Really, interrupted Malvina, with some degree of warmth, is it Mrs. Burton herself, who, at such a moment as this, when the life of a man, of your own nephew, is perhaps in danger, that could harbour the unnatural idea that any one should think of self?

Good Heaven, my dear cousin, replied Mrs. Burton, are we not perfectly certain that there are persons who seldom think of any thing else? Yes, without a doubt, said Mr. Prior, and I cannot conceive why Madame de Sorcy can yet have a doubt remaining on that point. This discourse, which Mrs. Burton had sufficient penetration to appreciate, very much offended her, and she was on the point of replying to it, as if she had taken it, when by a happy presence of mind, she felt, that to be angry, would immediately shew in what manner she applied it, and unwilling that any one should have the slightest idea that she even understood such an insinuation, she replied, with great mildness, it appears, my dear Malvina, as if I had been unjust; but when I have far more reason than any other person to be uneasy, as it is impossible any one here can love my nephew equal to myself; it appeared rather strange to me, that you should dictate what I ought to do, and then tax me with calmness and prudence, for a refusal which was only prompted by humanity. – Humanity! cried Malvina, with astonishment. Certainly, continued Mrs. Burton, for I have no right to sacrifice several persons for the safety of one. It was, therefore, from a motive of duty alone that I gave up the almost ungovernable desire of sending my people to seek for Sir Edmond. And believe me, my dear Malvina, that not any thing should have prevented my doing so, but that I felt it would not be acting justly.

Mrs. Burton, however, had not once thought of any one of these particulars, 'till the idea had been given by another, which, to adopt, was a proof that Malvina was more affected than herself; and this was the true reason why Mrs. Burton would not give her consent.

It was very late when the company separated. Malvina, when alone, became a prey to the most painful solicitude. – She sent Mrs. Tomkins to bed, and remained by the fire – anxiety kept her awake; and agitation prevented her from amusing herself. Terrified at the violence of the wind, which made her casements[243] rattle, she arose and went to the window, and found that it still snowed. She imagined that it must at least be two feet deep, and that Sir Edmond might be buried in it where it drifted. The torrents, which murmured from a distance, seemed to her like the cries of distress:[244] she wept, and prayed for his safety.

Malvina had been so much used to anxiety, and she knew so little how to be otherwise, that though, on this occasion, she experienced an extreme degree of solicitude, she was so far from attributing it to the real cause, that she had not the idea, but that she should have felt just in the same manner for any other person; and that Sir Edmond, in particular, had no share in her anxiety, more than the natural degree which all those in affliction inspired.[245] There are some minds which are so susceptible of humanity, that it evinces itself as plainly as the most powerful emotions of affection. It was near an hour after daybreak, that Malvina, exhausted by fatigue, had thrown herself upon a sopha, and a light sleep had just closed her eye-lids, when she was disturbed by the gate-bell resounding through the castle: she immediately got up, and left her room, to look out of the casement which fronted the court; and the first person she saw, was Sir Edmond, covered with snow, surrounded by the servants, who, as they advanced, seemed to question him with earnestness and affection.

She hurried back to her chamber; and, with tears, thanked Heaven for his safe return.[246] A short time after, she heard a general stir in the house; and, amidst the confusion of voices, she could distinguish those of Mrs. Burton, Mr. Prior, and Miss Melmor.[247] She wished, though she felt a disagreeable sensation at the ideas of going down. She recollected the solicitude she had manifested; and it made her blush at the idea of appearing before so many witnesses of it. Besides, she feared Mrs. Melmor, and her daughter might inform Sir Edmond of all she had suffered; and though she did not allow there was any thing uncommon in what she had felt, perhaps Sir Edmond, whose ideas were not so delicate, might think differently. She had been told that he was presumptuous; and such a character very likely would treat such feelings with contempt.[248]

While she was reflecting thus, her door was suddenly opened, and Sir Edmond appeared before her; his cloaths wet and disordered, his face pale, and his whole appearance evinced fatigue; except his eyes, which were brilliant, and animated with all that hope, and the most lively tenderness could express. Ah, madam! cried he, may I really hope they have not deceived me. Is it true that you have been interested in what became of me? That your generous mind condescended to think of me? That hope, had I dared to imagine it, would have made me forget all my difficulties, and have even rendered them pleasing. Ah, do not refuse to confirm it? Let me but hear from your lips, that I have been present in your thoughts, and the object of your pity?

In pronouncing these words,[249] he had taken the hand of Malvina, and fixed his eyes on hers,[xxiv] with an ardour and tender solicitude, which made her blush. She felt surprised, and confused; and hesitatingly replied: certainly I have been under some anxiety; but who is there who has not felt the same? The night has been so tremendous, and you walked so fast, that we feared that—. Sir Edmond! cried Miss Melmor, as she came in half breathless,[250] I am tired with following you; and there was not the least necessity for your saying much, to cheer Madame de Sorcy's spirits.

Has she been pathetic in the recital of her uneasiness? But, God bless me, added she, observing Malvina's bed had not been occupied – I believe she has never been in bed. Really, I could have done no more. But, good Heaven! my dear madam, how you are altered; your eyes are quite heavy and dull; you do not look like yourself. Ah! cried Sir Edmond, transported, and looking at Malvina with a tenderness he could not conceal, he thought that she had never appeared so beautiful. Malvina, all confusion, stammered out a few sentences, saying, her anxiety had not been particular; and that it had been exaggerated.

Miss Melmor, piqued at the preference which Sir Edmond evinced for Malvina, endeavoured to revenge herself, by rallying her in the severest manner. She tried to imitate her pleasing voice; and, with some delicacy, threw a vein of ridicule into her discourse, in order to render herself more amiable[251] in the eyes of her lover; and, perhaps, she might have succeeded, if the hope of being loved by Malvina had not, for the present, absorbed all the faculties of Sir Edmond. He interpreted her embarrassment, which became every moment more visible; and her blushes created the most delightful sensations. With true affection, delicacy glides into the heart, and it does not wish to receive one pleasure, at the price of creating a pain to those we love. He therefore endeavoured to conceal the joy he felt, and hastened from her, without appearing to remark her agitation, intreating her to pardon the liberty he had taken of so abruptly entering her room.

For some days Miss Melmor took a malicious pleasure in teazing Malvina, by continually recurring to the same subject; but Sir Edmond always changed the discourse, with so much delicacy, that Malvina could not avoid remarking that, in that point, he perfectly coincided with her. One day, when the same subject had been again resumed, and chance had left them alone in the drawing-room, Malvina seized the opportunity, when freed from their raillery, to ask a few questions concerning that day's encounter; and if he had really walked all the way there and back?[252] Yes, replied, Sir Edmond; the snow and the tempest increasing, prevented my reaching the castle 'till morning; and I continued walking all the time, as I had lost my path.[253] I sacrificed the pleasure of remaining with you, to that of helping a poor old man; and I would have risqued my life to have returned a moment sooner.

This was not said with the air of a compliment; neither was it meant as one. – Sir Edmond felt what he said: yet, the recollection of Miss Melmor, preserved Malvina from believing him; and she sighed at the idea of his regarding her in the same light as other women, which she could not but think, from his addressing such unmeaning and ready compliments to her, which she had heard him often ridicule. The sigh did not pass unnoticed by Sir Edmond; he looked at Malvina with an anxious tenderness, and endeavoured to develope her silence. What is it that absorbs your thoughts? enquired Sir Edmond. Ah! if I could but read your heart. You would have nothing to read in it but mourning and sorrow, replied Malvina; for the more I know of the world, the more severely I feel the loss which I have sustained.[254]

My beloved friend possessed a soul where purity and candor resided; I might say, with truth, all the virtues had taken refuge there; for she was a living temple of goodness. – And in losing her, like Eve, in Milton, I am chased from Eden, and feel as if I was disenchanted by painful comparisons.[255] Ah, replied Sir Edmond, with emotion, are you then ignorant that there is another Eden, besides friendship? and infinitely more delightful, more enchanting – as much above it as happiness is superior to repose. If I could believe it, I should not be the happier, since I have vowed never to resign myself to it.

Ah! and can you think yourself bound by a vow which nature revolts at? asked Sir Edmond. You was wrong in making it, and will be still more culpable in keeping it. I break it,[256] replied Malvina, it is a subject on which I do not know how to jest; and therefore it is too serious for you. And do you imagine I cannot be serious sometimes, madam?[257] You are certainly the best judge of that, Sir Edmond, replied Malvina, smiling; and I will not dispute it with you.

If it is so, added she, I ought to congratulate Miss Melmor. Miss Melmor! interrupted he, astonished; why, Miss Melmor? What concern is it of hers?[xxv] I do not think that I need to inform you of that. I see, madam, replied he, gravely, that I have been slandered by someone. Slandered! Sir Edmond – What! in supposing that you was very naturally attracted[258] by the graces of a charming young lady. I think it has rather all the appearance of truth! Without wishing to derogate from any charms which Miss Melmor may possess, madam, I must say, that if during my residence here, if she had been capable of fixing me, I should have appeared contemptible indeed, in my own opinion. I in love with Miss Melmor! Oh, Heavens! my heart revolts at such an accusation.

However that may be, added Malvina, I believe you are the only one who doubt it. I should be very sorry if Miss Melmor believed it, madam; though infinitely more so, if I thought you really did. Dare I ask, if it was yourself who remarked the inclination which you suppose I have for her? No, sir; and I believe I should not have thought of it, if every body had not mentioned it. And this every body is, madam –; but very seldom with those whom you see.[259]

As to that, added she, it is of little consequence; I only wonder why you should deny it, as if it was a crime, so very natural a sentiment.

Miss Melmor is pretty and amiable; her character is gay and lively, like your own. Yes, madam, interrupted Sir Edmond, I know that I am often reproached with being so, even to folly; but, believe me, I possess a mind capable of being otherwise. And this was exactly the reason, though unknown to Malvina, which had insensibly subdued her. While she thought that she had nothing to fear, in that respect, from Sir Edmond, as their dispositions were so very opposite; she had not foreseen that there are attractions for a sensible woman in a mind naturally gay, when she is conscious that she can render it serious; and, from being a flighty character, teach him to be a steady one.

The turn which this conversation occasioned, began rather to embarrass Malvina. The rest of the evening she was thoughtful and absorbed; and continued the same during the next day. The remembrance of her friend, though ever present, had lost that poignancy in the grief she felt; and though always indulging the same sentiment of friendship, she now found herself more agitated, particularly when she thought of Sir Edmond, which she more frequently did, though she did not yet suspect her own heart of so great a preference. She did not perceive, that when the mind has been deeply affected by sorrow, it is more liable to imbibe an evil, which will cause it infinitely more pain than what it has already experienced. That at the very moment when it ought to be resisted, it is already too late.[260]

How could Malvina develope the cause of the enchantment, of which she found herself susceptible? not from experience, for she had not any from friendship. Lady Sheridan no longer existed;[261] and Mr. Prior could not replace her. He was not, nor ever could be, that second self, which that lady had been.[262] Besides, in her situation, the friendship of men generally appeared to be influenced by interested motives. They did not possess that delicacy of feeling and sensibility, which gently forces a friend to tell what she wishes to disclose;[263] which can penetrate into those feelings, delicacy does not wish to acknowledge, and sympathise with that sensibility, without causing it to blush.

Mr. Prior had never imagined it was possible for Malvina to have a regard for Sir Edmond, their characters were so perfectly opposite; that the more he endeavoured to develope them, the greater he found the dissimilarity. One was so constant; the other so changeable. The one treated with so much frivolity, what the other regarded as sacred. Sir Edmond wished only for pleasure; Malvina required only affection. The gratification of the moment was quite sufficient for the first; but a whole life would be scarcely enough for the constancy and delicate sensibility of her heart. Where there is not the least congeniality of mind, can she feel an attraction, and love one whom she really does not understand? Thus thought Mr. Prior.

But he was not sensible, that if love is the offspring of sympathy, it is also the child of contrast. That sometimes they are united, by the most indissoluble ties; while those who appear by nature to be formed for each other, never meet.[264]

END OF VOL. I.[265]

H. Reynell, Printer, 21, Piccadilly.

MALVINA,
by Madame C****,

Authoress of Claire d'Albe, and Amelia Mansfield.

Translated from the French,

by Miss Gunning,

in four volumes.

VOL. II.

London:

printed for T. Hurst, Paternoster-Row;

C. Chapple, Pall-Mall, and Southampton-

Row, Russell-Square; and R. Dutton,

Gracechurch-Street.

H. Reynell, Printer, 21, Piccadilly.

1803.

MALVINA.

CHAP. 1

The intrigue understood.

It was very seldom that Sir Edmond had the opportunity of being alone with Malvina; who, though she did not seclude herself so much as she had done, yet continued to consecrate part of each day to the education of Frances; and whenever she went down, she generally found Mrs. Burton or Miss Melmor in the saloon. An indifferent person was sufficient to throw a restraint over her,[1] consequently, the presence of such interested observers, must have rendered it disagreeably irksome. The restless ambition of Mrs. Burton, and the scrutinising jealousy of Miss Melmor, who was continually watching the motions of Sir Edmond, and maliciously interpreting those of Malvina, if she was seated by chance near the object of her wishes. One look from Mrs. Burton created a blush on the cheek of Malvina; if Sir Edmond seized an opportunity of conversing with her, Miss Melmor immediately bent forward to hear the reply.

As Malvina did not say any thing that she did not wish every one to hear, it was of little importance to her what Miss Melmor heard. Malvina, without ever penetrating into the motive which induced her to wish to go down, went earlier every day and retired later: she never particularly avoided being alone with Sir Edmond, yet when it happened, which was very seldom, they conversed the same as when they had witnesses present; only we may suppose there might have been a different expression, and a more lively interest betrayed.

When alone with those we love, the thoughts may sometimes be guessed, without revealing the secret. But the same countenance will endeavour to conceal that expression before a third person, and therefore, the presence of those who have particular reasons for remarking the actions of others (in such instances) are generally dreaded. Sir Edmond was however not a little impatient, under the severe restraint which he was obliged to undergo before Mrs. Burton, and the teazing watchfulness which he continually suffered from Miss Melmor; his haughty spirit being little accustomed to contradiction: it was at this time particularly painful, as it regarded a woman who interested him, and the being compelled to disguise his partiality for Malvina, became every day more insupportable; and he resolved to rid himself, at least, of that witness which he was conscious was the most dangerous.

As his sole intention was to gain Malvina's affection, in order to succeed, the most essential step would be, to send away Miss Melmor, whom he knew he had injured, without considering or feeling the least concern for what might ensue from it; or from the anger of Mrs. Burton, who would have only him to reproach.[2] He had observed that the passion he had pretended from Miss Melmor, in the absence of Malvina, when Mrs. Burton was present, had not had the desired effect on his aunt, and therefore not obtaining the success he had promised himself,[3] he thought he must devise some other stratagem, in order to accomplish his wishes.

His behaviour had caused Miss Melmor to assume a haughtiness and freedom in her words and actions, which a person of Mrs. Burton's overbearing disposition, would not long support; while she, proud of the attentions of Sir Edmond, not doubting but that he would marry her, followed his advice, which was never to acquiesce with Mrs. Burton in any of her capricious whims, as she had been accustomed to do. She consequently treated her with all the haughtiness of a person who was confident of success.

Mrs. Burton must have been perfectly metamorphosed, if she could have submitted to this arrogant treatment: Miss Melmor's humiliation or removal was therefore necessary to her existence. She did not particularly fear that Sir Edmond would marry her; but she clearly perceived that was expected, and the pride which this idea had created, was become insupportable; she therefore resolved to put an end to this proceeding.

By the promise of a tolerable fortune, she soon found a husband, which she thought more eligible for her ward. She desired Mrs. Melmor's attendance, as she had something particular to communicate to her. This request was immediately complied with; and she abruptly declared in the presence of Sir Edmond, that she desired Mrs. Melmor would immediately obtain the consent of her daughter to a marriage she should propose; and if she refused to comply, they must both of them instantly quit the house. Sir Edmond, though he hoped to reap the advantage of his scheme, yet did not expect the accomplishment of it so early. He was, in consequence, so agreeably surprised at Mrs. Burton's declaration, that he affected a concern, which he pretended to hide by covering his face with his hand; but secretly to conceal the joy it had occasioned.

As to Mrs. Melmor, her daughter had assured her that she should become Lady Burton, as Sir Edmond had promised to marry her: with this idea, on hearing Mrs. Burton's proposal, she remained as if petrified, 'till recollecting Sir Edmond was in the room, she fixed her looks on him, and her astonishment increased on marking his silence. The angry discontent which Mrs. Burton expressed in her countenance, united with the menace she had just uttered, seemed to have annihilated the small portion of sense with which nature had endowed her, without offering a reply, as her tongue appeared chained by fear.

Her friend was so little accustomed to find her hesitate whenever she spoke to her, that she repeated her commands with more severity. When Mrs. Melmor endeavoured to answer, and stammeringly said, I thought my dear Mrs. Burton, that is I supposed, in reality, I had imagined, that you had destined my daughter for Sir Edmond.

How Miss Melmor could have the ridiculous vanity to such a pretension, replied Mrs. Burton, disdainfully, is what I am really at a loss to conceive; but it is still more strange, that she should have succeeded in making you a partner in her folly – Sir Edmond is here, and if it had been any thing more than an idle fancy of her own, he would explain himself; it was for that reason that I have spoken to you when he was present: but, I think I may venture to assure you, that he will never renounce the advantageous union which awaits him, for the caprice of a day: for if he should, neither himself or your daughter will have any thing to expect from me.

On any other occasion, Sir Edmond would have revolted at such a threat,[4] but the advantage which he should gain by pretending to acquiesce in the views of Mrs. Burton, coincided but too well with his secret wishes; he therefore formally renounced all pretension to the heart of Miss Melmor. Why then did you tell my daughter that you would marry her? said Mrs. Melmor, in a passion – why desire her to visit in your own apartment – was it to abandon her after having seduced her?

Sir Edmond was confounded on finding Mrs. Melmor acquainted with all the affair; and thus exposing her daughter's shame so publicly. Mrs. Burton immediately demanded, with much indignation, what was meant by such an accusation, and if it was really possible he could have the audacity to prophane the house in such a manner; and render it an asylum for his intrigues?

No, no, replied Mrs. Melmor, my daughter has not any thing to reproach herself with, that I am certain, for she told me so. But I cannot help blaming Sir Edmond for having enticed her to his apartment, that they might consult together on the preparations for their marriage, before he had obtained your permission to marry her. Do you not think I also have reason to blame him, said Mrs. Burton.[5] You are convinced that your daughter has had the imprudence to visit Sir Edmond alone, and yet do not believe she is lost, dishonored, and unworthy to breathe the same air with me? elevating her voice at every word she uttered. Ah! good God, my dear friend, said Mrs. Melmor, trembling; I assure you that you terrify me, indeed you do. Yet permit me to say, that if every person was ruined by being in the room alone with a gentleman, I do not know what we are to think of Madame de Sorcy.

At these words, Sir Edmond was so violently agitated, that it prevented him from speaking: when Mrs. Burton said, with quickness, in the name of Heaven! explain yourself, what has passed there? Is it possible that my cousin, one of my own relations, under my eyes, she who possesses such an air of innocence. No, no, it is not possible, I cannot believe it! I do not directly assert, returned Mrs. Melmor, that Madame de Sorcy is in the least guilty; but it is certain that every morning Mr. Prior goes up to her room, where he stays at least two hours; and they appear to be very agreeable to each other. He is not so haughty when with her; I suppose the gentleness which is so conspicuous in her behaviour, will render him less severe.[6] We know there is nothing to fear in still water;[7] and I should not be surprised if her fine sentiments had alienated the heart of Sir Edmond from my daughter. – But Heaven is just, and I hope I shall live long enough to see her used in the same manner.

Mrs. Burton continued silent some moments, then sighing deeply, she exclaimed, it is really a truth then, that a virtuous example has not any influence; I had imagined that in my presence, vice and indecency would have blushed; and that I should have inspired the love of wisdom and morality. But I observe with sorrow, that there is no defence against general corruption; and that there is not any, unless I speak for myself, that I can believe is really virtuous.

Sir Edmond, who cared very little for Mrs. Burton's perfection, had waited with the utmost impatience for the conclusion of her speech, to enquire of Mrs. Melmor, what was the motive of Mr. Prior's visits every day to Madame de Sorcy's apartment? He pretends, she replied, that it is to give her some lessons, in God knows what; for my part, I do not know what passes between them: I am good myself, and God preserve me from speaking ill of any one. So it appears, replied Sir Edmond, with agitation; and if it was so, you would not form such wretched motives; have dared to attack the reputation of Madame de Sorcy. Though this was said with an assumed indifference, his heart was torn with jealousy: for it is the misfortune of those men who have been most conversant with the vicious and depraved part of the sex, to have the least reliance on their virtue.

But, though he could not prevent himself from being uneasy at Malvina's intimacy with Mr. Prior, yet, the idea that any other should have the least doubt of her, was insupportable to him. Mrs. Burton was astonished at the vehemence with which he expressed himself on the occasion; and said, I do not know, Edmond, why you should speak so highly of Madame de Sorcy's wisdom? I acknowledge that at her age, and also Mr. Prior's function,[8] renders her much more excusable than Miss Melmor; yet, she is censurable in having such appearances against her; and I shall take care to inform her, that I think so. As to your daughter, my dear, said she, turning to Mrs. Melmor, I shall, from the regard I have for you, and the long friendship which has united us, never divulge this shameful affair; but she must on this condition, consent to obey me without hesitation, or she will have to repent all the days of her life.

Mrs. Melmor assured her friend in the most submissive manner of her daughter's perfect obedience. And Sir Edmond, fearful (and with reason) of Miss Melmor's reproaches whenever he met her, determined to leave the castle as soon as possible; and immediately told Mrs. Burton, that in consequence of what had happened, and to avoid the regrets on both sides, he would absent himself 'till the ceremony was performed. Mrs. Burton was however not to be so easily deceived by the air of affected sorrow, which he assumed as he pronounced these words.

She looked at him with an expression of incredulity; but she was so rejoiced at the idea of his departure, that she was regardless of the motive from which it proceeded. It was therefore agreed between them, that not any thing of the above should transpire to Miss Melmor, 'till after his departure; which was fixed for the next day.

He retired to his chamber, a prey to the most painful sensations. Malvina's intimacy with Mr. Prior was insupportable to him. He wished to penetrate into the cause, as well as the effect. He could only judge by the pleasure he experienced in the company of Malvina,[9] not that he had an idea of any thing improper, with regard to her; but the slightest expression of her esteem for any other, he considered as an unpardonable deprivation, which seemed to despoil him of his right. He wished to be the sole object of her thoughts, and that her heart should alone feel for him. He would have been jealous of Lady Sheridan, had she been living.[10] He would have sacrificed his life to have penetrated Malvina's private sentiments. – Nevertheless, from an inherent pride, which was increased by the conquest of so many women; for the moment[11] he was in doubt of the affection of a woman, he disdained to stoop for it, or acknowledge an attachment, without he was conscious of its being reciprocal: however jealousy might torment him, it would never force him to complain; and if it sometimes pierced his bosom, it was involuntary – against his inclination, and only in those moments when nature proved more powerful than vanity.

Certainly the sentiments which Malvina inspired, bore not the least resemblance to any thing he had ever experienced; but all powerful as it was, he would never have made the slightest confession of his affection, if he had not read in her eyes, that what he uttered did not offend her. He therefore waited, though impatiently, for the moment which might elucidate this; when Mrs. Melmor put a stop to this overflow of tenderness, and he determined not to open his heart, before he was convinced if her accusation had any foundation. And if he found it confirmed, that any other could for a moment leave a doubt of preference in the heart of Malvina; he resolved to forget her.[12]

CHAP. II.

The eve of a departure.

In the evening, as they were all sitting at the tea table, Mrs. Burton occupied by the pleasure of humbling Miss Melmor, by the marriage she intended: at the same time she was rather uneasy on Malvina's account, and dubious in what manner to act with respect to her.[13] Mrs. Melmor was endeavouring to recollect something that might amuse her more than dwelling on the anger of Mrs. Burton, and the fear of her daughter's disappointment: and she was supposed to be in deep reflection, because she was silent.

Sir Edmond was thoughtful and melancholy, leaning with his elbow against the chimney-piece, as he held a newspaper in his hand, which he was pretending to read; though entirely absorbed by his affection for Malvina, yet unhappy at the idea of leaving her – and the fear of not possessing her heart. On the opposite side of the table, was seated Malvina, by her little girl, shewing her some prints, and explaining the different subjects to her. Miss Melmor was with much negligence looking over Frances's shoulder at them: and Mr. Prior pacing the room, absorbed in reflection.

This silence was interrupted by Miss Melmor, who being the youngest, drew near the table to make the tea. When she had offered it round, Malvina was holding the cup in her hand, Mrs. Burton addressing Sir Edmond, said, you do not mean to go 'till after breakfast tomorrow, I suppose? He bowed. Where are you going then, asked Miss Melmor, with quickness? Some very particular business requires my attendance in Edinburgh. Oh, mama, you have scalded me, cried little Frances, with tears in her eyes; and shaking the tea from her fingers. Malvina was vexed at spilling her tea on the child.[14]

Will you make a long stay there, enquired Miss Melmor? with visible vexation. Yes, replied Sir Edmond, fixing his eyes on Malvina, I am not certain whether I shall not be obliged to go to England.[15] On hearing this, Malvina turned pale, and she felt her heart flutter.[16] Sir Edmond had marked all these emotions, he went to her under pretence of taking her cup, and touching her hand, he felt it cold and moist. Such a sudden and lively sensation in an instant, removed all his doubts. He was perfectly convinced that he was beloved – he seated himself by her, and was sincerely grateful in possessing the affections of so lovely a woman.

Malvina, who was overpowered by the most melancholy sensations, continued silent, and did not even imagine that she was observed. The idea of his departure, which she had never heard mentioned, gave her a sudden shock, which awakened a thousand painful ideas, and which as they succeeded each with rapidity, she was fearful of investigating, and wished to remain in doubt; but she could no longer conceal it from herself. The more wretched her heart felt, the stronger was her conviction. It is when the mind is overshadowed by sorrow, that certain truths, like a flash of lightning, darts from the darkness, and throws a gleam of light on some obscure point, which like this flash, strikes conviction to the heart. Oh! fatal light – unpardonable weakness – Oh! my dear Frances. Such were the mental spontaneous expressions of Malvina, and the first time she had felt the fatal presentiment: and on repeating the last, she eagerly pressed Frances to her bosom, as if to prevent the intrusion of any other sentiment.

Sir Edmond easily penetrated into the cause of this last action; which served to increase his affection, as it made him more vain at the idea of conquering in such a heart, the remembrance of a friend, the conscientious scruples of a vow, and a sentiment of duty. This mute scene had not lasted above a minute; but it was one of those critical minutes of existence, when these new sensations pour like a torrent on the mind, and mark its future course, and which has given life to the embryo seed, that was enclosed in the bosom, and lay dormant, 'till this critical moment[17] informed us that we possessed that, which alone decides our present and future destiny, while they glide unperceived by others, like a passing cloud.

Thus, while Malvina in idea had ranged so great a space, Miss Melmor had remained immoveable with astonishment, on hearing Sir Edmond's reply. To England,[18] she at last exclaimed, what can be the business which calls you so unexpectedly to so great a distance? Sir Edmond is not accountable to you for his actions, Kitty, said Mrs. Burton, imperiously – why am I always obliged to reprimand you for the rudeness of your questions? Whatever may be the motives which have determined me, replied Sir Edmond, to this journey, they ought to be very powerful, since they force me to leave this place and the most amiable society, which would be an inducement for my stay; and also to make me wish a quick return. Sir Edmond, hastily interrupted Mrs. Burton (who feared that both Malvina and Miss Melmor might each of them apply the compliment).[19] To prevent you from dwelling on what we shall mutually feel at parting, would it not be better to amuse yourselves with a little music?

Most willingly, replied Sir Edmond, with eagerness, in the hope that in going from the saloon to the music-room, he might find an opportunity of speaking to Malvina. You must not depend on my singing, said Miss Melmor, with vexation, for I am not at all disposed. We can dispense with that, replied Mrs. Burton, in the same tone. Mrs. Melmor who saw that her friend was displeased, made a motion to her daughter, to inform her there was a particular reason for this behaviour; but that she need not make herself uneasy, as she would soon be informed of it. Dear aunt, said Sir Edmond, will you be so good as to let us have that new selection of French songs which you received this morning?[20] – Seeing that she hesitated, he added, in a whisper, because if they are pretty, I shall intreat you will permit me to present them to Lady Mary. Mrs. Burton went immediately to fetch them. For ever this detestable French, said Miss Melmor, rising from her seat with ill humour. Sir Edmond approached her, and looking tenderly at her, as they were at a distance from the rest of the company, said, in a manner which could only be understood by her – Of what consequence is all this to you; cannot you remain here alone? I shall soon return. Miss Melmor imagined she understood his meaning, and, re-seating herself, declared she would not go with the others. Mrs. Melmor thought by following her example, to satisfy her daughter's curiosity, saying, she did not fancy music. Sir Edmond was delighted to get quit of both of them;[21] and taking Malvina's silence for consent, he presented his hand to lead her to the music-room, but being not the least disposed to sing, and Tomkins just then entering, to take Frances to bed, she rose up to follow the child. Sir Edmond, perceiving her intention, endeavoured to detain her;[22] she had no sooner stood up, than she felt a tremor all over her, and seemed near falling; she caught hold of Sir Edmond's arm to sustain herself. He immediately guessed the cause of this agitation; determined not to give her time to deny him, and taking advantage of her weakness, lead her to the music-room. Frances, on finding her mother did not follow her, as she thought she meant to have done, began to cry from the disappointment. Malvina instantly turned to yield to her intreaties, when Sir Edmond, turning to Mr. Prior, who was following them said, as he gave him a paper of sweetmeats,[23] dear sir, will you endeavour to appease that dear child with these sweetmeats, as I am positive you will succeed best, for Frances loves you tenderly, and you are the only person here who can console her in the absence of her mother.

Mr. Prior was flattered by a compliment which he thought might render him more agreeable to Malvina, immediately went back, and taking Frances in his arms, carried her up stairs. By this stratagem, Sir Edmond was alone with Malvina in the music-room. He prevailed on her to place herself at the piano, which she did mechanically; but, from the confusion of her thoughts, she could not distinguish a note. Sir Edmond opened the part of Armida[24] which is the duet[25] at the conclusion; and fixing his eyes on her, he sung this air in the most plaintive and tender manner. 'Armida, I am going to leave you'. These words, which were so applicable, and the tone in which they were expressed, so greatly augmented her agitation, that all her efforts were vain, and her tears betrayed what she attempted to conceal. Sir Edmond, on observing this, seized her hand, and pressed it to his lips with ardor, exclaiming as he held it, ah! is it really true? can it be possible that my departure is not indifferent to the most charming, the most adorable of women? – Ah! what a severe punishment should I have considered it, had I left this place without having dared to express all which you have inspired.[26] I have been a prey to the insinuations of others; and possessing a character naturally ardent and impetuous, it occasions inconsistences, which originate from the anxiety of a passionate heart, who only wished to be convinced if its affection was returned. Ah! was I not also to leave you with an amiable, virtuous, and worthy man, capable of appreciating all your merits, and who is permitted to visit you every day alone. At these words, Malvina looked at Sir Edmond with astonishment, and then said, have I done wrong in admitting Mr. Prior's visits? You cannot do wrong, he replied, with vivacity; but you can give me infinite affliction. Ah! exclaimed she, spontaneously from her heart, I do not wish to afflict *you*![j] Sir Edmond, delighted at the expressions which had escaped her, was just going to answer, when the entrance of Mr. Prior prevented him.

Malvina was so little accustomed to disguise her emotions, that had she attempted it, she would not have succeeded, at least not from the penetrating looks of Mr. Prior. But Sir Edmond was so well versed in deceit of this nature, that it was become habitual; he therefore immediately changed the conversation, with so much ease and gaiety, that the most scrutinizing observer would never have discovered that the moment before he had been affected. Malvina made no reply to all the disagreeable nothings[27] which he uttered; but kept turning over the leaves of the music-book,[k] and appeared to be looking for a song, without knowing what she did. Mr. Prior seated himself opposite to her, and looking steadily at her, he immediately asked what had been the matter – why do you look so pale? This question occasioned a blush. She who had so lately developed her own feelings, was fearful that every one else would penetrate them; and because she was exclusively absorbed by one object, and imagined the thoughts of every other was directed to the same subject; and she supposed it impossible but that they must read in her eyes what she so poignantly felt in her heart.

Mr. Prior having waited in vain for a reply, fancied Malvina had not heard him, and enquired a second time with greater earnestness, why she was so changed, and what had occasioned it? Malvina, thus questioned, hastily answered that she was perfectly well, and just as usual: but as she pronounced these words, a blush of the deepest shade dyed her countenance, for she had uttered an untruth:[28] she told it Mr. Prior who she regarded as a friend; and Sir Edmond, whom she could not deceive by such answer, she included in the secret.

At this instant, Mrs. Burton returned, and Malvina appeared in haste to begin the songs; but each person was absorbed by their particular ideas; every one seemed at cross purposes, and sung without attention, while the rest listened without pleasure. They were on the point of concluding, when Mrs. Burton, in turning over the songs, and yawning at the same time, said, I have found one, which was written by a woman. Mr. Prior taking it, told Malvina she could not conclude without playing it, in compliment to her countrywoman. Sir Edmond smiled approbation, and placing the song before her, she began it, as she would not deny him. The words were very trifling,[29] yet, they made such an impression on Malvina, that her voice could scarcely be heard. Come, said Mrs. Burton, I think you had better leave off, as I observe you are not in a humour for music this evening, for I never heard you sing so ill. A look from Sir Edmond informed Malvina that he thought very differently, and stooping forward as if to read the song, he said, in a low voice, which no one heard but Malvina, your singing this evening was delightful, as it gave the promise of supreme felicity. I was going to leave you without hope; but one word, one look, can raise me to ecstacy. Malvina's eyes were instantly cast down, as she was conscious a look would have been an answer; but she was ignorant that her silence was equally so – and Sir Edmond construed it as such. On leaving the saloon,[30] Malvina, overcome by the sensations she felt, begged her cousin's permission to retire, which was instantly granted. Ah! why will you leave us? demanded Sir Edmond, with vivacity. But,[31] if you should not come down to breakfast, will you permit me to pay my respects to you in your apartment? Malvina desired he would not give himself that trouble, as she certainly would go down in the morning. –She went up to her room, and walking hastily backward and forward, she trembled at the idea of investigating her heart; and in the tumult which her agitation occasioned, she uttered this soliloquy:

Happiness is departing from me[32] – Why am I so agitated? I tremble, and cannot connect my ideas – Why have I beheld a being who has such a sudden power over me? – Why is he the cause of such poignant sensations? – Do I love? no, no; I think I do not, I am sure of it; for do I not rather wish to avoid, than to see him? Depart, oh! depart, Edmond, and deliver me from thy sight – I have beheld you too long. Then pausing a moment, she continued – Is this a dream? Art thou not before me every moment? perhaps to-morrow.[33] The voice of Frances recalled her ideas; and throwing herself by the side of the bed, she exclaimed, ah! have I not promised to consecrate my days to this child? – Did not my beloved Clara, on her death bed, receive my vow? Methinks, that from the seats of bliss she looks down upon me; but, can she know me in my present situation? – Oh! thou guardian angel, sainted holy spirit, behold my tears, and have pity on me – Shield me from this weakness! Ah! it is certainly for my repose that this dangerous being is going to leave us. I fancy I hear thy sweet voice, which warns me not to see him any more; and I will obey it. She threw herself upon the bed, and in silent reflection, endeavoured to overcome her sorrow.

CHAP. III.

Agitations, confidence, and explanations.

The next morning she retained her resolution, and did not go down: also to avoid Sir Edmond's visit, she sent to inform them she was indisposed. He deferred his departure in vain for some hours, in the hope of seeing her; but as she did not appear, he found he must resolve to quit the house without again beholding her, who was become the arbiter of his destiny. This resolve was not executed without pain, and he was also hurt that Malvina had not performed her promise; and still more so, that she could resist the opportunity of bidding adieu.[34]

Malvina had not a doubt after what had been said the evening before, but that he would have been tempted to see her, and all the morning her heart was in a constant flutter from this expectation:[35] but the noise of the carriage rolling through the court, put an end to this expectation, and her hopes. She fancied perhaps, Sir Edmond had imagined he would not have been admitted, and perhaps had left her a billet. She therefore expected every time that Tomkins made her appearance, that she came to present one; and her looks were so intelligent, that Tomkins enquired each time if she wanted any thing. At last, as the evening began to throw her dusky shades on all around, she could no longer doubt Sir

Edmond had departed without thinking of her. A hopeless and gloomy anxiety took possession of her soul; and notwithstanding the duties which occupied her, she could not prevent her thoughts from dwelling on him. And he who had no motive, had departed as if he had quite forgot her.

From this she thought they must be very differently affected, for in his situation how differently would she have acted. Thus thought Malvina: and this was the first proof which taught her, that a tender woman, who expects to receive as much attention as she pays, and who judges of the heart of a man by her own,[1] is in an error; and that dear-bought experience will sooner or later convince her of it.

The indisposition of which she had complained in the morning, served as an excuse for keeping her room all that day; and the fear of intruding, prevented Mr. Prior from going to visit her. But what infinite pain was it to him to prevent himself from seeing her. One day passed without beholding Malvina, was not a day but an age to him; nothing could compensate this loss; and though he felt that even to breathe the same air with her was a felicity. But how much more could a word or a look from his friend bestow. Yet he was not the least alarmed at the consequences of such a friendship.

The impossibility of his pretensions to any other sentiment, precluded every idea of danger. His vows, his religion, appeared to him an insurmountable barrier that not any power on earth could subdue. Thus he stood fearless, though tottering on the brink of a precipice, little imagining that only a single thread held him to Heaven; while an unfathomable abyss was at his feet. The idea of obtaining any thing beyond the friendship of Malvina, had never entered his imagination. But we may doubt whether he could have supported this by that reason, which is ever so watchful and quick sighted, that its investigation sometimes creates fear.

It appears as if we might be dazzled by the idea of a happiness, which is so great that it defies the weakness of our senses, and yet our souls fear as much to rest on the enjoyment of it, as our eyes do to gaze on the sun. Mr. Prior, under the sanction of his vows, looked forward to the next morning, when he should see her with all the temerity of self confidence.[36] He rose early and went to pay his visit at the hour she usually came down stairs, but all was silent in her apartment, and he was obliged to return to his own. At last, after the clock had struck twelve, as he passed for the seventh or eighth[37] by her door, which he so much desired to find open, he met Tomkins coming out, and he enquired if Madame de Sorcy was up, and if he might go in? Ah, sir, said Tomkins, she has been ever since it was light, up, walking her room; and the dear lady has slept so little, that I am sure she will make herself ill. For two nights she has obliged me to go to bed, and God knows at what hour she went herself; she has never ceased weeping: what can have produced this change? Indeed my good sir, if I am always to behold her thus, I can have no longer any pleasure in life.

Mr. Prior made no reply, but went in to Malvina, she was seated with her elbow resting on her knee, and her hand before her face in a melancholy attitude. She arose the moment he entered, and came to meet him. He observed her eyelids were red and heavy. You are not well my friend, or else you are much afflicted. Will you not let me sympathise in the sorrow that oppresses your heart? It is true that I am a little indisposed, replied Malvina, it was that cause which made me keep my room yesterday, and not admit any one. Though I was fearful my conduct might appear rather extraordinary or unpolite.

Who could have thought so, said Mr. Prior? Sir Edmond particularly, replied Malvina, but fearing this might be observed, she stopped, without asking a question. I was very uneasy all day, said Mr. Prior, after a moment's silence,[xxvi] but the fear of intruding, prevented my coming up. The day appeared to me tedious and very long, from not having seen you – But, dear madam, did you not pity your friend being deprived of your presence? I believe I must open my heart to you, Mr. Prior, replied she, certainly your friendship is very dear to me, and you must be conscious of the pleasure I derive from conversing with you; but do you not fear, that we may be liable to have false construction imputed to our seeing each other so frequently?

Good God! exclaimed Mr. Prior, looking at her with astonishment, what can have given rise to such an extraordinary idea? But in the nature of things replied Malvina blushing, such constant visits in my apartment may appear particular. But who can think so – who remarked it[38] – who has told you so? This pointed question rather disconcerted her; but as she preferred naming Sir Edmond to telling an untruth, she instantly informed him.

At the mention of Sir Edmond, Mr. Prior was struck with astonishment: and immediately exclaimed, ah, what right has Sir Edmond to pass any remarks on your conduct. How dare he tell you this, and from what interested motive is it, that my friendship must be sacrificed to such a man as he is? The air of contempt with which the last sentence was uttered, made Malvina recover herself, and she hastily replied, whatever may be the opinion of Sir Edmond in other respects, you do not I suppose, think him incapable of making a just remark? And I am considered guilty in having listened to it? But, replied Mr. Prior, such kind of advice must suppose there exists an intimacy between him and you, which you have never mentioned to me.

I do not imagine it will any longer exist, replied she with an air of confusion. You do not believe it will, oh, Malvina! you are not then certain? What am I to imagine, what ought I to believe? Can this be the cause of your melancholy? Of the distress which I observe you in. Malvina you are silent, what a dreadful conviction has burst on my soul. Oh, Malvina, dear and unhappy friend, take care of yourself! Beware of this perfidious man: ever active and ingenious in every thing that can gratify or promote his wishes, he knows well in what manner to disconcert the wisest plans, to ruin the most unsullied virtue: for his words are like honey, whose melting sweetness charm the ear, and touch the heart.[39]

I now penetrate into the cause of his whimsical and mysterious conduct. He wishes to please and seduce your affections, without altogether relinquishing Miss Melmor. As he knows when you are present, the others are merely non-entities; and when he cannot see Malvina, he can amuse himself with Miss Melmor. For though he has not evinced so much eagerness to be alone with her since he has beheld you,[40] yet I have observed that when you are present, he always changes his behaviour, and in your absence, she was every thing to him; and he was so very particular and prodigal of his attentions, that they appeared passionate, even to adoration.

At these words, Malvina turned so pale, that Mr. Prior was alarmed. Oh my dear friend, said he, after she was a little recovered,[41] do not imagine that the fear of losing your friendship has occasioned me to transgress the confines of truth, with regard to Sir Edmond; no, if he was not inconstant, deceitful, and unworthy of possessing such a heart as yours;[xxvii] if he was but formed to make you happy; or could he feel the excellency, or appreciate such a character as yours,[xxviii] I would with pleasure be the first to lead him to your feet, and offer my fervent prayers for your united happiness, though you should from that moment lose the remembrance of such a being as myself.

At this moment Mr. Prior was interrupted by the entrance of Mrs. Burton; the agitation which was visible in Malvina, and the serious interesting expression of Mr. Prior's countenance, might have excited a suspicion of something particular in a common observer: what then must it have produced, and also confirmed, in a mind so little inclined to judge favorably of any one. She stood silent for a moment, as if deprived of the power of utterance; then regarding them for some time longer, she at last exclaimed, I have been informed of this; but I disregarded the insinuation, and scorned to believe it: but I now see plainly that I have not been deceived.

And what have you been told, madam, interrupted Mr. Prior, with quickness? What suspicions have you dared to form? Suspicions, replied Mrs. Burton, disdainfully, are they not confirmed beyond a doubt – from the situation in which I observed you both: has it not convinced me of the subject that occupied you entirely? Take care, replied Mr. Prior, raising his voice, take care, madam, that you are not biassed by unworthy passions; for they pervert the judgment, veil the conscience; and the virtues of the heart are enveloped in darkness. Where have you learned so much presumption, Mr. Prior, replied Mrs. Burton, regarding him with a look of the utmost contempt; how long is it that you have been authorised to reprimand me? I likewise inform you, that I think it is quite sufficient if you answer for yourself: I do not imagine that you will pretend to answer for that lady.

With regard to myself, he replied, it is very immaterial, what judgment is formed of me by any one in this world; to God alone belongs this right. Heaven is my witness, and my support is from it alone. But as to that amiable creature, who by her sex, is liable to be hurt by the perverse and too often wrong judgments of men; if I have not the power of defending her against those who possess the sting of the serpent in their tongue, and from whose lips flow the poisonous exhalation of the viper – Yet, O God, thou will be her resource, and thou wilt deliver her from those who meditate evil in their hearts.

Leave the room, sir, exclaimed Mrs. Burton, pale and trembling with rage, unless you wish me to infer, that you have a greater right to remain here than I have? Notwithstanding this threat, Mr. Prior, appeared undetermined whether he would go, and continuing in the room, evinced his unwillingness to obey her command. When, Malvina coming forward, with a gentle, though dignified calmness, which rectitude and virtue ever gives; said, be kind enough to retire Mr. Prior, as you observe my cousin wishes to be alone with me; retire my friend, and do not make yourself the least uneasy, for such reproaches do not deserve to occasion it, not even in the slightest degree.

Her manner persuaded much more than her words, and it almost produced the same effect on Mrs. Burton; though she pretended to continue her suspicions, yet in her heart, she was convinced there was no reason for them. The conviction did not escape Mr. Prior, and gratified by Malvina's superiority, he went out without speaking.

Malvina immediately desired an explanation of Mrs. Burton, of the strange ideas she entertained concerning herself and Mr. Prior. Her cousin, rather confused, said, indeed my dear, you may be assured that I have never encouraged all the suspicions which have been suggested to me concerning you, because I could never be made to believe that a relation of my own could be guilty of an imprudence. At the word imprudence, Malvina's countenance was suffused with a blush of indignation, and interrupting Mrs. Burton, with a voice and air of astonishment, she continued, whatever honor may devolve to me, from being related to you, madam, I should indeed be degraded in my own opinion if I did not know that I had a right to the esteem which I ought to receive from you. Let me then, madam, hear you particularise all the doubts which you have supposed; and also, I desire to be acquainted from whom they have originated, that I may confute them.

The words and manner of Malvina, serious and modest, possessed a power so forcible, that Mrs. Burton could not resist its persuasion; and the truth was compelled to escape her,[42] though she came with the intention of rejecting every thing which could remove her doubts. She was forced to confess that Mrs. Melmor was the person who accused her; and subdued by that superiority which innocence gave Malvina, she said that she did not believe this slander, and should not have mentioned it, had she not thought that in future it might be a preventative for her giving the slightest occasion for the malicious interpretations of the world.

I never considered this castle as the world, replied Malvina; or certainly I should have been more attentive to appearances. I had not an idea that I should have been so severely judged, by persons under your observation, and in your house. We are never out of the reach of evil speakers, my dear, replied Mrs. Burton, and I am much deceived if the insinuations of Mrs. Melmor has not prejudiced Sir Edmond against you.; and who can tell but that he may divert himself with this tale, in the world, at your expence.

Do you then suppose him capable of such behaviour, said Malvina, blushing! as to myself, whatever may be your opinion of him, I should imagine that he possessed too great a share of sense, than adopt the same ideas as your friend, and if he did, he surely must possess more honor than to expose them. Indeed, my dear cousin, interrupted Mrs. Burton, I must inform you, that you judge much more favorably of him, than he does of you; and allow me to say, that you must be particularly partial, to attempt excusing him on this occasion. He who has dared to make my house the scene of his debaucheries, and under my eyes, have an intrigue with a young girl whom I protected.

Perhaps, interrupted Malvina, with quickness, Miss Melmor has only been condemned from appearances[43] – because she may have been imprudent, she is believed criminal. Who has been her accuser? Her mother, replied Mrs. Burton, who, deceived by the artifice of her daughter, believes she may yet be innocent. But, when convinced of her frequent interviews with Sir Edmond, how is it possible to think as she does. If he knew she was thus accused, he certainly would vindicate her, replied Malvina, timidly.

It was in his presence that I told Mrs. Melmor her daughter was ruined, and he never denied it. He did not deny it, replied Malvina, irritated – Then he at least promised to make a reparation by marrying her whom he had seduced? If he had, he would have been less guilty than Miss Melmor; and it would certainly only have encouraged vice, by rewarding that unworthy girl by a marriage so much above her hopes. If I am silent on this scandalous affair, it is chiefly from respect to myself, not from any sentiment of pity she has inspired.

Thus it is, said Malvina, she will have merited your utmost contempt; yet, you retain your kindness to the man who has ruined her? Young and inexperienced, she did not foresee that such a fault would constitute her misery for life; and the world will disown and discard her; while her seducer, who premiditated her fall, and who glories in her dishonor, will be received, caressed, and distinguished by every one.

You are an able advocate in the behalf of guilty females, interrupted Mrs. Burton. Rather say unfortunate, cried Malvina. Well my dear cousin, replied she, with an ironical smile, whatever may be the motives which induce you so generously to defend them, know, that the one you plead for, though she will not obtain the reward you wish her, will not be condemned to the disgrace which she merits: but, in a few days she will be married. Marry any other than Sir Edmond, and does he permit it? He will be rejoiced to find that such a contemptible conquest is placed out of his way; as he is now gone to Edinburgh to facilitate his marriage with Lady Mary Summerhill; and it is my intention to join him very shortly, to assist at a union, which will place my nephew in one of the first stations in the kingdom, and will render him deserving of the fortune I intend to leave him.

Malvina had received so many successive shocks, that her heart was so overpowered by the various sensations they had occasioned, that she could make no reply.[44] Mrs. Burton, who had marked her change of countenance, said, I see this conversation has fatigued you; but before I leave you, I must inform you that I do not intend to keep Mr. Prior much longer in my house; though I am convinced there is not the least reason to suspect any thing in your intimacy with him; yet, the haughty insolence which your friendship has made him assume, renders him unbearable; therefore, I think you will have no objection to his departure. Me, madam, replied Malvina, astonished, are you not entire mistress here? Has any person a right to dispute your will? But I believe, if I did wish such a thing, it would not be on this occasion (recollecting that Mr. Prior had informed her at the beginning of their intimacy, that he only staid with Mrs. Burton per force). This answer appeared perfectly to satisfy her cousin, and embracing her with every mark of sincere reconciliation, she left her.

CHAP. IV.

The interior state of each person.

The grief and astonishment which Malvina experienced from the conviction of Sir Edmond's intimacy with Miss Melmor, will perhaps, appear rather surprising, when we consider what she had heard from Mr. Prior; not that she had forgot the circumstances with which he had acquainted her; but in fact, she did not entirely believe them; and flattered herself that he might be misinformed, or judge erroneously; and consequently unjust.

She had therefore never mentioned the subject since,[45] as she had placed an entire confidence in the tender and passionate behaviour of Sir Edmond towards herself. If it should be thought reprehensible, that Malvina should have been so easily deluded by an attachment, which her reason must have condemned; the only extenuation which I can offer for this seeming paradox, is, that it has been generally remarked (without even excepting Clarissa)[46] that many women of the strictest virtue have a partiality for those men who are of an ardent and passionate character.[47]

Whether it originates from the latent hope of reforming their errors, and changing the activity of their passions, by leading them to the pursuits of virtue; or that the equity of nature requires the union of contrasts, that there may be no evil without remedy, as there is also no good without its alloy. Such are the wanderings of the human heart. That of Malvina's followed the general rule, for though the world could produce but few women that would bear a comparison with her, yet she, even Malvina, was but a mortal.

It would be impossible to pourtray the melancholy reflections of Malvina. She vainly endeavoured to attribute them to the regret she experienced, from having forgot her vow, and permitting these new sentiments to usurp its place. She endeavoured to gain force to expel the latter from her remembrance, but in vain, and the most predominant was continually presenting itself, which was, that of Sir Edmond's having thought so lightly of her; and being included also by him with the generality of women; as he could act with so much deceit in her presence, as to feign so tender a regard when he was on the verge of marrying another; and at the same time occupied in seducing Miss Melmor.

She might perhaps have excused the deceitful sophistry of his language, but for his countenance she could find no extenuation; for when the eyes, those last asylums of truth, when they become false, then indeed the heart must be corrupted, and its depravity incurable. But Sir Edmond was not quite so perfidious as he appeared to Malvina, and she was not entirely deceived in him. Her reason undoubtedly made her believe it, and it was that which induced her to condemn him; yet, notwithstanding this, an instinctive feeling seemed to convince her of the contrary, and this cause induced her to love.

A prey to so many different sensations, she more than ever regretted the misfortune she was to experience, in losing her friend; for it is generally found, that when under the pressure of one sorrow, it recalls every other to the heart, and we unite them all, that our sufferings may be more acute. She thought that by allowing the recollections of the past to press on her mind, it was the original cause of the sorrow which overwhelmed her. It was also more congenial to dwell on the remembrance of the past, as Sir Edmond had deprived her of every present satisfaction.[48] Thus, by flying to the recollection of her friend, she sought consolation from Heaven, as there was not any for her upon Earth.

As to Miss Melmor, she heard the proposal of Mrs. Burton, from her mother, with much more tranquillity than could have been expected. The sudden departure of Sir Edmond, had taught her that she had nothing more to expect from him; the loss of such an alliance was certainly a great misfortune, but to find another who would marry her, was some consolation; and she pleased herself with the idea of his taking her into public, where she would be seen to such advantage.

The prospect of dress, pleasure, and conquest, soon filled her giddy imagination with a thousand fluttering hopes, and excluded every thought of Sir Edmond. But on reflecting within herself, with more attention than her habitual levity would lead us to suppose, she recollected, that in order to possess a greater latitude for the gratification of her vanity, it would be a necessary piece of policy to regain the favor of Mrs. Burton; and the most certain method of succeeding was by an entire submission to her will.

The fall of her hopes, by enlightening her mind, pointed out the cause of her errors; and she endeavoured to find the means of repairing them. Thoughtless and giddy, yet self interest taught her to form a plan, and gave her constancy to pursue it. It is thus, that when folly is guided by a bad heart, she has sufficient discernment to seize what is most advantageous; avoid that which is gloomy, and make her way in the world.

The hope of a brilliant conquest had made Miss Melmor arrogant; and adversity would render her a hypocrite. She consequently went to Mrs. Burton's apartment, and assumed a timid modest air, and with down cast eyes, she said, my mother, madam, has informed me of your intention towards me; and you will find me ready to submit to your commands, and by my obedience, expiate the imprudence of my conduct. But believe me, madam, thoughtlessness has been my only fault; and I have never forgot myself so far, as to render myself undeserving your kindness, and the virtuous example which I have ever beheld in you. Mrs. Burton, softened by this submissive introduction, was disarmed by the flattery so artfully applied. She was so extravagantly fond of adulation, that she never had a doubt of its sincerity, therefore, Miss Melmor was believed.[49] For in characters of her description, self-love, resembles a voracious animal, which devours without distinction, every thing which is offered it.

At the end of a month, Miss Melmor was married to Mr. Fenwick; Mrs. Burton determined to set out for Edinburgh; and Mr. Prior was dismissed from the castle. Six months earlier, he would have quitted it with rapture. But now, every thing was changed with him, when he was to leave Malvina. Nevertheless, he would not degrade himself by any solicitations. The first word from Mrs. Burton determined his departure; he continued not a moment longer in the house, than what was sufficient for the necessary preparations for his departure, and to bid an adieu to Malvina.

When he went to take his leave, she, without hesitation, gave him the most sincere promise of her unalterable friendship, in some measure to relieve the pain it occasioned him to leave her. On quitting you, said Mr. Prior, I feel as if I was going into darkness, and my soul is low, and without courage. Oh! Malvina, do not disregard me in this day of my affliction: alas! on leaving you, I have not any thing left but your remembrance, and your letters, that can console me. – The first is so interwoven with my heart, from which nothing on earth can ever tear it; the other, I request as a favour, and will depend entirely on yourself. You will not refuse me?

Ah! could Malvina, from a respect to the opinion of a haughty woman (and a depraved man) have rejected this affecting prayer; she would no longer have been the good the excellent creature, who always forgot herself for the benefit of others; and in this she gratified her reason and her heart at the same time. We should ever give more to the duties of friendship, than to social convenience; and it had ever been her idea, that public opinion should only be regarded when it respected self alone;[50] and never be brought in competition with the most trifling circumstance that would give a moment's pain to friendship.

Mr. Fenwick was a writer to the Signet,[51] at Edinburgh – he was a little more than forty years of age, of a dark complexion, short, and thick-set; whimsical at home, but gay in company; a bankrupt in ideas, but possessed a good memory; a very trifling portion of wit, yet could create a general laugh by his method of telling tales. He flattered all the world, and liked no one in it. In marrying Miss Melmor, he had not even thought of her person, or whether her disposition of character would correspond with his own; and as to rendering her happy, it had never entered his imagination. But what was of infinite more consequence, he had maturely reflected, that Mrs. Burton was vain, rich, without children; and that a union with one who was connected with her might prove peculiarly advantageous; and he was conscious of possessing those qualities which would enable him to draw with interest from such a character as Mrs. Burton's. Some years preceding, when Mrs. Burton was in the zenith of her youth and beauty, and accustomed to the most refined flattery, she would have despised such as Mr. Fenwick's; but, as her age had forbid her to expect it, she felt the deprivation so acutely, that she condescended to receive it, though less delicately offered, than be entirely deprived of it. Mr. Fenwick treated his wife as a child; her mother as an ideot; and Malvina as a visionary. He preserved all his praise and esteem for Mrs. Burton, and she attracted so much of his regard,[52] and reposed so much confidence in him, that it must have been an enigma to all those who knew the artfulness of her character, had not her devotion to self love constantly betrayed her.

By dismissing Mr. Prior so suddenly, her intention was not only to be revenged, for the severe truths which he had dared to utter, and the enthusiastic opinion which he had conceived of Malvina; but her secret aim was to insinuate to Sir Edmond, that his sudden rupture proceeded from no other cause than the scandalous intimacy which existed between Mr. Prior and Malvina. She had already, under the seal of secrecy, confided what she termed her discoveries, to Tasse[53] her maid, and Mrs. Melmor; and this, repeated by her two echoes, was whispered to every one in the castle. But this did not satisfy Mrs. Burton, it must be conveyed to the ears of Sir Edmond; she therefore determined to send Mrs. Melmor and Tasse before her to Edinburgh, with the excuse of preparing the house for Mrs. Burton's reception. Both were properly instructed in the information they were to give Sir Edmond of Mr. Prior's dismission; though she knew perfectly well that her nephew would not believe any thing she asserted. This was only to convince him that Malvina was stigmatised in every one's opinion; and she was certain his pride would never let him marry a woman that was even suspected.

CHAP. V.

New acquaintances.

It was the beginning of April, when Malvina set out with a party (to not one individual of which she was very partial) for Edinburgh, a place she was not very anxious to visit, and where she might meet the person, who, more than any other, she most feared to behold.[54] She however determined to accompany Mrs. Burton, from the conviction which her reason offered, which was, that the idea of a beloved object is much more dangerous at a distance, for then we embellish it according to our wishes; but, when present, we behold it as it really is. She imagined that when she would witness Sir Edmond's attentions to so many women, and also his union with Lady Mary Summerhill, she should then have nothing more to fear on his account. Such were Malvina's ideas. When passion endeavours to find a pretext for its weakness, the imagination is always ready to offer one; but of all the subterfuges to which it is most liable, that is the most to be feared, which bewilders it so far, as to occasion us to lose ourselves by its delusions. It is of less importance when it only yields itself to fancy, than when it endeavours to justify them; and the excess of its delirium is less to be feared than the sophisms of its logic.

On the third day of their journey, Mrs. Burton informed her companions that they should stop that evening at a Mrs. St. Clare's,[55] whose mansion they should have to pass. I formerly knew this lady at Edinburgh, she continued; at that time a very advantageous marriage introduced her to the great world. She is now a widow, and having nearly lost all her fortune, she has retired into the country, and resides with her father. – I cannot sufficiently praise her for the fortitude she has evinced in her misfortunes, and also for the use she made of her liberty. But, I have lately heard she has commenced authoress, and this information has lessened her very much in my opinion; for I think that a woman who has once given herself up to this pursuit, will never be any thing in future but a pedant or a belle esprit.[56]

I rather coincide with your opinion in this respect, replied Malvina: nature has imposed so many duties upon women, that it appears the time which they must devote to the public, must generally be at the expence of neglecting some of them. At the same time, a mother should have a mind well informed, that she may instruct her children; but the possession of any useful science will never compensate for the evil which her neglect of them will occasion. While she is perhaps writing on education, she leaves her children to the care of mercenaries; and while she is writing a dissertation on the importance of fulfilling her duties, it is another who must perform them for her. The conversation continued some time on this subject; and in the evening, they arrived at the house of the lady who had given rise to it.

Malvina beheld a woman still young, whose manners appeared simple, and her conversation not the least above what is generally termed common, which did not in the least coincide with her ideas of an authoress. At the first introduction she appeared cold and distant, but in the course of the evening she became more affable. Malvina received several instances of her partiality, which appeared to be offered from her heart. Whether it was from sympathy or gratitude on the part of Malvina, she could not ascertain, but she felt a preference for Mrs. St. Clare; and the next morning she joined her at a very early hour in the parlour, where they conversed with an intimacy which does not often result from so transient an acquaintance.

Mrs. St. Clare mentioned her predilection for study and retirement; and her partiality for the country, and all the pleasures it afforded; but never mentioned her literary pursuits. Malvina ventured to mention the subject.[57] A deep blush overspread the countenance of Mrs. St. Clare, and hesitating for a moment, she said, I am sorry to find how very difficult it is to prevent the world from being acquainted with our follies; every one is so eager to know, so capable in their own opinion to discern, and so ready to circulate them:[58] but I am less concerned at that, than I am to find that you should have been prejudiced against me, before you had seen me. It requires only to know you to destroy it, replied Malvina; and I have already reproached myself for it. Ah! do not endeavour to deny it, said Mrs. St. Clare, for you would not be the woman I think you, if you have not disapproved my conduct, unless you had been acquainted with the motives which occasioned it.

If I dare take such a liberty, replied Malvina, you perhaps might attribute my enquiry to curiosity; yet believe me, when I assure you, that the interest you have inspired, is the sole cause which dictates it. Your eyes have already informed me of that, replied Mrs. St. Clare, smiling, and there is no occasion to add entreaties to induce me to gratify you. If it is perfectly agreeable, we will retire into the garden; we shall be less liable to be interrupted there, and we can converse while walking. Malvina consented to this proposal with pleasure,[59] and they went to the shrubbery, where the first budding blossoms, and a pale verdure, had just began to deck the trees.

CHAP. VI.

Preface.[60]

I must draw a veil, said Mrs. St. Clare, over some particulars, which, on my retiring from the world, has taught me to love solitude. We are too little acquainted, for you to find any pleasure in hearing my resolution, and it is almost intruding in me to speak on such a subject; and though the preference which induces to this confidence would require some hours to explain it in,[61] yet, if I relate some of the particulars, it will be only to justify myself from an imputation which you have already heard; and the circumstances from which it originated, can only excuse.

You must imagine, in this retirement, I ought to have sufficient leisure for any amusement, without children,[62] and few duties to perform that interest me. Disgusted with the world, and all its pleasures; never could the remembrance of it afford a gleam of satisfaction, or occupy one moment of my retirement. I had but few friends with whom I kept up an intimacy, and was never troubled with the intrusion of visitors. I was therefore to find resources in myself, and endeavoured in a variety of ways to employ that leisure, which each day became more insupportable to me.

I alternately changed them from the fine arts, to domestic cares; from rural pleasures, to serious reading; and I thought no more blame could be attached to my writing a few things which pleased my fancy, than in singing or playing an air, or painting a landscape. Yet, I must acknowledge, I found this new employment very seducing; it was delightful to pourtray with my pen, those imaginary pictures, the reality of which, I had sought for in vain in the world. And if I indulged myself in that which most pleased my taste, it was in some measure, giving both a proof of it, and also that I never prejudiced any one. I really think, that whether a woman writes a romance, learns a science, or works with her needle, they are all nearly equal, provided she lives in obscurity.[63]

It is not the employment, but the use which is made of it, that ought to be censured. If she can amuse her friends by a tale which she has pictured with her pen, no one has a right to condemn her, if she stops there: but when she permits it to be printed, she then publickly acknowledges the value she thinks it merits; and from that moment she must depend upon the critics severity, without the pleasure which she had received from the indulgence of friendship. Besides, in laying a work open to public inspection, not only the book, but the author must submit to their fiat.

If a woman mentions the foibles of her sex, they are attributed to herself; if she paints their virtues, she is taxed with arrogance; and it is universally supposed that she only delineates the passions of her own heart, and those situations which she has peculiarly remembered.[64] How many dangers does a woman court, when she undertakes such a pursuit; and she should possess an uncommon degree of temerity, to attempt it.

Oh! Heaven, said Malvina, you appear to know and feel the inconveniences attending it, so sensibly, that I will desist from enquiring the cause which has induced your undertaking this pursuit; for I am convinced it must be very extraordinary; and I should condemn myself, in requiring you to reveal it. I perfectly comprehend your delicacy, replied Mrs. St. Clare, and it places me quite at ease, for I have gone too far, by wishing to explain the motives of my conduct, which relates to a secret, so very particular, that not one being living, not even my father, is privy to it.

That is sufficient my dear madam, interrupted Malvina, let the subject be buried in oblivion; only inform me, why, instead of writing romances, you did not exercise your pen on more useful subjects? Because those were most congenial to my mind, replied Mrs. St. Clare, I was not capable of any other; and I thought romances were most calculated for women, as they begin to read them as soon as they are fifteen. They, in some measure, realize them at twenty, and having nothing better to employ them, they write them at thirty. Also, I believe, that with a few exceptions of great writers, who have distinguished themselves in this line, women are the most proper, for undoubtedly they can more particularly understand and delineate all the characteristics of sentiment,[65] which is in some degree the history of their lives; while it is an effort for men to write their episodes.[66]

Then, said Malvina, you limit our talents only to the knowledge of describing affection, and you do not imagine that we can attain any thing higher? Perhaps there may some day be exceptions, replied Mrs. St. Clare; it would be a great temerity to set limits to our capacities. But at the time, I do not know one;[67] for those women[68] whose perceptions are not sufficiently penetrating, or who cannot connect their ideas, can never possess genius. This truth which has been demonstrated by facts, has been ascribed to the faulty education which they receive.[69] For how often do we see men born of the poorest parents, of the lowest extraction, surrounded by prejudices, without any resources, and as uninformed as women,[70] raise themselves by the force of their genius, from the greatest obscurity;[71] enlighten the age they live in, and search into the immensity of futurity. Not one woman, that I have ever heard of, has ever stept in such an original path.

But, replied Malvina, from the moment that women only write to display their talents,[72] would it not be more commendable to relinquish it, and consecrate themselves to the cares and duties of their sex? Certainly, returned her new friend; but remember, I do not allow any to write, but those who are in a similar situation with myself; and those will be very few in number. As wives and mothers of families constitute the greatest part of our sex, the importance of these duties will not permit them to employ their time in works of imagination; occupied in the care of forming the minds of men, they should leave others the power of amusing them, and recollect, that the same hand which can form a statue in marble,[73] should not amuse itself with toys.[74]

CHAP. VII.

Curiosity not gratified.

In so pleasing a conversation, Mrs. St. Clare had nearly forgot that her visitors might be waiting; and if she had remembered them, she was of that character who would have neglected them, when in conversing and listening to Malvina, of whom she thought so highly. But Malvina, who could never forget any one, and who thought that kindness should oblige the mistress of a family, as well as politeness,[75] to interest herself in these little attentions which were necessary to her friends; and she intimated to Mrs. St. Clare that it grew late, and perhaps Mrs. Burton might be surprised at their long absence; she acquiesced immediately with Malvina, and they returned to the house.

They found the party all assembled in the parlour; and they had been waiting some time. Mrs. St. Clare made a trifling apology, with an air of coolness, which Mrs. Burton received in the same manner, adding, without doubt Madame de Sorcy had found it very agreeable, as she had detained Mrs. St. Clare entirely to herself. I candidly confess, replied she, that your charming cousin is the cause of my negligence, and I have to thank her for reminding me of the time, or I might have entirely forgot myself in her company. But I imagine it is not necessary to explain this; such happy friends as you are, that have the felicity of knowing her, as she deserves, will not be astonished at the effect Madame de Sorcy has produced on me?

This eulogium, which was pronounced with energy, served to increase, instead of diminishing Mrs. Burton's ill-humour. But Mr. and Mrs. Fenwick, attentive to every thing which they considered pleasing to her, and coinciding with her opinion on every subject, the conversation soon became constrained and tiresome. Ennui appeared in the countenance of every one; and Mrs. Burton, who had at first intended to spend a few days with Mrs. St. Clare, determined to depart the next morning. Mrs. St. Clare endeavoured by every persuasion, to detain them, not from the pleasure she found in their society, but only that she might enjoy Malvina's some time longer. But all her efforts were useless – Mrs. Burton persisted in going, and gave as a reason for her quick departure, that her impatience to accelerate the marriage of her nephew with Lady Mary Summerhill, required her immediate presence.

Sir Edmond going to marry,[76] repeated Mrs. St. Clare, whose cheeks at the moment were suffused with a lively blush. Did you not know it?[77] enquired Mrs. Burton, looking at her with surprise. I knew them both, a few years since, at Edinburgh, replied Mrs. St. Clare, with less agiation; at that time, I did imagine that such a thing would have happened,[78] but since then, I have had many reasons to think otherwise, and your information confirms it. Did you not think it was suitable? asked Mrs. Burton; angrily? they are both young (she continued) amiable, rich, and descended from the first families in Scotland; they seem formed for each other.

Ah! madam, I have not a doubt in that respect, replied her fair hostess, with a smile of anguish, and I have observed likewise, that they resemble each other in many respects, besides those you have mentioned. Not to their disadvantage I hope, said Mrs. Burton; they have ever possessed the applause of the world, therefore no one can suppose otherwise. Mrs. Burton did not make any farther enquiries; and Mrs. St. Clare changed the conversation.

But transient as this discourse had been, it affected Malvina. What would she not have given for a solution of Mrs. St. Clare's evasive answers. How much she wished to be alone with her, that she might have an opportunity of introducing the subject; but how could she do this, without giving her cause to suspect the interest she took in it herself? In short, of what consequence was it to her, to interest herself in the union of Sir Edmond, and Lady Mary Summerhill; or to wish to develope the insinuations of Mrs. St. Clare!

Had she not determined in her own mind, that a man of such a character did not deserve to occupy her thoughts: though while thinking this, she seldom thought of any thing else, and it appeared as if she felt a pleasure in recollecting his vices, that she might have an excuse for continuing to remember him; and preferred painting him in the most odious colours, than entirely to forget him.

Notwithstanding all her resolutions, a secret instinct prompted her to seek every opportunity of being alone with Mrs. St. Clare, but in vain, for Mrs. Fenwick, curious and intruding, never left them all the day, and she was obliged to retire in the evening, without having satisfied those surmises which gave such pain to her heart.

The next morning she was at her window at day break, impatiently waiting the time which would assemble the family together.[79] As soon as she thought her appearance in the parlour would not be considered singular, she went down, but found the servants setting it in order, and Mrs. St. Clare not up. She therefore strolled into the garden, and walked near half an hour (rather impatiently) before her friend joined her. I know that you have been an early riser, said she, and when I add this to the amiable and interesting eagerness of your reception, and also those particular looks of surprise, I remarked yesterday, and your expressive though silent wish to speak to me; all this allows me to imagine that you have something to say to me – am I deceived in my conjectures?

This question prevented Malvina from making the so much desired enquiry. Mrs. St. Clare's remarks convinced her that if she interrogated her in respect to Sir Edmond, it would be confiding the interest she took in him; and she preferred continuing silent, rather than to expose herself to this suspicion. She therefore replied in an evasive manner, and entered into one of those disagreeable conversations where we speak on every other subject but that which is nearest the heart.[80]

They were soon joined by Mrs. Fenwick, to whom the pleasing ideas of leaving the present society, and perhaps arriving at Edinburgh that day, had awakened early for the first time in her life. She eagerly hastened to them, that they might be sooner ready to set out. Mrs. St. Clare very easily penetrated into the mind of this lady, and thought it only natural at her age, that she should be fond of pleasure. There is not a doubt, she added, but the marriage of Sir Edmond will produce balls and entertainments of every kind; and you possess personal advantages sufficient to be one of the most brilliant ornaments among them.

Ah! that is all I wish, said Mrs. Fenwick, with giddiness; I shall not be satisfied without I eclipse all the women in Edinburgh; particularly that odious Lady Mary. Why do you wish to do that; said Mrs. St. Clare? Do you envy her the honor of having fixed Sir Edmond? I do not know that she has any reason to be proud of such an honor, replied Mrs. Fenwick, from the manner in which he last mentioned her to me, I am convinced that her fortune is the sole charm which attracts him.

I think your supposition very erroneous, madam, replied Malvina, sharply, for of all the faults with which Sir Edmond is reproached, I have never heard him accused of being interested; and it appears to me on the contrary, that a noble generosity is the peculiar trait of his character. Do you know him, madam? asked Mrs. St. Clare, rather amazed. Can you doubt it? replied Mrs. Fenwick, ironically; from the manner in which she has drawn him, should you not have guessed it was done by a friend? – Yes, Madame de Sorcy knows him very well; they have passed nearly three months together this winter, at Mrs. Burton's.

But the only thing which astonishes me, is, that notwithstanding the charms of this lady, and the distinguished regard she has for him, and the peculiar fancy which he has for women, that she did not fix him for one moment seriously. Is it not true, my dear, that he was only jesting, when he spoke to you of love? at least he told me so. Mrs. St. Clare pretended not to observe the distress which Malvina appeared in, at this account; and addressing Mrs. Fenwick, she said, I am sure he could not have dared to speak to her in jest. Sir Edmond must know her better than to feel at his ease near Madame de Sorcy; and he ought to have felt that the general lover of all women should never be hers.[xxix] Her character reminds me of those verses I have read in some poet – I have forgot who.

> What, shall I support such a degradation,
> Among a crowd? shall I dispute for my lover?
> No, my heart disdains a frivolous admirer,
> He who does not know so pure a sentiment.[81]

The manner in which Mrs. St. Clare recited these lines, gave Malvina pleasure (I am very fond of poetry, said she, glad to change the subject) particularly if it is spoken with feeling and animation – it is then music to the soul. If you approve them, replied Mrs. St. Clare, looking at her attentively, I will repeat you a few more lines, which will please you still more.[82]

On hearing these verses, Malvina experienced a peculiar sensation of distress oppress her heart, without daring to search into the cause, or know why she felt it. She found it was impossible to answer Mrs. St. Clare; and as they were near the house, she hastily entered it. From that moment, her hostess became melancholy, she looked at Malvina with the most tender solicitude, and scarcely paid any attention to what was addressed to herself.

Breakfast being finished, the carriages were brought into the court-yard, and in a few minutes, Mrs. Burton rose to go, as they were all ready. Mrs. St. Clare took the opportunity of their taking leave, to approach Malvina, who stood motionless by the fire, and pressing her in her arms, she whispered, if I have guessed right, how I pity you, and how much do I regret the not having spoken to you. Why cannot you consent to remain here, it would perhaps be an asylum against the dangers which you do not foresee. Yet just now, probably it might appear whimsical, or capricious: but will you promise me (if any thing should occur that may induce you to leave Edinburgh, before Mrs. Burton chuses to quit it) that you will come here, and wait her arrival?

Malvina assured her she would; and returned her many acknowledgments for the interest she expressed in her welfare, and bidding her a last adieu, she was hurrying to the carriage, when Mrs. St. Clare said, with an air of confusion, I have one more favor to request, which is, that you will not inform Sir Edmond that I have ever mentioned him; and I entreat you will not question him on any thing relative to me? Malvina promised to conform to all she required, though accompanied with a look of astonishment, which might be translated that she considered this prohibition both particular and mysterious. It is possible Mrs. St. Clare might have added something more, if Mrs. Burton, shocked at their long tête-à-tête, had not prevented the intention, by taking leave of her amiable entertainer, with the most distant politeness; at the same time, entreating Malvina not to detain her any longer.

CHAP. VIII.

Some scenes in the world.

They arrived the same evening[83] at Edinburgh; and the following morning Mrs. Burton and Mrs. Fenwick went out to make some purchases. Malvina remained at home, from choice, but not from a particular reason[84] for secluding herself. She therefore went down to find a book, when, crossing from the hall door, she heard Sir Edmond's voice, enquiring of Tasse when the ladies arrived, and if they were yet visible? My lady is gone out with Mrs. Fenwick, replied the maid, but Madame de Sorcy is at home; if you chuse, I suppose you may see her?

By no means, that would be useless – I shall call another time. Certainly Malvina did not desire to see him, as the idea of it only had occasioned a tremor; and she would have undoubtedly avoided him.[85] But his refusing to see her when she was at home, and alone; what could she surmise from such behaviour? Could she now doubt of his indifference; and did it not appear that he wished her to be sensible of it?

What insupportable wretchedness at that moment oppressed her heart; one part of which arose from the conviction of having been deceived, and the sorrow this blameable weakness had produced, from having been guilty of such an error. She wept bitterly, but suddenly recovering herself, and wiping away her tears, she exclaimed, ah! Sir Edmond, if it was your design by pretending sentiments which you never felt, to render me your victim, and enjoy my unhappiness, your intention has not been accomplished, for I am perfectly cured of such a weakness.

Mrs. Burton soon after returned, accompanied by a young gentleman of a very pleasing figure, though there was something forbidding and contemptuous in his manner. On seeing Malvina, he appeared surprised, and saluted her with great respect. This lady, said he to Mrs. Burton, is certainly the amiable relation which you have mentioned; I am certain my sister will be charmed with her acquaintance. My cousin will be much flattered by such a favor, replied Mrs. Burton, looking at Malvina, with an expression which desired she would confirm the assertion; but not receiving any answer, she added, with some asperity,[86] do you not know that it is my Lord Stanhope, the brother of Lady Mary Summerhill, who I have the honor of introducing to you?

Malvina bowed, but continued silent. As I hope Madame de Sorcy will grace the entertainment my uncle is preparing, said Lord Stanhope, and as I make no doubt the honor of dancing with her will be disputed, may I be permitted to request the favor of her hand for that day, that I may not be anticipated by a rival? Excuse me, my lord, replied Malvina, but as I do not intend to frequent any entertainments during the short stay I shall make at Edinburgh, I cannot therefore accept your very polite invitation. On saying this, she respectfully bowed, and left the room.[87] Whimsical, perhaps, replied Lord Stanhope, but divinely handsome. Dear Mrs. Burton, you must prevail upon her to accompany you to my uncle's – absolutely you must. I wish to be acquainted with such a woman. Heaven confound me, if I have ever seen one who interested me so much.

You do my cousin infinite honor, my lord, replied Mrs. Burton, and I promise to use all my powers to engage her to accept your very flattering invitation, but though she is naturally gentle, yet she is very opinionated in some particulars, which makes her appear rather unpolished, and her disposition rude. So much the better, interrupted Lord Stanhope, laughing, I know nothing so seducing as these scornful beauties, when we know how to tame them.

Take care, my lord, said Mrs. Burton, she is not one of those that can be acted upon in that manner; she is a relation of my own, and a woman of condition, which ought to place her beyond the reach of any but honorable attempts. Go, go, Mrs. Burton, replied Lord Stanhope, with an air of superiority, which is never so disagreeable as when it wishes to appear affable; only give me an opportunity of seeing her frequently, that I may appear as amiable to her,[88] as she is handsome, and then I am at liberty you know, and who can answer for the future? perhaps I may be destined to double the alliance with your family. But I conjure you to go to her, and endeavour to prevail, that I may have her answer before I leave you.

Mrs. Burton, ready to facilitate the wishes of Lord Stanhope, and elated with the hope of contributing to the aggrandizement of her family, hurried to Malvina. You cannot, my dear, said Mrs. Burton, dispense with appearing at my Lord Stafford's entertainment; nor from being introduced to the charming creature who is soon to constitute one of my family. I have a presentiment in your favor,[89] that she will be anxious to commence an acquaintance with you.

Malvina wished to excuse herself, by intimating, that entertainments neither suited her taste, or her situation. But I entreat that you will not refuse me, replied Mrs. Burton, for I have promised for you, and Lady Mary will expect you. If it is your earnest desire, interrupted Malvina, perhaps I would acquiesce to oblige you; but, to satisfy Lady Mary's whim – You have resolved then to disoblige me, replied Mrs. Burton, hastily? and I observe that you conceal, under the veil of gentleness, a very perverse disposition. It is very unfortunate, she continued, and clasping her hands, that one never can prevail or obtain any thing of some people.

It is because these kind of people, replied Malvina, that are so determined in their refusals and caprice, would yield immediately to a kind word, or an obliging entreaty. Mrs. Burton was surprised at the manner in which this was said; for she was unconscious that Malvina's heart was distressed by Sir Edmond's conduct, and the idea of being noticed at Lady Mary's fête, had given a degree of asperity to her naturally sweet disposition. So far from offending, it had a contrary effect on Mrs. Burton; for in general, the most violent characters are the soonest overcome, when they meet with resistance, and submit to severity; when gentleness could have no power over them.

Mrs. Burton again made use of every persuasion; and Malvina, sorry that she had appeared ill-humoured, was consequently obliged to yield to her cousin's entreaties, in order to compensate for it. As the gala was not to take place for eight days, Malvina obtained permission to pass the intermediate time without appearing in public.[xxx] Her reason for this was, not merely to gratify her own taste for retirement, and her duty of attending Frances, but rather to satisfy a sensation of pride, by letting Sir Edmond know that she did not even wish to see him.

For several days, Mrs. Burton and Mrs. Fenwick were continually from home; they never saw Malvina but at table, and that time was generally employed in conversing of what they had seen. Mrs. Fenwick in particular, was never tired of speaking on pleasures so congenial to her taste. Malvina, who had hoped by not mixing with the world, that she might have enjoyed the same repose at Edinburgh as she had experienced at Burton-Hall, perceived at the end of a few days, how little the solitude of a city was to be compared with that of the country. There, her distance from society occasioned her entirely to forget it, or, if remembered, it was only to appreciate it as if deserved, and congratulated herself, that she was separated from it.

Instead of which, the living secluded in a city, renders us liable to have our tranquillity disturbed, by hearing of deceitful pleasures, and observing the unthinking giddiness which they occasion. The flattering praises they give rise to, create too often, instead of pleasure, uneasiness; and when we hear the sounds of mirth and rejoicing around us, our solitude appears only a name, and the silence of a frightful desart.[90] But what we experience in the bosom of nature, that is isolated, pure and tranquil.

The hours had ceased to pass with their usual rapidity – with Malvina, her occupations had lost their charms, and she could not abstract herself from the noise and hurry which surrounded her. Not a person entered the house, but she listened attentively to hear who it was.

Fancying she knew the step of Sir Edmond, her anxiety prevented her from fixing on any other idea, and she could not hear him come up stairs without a tremor; in short, the fear of meeting him, and the uncertainty she was under, on account of the motive which kept him from wishing to see her, accompanied by a desire to know if he had ever mentioned her, was the continual subject of her thoughts. In these moments, she frequently regretted the loss of Mr. Prior. It was from him that she became acquainted with many particulars relative to Sir Edmond, while Mrs. Burton and Mrs. Fenwick seemed carefully to avoid mentioning him in her presence.

As the evening for which the ball was fixed, drew near, Malvina heard that Sir Edmond was with her cousin, and she had never yet seen him; she therefore determined not to go down, if she could possibly avoid it. Soon after this determination, she was sent for by Mrs. Burton and Mrs. Fenwick, to assist in the choice of some head dresses, which the milliner had brought for their inspection. Not having any plausible motive for denying, she sent word she would wait on them, but as soon as she had given her promise, the idea of meeting Sir Edmond created such an agitation, that her countenance appeared changed; ashamed of feeling so much, she wished for more time to collect herself, but this was vain, for the more she reflected on this interview, the more her agitation increased; she therefore determined to go down immediately.

As she was passing through an adjacent room to go to Mrs. Burton, she observed a woman who appeared to be in the middling rank of life, and whose countenance was very prepossessing, weeping bitterly. She instantly went to her, and, with an air of infinite goodness, enquired the cause of her affliction. Ah! madam, said she, I came here with the hope that Mrs. Burton would have assisted me. I was told she is benevolent! but she says she has done so much for the poor – and Heaven knows I did not come to ask charity; I only intreated her to speak to my Lord Stanhope. And what business can you have with Lord Stanhope? asked Malvina. Ah! madam, you are very good to wish to be informed of it; if all the persons in this house had such a heart as yours,[xxxi] I should not have been repulsed with so much harshness.

Have they all treated you equally ill? said Malvina, with some uneasiness, fearing Sir Edmond was of the number. – Mrs Burton, madam, rang the bell, and reprimanded the servants for permitting me to go in. I observed a young lady who was employed in choosing caps: without deigning to look at me, my Lord Stanhope, to whom I wished to address myself, repulsed me with haughtiness, telling me, that this affair belonged entirely to his steward. – At last, a little man took me by the arm to turn me out of the room, when a young gentleman, God bless him, came up to me, and slyly put this in my hand (shewing a note for ten pounds) asked for my direction, and promised to take care of me. Well, my good woman, said Malvina, her heart relieved by this last sentence; has not the generosity of this young man eased your distress? Certainly, madam; but I do not know when I shall see him; and after to-morrow, we must be sent away. How do you mean – who will send you away?

Why, madam, I let ready furnished lodgings, in a house which belongs to my Lord Stanhope, and it is situated in a commercial part of the town; I have hitherto gained a livelihood by it, and brought up a large family. – For this reason, my lord's steward, Mr. Bingham, refuses to let me renew the lease of this house, and wishes me to quit it, that he may have it for his nephew. But, as I had the hopes of continuing in it, I have been at the expence of many repairs, which they refuse to pay me for; so that now, both myself and my poor children will be ruined.

Be comforted, my good woman, said Malvina, affectionately; since Lord Stanhope is with my cousin, I promise you, though I scarcely know him, to speak in your favour. Mrs. Moody, much affected by such kindness, took Malvina's hand, and pressed it to her lips. Just at this instant, Sir Edmond came out of the room where Mrs. Burton was; and seeing Malvina, he started; but recovering himself, he only bowed with much coolness, and passed on without speaking to her.

Malvina remained motionless – so many different thoughts and sensations overpowered her, that she could no longer think of any thing else. It was not merely the indifference which she remarked in the behaviour of Sir Edmond, but a peculiar degree of unpoliteness, which she could not account for. Not to speak to her, and to leave the room at the time he knew she was coming down to Mrs. Burton. Was there not a degree of insolence in such behaviour? And did it not appear as if he wished her to imagine that he had authority to treat her as he pleased? And what could have given him this licence? And was it not degrading in her to allow him to perceive that she would put up with it?

Reflecting thus on what had passed, she recollected, with some confusion, those moments of kindness (for she termed them so) when she had let him perceive the interest she felt towards him. The dissatisfaction she experienced on her having distinguished him, and also in being deceived by the pretended preference which he had endeavoured to make her suppose he had felt, while at Burton-Hall, alternately pressed upon her heart, and loaded it with bitterness. Certainly her credulity had not escaped the supercilious eyes of Sir Edmond; and might she not justly fear that he had made a jest of it. – And it was certainly to undeceive her that he acted at present with such marked coolness. What an agonizing idea, for such a delicate and dignified mind as Malvina's!

She remained absorbed by these distressing sensations, when Mrs. Fenwick[91] appeared. – Ah! what are you doing there? she[92] exclaimed – I am come to fetch you – we have been waiting hours for you. These words recalled Malvina to herself; and bidding Mrs. Moody farewell, with the utmost kindness, she went into the drawing-room.

You will never be able to guess, madam, if you was to try for fifty years, said Mrs. Fenwick,[93] who has occasioned Madame de Sorcy to make you wait so long. Will you believe, that I found her, tête-à-tête, in the anti-chamber with that crying old woman who came to plague us a little while ago. That does not surprise me, replied Mrs. Burton, ironically; for I have long known that my cousin has a peculiar regard for such kind of people.

Say rather, madam, replied Malvina, with a little asperity, that if I do find any pleasure in it, I am perfectly certain I shall not deprive any one here of such a felicity. You certainly must imagine, replied Mrs. Burton, colouring, that there is no person but yourself who knows how to listen to the complaints of the unhappy? Is that the request of old Moody, that Madame de Sorcy is so particularly interested in? interrupted Lord Stanhope. If that is the case, she could not have chosen a better advocate; and immediately, without knowing her wishes, he said, I will give orders that all she requires shall be granted.

But I thought, my lord, replied Malvina, she had explained to you all that she wished to obtain. Faith, it may be so, said Lord Stanhope; but may I die if I listened to one word she said to me; for these old figures make such ugly faces when they are crying, that I always turn away when they begin.

Good God! my dear, when will you have done with that tiresome conference? said Mrs. Fenwick: – come and look at all these charming things; shewing her several headdresses. – Here is a cap for the ball – is it not enchanting? But you are come too late; there only remains this, giving her one in a very bad taste.

Malvina took it; and though so much occupied with different thoughts, yet, with the assistance of a few pins, and her own exquisite taste, she gave it so graceful an appearance, that Mrs. Fenwick was mortified. Certainly, said she, making likewise some alterations in one of the caps, you have the art of rendering it the most elegant of them all, which will be seen in the party to-morrow.

What party? enquired Malvina. We have planned a trip to the gulph of Edinburgh,[94] said Lord Stanhope, that Mrs. Fenwick may view the sea; and I hope I shall be permitted the honor of taking you in my phaeton.[95] I shall go with you, cousin, said Mrs. Burton; observing that she hesitated – Malvina then replied that she would go with pleasure; and went to the milliner[96] to make choice of a hat. Mrs. Fenwick, leaning towards her, said, in a whisper, you are to go with Lord Stanhope, because Sir Edmond has insisted that I shall accompany him in the phaeton in which he takes Lady Mary; and he appeared fearful that they would not have offered you a place, as he certainly seemed averse to have you with him. Was it not whimsical?

No really, replied Malvina, with an assumed calmness; he has many reasons to think your society more agreeable than mine. And what are those reasons? enquired Mrs. Fenwick, with an air of raillery. – It certainly does not proceed from any value that I attach to them, or any alterations on my part to please him. I believe the hand which has so elegantly arranged this hat (returning it to Malvina, with an air of envy) is much more occupied than I am with that concern. If you prefer this to the others, said Malvina, who penetrated her thoughts, you had better take it; or if you wish that I should alter yours more to your taste,[xxxii] I will do it with pleasure?

Ah! you will oblige me infinitely, said Mrs. Fenwick, eagerly; really, my dear, you are extremely kind. Malvina smiled; and while she was employed in pleasing Mrs. Fenwick, Lord Stanhope approached her, and kissing her hand with the greatest respect, said, it is the French alone who can give a finishing grace to all they touch. And it is only the English who are inviolable in adhering to their word: is it not so, my lord? said Malvina, smiling.

I understand you, madam, replied he; and you shall see that I have not forgot your petitioner. – And taking a sheet of paper, he wrote the following words with a pencil –

'I desire that Bingham will fulfill all the arrangements which are most agreeable to Mrs. Moody, relative to the house which she rents.

Stanhope'.[97]

Will that satisfy you, madam? said Lord Stanhope, presenting her the paper. Me, my lord, said Malvina, blushing; but certainly it was from the kind intention of serving and relieving the good mother of a family, and not to please me, that you have written this? On my honor you deceive yourself by such a supposition; for I candidly acknowledge I thought only of you.

What! my lord, in performing so good an action, do you relinquish the sweetest reward that can be offered to the heart; the silent satisfaction of giving joy to this poor family, who believed themselves ruined; and who will, by your intercession, be rendered happy for life? May I die if ever I trouble myself with such affairs; but you speak of it with so much animation, that you almost incline me to wish to think in the same manner, if I had time, but I have not a moment to spare; and I have even forgot myself while with you, that I am expected to take a ride on horse-back. What, is it already two o'clock? cried he, looking at his watch.[xxxiii] Ah, good Heavens, how I shall be rated! I must make fifty thousand excuses, and be extremely sorry, at the same time, said he, with a gay air; and kissing the hand of Malvina, he continued, to-morrow, ladies – remember to-morrow.

Malvina, in a few minutes, went to see if Mrs. Moody was yet in the house; but not finding her, she immediately sent Tomkins to her, with Lord Stanhope's order; who, on her return, gave so lively a picture of Mrs. Moody's joy, and also that of her children, that Malvina was delighted; and she also humbly requested that her generous benefactress would call on them at that house, which she owed to her intercession.

Malvina did not hesitate to comply with her wishes, which were perfectly agreeable to her own; and the same evening, as soon as her cousin was gone to the play, she set out for Mrs. Moody's. On her arrival, the good woman, as soon as the first effusions of her gratitude had subsided, said to Malvina, ah! madam, one piece of good fortune never comes alone; for the moment before you arrived, I had a visit from that good young gentleman – Sir Edmond, interrupted Malvina: I do not know his name, madam; he came to enquire in what he could serve me; and was much surprised, I assure you, when I shewed him Lord Stanhope's letter.

He instantly desired to know by what means I had obtained it? I told him I was indebted for it to one of the ladies that was at Mrs. Burton's. – Which, which, said he, with quickness? But as I could not inform him of your name, I could only assure him it was the best, and, I believed, the handsomest. It can be no other than Madame de Sorcy, replied the gentleman (perhaps, madam, that is your name) as he appeared to be very well acquainted with you; and I am certain he is attached to you; for he continued – My good creature, listen to me; whenever you are afflicted, inform Madame de Sorcy of it, and she will comfort you. – If any unfortunate person is in distress, apply to her, and she will relieve them; in short, if you wish to express in one word all that is good, generous, amiable, and celestial in this world, name Malvina de Sorcy.

Really, madam, I fancied he had tears in his eyes as he uttered this, he appeared so much affected.[98] But do not mention a word that has passed, said she,[99] when I told him that I expected you. But as soon as he had requested this,[100] he flew away with such precipitation, that he did not allow me time to thank him for his goodness, as he had brought me more money.

What was Malvina to conclude from this recital? What was she to think from the praises Sir Edmond had bestowed upon her? – Did they in the least coincide with the evident proofs she had observed of his wishing to avoid her? But without wishing to penetrate into the motives of this whimsical conduct, and too proud to condescend to trouble herself concerning him, as he did not appear to wish it; she therefore left Mrs. Moody, without enquiring what it was he had come to tell her,[101] or mentioning his name.

The next morning, before she had quitted her room, she heard the noise of carriages, which appeared to be near the house; when stepping to the window, she observed the two phaetons of Lord Stanhope and Sir Edmond's, just entering Mrs. Burton's court-yard.[102] She immediately went down, and at the bottom of the stairs she met Sir Edmond, who was giving his hand to Mrs. Fenwick, and said, as he hurried away,[103] we must set out first, to take Lady Mary; but do you hasten to make your appearance, for your humble adored Lord Stanhope is waiting for you. Sir Edmond, after slightly bowing, added, what he intended should be thought coolness, was in reality only pique.

Ah! who would not be one to such a lady; in paying her his vows, my Lord Stanhope submits only to the general rule. Malvina did not wait to hear the conclusion of this sentence, but bowing to Mrs. Fenwick,[104] she entered the saloon. During the ride, she had no opportunity of seeing Sir Edmond, nor of being introduced to his intended bride, as not any of the ladies chose to quit their carriages,[xxxiv] to walk. Malvina absolutely determined to banish the idea of Sir

Edmond from her mind, to endeavour to amuse herself with all around, and not permit herself to think; she forced herself to join in the conversation, which so much delighted Lord Stanhope, that he involuntarily said in whisper, to Mrs. Burton, really I am more than half a fool; and if this fancy continues, I shall not be very unwilling to resign my liberty.

But, notwithstanding the appearance Malvina assumed, to render herself amiable, it is certain she had no other motive than to endeavour to dissipate the remembrance of Sir Edmond. Ought the hope of exciting his self-love and jealousy to be accounted as nothing? Yet Malvina possessed so pure and refined a mind, that I cannot believe this could be the reason.[105]

CHAP. IX.

The ball.

The destined day at last arrived, on which the ball was to be given. Perhaps Malvina was not extremely sorry; and perhaps also, without being conscious of it, she had employed more pains at her toilet than usual.

As she went down to her cousin, she learned from Tasse, that there was a great deal of company assembled in the drawing room; but as she knew Sir Edmond was not there, she entered without the least embarrassment. She observed several gentlemen standing near Mrs. Burton's chair, and near Mrs. Fenwick. But on the entrance of Malvina, all eyes were fixed upon her, and she excited general admiration. Her dress was neither rich or particular; a simple robe of crape constituted all her ornaments; but in her air and manner, there was an undefinable grace, and a taste which cannot be acquired, which is very seldom well imitated, and is similar to an artificial complexion, when compared with the bloom of nature.

When Mrs. Burton rose to go, Lord Stanhope offered his hand to Malvina to conduct her to the carriage, and took this opportunity of reminding her of the promise she had given, of accepting himself as a partner for the evening. She begged he would excuse her from dancing, particularly as she did not know any of the Scotch dances. On entering the assembly-room, Mrs. Burton placed herself near Lady Mary, and introduced Malvina to her. Her ladyship was near twenty;[106] she was one of those regular beauties, which possess neither expression or animation, and excites only the momentary admiration of others, without inspiring any interest in the possessor. – She examined Malvina with a scrutinizing attention, that nearly amounted to rudeness; then taking her hand, with much vivavity, she told her she was delighted to see her, and should rejoice to be acquainted with so charming a person: – and after this, never exchanged a sentence with her the remainder of the evening.

Malvina, surrounded by a brilliant circle with whom she was unacquainted, felt not the least interested in any one that composed it; and was tired, though

Lord Stanhope was incessantly near her, and prodigal to excess of his attentions. But he soon observed that she answered with reserve, to all his compliments. He then endeavoured to amuse her, by relating several entertaining anecdotes of the different persons who passed before them; and as this was a conversation in which he most excelled, he by this means obtained, for a few moments, a faint smile from Malvina. Notwithstanding she was so dissatisfied with the ball, yet she did not evince the least desire to leave it; when every thing changed its appearance by the entrance of Sir Edmond.

He went up to Lady Mary with a gallant and easy negligence, whispered a few words, which she appeared to listen to, with visible pleasure. Then turning towards the place where Mrs. Burton was seated, he perceived Malvina. But it was not the melancholy, pale Malvina, whose negligence veiled her charms. – Now she appeared with all that dignity and elegance so natural to her; the lights, the heat, and the agitation, had animated her eyes; and she appeared so fascinating and beautiful, that he was not master of himself; and instead of engaging Lady Mary to dance with him as he had intended, he instantly intreated Malvina to honor him with her hand for the evening.

Malvina, surprised at this invitation, and distressed to observe the same expression in his eyes, that she had formerly seen, was hurt, at the same time, by the behaviour of a man who constantly appeared to make a jest of her suspence. – She therefore very coolly answered, that if she had determined to dance at all, she was already engaged to Lord Stanhope. But, replied Sir Edmond, allow me to hope, surveying her with the most tender anxiety, that if Lord Stanhope must be the happy mortal whom you thus favor, that after supper, when the French dances commence, which are as changeable as all those who come from that country; that then we may be permitted to change partners. Malvina gave him a look of disdain, without replying. He added, you are silent madam; must I translate it as a refusal, to the only hope I had indulged of aspiring to the favor of your hand, for one dance only?

As Sir Edmond, replied Malvina, is apparently so universally distinguished (forcing a smile) he has not an idea it can ever be otherwise: but, that I may not follow his example, I agree to dance with him, just as I would with any other person. And as any other, madam, replied he, rather piqued, I shall call upon you for the first country dance? Malvina bowed, and Sir Edmond left her.

It should be remembered, that Sir Edmond had quitted Burton-Hall, irritated against Malvina, from being dubious of her affection; but as he confided in the virtues of her heart, he anxiously looked forward to the moment when he should again behold her.

Since his return to Edinburgh, the women who used to please him, now appeared indifferent, and if from habit he was still attached to their company, yet his heart was so entirely occupied by another object, that he was at some pains to abstract his mind sufficiently, to find any thing to say to them. His friends were astonished to observe him so often thoughtful, and sometimes melancholy. They imputed it to the gloomy retirement in the mountains, which they supposed had undermined his spirits and gaiety; and their conjectures were not without foundation; but he could have dispensed with their pity, which they were so ready to bestow; for he had become more happy since he had thus lost himself.

He was in love! Ah! with what new charms had this passion embellished the universe to him. He loved! and when that was the case, of what importance to him was all the gratifications of self-love; and the most exquisite voluptuousness. Where could he find a pleasure that was worthy of occupying a heart, which was absorbed by the image of Malvina? The most amiable only attracted his attention, as he thought they possessed any qualities which resembled her.[107]

All that the world could produce of perfection,[108] in his opinion, was the portion of Malvina. And though he was so distant from her, yet he was ever with her, saw her every where, without ever being separated from her. For as it is the excess of devotion to see God in all things; that of passion, is to see every thing in the person we love. He was no sooner apprised of Mrs. Melmor's arrival at Edinburgh, than he hastened to inform himself of what had passed during his absence at Burton Hall.

The old lady, after having acquainted him with her daughter's marriage, added some reproaches on his behaviour to her, accompanied with many particulars of Mrs. Burton's anger. But, continued she, this violent passion soon found another object: and the misconduct of my daughter, was a mere bagatelle, when compared with the indiscretions of Madame de Sorcy. Indiscretions of Madame de Sorcy, interrupted Sir Edmond, in a rage. How dare you say so? –What an infamous falsehood! Oh, dear me, replied Mrs. Melmor, this is no secret, every body will tell you the same. It was a sad disaster. She was obliged to send away Mr. Prior; and if it had not been for the great respect Mrs. Burton has for her own family, I do not know if her cousin would not have—

At these words, Sir Edmond abruptly left her, assuring her, he did not believe one word of what she had asserted. But in going, he met Tasse in his way out, who being faithful to the orders she had received, confirmed all that Mrs. Melmor had been relating. He heard also in addition, that Mrs. Burton had surprised Mr. Prior and Madame de Sorcy, in a tender tête-à-tête. That she had forbid Mr. Prior her house, and very severely reprimanded the lady; but had forgiven her, on her promising, as a reparation, never more to see Mr. Prior: but, that she certainly consoled herself by writing to him. This is an undoubted fact, she added, for I have a letter, taking one from her pocket, which has been this instant delivered for her, and which is from him, or I am much deceived.

Sir Edmond, almost annihilated by what he had heard, and shocked, as he recollected Mr. Prior's hand writing on the superscription of the letter to Malvina. His mind became a prey to agonising suspicion, and he began to credit all he had heard.[109] The first effects of this was dreadful. Frantic, at the idea of having been deceived by a woman; his pride was wounded, and tearing her from his affections, he swore not to think of her any more, resolved to make her feel the effect of his contempt, and convince her that she no longer possessed any power over his heart; and, that if he had said any thing to the contrary, it was merely from habit, not from any particular preference.[110]

Therefore, while he did not see her, he retained his anger: but the first look he received from Malvina, his resolution failed, though he had the force to avoid the opportunity of speaking to her: also the praises Mrs. Moody lavished on her so deservedly, had affected him extremely; yet, he still persisted in his determination; when, on entering the ballroom, the instant he beheld Malvina, he felt entirely subdued; and the charms of this interesting woman acted upon him like an electrical shock; and except herself, all the world was forgotten by him.

But the repulsive coolness of her reception, recalled his bewildered senses; and as soon as he had quitted her, Mrs. Melmor's information rushed to his memory, and caused him to repent having so easily forgot his anger. He was also ashamed of his weakness, as it might probably convince Malvina of the power she yet had over him, and determined to extirpate such an idea from his mind;[111] he pretended to have entirely lost the remembrance of the engagement he had made to call upon her; and the moment the country dances began, he immediately passed before her, and offered his hand to Lady Mary, which she eagerly accepted; and as they went to take their places, Sir Edmond looked at Malvina with an air of triumph. But this had not the least effect on her, and she regarded them with a look of cool indifference, which entirely discouraged him; and instantly accepted the hand of a young French gentleman with whom she had been conversing.

The figure, and particularly the grace of Malvina, soon attracted the attention of all the spectators;[112] and if her dignified air and modest deportment had not inspired an awe, they would have repeated her praises aloud. Lady Mary Summerhill was soon deserted; and though her self-love was cruelly wounded, yet, Sir Edmond was mortified beyond expression. The superiority which Malvina displayed – when he wished to humble her, she triumphed; and in the midst of such unanimous applause, what regret could she experience at his indifference.

Absorbed by such thoughts, he did not hear one sentence of what his fair partner said to him; his answers were quite contrary, and his agitation increased so violently, that he wished the country dances concluded a thousand times. At this instant the Marquis of Weymouth, a young man as much distinguished by his wit and figure, as by his rank, went up to Lady Mary, and said, with some agitation; in the name of Heaven, madam, can you inform me who that charming creature is? Is she fallen from Heaven to enchant us all? Ah! if this is the fate she has destined us; I feel that I have already submitted to her empire; and so far from resisting it; I only desire to receive it from her.[113]

Sir Edmond, who could not support the idea, that any person should dare to have the hope of obtaining the heart of Malvina, replied to Lord Weymouth's enquiry, very dryly, by informing him that Madame de Sorcy lived very retired; that this was her first appearance in public; and, that consequently she would be very much distressed by the eclat of such a conquest as Lord Weymouth's.

You are particularly acquainted with her then? said the Marquis. Yes, my lord; I have passed above two months with her in the country this winter. Ah! replied the Marquis, that is the worst news I ever heard in my life; but it does not signify, I shall make the attempt. On saying this, he left them: Sir Edmond followed him with his eyes, and perceived him stop near Malvina, and appeared to address a few words to her, which she answered by a bow. He trembled, lest he should engage her to dance with him; for he was very sensible that the attentions of Lord Weymouth were much more likely to succeed than those of Lord Stanhope; and he had the mortification to see them stand up for the next country dance.

From that moment, his agitation was so extreme, that he could not attend to his dancing; and yet, he had not the force to leave the spot where she was; though, but the moment before, he thought he could have renounced her for ever. He watched all her looks, and interpreted every action; and though he was subdued by her graces, yet, he could not pardon her for appearing amiable in the eyes of any other. A thousand times was he tempted to go to her and obtain her pardon, and the favor of a few moments conversation, that he might explain the motives of his conduct; but the fear of a refusal prevented him. For his pride had such an ascendency over him, that even the fear of losing Malvina, would not permit him to descend so far.

When the dance was concluded, he followed her to her place, and stood directly opposite to her, as if he wished to prevent any person from coming near her. Whether Malvina had been accustomed to praise from her infancy, or whether she was absorbed by a different object, I cannot altogether determine; but it was certain, that she had not heard any of the flattery which had been bestowed upon her, and seemed to be quite ignorant of the admiration she had inspired. It was the first time that Sir Edmond had ever seen a woman insensible in such an instance.

Notwithstanding this had excited his utmost astonishment, yet, he did not doubt a moment of its sincerity; for there was something so natural and ingenuous in her countenance, that on seeing her, it was utterly impossible to have a doubt of her candor. She was very much offended at the conduct of Sir Edmond, and determined to resent it, by treating him (in future) with the most distant contempt; and collect all her fortitude, to conceal the pain she experienced from it: and she so far succeeded, as to deceive every person.

But while all the women who surrounded her, were witnesses of the power of her charms, and rather envied her, Malvina was reflecting that if her retirement appeared so insupportable in Edinburgh, the world was infinitely more so, and she had no resource left but to accept the kind invitation of Mrs. St. Clare, and that as soon as possible. She had nearly determined upon this plan, when Mrs. Burton intimated her wish of retiring, and Malvina immediately arose to accompany her. As Lord Weymouth advanced, with the intention of offering his hand, Sir Edmond, who observed it, and who was not master of himself; by a motion, as sudden as it was involuntary, seized the arm of Malvina, and placing it within his own – At least, cried he, no person shall have this. No sooner had these words escaped him, than she was petrified at what he had both said and acted. Malvina, who was equally surprised, went on irresolutely, reflecting whether she ought to go or leave him. They both remained silent, and found themselves in a painful and distressing situation.

At the bottom of the stairs, they encountered the crowd, which obliged them to keep back a little, until the carriages could draw up. This circumstance tended to render her situation more irksome.[114] In vain did they endeavour to forget the past,[115] and to increase their distress – they might read it in each others looks. At last, Sir Edmond could no longer command the agitation he was under, and pressing the hand which he held, he said in a whisper, ah! why, why am I ever separated from you? Malvina, who could not penetrate his meaning, and who only considered this as a continuation of his capricious behaviour, withdrew her hand with evident disdain, and turned her head aside, without making him any reply.

Sir Edmond, wounded by this contemptuous look, made no attempt to regain her hand; and only said, your triumph has been complete this evening, madam; and every time you appear, you will undoubtedly gain new conquests. I shall in a very short time leave Edinburgh, replied Malvina, and I do not intend to frequent any other entertainments. How, said he, with eagerness, does not Mrs. Burton stay all the season in this city? That I believe is her intention; but mine, is to leave it as soon as possible. And will you then return again to the gloomy mountains? No, replied Malvina, I shall not go to any distance. Sir Edmond said it certainly would evince rudeness in my enquiring any farther.[116] Malvina, to avoid any more questions, forced her passage through the crowd, and joined Mrs. Burton.

CHAP. X.

The explanation interrupted.

The next morning, Malvina finding herself alone at breakfast with her cousin, acquainted her with her determination of leaving Edinburgh, and passing some time with Mrs. St. Clare. Ah, what has occasioned you to be so partial to that woman? said Mrs. Burton; and from what unfortunate whim is it that you do not like to remain where you are?[117] Malvina was that instant going to answer, when Sir Edmond entered the room.

Lord Stafford and myself are come to breakfast with you, aunt, said he to Mrs. Burton. But, before we seat ourselves, he wishes to have a little conversation with you, and will attend you to your dressing-room. Malvina immediately arose also to retire, but Mrs. Burton prevented her, that she might hear more of her intention, by saying to her, you are not at liberty to leave us, for Lord Stanhope intends to give a superb entertainment; and it will be utterly impossible for you to avoid making your appearance there. I assure you, madam, replied Malvina, you must dispense with my compliance, and, if you knew how little pleasure they afford me, you would not press it any farther.

Did ever any one hear of such caprice? exclaimed Mrs. Burton, and addressing Sir Edmond – As I suppose you must have remarked, as well as myself, the very particular attentions which my Lord Stanhope has paid my cousin; and by the frequent hints he has given me, I am almost sure, that he would not do it, if he did not mean to become serious;[118] and you know what a very honorable alliance it would be to our family. Yet, instead of being flattered by it, and endeavouring to secure such a conquest, by appearing at an entertainment, which is given entirely on her account, she is so ridiculous and obstinate as to resist all my entreaties, and is determined to depart: and who do you think she is going to? Why, no other than that eccentric and vulgar woman, Mrs. St. Clare.

Mrs. St. Clare, repeated Sir Edmond, with an expression of sorrow, which he could not disguise. Is it to Mrs. St. Clare then that you are going? are you intimate with her? No, replied Malvina, I know very little of her, but her character pleases me. Besides, it is not necessary, was it otherwise, that her society should be so very pleasing, to be in my opinion preferable to all the amusements which I find here. I observe, added Mrs. Burton, with visible ill-humour, all the reasons which I have pointed out, have not the least weight with you.

If it was possible for me to believe they had the slightest foundation, said Malvina, that would be a still more powerful inducement for my absence. What, exclaimed Mrs. Burton, the idea of securing the affections of Lord Stanhope, of making him your own, and being called by his name. Does not your soul aspire to such a hope? I have not the least ambition, replied Malvina; and if I was at liberty to make a choice, it would not be a title that could gain my preference. But as I have devoted my days to the child of my friend, the only wish I had formed, is the power of fulfilling that duty at a distance from the world, and from men.

I have not any patience with you, said Mrs. Burton, nor this affectation of singularity, which, to me appears despicable: but as I must attend Lord Stafford, I shall leave you with Sir Edmond, and hope he will endeavour to point out the absurdity of such romantic fancies, and delicate refinement, which you carry too far. I charge him to undertake this office, and shall be very happy if he can succeed: on saying this, she left the room.

I do not think, said Malvina, as soon as they were alone, that you will believe yourself entitled to speak to me on such a subject, particularly as it would be useless. For characters, which are so very different from our own, can never reconcile us to their opinion, or understand us on any point. Not on any, replied Sir Edmond, looking at her steadily – Alas, there was a moment when I once believed you thought otherwise. At these words, Malvina blushed so deep, that he was convinced that she understood him; and drawing near to her, he added, I had determined to refuse the hand of Lady Mary Summerhill, in contradiction to all the solicitations of my family; when a union, which was not congenial to my heart, appeared to me the most heavy of all chains. I have ever detested marriages of convenience, and I believe you will allow that we think alike on this subject. But there are others much nearer and dearer to me.

Is it possible, said Malvina, that you have refused the hand of Lady Mary? Gracious Heaven, what will Mrs. Burton think who came to Edinburgh on purpose to see the marriage celebrated? And do you seriously believe it, said Sir Edmond, with apparent anxiety? Why should I doubt it, replied Malvina, blushing, when there are so many reasons to confirm it. But, replied he, perhaps on this subject, there are a thousand reasons to persuade; but one only which is sufficient to destroy it.

Malvina, who felt much distressed at the turn which the conversation had taken, got up with the intention of retiring; when Sir Edmond, taking both her hands, said with uncommon animation, Ah! I conjure, I entreat you will not leave me? Hear me only for one moment! and when you have heard the confession of my faults, grant me your pity, for the torments which I have endured, and do not refuse to hear me explain the infamous accusation which they have dared to sully you with. Oh! good God! exclaimed Malvina, shocked at what she had heard – I did not imagine that any thing concerning me could give you uneasiness, or that any one should trouble you with my concerns.

All – every thing reminds me of you, cried he, with energy, in the world, as well as in retirement. The idea of you accompanies me every where; my eyes are ever in search of a resemblance to the form of her I love; and the whole universe appears to be animated by that sensation, which absorbs my heart. Oh! pardon me, continued he, on perceiving that she had turned from him, to hide her face with her hand – this confession cannot offend you; never was there one more true, or involuntary. I do not, cannot resist the peculiar ascendency which you have over me; it frustrates all my intentions, and dissipates all my suspicions, and forces the truth from my heart.

Beloved, and revered Malvina; slanderer has dared to let its voice be heard against you; and the being who is now before you, confesses he also has encouraged a doubt that was injurious to you: but Heaven can witness, from the moment I again beheld you, it has been obliterated; and I should blush to explain it to you. Should not such purity as Malvina's have expressed a desire to be acquainted with what he alluded to? But she had no occasion to vindicate herself; for the innocence and candor of her countenance was an emblem of her heart.

At this moment, Mrs. Fenwick entered in her usual giddy manner, and presented Malvina a letter, which had been just received. A flash of lightning could not have had a more instantaneous and powerful effect, than the sight of the hand writing had on Sir Edmond. It was from Mr. Prior – from that man whom Malvina honored with her friendship, in opposition to her cousin, and the censure of the world. Incensed at this apparent obstinacy, he could not attribute it to any thing but the most detestable motives. The desire of revenge was again kindled, and while his bosom was torn by rage, for the gratification of the moment, he went up to Mrs. Fenwick, and uttered in a voice loud enough to be heard, the most tender and flattering sentiments he could think of.

Malvina was leaning with her head supported by her hand, pretending to read, but rather shocked at the impassioned looks of Sir Edmond, she listened with inconceivable astonishment to his conversation with Mrs. Fenwick, and the extreme surprise it occasioned, prevented the pain she would otherwise have felt from it. Such unparalleled licentiousness appeared to her beyond all belief: she saw, but could not comprehend it, and was quite overcome, without the power of resolving to credit it.

Sir Edmond, who observed the deep meditation in which she appeared to be absorbed, and attributing it to the letter which she had in her hand, his rage increased at Malvina's reverie, and was determined to excite her attention, at the risque of offending her; and continued his pointed marks of preference to Mrs. Fenwick. But the more his animation increased, the more absorbed Malvina became; and while she was supposed to be thinking of another, she was at a loss for ideas, to understand what she witnessed.

Mrs. Melmor and Mrs. Fenwick[119] were alternately going out of the room, and returning instantly; yet nothing could rouse Malvina's attention, which continued so long, that it appeared singular; and Sir Edmond, who could not longer prevent himself from endeavouring to recall her ideas, took the opportunity (when he thought no one observed him) to lean over the back of Malvina's chair, saying, that letter appears to have claimed all your attention. Gracious Heaven, exclaimed Malvina, as if she had been just awakened from a deep sleep – you have reminded me that I have it, for I had entirely forgot it.

Sir Edmond then observed that the letter had never been opened: and he continued, Ah! who was the happy, the fortunate being, which so entirely occupied your attention? I was struck, replied she, looking at him, in contemplating; for I can not account for the prodigy, a falsehood the most uniform, united with frankness and candor, and all the energy of sentiment, to the most contemptible licentiousness. I have been reflecting upon this unheard of medley of contrarieties; the incomprehensible assemblage of which confounded all my ideas. Ah, madam, replied Sir Edmond, mournfully, how much does your severity make me suffer for the injury I have been guilty of towards you. I do not pretend to accuse or punish you, she replied, disdainfully. You do not think me worthy your anger; yet, if I had but the opportunity of explaining myself, and the motives—.

I can dispense with both, interrupted Malvina; I have not the least curiosity to be acquainted with them, as what I have seen is quite sufficient; and from this moment I relinquish the idea of ever comprehending you. On saying this, she quitted the room, and returned to her chamber.

The moment she was alone, she burst into tears. The more energy Sir Edmond had used in his expressions to her, the less could she pardon him for having counterfeited it; and even supposing that he had not deceived her, and that his behaviour had been the effect of thoughtlessness, she felt, that from henceforth it would be impossible to place the least confidence in a man whose sentiments could change every moment; and perhaps the most painful feeling which her heart could reproach him with, was, that he had placed it out of her power ever to believe any of his protestations.

Nevertheless mortified at a prepossession, whose reality she could not conceal, she confessed, that all the vices of Sir Edmond could not diminish this, so much as the sight of him augmented her partiality; therefore, to exclude it for ever, it was necessary that she should absent herself from his company. She then fixed her determination to set out for St. Clare-Hall, in two days, whatever might be Mrs. Burton's remonstrances against it. In the evening, when she retired to her chamber, she found a letter on her table, the hand-writing of which was perfectly unknown to her. Calling Tomkins, she enquired of her, from whence it came? She replied, that a strange man had brought it, and charged her to deliver it herself – to her mistress.

Malvina, at a loss to guess at the author; and before she opened it, looked at the seal, but there was no cypher on it – when she had, before perusing the contents she saw,[120] at the conclusion of the fourth page, the signature of Edmond Burton. She felt her cheeks glow, and her heart was uncommonly agitated. Uncertain whether she ought to read it – yet she had run over the first page, and had nearly got to the end of the letter, before she had concluded to peruse it.

CHAP. XI.

'Sir Edmond Burton to Madame de Sorcy[121]

'You left me overwhelmed by your indignation, and truly wretched from my repentance. Words are inadequate to express what I have suffered from that moment. – The new existence which I have derived from you is too novel for me to describe. – Till this day I was ignorant that there were pains and pleasures almost above human strength to support. It is certainly only yourself who can occasion me to feel the first, and conceive the hope of the latter. But my vices and your severity lessen this hope daily. – This hope, which will become my greatest punishment from having had the temerity to encourage it; and then finding it vanished as an airy phantom.

'May I be permitted to inform you that it was the violence of my passion which has rendered me guilty. Oh! Malvina, must I then relinquish this fond hope? Do not imagine, that from my being so solicitous of gaining your affection, that I believed myself worthy of such a blessing? But if the being must be deserving – who is to obtain such a felicity? – What mortal can have the presumption to aspire to you? Oh! Malvina, I am but too sensible of all that you possess. I behold myself – and then the distance between us is immense. But I love you, and this word brings me nearer to you. Deign to guide me – make me a new creature, that I may unite all that can please you.[122] There are no efforts which I would attempt, nor any proofs which I would not undergo to deserve you.

'My errors are innumerable I acknowledge – many guilty flames have profaned my heart; but the image of Malvina has purified it. – Will she then deign to accept that heart which is exclusively entirely her own? from that moment it may become more worthy of her acceptance, by humbly endeavouring to imitate her.

'One word from Malvina will perform wonders – she can transform my vices into virtues. I could do any thing by her commands – yes, every thing, except ceasing to love her. Oh! Malvina, most amiable, most adored of women, do not reject my vows,[123] but believe that such a passion as mine, with you for its object, is infinitely more capable of exertions and heroism than all those men who are only coolly virtuous. Ah, Malvina! pardon a being who had the temerity, before he had acquired the least right over your heart, for daring to be jealous. But the idea of Mr. Prior, of that man, for whom you have preserved so tender and unalterable a friendship, pursues and torments me. It is already too much to support the idea of being indifferent to you; but to see another preferred, is torture. This supposition alone renders me furious, and I am uncertain to what lengths revenge might force me.

'Malvina, you possess much sensibility, and that sensibility is lavished on another. Ah! what intolerable agonies has this occasioned my heart. May I hope to obtain my pardon from the gentle, the generous Malvina. But let me soothe my torments, with the consoling idea, that perhaps the tender sentiment of pity will overcome her anger. If I could but describe (but that would be impossible) all I have suffered from what Mrs. Melmor acquainted me with relative to Mr. Prior's being dismissed from Burton-Hall, on account of his affection for you; and also, that it was returned by Malvina.[124] Gracious God! could I ever have believed this?

'Oh! Malvina, on the evening of my departure, when I could not longer conceal what I felt, and I dared to let you perceive the pain your intimacy with him occasioned me, did you not answer me in a manner and with a voice which always penetrates my soul? and which you alone are capable of, in words which are engraven on my heart – 'Ah! I do not wish to afflict you.' This was sufficient to exclude for ever all that the insinuations of calumny could sully you with. But, Malvina, are we always just, and cool, when we are severely affected by what is nearest and dearest to the heart?[125] Oh! Malvina, the penitent Edmond can only deserve your forgiveness, and become worthy of you, by the remorse which he suffers – If you knew the promises he has betrayed. But the past seems to be annihilated from my existence; and I only begin to live since I have known and loved Malvina.

'You have enlightened my days, and changed every thing around me. What I have called pleasure and love, I now feel did not deserve the name; and my mind is exalted and enlarged since the fortunate moment that my heart has had the temerity to aspire to so superior a being: can I then dare to suspect such a one?[126] – Oh! Malvina, whatever may be my crimes, and the injustice I may have been guilty of towards you,[127] you shall be acquainted with every thing.

'You must know, that when I at last gave credit to Mrs. Melmor's information, I determined to renounce you for ever – that I even endeavoured to hate you; and I should have had a secret pleasure in your knowing it, if I thought it would have given you pain. But, on your appearance, all my resolutions vanished,[128] and my love seemed to increase from the sacrifices which I imposed on myself. – And I had only to behold Malvina – to believe her innocent. But this morning, when I beheld that fatal letter, it seemed to freeze all the ardor of my soul, and I was no longer master of myself. I had recourse to a blind and foolish revenge to allay my torments, which has now terminated in despair.

'At such a moment, how despicable do I appear in not making a distinction between Malvina and all the rest of her sex. To have the vanity to think I could *offend her*, by affecting to appear gay and frivolous with another woman. Alas! what have I gained by this painful dissimulation? an answer, which, severe as it was, was infinitely less painful than your contempt; and the look with which it was accompanied – Malvina hates and despises me.

'Malvina, perhaps, believes that I have deceived her, and therefore thinks me unworthy of her notice.[129] – She detests and flies me; yet I have no right to complain, as I have undoubtedly deserved it. – But at least do not doubt my affection – my love is my only consolation, and my only merit, for by that I shall live in hopes of softening her, who alone can make me attach any value to my existence.

'Edmond Burton'.

When Malvina had finished reading this letter, she, for some moments, gave herself up to the most pleasing ideas; – and she imagined, that if Sir Edmond could once experience a perfect detestation for his former pleasures, he might for ever renounce all those pernicious errors which had so long led him in the flowery paths of vice. That perhaps, on her account, he might as it were begin to live; and the pursuit of virtue would constitute his happiness. She easily pardoned him for the caprices his jealousy had occasioned.[130]

Oh! what infinite pleasure would it give me, said she, if I could be instrumental in saving such a mind from vice; to train those passions which are now so violent, to goodness and purity, by that tender and delicate sentiment which constantly leads to the practice of every virtue. And it is really myself who am, as it appears, called upon to undertake and accomplish the glorious task which is to be rewarded by the love of Edmond. And dare I deliver myself up, without blushing, to the sentiments which force me onward, and triumphs over me, in opposition to myself, and which, till this moment, has produced only sorrow and remorse?

O God! why, alas, cannot I free myself from it? But my soul seems dead to the remembrance of its duty, and its vows. Clara, my beloved friend, thou shouldst not have confided thy daughter to a woman who could submit to a tyrannic passion. At this moment I recollect, with terror, when delivering her into my arms, thou saidst, be thou her mother, Malvina; let her always live with you, a stranger to any other authority. Ah! I may impose a severe duty on you, but it is not from such a one as Malvina that I exact a common sacrifice. Clara, I will keep this promise, I will reject every connection which may in the least invade its rights, deprive me of my independence, or divide my heart. I will suppress the intrusion of every pleasing idea.

Oh! Edmond, at the moment when you have shewn yourself most deserving my esteem, must I bid you adieu for ever? But if I wished to avoid you, when I thought you perfidious and inconstant, how much more urgent are the reasons for my flying from you at this moment, when I have proved your affection and sincerity. It was infinitely more easy to resist it before this confirmation of your tenderness. But now – Ah! I will depart, without losing a moment; and be particularly careful to conceal this secret from him, which would only add to my grief and betray my weakness.

Malvina therefore resolved to set out for St. Clare-Hall, the following day,[131] without seeing Sir Edmond, devoting herself a victim to a fastidious delicacy,[m] which her friend would have been the last to require her adhering to, under such circumstances. But she imagined it was the dictates of duty; and with that idea, her determination was invincible.

Those who imagine they have authority to condemn Malvina, ought to remember such an example does not frequently occur, and seldom exists but in minds that possess the most exalted sentiments of virtue.

CHAP. XII.

The surprise.

On the following morning, on hearing Sir Edmond was below, she staid in her room longer than usual; and was preparing to go down, when she heard him bidding Mrs. Burton good-day – and immediately the latter entered Malvina's apartment, with her countenance inflamed, and every feature distorted by rage.

I was ignorant, said she, to whom I should attribute the singular behaviour of Sir Edmond; but if, what Mrs. Fenwick has acquainted me with is true, that his disobedience is the effect of your artifice, I shall never cease to regret having received you in my house – I who opened my arms to welcome an ungrateful relation, who ever since she has been here has endeavoured to distress and afflict me in the most unkind manner, and who, to-day, has given the finishing stroke to the whole, by engaging my nephew to refuse the honorable establishments which I had gained for him.

It is unfortunate, extremely unfortunate for me, who have been flattering myself with the hopes of such a noble alliance; and when I had exerted every means for its accomplishment, to see all my projects vanish, by the insinuations of a woman, who, under the appearance of candor, uses all the arts of coquetry.

Oh! good God, madam, exclaimed Malvina – of what is it that I am accused? that you have thus loaded me with such a torrent of reproaches, before you know whether I have deserved them?

Do not imagine that you can deceive me also? replied Mrs. Burton, with vehemence – I know you now, and all your intrigues are discovered. It was not sufficient to attach Mr. Prior by your wiles, but Edmond must also feel them.

It was very plain to be seen at the ball that you particularly endeavoured to eclipse Lady Mary Summerhill; and it was observed yesterday morning, that by an affected reverie, and sentence only half articulated, with a peculiar expression of countenance, that you attempted to inspire Sir Edmond with that spirit of disobedience which he has just now manifested.

All the preliminaries were settled, and Lord Stafford was on the point of obtaining the title for me, which I have so much desired. Lady Mary was ready to give her consent; accordingly I intreated Sir Edmond to attend me this morning in my closet, and informed him what had been concluded; and also that he was expected to perform his promise. Instead of the eagerness which I expected he would answer me with, he rejected all my proposals, and absolutely refused the hand of her ladyship.

I cannot love her, he replied, and therefore it would be sacrilege to form a union when the heart is not interested. How ridiculous to hear him talk of love, who has ever made a jest of such a sentiment, to think of sacrificing such a glorious and honorable alliance for this sentiment; and any one may observe, from this instance only, that he had been influenced by a romantic woman, who only yesterday despised, with an air of indifference, the marked attention of such a man as Lord Stanhope. But it is of no consequence, she continued (without giving Malvina an opportunity of speaking) who has instigated him to this; if I fail in my projects, I shall succeed in my revenge.[132] From this moment I shall give that fortune to another which I have hitherto always reserved for him. As to you, madam, you shall leave this house; for all the civilities I have shewn you, I have been recompensed by your having occasioned confusion, sorrow, and disobedience.

I had determined to set off to-morrow, replied Malvina, calmly; my plan has been uniform, and whatever may have been the civilities you allude to, the moment of my departure will be the most agreeable of any I have passed with you. Yet, if I do not condescend to vindicate myself from the slander which has been maliciously circulated concerning me; the interest of Sir Edmond so far engages me, that I solemnly declare that my intention of leaving this place is never to see him more.

Thus, madam, if the sentiments you suspect he possesses, and which has rendered him culpable in your opinion, the moment he has lost the object, you are to renounce the punishment.

Yes, madam, replied Mrs. Burton (regarding her with a look of anger) as she was leaving the room, I see very clearly, by your readiness in defending him, and your carelessness in what regards your own justification, how very dear he is to you; and also, how certain you are of your power over him. But do not imagine your triumph is complete; the truth may even reach him, and knowing what you are, he will estimate you accordingly.

Alas! said Malvina, as soon as she was relieved from her presence, what evil is it that she wishes me? Is it not sufficient that I have for ever renounced Sir Edmond? But must she endeavour to deprive me of his esteem; and may she not very easily succeed in that attempt? In my absence he will be surrounded by those who are my enemies – who will meditate my ruin – who will then vindicate me.[133] His heart will no longer answer mine, and he will no longer believe that virtue.[134]

Oh! cruel Mrs. Burton, why have I ever known you? – and what can I have done to excite such invincible hatred? – What she had done, was to be her superior in every thing. She was as conspicuous in her figure, as her mind was exalted, and no other was noticed when near her; and this was entirely the effect of that genuine simplicity and unassuming modesty, that she paid no attention to the praises she received, and despised such empty distinctions, from persons whom she could not esteem. This visible superiority Mrs. Burton was so conscious of; and from being forced to treat her as she deserved, she felt her hatred to Malvina increase, without the possibility of finding any thing to blame her for, with justice.

Without perfectly comprehending the reason, Mrs. Fenwick had conceived an instinctive dislike to Malvina; she sought every occasion to speak against her, and was encouraged in it by the advice of her husband. They had both determined for some time to ruin Malvina if possible, and also Sir Edmond, in the opinion of Mrs. Burton; at least sufficiently to deprive him of her fortune, and her confidence. By such artifices, they had gained an ascendency in the house; and guided by his advice, Mrs. Fenwick had prevailed on Mrs. Burton to send away Malvina, hoping by this means, in a short time, to gain as much influence over her, with respect to the destiny of Sir Edmond, that he might severely repent the having abandoned her.

While all these plans were projecting, Malvina was preparing for her departure, though undetermined where she should fix her residence; but retained her first intention of visiting Mrs. St. Clare, and when there, reflect what would be most eligible for her future destination.

She did not make her appearance at dinner, but as soon as she heard all the party were set out for the play, she went down to the garden. It was large and solitary. She sought the most retired part, that she might indulge the melancholy reflections which her situation produced. But notwithstanding all her endeavours, the idea of Sir Edmond would intrude on her thoughts. She wept on their approaching separation, and sighed with regret, when she imagined how bitterly he would reproach her, on hearing of her departure. Taking his letter from her bosom, and bathing it with her tears, she said, Ah! it did not deserve such an answer as silence and neglect; but whatever may be the ill opinion he may have of me in future, on my appearing insensible and severe, I shall at least not have deserved it.[135]

Oh! Sir Edmond, continued she, holding her handkerchief to her eyes, and resting her head against a tree; could you but read my heart: but I should rather say, why cannot I conceal from myself the distressing conflicts I have endured in order to forget you. Just as she had finished these words, a slight noise made her start, and turning to observe what had occasioned it, she perceived Sir Edmond at her feet.[136] The unexpected sight of him occasioned her to utter a faint cry; and alarmed also, at the idea that he might have overheard her, she wished to fly from his presence. But the first step she advanced, Sir Edmond's letter fell, and on stooping to take it up, the wind blew it towards him, he caught it, and returning it to her, he found it was still wet with her tears. Oh, God! he exclaimed, is this an illusion? Is this Malvina whom I behold, and is it her whom I have heard? Is it Malvina who possesses sensibility? Malvina, who really loves? What unexpected happiness! for the object of her preference, who is now before her. On uttering this, he surveyed her with that look of eloquent silence, which infinitely more than words expressed the excess of his felicity.

Ah, I am ruined, interrupted Malvina! half terrified; where shall I fly? Where hide my weakness? Ah, what do I hear? exclaimed Sir Edmond, with impetuosity. Fly me, hide yourself. – Can I believe it possible? I who adore you! when you love me, what power on earth shall tear you from me? Before I had an idea of your tender sensibility, I would have contended for you with the whole universe; and now thy heart acknowledges its attachment, when I have heard the confession from your own lips, in opposition to yourself, the sweet sensations I experience, confirms me we are destined for each other.

No, Malvina, from henceforth you are mine; I am interwoven in your destiny; I must in future tread in your path of life; I will never leave you again. Fly, if you wish it, to the end of the world, there also will you find me. I shall follow you every where, claim you every where, and you will behold me at your feet, as I am now, loving you to madness. But Malvina loves me, Malvina is mine: saying this, while on his knees before her, he folded his arms round her with the most profound respect; and though in this delirium, he only dared press his lips to her robe, from an instinctive delicacy, which proved beyond all he could have uttered, that he now loved for the first time in his life; as it was a degree of respectful awe he had never before felt.

Malvina wept, but continued silent. What could she say? What more could she add? Sir Edmond had inadvertently heard the confession of her affection, without her wish or knowledge. She was now certain of his adoration,[137] and his passionate determination of never leaving her, though she blushed to have her secret known, yet she could not wish to recall it.

Sir Edmond, intoxicated with the pleasure of an attachment which had always been so dear to him, and folding the object in his arms, certain of being beloved. He was now enjoying a few of those moments which afforded the sweetest and most refined pleasure, and which are so seldom ever realized in the course of our existence. He was astonished at finding his eyes bathed with tears, when he was so happy; and for the first time in his life, found they were produced by the effect of those exquisite sensations which he never had an idea of; and pressing Malvina's hand to his heart, exclaimed, Ah! I now am convinced, that if there are a thousand pleasures in life, there is but one kind of happiness; as that which I feel at this moment is so pure and transporting, that perhaps it is not even in your power to augment it. Oh, my beloved Malvina, condescend to determine my fate,[138] and by consenting to unite your destiny with mine, confirm that confession, which my love dares not again intreat from your delicacy.

Malvina was confounded by this sudden proposal, which her heart perhaps accorded with, though it appeared irreconcileable with her duty. She was hesitating for an answer, when she heard somebody cough near them, and she was certain it was Mr. Fenwick.[139] This immediately recalled her to the world, which she had forgot. She then recollected with terror, that she was in the gloom of the shrubbery, and almost in the arms of Sir Edmond. Leave me, she exclaimed, I have been here too long, and my inexcusable imprudence will authorise all their malicious suspicions; complete their triumph, and perhaps, embitter the rest of my life.

Why, interrupted Sir Edmond, with quickness, will you value the opinion of a ridiculous and misjudging world, which can never understand your character or your actions? I who love you only, wish to live for you alone. Of what consequence is their idle malice? Oh, Malvina, before Heaven, who can behold and judge our intentions; Oh, say that this beloved hand shall be mine; and then let the storm rage – it cannot affect you.

Ah! exclaimed Malvina, hurrying towards the house; in the distress my mind is in at this moment, you must not exact any promise from me? I am not perfectly my own mistress; for does not the child of my Clara claim all my attention? Did I not on the death of my friend, give her my solemn promise never to engage myself? Yes, Sir Edmond, let me fly, and endeavour to forget you, that I may not have to accuse the memory of that beloved friend, as being the only obstacle which separates me from you.

Dearest Malvina, said Sir Edmond, stopping her against her inclination, must such considerations always rule over every other? But love will usurp its power, and overthrow such reasons, and even soften Malvina. Why will you leave me? You wish to depart to-morrow; and you must go to Mrs. St. Clare's, to that Mrs. St. Clare's, whose doors are for ever closed against me. In the name of Heaven change an intention which will drive me to despair? But what is it that you require, replied Malvina, violently agitated (and attempting to go forward) I really cannot stay here any longer, I will not stay another day with Mrs. Burton; and at present I have not any other asylum but Mrs. St. Clare's house; she is the only woman that I know.

Well, Malvina, replied he, I do not wish to oppose your design, and however miserable your absence will make me, if you can be at peace, I will not murmur. But grant that I may at least be permitted to see you once more, that I may anticipate all the wishes of your heart,[140] and inform you of all that agitates my own. Will you consent to stop a few hours to-morrow at Falkirk? where I will meet you. There I can explain myself with more propriety, dissipate all your doubts, and banish your scruples; and when I leave you, may it be with the flattering hope that it will not be for ever.

Do not refuse me? he added in a commanding tone; and detaining her a second time, fearing an interruption by the voices which they heard at a little distance; for if you deny me so simple a request, I declare that I will not be submissive, but employ force, and even violent means to see you. But what do I say? Malvina, pardon me, I am wild: I will relinquish these rash intentions; you are at liberty, and I submit. But if my happiness is dear to you, do not pronounce a refusal, which I will not survive.

Malvina, trembling, alarmed, and overcome by solicitations which were congenial to her heart, promised Sir Edmond to wait for him the next day at Falkirk; and then flying from him with the rapidity of an arow, she passed Mrs. Burton and Mrs. Fenwick on the stairs, who were going up with Lord Weymouth, without either saluting or seeing them.

CHAP. XIII.

A duel.

The ladies, astonished at this sudden appearance, were at a loss to account for the cause; when, about a quarter of an hour after, they saw Mr. Fenwick enter pale and agitated. He had met Sir Edmond in the garden, who, surmising that he might make some malignant reports, injurious to the peace of Malvina, seized him by the arm, declaring on his honor, that if he suggested the slightest suspicion, or uttered one word against Madame de Sorcy, he should feel the severest marks of his resentment. Mr. Fenwick, terrified at such a threat, very readily promised to be silent, that he might be relieved from the presence of Sir Edmond, whose very looks made him tremble.

In vain did Mrs. Burton and his wife question him on the cause of his agitation. He was yet under the dominion of his fears, much more than a regard to his promise, therefore, he would not let a word transpire while Sir Edmond was in the house. He soon after heard him talking below, and the house door being fastened for the night, the servants were intreating him to go up to their mistress. Mrs. Burton, ever suspicious, immediately went to the staircase, and elevating her voice, she said, by what chance is it Sir Edmond, that you are here at this late hour? What could have induced you to come here while I was absent, and afterwards leave the house without wishing to see me? Take care you do not accuse me of any indiscretion, said Mr. Fenwick, running hastily to the stairs, for these ladies can witness that I have never mentioned one word of what passed between us.

And for your own sake, I hope you will continue to be silent, said Sir Edmond, coming up stairs, and giving him a furious look. What mystery is all this? asked Mrs. Burton. What has passed between you? And what right has Sir Edmond to threaten, or give laws to any person in my house? You shall hear all, cried Mrs. Fenwick, going up to her, followed by Lord Weymouth – I will inform you, dear Mrs. Burton, of all I have learnt from Jenny, which accounts for the distress of Madame de Sorcy, and the anger of Sir Edmond.

They were seen both together in the garden, Mr. Fenwick went to walk there also, and he was so unfortunate as to interrupt a charming tête-à-tête. Ah! what a flash of conviction bursts upon me, said Mrs. Burton; I can no longer doubt but that my unworthy relation has dishonored my house, and I will this instant go and—

Stop, cried Sir Edmond, retaining her by force, no person here will have the rashness to disturb that lady, or even dare to breathe a suspicion that can sully her fame. What is the meaning of this insolence, said Mrs. Burton, colouring with rage, and endeavouring to get from him? Is it proper in you to dare to prevent me from going where I please in my own house? Let me pass, sir – let me go and send away her whom your shameful licentiousness has encouraged to such audacity.[141] Neither you, or any one else are worthy of her regard, replied Sir Edmond. Know, that while the breath of life animates my bosom, I will defend her from your rudeness, and render the rage of malice impotent.

Will you, Lord Weymouth, permit a woman to be treated thus in your presence? said Mrs. Burton, addressing herself to him; will you not release me from the hands of a madman? Do not advance a step, my lord, exclaimed Sir Edmond, on your life do not, or you shall repent it. I never yet put up with a threat, replied Lord Weymouth, haughtily, and I am not in a disposition to slumber over yours.I am not in a disposition to slumber over your's.] I am not in a disposition to slumber over yours.[xxxv]

I am ready to support it, replied Sir Edmond, drawing his sword with one hand, and holding Mrs. Burton with the other; happy to have the opportunity of fighting with a man that he considered rather as a rival. Lord Weymouth parried the stroke of his adversary, and gave another in his turn; while the rest, terrified, were silently gazing at this dreadful scene; when the room door was suddenly opened, and Malvina rushed in pale and disordered, and threw herself between the combatants.

Stop, said she, wildly, it shall never be said that blood was shed on my account; Oh! save me from such a horrible idea? and if my sorrows, my tears, cannot restrain you, let me fall the first by your hands? On saying this, she advanced before Sir Edmond, and to defend him, presented herself to the sword of Lord Weymouth, who, struck with her courage, and also surprised at the action, was overcome by that beauty which the agitation and distress of her mind had rendered still more interesting. He instantly threw down his sword at her feet, saying, Ah, madam, who can resist you, who can behold you, and not obey? It is in your power to calm rage, command the passions, and attract the love and admiration of every one.

Malvina, said Sir Edmond, with a mixture of jealousy and tenderness, is this your place? – Ought you to prophane your angelic purity, by coming near beings who wish to sully your honor? Mine is not in their keeping, replied she, haughtily; and when I have no cause to reproach myself, I do not fear it from any one else. Do not exhibit any of those assumed airs of haughty behaviour, said Mrs. Burton, who was now a little relieved from her terror.

Neither do you, madam, interrupted Malvina, with a dignified air of energy, any more affront me, whom the laws of hospitality, at least, should have allowed you to treat with respect. Your behaviour to me has been uniformly unkind; you have endeavoured to distress, when you ought to have protected me. And if I disdain to mention particulars, it is because I leave you to the remorse of your own conscience.

I have heard you, madam, and do not imagine that I wish to remain another moment with you;[142] for I shall think myself more safe any where than in this house. On saying this, she called to Peter, directed him to order a chaise, and desire Tomkins to bring Frances.

But what is your intention, Malvina? (said Sir Edmond, alarmed) where can you go at this late hour? and what will become of you? That I am a stranger to, replied she; but I am absolutely determined to go – and Heaven will direct me for the best. Dear Malvina, said Sir Edmond, I cannot – will not suffer you to expose yourself to danger; at least permit me to accompany you? No, sir, not either you or any one else shall accompany me;[143] I wish to fly from this detested place, and not any one here has a right to prevent me.

Will you allow me, madam, the permission of conducting you to my mother's? said Lord Weymouth, where you shall be treated as you deserve; and if you desire it, I will give you my honor that I will not enter the house while you remain there.

A thousand thanks for your kind obliging intention, my lord, said Malvina; but I confess if I was to choose a protector from here, you would not be the person I should select. You had better take pity on her, said Mr. Fenwick, addressing Mrs. Burton; her situation is distressing, and you are so very good. Well, said she, to favor your intercession, and on account of her being my own relation, I *consent* to *permit* her to pass the night here.

Do you judge of me by yourself? (said Malvina, with contempt) and can you think me capable of accepting, as a favor, that which I have rejected from intreaties? I shall leave you, madam, to distribute your favours to those who can, without blushing, degradingly stoop to all your wishes and commands; but learn, at the same time, there are characters which no situation or change can debase.

As to you, Sir Edmond, and Lord Weymouth, added she, with energy; and taking a hand of each – if my situation in the least affects you, spare me the only misery I cannot support, and give me your words, that you will not renew a scene, of which only the idea stabs me to the heart? Malvina, as she spoke, had something so affecting in her voice, and so sweetly interesting in her look, that it was impossible to resist her intreaties. – Sir Edmond, and Lord Weymouth, whatever anger remained, acceeded to her wishes; and immediately both promised to obey her.

As soon as she was relieved from this fear, being informed that Tomkins was ready in the carriage with Frances, she instantly followed them, leaving Mrs. Burton, and all the rest, petrified, at the empire which timidity and innocence sometimes has the power of assuming over arrogance and presumption.

Sir Edmond, however, prevailed on Malvina to allow him to lead her to the carriage, and snatched that opportunity, to enquire where she meant to go, and if he should meet her the next day at Falkirk? I shall endeavour to go somewhere[144] for the present, she replied; but I promise to wait for you there.

As soon as they had left the house, Sir Edmond, out of respect to her, and to prevent all suspicion,[n] did not leave Mrs. Burton's for some hours after. He had witnessed the ill treatment by which a despicable vanity had been capable of afflicting so gentle a being. But Lord Weymouth could not contain his resentment, when he spoke to the ladies; but the man he considered as a detestable wretch, to whom he did not condescend to exchange a sentence[145] –and he left the house, the instant delicacy would permit him, to fly from so detestable a place.

CHAP. XIV.

One day of happiness.

By the assistance of a few guineas, Malvina easily prevailed on the driver to convey her immediately to Falkirk, where she arrived at midnight,[146] and alighted at the best inn. She immediately put Frances to bed; and, conscious that the recollections of the evening, and the thoughts of the ensuing day, would banish Morpheus[147] from her pillow, she opened her window, which presented a beautiful view of the country, and gave way to the various sensations and reflections which her present situation naturally created.

She beheld the first beams of that day appear which was to decide her future destiny. Little Frances continued in a sweet sleep till late in the morning; Malvina was uneasy, and agitated, listening to the sound of every carriage, fearing it might be Sir Edmond – and still more fearful that he would not come. She contemplated the sweet repose of her child with a heavy sigh, and envied those tranquil slumbers, which she was incapable of enjoying; when Sir Edmond suddenly presented himself. – I am come very late (said he) but the fear of exposing you to the slightest suspicion, determined me to come alone; I therefore came part of the way on foot; and though I walked very quick, yet I observe I have lost, to my sorrow, some hours of that inestimable day which you had consented to grant me.

It is far from its decline yet, said Malvina, effected by seeing Sir Edmond overheated and covered with dust, and more so at the motive which occasioned it, we have time sufficient to be together; and, as you appear to be fatigued, it will be much better if you take a few minutes repose, and I will see you afterwards.

Malvina, said Sir Edmond, seating himself by her, and taking her hand, which he pressed between both his – when I behold you, when I am with you, not by chance, but by your own consent; when I have no reason to fear the intrusion of the malicious to disturb those sweet moments, can you believe it possible, that I would voluntarily lose one of them.

Ah! let me enjoy, without interruption, the felicity of contemplating the mistress of my heart, the confidant of my thoughts, and the arbitress of my destiny. She whose gentle pity is moved in my favor, and whose generous and exalted goodness can lead and form me to all those virtues which can please her.

Stop, Sir Edmond, interrupted Malvina, turning aside her face to conceal her emotion, those epithets do not belong to me. The respect which I owe my friend, the last promises which I gave her on her death-bed, makes it my duty to renounce you. – Do not hope to induce me to forget it. Besides, that is not the only objection which can separate us. – Do I not know, that as you have so generously resigned your fortune in favor of your sister, that Mrs. Burton has reserved hers for you?[xxxvi] Do you think it possible that I ever could consent to be the cause which would deprive you of it?

Hear me, Malvina, replied he, with an energy which he endeavoured to moderate – when I am actuated from what must concern the future happiness of my life, I must banish all fastidious and superstitious prejudices, and only endeavour to follow nature, and listen to truth. It is true that I have given away a part of my fortune to my sister, and it is a sacrifice which will ever afford me the utmost gratification, because it has contributed to her happiness, but I shall indeed think it a still greater, if it has also contributed to gain me a share of your esteem. – Yet do not appreciate it too highly. As from the slight value which I set upon riches, it gives me less concern than any thing else might.

As to Mrs. Burton's fortune, I never paid the least attention to such a concern, when I was conscious it was only to be obtained at the expence of flattery and submission to her will. And I hope that I possess so much of Malvina's esteem, as that she will believe, that from the purity of that affection which she has inspired, I have long renounced all claim to such advantages, as can only be acquired at the expence of truth and honor.

Ah! Sir Edmond, replied Malvina, much pleased with such a congeniality of sentiment,° I also wished to speak to you of those youthful errors – those transient amours – the sole recollection of which ought to frighten and deter every woman who might dare to have an affection for you. But surely such errors may be conquered, as you have had so much strength of mind as to retain those noble and generous sentiments, in a world where they are but too often obliterated; yet, without degrading them, you may still preserve Mrs. Burton's favor, by relinquishing me. For she both loves and fears you, and will listen to truths from you without being offended; and all the return she requires for her kindness, is, that you unite yourself to a beautiful and opulent young lady, whose favor and protection may raise you to the first rank in the kingdom. These are not your own sentiments, Malvina, said Sir Edmond, gravely, I cannot believe that you would advise me to sacrifice the woman whom I love, for her whom I do not?

For a little dross,[148] and a few vain titles, can you convince me, that if you was in my situation, similar motives would induce you to act in such a manner. If, therefore, your heart would repulse them with contempt, why have I deserved such degradation in your opinion, as to imagine that I was capable of yielding to them?

I acknowledge my injustice, Sir Edmond, I have done you an injury, by supposing I could convince you by those arguments which make so deep an impression upon common minds, replied Malvina. Alas! why did I even think of such, when there are others so much more powerful?

There are not any, cried he, with ardour, which can or shall separate me from my beloved Malvina! And surely there are not any which should induce her to leave[149] the man who adores her. – Ah! Malvina, I think you will approve of the plan I have fixed upon; and if it does meet with your approbation, you will anticipate the pleasure of which such a perspective gives the idea. – I have a paternal estate, which is situated a few miles from Glasgow, on the banks of the Clyde,[150] in a most pleasant and fertile country.

The mansion is large and commodious, and the lands belonging to the estate, bring in a revenue quite sufficient for all the necessaries of life. Do you think you could live there, Malvina? Will you consent to unite your destiny with mine, become my wife, my friend, and the sovereign of my existence? There we may forget the world, and never once regret those vain and transient pleasures, which I have but too often found illusive. There I shall have no other desire but to please you; all my ambition will be to imitate you, by adopting those sentiments which are so dear to you.[151] – There, when guided by you, virtue will become a pleasure to me.

And as we, together, visit the cottages of the poor, our only dispute will be, who shall do the most good, and all our rivalship will be in virtue, and love for each other. Ah! it will be there absorbed by my love, and my happiness, neither knowing, seeing, or loving any but you, feeling that you are the source of all my affections, my thoughts, and the end of all my actions.[152]

Oh! Malvina, do not therefore reject my intreaties, my wishes, and my tears. I have no other idea of happiness but what is inspired by you, nor the least desire for life, unless you will partake it with me. His agitation prevented him from saying any more. The tears rolled down his face, and the energy of his looks and discourse, animated by his passion, gave him an eloquence which had nearly subdued Malvina; when, to hide her distress, she turned her head aside, and chancing to cast her eyes towards Frances, she ran and took her in her arms, saying, come my beloved child, and shield me from the most powerful of seducers; let me press you to my bosom, that I may fortify my courage. And, ah! recall me to fulfil the promise which I made to thy angel mother. Secure my heart from being overcome by its own wishes, and harden it, if it is possible, against the insinuations of an object too much beloved.

No Frances, no, cried Sir Edmond; rather lend thy innocent voice to assist me in my endeavours to touch the heart of this insensible woman. Tell her, that her conscientious scruples lead her astray, and deceive her. Tell her, she did not promise thy mother to remain free, but while it conduced to her happiness;[153] for her duty rather prescribes that she should give me her hand. Tell her, that you will also become the object of my care, the child of my heart, and my adoption; and that my days shall be dedicated to you as well as herself.

And you, Lady Sheridan, said he, falling on one knee, and raising his hands towards Heaven; if it is permitted the blessed, in the ethereal regions, to read the hearts of those on earth; you then can be a witness of the sincerity of my vows. Ah! blessed spirit, dispose the heart of your friend to listen to them, and your dear infant shall be the solemn pledge between us.[154] Oh! my dear, good mama, cried the little creature; what does he cry so for in this manner? Is it because you have been scolding him?[155] Only see then how he begs you to forgive him; I will kneel too, and beg, and then you, and are so very, very good, will surely give him what he wants?

Ah, what is it I hear, said Malvina, agonized; Clara, my tenderly beloved Clara, thy daughter seems to speak for thee! And can it be? Am I then at liberty in reality to give my hand? And you, added she, permitting Sir Edmond to take her hand; you, who possess such power over me. Ah! I am not perfectly conscious whether I am in an illusion, or blinded by a superstitious presentiment which leads me wrong, or deceived by my own heart: but I cannot resist their united, perhaps fatal, importunities any longer; and if I am not guilty in thus yielding my hand to you, I do consent to be yours.[156xxxvii]

It is then mine, really mine, cried he, with transport. Thou beloved, and best of women, whose very first look subdued me, and rendered thee the arbitress of my destiny. She is then mine, she, who alone taught me to know love; I see, I press her to my heart; she loves me, she belongs to me! His happiness was too great to allow him to say any more.[157] Their tears fell in unison, as the only testimonies suitable to such a scene. The emotions experienced in such a scene, seemed as if they had once belonged to beings of a higher order; or that they were infused into some natures, to give them an idea of the felicity which is to be the eternal lot of the virtuous in Heaven.[158]

Sir Edmond did not wish to leave Malvina if he could have avoided it. He intreated her to name the day, the moment when she would bless him with her hand; but she denied him in a tone that convinced him that she would be obeyed. It is my desire, said she, that for the space of one month, you will return and partake of all the pleasures and enjoyments of the fashionable world, and after that time, if you can leave them without regret, and are not alarmed at the idea of being deprived of them for ever, you will let me know it Edmond, and Malvina will believe you.

She thinks you will not abuse the confidence she places in you, and that the facility with which you might do so, will be the most powerful inducement for you to avoid it. From such a proof as the one I have mentioned, and not till that has convinced me, should I dare to become your wife: equally as much on account of your happiness as my own. As I do not wish to owe the sacrifice which you intend to make for my sake, to the feelings of the moment, but to your deliberate and mature choice and determination, which can only be ascertained by absence.[159]

It shall be so, Malvina! I will obey you! Not that I have a doubt of my own sentiments ever being different from what they are at present. But what would I not undergo to obtain the blessing to which I dare to aspire. Certainly I am unworthy of you at present, and I shall be more capable of appreciating the felicity, when I have better deserved it. Yet, how tedious, how irksome, will this long month appear, while absent from you! You! who are going to Mrs. St. Clare; to a woman who detests me, who may prejudice you against me.

What reason has she to hate you? demanded Malvina; how can you have deserved such an epithet from so amiable and interesting a woman? Alas! Malvina, I am not at liberty to inform you of the particulars. I certainly have injured her greatly; the part I have acted with regard to her, is not quite inexcusable; but I shall render it so, if I divulge the secret which I have sworn to keep, as Mrs. St. Clare alone has that privilege. And yet, Malvina, she is unacquainted with all the motives which might plead as an extenuation of my conduct! Though by revealing this mystery to you, she may ruin me in your good opinion; instead of which, could I dare to inform you, I might hope for your indulgence. But it is no matter, I will abide by the consequences. – And the lover of Malvina will rather prefer the fear of being judged guilty, to the dishonor of being so in reality.

Do not alarm yourself by any fears of that kind, replied Malvina, I never give my confidence by halves, and I therefore promise to avoid any conversation upon that subject, which Mrs. St. Clare may think proper to relate to me. I shall therefore wait till you are permitted to inform me yourself. Ah! Malvina, said he, much affected, what being in this world is there that could be so despicable as to abuse so generous a confidence, that even in this extreme, cannot be termed a weakness, as it proceeds entirely from the purity of your own heart.[160] That conviction alone would ever deter me from deceiving you, even was it so, that I could not obtain you without it.

Excellent, amiable woman, rest assured that such a confidence will never be abused. For, by raising me to thyself, Malvina, you have placed me in so exalted a situation, that I cannot descend without debasing myself. And by that sacred altar which I have raised to you in my heart, I vow to communicate all my thoughts, or rather[161] never to form any which shall give me cause to blush. But Malvina, added he, with some confusion; since I have thus laid open my heart to you, may I not ask why you have been so uniformly silent[162] upon a subject which I am almost fearful of enquiring into, though it so much concerns my peace? you have ever concealed[163] your correspondence with Mr. Prior from me, which has caused me many moments of real pain; indeed, I shall not taste my present felicity without an allay, till you have desired him to relinquish that privilege.

This confession rather astonished Malvina; but taking the letter from her pocket-book, and looking steadily at Sir Edmond, you shall hear if you have any cause for uneasiness, said she; and opening the paper she read what follows:

'My situation becomes every day more wretched. The distress which I behold my parents labour under, rends my heart! Alas! it is in vain that I have tried every possible means to assist and comfort them; but every thing which I undertake fails in its success; it seems as if the vicious, and impiety alone, were permitted to prosper in this world, for they daily accumulate riches, while I may keep my heart pure to no purpose. 'For verily I have cleansed my heart in vain, and washed my hands in innocency.' Alas! I am agitated and distressed even to agony; my days glide without hope, and my nights are passed in sorrow, and my eyes can no longer behold comfort.[164] We live solitary and neglected, while misery and despair seem to dispute their right to our asylum; and I should soon sink under their united efforts, if it was not for your letters, which for a moment recall my attachment to life'.

Thus interrupted, Sir Edmond,[165] with some asperity; this man owes what happiness he does enjoy to you alone? It is you who form all his comfort; he receives your letters with emotion, calls you his dear Malvina, and perhaps pure as he may imagine himself, his heart may have formed hopes, which these marks of your friendship will but serve to increase; and yet you do not even offer to desist, but are rather strengthening his hopes by constantly granting—.

Stop, for Heaven's sake, Sir Edmond, replied Malvina, hastily; and reflect a moment upon the misery of this unfortunate being, who has no other comfort to flee to, but the sympathy of a friend. And shall I, at such a time, refuse to hear his sorrows, and perhaps endeavour to sooth them? It is but merely the office of charity.[166] Oh! then, you, who are from henceforth to be my director and guide, do not wish to render me hard, unfeeling, and ungrateful, but make a generous use of that power, and rather say that you approve of my addressing a few friendly words of soothing consolation to an unhappy man, who feels comforted and relieved by them. And do not so far injure either yourself or me, by indulging the idea that they can have the least tendency or connection with those sentiments which you inspire.

It is not you, Malvina, said Sir Edmond, of whom I have the slightest doubt. But when I am conscious that any other in the world but myself dares to love you, to think of you with rapture, and perhaps – and that still you do not forbid him from[167] – Malvina, forgive me; but I should really deceive you if I was silent upon a subject that alarms and embitters my existence! Perhaps, replied Malvina, I was imprudent in accepting the friendship of Mr. Prior? Perhaps, I should have reflected that notwithstanding his religious and virtuous character, and situation, his sex alone should have deterred me from forming any intimacy with him. But to desist, just at this distressing moment, would be only increasing his misery, and perhaps drive him to a state of desperation, for he will immediately conclude that he is entirely obliterated from my memory; and perhaps, we may both be sorry for the consequences.

You make me tremble, Malvina, cried Sir Edmond, for I certainly do not wish to reduce that good man to such a state of despair; but to-morrow, when I return to Edinburgh, I will make it my business to find out a situation or employment, which may be so beneficial, as to place both him and his family above want. And when I have seen so fortunate as to accomplish this, my own Malvina – I understand you, said she, and I promise from that moment to desist from any farther correspondence with him. But in the mean time, you shall read all the letters which pass between us.

No, replied he, if I had any doubts, I would have mentioned them; all my anxiety proceeds from the tender manner in which he addresses you, and from his writing so frequently.[168] Believe me, my only love, I do not require more from you. On your affection alone, I will perfectly rely, for your relieving me as soon as possible, from an idea to which neither reason or pity can reconcile me. You will also believe, Sir Edmond, that this generous reliance, will make every line I write painful to me, and every word, which from kindness and humanity I am forced to adopt to Mr. Prior, make me wish for the moment which will put an end to it.

Such were the terms upon which they separated, though not before they had previously given a mutual promise to write and even see each other, if any unforeseen circumstance should render such a step necessary.

CHAP. XV.

How little are the hopes of happiness to be depended upon.

Mrs. St. Clare was as much surprised as delighted, to again behold Malvina, and not a little pleased that she had returned so soon; and after expressing the most affectionate marks of the satisfaction it gave her; I should be too much flattered, said she, if I could hope that you have thus gratified me from a dislike to public life only; and that your fondness for retirement is not owing to any other cause?

I wish I had the power of expressing my acknowledgments, said Malvina, and that I could say, that my sudden appearance was only prompted by the great interest which you have inspired. But this would be an untruth; for I really had not the choice of an asylum, and in the situation to which I was reduced, the offer which you had so kindly made, was the only one I could adopt.

Ah! what is it I hear? What is Mrs. Burton's house,[xxxviii] as well as those of her numerous acquaintance, no longer yours? Are they not happy to receive you? I have left Mrs. Burton for ever, and I do not desire to behold her again, said Malvina. You have left Mrs. Burton, then? replied Mrs. St. Clare, astonished. There must have been some very powerful motive to induce you to take such a step? My dear friend, replied Malvina, affectionately, do not ask me, as from the peculiar attentions you have shewn me, I should be sorry to deny you any thing; but under the present circumstances I have promised to remain silent, whatever it may cost my heart, which would otherwise with pleasure repose all its griefs in your friendly bosom. That is sufficient, returned Mrs. St. Clare; I have but too often myself been taught by experience, that from reasons the most trivial in themselves, we are sometimes, from particular circumstances, forced to appear whimsical and mysterious. Therefore, my dear madam,[169] as I perfectly understand your wishes, you may be certain of my compliance in every thing which can contribute to your satisfaction.

The following days passed with rapidity. Mrs. St. Clare's father having been called to London upon business, she was more at liberty to enjoy the society of Malvina. And Malvina was perfectly at liberty to dispose of her time as was most agreeable, without fearing to meet any of those inquisitive looks which seem to enquire how it has been spent; or those formal and constrained attentions which oblige you to answer them, however ridiculous.

Mrs. St. Clare spent part of the day in her own apartment; and Malvina occupied part of hers[xxxix] in attending to the education of her little girl, in reading and sometimes in the indulgence of the most delightful reveries in the pleasant gardens of St Clare-Hall. It cannot be imagined that Malvina had all at once forgot the vices to which Sir Edmond was addicted. She, on the contrary, frequently recollected them, and all which had happened at Burton-Hall. For though he had not absolutely acknowledged his intrigue with Miss Melmor, yet he had said sufficient to prevent her from having any farther doubts; but that prudence and honor forbade him to be more explicit.

But the sentiment which now governed her heart, placed him in such a point of view, that she could only look upon those vices as transient weaknesses:[170] for she sometimes had heard of those who were free from such errors as Sir Edmond's, who were also devoid of his best qualities.[171] But, in the midst of these reflections, if she had been told that he had been wise and reserved in his youth, she would have undoubtedly said that such a character could not possibly err; because such a one was endowed by Heaven with such an exalted mind, that it could repulse every idea which could in the slightest manner degrade it; and therefore could never enjoy a pleasure which was not allied to virtue.

For above fifteen days had Malvina dared to indulge her tenderness without contradiction, and without blushing.[172] Though she was not happy, she thought that she was going to be so, and the present scene was embellished by the rays of hope which illumined the perspective. She could not yet enjoy that serenity which happiness gives; but that sweet agitation of the heart, which exists only in the expectation of it. Sometimes her thoughts were absorbed by the certainty of being beloved by Sir Edmond, that she alone was the object of his attachment, was a pleasure which harmonized her soul, and vibrated to her heart.[173]

During the silence of night, her thoughts still reverted to the same object, and when she did recollect herself, she would forget that she was beloved for the pleasure she found in loving; and at such moments she felt happy in the idea of the affection she bestowed. For this delicate and generous sentiment, when real, does not always depend upon a return for the pleasure it finds in its attachment to a deserving object.

But her heart indulged the hope that he might become the virtuous being she wished him.[174] After many hours passed alone, under these pleasing illusions and delightful hopes, Malvina, though apparently far from happy, yet felt that her existence would be a pain to her, was she now to be deprived of them.

The month of trial was now nearly elapsed, and Malvina flattered herself, that it had served only to strengthen Sir Edmond in his resolution of giving up every thing for her sake. She already, with a blush, began to anticipate the moment when he would return and claim her as his own. When one morning, as she was at breakfast with Mrs. St. Clare, two letters were brought to her; one of them, the agitation of her heart convinced her, was from Sir Edmond. The other she saw was from Lord Sheridan.

But as his lordship seldom or ever wrote but a few lines of mere enquiry concerning his daughter, and politeness to herself,[175] she was not under the necessity of opening his, but at her leisure; and therefore laid it on one side till she had perused the one from Sir Edmond, which was as follows—

'Though Mrs. Burton, ever since my return, has been made acquainted that you was the only object of my tender affection, yet she could not resist from attempting a last effort, yesterday, to entice me back to Lady Mary Summerhill, by informing me, that her fortune was to be the alternative. In answer to which proposal, I positively declared to this ambitious woman, that I most willingly renounced all her benefits, that the hand of Malvina was all that I coveted, and that we both should be happy without wishing to receive any thing from her. These words irritated her to the last degree.

'Then, said she, if you were both to come begging at my door, I would not stretch out my hand to save you from misery. Go, ungrateful man, go to that deceitful creature, for whom you are going to sacrifice my friendship and fortune. Go, and receive from her lips, the tender affection which Mr. Prior received from her before you did. But should you reach the altar, do not imagine yourself so secure, but that I may find means to separate you. I shall punish you for your insolence and contempt; and when you are separated for ever, you will repent.[176]

'Ah! I shall not be long,[177] said I, flying from such a fury, who, not satisfied by endeavouring to part me from her I love, would wish to poison my happiness, by for ever recalling the idea of your attachment for Mr. Prior, and that particular moment when she surprised you both in a state of agitation – when your sorrows were so great – and your constant correspondence –

'Cruel, barbarous woman! this was the venom she wished to shed over my soul, and her malicious heart enjoyed the power of tormenting me. Oh! my gentle, my dear Malvina, come, and, by your presence, banish these fatal ideas; and as I have fulfilled your commands, I may know that you are my own. The moment which was proposed by yourself is arrived, though Mrs. Burton will, I am sensible, employ all the arts she is mistress of to separate us; yet, if it is true that you love me, and my repose is dear to you, delay not, my Malvina, to come; and let the inestimable gift of your hand be instead of an answer[178] to this letter.

'I am at present at Kinross, about twelve miles from Mrs. St. Clare's; there I shall impatiently wait for you. It is from thence I have sent the express, which will certainly, in a few hours, bring back at least a line from my Malvina, which I shall trace without agitation.[179] For in this I shall hope to find the assurance of her consenting to fix to morrow as the fortunate day which is to unite our destinies. If Malvina can hesitate; but no, she knows me; and since I am dear to her, she will not disappoint me. This to-morrow – what shall I behold! that day in which she is to pledge her faith, and receive my solemn vows, that I will never love any one but her. In short, to become for ever happy.

'Oh! Malvina, by the love I bear you, hasten to me;[180] I am writing this at midnight,[181] that my express may set out at day-break; and I shall wait his return, a prey to all those tumultuous agitations which exhaust life by the excess of our feelings, and which I could not exist under, if the hopes which created them, should deceive me'.

Malvina read this letter several times[182] without knowing what step to take, or what answer to return Sir Edmond, when she was informed the man who had brought it was waiting for her answer, and that he intreated she would be as quick as possible, for the gentleman who sent him was in such haste, that he had threatened him severely if he did not return at the appointed time, and promised to reward him handsomely if he was punctual.

These words surprised Mrs. St. Clare; she fixed her eyes on Malvina, who instantly cast hers down,[xl] and blushed; much distressed by Sir Edmond's anxiety, the impatience of his express, and the particular looks of her amiable friend. She hastily snatched the first sheet of paper she could find, and traced a consent, which she would have been unjust in refusing. She was quite agitated when she had given it the messenger, that her voice was so tremulous she could scarcely be heard.

When he was gone, her distress increased, on being alone with Mrs. St. Clare. Malvina was sensible this scene wanted an explanation; but how could she do that with propriety, after the promise she had given Sir Edmond not to mention their present situation? Yet, she remembered that Mrs. St. Clare observed her very attentively, but remained silent, as if expecting her to speak on the subject. Fearful of disobliging her by conversing on any other, and not daring to mention her departure, fearing her enquiries, Malvina continued silent, and the longer she remained so, the more irksome the tête-à-tête became.

She at last became so oppressed by her sensations and situation, that she breathed with difficulty, and her eyes fixed on the ground. Mrs. St. Clare, affected by the distress she observed her in, endeavoured to recall her to herself, by those interesting attentions which the heart prompts us to offer; and was just holding out her hand to take Malvina's, who, in order to avoid it,[183] immediately took up Lord Sheridan's letter which she had laid on the table, and hastily broke the seal, in order to conceal her embarrassment, under this pretended employment.

She had no sooner perused a few lines, than every other idea vanished. A sudden paleness overspread her countenance, a cold chill enervated her whole frame; she felt her strength fail her; and had scarcely reached the conclusion of the cruel mandate which she held in her hand, when she sunk under the heavy pressure of the sorrows it announced, and fell, without sense or motion, into the arms of Mrs. St. Clare, faintly murmuring – Ah! it is done – my Edmond, we are ruined for ever.

END OF VOL. II.

H. Reynell, Printer, 21, Piccadilly.

CONTENTS OF VOL. II.[184]

MALVINA,
by Madame C****,

Authoress of Claire d'Albe, and Amelia Mansfield.

Translated from the French,

by Miss Gunning,

in four volumes.

VOL. III.

London:

printed for T. Hurst, Paternoster-Row;

C. Chapple, Pall-Mall, and Southampton-Row, Russell-Square; and R. Dutton, Gracechurch-Street.

H. Reynell, Printer, 21, Piccadilly.

1803.

CONTENTS OF VOL. III.

CHAP. I.

MALVINA.

Explanation of the preceding chapter.

Mrs. St. Clare was most sensibly affected at the situation of her amiable companion; she instantly used every method to recover her, but finding all her endeavours ineffectual, she assisted in having her conveyed to her chamber. They laid her on the bed, and she continued for some time longer insensible: at last, after Mrs. St. Clare's repeated efforts to recover her, she had the felicity to see her open her eyes, and giving a deep sigh, she continued silent. Mrs. St. Clare pressed her in her arms, and her silent tears fell on the face of Malvina.

Calm your agitated spirits, my dear Malvina, said she, in the softest accents, a little repose will be necessary; I will leave you for a short time, but do not let it be long before you recall me. Ah, madam, I wish to open my heart to you;[1] little did I imagine how much you was to be pitied – Ah! how infinitely do I feel my friendship for you increased. Mrs. St. Clare's distress augmented, on saying this, to find Malvina remained silent;[2] therefore, fearful of increasing her painful sensations, she retired.

As soon as Malvina found herself alone, she looked mournfully round her, and perceiving Lord Sheridan's letter, she trembled, and pushed it from her; but soon after took it up and re-perused it, perhaps with the idea that she might have misconstrued it, or that some hope might beam from it on a second perusal.

'Lord Sheridan to Madame de Sorcy.

'Madam,

'As I have just been informed that you are on the point of marrying, without wishing to investigate the motives which have induced such a determination, I shall not even enquire why you have remained silent on this subject in all your letters, neither will I reproach you with the imprudent and public manner in which you have separated yourself from your respectable relation, who had so obligingly received you in her family, and who is so extremely distressed at your strange conduct.

'I shall only observe, that as you have thought proper to invalidate the promise which you made your friend, I have certainly a right to retract from mine. I therefore inform you, that I do not intend my daughter to be brought up in the same house with such a man as he is, whom you have selected for your husband; nor shall she remain under the protection of one to whom I am a stranger.

'It was to you alone that Lady Sheridan confided her child; and from the moment you resign your liberty, she is, from that instant, no longer under your direction; and I shall then exercise my authority.

'You will be so obliging then, madam, the moment you are united, to place my daughter under the care of your respectable relation, Mrs. Burton, who has consented to take the charge of her, until my affairs permit me to send for her. Without wishing to give you the slightest offence, allow me to say, that we must not always rely too much on appearances.

'Your friend, when on her deathbed, bathed by your tears, confiding entirely in your friendship, and complaining of my want of affection, little imagined I should be more faithful and attentive in fulfilling all the duties which she wished to her child.

I am with respect,
Madam,
Your obedient Servant,

Sheridan.[3]

P.S. It will be quite useless for you to give yourself the trouble of answering this, as I am on the point of departure for Ireland, and shall continue there during the Summer.

Malvina was astonished at this letter, as she had not an idea he would have taken the trouble to write on this occasion, as it was very seldom she could gain an answer, of a few lines only, to any particulars relative to his daughter, which she had informed him of; and his negligence in this particular was remarkable.[4] That he should be so suddenly alarmed, at the idea of a marriage which she supposed to be so perfectly indifferent to him, that she did not think it necessary to inform him of it. But from this letter it was plainly to be seen, that the whole proceeded from Mrs. Burton; and she was convinced it was to her she was indebted for this misfortune.

She was not deceived; for the moment she left the house, Mrs. Burton immediately wrote to Lord Sheridan, and acquainted him with it, that she might gain him in her interest. She therefore insinuated every thing which she thought might prejudice him against Malvina; and, under the mask of friendship to him, described the imprudence of Malvina's conduct, also her being so extremely obstinate and conceited, as easily to be deluded by it.

It is in your power, said she, in her letter to Lord Sheridan, to prevent this misfortune from overwhelming both her and me, as my cousin's only objection to this marriage, is the child Lady Sheridan confided to her care; therefore, by informing her that you will take it from her, if she persists in fulfilling this unworthy union, you will not only save the friend of your wife from ruin, but the first family in Scotland from despair. – Besides, as a father, there is another consideration which ought to encourage you to this proceeding, which is, the interest your daughter demands. For if my cousin should retrieve the good opinion which she has so nearly lost – as she has been the occasion of a duel, and quitted my house in so public in manner, she will then inherit, with my will, part of my fortune, which, added to what she possesses of her own, if she should not marry, will become the inheritance of your child.

Lord Sheridan, from having possessed an immense fortune, had so much impaired it by riot and debauchery, that the residue of it was scarcely sufficient to pay his debts.[5] His conscience frequently reproached him, even when surrounded by the most alluring pleasures, with the torturing idea of having ruined his daughter. Under these circumstances, which oppressed his mind, it will not excite so much astonishment, that he so instantaneously coincided with Mrs. Burton's scheme, in order to soothe his remorse;[6] therefore, he wrote in the very terms she wished, and which so much affected Malvina.

Ah! cried Malvina, shedding a torrent of tears; do not fear, my beloved Clara, that thy child shall ever be placed under so unworthy a woman's care as Mrs. Burton's. For if her unfeeling father persists in his intention of taking her from the wife of Sir Edmond, never will Malvina accept that title, for she will have fortitude sufficient to renounce all that she loves, rather than deviate in what she owes thee.

Oh! Edmond! dear and much loved Edmond, an eternal separation will take place of our intended union; and instead of the happiness which you expected from my love, I shall plunge a dagger to thy heart by this fatal change. Unhappy Malvina! wretched Edmond – how swiftly have the days of hope and joy fled. Distress approaches like the darkness of night and heavily clouds our existence. Adieu, sweet and flattering chimeras; through whose brilliant medium I had beheld the sunbeams of happiness enlighten the perspective of my future horizon. Adieu to that felicity, which I had vainly imagined I was so near realizing. Thou hast now fled from me for ever! But I have been taught in what manner to appreciate it.

How does my dear Malvina find herself? said Mrs. St. Clare, opening the door; may I be permitted to come in, will my presence be an intrusion? Malvina made a sign with her hand; Mrs. St. Clare approached, and pressing it between both hers,[xli] looked at her in the tenderest manner, and said, do not be the least alarmed at the idea of my making any enquiries concerning your situation, this morning; I too well know there are some chords of sensibility which cannot be touched, without their vibrating through the whole frame; and I respect your sorrows too much to penetrate their source. But let me hope my amiable friend, that the wing of time may burst away your reserve; and that I may obtain that confidence, I would not wish in your present weak state.

Ah! what do you say? replied Malvina – What do you hope from time? To-morrow I must leave you, for him who expects me. You leave me? You are expected? Where are you going? and when shall I see you again? Alas! I do not know myself, replied Malvina, weeping. I have been indulging the hopes, that when I left this place, the enchanting retreat to which I was going, would have compensated for the regret I should have felt on leaving you, my dear friend. But all, every hope is vanished,[7] one moment has deprived me of them.[8] I am a wanderer, without a home, without a protector; I know not where I ought to direct my steps. I am uncertain whether I am to leave you, or whether I may not return and expire on your bosom! But where do you go to-morrow? demanded Mrs. St. Clare, with the greatest earnestness; why can I not company you?

Ah! exclaimed Malvina, do you believe he would not imagine that I wished to expose his grief, and would think my taking a witness with me an insult to it. Who is this person? asked Mrs. St. Clare. In the name of Heaven, of whom are you speaking? Of him who possesses all my affection, cried Malvina; of him who occupies all my heart.[9] Has he not renounced every thing for me; riches, titles, and the world? and when he expects to receive my hand, will only hear from my lips an eternal adieu, which can only terminate with life. You alarm and terrify me, Malvina, replied Mrs. St. Clare, more and more agitated. – Oh! quickly inform me, I conjure you, tell me who is the happy being that possesses all your affections? Is it not Sir Edmond Burton?

And who but him is worthy? exclaimed Malvina, with a degree of enthusiasm. Why should I conceal a sentiment which exalts me? Yes, it is he alone whom I love, and who must ever possess my heart.[10] To have been thine Edmond, my life would have been a continued blessing; but now, if I must in future live without seeing thee more; rather let me sink into the silent tomb.

Ah! what have you said, dear unhappy, unfortunate woman? exclaimed Mrs. St. Clare, in an agony of tears. Is it to this vile man, that the gentle, the tender Malvina has given her heart, is it to this perfidious wretch[xlii] that she wishes to unite her angelic mind; and is it to Sir Edmond Burton that she wishes to go to-morrow? No, Malvina, you shall not stir. No duty ought to carry you there, but rather keep you from him.[11] You do not know what stratagems this wretch employs to seduce virtue. If you are once with him, I shall never behold you more; you will be ruined, Malvina. Oh! my beloved and innocent friend, let me acquaint you with every thing if there is yet time for it? To you alone I will reveal this fatal secret. – You will see the shades of death surround the living; you will behold the coffin which yet encloses the sweet companion of my early days, who was mowed down in the bloom of life, by the vile seductions of Sir Edmond.

I do not wish to hear or know any thing, said Malvina, rising and going some distance from Mrs. St. Clare. I have promised that I would not listen to any but him; and to believe only him. Therefore I will not forfeit my promise, to listen to your accusations. No, Edmond cannot be so culpable, his heart is too noble to be sullied by such a crime: if the whole world was united against him; one word, one look from Sir Edmond would make me discredit them all. Do not imagine that you can prevent my meeting him to-morrow, I will go, and if it is possible, endeavour, by the utmost tenderness to alleviate and urge him to acquiesce, in the painful trial which rigourous duty compels me to perform.[12] I am at the same time determined to separate myself from Sir Edmond; yet, that will not induce me to believe her who hates, and tries to scandalise him.

Oh! cruel Edmond, interrupted Mrs. St. Clare, weeping, were you really born for my punishment, by what fatality is it, that thy insinuating arts must ever strike at what is nearest and dearest to my heart? Was it not sufficient to have deprived me of a sister, without adding to it the hatred of Malvina?

This was uttered in such a plaintive and affecting manner, that it touched the soul of Malvina; and she was so much affected, that she threw herself into the arms of Mrs. St. Clare, who eagerly pressed her to her bosom, and they mingled their tears in silence together, and each feared to interrupt it, lest it might disunite them again.

However alarmed Mrs. St. Clare was at the symptom with which passion had inspired Malvina, she knew that it was in vain to attempt to conquer it by reason: the knowledge she had of Sir Edmond occasioned her to regard her fair friend as his victim; and she considered it as her duty to endeavour to save her if possible. For this purpose, she was confident she must use the most forcible means, by powerfully striking upon the imagination, and touching the heart; she knew this was the only probable way of accomplishing what she desired.

She therefore no longer attempted to dissuade her from going, but only requested permission to accompany her the next day, part of the way. A sacred duty, said Mrs. St. Clare, calls me to assist a friend, which lies in your way, where I shall stay while the carriage takes you to Kenross; and since you are determined to leave Sir Edmond, you can resign your little charge to me; and we can both wait your return at the same place where you will take leave of us.

Malvina thought this arrangement perfectly agreeable; it was therefore agreed that they should set out the next morning at eight o'clock.

CHAP. II.

An unexpected meeting.

Though Mrs. St. Clare was perfectly satisfied with the plan she had formed, yet she was rather alarmed at the effect it might produce on Malvina. This anxiety prevented her from sleeping part of the night; and rising with the sun, she strolled into the garden, to reflect more maturely whether she could conscientiously justify herself for the step she was about to take. But all these reflections only served to confirm her in the goodness of her intention; and she anxiously wished to set out.

The clock had struck eight, and Malvina not appearing, Mrs. St. Clare became uneasy, and going up to her chamber, she found her seated on the bed, in the same dress that she had worn the preceding evening;[p] she appeared motionless, with her eyes cast down. Her countenance had no longer that sweet, gentle, and pensive expression, which added charms to her whole appearance. Instead of this interesting tout en semble,[13] she appeared oppressed by a gloomy dejection, which had altered her in a most surprising manner. The ravages of the passions are totally different from the tender regrets of friendship; and they too often leave the traces of their progress on the countenance for life.

They undermine the soul, similar to a volcano, which consumes while it burns, and creates so frightful a void, that the cold hand of death can alone extinguish it. Malvina had passed the night in anticipating all the distressful struggles which she expected to undergo the ensuing day. Thus, she had already suffered nearly as much as the evil she apprehended; and her destiny was preparing heavy sorrows yet to come.

Oh! why was she not one of those beings, whose inactive mind never dives into the future, who never knew what reflection or presentiment meant?[q] but who, when it is day, never think of the morrow, or remember evening till they see it dark.

Mrs. St. Clare taking Malvina's arm, conducted her to the carriage, and getting in after her, she took Frances on her lap.[14] She was sometimes tempted to reproach herself for deceiving Malvina; but the next moment she was pleased with the idea of saving her. Mrs. St. Clare was absorbed by her own reflections; while her melancholy companion was following the image of Sir Edmond, picturing his despair, and every other attendant that could depress her mind, or make her lose the remembrance of her present situation, or where she was going.

After they had travelled near two hours,[15] she at last noticed that they were not in the same road which led from Mrs. St. Clare's. Stupendous mountains environed them on every side, and the carriage rolled through a gloomy and solitary glen. Where are we going? enquired Malvina, hastily. To the house I mentioned to you, replied her companion, a little agitated; as it lies out of the great road, we were obliged to take a cross one to reach it.

I fear it will detain me later than I wish, said Malvina, with visible anxiety; Edmond will be waiting for me. Ah! replied Mrs. St. Clare, mournfully; do not pity him; let him to day experience a few of those torments which he has so often occasioned the innocent to suffer. Heaven, in its justice, will some time make him feel what he deserves. – I will not go any farther, exclaimed Malvina; I will get out of the carriage, madam, if I am obliged to go on foot, without a guide or support; no power on earth shall prevent me from going to the unhappy being who expects me.

Do not make yourself the least uneasy my dear, said Mrs. St. Clare, suppressing her agitation; this road is not so much out of your way as you imagine; and the house I shall stop at, is not more than an hour's drive from Kenross. Malvina believed her; in about a quarter of an hour they stopped at a farm, which was in the most lonely situation imaginable. While the horses were resting, Mrs. St. Clare desired Malvina to remark the house, that she might know it again on her return; and taking her arm without waiting her reply, they went towards a rock which was very steep, and its sides were decorated with festoons[16] of brambles, and a variety of wild flowers, which partly concealed a small door, made with great art in the rock. Mrs. St. Clare put her hand under a projecting stone, to reach a string which belonged to a bell.

Soon after, a little child about seven years old, opened the door, and said, dear Mrs. Cecilia,[r] how good you are to come just now – my poor mother is so very ill, that we think she is going to die. Oh! my God, let us hasten to her, said Mrs. St. Clare, rushing in with such precipitation that she forgot to fasten the door. She was soon after met by a middle aged woman, who, lifting her hands to Heaven on beholding Mrs. St. Clare, said, blessed be the chance which has conducted you here, madam; my poor mistress has been so extremely ill all night, that she believed herself dying, and requested that we should send for a priest to be with her in her last moments. We luckily met with one at Kenross, and he is at present with her. She is rather better now, and I will go and prepare her; for your arrival will rejoice her. That is very proper, Mary, replied Mrs. St. Clare, so agitated she could scarcely articulate a word. I will wait in the next room, and you will acquaint me when I may be admitted.

Mary went instantly; and Mrs. St. Clare taking Malvina's hand, led her to the casement.[17] Do you notice this dismal retreat? said she – this gloomy solitude; but infinitely less so than the soul of her who inhabits it. Would you not imagine that every thing was moistened by tears? and that the very air was impregnated with grief? Do you not hear the groans of that unfortunate, who is perhaps now expiring? Do you guess who this dying victim is? It is my sister, my friend, she who lives in my heart. Do you know who is her murderer, and the father of that child? – It is Sir Edmond.

Oh! why did I not expire before I heard it? exclaimed Malvina, with an agonised shriek, and sinking into a chair, nearly deprived of life. At this noise, a door suddenly opened, and a man rushed into the room, crying, it certainly was her that I heard, if I may believe my senses? It is her, it is Malvina, whom I behold. By what strange fatality is it, that I find you in this house of mourning?

Edmond, Edmond, what have you done? exclaimed Malvina, sobbing; who had not perceived the entrance of Mr. Prior: alas, you have then deceived me! What name is that you have just mentioned, asked Mr. Prior? Can such a perfidious man be yet dear to you. Ah! I have not a doubt but it is the hand of the Almighty which has conducted you to her; whose sorrows and sufferings will give you a more just idea of the character of Sir Edmond.

Ah! Mr. Prior, it is not now a proper time; whatever Sir Edmond may be, my lot is ever to love him; and his crimes cannot tear him from my heart.[18] Unhappy being! she continued, what a source of remorse has he accumulated on his head; where will he find a gentle hand to soothe him under it? Sir, said Mrs. St. Clare to Mr. Prior, who appeared much astonished at what Malvina had inadvertently uttered. Since I have unexpectedly met so estimable a character, who also possesses the esteem and confidence of this interesting creature, remain with her; and like the angel of peace, speak comfort to her soul. Prevent her, if you can, from rushing into that fatal gulph,[19] which will in the end, overwhelm her. Endeavour to fortify her mind, and rouse it to that noble love of virtue, which a fatal passion seems nearly to have annihiliated. I am going into the next room. – I am going to wipe away the tears of another. Oh! may Malvina never have reason to shed such tears of bitter repentance.

Mr. Prior permitted Mrs. St. Clare to depart without returning an answer. Then, looking steadily at Malvina, who appeared absorbed by grief; after a long silence, he exclaimed, Was it in such a situation, O Heaven, that I was to behold my friend again; giving way to an unruly passion, without blushing at the selection of her heart, and daring publicly to avow it; who has not even a word to bestow on a friend who has been so long[20] absent from her?

Is it then really true that the friendship of a woman is only the phantom of a few days? which blooms only like a flower, and which is alas, as soon withered; and which flies like the shadows of the field; to render that mind a prey to anguish; whose deep and unchanging sensibility, time, place, distance, and such impalpable things can never alter.[21] Ah! Malvina, why are you silent? Are you even a stranger to pity? Alas! I only supported a painful existence by the hope of seeing you again; and I now behold you in a situation which renders me infinitely more wretched.

What would you have me say? replied Malvina, with gloomy calmness. I have nothing to offer you, do not longer think of friendship, or any thing else: do you not know that all is destroyed? Edmond has deceived me. What, exclaimed Mr. Prior, with quickness, because he is false, do you imagine there are not any who are sincere? and that no one is capable of friendship, because so many are deceitful? Ah! Mr. Prior, when I have lost all the happiness I valued in this world, of what consequence is the reality of any other?

Oh! Malvina, what have you asserted; my friendship is from henceforth indifferent to you, and you no longer esteem me? Yet, I shall hope, said he, raising his hands towards Heaven, I shall find it then, in thee, O my God; oh! deign to look down on me, and pity me; for I am bereaved of comfort, and my soul is heavily afflicted. Ah! Mr. Prior, said Malvina, forgive me, if I have been the occasion of a moment's pain;[xliii] but, added she, pressing both her hands upon her heart, there is not any room here for confidence or belief, or any place to love any thing.

Oh! dear Malvina, said Mr. Prior, seizing one of her hands, and bathing it with his tears; ah! why will you thus torture me by those words? But, no, no, I will not believe you; your unhappy friend cannot have become quite a stranger to you. A merciful Creator adapts our sorrows to the strength we possess to support them.[22] Ah! do we not rather fear those only, which are insupportable? replied Malvina, with the most melancholy tone and manner; yet there is nevertheless. – She had scarcely pronounced these words, when a hasty step announced the approach of some person. The door was suddenly opened, and Sir Edmond appeared before them.

CHAP. III.

The storm of the passions.

Sir Edmond drew back with amazement, on observing Mr. Prior with Malvina; and then standing motionless for some moments, he exclaimed, Great God,[23] am I then under an illusion; is it possible that Malvina has betrayed me? Edmond, is it you? you here! she would have said, but he did not give her time to finish the sentence; but interrupting her with vehemence, he said, Take care Malvina, of uttering a word, or making a sign that may recall me to myself; do not let me know that I am awake; for my revenge shall be as dreadful as the tortures which has occasioned it.

And on whom is your fury to fall? said Mr. Prior, haughtily, and going up to him. On thee, replied Sir Edmond, trembling with rage; on thee, who hast robbed me of Malvina's love; and thy life shall answer for this perjury. Come, follow me, putting a pistol into his hands, I must have blood to satisfy my despair. What are you going to do, cruel Edmond? cried Malvina, flying after him, and holding him with both her arms. What is it that you suspect? what is it that you dare to say?[24] violent and barbarous man. Look and recollect where you are, blush for yourself, and do not judge of Malvina's heart by thy own.

The noise which this scene occasioned, soon drew Mrs. St. Clare into the room. She appeared, and perceiving Sir Edmond, she exclaimed, Oh! merciful Providence, is it then as a punishment for his guilt, that thou hast sent here the murderer of Louisa, to witness the last sighs of his victim? Is this the place where Louisa is? said Sir Edmond, with a wildness in his manner. Am I then under the same roof with Louisa? Is it here that Malvina came, without any regard to the promise she made me never to become acquainted with this secret, from any one but myself? When I have been waiting for her on that very day which was to have seen us united; yet she could forget her vows, despite her engagements, and betray her faith. When I have been expecting her with the most agonising anxiety, and finding it exceeded the promised hour, I vainly traversed every road which she was to have come; I questioned every one whom I met, and guided by one of them, I found her under the same roof with Louisa, and alone with a detested rival. The punishments of hell are in my bosom, and I carry their torments in my heart.

Edmond, unhappy Edmond! exclaimed Malvina, the most dreadful of them is to be thus accused by thee; stop, oh! stop these unkind reproaches. Go, I have never ceased to love you; but do not look upon me, it freezes and oppresses my heart: even my life could not long sustain thy anger. Ah! enquire of them? added she, melting into tears, and pointing to Mrs. St. Clare and Mr. Prior. Unjust, though unworthily dear, hear from them, whether I have deceived you?

Malvina, irresistible Malvina, exclaimed Sir Edmond, with quickness, you have conquered; for whatever appearances may indicate, I will not demand any other explanation, and I will believe you alone. I thought that you had been brought here without your knowledge, that your meeting with Mr. Prior was entirely the effect of chance; but the value I affix to such a confidence which you only could have obtained from me, is, that you will from this moment consent to be mine, and from this place follow me to the altar.

Oh! my God, what is it that you ask of me? exclaimed Malvina, retreating from him, and renewing her grief. Ah! Malvina, you fly me; you hesitate? replied he, with a gloomy rage. In the name of Heaven, hear me, Edmond? said Malvina, let me acquaint you with the powerful motives which restrain me, and you will then find that the menaces of Lord Sheridan have compelled me to retract my promise.

I will not hear any thing, interrupted Sir Edmond; I shall depend on your affection; that I shall receive your hand from it alone. If you love me, not any consideration or any power on earth ought to have the precedence of me, Ah!

do not resist my entreaties, adored Malvina; following and throwing himself at her feet.[25] I feel that the idea of losing thee will deprive me of reason; I therefore cannot command my actions, neither can I tell to what their excess may reduce me; when you are the object of them, and the reward I wish to gain.[26]

Pardon me, Malvina, I fear the violence of my behaviour shocks you; but remember, that love – love for you alone deranges me; and it is from that which I hope to obtain my pardon. Oh! thou best loved of my heart, let it be to love alone that I am to be indebted for thy hand. Come then, my Malvina, do not delay any longer; give me your hand, and consent to receive.[27] On saying this, he folded her in his arms, and drew her without her having the power to consent or defend herself.

Mr. Prior considered this proceeding evinced too much force, and happy to find a reason to prevent it, placed himself before Sir Edmond, to prevent his passing. What authority, said he, have you to carry away that lady? And by what right dare you prevent me? replied Sir Edmond, trembling with rage. That right which the Deity has given to every one to relieve each other, and protect weakness, returned Mr. Prior. This lady is not yours,[xliv] she refuses to follow you; did she not tell you as much? Is this true? exclaimed Sir Edmond, Is this really true? Malvina, that you refuse to follow me; Do you not belong to me? Are we not contracted to each other? Have you not acknowledged before Heaven and man, that you are my wife; the perpetual companion of my future life?

No, no, I cannot, replied Malvina, faintly. You cannot, Malvina, you cannot,[28] and yet, only yesterday, you consented: Ah! have pity on thyself, and do not drive me to desperation; for the prospect of futurity is too horrible. Stop, interrupted she, taking Lord Sheridan's letter from her bosom; read that fatal paper, and then judge if I am permitted to be yours.[xlv] I will not look at it, said Sir Edmond, tearing the paper to atoms, and pushing Malvinas so rudely from him, that Mrs. St. Clare had scarcely time to save her from falling.

I will not see, hear, or believe any thing; you are a mixture of perfidy and deceit. I sent you that letter yesterday, at the same time with mine, and it did not prevent you from sending me your promise. But you have seen that man to day, and that is the reason why you refuse to fulfill it. That is the whole; why should I seek to know any farther? Yet, you had such an ascendency over me, that I consented to forget every thing; but you have now refused to follow me. Well, Malvina, you shall witness the course of my revenge, which will be as dreadful as my torments are; you will repent some day, when it is perhaps too late, and when there has been bloodshed.

And now, continued he, dragging Mr. Prior violently by the arm, come and receive the just reward of thy deceit, or take from me a life which this perjured woman has rendered hateful. On seeing them both go out, Malvina flew after them;[29] but though despair had given her additional strength, she had not sufficient to prevent two men, who were overpowered by rage and jealousy.

Pale and terrified, she followed and perhaps would have overtaken them, if they had not closed the door in the rock after them. She tried every method to open it, but in vain; a secret spring which she did not understand, rendered all her endeavours abortive. She called after them as loud as possible, and then for some person to open the door.

Mrs. St. Clare was the first who came to her; and Frances, who had been, during these transactions, playing in the garden with little Edward, hearing Malvina's voice, came running to her,[30] and wanted to go with her.

In the name of Heaven, said Malvina, take away the child, giving her into the arms of Mrs. St. Clare; and prevent her from following or detaining me.[31] Malvina had scarcely concluded these words, when they heard the report of pistols[32] at a little distance. She stood petrified with horror, and exclaiming, it is all over, fell senseless on the floor.

CHAP. IV.

Of a more tender nature.

Mrs. St. Clare, alarmed and agitated by her fears, confided Malvina to the care of Mary, and ran to the farm in order to send some relief to the place where they heard the report of the pistols. She had not advanced above a hundred paces, when she observed, at a little distance, some men, who were carrying a person between them; and seeing Mr. Prior coming towards her, shuddering, she exclaimed, He is killed then? and by you, a clergyman! your hands are stained in human blood!

He is but very slightly wounded, replied Mr. Prior; but that is no relief to me, for I shall ever consider myself as a homicide.[33] Destruction appears to surround me on every side; and I feel as if all nature was risen against me to publish my iniquity. Where are they conveying Sir Edmond? enquired Mrs. St. Clare. To his carriage, replied Mr. Prior, which is a quarter of a mile from hence; he desired to be taken there immediately. – Are you not fearful that the motion of the carriage may be detrimental? No, replied Mr. Prior, the ball only grazed his shoulder; and the bleeding was stopped instantly. Who are those that are with him now? His servants,[34] who were waiting at the farm, one of whom understanding a little of surgery, asserted that the wound would be cured in two days. No, said Mrs. St. Clare, we must not suffer him to go; I will go and order every thing for his reception at the farm, where he may be recovered without being moved.

It will be useless, replied Mr. Prior, for we have already used every effort for that purpose, which has been ineffectual, and only served to irritate him; and the manner in which he insisted upon going was so decisive, that his people dared not disobey. But where is he going? – To Edinburgh. – So far! Never shall I be far enough from Malvina, said he; and yet it is to Mrs. Burton that he desires to be conveyed, that he may increase the hatred she bears Malvina;[35] and he will also be surrounded by her enemies. Oh! what a fatal present did Heaven bestow on man, when it gave them such violent passions, said Mrs. St. Clare. But let this fury pursue his destiny, while I endeavour to recover his two innocent victims. As to you, Mr. Prior, you must not appear before Malvina after this affair, she will only behold you with horror.

Ah! exclaimed Mr. Prior, shuddering, I know it. Malvina hates me! I have[36] – O God! who hast made my days miserable, and before whom I am nothing. Oh! do not plunge me into still greater misery than that of being hated by Malvina!

Mr. Prior, replied Mrs. St. Clare, gravely, perhaps you have deserved the loss of that friendship which seems so dear to you. Search the secret recesses of your heart, and it will inform you whether a bitter stream can run from a pure source; and if it had not been for the friendship of Malvina, do you not think you would have avoided this duel?[37] Stop, Mrs. St. Clare, interrupted Mr. Prior – do you not know that the time of affliction is that of mercy also? Do not then, at this moment, lay open the iniquities of my heart; let me be at pea ce a little while, that I may regain my fortitude, before I enter this retreat, to which I can never again return.[38]

No, Mr. Prior, replied Mrs. St. Clare, it is not permitted us to die while we can be of use to one unfortunate being. Go into Louisa, as the woman[39] who attends her, deceived her, relative to the noise which she heard, be kind enough not to undeceive her; that she may never know Sir Edmond has been here. – Do not leave her while your pious exhortations can recall her to life, or give her resignation.

She immediately went to Malvina, whom she found just as she had left her, pale and inanimate. Frances was weeping on her knees by her side, and saying, Oh! my dear Mama is so cold – just like my other mama: – Is she then going to her also? Ah! pray do not let her go without me. Oh! let her take Frances with her, she will be so glad to see me; and I will never, never leave my two mamas.[40]

Mrs. St. Clare could not restrain her tears at the sight of this little innocent, whose existence had occasioned Malvina so many sorrows; but wishing to prevent her young and artless mind from dwelling too long on the melancholy sight of her mother, she desired Mary to take her in the garden to play with Edward. But Frances, bursting into tears, hid herself in the bed curtains, crying no, no; I do not wish to be taken away, I had rather stay here; and if I must go, we will all go together.[41] I can remember when they carried me from my other mama, and I have never seen her since. Oh, pray let me stay here, I beg of you – I will keep in a corner – and I will not make the least noise, nor cry any more. The little creature immediately began to wipe her eyes, scarcely daring to breathe, lest they should send her away.

Mrs. St. Clare let her remain in the room, and endeavoured, by every method, to recover Malvina; which, after some time, she accomplished. The instant she recovered her senses, she started from her seat; – she looked wildly round the room, exclaiming, where is he? – where is he? – Do not alarm yourself, my dear Malvina, he is not in the least danger, you may believe me, for I would not deceive you. Why then does he not appear? replied she, with quickness. He is not here, he chooses to return to Edinburgh. Ah! that is certainly to avoid me! My dear Malvina, he does avoid you, because he supposes you guilty; but you can easily undeceive him. Let his passion have time to cool; and endeavour to compose yourself. Me! – Me! – What! shall I stay to repose myself, when he thinks me guilty? No, madam, I wish to depart instantly – I will follow him.

But, my dear, said Mrs. St. Clare, it is now two hours since he set out for Edinburgh;[42] and he is gone to Mrs. Burton's. Why do you think so? asked Malvina – he does not live with her. Because he desired to be conveyed – To be conveyed; Ah! he is then wounded; very slightly. Edmond is wounded – and it is at Mrs. Burton's he is going to die. He will not die, my dear Malvina; it is only a slight flesh wound. No matter, I wish to go, whatever may be his situation, or wherever he is, nothing shall prevent my seeing him.

Well, my dear, you shall go, replied Mrs. St. Clare, who perceived it was in vain to persuade her from her determination; but the evening is now closing in, and these mountainous roads are very dangerous, and quite impassable in the dark; therefore, if the carriage should meet with any accident, that will impede your journey. Wait then till to-morrow, my horses shall be ready as early as you please in the morning, to take you to Kinross; when there, you will be supplied with others to convey you to Edinburgh. I would attend you, if the dear unfortunate who is here did not claim all my attention; but I will take care of your little girl, which would be rather inconvenient on your journey.

On hearing this, Frances came from behind the curtain, where she had concealed herself; and kissing the hand of Malvina; mama, said she, pray do not go without me, they wanted me to leave you just now, when you was almost as dead as my other mama, and now you see that has prevented your dying, because I stayed. Oh! mama, pray always keep me with you.

Malvina, affected by her voice and manner, looked at the child; and marking the same sweet expression in her eyes, which had once animated those of her mother, her tears fell in profusion at the remembrance of their friendship.

Clara! exclaimed Malvina, dear Clara – Oh, what moment can ever be more fatal than that which separated us? Alas! when I lost thee, I fancied I should never have any thing more to weep for than thy death; little did I imagine that this misfortune alone would be the source of all my distresses. Ah! my beloved friend, Heaven, which had formed us to live together, poured its wrath upon me when I dared to be happy without thee. But since it prohibits me from a happiness which you cannot now partake with me, assist, and implore for me, that Heaven will call me to you; and when we are permitted once more to be united, I shall then no longer count the hours and days; and when the present will not be imbittered with the ever painful idea of change.

Mrs. St. Clare silently rejoiced on observing Malvina weep; she was therefore fearful of interrupting her. She had experienced too many sorrows herself, to be unacquainted that each have their calm moments; and that these are generally preceded by tears. She was not deceived; for those which Malvina now shed so profusely, relieved her. Then again she became the tender, the gentle Malvina; and folding her arms round Mrs. St. Clare, I fear, she said, I have hurt you much? No, replied her friend, it is I who ought to be fearful of that; and I have to-day been convinced there are some particular incidents which we vainly endeavour to strive against, and sentiments which we cannot overcome.

Oh! my dear Malvina, pardon me for having brought you here – I flattered myself with the deceitful hope of recovering you from this fatal prepossession.

And you are convinced, interrupted Malvina, that it had taken too deep a possession of my heart, and can only be eradicated with my life. Let us for the future, continued Malvina, resign the care of our sorrows to Heaven, without creating more, by endeavouring to avoid those which the heart feels sufficiently oppressive.

The remainder of the evening was passed with tranquillity. Malvina never required the least explanation concerning Louisa, and Mrs. St. Clare did not intrude the subject, as her mind had already been sufficiently shocked; and Malvina had undergone, in the course of that day, so many painful incidents, that her kind friend avoided every thing which might tend to increase her sorrow.

CHAP. V.

The road to Edinburgh.

Day had but just partially enlightened the surrounding scenery, when Malvina enquired if her friend's carriage was ready to take her to Kinross. Mrs. St. Clare promised that in case she should prolong her stay in Edinburgh, she would join her with Frances, as soon as her sister's health would permit her to leave her. At this epithet Malvina looked at her steadily, and pressing her hand; do not imagine, said she, that I shall forget you have a sister; or the right she has over the man I am now going to? I am only going to him that I may vindicate my conduct: but the instant he has acknowledged my innocence, I shall leave him for ever.

You think so just now, replied Mrs. St. Clare; but when you behold him intreating at your feet, all these resolutions will vanish. As to any thing on my account, my dear Malvina, if I wished so earnestly, that you might be fortunate enough to renounce him, it was entirely on account of your peace and happiness; that alone was the sole motive; not for any thing which can regard my sister. My unhappy Louisa is dead to the world; the secret of her being yet in existence, is only known to Edmond and myself. Even those who attend her, are not acquainted with who she is.

Why did she thus bury herself, did Edmond refuse her his hand? Edmond, replied Mrs. St. Clare, could not, my sister is married, her husband is still alive;

if he was informed she was living, he would usurp all his authority over her, and this would be to immure her in an ignominious wretchedness, and her only consolation, her child, her Edmond,[43] would be taken from her. And why could not your father vindicate his unfortunate daughter?

My father is very good, but severe and inflexible where his honor is concerned. He knew that Louisa was guilty, he blessed the hour of her death: but if he had known that she had deceived him, he would not have saved her from the vengeance of her husband. And can your father yet be ignorant of the existence of his daughter? But as she entirely depends on you, how can you support this unfortunate victim? Ah! undoubtedly Sir Edmond in some measure compensates by his benevolence for. –

Do you imagine, said Mrs. St. Clare, that my sister would condescend to accept of any thing from her seducer? No, no, it is I alone who have the inexpressible felicity of providing for all her wants. I observe your astonishment; as my situation with my father seems to put it entirely out of my power; but have you quite forgot those works which you reproached me for? – This is my excuse.

On hearing this, Malvina melted into tears, and pressed Mrs. St. Clare in her arms; who thus continued, justice forces me to say, that Edmond is not what he was formerly; his pride appears to be lessened, and he does not blush to submit to a woman; he loves at last! Though I may detest the frenzy of his passion, I believe it is sincere. Malvina, if you do not fear the being unhappy with him? Ah! what should render me unhappy? replied she, provided he continued to love me! Poor creature! exclaimed Mrs. St. Clare, looking at her with the most tender solicitude. What an unbounded passion must that be, which could dictate such a reply!

But this child, Mrs. St. Clare, this child of Sir Edmond's, is its existence unknown also? He now must submit to the same destiny as his mother: when my unhappy sister gave him birth, her husband was ignorant that he was not the father of him, and both would have been the victims of his rage, if by a particular artifice, too long at present to relate, I had not been fortunate enough to prevent it. But I wish to leave Edmond the means of expiating his fault, by confessing it at your feet.

As this tragical recital, may perhaps awaken his remorse; cause him to blush at his conduct, give him a detestation of vice, and render him, if possible, worthy of your love. I sincerely wish it, Malvina, for his tenderness for you, has in a great measure eradicated the hatred which I felt towards him. Malvina deeply penetrated by this kindness, once more pressed Mrs. St. Clare in her arms, then tearing herself from her, kissed, and bidding her adieu, stepped into the carriage, and departed for Kinross.

On arriving there, she took a post-chaise,[44] and the next evening arrived at Falkirk, at the same inn where the preceding month she had been met by Sir Edmond.[45] On entering it, she trembled so much, that she could scarcely get up stairs, which being observed[46] by the girl of the Inn, she offered her arm to assist her. The lady seems but poorly, said she, what a pity that the handsomest and richest persons should always be either melancholy or ill!

Have you many here then? said Malvina, carelessly. Pardon me, madam, I cannot say exactly, for as I have only been here fifteen days, you may suppose I have not had time to see many; but I was thinking of a young gentleman who was here yesterday, just as handsome as yourself, madam, but so melancholy, and so dull, that he sighed enough to break ones heart. Was he wounded? interrupted Malvina, with quickness. Oh! my God, yes; but dear me, madam, how could you know it?

No matter, only inform me how he is? Why, madam, the surgeon who has been to see him, says, that he will not die. What! that he will not die? replied Malvina, alarmed. Yes, madam, so he thinks if the fever does not increase, for then. – What then? said Malvina, trembling. Oh! madam, he is a very skilful man, is Doctor Sandwich; and yet he said with all his skill, he could not tell how to save him if the delirium continued. What! is he delirious? Yes, madam, and he says such strange things, that nobody can understand what they mean. – He talks so loud to himself, and seems so angry with some woman, who, he says, wished to kill him; he calls her ungrateful and perfidious, and a great many other vile names; then afterwards he says he loves her, begs her to come to him, and says, he should be contented if he only saw her once more.

I will go directly, said Malvina! Ah! good gracious, at this hour? replied Peggy, astonished; I thought that you would have slept here, madam? No, I wish to go directly to Edinburgh. But, madam, you will arrive there in the middle of the night, and all the inns will be shut. No matter, I shall be nearer to him. You know the young gentleman then, madam? That is of no consequence to you Peggy, your business is to order me a chaise immediately. But madam, had you not better rest one moment, here is a room quite ready, which that gentleman last night occupied? Let me see it, said Malvina; in hopes of finding some traces of Edmond: she perceived that it was the very same room[s] were a month before they had passed some of the happiest moments of their lives.[t]

The impression this recollection occasioned, very nearly overpowered her; and leaning her hand against the sofa,[47] she desired Peggy to fetch her a glass of water; and putting a few drops[48] into it, she recovered; and absolutely determined to be in Edinburgh that night, and sent Peggy to order the chaise immediately.[49u] She carefully searched every part of the room, in hopes of finding some paper which might have been left by Sir Edmond; she then examined the windows,[50] to see if she could find a line or word expressive of his grief;[51] but not finding any, she was convinced that he was too ill to write. Her anxiety increased every moment, and her sickly imagination tortured her with the most alarming fears;[52] though her reason condemned this, her heart construed them as a presentiment of misfortune.

Affection is acknowledged to be liable to superstitious fears, and those who have experienced real misfortunes, are apt to imagine all they fear may be realised. The terrors of Malvina seemed to increase with the shades of night; the murmuring of the wind, the shrieks of the owl, the dull reverberation of a bell, the very echo, and the distant sound of voices, all appeared to her diseased mind, omens of death. Incapable of supporting these horrors any longer, she rushed out of the room,[53] and ran down stairs to see if the chaise was ready. But all her endeavours were ineffectual; the master of the inn was drinking, his wife scolding, and the servants running backward and forward, quarrelling with each other. Malvina saw the impossibility of making herself heard amidst such a noisy scene; she was therefore obliged to defer her journey 'till the next day, and consequently she would not reach Edinburgh before eleven the next morning.

CHAP. VI.

Illness.

Malvina desired to be set down at Mrs. Moody's, whose house was not very distant from Mrs. Burton's. This good woman, who had never forgot the essential service which she had received from Malvina, was both surprised and rejoiced to see her benefactress. Malvina checked her protestations, held her finger on her lips as a token of silence – and going up stairs with her to look at an apartment,[54] desired that her residence in Edinburgh might be kept a profound secret.

Ah, certainly, madam, said Mrs. Moody, you shall be obeyed. But may I not at least know the cause which has brought you to me? Well, you shall be informed, I shall even require your assistance, if you will oblige me so far. – You may depend upon me, madam, replied the good woman, I shall esteem myself happy, if I can be of the least use to you. Sit down by me, my dear Moody, said Malvina; without doubt you have heard of my leaving my cousin? Yes, madam, I heard it from the servants, particularly from Ann, who is a relation of my poor husband; and as your kindness made you as much beloved as Mrs. Burton's pride made her disliked, all the accounts I have heard were in your favour – and Ann wept at your departure.[55] But, said Malvina, as you are no stranger to what has passed, I suppose they did not forget to inform you that Sir Edmond is dear to—.[56]

Mrs. Moody nodded assent, and Malvina continued – I do not pretend to disguise it, Moody; for it is but too true that he is very dear to me. Both at our own disposal, we were on the point of being united, when a dreadful circumstance occurred, which entirely prevented it. Since he has been wounded[57] – Well, madam, said Mrs. Moody, observing Malvina's tears, what is to be done? only tell me, I am ready to undertake any thing.

I wish to know first, Moody, if he is at present with Mrs. Burton? He arrived there yesterday morning, madam; and I heard that Mrs. Burton was very much surprised to see him return in such a situation; and that after abusing you very much, she was taken very ill; and the physician, which was sent for to her nephew, attended her great part of the morning.

But did you hear what was said of Sir Edmond's situation? – Do they say his wound will prove dangerous? No, madam; it would not have been the least so, if his fever had not been occasioned by the violent perturbation of his mind. Ah! gracious Heaven, it is then I who am sending him to his grave. My dear Moody, endeavour to be informed how he is at present,[58] as I wish to know what he feels; and particularly if he enquires for me. As I would dare any thing, I will go to Mrs. Burton, and intreat her to let me see him, for the last time.

Oh! my dear madam, replied Mrs. Moody, do not thus alarm yourself, I will go immediately to your cousin's, and enquire all the particulars which you wish from Ann; and in less than an hour you shall be acquainted with all that has been said and done in the house since yesterday. Ah! said Malvina, only let me know the particulars relative to Sir Edmond; the rest are of no consequence to me? Mrs. Moody replied that she might depend on her zeal and delicacy in the management of this affair.[59]

The situation of Malvina may easily be imagined during the absence of Mrs. Moody;[60] and the pain of suspence, which occasioned her to fancy she staid longer than the time proposed, increased her fears. She was continually walking to and from the window, counting the minutes, fancying time had made a pause in his flight. At last, Mrs. Moody returned, and went very leisurely up stairs, where Malvina had come to meet her. – Well, Mrs. Moody, how is he? said she with quickness. I am going to tell you, madam; but I must go in with you – we may be overheard here.

Oh! Mrs. Moody, only speak, one word is sufficient – only say how he is? Good God, madam, why, you are all of a tremble, you will make yourself ill. – Ah! Moody, exclaimed Malvina, impatiently, never mind me, only tell me, I beg of you, how Sir Edmond is now? Why, madam, you must know that I am told that the physician, this morning, after feeling his pulse, examined his eyes, looked at his wounds,[v] shook his head, but did not speak. Said nothing, and shook his head, Moody; did not any body ask him a question? As to that, madam, I cannot say; Ann did not follow the doctor out of the room.

But what have you heard then? I am going to tell you; at first, madam, Ann seldom left Sir Edmond's chamber; for though he had a nurse, it was her who chiefly attended him. She is very sorry for him indeed; and says he is such a good young gentleman; and there is only one person who is better, and that is Madame de Sorcy. Poor Ann would be quite satisfied if you was but united.[61] Ah, dear Mrs. Moody, if you knew what I felt, said Malvina, you would not mention any one but Sir Edmond.

Pardon me, madam; this morning his fever increased so much that he was delirious, at least Ann supposed so, as she could not believe that you had wished

Mr. Prior to kill Sir Edmond, which he accused you of; and then again, he calls you Malvina, his dear Malvina! He then intreats that you will not refuse his prayers, and says, that the altar is ready; and then he immediately begins to tear the bandages from his wound, saying, his death alone would please you. However, yesterday evening he had a calm interval, when Mrs. Burton took the opportunity of seeing him, and Ann overheard all their conversation; for she concealed herself behind the folding screen. Mrs. Burton seated herself by his bedside, and after slightly enquiring the state of his health, she said to him, I hope we shall at last agree on one point, now you are convinced of the spirit of intrigue and coquetry which Madame de Sorcy has evinced; that you will entirely obliterate her from your remembrance, and only recollect those engagements which I have made for you with Lord Stafford, as this is the only condition upon which I will forgive you.

Then, madam, I shall forfeit your pardon, said Sir Edmond, with a voice of anger; for I will never give my hand to any other woman. What! replied Mrs. Burton, with an impatience which she could not conceal; what! do you renounce every woman, because you have been deceived by the artifices of – Madam, interrupted Sir Edmond, I am but too sensible Madame de Sorcy has deceived me, for that reason I ought to detest her; and it was from a motive of revenge to her, that in the first moment of my anger I desired to be brought here, hoping that such a step would render her as miserable as myself.[62] If I had thought my blood would have cost her one tear, I would have shed it all. But, added he, after a pause of a few moments, however I may detest her crimes, I will never permit any lips but mine to reproach her, even with a shadow of blame. I only have that right – she has injured only me! every one else ought to revere her; and while the breath of life animates me, no one shall dare to treat her with less respect than she merits.

Oh! dear Edmond, exclaimed Malvina, melting into tears, when you suppose me guilty of the blackest deceit, can you vindicate me with such generous energy? and would readily expose your life for my sake, at the time you believed that I wished your death. How shall I ever repay the generosity of such a noble heart, and make those blush who can doubt thy virtues? But proceed, Moody – what said Mrs. Burton?

She appeared very much enraged, madam, but endeavoured to suppress it; and told her nephew that she hoped his reason would return with his health; and she should wait for that moment, to come to a conclusion with him relative to the affair in question. She then took leave of him, and very coolly desired him to avoid all those ideas which might affect him too much, and retard his recovery.

Ann, observing she departed with a threatening aspect, followed her on tiptoe, and perceived Mrs. Fenwick running to meet her. Well, madam, said she, what says Sir Edmond? A greater fool than ever, Kitty. What! said Mrs. Fenwick, will he not relinquish, and avoid her? Perhaps not, replied Mrs. Burton; but I am certain of separating them, and then it will be of no consequence whether they love each other or not.

But in what manner will you draw him back to Lady Mary Summerhill, if Madame de Sorcy continues to be so very dear to him?[63] They were soon out of hearing – Ann therefore could not hear the conclusion of this conversation. I could not help enquiring, madam, why Mrs. Fenwick was so inveterate against you. Ah! dear Mrs. Moody, replied Ann, every one here is for ever endeavouring to deceive each other; and those who possess most art, are those who gain most belief.[64]

Mrs. Fenwick once hoped that Sir Edmond would have married her; and, perhaps, he might, if he had not liked Madame de Sorcy better; and every body must be of his opinion. But she is so enraged at having lost him, it is from that cause she aggravates Mrs. Burton against them, and is perpetually talking of Lady Mary Summerhill, whom she detests in her heart.

This is quite satisfactory, dear Moody, I do not desire to hear any more of her; and from what you have said of Mrs. Fenwick, I now have not a doubt but I have been the object of her revenge ever since she was married.[65]

Well, madam, I have informed you of all I have heard; and I can assure you, Ann has spoken the truth; for she told me she heard many things from Jenny, to whom Mrs. Fenwick communicates all her thoughts. There is not any thing, replied Malvina, that passes in that house, except what relates to Sir Edmond, that is of any importance to me. With your leave, Mrs. Moody, I wish to be alone; I shall not go out, and hope you will not mention me to any person; let me hear, as frequently as possible, how Sir Edmond is.

The remainder of the day was passed with tranquillity,[66] and she heard nothing more concerning Sir Edmond. At night she was disturbed by disagreeable dreams; if sleep does not suspend pleasure, there are distresses which it cannot ever relieve. They are a part of ourselves, which wear and corrode to life's latest hour.

When we are covered by the mantle of sleep, our ideas are ignorant from whence the evil proceeds; but the heart, while it beats, will ever feel them. – It can only cease to suffer, when we cease to exist.

CHAP. VII.

New alarms.

Malvina, more fatigued than relieved by a tiresome night, had but just arose, when Mrs. Moody entered with her breakfast. Well, madam, said she, with an air of satisfaction, I was very certain that what I told you was all true.[67] Is he then supposed to be out of danger? exclaimed Malvina – and will Edmond, my dear Edmond, live? As to that, madam, I have nothing very pleasing in that respect to tell you, as it appears the fever has taken rather an alarming turn; the doctor thinks it will prove malignant, which occasions Mrs. Burton great uneasiness, as she is fearful that it may be contagious.

A malignant fever! repeated Malvina, with terror – and who is with him? – who has the care of him? He has a very good nurse, madam, I know her very well. You know her? Moody, replied Malvina, considering for a moment. Could I see and speak with her, do you think? Why, I do not know, madam; I fear you could not, as Sir Edmond continues so ill, I should suppose she cannot leave him.[68]

Moody, said Malvina, if they should wish to have another, I will procure one. You, madam, replied Moody, with surprise. Yes; only let me know if Mrs. Burton goes often into the room to see her nephew. She! madam, Oh! dear no; since she has been informed that it was malignant, she has declared that she is fearful of going near him. So much the better, replied Malvina; and you say that Ann is the only person in the house who goes into his room?

Yes, madam, but it is a question whether she is permitted to attend now; as Mrs. Burton is so much alarmed at its being infectious. I am glad of that, said Malvina: well, dear Moody, return there immediately, and tell the nurse that you know a person whose care may be depended on; who will relieve her by sitting up every night; and will with pleasure exempt her from so dangerous an office. Yes, madam, I will; but then I do not know this person. Oh, never trouble yourself concerning that, she will be ready whenever she is wanted. Thus, Moody, for your own interest, as well as my repose, be punctual in executing my directions. Mrs. Moody readily promised. Malvina hastily paced her room; she did not weep, though she breathed with difficulty.

Mrs. Moody, who considered tears as the only sign of grief, and who had never known it under the form of despair, had not an idea that Malvina was at that instant agitated and distressed.[69] She therefore began with the first idea which had dwelt on her mind in the morning; and smiling said, another time, madam, you will believe me; for this morning as I appeared rather scrupulous[70] of believing what Ann said, concerning Mrs. Fenwick; to convince me, she took me into Jenny's room, which joined her mistress's, and from the closet[71] we could hear all what they said.

Mrs. Fenwick was still in bed; she enquired of Jenny how Sir Edmond was. He is worse, madam, replied she; the doctor is in despair. At these words, Malvina shuddered; and going close to Mrs. Moody's chair, she supported herself on the back of it. Flattered by this apparent attention from Malvina, she continued. Well Jenny, said Mrs. Fenwick, notwithstanding the injuries I have received from Sir Edmond, what you have told me really afflicts me. He gained my first affection, and I never shall love any other so well as him.

Yet, madam, replied Jenny, you appeared quite satisfied the other day, when Mr. Fenwick assured you that he was certain Mrs. Burton would disinherit him. Certainly, Jenny, I wish to possess all the fortune which she has destined for him; but that does not prevent my regreting the moments that I passed with him at Burton-hall; nor from employing all the means in my power to regain him to myself. Why then, madam, are you the first in constantly boasting of the advantages which an alliance with Lady Mary Summerhill will afford? What an idiot; do you not see that it is in order to deceive Mrs. Burton, by pretending to admire her idol, I avoid all suspicions, which might otherwise be formed concerning my former connection with Sir Edmond; I aggravate her aversion for Madame de Sorcy; and I have not the least fear of Lady Mary becoming my rival. With her stiff airs, her prim and affected manners, and inanimate beauty, she can never eclipse me.

Certainly, madam, you do grow handsomer every day, replied Jenny, in a softer voice; and if Sir Edmond was but in a situation to pay attention to you, he might think if Miss Melmor's charms had power to attract him, those of Mrs. Fenwick ought to fix him. I do not yet despair, Jenny, if he gets the better of this illness; Oh, what pleasure shall I enjoy, if I have the power of triumphing over that hateful Madame de Sorcy.

You hate her then? said Jenny, I am astonished that any one can like to do that. How, Jenny, should I not, when Sir Edmond loves her? Was she not the cause of his neglecting me? Yes, yes, I do hate her; for the men admire her, and all the world speaks well of her. But madam, replied Jenny, that is because she is so good, so charitable; she appears to receive so much pleasure in serving others, and is so willing to oblige every body. I am sure she has done so much good without ever stirring out of her room; she succours and assists the unhappy. She no sooner arrived in Edinburgh, than she found means to relieve that poor Mrs. Moody.

Jenny, said Mrs. Fenwick, dryly, make an end of your praises, and let these be the last I ever hear, if you wish to remain with me. Jenny, who was confused at the folly she had been guilty of, endeavoured to repair it, by praising her mistress in the most extravagant manner, which had the desired effect; and she resumed her good humour again.

Do you think they will conclude to have one? interrupted Malvina, who had for some time been buried in thought, and had not heard what Mrs. Moody had been saying. Who do you mean, madam? said she. The nurse we were speaking about just now. Oh! dear madam, I had quite forgot it; I beg your pardon; I was so taken up with recounting what Mrs. Fenwick said.[72] I have heard quite sufficient of Mrs. Fenwick, said Malvina, seating herself, and supporting her head with her hands;[73] I did not know what you were talking of; I do not know where I am. – Every thing vanishes but the pain which at first touched my heart; and which has gained such an ascendency over me. I am no longer myself: it exhausts my strength: Oh! Heaven, that I should lose it at the moment when I most wish to retain it, and if possible, gain an increase.

But dear madam, you ought to take something to strengthen and support you, said Mrs. Moody, with tender anxiety. Yes, replied Malvina, without changing her posture, make haste and bring me something that will do so. Mrs. Moody immediately went and returned with some jelly,[74] which Malvina endeavoured to take, but could not; she tasted and set it down; arose and went to the window, opened it and looked towards Mrs. Burton's; that is where he is, she exclaimed, where he is at this moment suffering; and where I have vowed never to go again. – Yet, where I hope to be to-morrow.

You, madam! asked Mrs. Moody. What do you intend? Why did you listen to me?[75] replied Malvina, I do not yet wish you to know my determination. Do not acquaint any one with what you have heard me say. Go, and leave me alone, I really want repose. Let me have materials for writing. But, madam, you are so weak, will it not add to your fatigue? Moody, replied Malvina, without attending to what she had said, bring me one of your caps and a gown, which you wear in common.

What, madam? replied she, all astonishment – Yes, I wish to try them on presently, said Malvina. But you are certainly in jest, madam? At these words, Malvina looked steadily at her, and smiling with anguish, took her hand, and pressing it with force, she said, Moody, there are situations in which it is easier to die than to jest.[76] Mrs. Moody, alarmed at the serious air of Malvina, obeyed her in silence, and returned instantly with the clothes, paper, and inkstand. Malvina desired her to lay them down and retire.

She made several attempts in the course of the day to write, but all in vain; she could not trace a line. Towards evening, she dressed herself in Mrs. Moody's clothes and large cap, which she thought would sufficiently disguise her; and surveying herself in the glass,[77] certainly, she said, thus arrayed, Edmond will never know his Malvina; and I may see and be serviceable to him. I shall avoid his looks, and suppress my grief; he will not know the hand which serves him.[78] – But how ridiculous this thought, in the situation he is in, I need not fear being known; his eyes may rest on Malvina, without knowing who she is.

While she was speaking, Mrs. Moody tapped at her door; Malvina desired her to come in; and on observing her thus metamorphosed, she uttered an exclamation of surprise. I came – I came, said she, but really, madam, looking at her with amaze, I scarcely know you. What did you want with me? enquired Malvina. I only came to inform you, madam, that as I was standing at the door, I saw Ann at a little distance, walking very quick; I called to her, to know where she was going in such haste; but, madam, you really are so completely disguised – You asked her where she was going? said Malvina, impatiently.[w] Yes, madam, and she informed me she was in search of a nurse for the night; as the doctor had declared the fever to be of the most malignant kind; and as this is the third day, consequently one of the most dangerous; and that it was necessary that some person should set up all the night with him that he may have his medicine regularly, and relieve the other nurse, who is very much fatigued.

Well, Moody, you see I am ready to take her place, said Malvina, collecting all her strength to conceal her despair. Ah! Madam, do you think I will suffer you to expose yourself thus? said Mrs. Moody; I cannot hide it from you that Sir Edmond's illness is mortal, and even contagious. Every body flies from him; the nurse is fearful of being long with him; and they are in doubt whether they can get another.

Do not say a word or lose a moment, replied Malvina, in a tone that commanded obedience; assure Ann, that in the course of an hour you will bring her a nurse; and prepare yourself to introduce me as such this evening, as a woman you can recommend. Mrs. Moody wished to excuse herself; but Malvina would not give her time; and not being able to command the grief which oppressed her, she forced her out of the room: Oh! hasten, pray hasten, and recollect that a moment's delay may render you answerable for both his death and mine. Why do you mention danger? what is contagion to one who is in despair? Go, only prepare the way, that I may receive his last sigh. Mrs. Moody, shocked at the melancholy tone in which she spoke, could not resist her commands; and they were so punctually executed, that the clock had not struck nine, when they arrived at Mrs. Burton's door.

CHAP. VIII.

Nocturnal tête-à-tête.

The servant who attended the door, immediately conducted them to Sir Edmond's apartment; and as they went up stairs, Malvina supported herself by holding Mrs. Moody's arm. On entering the room, where the light but faintly gleamed, and perceiving the only person she loved in the world, languishing on the bed of sickness, she trembled so much, that without Mrs. Moody's assistance, she would have fallen. The nurse, who perceived her distress, came up to her, and addressing Mrs. Moody; This woman appears very weak, said she; I much doubt if she can support the fatigue of the night. The gentleman is very low, and perhaps he may not live longer than to-morrow.[79]

As to what you have to do, continued she, looking at Malvina; you have only to be very particular in giving him his medicine every quarter of an hour; and when he appears unable to take it himself, you must give him the draught, which is here, with a spoon. Come and hold it for me, and I will shew you how you must give it. Malvina approached with a gloomy tranquillity, she felt a cold chill, her blood seemed frozen, and she thought her soul would be ready to attend Edmond's. If the symptoms should become more alarming, continued the nurse, putting on her spectacles to arrange[80] the phials[81] which stood on the chimney piece, and you should find yourself at a loss for any thing; you have only to call me as loud as possible, for I sleep pretty sound, when I do sleep, for I have not had any these three nights: I shall be in the closet close by.

Malvina, who could not speak, bowed her head, and attempted to take the spoon;[82] but the nurse preventing her, said, Are you then dumb? Ah! Lord, how you tremble; one may soon know you have never seen a dying person. The last sentence – the chamber, the glimmering sickly light; all reminded Malvina of the last moments of her beloved friend, and supporting herself by the bed-post, she said, no one has perhaps been more used to such scenes than myself.

Faith, one would not believe it, said the nurse; why then are you so serious? that is not very common in our situations; for if we were to afflict ourselves about all those whom we see die, we should soon come to an end ourselves. But come, continued she, approaching the bed; open the curtain, hold up the patients head while I give him some drink. Malvina obeyed, it was only then that she perceived Sir Edmond, with his eyes shut, without motion, pale and disfigured; his respiration short and oppressed, was all that shewed any remains of life. She saw, and felt her courage increase with the danger of her lover; putting her arm under his head, she laid it on her bosom, and taking the spoon in the other hand, she gave the sick man all its contents.

That is well, very well, said Mrs. Goodwin; I see you are not quite such a novice as I at first thought you; really I could not have done better. Well, good night, I will leave you, for I have been a long while on my feet, and sleep seems to gain upon me. You will find some vinegar in that bottle, which you must remember to burn frequently. What! Mrs. Moody, are you there yet? come, make haste and get away; do you not know that the air is infectious?

Saying this, they both went out, and Malvina was left alone in Sir Edmond's chamber. What a moment! What a situation was hers![xlvi] She again beheld that beloved object; but how did she behold him? – In the gloomy chamber, on the bed of sickness, inanimate, without the power of distinguishing any person, without even knowing Malvina; in short, half expiring. She approached the bed, undrew the curtain, took hold of his hand, which she found of an icy coldness. She touched his forehead, which was covered with a cold sweat. His discoloured lips were dry and half open.[83] She fancied she heard him endeavouring to articulate some words – she held her breath and listened – she was not deceived.

Malvina, said he, in a dying voice – Malvina. At this name, she could no longer suppress her sobs; but they were not heard or understood. She wrapt her head in the curtain, fearful that her crying, should have informed him she was present; and that she might become more useful to him, she determined in future never to complain. She would not weep; her heart should cease to flutter. She fixed her eyes on the watch, and counted the minutes with such anxiety, that as one passed, she shuddered at that which was to follow.[84] She was on her knees by the bed of Sir Edmond, with her head leaning upon that cool hand; then holding it between both hers,[xlvii] she endeavoured to warm it.

At the solemn silent hour of midnight,[85] she implored the God of mercies to restore him whom she loved. How sincere was her faith, how fervent her prayers. She believed that she should not supplicate in vain; for the confidence which our Heavenly Father inspires, augments with the occasions we have for his interposition. Ah! who has not sometimes experienced those oppressive dreadful moments, when the extreme of misery gives a powerful voice to religion; when no power on earth can relieve our despair: then it is that our only reliance is on Heaven, and its mercy alone enables us to sustain life.

It was scarcely day, and Sir Edmond continued in the same state as Malvina found him the evening before, when she heard some person knock at the door, she immediately opened it; it was Ann, who came to inform her that Doctor Maxwell[86] was there: he entered soon after, and adjusting his wig, he said, well Goodwin, how is your patient?

Mrs. Goodwin is still asleep, Sir, said Malvina; I took her place last night. The doctor observed her more attentively, and discovered her, notwithstanding her aukward head dress (indeed she did not in the least resemble Mrs. Goodwin) and taking her hand in a very affable manner; well upon my word, said he, here is the most delicate white hand imaginable, just fit to assist the sick without hurting them.

Do you not wish to see Sir Edmond? said Malvina, retreating from him. Oh, yes, I shall look at him; but first my pretty child, tell me how long you have practiced this way of life? – God's mercy, Doctor Maxwell is so well known in Edinburgh, that there is not a nurse but has asked for his recommendation; and among them, you have never applied.

Oh! sir, replied she, wretched at finding Sir Edmond under the care of so indifferent a person; when Sir Edmond is dying, have you leisure to think of any thing else? in the name of humanity attend to him. She then acquainted him with every particular so minutely, of all that had passed during the night, and was so animated during the recital,[87] that the doctor looked at her with surprise; exclaiming, Faith, if all my patients had such women as you to attend them, I do not think I should lose one; and I shall not despair of Sir Edmond, now you are with him. – Well, we will now see how he is. He then felt his pulse, and appeared to reflect with some attention. Malvina watched him attentively, and endeavoured to guess his thoughts, by the expression of his eyes; she suppressed her respiration, fearful of disturbing his reflection.

At last, after a long silence, he replaced the hand, saying, his pulse is something better. But really, sir, replied Malvina, concealing her agitation, what do you think? – Do you believe him in danger?[88] The doctor, who had not an idea that there was a necessity for concealing his sentiments, said carelessly, Ah! I cannot yet answer, I cannot say how it will be; we shall see. There is nothing decisive can be said till the ninth day, which is the crisis; but if he survives that, then I shall have foundation for hope.

But child, you appear to be too young and delicate to sit up thus every night, particularly as this disorder is contagious. It is really a pity, my conscience will not permit it, and I beg that you will endeavour to procure another situation.[89] Me, sir, said Malvina; no, no, I am very well here, and will not change it; have you no orders to leave, sir? Do you not prescribe any thing?

The fever is on the decline, replied the doctor, examining his pulse again; his senses will return. I will write for him, and desire it may be punctually followed. While he was writing, Malvina was distressed to know how she should act, if Sir Edmond recovered his senses, as she was fearful he would recognise her; and the emotion it might occasion, would perhaps be injurious to him.

Here child, said the doctor, rising from his chair, read this paper with attention; and observe, that every particular is regularly obeyed. I shall call again in the evening; but if you will take my advice, you will not expose that pretty person among the dying, when the living might make a better use of it. Satisfied with the compliment he had made; the doctor, rubbing his hands with an air of self-complacency, left the room.

Malvina seated herself by Sir Edmond, and attentively watched for the first movement he should make. She had carefully closed all the curtains to darken the room, and anxiously waited for the moment when his beloved voice should arrest her ear. In about an hour he opened his eyes, and raising his hand to his forehead, he said, in an oppressed voice – Ah! my god, how much have I suffered, my lungs seem to be on fire. Goodwin, give me something to drink, to quench this devouring thirst which consumes me.

Malvina immediately gave him a refreshing draught, but he was so extremely weak, that she was obliged to support him in her arms, and sit on the bed to support his head on her bosom, while she gave it him. Let me remain thus a little, said he; I feel better with this change of posture. Malvina, happy to obey him, did not move, or utter a word; and stifled her tears, fearful they might betray her.

While she thus supported the person she loved in her arms, she thought herself blameable in not permitting him to know her[90] – perhaps he might expire in her arms, without her daring to say Edmond. – I am here, condemn me. Alas! she mentally exclaimed,[91] he has not an idea that it is Malvina whom he no longer loves,[92] who now supports him in her arms, and sympathises in his sufferings; who vows never to survive him; and who only petitions Heaven to lend her strength, till he has no longer occasion for her.

These melancholy thoughts sunk deep into her soul, and overpowered her so much, that it was with the utmost difficulty she suppressed her agonising grief. – Yet, even under this constraint, there was still a something of Malvina; and Edmond, weak as he was, felt a particular sensation which he could not account for. It was late in the morning when Mrs. Goodwin appeared, and Malvina immediately resigned her charge; for she found that the sound of her voice, though low and disguised, had been remarked by Sir Edmond; and she was in pain lest it should betray her.[93]

She trembled at the idea which the effect of his knowing her might produce on him, and the danger she was in of being discovered by the whole house. She retired to the foot of the bed, that she might hear without being observed. Are you not going to sleep? said Mrs. Goodwin. No, replied Malvina, in a low voice, I have lost my sleep for some time, but I can take a little rest in the chair very well.

After some time, Mrs. Goodwin, fatigued with supporting Sir Edmond, laid him on the pillow. This motion seemed to awake him; he asked, in a faint voice, are you there, Goodwin? Yes, sir, she replied, going to him.[94] Is it you who have been with me all this time? No, sir. Who then gave me this drink? The woman who sat up with you all night. – I thought it was not your voice; this woman has such a particular voice. I thought there had been but one like it.

Where is she now, Goodwin? I believe she is gone to sleep, sir, replied she, seeing Malvina with her eyes closed.[95] That is well, replied Sir Edmond, let her remain so, do not awake her – he said no more.

CHAP. IX.

The ninth day.

Several days had elapsed in a similar manner. – Malvina sat up every night, and concealed herself during the day; and was therefore not observed by any one. Sir Edmond soon forgot the impression which her voice had made. At last, the ninth day arrived; that fatal, that dreaded day at length appeared.[96]

Malvina, with her face hid behind the curtain,[97] pretended to be asleep, though anxiously attentive to every movement which Sir Edmond made; she perceived that his respiration became more quick and difficult. It was not anxiety, it was not fear, that alarmed her; it was that heart-corroding grief which chills all the blood, relaxes every nerve, and is as dreadful, when inanimate, as in its frensy;[98] because it has then attained that silent gloomy period, when all the powers of life seem to be annihilated, and the phantom hope flies from us.

While the fever raged, it gave Sir Edmond a momentary degree of strength. When the doctor entered, the patient knew him, and made a sign for him to come to him; saying, doctor, I feel myself so extremely ill, if you think I am near death, I intreat you will not conceal it from me. Come, come, said the doctor, there is no occasion to disturb yourself thus; you are very young, and possess a strong constitution; we shall save you, never fear.

I beg, doctor, that you will not deceive me, as it is of importance to me, much more than you can imagine. If, replied the doctor, you have any affairs to settle, there would be no impropriety or inconvenience attending it, supposing we could not pronounce[99]—. I understand you, doctor, and thank you. Do not imagine that I possess so timid and weak a mind, that I do not know how to submit to my fate. Many vices and follies have, I acknowledge, sullied my life; but if they were blended with some virtues, may I not rest in peace, and rely on the divine mercy? He then ceased speaking, and raised his feeble hands towards Heaven.

After a moment's emphatic silence, he said, Oh! Malvina, since I am destined to die at a distance from you, and that thy presence could not alleviate my sufferings, at least my last thoughts shall be dedicated to you; and if my hand is too weak to write an everlasting adieu, another shall supply its place. Goodwin, will you undertake to write for me? and get the materials ready. I do not know how to write, replied she, rather confused, and going out to fetch the paper and pens. No matter, said Malvina, speaking low, and in a feigned voice, I will write for you. But, continued she, addressing herself to the doctor, in the same tone, do you not fear it may fatigue him?

Faith, replied he, in the situation he is in, we may permit him to act as he pleases. Besides this, Malvina appears to occupy all his thoughts; and I do not know whether unburthening his heart may not in a great measure accelerate his recovery. Indeed, I think he is too good to think so much of her; for I think she must be a very wicked woman to act in the manner she has done, to be the cause of reducing this young man to so deplorable a situation.

Ah! doctor, said Malvina, with an exclamation she could no longer suppress; if it was possible to read her heart. Who uttered that exclamation? asked Sir Edmond, with some emotion. It was nothing, replied the doctor; I was only speaking to your nurse, that you had better forget a creature who had done so much mischief, as that Malvina has.

Take care, doctor, how you insult that angelic woman. Take care you do not believe any thing you may hear against her. It is I alone who have been cruel and unjust. – It is myself only. But I will not exhaust my strength in vindicating her, as I fear I should not have any left to dictate what I wish to have written. Are you ready, Goodwin? I am here, sir, replied she; and Malvina, gliding softly to the head of the bed, and concealed by the curtains, wrote what follows, dictated by her lover. –

'*Sir Edmond Burton to Malvina de Sorcy.*

'I am dying, Malvina; but though my love for you is the cause of it, do not, I beseech you, accuse yourself of my death. It is entirely my own fault, and has originated from the violence of my passions, which has occasioned a fever, which is conducting me to the tomb. I think I can assure myself of your grief on my leaving you. – That is sufficient to vindicate you, Malvina. This will convince me that you have never ceased to love me; and that your tears will fall over my grave.

'Malvina, I acknowledge that I regret life, when I think I should have lived for you. I regret leaving a world where you remain! – but I feel the deepest anguish for having doubted you a moment; and actuated by the most unpardonable rage, I have exposed myself to die, surrounded by your unworthy and cruel enemies. Oh! Malvina, can you pardon this guilty behaviour? Alas, how much am I punished for it! Had it been otherwise, I would have sent for you to be near me, that I might once more have pressed your hand, fixed my last looks upon you, and told you that I still loved – loved only Malvina; and I die in adoring you.

'Say! oh! say, Malvina, that you would have come – would you not? You could not have resisted the dying entreaties of your lover. – You would have been at present with me – I should have beheld you – I should have heard you – I should have been comforted'.

Who is it that weeps? said Sir Edmond. Every where I think I hear her step. The hand which touches me seems always to be hers.[xlviii] That murmuring voice which I hear is also hers;[xlix] these stifled sighs and groans appear to proceed from her heart. Oh! Malvina, if it is thy soul that breathes round me, and is come to unite with mine, that we may together take our flight; press thyself on my bosom, and exhale its last sigh.

At this tender appellation, Malvina threw herself into the arms of Sir Edmond; and his delirium immediately returned. He exclaimed, with fury, no! no! leave me, perfidious woman! do you wish to shed my blood a second time? Why arm the hand of my rival with that bloody dagger? Why order him to plunge it in my bosom?[100] Did you not bid me die? – and you shall be obeyed.

Oh! my God! my God! exclaimed Malvina (striking her hand against the wall in the most inexpressible agony) when wilt thou put an end to my torments? – they cannot be increased!

There is something very extraordinary in this, said the doctor. Poh, replied Mrs. Goodwin, in a whisper; I am certain this woman is only one of those fools whom Sir Edmond has deceived. Fie, Mrs. Goodwin, replied the doctor, on the contrary, I think she has the air of a very sensible person; but there are some women, whose nerves are so irritable, that they weep merely from seeing others do so.

Why for that matter, said Mrs. Goodwin, it is of no consequence who she is, it is sufficient for me that she is here; for I can now sleep all night, and even in the day she relieves me of half my business. Sir Edmond's delirium lasted till evening. Malvina's sufferings, during the course of that day,[l] were beyond expression; and in order to gain strength, she was obliged to recollect the dreadful night which was fast approaching; for which she would require supernatural force to support her through it.

At midnight, Edmond ceased talking; and the doctor having felt his pulse, said to Malvina, the crisis draws near; if he does not die in six hours, I will answer for his life. Watch him very carefully, I shall not leave the house; if his senses return, accompanied with a gentle perspiration, and if the oppression diminishes, let me be called, for he will be saved.

This then is to be the hour which will decide my fate, said Malvina, as soon as she was alone. She traversed the chamber with her heavy eyes fixed on the ground. Then, suddenly starting with terror, she would say, Yet, a few moments perhaps, and the cold clay will be all that remains of my Edmond; and he, who was lately blooming in health, and animated by love, will soon be laid silent and motionless, in the dark, deep, and silent grave.

She then approached the bed, with the countenance of despair, fixed her eyes on the face of her lover, and continued thus: – Yet a few moments, and perhaps thy form and my happiness will be buried in eternal night. We have had only a moment to love each other in, and fate is going to snatch that and your existence from me. Oh, my God! if I have only received my life to behold those die whom I best loved. Ah! why didst thou bestow it? Oh God! I did not desire it. Edmond, I shall never hear thy voice again! – That beloved voice, whose sound yet vibrates to my heart. Shall mine, never again arrest you? Edmond, my Edmond, you are then going to leave me. – All powerful God, permit him at that moment to answer his Malvina.

Dear Edmond, at least hear my last adieu; it is thy Malvina who calls thee; who would die with thee: already the icy hand of death has chilled all thy frame. I feel it has also reached my heart. Edmond! Oh Edmond! do not go without thy Malvina, wait for her, and she will follow thee. – Perhaps the same grave may receive us both; and pressing the body of her Edmond in her arms, she fell inanimate near him.

Edmond yet lived; possessing a strong and vigourous constitution, he had struggled for some instants against death, and the victory was decided in his favor. The flame of life was rekindled in his bosom, and life's vital current began again to circulate in his veins. Exhausted by his sufferings, he half opened his eyes, raised his head, and by the light of the lamp which shone directly on the bed, he perceived a woman extended near him. Astonished, he looked at her; her head-dress had fallen on one side, and her hair floated round her neck. He could not mistake, they were the features of Malvina. Where am I, he exclaimed; is it really her whom I see? At the sound of his voice, Malvina was re-animated, and looking at him in silent extacy, she extended her arms towards Heaven, without the power of uttering a word. Malvina near me – is it a dream that deceives me? Can I believe it? Is it really thee, Malvina?

Oh! my Edmond, replied she, are you given back to life. Malvina, said Sir Edmond, in a languishing voice, I cease to suffer since I behold thee. But tell me, by what miracle do I behold you here? Have we really quitted the earth, and are we united in eternity? On concluding these words, his ideas began to wander, and his eyes closed; but he breathed more freely, and the moist warmth of his hands, comforted Malvina.

She beheld his faded lips regain a degree of colour; the shades of death were retreating, a gentle sleep suspended his sufferings; and overpowered by gratitude, she fell on her knees, and offered to the Father of Heaven, who had saved him, her silent eloquent tears of gratitude and joy. She looked around, with the idea that every thing should respect the repose of Sir Edmond, and the solemn silence, whose gloomy horror was so frightful a few hours before, she now thought was not sufficiently still.[101] The very air made her fear, she scarcely breathed; she wished the life of the world was suspended, and that nature would not awake till her lover did.

CHAP. X.

Joy after grief.

Aurora had already began to illumine the horizon, and Sir Edmond continued to sleep. Malvina, with her eyes fixed upon him, was kneeling at the side of the bed,[102] when she heard the heavy step of Doctor Maxwell; she flew instantly to open the door, as gently as possible; as he entered, she informed him his patient was then in a tranquil sleep. He sleeps, replied the doctor; are you certain of it? Ah, doctor, do you think I can be deceived? Faith, said he, this will not be the first time that it has so happened; nevertheless I will look at him, for if he is asleep I can answer for him.

Malvina flew as light as a bird, and guided him in silence to the bed. The doctor examined his patient with his usual attention, and then looking at Malvina with an air of surprise, he said, Sir Edmond is out of danger. At these words, less mistress of her joy than she had been of her grief, she could not contain herself, but ran out of the chamber to relieve the violence of her agitation.

The doctor was astonished at this sudden flight; called Mrs. Goodwin to come to his patient, and then followed Malvina, whom he found in the next room bathed in tears, and carefully overcome with joy. On seeing him, she went up to him, and pressing both his hands between hers.[l] – It is then you who have saved him, she said; angel from Heaven! – Benevolent man! Who, after God, possesses all my gratitude. He is out of danger, you say? Oh! once more repeat those words; which recalls me from the abyss[y] of despair, to Heaven.

Certainly you are a very extraordinary woman, replied the doctor, wiping away a tear. Undoubtedly I appear so to you, but I intreat that you will not mention it to any one? Doctor, I conjure you not to disclose me to any person. Tell me, however, said Malvina, with an agitation which scarcely permitted her to breathe; do you think when he awakes he will know those who are with him?

There is not a doubt of it, the fever is abated, consequently the delirium will subside. The moment of convalescence approaches, and his chief symptom will be weakness. But from this weakness, doctor, will any violent emotion prove dangerous? Certainly, if the powers are too much exhausted to support it; therefore I cannot answer for the consequences. – But why all these questions, what interest can excite you to make them? What interest, doctor, exclaimed she, with animation; there are no expressions which can delineate it. – But once more I entreat that you will not discover me? I am a very weak creature, that could not longer conceal my feelings. But I have suffered so excessively; pity me, doctor, the unexpected change from death to life, has weakened all my faculties.

I can guess, he replied, that you are not what you appear to be; and that some very particular motive must have induced you to come here. Sir Edmond is the farthest from being indifferent to you; and there is some mystery which you do not wish to disclose. Perhaps so, but do not deceive yourself, doctor, said she, smiling with satisfaction at his penetration. Let us return to your patient, I shall conceal myself in a corner of the room till he awakes; I shall anxiously wait for the first word he utters. Beware that you do not say I am there, and particularly do not pronounce my name.

Faith, replied the doctor, I shall find no difficulty in complying with this last request, for you know I have never heard it. Well then, permit me still to continue silent, and the secret will be very easily kept. Nevertheless, I am not a little curious to know it, said the doctor.

Do not, dear sir, said Malvina; I intreat you will not ask me; you are a good and excellent man – have compassion on my long sufferings, and do not increase them, by obliging me to acknowledge who I am. Well, my child, it shall be as you please; you appear so good and so gentle, that it would pain me to afflict you. My God! I think I hear him, said Malvina, listening. I am not deceived – Edmond is awake. Do you go alone, doctor, I am fearful he should see me. I will listen at the door, where she immediately placed herself,[103] and heard all Edmond uttered.

Ah! good Heaven, said he, on seeing the doctor; what has happened to me? a refreshing slumber has cooled the burning heat which seemed to consume me. What a sweet sleep have I enjoyed, and what pleasing delusions have attended me – I have seen, I have touched Malvina! I think I still hear her voice. Hush! hush! said the doctor; I will not allow you to think of her: this tormenting idea may again throw you into the same danger from which I have just rescued you. No, doctor, you deceive yourself; it is she alone who has saved me. This night I should have died, I suffered so much; a devouring grief seemed to consume all the ties of life, which were on the verge of separating, when her beloved voice appeared to arrest the stroke of death, and save me from the tomb. Edmond!

Edmond! she repeated – and the accents of Malvina vibrated to my heart. I opened my eyes, and she was there; she pressed me to her bosom, and I experienced through my whole frame that sweet fluttering sensation, which her approach always creates. I had no sooner wished to make the effort of embracing her, than she disappeared like a shadow.

Well, sir, said Mrs. Goodwin; such sleeps are not very good, for they give you a fever. She says very true, replied the doctor, for they are the phantoms of a delirious imagination; your pulse is already much agitated, and if you continue talking thus, you will have a relapse. Sir Edmond had not much occasion to be desired to remain quiet, for he was so languid, that though the image of Malvina was stamped on his heart, she soon escaped his recollection, and by degrees, the remembrance of that night was obliterated from his memory; as the shades of darkness vanish before the rays of the sun.

Malvina took the opportunity of Sir Edmond's repose, to clandestinely enter the chamber, and carefully avoided his looks, by concealing herself behind the curtains. As Ann had circulated the report of Sir Edmond's recovery throughout the house, Mrs. Fenwick, whose heart had never been touched by any person, or felt, but for him, experienced sincere joy; and Mrs. Burton, for the first time, expressed the most lively marks of sensibility. When the gloom of evening began to obscure every object, Sir Edmond being asleep, Malvina was seated near the window, making lint for her lover's wound, when some person tapped at the door. See who it is, said Mrs. Goodwin, who was half asleep in her chair? Malvina arose – Who is there? said she, in a low voice. Can I see Sir Edmond? asked a voice, which she instantly recognised to be Mrs. Burton's. No, no, replied Malvina, so disconcerted that she could scarcely recollect one idea; he is asleep. Go out, and speak to the lady, said Mrs. Goodwin. What now?[104] replied she, trembling. To be sure, when the lady is so kind as to come herself, you wish to make her wait – Go, I say. Really, replied Malvina; I shall not – I do not know her.

Oh, the foolish creature, exclaimed Mrs. Goodwin, scolding, you will not; and what is it that prevents you? when you see that I must discompose myself. On saying this, she observed that Malvina, instead of opening the door, had retired to the most obscure part of the room. She got up, and shaking her head, set her cap in order, and went into the next room, to acquaint Mrs. Burton with the state of her nephew.

Malvina followed her, from a very pardonable curiosity; to overhear their conversation. I shall come and see him to-morrow, said Mrs. Burton; and take particular care to purify the room with vinegar; and also I desire another time, I may not be obliged to wait so long. I hope you will excuse me, madam, said Mrs. Goodwin; it was the fault of the other nurse, who is so timid, that she never has the courage to speak to a lady. But she might have opened the door at least. Why, to tell you the truth, madam, though I have never mentioned it, this woman appears to have fits. Pray then, why was such a fool permitted to attend my nephew?

It was Mrs. Moody, madam, who recommended her; and to speak the truth, I must confess she is very clever in her situation; and I could not have shewn more zeal and attention myself, than she has. But she is so serious and distant, that it is impossible to make her smile. That is very whimsical, replied Mrs. Burton; Ann, has informed Tasse, that the doctor was surprised at her sensibility, which is not a very usual fault in women of your line. – I should like to see her, is she within?

Yes, madam, but Sir Edmond is asleep, and we have not a light. Well, I shall come to-morrow, replied she, going away. These words seriously alarmed Malvina, she knew one glance was sufficient for Mrs. Burton to discover her; would it not be best to avoid such a meeting? Edmond was out of danger, and her attendance was now useless. She ought to depart as soon as possible. She however passed that night with Sir Edmond.

His sleep was calm, and towards morning, particularly tranquil; she ventured to undraw the curtains, and gently pressing her lips to his hand, which laid out of bed; adieu, said she, in a whisper. This day I must leave you! A merciful God has saved you! You no longer require my cares. Thy Malvina departs without leaving any traces of the moments she has passed near thee, but a faint and confused idea, which will only be remembered as a transient dream. Adieu, my Edmond! Perhaps we may never behold each other again on this wretched earth.

With thy returning health, I shall recollect the duties I have to fulfill; but when the tumult of passion shall have subsided, and the touch of time shall have silvered our heads, shall I not then be permitted to press thy hand with mine; though it may then be feeble and withered? Then I may ask, Edmond, do you remember that night of agony; that dreadful moment, when the tomb seemed ready to open and receive us both? Has thy ear forgot that accent, which repulsed me; and then relapsing into a state of forgetfulness; by the gloomy light of a lamp, you thought you had seen Malvina. – But thy languid eyes were soon closed, and you believed it was a phantom of the night; a child of your delirium, that had taken her form, and her voice.

No Edmond, it was not her shadow. – Who, but Malvina, would have died with you? and those sounds of despair, were they not from her heart? Ah! the day advances, and I must fly! I must go without beholding one look from Edmond to his Malvina. Thy eyes will dwell on every object in this room, but I will be no longer there. Adieu, Edmond; my heart is torn at leaving you, but no matter. Thy repose requires that I should depart. Once more, applying her lips to the hand of her lover, she started up to desire Mrs. Goodwin to take her place; but her moving, awakened Sir Edmond.

Who is there? he faintly enquired. She was motionless; she was uncertain whether to speak, or continue silent; she waited. Alas! said he, must I always be pursued by this lovely phantom? Shadow of Malvina, can I never escape you? I fancied I heard thy sweet soft voice murmuring some plaintive words. – I fancied

I was on the verge of happiness; but it was only in my sleep. Oh! sweet and transporting dreams, I implore thee to close my eyes, and give me back Malvina: on concluding these words, his voice died away, and he again slept.

Malvina stood a few minutes motionless, a prey to the most violent agitations. How much did her heart wish to gratify him, by discovering herself.[105] It was not the fear of Mrs. Burton, which alone prevented her; but the languid stage which Sir Edmond was in, which deterred her; he required rest, not pleasure. She owed him this sacrifice, and extending her arms towards him, she faintly articulated a last adieu, and rushed out of the chamber.

She awakened Mrs. Goodwin, went gently down stairs, found the streetdoor open, stole out without being observed by any person, and returned immediately to Mrs. Moody's.

CHAP. XI.

An accusation of magic.

God be praised, cried the good woman, as soon as she perceived her; that you are returned. Ah! madam, I have not had one moment's peace[li] since you have been at Mrs. Burton's. But good Lord, madam, how you are altered. I am very well for all that, dear Moody; Edmond is saved. Ah! my dear madam, replied she, shaking her head, how much I feared your having caught the same illness; and who knows yet but he may have been saved by your having taken it from him.

Do not fear any thing, Moody; Edmond is saved – How then can I die? But while I take some rest, go to Mrs. Burton's, and find an excuse for my departure. Say that I was taken suddenly ill, that my head was deranged; in short, say what you please. I only wish to conceal my name; it is a secret which must ever remain between us. I know you will rely on my discretion, madam, and the manner in which I shall endeavour to elude all suspicions.

Has any one conceived any, Moody? As to that, madam, I do not think it possible, but some must have been formed; you could not hide your figure, your language, and particularly the grief by which you were absorbed. No one could suppose you to be a common nurse; and Ann told me – Oh Heaven! she knew me then? No, madam, but she said that you neither ate or slept; that you was continually weeping, and that consequently, she was certain you must be foolish; and she could not think how so reasonable a person as myself—

That is sufficient, Moody, interrupted Malvina; I will hear another time; at present I have great occasion for rest: on concluding, she tottered, for not being longer under the necessity of exerting herself, she felt her extreme weakness and want of rest; having undergone eleven painful nights of severe watching, and agonizing anxiety.

While she was reposing her harrassed mind and body, Mrs. Goodwin had searched and enquired all over the house for her. No one could give any account of her. Ann then told some idle tales of her own coining; that she had seen her one night through the key hole making such odd grimaces, twisting her arms about, and forming circles, which were certainly to invoke the devil.[106] All this was circulated among the other servants, who heard it with terror; their imaginations took wing; and they all were convinced that Malvina was a witch; who, by her enchantments had so speedily cured Sir Edmond of an illness, which Doctor Maxwell had pronounced mortal.

Mrs. Moody happened to enter as they were listening to these idle tales, and they immediately told her the same nonsense;[107] not doubting but that she would give implicit belief to all that was reported. Jenny was impatient till she had acquainted her mistress of these wonders. Mrs. Fenwick, rather astonished at what she heard, questioned her more particularly; and to convince her mistress, Jenny added a few novel exaggerations; and the reality was no longer doubted.[108]

Mrs. Melmor, who was as superstitious as the most ignorant domestic, augmented her daughter's terror, by saying she was miserable beyond measure, at their having lived so long in the house with a sorceress. These ridiculous fancies were at last related to Mrs. Burton. She was not to be duped by such an absurd account; and she had particular suspicions; she therefore treated it as a mere bagatelle; desiring, if that woman appeared again, they would immediately conduct her to her presence.

What strength of mind! what penetration! exclaimed Mrs. Fenwick, as she listened to Mrs. Burton, as if struck with admiration: who, but a woman who is so superior to the rest of her sex, would have so quickly discovered truth from error; and rejecting those vulgar prejudices, by her philosophic and enlightened understanding, have guessed that some extraordinary cause must have given rise to this affair. – But there is only one Mrs. Burton in the world.

Malvina was informed of all these particulars, from Mrs. Moody. She heard them with indifference, she was satisfied with remaining unknown; and hearing that Sir Edmond daily gained health and strength. This, diffused a soothing tranquillity over her harrassed mind. Hope, deceitful flattering hope, seemed again to hover near her; though unconscious as yet what to hope for – whether its eagle eye would not rest on some pleasing distant perspective; or soar beyond the dark clouds, which too often obscured her view, and eclipsed the orb of day; or whether to securely rest, alone on Heaven.[109]

Thus the limpid stream, which the rain and storms has occasioned to overflow its banks, yet soon subsides to its own course; becoming calm by degrees, reflecting on its glassy bosom each fair flower, that buds, blooms, and pendant decorates its borders; exhibiting a nile in miniature, on the floating mirror of its waters.[110]

Thus, while Edmond was rapidly recovering, and his renewed strength permitted him to reflect, his first care was to demand of every person in the house, if Madame de Sorcy had sent to enquire concerning his health, while he was ill; or if any person had come from Mrs. St. Clare? No one could inform him, they had never seen any one; or heard of Madame de Sorcy, or Mrs. St. Clare.

This cold indifference with regard to him, created the most painful discontent; and all the anger of Sir Edmond was renewed against Malvina. What, said he, did I not leave her, wounded by Mr. Prior; and yet she has not condescended to trouble herself, to know whether I live or die? She, who is so good and humane to all who are afflicted, remains frigidly indifferent to my sorrows.

Does not this conduct evince the influence of some different, or altered sentiments? Can she have given them to Mr. Prior? But no, did she not consent to be united to me? – Did she not confess that she loved me? Can I then ever doubt Malvina's sincerity? Yet, I have been dying, and not a word or a line to inform me of her regret.[111] But that letter which I dictated to her, what has become of it? – who was ordered to send it? In this suspense, he rang with violence. I want Mrs. Goodwin, said he to his servant – I desire to speak to her immediately. Sir, do you not know she is gone? No matter, I suppose she is to be found, and you must fetch her without delay.

It was rather difficult to find Mrs. Goodwin; for on leaving Sir Edmond she had been sent for into the country, to attend a person who was very ill; consequently several days must elapse, before she could obey the commands of Sir Edmond. At last, she arrived. Goodwin, said he, very gaily; did I not dictate a letter which you wrote for me in my illness?[112] Excuse me, sir, she replied, in some confusion, but I know nothing of it indeed. The truth is, it is not my fault, for I do not know how to write, and can scarcely sign my name.

Who then did write it? hastily demanded Sir Edmond. Sir, it was that unhappy woman whom I hope God will have mercy on. What woman? replied he, impatiently; of whom do you speak? Mrs. Burton has forbid my mentioning her to you, sir; she very probably imagined that you would not think yourself cured, if you were acquainted that it was the effect of witchcraft. What is all this stupid nonsense? Ah! sir, replied the nurse, who was dying to inform him of all she knew; if I was but certain that Mrs. Burton would never know that I had told you, I could acquaint you with such wonderful things.

I am not at all disposed to hear them, Goodwin; only tell me if you know whether my letter was sent? Sir, that woman took the charge of it.[113] Where is this woman to be found? Holy Virgin! said she, making the sign of the cross (for bigotted to her own faith, Mrs. Burton admitted no Protestants to her house)[114] at the nightly meeting of witches, certainly; and it is not I who can go and fetch her. Only tell me where I can direct to her? Lord bless me, sir, the devil only can tell.

But who sent her here then? added he, with anger. Mrs. Moody. Oh, very well: then Goodwin, go and beg Mrs. Moody to come, I wish to speak to her. Mrs. Moody went instantly, proud of being in the confidence of Malvina; as it gave her infinite consequence in her own opinion.[115] Sir Edmond enquired of her concerning that woman; but she returned him only vague and unsatisfactory answers, assuring him she did not know where the woman lived, whom he wanted, and that she had not any directions where to find her.

Thus, he was obliged to remain in his former irksome state of suspense, which he could not any longer support; and determined though weak, to go and enquire what was become of Malvina, and the reason of her silence. With this determination, without having informed any one of his plan, he went down one morning to Mrs. Burton, and making many polite and cool apologies for the trouble which his illness must have occasioned, he pretended that he was going to pass a few days with a friend, at a little distance from Edinburgh, as he thought change of air might be of service to him.

Mrs. Burton, who was always suspicious, fancied there was some mystery in this projected journey, and made several attempts to oppose it. It was quite sufficient for such a character as Sir Edmond's, to have informed his aunt of his intention; therefore he did not condescend to hear any objections she could make to his going. He set out the next day, and did not stop till he arrived at Aberthay, the nearest place to St. Clare Hall.

It was from thence, that letters were directed for those who inhabited that house. That he might be certain Malvina was there, he enquired of the postmaster, how long it was since he had received any letters, directed for Madame de Sorcy, addressed to Mrs. St. Clare? For Madame de Sorcy repeated the good old man, putting on his spectacles, and examining the register which lay before him; yes, here is one which I sent to St. Clare Hall, yesterday. It is there then![116] cried Sir Edmond, flying out of the house, without speaking to the old man; whom he left astonished at his abrupt departure. She is yet there very calm, and at peace – while I – But I will not yet form any judgment, or condemn her unheard. I ought to have the strongest evidence, before I have the temerity to doubt Malvina.

While he was thus mentally conversing, he arrived at the gates of the park; he dismounted from his horse, and giving it in care to the servant, desired he would wait there; and proceeded on foot to the house: as he passed on, he was intercepted by a railing, through which he could discover the gardens. He stopped, and fancied he saw – no, his eyes did not deceive him; it was Frances, he recollected her voice; Malvina was certainly near. His heart beat violently; he seated himself on a large stone, and watched, with inexpressible anxiety, the development of his destiny.

Frances, who was running about the grass, advanced to that side where he was, and amused herself with gathering the flowers which grew on the side of a little rivulet, which was close to the railing. Suddenly, he heard somebody call her; Sir Edmond shuddered; it was Mr. Prior's voice, he was convinced. He saw and heard him very distinctly speaking to Frances, thus: – Why do you wander so far from this side, my dear? Have you forgot how you frightened your mother, by being alone near the water?

Oh! my dear mama, where is she now? cried the little creature. Come with me, my love, and it will not be long before you will see her, continued he, raising his voice, and addressing a lady, whose white robe distinguished her among the trees, and who was moving towards them. Francis, perceiving her, ran to her; who, by her air and form resembled Malvina. She took the child in her arms, and turning another way with Mr. Prior,[117] they went into the house.

This sight so shocked Sir Edmond, that he remained motionless; a cold chill ran through his veins; he then kindled into rage – he rushed from the place, and ran towards the town he had quitted. He could not think or reflect; his heart was oppressed, his ideas stagnated. A gloomy veil seemed to overshadow all nature; every object appeared changed; and the weakness of his frame was unequal to this violent shock; he tottered, and fell senseless on the pavement, at the entrance of the town.

Several persons surrounded him, and some of them carried him to the first inn they came near, where they endeavoured to recover him; and it was some time before he re-gained his senses. Silent and gloomy, he made a sign, which indicated his wish of being alone. He sat motionless at the window, without attempting to overcome his weakness. Entirely absorbed by the weight of one sensation, the whole universe was a blank to him; and he did not even observe that a tempest was gathering in the lowering sky.

The hours passed, night approached, the distant thunder rolled, but he did not hear. The jarring elements might have clashed together; nothing had power to rouse him from his dejection. He remained fixed in the same place, without changing his attitude; his head leaning against one of the iron bars which crossed the window, which he had pressed his forehead against with such force that it was covered with blood.[118] He was roused at length by the sound of a voice which he detested, and he flew towards the door.

The thunder had pealed loud, tremendous and unheard; but the sound of Mr. Prior's voice had acted as an electrical shock; and, in a moment, roused him to himself, by producing again his torturing sensations. He heard him asking a lodging for the night, as he was come to fetch letters for Mrs. St. Clare, and Madame de Sorcy. The storm had overtaken him, and prevented his return that evening.

They said they could accommodate him with an upper room. Sir Edmond, undetermined how he should act, and a prey to the rage of jealousy, was walking furiously about the room. Mr. Prior, is come for letters for Malvina, said he; perhaps he will carry one for me; she will receive it from the hands of Mr. Prior. Will she condescend to read it? Does she even know that I exist? Perhaps, at this moment, she is only anxious for Mr. Prior's return. As he finished these words, he fixed his eyes upon his pistols, and seizing one of them with a ferocious pleasure, he charged it immediately, without knowing for what purpose.

The idea of bloodshed made him smile, and seemed to soothe his grief. He was so intent on his gloomy projects, that he never knew that the lightening had struck the house, that the roof was on fire, and threatened to consume the building. They ran to his door, and begged him to save himself. But insensible to all which did not concern his love, he perceived no danger; he thought only of revenge. He would not have stirred, if it had not been to seek for Mr. Prior.

At this moment, he heard the groans of an unfortunate being, who was on the point of perishing in the flames. His rage gave place to a more noble sentiment; he enquired where the sounds proceeded from? It is certainly, they replied, from the gentleman who is above; the lightening has caught the hay-loft, near which he lays. The smoke must suffocate him, for the stairs are on fire, and no one dare venture up them. On which side is he? asked Sir Edmond, hastily, dashing his pistols from him. On this side, said the landlord; Ah! if there is any time, endeavour to save that good Mr. Prior.

Oh! Mr. Prior, replied Sir Edmond, looking angrily; I know very well that it is Mr. Prior; do you believe that name will prevent me? Is not Mr. Prior also a man? and without hesitating, he flew to the stairs. At this moment, it was generosity which excited him,[119] for he had forgot his hatred. Malvina was not even remembered. Every other sentiment was suspended, and humanity alone triumphed.

He had no sooner ascended the stairs, than they gave way behind him; but nothing could prevent his intrepid mind from rushing forward. He saw the danger without losing his coolness. He broke open the door, and almost overpowered by torrents of smoke, he observed Mr. Prior, motionless on the floor. He raised him on his shoulders, and bending under his burden, he endeavoured to find a passage, but in vain; every opening was interrupted by the flames; he rushed towards a window which looked into the street, where many persons were collected; they perceived him, and hastened for materials[120] to receive them; but in the state Mr. Prior was in, it would be dangerous to throw himself out with him; and every thing was on fire around him, the beams breaking in; one moment longer, and it would be too late.[121] He rested him on the window, and using every possible precaution in directing the fall, he threw him as gently as possible, and courageously waited to jump out after him.

Before he could escape, the fire burst out with redoubled violence, and entirely enveloped him. He was obliged to stand on the end of a beam which trembled under him,[122] and from which he threw himself to the ground. Happily, a long piece of cross bar iron caught hold of the bottom of his coat, and broke his fall; he immediately recovered himself, and ran to Mr. Prior, who was just beginning to discover signs of life; being revived by the fresh air.

Sir Edmond's dislike had not lessened by having saved him, and perhaps it was rather increased; for now he had preserved his life, he could never in future wish to kill him.[123] He, however, did not desire that Mr. Prior should ever be acquainted by whose interposition he was saved; that he might avoid his acknowledgments; and for ever bury in oblivion an action, which connected him against his will, to a man he detested.

For this reason, as soon as he had given a draft on his banker for five and twenty pounds, to the unfortunate proprietor of the house, he departed without being known, and arrived the next day at Mrs. Burton's, without having determined to return to her, or having taken any rest.[124] He entered the saloon, quite in dishabille,[125] where he found a numerous company; among whom, he remarked the beautiful, the insipid, the cold Lady Mary Summerhill; and the pretty seducing Mrs. Fenwick, whose coquetry increased daily, and added to her charms.

On beholding him, all the ladies uttered an exclamation of joy and surprise. The noise, the company, recalled Sir Edmond a little to himself; and in the distress of his heart, he cast a look of satisfaction on those who were round him, vowing and hoping to render them the victims of that hatred, which the perfidious Malvina had given him to her whole sex.

With this idea, he indulged the sallies of his imagination; a forced gaiety animated and gave an energy to his discourse and manners, which rendered him uncommonly amiable and brilliant. He replied, with vivacity, to all the airs of Mrs. Fenwick; and even appeared to give animation to Lady Mary. Each woman received his homage; all imagined they had the preference; and without scarcely looking at Mrs. Fenwick, he told her she was adorable[126] – and she believed him. Lady Mary was applauding herself for having brought him to her feet. Thinking she ought to punish him for his inconstancy, she pretended to treat him with a severity, which was foreign to her present feelings; but which she thought would make a great impression upon him, though he never perceived it.

Thus, each deceived themselves, imagining they were nearest their wishes; when at the same time they were as distant as the antipodes. The following days still confirmed them in their illusion; for Sir Edmond,[127] a prey to stifled rage,[128] premeditated his perfidious projects of seduction; and he wished to have the power of uniting all their hearts in one, that he might have the barbarous pleasure of tearing them at his ease; and thus revenge himself for all the torments which he suffered.

CHAP. XII.

Mutual resolutions.

While Sir Edmond was resigning himself to the most violent sensations, how very different was the soul of Malvina actuated. She had remained in Edinburgh, not only that she might hear frequently of Sir Edmond, but that she might find a favorable moment, either to see or write to him, without endangering his health, by any premature emotion. It was her intention to give him a particular explanation of their last meeting, and Lord Sheridan's letter; and enforce her determination of maintaining inviolable the promise she had given to her dying friend; and appeal both to his generosity and honor, if there was not an indispensible necessity for their being separated for ever.

Before she had executed this intention, she was informed that Sir Edmond had left Mrs. Burton's. If she was astonished at his sudden departure, she was infinitely more so at his quick return. She soon heard that he was more gay and frivolous than ever; and resigned himself entirely to all his former dissipation, even to excess.

It was asserted, that Mrs. Burton had named the day which was to unite him to Lady Mary Summerhill; while Mrs. Fenwick boasted continually of having captivated and chained him with new fetters, which afforded her the most supreme gratification. All this was circulated by Jenny and Ann, to Mrs. Moody. How deep did this account pierce the heart of Malvina; she relinquished all her intentions, and totally absorbed by her grief, neither complained or accused any one. Sir Edmond believed her guilty, and therefore had determined to forget her, as he had now done with her entirely.

By vindicating herself, she perhaps might recall him; but since he had vanquished his affection, and she had determined to maintain her vow, why endeavour to re-kindle sentiments, which would only render him unhappy? Also, she had a secret presentiment, which informed her such an attempt would be useless. Edmond was susceptible of a violent passion, but incapable of a lasting attachment; he therefore no longer deserved her confidence. She could believe the energy of his love; but no longer depend on his stability.[129]

From the time she was at liberty to fulfil her duties of friendship;[130] her resolution was taken; she would remain silent with regard to him; and suppressing her affection,[131] she would go farther and absent herself; devoting all her days to her little charge, in solitude and retirement; and bid adieu to a deceitful world, where she had only experienced disappointment, sorrow, and pain. Before she resigned it entirely, she gave a last glance mentally to the being in it, who was so dear to her. Oh! thou, said she, whom I love – I never can again[132] (for the first excess of a sentiment, which expects to receive as much as it gives, can never be felt twice) be happy,[133] since thou canst be so without Malvina.

Alas, in absenting myself from thee, I relinquish for ever the idea of happiness. But at my age, when the heart is rent by so many sorrows, will it not require all the remainder of my future life, to calm and soothe the sufferings I have experienced? In renouncing Sir Edmond, she determined never more to see Mr. Prior. At any other time, she would have blushed at thus sacrificing friendship, to an unworthy and false suspicion. But in her present situation, she was not sensible that it was a secret gratification to herself,[134] that Sir Edmond should know that she had left the world on his account; and also broken every band which had united her to it. In this disposition, she wrote to Mrs. St. Clare.

'I shall set out to morrow, and once more re-join you and my dear girl, that I have so long neglected. You shall read my heart, you shall be acquainted with[135] my future determination – your kindness will assist me in the execution. By that affectionate interest which you have so kindly expressed, and evinced in all your actions for me, I intreat that you will be alone, absolutely without any company, when I meet you.'

At this moment, when Malvina was alone in her apartment, a prey to that silent corroding sorrow, which embittered her life; and resting on that insurmountable barrier, which was to separate her from the world. How differently were they engaged at Mrs. Burton's house; noisy pleasure and rejoicing reigned there, uncontrouled by any reflection. A splendid dinner, to which all the first persons in Edinburgh had been invited, was terminated in a superb evening gala. The gardens were illuminated, the company dispersed in groups, wandering through shrubberies of the sweetest and most blooming flowers.

Sir Edmond, almost fatigued by lavishing so profusely his incense on every woman, and perhaps[136] successful in making them believe him sincere in his admiration, was nearly giddy with his conquests; and devoting himself to gaiety and pleasure, replied, with rather too much animation, to the seductive graces of Mrs. Fenwick; and chance conducted them both to one of the most distant and retired alcoves. It may be imagined that Sir Edmond would have been perfectly at his ease with his Kitty, if he had not at that moment recollected that it was the same in which he had been surprised in his first interview with Malvina. This remembrance, by re-calling her beloved image, caused him to shudder, and he regained his scattered senses. His assumed gaiety vanished; he leaned mournfully against a tree; and Mrs. Fenwick, though near him, felt herself alone and deserted.

Piqued at the sudden change, which she could not account for, she went to Doctor Maxwell, whom she observed at a little distance, and said to him ironically, Doctor, be quick, and hasten to your patient, for I think there is much required to complete his cure, while he is subject to such starts and whimsies. What does all this mean? said the doctor joining Sir Edmond; are you really indisposed? Faith, between ourselves, it is not overwise,[z] when every beauty is disputing for your heart, and see only you; is this a time to be ill? – though then, even then, you have the power of attracting them near you, and render them callous to the danger of infection; and I acknowledge all the fine ladies, decorated by all the powers of art, not one of them can boast more charms than your pretty nurse, who expressed so lively an interest in your fate.

But doctor, said Sir Edmond, rather astonished at what he heard; pray inform me of a few particulars relative to this woman? No, no, I assure you I shall not. – Mrs. Burton has expressly forbid me never to mention the subject[aa] to you.

Mrs. Burton, replied he, with surprise; and by what authority, does she pretend to controul my curiosity? Mrs. Burton, doctor, is a stranger to what regards me, and ought not to prevent you from answering me. I beg you will immediately acquaint me who that woman is, of whom I have heard such strange accounts?

What, have you not seen her? No – But you have not a doubt who she is, I suppose? No – I really cannot guess. Well then, Sir Edmond, you will smile, for I am certain that woman must have been one whom you was too much attached to not to have known her, notwithstanding her disguise; for she possesses one of those figures which are not easily forgot. Really, doctor, you have roused my curiosity; and it will not again slumber till it is in some measure gratified. – You will then at least inform me of her name? Yes, that which she was called, but not her real name.

What, did she conceal it then? I alone possess her confidence in that respect. – Dear doctor, she said, in the softest tone, and with the most enchanting expression, do not betray me, do not mention my name. As to that, she may be perfectly satisfied I shall keep her secret. So then you do know who she is? No; she desired me not to ask her; and who would have had the cruelty to hurt her, who was already so much afflicted. But what could affect her so much? What, can you not find that out neither? – Why, she wept at your sufferings, and the fear of your dying; Oh! how many tears the poor thing shed. Though so delicate, she would never permit any other to sit up with you at night.

Well, it is inconceivable, exclaimed Sir Edmond, much agitated; and I have not any method by which I can ascertain who she is. – Do you not know what is become of her, doctor? Oh, dear no, as soon as you was pronounced out of danger, she disappeared very early one morning, without speaking to any person, or requiring any recompence for her trouble; and she has never been heard of since. But certainly she must have been seen by some one in the house; did no on know her? No, for she never left your apartment; and no one ever entered it, but myself and Goodwin. Though Ann pretends to have seen her through the key hole, making strange gestures; so that since, she is convinced she was a witch. But I never credit such nonsense;[137] those eyes so gentle, and so tender, perhaps –

I must absolutely endeavour to penetrate this mystery, interrupted Sir Edmond, speaking to himself. A woman so disguised, who was so distressed! – it must – ! it can be no other! But what a recollection arises to damp this hope, whose distant ray gleamed o'er my heart. Did I not hear at Aberthney that she had never left Mrs. St. Clare's? Did I not myself observe her walking under the trees with that hateful – ?

But when you was dictating the letter to that Malvina, of whom you was perpetually talking, continued the doctor, her grief appeared much increased, and she sobbed aloud! I fancy there was some little jealousy lurking! – for she was then most affected and wept the most, when you addressed any tender epithets to that favored lady.

This name always follows me, said Sir Edmond, rising and returning to the walk which led to the house. From all that I hear, and all that I feel,[138] the remembrance of Malvina will ever rise superior to every other pleasure; and notwithstanding all my efforts, she will always maintain her station in my heart.[139] But there is a necessity for an immediate elucidation of this enigma, which certainly conceals something very extraordinary. Yet, what interest can I have in it? It was not her who was thus concealed; but no matter, I will be certain at least.

As he ended these words, he entered the ball-room, and was silently crossing it, in order to go out; when Mrs. Fenwick, who penetrated his design, immediately flew after him, with an intention of detaining him. Where are you going? said she, with a kind smile; you will soon return. Certainly, he replied; without knowing what he said. You will be my partner, will you not? She was going to say, that was what she most wished; when she perceived Mrs. Burton coming towards them, to speak to Sir Edmond. She therefore retired.

I hope, said she, with an air of authority, you will not forget that Lady Mary Summerhill expects your hand for the evening. Present my compliments to her, he replied, quite absorbed, I shall be with her in a moment. He walked out of the room, ran down stairs, and in less than five minutes he was at Mrs. Moody's.

CHAP. XIII.

The shortest and happiest.

I wish to speak with your mistress directly, said Sir Edmond to the servant, who opened the door. I will inform her, sir, replied she; will you please to walk into the parlour? Shall I find Mrs. Moody there? no, sir, she is up stairs – looking more at him, than attentive to what he said; but I will go and let her know. I shall be with her sooner than you, said he, impatiently; and running up stairs, he opened the first door he came to. The room was nearly dark, except the faint glimmering of a lamp, which hung on the staircase, which, as he opened the door, permitted him to distinguish a woman sitting near the window, with her back towards him, and her arm resting on a table, as if lost in the deepest reflection.

Is Mrs. Moody here? said Sir Edmond, in a gentle voice: at the sound, the person uttered an exclamation! and, rising with precipitation, overturned the table; and raising her hands to Heaven, Oh! Great God, I thought it was him. Sir Edmond was struck at the sound of that loved voice, and knew it was Malvina. He fell at her feet, and rising again, pressed her with transport to his bosom, repeating a thousand times, it is her! – it is Malvina! my tender, my beloved Malvina! she did not withdraw from him; mutual sentiments united them.

Suspicion, reproach, grief,[140] all were obliterated. – Without being mentioned, every thing was understood intentively; what occasion was there for an explanation? – they loved each other, they were certain of it, and that was sufficient; their tears fell together, love absorbed them;[141] and the universe was annihilated.

I do not pretend to describe the scene, as it is one of those where expression must fail, and which a refined and delicate soul, such as Malvina possessed, could alone feel.[142] It is the great passions which can call forth the energy of eloquence, but when they have arrived to their particular height, expression makes a pause, and silence is most eloquent; and these mute scenes give the sublime of happiness. – It may naturally be imagined, that on Sir Edmond's finding Malvina, he soon forgot that he was expected at Mrs. Burton's.

With what rapture and gratitude did he contemplate that beloved woman! whose generous tenderness could find force sufficient to return to a house, which she had been partly compelled to leave; and who, for his sake, had braved[143] even death. When the first effusions of their joy was a little calmed, they mutually relieved their oppressed hearts; they wept at the recollection of those moments, when Sir Edmond had nearly recognised his attentive nurse: she explained the reasons of her silence, and her lover approved every thing.[144]

At such a moment there was no cause for blame; all appeared perfectly right; they felt so happy, that not any additional circumstance could have rendered them more so. He quitted her with extreme reluctance for the present, but it was only to see her again. Without saying it, they each felt they could not live separate any longer. They were conscious that a thousand obstacles must prevent their union, yet they imagined they might be overcome.

On his return to Mrs. Burton's, he had to sustain her haughty reproaches, the tender complaints of Mrs. Fenwick, and the disdainful silence of Lady Mary Summerhill. He paid not the least attention to any thing; he never answered any of them, every thing appeared indifferent to him; he had ceased to live for that day – he should not see Malvina till the next.

He went therefore every morning to see her, and the exquisite pleasure of being together, was so much increased by the pains they had endured, that they thought only of enjoying it. They were sufficiently happy in beholding, in loving, and in expressing their affection. In this sweet intercourse the time passed so swiftly, that they never remarked[ab] with what velocity he winged his rapid flight; and days that appeared but as moments, succeeded to those hours, which seemed as ages. Though Malvina was so much absorbed by her affection, yet the idea of Louisa often obtruded itself; she could never forget the melancholy situation of that unfortunate woman, and more than once, these painful recollections deprived her of the pleasure she enjoyed in Sir Edmond's conversation.

She at length could no longer conceal how much these thoughts occupied her attention, and resolved to speak to him on the subject. On hearing her enquiries, he blushed, hesitated, and, taking both hands of his friend, and pressing them to his heart, he said, you shall know every thing; from henceforth I will never conceal any thing from you.

But, Malvina, on hearing what I formally was, do not forget what you have made me at present. Do not forget that Edmond, now esteemed by Malvina,[145] is no longer that giddy, inconstant, perjured, insensible Edmond, which he was formerly. Oh! my Malvina, thanks, ten thousand thanks, as a preface to you, for the vices which you have so completely cured in me. What is it you require? and what is it you fear? Edmond, replied she sighing! Do you not know what lengths my heart has gone for you?

Alas! whatever may be the vices which you are to acknowledge, though they may undoubtedly afflict me greatly, they cannot obliterate my affection. Recollect also, Malvina, continued he, that it is to her, whose esteem I prize more than existence, that I have the courage to confess my crimes. But sooner than not avow the truth, I am resolved to run the risque of your contempt, that I may at last be more deserving of you: I perhaps expose myself to the hazard of losing you for ever.

Edmond, said she, smiling; is there any occasion for your wishing to seduce your judge? Confide alone in my tenderness, as a shield for your defence; it is that which will extenuate your faults, and excuse your errors. No one will be more ingenuous than myself[ac] in diving for reasons, to make you appear less guilty; and certainly, no one has more sincere wishes to find you so.

Edmond, then certain of his power, seated himself by Malvina, with his eyes fixed on her face, that he might observe and penetrate the slightest of her feelings, which would be reflected on the mirror of her expressive countenance, by the recital which he was going to communicate.

CHAP. XIV.

The history of Louisa.

It is now above seven years since Mrs. Burton made a journey to London. As she was the only one I ever had to observe my conduct, I led a dissipated and giddy life, indulging in every pleasure to excess, though I was scarcely nineteen, and my aunt trembled for the consequences this might produce in future. She consequently wished me to attend on this journey, and I should have consented with pleasure, if Mr. St. Clare, one of my friends, had not prevailed upon me to remain with him in Edinburgh, as he was to be married in a few days. I therefore bid adieu to Mrs. Burton; and in a little time after, my friend presented me to his wife.

Mrs. St. Clare was then of the same age with myself, and in all the bloom of youth and beauty: she pleased me, and I determined to make her love me. Do not exclaim against me, Malvina; at that time I had no idea of the virtue of woman; I only thought that the best of them were those who had the fewest lovers; and with such ideas,[146] it appeared a matter of little importance I thought for my friend, whether it was myself or any other who was in love with his wife. However, Mrs. St. Clare resisted all my attempts: I found she possessed a mind fraught with an enthusiasm for virtue, which I considered as prejudice, and which I imagined would be very easy to overcome. I found she was tenderly attached to her husband, and so far from my making any impression on her heart, I was every day more distant from succeeding; and as I loved her, it afflicted me extremely.[147]

At that time, I was firmly persuaded there was not any woman who had not moments of weakness,[ad] or any virtue which would not yield to perseverance and opportunity: I therefore had not a doubt, but that if I would take the trouble, I should in the end triumph over Mrs. St. Clare. I had not made the least progress in gaining her affection, when a new object created new desires in my heart. Mrs. St. Clare had sent for her sister to be with her. I then, for the first time, saw Louisa; she was only sixteen; she was beautiful, innocent, and tender; her large blue eyes expressed a voluptuousness which her heart was unconscious of. I had only to speak, to gain her affections; and she returned my love so cordially, that the facility with which I gained it, might, perhaps, have cooled my ardor, if Mrs. St. Clare, uneasy at my attention to her sister, believing that she could not rely upon my principles, had not nearly prevented her from speaking to me. This obstacle immediately re-animated all my tenderness. – I spoke, I pressed, I complained, and Louisa was very soon all my own. But possession, in a short time, extinguished that irritation of the senses,[148] which I had falsely mistaken for love; and I was soon powerfully convinced I never had loved Louisa. I saw her but seldom; she was consequently alarmed at it, and imparted her fears to me. Her reproaches fatigued me; I relinquished seeing her; she became desperate and half distracted; she made her sister a confidant of all that had happened, deeply repenting her weakness, and the consequences which she suspected would follow.

The instant of her being acquainted with it, Mrs. St. Clare wrote to me with all the indignation of unsullied honor, in order to make me blush for my conduct; pointing out the only way which I could repair it. The absolute manner in which she expressed herself, offended me extremely, for I was resolved not to marry so early, and particularly a girl who had yielded to me with so little reluctance; yet, I wished to save her from dishonor, and I found means to marry her to another. Mrs. St. Clare's letter reached me at a relation's, where I had gone to pass a few days.

Lord Westbrook,[149] a near relation of my own,[150] was a batchelor of sixty years of age, very rich, and who had promised me all his fortune. He had remained unmarried, from his being of so changeable and capricious a character, that he never could meet with a woman who pleased him two days together. I formed the idea of his marrying Louisa.

I began my attack by praising her; I attributed to her every quality which I knew was most agreeable to Lord Westbrook; and I concluded, by giving him so animated a picture of the happiness which such an event would spread over his future life, that notwithstanding his whimsical character, the picture touched him which I had painted; and particularly with a proposal, which was in his opinion, the greatest, the most convincing proof of disinterested friendship; in recommending his marrying, and by that means deprive myself of his immense fortune, which was to have been my inheritance. This, which he stiled my noble generosity, was the only reason which determined him. He imagined that I must be positively certain that he would be happy, since I could so willingly sacrifice all his fortune, to contribute to it.

Possessed with this idea, he became as eager as I could wish him, to be introduced to Louisa.[151] He wished to set out immediately for Edinburgh, and we no sooner arrived there, than I waited on Mrs. St. Clare, to know when he might be introduced. I found her alone: Louisa had set out that day for her father's seat; and Mrs. St. Clare was to join her in a short time. I made the most of this interview, and acquainted her in the most delicate and polite manner, that I never could make Louisa my wife; and intimated Lord Westbrook's proposals. She rejected them with contempt. She said as I was the person who had ruined Louisa, I was the only one who ought to shield her from dishonor. That the reasons which I gave could not excuse me, or extenuate the injury; and the reparation which I had dared to offer, was mean, despicable, and beneath a man of honor. She said that she would never consent to witness her sister's being united to another, when she knew she was solely attached to me.[152]

Irritated by her refusal, which was increased by the manner in which it was expressed; I replied that I never could love Louisa again, as she possessed but little of my esteem; I therefore never would marry her; and she ought, for the sake of her sister's honor, to endeavour to press her to accept the only resource which was left. That I would myself speak to Louisa, and I was certain I should gain her consent to the union.

At these words, Mrs. St. Clare regarded me with a look of the utmost contempt, saying, as I could not prevent the shame, nor all my efforts save her from your fatal seductions, or even incline you to render her the justice which honor demands; you may at least be certain that I will save her from the disgrace you intend her. I shall endeavour to prevent her from concealing her fault by a falsity. I am going to her, and will use my best efforts to strengthen her by all the fortitude I am mistress of, and we shall see whether you can have equal power over her a second time. Finding Mrs. St. Clare so resolute, I discontinued my persuasions, for, according to the principles which I professed at that time, hers only appeared to me as romantic in the most extravagant degree:[lii] I therefore made not the least scruple of deceiving her, and, to prevent her from having any influence over her sister, I engaged Lord Westbrook to set out at the same time for the seat of her father, Mr. Transuley.

We travelled all night, and arrived there early the next day. Happily, Louisa was in her own room when we were introduced to her father, and she had time to recover her surprise prior to her appearing before us. Though she did not make her appearance till several hours had elapsed after our arrival, yet, on entering, she was so extremely shocked and astonished at seeing me, that she had not the courage to raise her eyes, or utter a sentence: her timidity, which Lord Westbrook mistook for delicate reserve; her guilty blushes appeared to him the modest bloom of innocence; in short, the embarrassment which was visible in her countenance, and the coolness with which she treated me, delighted him so much, that I could scarcely prevent him from making proposals immediately to her father for his charming daughter; but the most important point was to be settled, which, in order to succeed in, it was necessary that I should be alone with her. I therefore secretly conveyed a note into her hand, wherein I informed her of particulars which were so essential to the happiness of us both, that I wished to have a little conversation with her some time that night, and that a nod of approbation was to be my answer.[153]

At midnight, I repaired to her room, and after the tenderest caresses, I explained the motive which prevented my marrying her, and my intention of introducing Lord Westbrook. At first, she loudly exclaimed against me, and shed a torrent of tears; I soon calmed her grief, and she at last seemed to acquiesce with my reasons, but chiefly from my entreaties, and perhaps the assurance which I gave her of seeing her very often when she was married.

The next day Mr. Transuley, on receiving the proposals of Lord Westbrook, blinded by his rank and fortune, called his daughter, and commanded her to receive the hand of this gentleman: he found her ready to obey him. She,[154] however, wished to wait the arrival[ae] of Mrs. St. Clare, and her father so far coincided with her, that he[155] would not conclude this affair without informing her of it. But, as I much feared the steady firmness of this young and virtuous woman might destroy all I had done, I pressed Lord Westbrook, who was as much inclined as I could wish to hasten the marriage. I informed her father, that, from the well known character of his lordship, it would be impolitic in him to give him time to reflect, as, perhaps, by to-morrow, he might relinquish the pursuit which he was so anxious to accomplish to-day: that he might very plainly perceive, throughout all this affair, that I was actuated by the most sincere and disinterested friendship, as by the marriage of Lord Westbrook, I should be deprived of all his estate: that I knew him sufficiently to be certain that if he did not marry Miss Transuley, he never would marry at all; and fearing he might change the fancy he had taken to her by one of those fits of caprice, to which he was so subject, he might renounce her as sudden as he had been eager in demanding her, if it was not concluded immediately.

These considerations determined Mr. Transuley, and, yielding to my advice, as well as Lord Westbrook's, he sent for his lawyer, and the settlements were signed that evening, and the next morning, at eight o'clock, his lordship received the hand of Louisa, in the chapel belonging to the mansion.

CHAP. XV.

Continuation.

The ceremony was but just ended, when Mrs. St. Clare arrived. It is impossible for me to describe either her astonishment, or her grief, on finding her sister married. The dreadful look which she directed to me was sufficient to understand what she felt; yet, as there was no re-calling what was passed, she was obliged to dissemble her uneasiness, and, during the rest of the day, assumed the appearance of tranquillity.

Towards evening, she withdrew to her room, with Louisa;[156] and desired that I would follow them. I went: when I entered, I found Louisa pale, dejected, and her eyes void of their usual lustre; she appeared smiling under despair.[157] Mrs. St. Clare seemed distressed, yet her countenance was animated by contending emotions, though her eyes were suffused with tears. She instantly seized my hand, and leading me to Louisa: Behold! and contemplate the victim of your perfidy, she exclaimed; feast your inhuman eyes on the sorrows which oppress her. Behold! there, the fearful contest between love and duty; and remain unaffected, if you can, at those evils which you have occasioned. Sir Edmond, my sister was innocent, and you have dishonored her; she was open and sincere; but now your perfidious advice has condemned her to the dreadful necessity of deceiving the man who this morning received her vows: yet that is not sufficient to satisfy you, but presuming on the licentious attachment which your insidious arts have inspired,[liii] you wish to embitter all the rest of her life, by engaging her in all the guilty horrors of an adulterous connection.

The unhappy creature, blinded by her passion, ceased to behold her crime, or rather you have made her cherish it; and she has thrown herself, with joy, into an abyss, when she thought you would be with her. But, since I have informed her, that so far from your wishing to ruin yourself on her account, you had confessed to me that you did not even love her: when I proved to her that if she had been dear to you, nothing could have prevented you from marrying her: now that she is convinced that it is merely from indifference that you have drawn her into this guilty snare, she trembles at the lengths she has gone; and that virtue, which was nearly extinguished, is now re-kindled in her bosom. Ah! you now behold her shuddering and agonised under the weight of her remorse; she is now endeavouring to rise superior to her weakness, and will for ever abjure her guilty attachment.

Edmond, will you attempt to prevent her? after having sullied the sweetest days of this unfortunate creature: Will you not consent to let her enjoy the remainder of her life in peace? Alas! I am but too conscious that neither my advice, her duty, nor even her virtue, can save her from your seducing arts; and that if it is your intention, you will yet complete her ruin. Therefore, what I have said, is not to be construed as threats, but as entreaties and prayers, which I fervently address to you. I no longer invoke your justice, I only implore your pity. Oh! Edmond, it is not as a passionate lover that I speak to you, but as a man of honor,[158] that I demand this as a favour for my sister; for as yet you have never evinced either one or the other, by her.

But, if every sentiment of humanity is not totally extinct in your heart, you will permit yourself to be touched by the despair in which you behold her; and by the humiliation which I have submitted to on her account. As Mrs. St. Clare concluded these words, she fell at my feet; I hastily raised her, with emotion and respect. Though I was rather hurt on hearing her accuse me of wanting honor, respecting my future approaches to Louisa.[159]

I replied, addressing myself to Louisa: You appeared, my amiable friend, to be convinced by the reasons which I assigned, and which prevented my marrying you; also of the superior advantages attached to your union with Lord Westbrook. I therefore cannot imagine how Mrs. St. Clare can have induced you to change your opinion in this respect. – Whatever it may be, yet, if[160] you think me guilty, I will not pretend to vindicate myself.

Your peace requires that I should never see you more. – I will to-morrow leave this place. Do you exact any more from me? said I, to Mrs. St. Clare. Yes, she replied, it is necessary that you should promise on your honor, carefully to avoid every place where you are likely to meet my sister; and that you will never betray, by a word or look, the slightest suspicion of the fatal connection which has existed between you.

I shall not see her any more,[161] replied I, haughtily; therefore, why do you think it necessary to caution me in this manner? I defy any woman, who has had an affection for me, ever to have reason to complain of my rectitude and honor, in that respect. And is it here that you dare to make that bold assertion? said Mrs. St. Clare, raising her hands with contempt.

Oh! my sister, cried the tender Louisa, sobbing; do not thus despise my Edmond, and recollect, that if he has not thought me worthy of sacrificing his liberty for my sake, at least he has made me one of an immense fortune. I know it, replied Mrs. St. Clare; I know, and allow, that in some instances, Edmond possesses a great and generous soul; for if he had not, how could he have seduced you? But they are even more pernicious than his vices, from the dangerous use which he makes of them; they almost render him hateful. But from henceforth all disputes of the kind will be useless. We have nothing more to say, Edmond; than, that you will depart as soon as possible. Go, fly to that brilliant world, whose deceitful pleasures will soon obliterate from your mind, the remembrance of our sorrows – Though I hope it may not always have the power of suppressing your remorse. Adieu; and may this moment be the last in which I behold you together.

I left them, and the next day, after taking leave of Mr. Transuley and Lord Westbrook, I set out for London, to join Mrs. Burton, where I passed several months in the most brilliant circles, and was so well received by the most amiable women, that I very soon forgot that Louisa existed. Towards the end of the autumn, my aunt proposed my accompanying her to Bath; as it was the season when all persons of rank resorted to that place. I therefore eagerly accepted her offer; for at that time, my dear Malvina, I was so profligate, that any thing which gave the idea of novelty and dissipation, appeared to me the only real enjoyment of life. I did not then know that dissipation was to be found every where; but felicity only in one place. My heart was then a stranger to love, and ever would have continued so, had I not beheld Malvina!

Oh! Edmond, said she, you can easily read my heart; and there behold that the affection with which Malvina has inspired you, absolves you against her will, from some of your vices. But continue your recital, and inform me in what manner this interesting Louisa proceeded; that she was obliged at last to conceal herself from every eye.

On my arrival at Bath, continued Sir Edmond; I was informed that Lord Westbrook was there, with his young wife. This distressed me greatly, yet I did not think their being there ought to oblige me to quit Bath. That I might keep my promise inviolable, I determined to see Louisa as seldom as possible; and not at all, if I could with politeness avoid it. But I was not permitted to execute my plan as I wished; for Mrs. Burton, who was ignorant of my connection with Lady Westbrook, asked me to attend her on a visit to her; and as I had no plausible excuse for my declining it, I was necessitated to accompany her.

As Louisa had heard of my arrival in Bath, she therefore expected to see me; yet the agitation she evinced at my entrance, gave an animation and brilliancy to her complexion, and a vivacity and grace to her manners, which I had never before observed, and which rendered her extremely alluring. She particularly avoided speaking to me, and affected to treat me with marked indifference; yet I could very easily see that this behaviour was not assumed without an effort; that I still retained her affection.

I regarded her more attentively; and she never had appeared to possess so many charms. She was grown taller, she had more assurance in her air; her countenance had more expression, and her complexion appeared more brilliant. Besides, she was advanced in her pregnancy,[af] which gave her an interest which I could not resist. I met her at all the public places, where she excited universal attention. I frequently went to see her, and several times found her alone. I shall not enter into all the particulars which again gave us an opportunity of being connected. I shall only say, that Louisa, more affectionate, more weak than ever; forgot every duty for my sake, and gave me all those rights, which her union had deprived me of.

You condemn me severely, Malvina; I can easily read in your eyes the indignation which my conduct inspires; but how much more blameable will you think me, when I inform you, that it was neither from any love which I felt for Louisa, nor from any interest which she inspired; but the mere vanity of daring to break my promise. I certainly could have resisted the wishes, which Louisa's charms had re-kindled; but as she eclipsed most of the women in Bath; and all the men boasted of her discretion, and complained of her indifference; that was sufficient for me, and the pride of triumphing in the eyes of every one, obliterated every other consideration. Our connection lasted some time; and the confidence Lord Westbrook reposed in her, removed every obstacle.

I began to be seriously disgusted, when an admirer of Louisa's, whom she had treated with some severity, found out her conduct, and developed our intrigue; and immediately acquainted her lord of it. He pretended to disbelieve this tale; however, he wished to ascertain the fact himself; and as his extreme confidence had made us neglectful of every precaution, it was very easy for him to surprise us. I cannot describe the excess of his fury; as he had not even suspected it, his misfortune was the more insupportable, and he was determined to publicly revenge himself.

But from his singular caprice, and whimsical disposition, which was the most conspicuous feature in his character, his rage turned almost entirely on his wife; and suppressing his fury for the present, he came to seek me, and told me, that if I would consent to assist him in procuring a divorce[162] from Lady Westbrook, and support before a court of justice, that I was the father of the child, with which she was now pregnant, he would still retain his former friendship for me, and that I should become heir to all his fortune.

I rejected his proposal with contempt,[ag] and endeavoured to turn all his anger upon myself; by assuring him, Lady Westbrook had for a long time been deaf to my intreaties; and that I had used every possible artifice to seduce her. – That she would have been yet innocent, if I had not made use of violence to triumph over her. That I was incapable of affirming what he required of me; for that the moment of weakness which I had surpassed her in,[163] was the only one she could reproach herself with – That the child which she was going to bring into the world, was as likely to be his, and consequently must be his only heir.

He would not give me time to finish, but interrupting me with fury, he said; As I still wished to deceive him, I should have better instructed my infamous accomplice; for she had not denied her scandalous adultery to him; and that I should at least have desired her to conceal, that she was dishonored, when you had the perfidy to engage me to give her my hand. I frightened Louisa by my menaces; and the weak and guilty creature has confessed every thing to me. I know when your criminal attachment and connection commenced with her, and you may rest assured, that I will never acknowledge the infamous fruit of your amours, as my child; and I once more propose it to you, to assist me in my revenge, and I will forgive all you have done. I have no other witness of Louisa's crime; serve me therefore; accuse her, and—

If any other but yourself, I hastily answered, had dared to make me such a proposal, I would have answered him with my sword; but as I have injured you, and more particularly from the respect I feel for your age, I decline to punish you, as I otherwise would the insolence of a demand, which insinuates, that you think me capable of dishonoring my name for the prospect of your contemptible fortune. Do not fear that I shall repeat this proposal a third time, replied his lordship, with a gloomy calmness; I have now done with you. But since you refuse to oblige me, by joining in a public trial; promise me at least that you will bury this infamous affair in oblivion?

I promised with an oath: when I in return, wished him to treat his wife with gentleness, and generosity. He pressed my hand with a convulsive emotion, saying in a terrible voice, accompanied with a frightful smile, that I need be under no apprehension for Louisa's fate. That he was convinced, by the sacrifice I made for her, how very dear she was to me; and that in a little time I should have nothing to fear on her account. I desired him to elucidate his meaning? He replied, he had no other explanation to give.

As I observed that all my solicitude respecting Louisa, only appeared to irritate him, I remained silent; he then left me; the next day I heard that he had set out in the night, with his wife, for a distant estate which he possessed in Northumberland.

This adventure depressed me for several days, so much, that I forgot every pleasure. Mrs. Burton, who had heard a faint rumour of my intrigue with Lady Westbrook, fancied I was distressed at her departure; and, in order to amuse me, she proposed our returning to London. I consented, and I confess to my shame, that I was not long in that capital before I soon lost every recollection of Louisa. I renewed my former connections, and engaged in new ones. – I also refused to accompany my aunt when she wished to return to Edinburgh. I acknowledge I felt a secret joy on seeing her depart. For though I never submitted very quietly to her commands; yet, she was the only check which could interrupt me in my career; and I was no sooner relieved from her presence, than I resigned myself, without reserve, to all those licentious pleasures, which wild and ungovernable youth calls happiness. But which, when the heart is really touched, it regrets ever having known; and must ever remember with contempt.

Oh! Malvina, deign to draw a veil over this dishonorable, shameful part of my life – That your chaste looks may turn from, and your pure thoughts never dwell on such scenes. Be assured, those insensible beings, who consume life in the pursuit of gross and voluptuous pleasures, deserve more pity than anger; for by resigning themselves to the gratification of the senses, they leave nothing for the heart; and there remains a void, which all their numerous enjoyments can never fill. Their licentiousness by degrading them, deprives them of the power of loving, without their wishing it.[164] – Mentally tormented, by the idea of their degradations, and their noble origin; they would wish to be less than men, that they might be freed from their own consciences; and plunge without restraint or remorse, into their vicious excesses. But in vain, for they cannot extinguish that spark[165] which will ever live in their bosoms, to their latest hour; they feel those sensations within, which pursues them continually, condemns, and ever reproaches them.

Oh! Malvina, my benefactress, and my friend; without you, such had been my fate – without you, my heart would ever have remained a stranger to love. It would never have known that supreme felicity of partaking in the virtuous interchange of mutual sentiments.[166] It is you who have saved me from ruin; and it is you, whom I alone contemplate, as the object of my most fervent love, as the most perfect of creatures. I ought to adore you, as one to whom I am more indebted than the Divinity himself; since He only gave me life;[ah] but you have given me happiness: and a desire to merit it.[167] In speaking thus, Edmond leaned his face upon Malvina's hands, bathing them with his tears.

She looked at him in silence, with such a look! – it spoke volumes. After a pause,[168] Sir Edmond continued his narration. I had been invited to a superb entertainment, given by the Duchess of Peterborough. This lady so much celebrated, and so handsome, easily enflamed the passions of a man, who was only delighted with novelty. At supper, I was placed next herself; I entertained her in whispers – I saw that she pretended to be affected; and desirous of gaining an attachment, which I did not feel; and I foresaw the moment when her coquetry would crown all my wishes.

At that instant, I heard some person near me,[liv] name Lady Westbrook. At this name I turned involuntarily, and shuddered with fear, on hearing them say, that she was dead. The particulars they gave of this fatal event, too certainly confirmed it. From that moment, I became insensible to the pleasures which surrounded me, and to all be polite and sparkling attentions of the tender duchess. It was not that I loved Louisa, but the idea of having blighted this fair flower in her early bloom; and having contributed to a premature death; occasioned me infinite regret and remorse. London had no longer any dissipations which could amuse my mind, and I determined to leave it.

As I had to pass through Northumberland, in my way to Scotland; the desire of knowing the particulars of the death of the unfortunate Louisa, determined me to pass near the estate which she had inhabited, in that county; and where I was informed she had died. I proposed to spend a day there, in case of Lord Westbrook's absence; after leaving my chaise at Durham, which was the nearest city to Westbrook-hall; and where Louisa was the object of universal regret. I went on foot to the castle, the road which led to it was intricate; I had also to cross high and gloomy mountains, and the road passed round in a serpentine direction, through dry brushwood; a thick fog coming on, rendered the way still more difficult – and I lost my path. I walked some time without seeing the vestige of any human dwelling. All appeared uncultivated and wild. Towards evening, the fog being a little dispersed, I espied a village at some distance, and I endeavoured to find a road that would lead me to it; when crossing some wild broom, which covered the mountains, I perceived a woman at some distance, who appeared very well dressed; and she was endeavouring with apparent difficulty, to reach a cottage, which was quite by itself, at some distance.

The form of this person agitated me in a very singular manner; and I fancied it was Mrs. St. Clare. I was tortured by doubt, and immediately flew after her. I soon reached her, and the noise of my footsteps caused her to turn; I was convinced she also knew me. She trembled, and uttered a fearful exclamation. Then said, Ah! my God, what fatal power is it which leads this infernal man to pursue me wherever I go?

Mrs. St. Clare, I replied, with an agitation which scarcely allowed me the power of speech; I was going to Westbrook-hall, a prey to the most poignant remorse; that I might shed those tears over the tomb of Louisa, which her death has caused to flow. I have lost my way; I am but too happy in meeting with you. Ah! since I see you here, a flush of hope has penetrated my soul, that Louisa still exists. No, no, no, said Mrs. St. Clare, with a hurried voice, looking round her with terror.

Do not conceal any thing from me, replied I, in a determined voice; the secret equally interests me as yourself, and I must know it; I will discover it whether you wish it or not. I have a presentiment, that I shall find in that low and solitary cottage, the information which you refuse to give me; I shall therefore hasten there. Stop, stop, said she; endeavouring to detain me, and letting my arm drop: she continued; well, go cruel man, and destroy all I have done; but do not hope that you shall ever return your victim again, into the tyrannical power of the man you forced her to marry. Your wish[169] is to hurry her to the tomb, from which I have by little less than a miracle, saved her, from being immured alive.

No, replied I, no; I do not wish to see her; I am satisfied to hear that she yet exists. Oh! my dear Mrs. St. Clare, is it you who have saved her? Is it you to whom I am indebted, for saving me from the terrors of such a repentance: blessed, a thousand times blessed may you be; my kind guardian angel. Leave me – leave me, she replied; your benedictions only shock me. I shall tremble all my life now, for having granted you a confidence which has saved your barbarous heart from the compunction and remorse, which I wished it to feel.

Dear Mrs. St. Clare, said I; why so much anger and vehemence; are the frailties of love such a heinous crime in the eyes of virtue? No, replied she; my unfortunate sister, on the contrary, is the dear object of my regard, and tenderest indulgence. But you, who are ever insensible; who have never felt love, have behaved with so much indifference, as to obliterate every duty. You, who from a motive of the most sordid and infamous interest, of which I believed you incapable till now; have exposed her frailty to her husband.

What a detestable falsehood, and scandalous slander, replied I, with warmth; who has dared to stigmatise me with so horrible an aspersion? Lord Westbrook himself, replied Mrs. St. Clare; and though such a proceeding appeared to me contrary to your character; yet, I am not certain whether it is not an atrocity which I ought to have expected from you. I then related all that had passed between his lordship and myself. I acknowledge, she replied, that the account you have given, appears more credible than that which I have heard. But whether you are guilty or not of the baseness which is imputed to you, neither my contempt or dislike can be increased.[170] Yes, Edmond, I must say, I hate you; as the destroyer of my Louisa; you have embittered the remainder of my life. I candidly confess, interrupted I, that I deserve it from you, and I will not even attempt to extenuate or excuse my conduct; the only favour I intreat of you is to inform me of the particulars of this fatal affair[171] concerning Louisa, and then I will for ever exile myself both from her sight and yours.[172lv]

As soon as her lord had brought his wretched wife to this place, said Mrs. St. Clare, speaking very fast, as if wishing to abridge the recital[173] as much as possible, he confined her in a lonesome tower of the castle, where he declared she should remain for life;[174] that she never should behold the child, of which she was going to be the mother; and she should also be deprived from ever seeing or hearing from any of those friends whom she most valued. These dreadful threats drove Louisa to despair, and sunk her into so gloomy a despondency, that it deprived her of the power of using the means of supporting her lot, or letting me hear from her.

I was then ignorant of what had become of her. I wrote to Bath, in vain. I enquired in Edinburgh of all those persons who were acquainted with Lord Westbrook; also of his servants; but every one was dumb when I mentioned Louisa. At last, by my unremitting endeavours, I gained the information of her being in Northumberland. – I immediately set out. On my arrival, my Lord appeared very much surprised on seeing me, and received me in the most cool and disagreeable manner. As I was determined to disregard this behaviour, I would not appear to observe it, as my anxiety for Louisa was so extreme, and my only wish was to see her: I therefore would not permit myself to be the least frightened at his menacing looks; and my fervent friendship at last prevailed, and I was introduced to my unfortunate sister.

On entering the dreadful apartment where she was immured, I shuddered. Lord Westbrook perceived my terror, and looking at me with a gloomy countenance, said – take particular notice of this asylum; it is where this infamous creature, who has deceived me, shall henceforth live and die; and if I have permitted you to enter it, it is only that your care may preserve and prevent her from dying sooner than she deserves to do. I wish her life to be prolonged, that she may have time sufficient to repent of her crimes. You may continue with her till her confinement, at which time[175] I shall leave this place for a short period; and on my return, you must then resolve never to behold her again: and also the infamous fruit of her dishonor shall be for ever deprived of her caresses. It shall live to be a stigma to its mother, but you shall neither of you ever know its future fate.

On concluding these menacing and terrific words, he left us, and I heard him lock the heavy doors of our prison after him. I threw myself into the arms of my sister, and we mingled our tears together; but these were tears which could afford us no relief in our painful situation. I reflected upon all the most probable means I could possibly devise to save her. I was conscious it would be a useless attempt to make any application to my father; I knew too well how very tenacious he was, and also his strictness and immoveable severity[ai] with regard to every thing relative to morals and behaviour; and, consequently, if he had been informed of my sister's imprudence, he would have been more liable to increase the anger of Lord Westbrook against her, than extenuate it. Yet, I was a prisoner, and deprived of communication with any person whatever.

At last, his Lordship left the castle.[176] This circumstance, added to my arrival, afforded my sister so much pleasure, that it advanced the time of her pregnancy. She was therefore taken very suddenly;[177] and, notwithstanding the dreadful injunctions of her husband to keep us strictly confined from all intercourse with any of the household,[aj] yet they could not refuse sending for a medical man; whom, on his entrance, I observed with particular attention. He appeared to be modest, sensible, and worthy. I therefore opened my heart to him, made him acquainted with Louisa's situation and destiny, and conjured him to assist me, if possible, in saving her from such a wretched fate. Affected, even to tears, at her misfortunes, he most readily promised to make use of every effort in his power to accomplish my wishes: in consequence of which, when he went down, he declared that Lady Westbrook was in the greatest danger, and that he did not think she could survive. This account very much alarmed the persons who were to guard us, and from that hour they began to relax in their vigilance. I was therefore permitted to go and come whenever I pleased; and by that means I made all the arrangements, and settled every thing which I could wish, or was necessary to the plan which I had determined upon. I procured a very honest and good woman as a nurse, whom I secretly engaged in my interest, and who is the owner of that cottage you see there.[ak]

As soon as Louisa was capable of being removed without danger,[178] our good doctor gave out that she was past all recovery, and that it was necessary he should pass the night with me and the nurse, as he could not think of leaving her in the agonies of death. This was the opportunity fixed upon for sending her away with her infant. A chaise, which the doctor had procured, and was ready at the park gate, carried her to the asylum which she now inhabits, and a figure, which we dressed for that purpose, replaced Louisa in her bed. The next morning, my sister's death was reported to every one in the castle, and I also gave out that I insisted upon being permitted myself to place her in her coffin; in consequence of which I did as I pleased, without being interrupted. I therefore carefully wrapt the figure in a shroud, and had it buried, to avoid all suspicion.

As soon as I had fulfilled the last duties to the supposed remains of my sister, I immediately left the castle, and hastened to my dear Louisa, whose weak state of health has never permitted her to leave that cottage, which is rather more than six miles[179] from Westbrook-hall. She has indeed been so very ill these three weeks, that I dare not suffer her to be removed elsewhere: yet I sincerely hope she may live, and that I shall find her a secure, though unknown, retreat, where she may pass the rest of her melancholy days in peace, and enjoy the only comforts which are now left her, which are the company of her son, and the visits of her sister.

On finishing this recital, Mrs. St. Clare burst into tears. Mine also fell at the idea of Louisa's wretched fate, and the existence of her son, who was also mine! I informed Mrs. St. Clare of my intention of providing for the mother and her infant, and hoped she would at least permit me to have that satisfaction; and I intreated her to take the trouble of receiving yearly whatever sum she thought proper to mention for that purpose, and to conceal it from Louisa, for fear it might give her pain, or create any disagreeable sensation from knowing who it came from; but she was so far from accepting such a proposition, that she immediately rejected it, saying, that as she alone had the consolation of saving her sister, she only should enjoy the sweet satisfaction of supporting her, and that if she should ever wish to divide that pleasure with another, that I could not surely have such an idea that it would be with the cruel author of all her misery. I then interrupted her, intreating that she would only suffer me to deposit a particular sum yearly, which I had destined for Louisa, that it might accumulate for the benefit of her son, and a certain resource for him. This proposal she at last consented to, and we then entered into a sacred promise, that no consideration should ever tempt us to reveal this dreadful secret which she had confided to me. I then took a melancholy leave of her, and went forward to Edinburgh.

Some months after my return, I heard of the death of Mr. St. Clare, and also that his widow, who was much distressed by the unfortunate situation of her husband's affairs, had, by the assistance of her father, just been enabled to re-purchase the estate of St. Clare[180] (for which she had a particular partiality) and which she determined to make her perpetual residence for life. Fearful that her dependent situation might put it out of her power to provide for the support of Louisa, I wrote to her, conjuring her to give me leave to be useful to her sister; but, in a few days after, my letter was returned with contempt, with only two lines, written by Mrs. St. Clare in the envelope, the purport of which was, that all my endeavours had not degraded her sister so low, as to condescend to receive any support from the hand of him was the author of her ruin; that I, of all others, was the last person she should ever wish to accept of any thing from; she therefore intreated me not to force myself on her remembrance, and to reserve all the obligations I wished to confer, for that time when they might be useful to my son. Since then I have never heard a word from Mrs. St. Clare, as she has always avoided answering every letter of enquiry which I wrote concerning Louisa; I did not even know whether that unfortunate victim still existed. I have never seen Lord Westbrook since, who resides on one of his estates, and never visits Edinburgh.

An interval of six years[181] had began to obliterate this mournful event from my remembrance, when your sudden acquaintance with Mrs. St. Clare awakened all my fears, and opened all my wounds. What more shall I add, my Malvina? You are acquainted with all that has passed since; you know the fatal interview I had with you at Louisa's, which has been some expiation for my crimes. Ah! you cannot surely have forgot the violent despair which I experienced there; that its effects rent my heart, and conducted me to the gates of death! You have beheld me dying, Malvina, and you have saved me! But how severely shall I regret that kindness which preserved me, if the recital I have been giving you should occasion you to think me so very guilty, that you judge me no longer worthy of you? Oh! Malvina, thou idol of my heart! if I am not to possess your affection, why did you not permit me to die?

Edmond, said she, bathed in tears, your guilt has been almost beyond forgiveness, and I am, without a doubt, equally so, in still retaining my affection for you; but whatever you are, why am I thus fatally attached to you? I can relinquish the idea of seeing you again, can renounce life and happiness, but not my affection! It is here, continued she, pressing her hand to her heart, it is here that it will exist for ever, from which death alone can obliterate it, whatever may have been your crimes, my duties, and my wishes.

Sir Edmond was transported at this affectionate answer. He pressed Malvina to his bosom; and while thus in the company of each other, the remembrance of the past, as well as the fear of the future, vanished before the enjoyment of present happiness; and the heart overflowing with tenderness, experiences every sweet sensation which this life can give, in favour of one object, and scarcely leaves a thought to bestow on the rest of the world.

END OF VOL. III.

H. Reynell, Printer, 21, Piccadilly.

MALVINA,
by Madame C****,

Authoress of Claire d'Albe, and Amelia Mansfield.

Translated from the French,

by Miss Gunning,

in four volumes.

VOL. IV.

London:

printed for T. Hurst, Paternoster-Row;

C. Chapple, Pall-Mall, and Southampton-Row, Russell-Square; and R. Dutton, Gracechurch-Street.

Stower, Printer, Charles-Street, Hatton-Garden.[1]

1803.

CONTENTS OF VOL. IV

MALVINA.

CHAP. I.

A love scene.

While Mrs. St. Clare was under the utmost anxiety and astonishment at not seeing her friend, she wrote to enquire the reason which detained her. This letter awakened Malvina from the pleasing dream in which she had been entranced, and informed her that Sir Edmond was not the only being which existed in the world. Malvina was also acquainted by Mrs. Moody,[2] that Mrs. Burton, surprised at the frequent absence of Sir Edmond, could no longer attribute it to the love of dissipation, as she never met with him in any parties of pleasure; and from that reason she had desired Mrs. Fenwick to follow him, and was assured that he passed whole days at Mrs. Moody's. In consequence of this intelligence, she had charged Tasse to enquire particularly who resided at that house. Malvina became alarmed and uneasy at Mrs. Burton's curiosity. She concluded to answer Mrs.

St. Clare's letter immediately, and felt from this time as if her happiest moments were past, and that it was time to depart. She impatiently waited the time of Sir Edmond's appearance. As soon as he came, she acquainted him with all she had heard, and her determination. And can my Malvina, my tender friend, said Sir Edmond, think of leaving me? – Are we not each of us at liberty, who then ought to prevent us from determining to enjoy happiness with each other? Intoxicated with the pleasure of loving and seeing you every day, I forgot there was any felicity which could exceed that; but the moment is now arrived that must convince me of it. Malvina must then agree to be mine, not only by the invaluable gift of her heart, but also accompanied by her hand and her faith. Do not blush my amiable friend; your delicacy ought not to be alarmed at the happiness of your lover.

Edmond, dear Edmond, said Malvina, I know it, and I am willing to oblige you; and if you require it, I will follow you to morrow to the altar. But when my courage forsakes me, I must have recourse to your generosity. It is from that I must intreat that you will not abuse the power you have over me; and that you will enable me to support my weakness, and recal me to the duties which you have caused me to forget.

Dear Malvina, replied Sir Edmond, who on earth could ever abuse your angelical sweetness? what is there which it cannot overcome? No, never, however I may suffer from my candor, I will never betray your confidence; and nothing shall be concealed from you. I must therefore inform you, that Mrs. Burton has got an order from Lord Sheridan,[3] which gives her the power of taking his daughter from you as soon as you are married. – Ah, my God! exclaimed Malvina, turning pale, Edmond, what is it you have said? It is then settled; I must renounce you! Renounce me, Malvina, fixing his eyes upon her, and pressing both her hands to his bosom, renounce me! what have you dared to utter? how can thy heart have conceived such an idea? – To be separated Malvina! – Ah! do you not feel that from henceforth we must live and die together? Edmond, replied Malvina, much affected – I do not think I could support the misery of never again beholding you. But it is of no consequence; if my life should be the sacrifice of our separation, I shall submit, sooner than behold Frances, that sacred pledge which was confided to me by the purest friendship, resigned to the care of Mrs. Burton. Oh! Heaven, the very idea chills my heart: I should expect the wrath of Heaven[4] would be the consequence of my perjury. What faith could you place in my vows, when you knew I had violated this sacred engagement? What confidence could you place in a woman, who was so weak as to allow passion to usurp the dominion over duty? What happiness could you expect from a being, whose conscience must continually upbraid her?[5]

Malvina, interrupted Sir Edmond, you are too dear to my heart for me to be happy, if I cannot render you so. No, no, do not imagine, that even to gain you, I would hurt the peace of your celestial mind, or irritate the dead, by having that child taken from you? But most beloved of women, you may, though my wife, keep the daughter of thy Clara always with you. I shall enjoy the affectionate attentions you bestow on her, and be happy if you will permit me to partake in them. Ah, Edmond! what a delightful scene do you pourtray; were it possible to realise it, Malvina would give herself to you with transport.

Well, then, Malvina, attend to me, he replied, with animation. If you will agree to meet me the morning after to morrow, at the break of day, at the distance of a mile from Edinburgh, on the sea side, there is an old church which is seldom used now; it was formerly built by the kings of Scotland; and now serves for those who profess our religion.[6] We shall find a catholic priest there, and there it is that I will wait for you; and at the foot of the scared altar Heaven will receive our vows – but the secret shall be known only by him and ourselves. When we leave the church, I will conduct you to a little country seat, which is in a very retired situation, some miles from Edinburgh; which I have purchased privately from one of my friends. I will leave you there, set out for London, fly to Lord Sheridan, introduce myself to him, and inform him myself of our union. He will be affected at our loves, accede to our wishes, by granting us leave to keep his daughter; I shall receive his promise from himself, and also bring a confirmation of it, from under his hand. I will keep it in my bosom as the seal of your happiness, and return to you on the wings of love. Frances will be with you, and you will be mine for ever; for even death cannot separate us, as we shall be united and happy in eternity.[al]

Malvina, astonished beyond expression at what he had been saying, remained motionless without the power of uttering a word; she continued for some moments with her head reclining on her hands, as if meditating what reply she should return.

Edmond, fearful that her reflections would not be favourable to his wishes, conjured her, by the most persuasive intreaties, to explain herself. Fearful of meeting a repulse, as he could not divine her thoughts, yet he could scarcely command the impetuous impatience of his nature from flying out; when Malvina, after a long silence, turned towards him with inimitable grace, downcast eyes, and the vermil tinge of delicacy on her cheeks: – This hand is yours, said she, presenting it to him; but not until your return from London can I consent to give it for ever. Go, then, Edmond, go, and endeavour to persuade Lord Sheridan, which you will very easily, of the false accounts with which he has been abused. It will only be necessary to elucidate every circumstance, to render him favourable to our request. Explain your generous intention in favour of his daughter, and you may be certain that he will resign her to our care. Then Edmond will return to his Malvina, and he will find when she is at liberty, that her heart and hand will both be his.

On finding that she resisted his intreaties, Sir Edmond became irritated on being thus deceived in his hopes. He permitted the violence of his passionate character to display itself without controul; and he exclaimed with vehemence,

Oh! – no no – do not imagine that I will thus leave you! do not hope that I will depart till I have acquired every sacred and inviolable right. Malvina, it is necessary that you should become mine, that if you are to be the victim, I may also. Yes, I declare that you shall be mine, in opposition to all the world.[7]

Edmond, replied Malvina with surprise, accompanied with dignity, what do you hope to obtain from this violent behaviour? Do you imagine I will yield that to fear, which I can withhold from love? Speak no more of love, interrupted he, in a tone of ferocity – I see plainly that you have never loved me. You dare to say that I have never loved you, exclaimed Malvina, joining her hands, and raising them to Heaven. No, you have never loved me, or else my despair would have touched you, my intreaties would have affected you! The remembrance of friendship would have vainly endeavoured to resist my love; in vain would it have arose from the tomb, to assert its power over mine: it never could have overcome the real force of love. But Lady Sheridan, though dead, can preserve a power over you, with which no other can be put in competition; and your tranquil mind has never felt any thing superior to friendship.

He yet dares to say, replied Malvina, in a melancholy tone, that I do not love him. No, you do not love me in the manner I do you. Love does not tyrannise in your soul. You can make it submissive to reason, to circumstances. It never renders you forgetful of any thing. Oh! Edmond, dare to tell me that. If I permitted it to rise superior to duty, could you really then esteem me? Why do you mention esteem; is that sentiment sufficient to engage your attention? Ah! that would never be the object of your regard, if you thought more of love. Have I not then a conscience Edmond, and can we enjoy one pleasure, which its silent reproach will not embitter? Malvina, when love is a flame, which not only warms, but burns, consumes, devours, and evaporates every other effort of the mind, even conscience itself is weakened.

Ah! Edmond, exclaimed Malvina, if you knew how injuriously you judge me, when you appear to doubt my tenderness, you would cease these reproaches. But, then only inform me Malvina, if you do love me, why suffer me to be the prey of such cruel torture? Why will you not accept my vows? Oh thou, dearer to me than life, continued he, pressing her in his arms, – if the sacred engagement, which I so much wish, only alarms you, from the fear that it will not be sufficiently secret, give thyself to me and let us have only Heaven to witness our vows and our happiness.

Edmond – Edmond, replied Malvina, flying from him with terror, perhaps I should be less guilty, as it would then only be the sacrifice of myself. Ah, why should you term it guilt, replied he, with an ardor he could no longer conceal, are you not at liberty? – Are you not your own mistress? – Who is it that dares to controul your actions? Do you fear the public opinion? What is that to the happiness of your lover? – Oh, thou insensible being, exclaimed Malvina, still avoiding him – insensible man, who in thy ungovernable mind, wishes to deprive himself of the most valuable good which can give peace to his life – to rob his wife of her virtue! Blind, thoughtless man, tell me, would you not blush to receive my hand upon such terms?

Oh my Malvina, interrupted he, leave, O leave to vulgar minds these weak and subtle distinctions, these pusillanimous fears;[8] we can follow other laws.[9] Are you to grant only to the laws instituted by man, what the excess of my love could not obtain? No, Malvina, the happiness of possessing you ought to proceed only from your own will![10] Do you not think thus my Malvina, circling his arms round her; but thy silence gives consent; it is understood by thy lover; he wishes for no other reply.

Stop, Edmond, replied she, endeavouring to get from his arms, but all in vain. He held her to his breast, and covered her lips with kisses. Stop, exclaimed Malvina, but he heard her not; his lips had touched hers,[lvi] and no power on earth could restrain his transports. The world was annihilated – he would not listen to any thing. At such a moment, the voice of offended virtue alone had power to restrain him. Leave me, cried Malvina, in that determiend voice which commands and awes into obedience, which phrensy itself can never resist. Edmond was confused, and instantaneously obeyed. She started from him without his daring to detain her. She covered her blushing cheeks and streaming eyes with her handkerchief.[11]

Edmond fell at her feet to obtain her pardon; but she was deaf to his intreaties, she even refused to look at him. Leave me, she said, depart, I will not see you any more until you have recovered your recollection.

In such an ungovernable character as Sir Edmond's, pride often suppresses tenderness. He felt degraded at being obliged to petition so long without effect; and in a voice which expressed both anger and despair, he assured her, that if he departed without obtaining her forgiveness, he would never return again. This threat roused the insulted dignity of Malvina, and without condescending to speak to him, she made a sign with her hand for him to retire. Surprised at observing a haughtiness which equalled his own, he no longer intreated, but immediately went out, nearly overcome by despair. When he got home, he sunk under the violence turbulence of his outrageous passions, and he was seized with a severe fever. Malvina was informed of it, and it overwhelmed her in a moment; every other consideration vanished. She fancied she again beheld him dying, and accused herself of being the cause of his death; and from that time there was not any sacrifice which she would not make, or any duty she would not have relinquished, rather than not preserve the sincerity of her affection.[12]

She wrote to him in these words: 'Edmond live for the sake of thy Malvina, for she exists only for thee. Appoint the place, the time, the hour, when you wish to receive her plighted faith; and she will fly to perform an engagement, which unites her to you for ever'.

Notwithstanding all the wonders and miracles which have been atchieved by love, this billet would not have had the power to effect the cure of Sir Edmond, if his indisposition had proceeded from any thing more than a transient fever, which had been occasioned by the unruly and tumultuous agitations which he had experienced. The next day Malvina saw him enter her apartment with rapture and gratitude; and though he was sorry and repented of his behaviour the evening before, and apparently submissive, yet he was always tenacious of his own will, and had previously taken all necessary measures to oblige Malvina to meet him early the next morning at the church, where they were to receive the nuptial benediction. She was petrified and overpowered on finding that the irrevocable moment was at last fixed; a thousand different sensations oppressed her soul: and the recollection of her duty, and the struggle it occasioned between her love, was extreme and severe: however the sentiment of love at last prevailed. She therefore declared that she would not retract her promise, whatever might ensue from it, and that consequently she would meet him the next morning at the appointed church.

The severe mental contest which Malvina had experienced, did not escape Sir Edmond's penetration; and he felt how much more delicate it would have been in him, if he had not abused the ascendancy which forced Malvina, in opposition to her wishes, to a proceeding which she could not undertake, without self-reproach. But Sir Edmond's affection, it must be acknowledged, was more ardent than generous; and notwithstanding all his scruples, his impetuous and ungovernable impatience would not permit him to sacrifice his wishes, to the peace and happiness of his friend.

Had it been possible, he much wished Malvina to accompany him to London; it would have been also agreeable to her: but she well knew of how much importance it was for her marriage to be kept a profound secret, until they had obtained Lord Sheridan's consent to it.

Ah! Edmond, said Malvina, recollect if he should refuse your solicitations. In such a dreadful alternative, it would be essential that our union should remain concealed under the veil of mystery, fearing Mrs. Burton should usurp her authority, and deprive me of my dear charge. Edmond perceiving these reflections were so painful to Malvina, that she could with difficulty suppress her tears, immediately endeavoured to change the subject, and replied, as he was conscious Mrs. Burton would have all his motions watched, he had deputed his friend, Sir Charles Weymund,[13] to procure a catholic priest, who would ratify their union. That this friend, with Mrs. Moody, would serve as witnesses; and that there would not be any more than those two persons who were made confidents, and also, it was this same Sir Charles who had sold him this little country seat he had mentioned, and bought in Malvina's name: and it was settled between them that she should pass for the sole proprietor of the place: that it would be imagined that she had bought it, that she might live in this retirement with her Frances, far from the world and its society – a plan perfectly according with her well known character. But if Edmond should be so fortunate as to prevail with Lord Sheridan, he would immediately publish his marriage, and carry Malvina in triumph to his estate near Glasgow. But if on the contrary the father of Frances remained inflexible, then Malvina was not to leave her retreat, and her husband was only to visit her (if there should be a necessity for this concealment) by stealth, and he was to enter by a private door, of which even the domestics were to be ignorant.

It was time now they should separate. Sir Edmond could scarcely resolve to leave Malvina, though so conscious that he was to meet her in a few hours, to be united for ever. He was fearful, that when she was alone, she would resign herself to the most melancholy reflections; and the idea that she did not equally participate in all his felicity, became insupportable to him; and he could not prevent himself from being tormented by his own jealous fancies.[14] It was both certain and natural to suppose that Malvina's joy was not unembittered by fear and remorse; but there was now no alternative: she had not the power of ordering her destiny, and she must now give herself to Sir Edmond. She was perfectly conscious of the dangers by which this union was overshadowed, and it required all her force to prevent his perceiving the slightest trait of disquietude; as she was certain he would immediately infer, that she resigned her hand to him with regret.

CHAP. II.

The marriage.

The beams of light, which told the approach of this awful[15] day, at last appeared, and in partial gleams touched the distant objects. Not that Malvina awoke to behold them, for her eyes had never been closed during the past night. Too much agitated to find any rest, she arose without the power of collecting her ideas: and after having hastily put on a simple robe of white[16] muslin, with a hat and black[17] veil, she stept into the carriage, accompanied by Mrs. Moody, and was carried to the appointed church. Sir Edmond was waiting at the door; he eagerly advanced to assist her in alighting from the carriage, and as he supported her, he founded she trembled. My best beloved, said Sir Edmond, with tender anxiety, collect yourself, this is the moment of our beginning felicity, the moment which will ease all my anxieties. It is your lover, the man whom you have selected, and preferred to all others; to whom you are now going to resign your beloved hand. Calm these useless fears, the altar is ready.

As he finished speaking, he led her into the church; but on stepping on the threshhold of this temple, Malvina's agitation increased. That altar was to receive her vows; the pale and trembling light which was emitted from the flambeaux which surrounded it, but faintly dispersed the dark shadows which were visible in different part of the church. The numerous tomb-stones that she surveyed under her feet, every one of which reminded her of her beloved Clara; the profound and solemn silence which reigned uninterrupted, except by the deep and hollow sound of their steps, which echo returning from the void beneath, resounded through the vaulted roof, and then died away in silence. Every thing contributed to increase in her agitated mind an awful terror, of which she could not divest herself. However, she slowly advanced, leaning on the arm of Sir Edmond, when Sir Charles Weymund joined them, and saluting Malvina with the most profound respect, he informed Sir Edmond that the priest was arrived, and ready to perform the ceremony. Malvina continued silent. Sir Edmond was alarmed at it, and enquired the cause of it. Why is my tender friend thus alarmed, said he, does she fear to behold me too happy? Is not this a moment to dissipate and banish all recollections, and every uncertainty? Dear Malvina, I intreat you, for my sake, rise superior to this weakness. I do not possess any, she replied, with a sweet smile; but what is very natural, the solemnity of the place, and the sacredness of our engagements, filled my heart with an awful and holy sensation; but I do not hesitate.

As they approached the altar, a small door opened into the choir, and the priest appeared dressed in his canonicals, with a prayer book in hand. The light of the flambeaux gleamed directly on his countenance; Malvina, whose eyes were cast down, did not perceive him; but Sir Edmond immediately recognised him, and shuddering – exclaimed, Mr. Prior![lvii] As soon as Mr. Prior heard his voice, he instantly suspected who the lady was that stood before him; and he feelingly anticipated his misfortune. A death-like coldness seemed to penetrate and freeze his heart: – the book fell from his hand. Shocked, he paused for a moment without approaching.

Malvina, uncommonly surprised, felt, that perhaps this was the critical moment in which she should for ever obliterate every suspicion relative to Mr. Prior in the mind of Sir Edmond, and determine his confidence in her. Therefore, suppressing her agitation, she went up to him with an air and manner peculiarly affecting, saying, I cannot suppose that chance alone can have contributed to afford us the pleasure of seeing you; I consider it as an additional goodness of the hand of Providence, which would increase my happiness, by directing that I should receive it from you; and likewise of its justice, that the same hand which had wounded Sir Edmond, will confer a blessing on his union, as an expiation of your fault. Ah! Malvina, what is it you say? Do you believe that my voice shall consecrate this bond? Why should I have a doubt of the contrary? interrupted Malvina – I have never ceased to esteem you! Mr. Prior, exclaimed Sir Edmond, with difficulty suppressing his anger, dare to stir from hence till you have performed the ceremony, for which you were sent for at your peril. Stop Sir Edmond, said Malvina, with an elevation of mind which was conspicuous in her countenance – recollect where you are; this holy temple is supposed to be filled with the peculiar omnipresence of the Deity, and ought only to echo to the words of peace and good will: and every sensation of haughty overbearing pride, which can never support the slightest resistance, should here be suppressed. Even you, Mr. Prior, if you examine your conscience, will you dare to assert, that it has no secret motive which deters you from performing the ceremony? And if there is one which is unworthy of you, endeavour to purify your heart, that it may be worthy of exalting itself to that Supreme Being, whom you are going to implore on our account. Oh! gracious God, exclaimed Mr. Prior, what have you asserted? Is it possible you can suppose that I have sullied my heart with one criminal wish? And is it not possible to expiate such a fault, if it had existed, but by sanctifying Malvina in the excess of her partiality for another? All powerful God, celestial Father! O turn this misfortune aside; and if it is possible, permit this stroke to pass from me.[18] As for myself, continued Malvina, whatever may be your determination, I declare here, before the altar of Almighty God,[19] that Sir Edmond Burton is the being which my heart has selected, and whom I implore Heaven to grant as my husband; and that I will avoid both the sight and the friendship of that man who refuses to give his benediction on our nuptials.

The words and lively enthusiasm which animated Malvina's features, overcame Mr. Prior; he could no longer resist her. I obey your voice, he replied, whatever it dictates; and I perceive that Heaven or my conscience has no power to resist this determination. I do obey; but remember, Malvina, that whatever may be the faults which the past may reproach me with, or all I may experience in future, the sensations of this moment ought to obliterate them all.[20] Malvina de Sorcy, and Edmond Burton, unite your hands, and approach the altar. He then began to read in an elevated voice, which became commanding, and thundered as he asked Sir Edmond these words: will you swear to love and protect this woman for ever? But on addressing the same question to Malvina, he modulated and softened his voice; the words came from his lips apparently with reluctance, as unwilling to articulate a sentence, the answer to which would agonise his heart. At length the vows were pronounced, and the awful ceremony concluded. He implored the blessings of Heaven (without which all must fall)[21] on the new married pair. Be happy, said he, as the tears involuntarily streamed down his cheeks, Be happy in each other! – and may the God of infinite goodness and mercy watch over your felicity, and render you every day more dear to each other. You are now united for ever. Depart in peace. He then came from the altar.

Excellent and worthy man, said Sir Edmond, pressing his hand with friendship, forgive my suspicions and my behaviour.[am] Become my friend, as you have ever been[22] to her who is now my wife, my Malvina. Let her see you frequently, I shall never forbid it; her friendship will repay you for the blessing I have this day received from you.

Mr. Prior, said Malvina, with that interesting grace which embellished all her actions, remember how often you have offered up prayers to Heaven for my happiness, you at last behold me so; and it is to you, my dear, my estimable friend, that I owe it.

Ah! returned Mr. Prior pressing both their hands in his, and bathing them with his tears, perhaps I may one day be called to enjoy the sight of your happiness, and mutual love; but it must not be yet. My fortitude is exhausted, for the moment in which I united Malvina to another, revealed to me my own situation: and I abhor myself. But in the deepest humility of a repentant heart, I ought to relinquish the object of my love, for the sins of my soul.[23] Perhaps I shall not survive it long; but of what consequence is a long life,[24] or all the blessings on this earth, which can be enjoyed by man, compared with an immortal crown? as this life is only introductory to that eternity, which may soon conclude this toiling scene of sorrow. Eternity rolls towards us like the waves of a mighty ocean, ready to overwhelm all that appertains to humanity; and only leaves us the remembrance of our virtue, and the deep repentance of our faults.

No, said Malvina, much affected, no, may you live long, as a consolation to the unhappy and unfortunate, and an example to your fellow creatures; and add to the happiness of your friends.

Oh! Malvina, said he, you have caused me to blush, by recalling me to a consciousness of my guilty wanderings. Leave me then to submit to my fate; and if Heaven in its kindness should think proper to take me to itself, will you not join me in blessing its mercy?[25] But you, Sir Edmond, have obtained the first, the only felicity, which this world has power to bestow; and which is so extraordinary, so rare to be met with – the possession of a virtuous and sensible woman. Show yourself worthy of the blessing you have obtained, by for ever abjuring your errors; and let all your endeavours be centred in contributing to the happiness of that angelic creature; may tranquillity ever appear in your countenance,[26] as virtue for ever lives in her heart; love her as she deserves to be loved, that the sound of her grief may never reach the deep and sequestered retreat where I am going to bury myself; nor ever let me hear, that the agonies which I experienced in uniting you, were the fatal presentiment of the unhappiness which was to befal her. Then, without waiting to hear an answer, he abruptly left them, and disappeared in an instant.

The last words which he had uttered, struck mournfully to Malvina's heart; but Sir Edmond was so transported with his joy, that he scarcely heard them. He could feel nothing but his own happiness; he saw only his wife; and the delight that name gave, was harmony to his senses. – My Malvina, my wife! repeated he, pressing her in his arms, and thanking her for her kindness; he blessed her a thousand times for her love, and could scarcely restrain the violence of his agitation. Malvina less ardent, but more tender and affectionate, did not love him more, but loved him better: she shed tears of gentleness, as she surveyed Sir Edmond; and mentally implored Heaven to take her from this world, the moment when a being, so dear and beloved, should cease to find all his happiness and satisfaction in her society.

The day now rolled on, and Malvina, begging Mrs. Moody's acceptance of a handsome and valuable present, and returning her also a thousand tender acknowledgments for her kind attentions, she bid her adieu, with many injunctions to keep this secret. – She then returned to the carriage with her husband and Sir Charles Weymund; and they set off for the country seat which had been purchased for her.

CHAP. III.

Conjugal happiness.[27]

The house was small, but elegant and commodious. It was situated in the centre of an extensive forest, which rendered it difficult of access; and surrounded with very large enclosures, bordered with excellent hedges and wide ditches.

Sir Charles, after having welcomed the new married pair to their little mansion, partook of their frugal repast; and promised to protect Lady Burton, during Sir Edmond's absence. He then wished them all imaginable felicity, till he saw them again, and left them. Sir Edmond's intention was only to have remained two days with Malvina; and eight had already elapsed, without his thinking of leaving his lovely wife; when he received a letter from Sir Charles, which informed him, that Mrs. Burton was very uneasy at his absence, and had sent every where to search for him. That last evening Mrs. Moody had shewn him a letter, which she had received from Mrs. St. Clare; in which she expressed so much uneasiness, and also was so alarmed at the silence of her friend, that she was determined to set out for Edinburgh, in order to inform herself what was become of her, unless she heard very shortly from her.

They both felt the moment of separation was arrived: without speaking they understood it; as if by mutual agreement their lips opened to utter the same fatal words. To-morrow, to-morrow, mournfully repeated Malvina. Yes, to-morrow, repeated Sir Edmond, with vivacity; but I shall soon return; a few days, and I shall hasten to you as happy as ever; neither wishing nor imploring any other blessing from Heaven, than that I may never more leave the wife of my idolatry, who occupies every recess of my heart. – Affected by these tender expressions, Malvina gave him her hand: he pressed her to his bosom; and while they appeared to be united by love and tenderness for each other, it might be said, that all nature seemed embellished for them alone.

Concealed in the leafy dwelling of the grove, the nightingale warbled her plaintive touching cadences; which seemed to proceed from the heart that could die, as if uttered these expressive notes of mournful melody. A running stream of the purest water, joined its indistinct murmurings to the lonely bird of evening, and spread its silver meanderings over the emerald coloured carpet of nature.

The glorious orb of day, as it slowly sunk beneath the west, overflowed that part of the horizon with a mantle of crimson, tinging the pure azure of the heavens with soft clouds of purple and gold, heightened by the vermil glow, which gives the rich warm colouring to an evening landscape. – While the first shades of night slowly descended on earth, as if reluctant to drop its veil, before the last rays of the setting sun had disappeared; and seemed in unison with this pair, that day left nature with regret.[28]

As they returned, after a delightful walk, towards the house, Malvina mournfully supported herself on the arm of Sir Edmond; and, as they were proceeding, she could not help shuddering, as she perceived some withered branches quivering in the air, and then suddenly falling to the ground near them. – A similarity between them and herself instantly pressed upon her heart, and made her tremble for her happiness; recollecting the dreadful and invariable law which governs all nature, has placed the moment of declension next the greatest and most elevated point of happiness. This idea filled her heart[lviii] with inexpressible terror, as a presentiment that her happiness was at an end. – Indeed there is much similarity between the moral and physical world. We behold stern Winter walking with his leaden sceptre over our fields, more than half the year; and his young successor, smiling Spring, reigns but a moment over her tender subjects, the beauteous flowers. Too similar to the constant anxieties, cares, and pain, which nearly occupies all the term of life; and if it permits one moment of tranquillity or pleasure, to enlighten our prospect, it only serves to render the gloom, which is to succeed, more dark and fearful, from the contrast. But we must ever remember, that if Heaven has granted to mortals hereafter, an eternal spring and unchanging felicity, we must not only desire to attain, but endeavour to deserve it.[29]

It was in vain, during the course of the evening, that Malvina attempted to overcome the melancholy impression which she had received – not all the efforts and caresses of Sir Edmond could succeed. Though he was with her, he was already departed in her mind; and notwithstanding the fair prospect of the future, which he pictured to her in such brilliant colours, yet she could not gain from hope, the sweet promise of his return.

Oh, Edmond! she exclaimed, I am destined never to behold you again; and if these are the only moments which I am permitted to pass with you, at least hear my best wishes.[30] – Remember that this heart, which beats for thee alone, will never cease to remember thee but with life; and if, in the future state, which Heaven has destined us to inherit, we should preserve the remembrance of what was most dear to us, eternity to me will be only the continuance of my affection. Oh, Edmond, perhaps when united there, never more to leave each other, we shall at last enjoy that supreme felicity[an] which can exist only there.

Why does my Malvina doubt that we will find it on earth? We who are so perfectly sensible of the blessing, may we not hope to enjoy it on earth for a length of time? – But the uncertainty, Edmond, do you not feel that it is alarming? It is not sufficient for me only to hope for your tenderness, but to be certain of it, or die. – My tender friend, this absence will be but of short duration: I shall fly to you[ao] – love has wings, you know. – Yes, Edmond, it has, replied Malvina, with a look of the most inexpressible tenderness and melancholy. Can you ever forget that it has? Unjust Malvina! Dear Edmond, pardon me, but you can never know what you are to Malvina. Love which, with you, is only a transient passion, is become the intuitive sentiment of my soul, and will terminate only with my existence.[31] Edmond, you will be the arbiter of my fate, and you must answer for my life. If any other should become dear to you, if it is but for a day or an instant, your error would never change my tenderness; I should not even require your repentance, before I should have pardoned you. Yet neither your return, or your caresses, or all the endeavours I could make, could ever obliterate the shock I should receive; and the stroke of death would enter my heart, at the very moment yours was unfaithful.[lix]

Dearest Malvina, why do you oppress your mind by these melancholy presages of our separation. Let me press thee to my heart, which will answer for me. O! let one of thy soft smiles evaporate the gloomy shadows which envelope thy mind; and one of thy tender kisses raise me from the earth; then pressing her in his arms, he endeavoured to enliven her by the joy he felt in being with her, and in their present happiness to forget the future.[32]

If it is already perceived, that Sir Edmond's regret was less lively than usual; and that Malvina's love appeared rather augmented, it is, alas, but the melancholy confirmation of the inconstancy of man.[33]

At length the day appeared – the carriage was ready – the fatal moment arrived. Edmond tore himself from his love: she wept, but was silent. Edmond looked at her, and fell at her feet again. They mingled their tears together: but Edmond, finding his fortitude fail him, roused himself, and, with a kind of cruel courage, forced himself from her. Malvina was overcome, she rushed after him: Edmond, she exclaimed, only one word more, only once more, adieu – it will be the last. Her address was in vain; the carriage was gone, and he heard her not. She perceived the traces of the wheels fresh on the gravel, marked the carriage as it passed among the trees, and observed the hand of Sir Edmond waving an adieu. Struck by the alarming presentiment, that she should never behold him again, she uttered a last adieu, and fell senseless on the grass.

On recovering, she recollected the anxiety which Mrs. St. Clare must be under, on her account; and that it was above two months since she had been separated from her dear Frances. Condemning her neglect, and conscious that the sight of her would sooth her grief, and mitigate the absence of Sir Edmond, she ordered every thing to be made ready for her departure; intending to bring Mrs. St. Clare and Fanny back with her, which she determined should take place on the following day.

Though she had so suddenly formed the plan of leaving her retreat, she could not think of quitting it, without visiting all the places where she had walked with Sir Edmond, frequently stopping to survey the scenery which they had together admired. Everywhere she met with something which excited her regret and her tears; and resigning herself to the mournful sensations which oppressed her heart – Oh! Nature, she exclaimed, whatever place I may inhabit, he will ever be present to my imagination; and may all thy productions ever produce the remembrance of me. Thou thick and impervious Forest, tell him, that when I wander through thee, voluntary and alone, I only behold thy glooms; but when together we roved amidst thy shades, thou wast a retreat of odoriferous flowers: let thy enchanting perfumes recal to his mind, the sweetest, the most gentle sensations. Ye little tuneful Tenants, let your sweet melody warble notes of love; and thou, fair River, let thy gentle murmuring course, be to him an emblem of constancy; and when Night, with her sable mantle, shall envelope every object, which may remind him of me, then let thy plaintive echo, from her airy cell, inform him, that it is a voice which replies to his own.

It was not without the deepest sensations the mind can experience, that Malvina found herself once more in the arms of Mrs. St. Clare, and her beloved Frances. But all the pleasure received, could not efface the melancholy impression which the parting with Sir Edmond had occasioned. It was too recent for her to overcome its shock.[34] It is not on a stormy day, that we can perceive the clear azure of the heavens.

But while the world could not afford any thing which seemed to relieve her anguish, was Sir Edmond equally concerned, by the remembrance of her? – Had he but one thought, of love and Malvina; but one wish, to see her again? Ah! we must doubt of such a thing; and it is necessary to recollect, that in such a character as he possessed, there existed more ardour than tenderness; that his passion was more violent, than deep-rooted, indeed is it not sufficient that he was a man![35]

The difference which is observed in the affection in both sexes, must always be objected to as a reproach.[36] These half of the species, which Nature destines to be men, receive with their sensibility, a mixture of ambition and glory; but those who are formed for mothers, ought to possess only the soft affections.

While Mrs. Burton was wondering at the sudden appearance of her nephew, and commanding all her servants to answer her inquiries, not one of them could give her any information. But Mr. Fenwick, who was more calculated to gain it from this class of persons, as he was only indebted to fortune for having placed him above them, could therefore descend to them without degrading himself; and learned from the domestics all the gossiping of the neighbourhood, and Sir Edmond's visits to Mrs. Moody; where a handsome young lady, who never went out, always received the visits of Sir Edmond.[37] That she never appeared at the windows but by chance, when she had neglected to draw the curtains, which otherwise were kept constantly closed.

When Mrs. Burton was informed of these particulars, she partly guessed at the truth; and was determined to discover the whole of this mystery.

In consequence, she sent for Mrs. Moody; had her ushered into her dressing-room, where she received her with the utmost affability; questioned her with the most consummate art, and mentioned Malvina and her nephew with seeming kindness. Complained that they had neglected her; that if they would have placed a confidence in her affection, she would never have opposed their union: – and *insisted* on knowing the truth[ap] of this affair, that she might grant them her pardon, before they came to require it. Then, addressing herself in a still more interesting manner to Mrs. Moody, saying, it would be of infinite consequence to all those who should contribute to this happy reconciliation; and spoke in the highest terms of the acknowledgments they would receive.

Thus she interested both the heart and vanity of this good woman; drew a secret from her, which neither bribes or threats would have had the power to make her confess, but which she could not refuse to the flattering idea of acting a part in such a particular case.

Mrs. Burton was then informed, of both the day and place where Malvina was married; and notwithstanding the anger she felt by this information, she never betrayed the slightest change in her countenance. – She took leave of Mrs. Moody with the utmost kindness, charging her to be silent with respect to what had passed between them, that she might not deprive her of the pleasure of surprising her nephew and niece.

But the moment she was alone, she gave way to her resentment, and endeavoured to devise every method she could think of, necessary to have the marriage annulled. She had not a doubt but that Lord Stafford, the uncle of Lady Mary Summerhill, would be so extremely hurt by this event, that he would be ready to assist her in revenging it. She determined and prepared immediately to go and consult with him; when Sir Edmond made his unexpected appearance, equipped for travelling, and inquired if she had any commands for London.

CHAP. IV.

The dangers of the world.

Sir Edmond had agreed with Malvina, that prudence required that he should go to Mrs. Burton's before his departure, and inform her of his intended journey, which she would undoubtedly hear of; also his visiting her would prevent her from forming any suspicion, which, perhaps, would have been the case, if Mrs. Moody's confidence had not preceded his appearance.

Mrs. Burton, who could so easily conceal her anger, made but few inquiries concerning his last absence, pretending to believe all he told her; and without knowing the real motives of his journey, she heard of it with pleasure.[aq] For though she had not a doubt but that Malvina expected something from it, yet she was too well acquainted with Sir Edmond, not to know this separation was most fortunate for the plan she meditated. Therefore, far from offering the slightest objection to it, she approved of his intention; saying, I am very glad that you did not think of setting out[ar] without seeing me. I am perfectly sensible of this attention; but may I hope you will enhance it, by having the kindness to call at Lady Dorset's, for a few minutes, whose mansion lays in your road; and you will be so good to deliver a letter of much importance to Mrs. Fenwick, who has been there near fifteen days, and I can no longer delay sending it. – Sir Edmond promised to take the charge of it, and she instantly retired to her closet to write it.

'My young friend, said she, I have this instant heard they are married; and from the conversation which I had last with you, it will lead you to imagine, that I cannot endure to be treated in this manner. But if I am not deceived in my hopes of revenge, I shall very soon be enabled to burst asunder a chain, which every way mortally offends me. – It is in your power to afford me great assistance in this affair: I wish you, by all means, to make use of every art, to detain Sir Edmond a few days at Lady Dorset's. I do not imagine that you will find the least difficulty in doing this, as you are at liberty to use all the means in your power: they will all be right if you can but succeed.

'While he is forgetting himself with you, I shall employ the time to advantage, in concert with Lord Stafford, to petition government; setting forth Sir Edmond, as being a zealous convert to the French principles,[38] as a subject that would bring dishonour upon his family, and they desired, for that reason, that he might be sent out of the kingdom,[39] to prevent this disgrace.

'Difficult as the execution of this plan may appear, yet by the assistance of our numerous connections, I am almost certain of its success: and when he is on board, and the vessel ready to sail, I shall then make my terms with him; and the only alternative shall be, that I will engage to procure him his liberty, provided he will consent to sign an agreement, by which the marriage shall be annulled.[40] Then I shall immediately intimate to Madame de Sorcy, that she must instantly send Miss Sheridan to me, unless she will acknowledge her marriage to be void.

'If they both submit to my wishes, I can soon annul the union, which has destroyed all my hopes. But if, on the contrary, they should refuse me, and dare publicly to defy me, I shall at last[41] be revenged by their despair, by taking Sir Edmond from his beloved wife.[42] The detested Malvina, from being deprived of both her husband and her charge, will be rendered so miserable, that I am certain of being successful in that point.

'Adieu, my young friend, I trust to your address; employ all your charms to detain Sir Edmond, that my petition may reach London before he can; that the friends which he may have in the political line, may not have time to prevent its taking effect.

Ann Burton'.

She returned and gave this letter to Sir Edmond, with an air of so much kindness and freedom, that it would have deceived suspicion itself. This dissimulation was almost useless, as she well knew she had not the least reason[43] to be under any anxiety with regard to its contents; for had he even doubted its tendency, he was so scrupulous in such cases, that she had not the slightest cause to fear his imprudence in this respect.

He then left her; and, according to his promise, he stopped the next evening at Lady Dorset's. He gave Mrs. Burton's letter to Williams, his own servant, to present it directly to Mrs. Fenwick; for it was his intention not to lose a moment, and to proceed on his journey without getting out of his carriage.

Mrs. Fenwick had no occasion for Mrs. Burton's commands, to induce her to make use of every art to detain Sir Edmond with her; for as she had conceived a real affection for him, in the solitude of Burton-Hall, she, though surrounded by pleasure, and in the midst of the gay world, yet preferred him to every other. Intoxicated with pride, from seeing herself the object of universal attention; yet, perhaps, she would have sacrificed them all, to have obtained a return of Sir Edmond's attention. – The knowledge of his marriage corroded all the joy she felt on his arrival: yet she was so well versed in the manners of the world, that she was a sufficient judge of the difference and situation of a lover who lives in hope, and the husband who is in possession. From these considerations, she well knew how to appreciate the slight obstacles which marriage, in general, places between infidelity and love.

While Sir Edmond was impatiently seated in his carriage, Williams was waiting at Mrs. Fenwick's room door for her answer, or if she had any commission for his master. – In the interim, this lady was reflecting what steps she should take, to detain Sir Edmond and ruin Malvina. She therefore called Williams into the room; examined him; made a few inquiries – observed that he appeared a character, that would coincide with, and assist her in her plans. She, consequently, spoke to him as follows:

'Williams, your master has fallen into disgrace with Mrs. Burton, by the most imprudent step he could have taken, and which will for ever deprive him of her kindness; yet, if you value your master, it is in your power to assist me in repairing his folly and imprudence. If you will follow my directions, we may, perhaps, prevent his aunt from disinheriting him; and, likewise, it will be above fifty guineas in your pocket'.

The last assertion was quite sufficient to determine Williams; it was, therefore, concerted between him and Mrs. Fenwick, that Williams was to acquaint her with all his master's actions and intentions; and, also, all letters which might pass, were first to be remitted to her.

As soon as this was settled, Mrs. Fenwick sent to inform Sir Edmond, that the letter she had received from Mrs. Burton, required her to write immediately to London, as it was of the utmost importance, and must be sent as soon as possible; and hoped he would be so obliging as to take the charge of it; and, as it must delay his journey a few minutes, intreated he would alight, and walk into the house during that time.

She immediately acquainted Lady Dorset with Sir Edmond's being there, who went herself to the carriage to invite him to enter the saloon; and, on his refusal, she taxed him with unpoliteness. This forced him to comply with her pressing invitation; and he followed her, in order to wait till Mrs. Fenwick had finished her letter. He however went with an ill grace, without wishing it, into a room full of company; composed of gay, fashionable,[44] and, some of the handsomest women.

Soon after Mrs. Fenwick entered, with a packet in her hand, which she presented to Sir Edmond, without attempting to detain him. He looked at her, surprised at her looking so handsome, and offered to depart that instant. But Williams had taken care, by his officiousness, to prevent him; for, as he believed that his master would of course stay the night there, he had sent away the horses, and it was too late to procure others.

Mrs. Fenwick pretended to be greatly distressed at having detained him so long, and offered hers, to take him to the next post;[lx] but so many delays had made it so late, that he deferred setting out till the next day.[45]

Lady Dorset and her company were rejoiced at his being detained. Mrs. Fenwick alone appeared sorry; she excused herself in a voice of so much apparent veracity, that Sir Edmond had not a doubt of it. She requested his pardon, with such a bewitching grace, that it was impossible to avoid granting it. His being obliged to stay, allowed him time to examine her at his leisure; and he was astonished at her improvement.

Every person repeated to him how much she was admired, and that the world acknowledged her among the most celebrated beauties.[46] She was no longer the Miss Melmor, whose inexperience prevented her from heightening all the advantages which Nature had endowed her with. Coquetry had rendered her quite another woman. Each day increased the charms of her figure, and her manners and wit became more alluring. Perhaps she had not one quality which could attach, but every allurement that could seduce. In solitude or retirement, she would not have been noticed; but in the world she attracted every one. Her witticisms were so apt, her sallies pleasant, and her ridicule pointed. Besides, how was it possible to escape those tender and brilliant eyes, which always seemed to dwell upon you;[47] that touching smile which expressed so much; those languishing and voluptuous looks;[48] those half sentences, which excite and interest the imagination;[49] those affected efforts, which feign to disguise what it wishes to utter, with a view to enhance the value of what has escaped the lips. In short, all those assumed reveries, those artful well-acted manners, that enchanting carelessness in the dress, which has purposely left something unfinished, as if by chance, which one would blush to show.

Perhaps, though I wish to delineate a coquet, I may not then give an adequate idea of Mrs. Fenwick. Yet, with so many advantages, she was allowed to captivate the senses, without ever touching the heart. Her figure might gain her admirers, for her character alone was formed to excite the passions.[50]

It was for this reason that Mrs. Burton, who understood it so perfectly, was conscious that she possessed exactly those attractions which inflame; but not one of those lasting qualities which attach. She, therefore, had selected Mrs. Fenwick[as] as the most eligible person, to divert and separate Sir Edmond from Malvina; to seduce, without fixing him.

We observe, from this trait, that Mrs. Burton, who was formerly so extremely severe on the conduct of Miss Melmor, was now totally indifferent with regard to that of Mrs. Fenwick. Such is the foundation which we must attribute to those who make such an ostentatious boast of their virtue, whose origin arises entirely from pride; and which is instantly effaced, when it is found to interfere with their self-interest.

Attractive as Mrs. Fenwick was, we should not have imagined that the happy lover and husband of the tender Malvina, was so near forgetting his vows. But it must be remembered, that the character was drawn from Nature, and is not an ideal one; that it existed in the eighteenth century. That, in general, Providence has endowed men with more of the sensual in their idea of love, than the refined affection of the heart; but that women, who possess delicate and sensible souls, feel the latter sensation in all its native purity and sincerity. Therefore, it is asserted, that a man, from the excess of his tenderness for one woman, feels a distant attraction for every other; but the instant that a refined and sensible woman has fixed her selection, all other men are as perfectly indifferent, as if they were not in existence.

CHAP. V.

Trial of coquetry.[51]

If a knowledge of the world had developed the graces of Mrs. Fenwick, it had also given her discernment, and an artful penetration, which intuitively taught her, the moment and opportunity when her plans would take effect, and best succeed. She was certain that Sir Edmond had promised his wife to remain faithful to her alone, and that he wished to keep this promise inviolable; consequently, any particular advances would be impolitic, as they would immediately put him upon his guard. On the other hand, it would be equally dangerous to appear as if she had quite forgot him; for it was by that point that she intended to draw him back.

It was a long road, and she was conscious she could not attempt to reach it at the first outset.[52] Therefore, in order to succeed, it required all her art to allure him, without his suspecting it; and to be sufficiently agreeable to tempt him, without letting him perceive that it was her intention to do so. To be continually with him, that she might lead him on imperceptibly, till she found she had entirely subdued him; without allowing him time to recollect what he had forgot, or a moment to reflect on what he felt. Accordingly, that she might succeed in this plan, she neglected no opportunity of being near him, without ever appearing to wish it. She was particularly careful not to speak to him first, yet had the art of obliging him to address his conversation to her. What was infinitely more dangerous, she used that finesse, which answers with that peculiar reserve, that excites inquiry and prolongs a conversation, by rendering the most indifferent interesting.

Sir Edmond consequently became more easily deceived from not suspecting it, and relied too much on the profound knowledge he thought he had of women; therefore, he believed it impossible to deceive him. He did not know that whatever penetration a man may possess in that respect, he could not, in the course of his life, acquire a sufficient share to develope all the varieties, and the deep arts of coquetry. He fancied he only perceived in Mrs. Fenwick's negligence, the certainty of her having lost the presumption of thinking herself superior to Malvina; and this thought afforded him pleasure. He cast a look of disdain on all the beauties who apparently wished to excite his attention, and only continued near her, who did not appear to seek for it.

This distinction did not escape Mrs. Fenwick, and she drew from it a favourable omen of her triumph. By this means she could speak with confidence, but this she most carefully concealed; and, by this, she had the power of rendering herself still more amiable.

It was not to Sir Edmond that she displayed the brilliancy of her wit; no, for him she reserved all those little interesting half sentences, which appear to escape with such indifference. But when she addressed others, her conversation betrayed that sparkling animation, which by some is considered so attractive, when uttered by lips of the brightest vermillion, and a countenance which was admired by the fashionable world. Yet this fascinating woman was no other than the pretty Miss Melmor; and it may be remembered, that Miss Melmor spared no trouble to please Sir Edmond.[53]

He observed her with astonishment:[54] if she had betrayed the least coolness in her behaviour, he would have perceived that she had some design; or, at least, he would have considered it as proceeding from jealousy. He observed she displayed her wit to others. With him she seemed only to speak her real sentiments, which she made appear natural and amiable:[55] this certainly was a flattering and very particular distinction, but it was involuntary. She slightly hinted their former connections, and the friendship which had succeeded it.[56]

This idea rendered Mrs. Fenwick still more interesting; he drew nearer to her, that he might converse more at his ease; and from curiosity only, wished to discover whether she saw him with any emotion. – But their conversation was soon interrupted by the festivity of the rest of the company; and Mrs. Fenwick was the first to assist in the general gaiety.

Dancing was mentioned. It was Mrs. Fenwick's delight: in that she displayed all her graces. If her manner of dancing was not so dignified as Malvina's, it was light and voluptuous; her steps and her looks were not adapted to attract the heart, but to inflame the senses. It was acknowledged that she only caused a momentary impression; but it is not always possible to resist momentary impressions!

By degrees Sir Edmond began to be elevated: Mrs. Fenwick, attentive to his every motion, perceived and took advantage of it, to ask for a waltz. She knew, from the success of her first attempts, that she might be permitted to hazard another. She let Sir Edmond observe, that she only wished to dance with him. How could he refuse her, even if he had not felt a wish to hold this charming creature in his arms: his self-love had been excited by the discourse of several of the young gentlemen during the ball, who had mentioned Mrs. Fenwick with rapture; and described her as the fascinating,[57] but the most indifferent of women.

In short, Burton, said Lord Wigby, a young man of high birth, and an agreeable figure, will you believe, that after having passed more than eight days with her, in all the freedom of old acquaintances, in the country; and tried every endeavour to render her sensible of my love, I could only obtain a few tender looks and kind sentences, which is all I can hope for: and there is not any one here, who has been more successful[58] than myself. I am also certain, that even you, Burton, with all the brilliant advantages which have given you success, I am confident that you will not succeed any better with her.

Me, said Sir Edmond, with a smile, which expressed how certain he was of conquering, if he chose to make the attempt.

Yes, yourself, replied Lord Wigby, and we shall soon be convinced; for I know you Burton, and I am certain of it: – if you take no pains to conquer, you will find how impossible it will be to succeed.

Yes, yes, added the rest of the young men, Wigby speaks from experience, and we shall now see if there is not one woman who can resist Sir Edmond Burton.

I will do more, continued Lord Wigby, encouraged by the applause of his companions, I will wager, if he will, two hundred guineas, that he will not obtain any more from Mrs. Fenwick than we have.

Sir Edmond possessed more delicacy and honor, than to be capable of revealing the intimacy which had formerly existed between Miss Melmor and himself; and we may imagine from his character, that he with difficulty suppressed that pride, which would only have been displayed from cruelty.[59] The remembrance of Malvina occasioned him to make this sacrifice; and he refused to bet with Lord Wigby, and preferred supporting the ridicule of his friend's pleasantry, rather than offend the woman he adored. This, from such a character as his, was the highest proof he could give; for it was not usual with him for the heart to vanquish his vanity. But that vanity, which in general is the cause of so much mischief, and in reality may be termed inhuman in its baneful effects, was going to be gratified in its turn. Sir Edmond, it is true, had refused willfully to seduce

Mrs. Fenwick, and determined to persist in his resolution; but at the same time he was highly gratified to receive so many public marks of her partiality.

It was at this instant she went up to him, and whispered the dance is going to commence, I am passionately fond of it, was I not a stranger to the gentlemen who are here; the only one who is to dance, is the only person Kitty would wish for her partner.[60]

He looked at Mrs. Fenwick to penetrate whether this was said with design. Never before had she appeared so lovely; and with a look of the utmost tenderness, he informed her she was always his Kitty. He saw his friends remark with surprise and envy, the preference which he received from her; and he could not resist the desire of triumphing in their presence. It was decided, that he should leave Mrs. Fenwick after the reels.[61] He advanced, and twining his arms round her elegant form, beheld the bosom of Kitty through the thin gauze which shaded it;[62] and they both began this dangerous dance, which the voluptuous imagine awakens improper sensations, creates courage, and emboldens innocence.

Soon after, this brilliant society sat down to a sumptuous collation, composed of every delicacy, and the most exquisite wines.[63] The light hand of Mrs. Fenwick helped to empty the flasks of champagne. She always began, and ended with Sir Edmond, and it might be said, that with her rested the sole power of animating him;[64] as she wished to employ other arms, besides those of beauty, in order to succeed.

As Sir Edmond had already felt her power, the mirth, and the company, the fumes of the wine, and the alluring looks of his charming neighbour, all, every thing conspired against his resolution, and the happiness of Malvina. This unprincipled man did not recollect how frequently it happens, that one moment may utterly destroy that peace of mind, which the longest life can never retrieve. But he no longer knew what he did; his hand met Kitty's, he pressed it with ardor: from this action, Mrs. Fenwick no longer doubted of her victory. She, however, was rather premature in the confidence she had inspired, and her sanguine hopes led her to fancy she might dare any thing. She therefore seized that opportunity of requesting Sir Edmond to prolong his stay at Lady Dorset's; but this imprudent request recalled him to himself, his journey, and the object of it, and he declared that he would not defer it for one day.

Without investigating the situation he was in, he found he was in danger; and fearful that he might not always have this command over himself, instead of answering Mrs. Fenwick, he went out, and desired Williams to be particularly punctual to have the chaise ready by six in the morning. This charge pierced Mrs. Fenwick to the heart: she felt she had gone too far: and to repair her fault, she pretended not to have understood Sir Edmond; without again mentioning his departure, she maintained her smiling countenance, occupying herself entirely in endeavouring to make him forget, what she had been so unlucky as to call to his remembrance. Certain that she must take advantage of the present opportunity, or risque the loss of it for ever, she consequently determined on the part she would act.[65]

She arose from table,[66] and proposed one of those innocent amusements which the country allows; but which, for those who have drank too much wine, is esteemed dangerous. She was consequently blindfolded, and ran about with her arms extended, though she first very dexterously lifted one part of the handkerchief from her eyes, that she might distinguish those whom she caught; and on perceiving Sir Edmond near her, she threw herself into his arms, with a laugh, pretending to have mistaken him for an old nobleman[67] who was there. Soon after, she was commanded, by an artful manoeuvre of her own, to pay a forfeit, which was to embrace Sir Edmond, which she declared she would not obey. He of course wished to sieze what was refused, and she endeavoured to prevent him, with that kind of faint resistance which is artfully assumed to enhance the value of what is taken,[68] and under this pretended reserve she knew how to grant many more than were asked; and turning her head at the moment he was near her cheek, by that means their lips met. She then pretended to be very angry, and punished his temerity with a slight blow with her hand, and ran away. He followed her to be revenged, while the rest of the company were taken up with their play, and were all running from one room to another, laughing and calling after each other.

Mrs. Fenwick, in the midst of this festivity, was careful not to lose sight of Sir Edmond; and when they entered the dining room, she pretended that she wished to be revenged on Lord Wigby, who had snatched away her bouquet, and taking a large glass of water, she endeavoured to throw it upon him, instead of which, she artfully let it fall on her own dress. She shrieked, and complained, and flew towards her own chamber to change her clothes. Every one followed her; Sir Edmond was before her, as he wished to shut the door that she might not enter. But she was so quick, that she got up to him, and artfully feigning that she wished to prevent any one from going in, hastily pushed Sir Edmond in before her, and closing the door after them, drew the bolt. Thus was she, as she wished, left alone with him in her chamber.

Lady Dorset had not been near enough to observe that they had entered together into the same room: therefore she imagined they had each retired to their respective apartments: and hearing this, the rest of the company followed their example. But Sir Edmond and Mrs. Fenwick remained alone,[69] and he must have continued there some time;[70] for when Williams went to call his master at six the next morning, he was not to be found in his own apartment.

CHAP. VI.

Journey to London.[71]

The sun had shone in all its splendor for some hours above the horizon, when Sir Edmond in some confusion, with a hurried step, went to call Williams, and enquired in an angry tone why the chaise was not ready?

Williams smiling, replied that the horses had been put to the carriage, and remained waiting for three hours; but that he had ordered them to be taken out, as he could not find his master in his own room, he supposed he had changed his mind. The smile of his servant, the lateness of the morning, and the recollection of Malvina, were all accusations to Sir Edmond, as they reproached him for his fault. Get my carriage ready immediately, said he, in a passion, to Williams, and acquaint me the moment it is at the door, and in future, I desire you will not act without my orders.

While it was preparing, he ran up to his apartment: and to soothe his misery, he endeavoured to write to Malvina. It was then he experienced how dreadful it was to use dissimulation with those we love. He dare not hazard a confession which would ruin the peace of Malvina, and the torture of having some concealment must destroy his own. If it was only her reproaches that he feared, he would have confessed his crime; but he well remembered what she had told him, and that it would certainly be fatal to such a mind as she possessed, if she heard of his being unfaithful. This recollection withheld his pen.[72] These letters, which were to have been the only solace for the absence of her society, were now become his punishment. Thus, when love and confidence have once been abused, its revenge is complete; when it has to descend to the mortifying constraint, it is necessitated to support; instead of that sweet intercourse of reciprocal confidence and pure affection, which is the only solid basis of happiness in this life. Edmond was conscious of the difference of this, in the expressions he made use of in his letter: they wanted that force, which the idea of having acted wrong, deprived them of; and they even tinged the assurances of his affection, though they were not the less true: but the remembrance of his guilt deprived them of that passion, that energy of expression, that sweet delirium which the heart delights to feel, when it loves with native purity and refinement, and beholds no other object but one, to whom it could attach itself. If he felt thus, how much more, and to what excess, would Malvina feel it. If he only wrote a few lines, he might betray himself less; but would not this brevity be more likely to expose him? for it would not be natural, he would not have acted so the evening before. One moment, then, might destroy confidence, and one fault his happiness. Ah, how much did the misery which he experienced, make him detest Mrs. Fenwick. He determined, that from henceforth his extreme coolness towards her, should repair the offence which he had committed against Malvina! This vow which came from his heart, allowed a momentary tranquillity to his conscience, and permitted him to write with more candor and facility.

He then began another letter, wherein he informed Malvina that he had been obliged to stay a few hours at Lady Dorset's, and how insupportable this detention had been to him. He slightly mentioned Mrs. Fenwick, accompanied with the utmost contempt: and never had he felt it so powerfully, as when he wrote it.

'Oh! my Malvina, he continued, I have no other wish than to meet you again. It is therefore as much on my own account, as yours,[lxi] that I wish to hasten with all possible speed, that I may repair the time I have lost here: and the sooner return to that felicity which I have enjoyed in such an exquisite degree, and which my most ardent wishes are, that I may enjoy in future'.

Whilst he was writing, Williams took that opportunity of informing Mrs. Fenwick, that his master was ready to depart, and this dangerous Syren[73] wished to ensnare him still farther. She ran into his room, threw herself into his arms, bathed in tears:[74] she pressed, she intreated him not to leave her so soon; she almost fell at his feet: her eyes full of languor,[lxii] her lips breathing voluptuousness, while pleasure had tinged her skin with its softest bloom.

Sir Edmond pushed her from him, and turning his head aside, leave me, said he, I have already staid too long.

Edmond, cried she, has Kitty then no right to your kindness? she only asks for one day, and she cannot obtain that.

Do you not think your behaviour rather ungrateful, Kitty? replied he, disengaging his hand from hers;[lxiii] an indispensible duty calls me to London, and were you more beautiful and seducing than any other in the world, I should be inexcusable to neglect it for you.

Well, replied she, with spirit, if such is your situation, that you cannot grant one day to her, who has given you so much, you cannot however prevent me from following you. I wish to go to London, Sir Edmond; Mrs. Burton's affairs require it; consequently she will consider it extremely attentive in me to undertake this journey, and then I shall at least have the pleasure of being with the only man I ever loved.

You think of going to London, Kitty? replied Sir Edmond, astonished and confused: but I declare it shall not be with me.

If it must not be with you, she answered, you have not the power of preventing my following you. Do you imagine that I have any fear of the opinion which may be formed of me here? You may undeceive yourself in that point, for I go on Lady Dorset's account also, whose business requires my immediate departure for London:[75] and yet, without having any regard for my youth, and the proofs of affection which I have given you, you have the inhumanity to repulse me so cruelly, and suffer me to take so long a journey alone.

Sir Edmond, much alarmed at Mrs. Fenwick's intention, was particularly fearful it might be made public, and Malvina would be informed of it. He endeavoured to appease and dissuade her, but all in vain. Mrs. Fenwick said she was determined to go with him, or complain of it publicly. In this cruel dilemma he promised to wait for her, though he was resolved not to keep his word. With this assertion she was so well satisfied, that she went to prepare every thing for her departure, and in the interim, he went gently down stairs, then into the stable, and had one of his horses saddled, fearing the noise of the carriage might inform Mrs. Fenwick of his intention, ordering Williams to meet him in London with the chaise; at the same time he gave him a letter to Malvina, which he was to send by the first conveyance; he then wrote a billet with his pencil in the greatest haste to Mrs. Fenwick, sufficiently tender to calm her anger, and permit him to depart in peace.[76]

Mrs. Fenwick was much enraged when she heard of Sir Edmond's being gone; but the billet which Williams presented her, gave her the hope of revenging herself. – The contents were as follow: –

Sir Edmond Burton to Mrs. Fenwick.

'I depart, Kitty, overcome with gratitude for your kind favours, though unworthy of them, since they have made me forget the most sacred of all duties. If you are as good as you are handsome, you will pardon me for a departure, which you ought to believe was absolutely indispensible, as I am determined upon it: and I acknowledge, when the recollection of last night presents itself, it requires nothing less than the impossibility of staying, to determine me to leave you'.

Mrs. Fenwick read this billet several times, she was not to be thus deluded: she became more exasperated, and determined to be revenged upon Malvina, for the contempt of Sir Edmond.[77]

By the agreement which had been made with Williams, she was in possession of the letter addressed to Malvina. She considered some time before she could decide what plan to adopt. She then called Williams in, and spoke to him as follows: – I shall set out to morrow for London, in the carriage which your master has left here; you shall go to day, and deliver this letter to Madame de Sorcy. Tell her that he waits for an answer at Lady Dorset's, that his plan was to have gone directly to London, but that Mrs. Fenwick had intreated him to wait for her, and he therefore immediately complied with her wishes. All these particulars must not be told as a natural recital, but as an imprudence which escaped involuntary from you:[at] and when you leave her, take particular care to drop this billet which your master wrote to me, and which I am going to seal again, that she may imagine you had it to give me, when he had determined to go: and that since his having yielded to my intreaties, his billet was no longer of consequence. Here is my address when I am in London, added she, giving him a card, come to me as soon as you arrive, to give me Madame de Sorcy's answer, that I may judge whether it is necessary for your master to see it. Now you may go; here are ten guineas to drink my health during the journey, and you may be assured, that if you faithfully execute my orders, you will be generously rewarded on your return.

Williams set out furnished with his instructions, and the next day Mrs. Fenwick departed for London. She had more than one motive for going there, for she meant to make a favour with Mrs. Burton of what her own inclinations alone had induced her to undertake: and she wrote the following to acquaint her with it.

'I wished so much to accomplish your wishes, that I have determined to follow your nephew to London, for I have recollected, that if your petition to the minister is found to be supported by a woman whom nature has endowed with some power of pleasing, it may be more favourably received; and the hopes of being serviceable to you on such an occasion, will make me easily despise the fatigue of so long a journey, and the malicious interpretation which may be given to it'.

Mrs. Fenwick, being steadily determined in a case in which she hoped entirely to seduce Sir Edmond,[78] and use every endeavour which her charms afforded, to ensure the success of Mrs. Burton's project; for the pride inherent in her character, added to her love, excited in her heart a degree of malevolence, even beyond what was natural to it; and there was not any thing she would not have attempted, and executed, to be revenged on Malvina. Such was her disposition, when she arrived in London, three days after Sir Edmond. She stopped at some hotel[79] which he inhabited, and enquired if he was within? She was informed, that he was just gone out, and, perhaps, he might not return till the evening. She congratulated herself on his absence, as it would afford her time to form such arrangements, as would be best adapted to her views. Therefore, as soon as she had settled herself in an apartment, which was next to that he occupied, she then desired, that, as soon as he returned, they would desire him to walk up to her, without informing him who she was.

Sir Edmond's first business on his arrival in London, had been to seek Lord Sheridan, and was informed that he was out of town, and would not return till the next day. He enquired the place to which he was gone, that he might follow him; but no person could inform him. Each following day, he met the same disappointment. Thus foiled in his attempts and wishes, he returned to his hotel, melancholy and dispirited, without having the power to write an account of his disappointments to Malvina, to explain the length of his stay in London; because, he was very conscious, that[80] those hours he had spent at Lady Dorset's, was the sole cause of his missing the opportunity of meeting with Lord Sheridan. As he was returning home, he reflected, that it would be much better for him to open his heart to Malvina, incur her reproaches, and implore her pardon, than always dissemble with her; and leave her to suffer from anxiety. Ah! why should I any longer defer confessing my crime? Can I doubt, whether she would forgive me?

Entirely occupied with these ideas, he was just going to enter his chamber, when he was informed, that a lady had lately arrived, who wished to see him immediately. His mind being absorbed by Malvina, he fancied that this must certainly be her, who was come to meet him. In consequence of this thought, he hurried into the above-mentioned room, and entered it with precipitation. It was nearly dark; he beheld the figure of a woman, reclined upon a sopha; he flew towards her, and pressed her in his arms; but he too soon was convinced, that it was Mrs. Fenwick; and, pushing her from him, he exclaimed, Ah! heavens! it is not her.

The artful Kitty did not complain, but she trembled; and, forcing Sir Edmond to seat himself by her, she took both his hands; and, looking at him for a moment in silence, she at last said, I see very plain, Sir Edmond, that it was not me whom you expected; but say, ungrateful man, has this rival, which thy heart prefers – can she have so many claims to thy love, as I have? To behold you, has she braved the danger of a long and tiresome journey, the anger of Mrs. Burton, the reproaches of an offended husband, and the opinion of a malicious public? In short, is she here?

Presumptuous Kitty! replied Sir Edmond, take care how you compare yourself with her, who is above all comparison; and do not imagine, that I shall ever attribute to love, what is the effect of your folly and obstinacy.

Kitty, who was much offended at such an idea, vainly endeavoured to obliterate it; but, finding that she could not succeed, she thought it would be much better to endeavour to amuse him; and set forth all the power of her attractions, to seduce him, and accomplish her views. Did she attain it? If I say, she did not, all the men will render themselves more justice than to believe me, and would disdain to interest themselves in a recital, which was so different from reality. If I say yes, the women, who had retracted their good opinion of Sir Edmond, from the commission of his first fault, would now entirely despise him. In order to obviate this inconvenience, and avoid displeasing any of my readers, I shall throw a veil over Sir Edmond's conduct; and, as a woman, I shall please myself with believing, that he resisted the seducing arts of Mrs. Fenwick, and remained faithful to Malvina.[81] Yet I must reproach him for not leaving the hotel, where she had taken up her residence, the same evening; and for daring to stay where she was, while waiting the arrival of Lord Sheridan.[au] For the readiness with which he had yielded to the seducing advances of this artful woman, should have caused a diffidence of himself, which might have produced the most salutary effects, as he could not be ignorant, that the first step was the most difficult; and that, being too confident, we are frequently liable to be betrayed into error. If the first fault does not alarm the conscience sufficiently for it to resolve never to become guilty a second time, it is, then, in danger of progressively leading us to the commission of a thousand others, which are the consequences that result entirely from the first; for, if we are so liable to fall on the first trial, may it not be deemed the excess of temerity, to permit ourselves again to be tempted by the same danger? This self-confidence too frequently proves but a slight barrier against the attraction of the senses; and, in the end, we must, from conviction, allow it arrogates to itself, what it never attempts to correct; therefore, can never expect to accomplish, while the veil of self-delusion is constantly worn. But that real humility, the invariable concomitant of merit, if it errs once, it errs not again; but, depending for support on a superior power, it rises above itself, and invariably pursues the path of rectitude.[82] If Edmond had doubted himself, would it not have appeared, as if he had doubted the sincerity of his affection? – No. As he had been led astray once,[83] he ought, therefore, to have armed himself against a second fault. But, on the contrary, had Malvina been surrounded by all the pleasures of the world; tempted by every alluring, seducing artifice that could have been devised against her, yet, from the strength of her affection alone, she would have blushed, if, in the most secret thought of her heart, she had found any reason for being obliged to use any precaution against herself. Why, then, did not the same sentiment produce the same effects with Sir Edmond? and, why must he be so inferior, as to be faithless? But, I must confess, in such a character as his, even a real affection could not act as a defence against the seduction of the senses.[84] How very different is this in women![85] When a pure affection occupies the heart, it is for ever fixed, and produces that uniform stability, which elevates it above all those pleasures which are tainted by vanity. It exalts, and refines the heart to the most celestial purity. It can devote itself to the most generous, the most heroic actions, when it has the full power of displaying itself in all its native force; and she, whose character is most conspicuous for its excellence and superior virtue, may be known to be also superior in the affections of the heart.[86]

CHAP. VII.

Fatal news.

Night had for some hours enveloped the world in darkness; and silence more than peace reigned in the sweet retirement where Malvina resided. Mrs. St. Clare, distressed at the anxiety which she observed oppressed her friend, had followed her, and in order to amuse her mind, proposed reading to her, which Malvina accepted, perfectly sensible of her kind intention; she was just interesting herself in what was reading, when Williams was shewn into the room. She uttered an exclamation, arose, and in a hurried voice, enquired if his master was near?

He, madam, replied Williams, smiling; no really, I left him at Lady Dorset's.

How, – is he not going to London?

As to that, madam, I believe he certainly did intend to go; but –

But what unforeseen accident has happened to prevent him?

No other than his own will, madam, and faith it was no wonder, that such a society of handsome women should detain my master.

Malvina turned pale, but scorning to interrogate a servant concerning the conduct of her husband, she only enquired if he had not brought a letter from Sir Edmond?

I beg your pardon madam, said he, here is one, giving it to her.

She received it in silence, and was going into the next room that she might peruse it at her leisure, when Williams prevented her by saying, if she meant to answer it, she would be pleased to do it that night, because his master was waiting for him at Lady Dorset's.

Your master waits for it, interrupted she, scarcely able to restrain her tears, the painful idea obtruding, that if Sir Edmond had time to wait for his servant, he certainly might have come himself, as he knew the pleasure it would have afforded her.[87]

Yes, madam, he replied; he desired I would make all the haste I possibly could, that I might not prevent his departure; yet, I think, Mrs. Fenwick will prevail for a longer stay at Lady Dorset's; for she is a lady, to whom he can never refuse any thing; though, to be sure, as she is to go with him to London –

My God, my dear, exclaimed Mrs. St. Clare, alarmed at the uncommon alteration she observed in the countenance of Malvina, you are not well! You must have something.

I can only find it here, said Malvina, almost suffocated by the oppression of her heart, shewing Sir Edmond's letter. Leave me, if you please, for a moment, that I may read it, and see if I can yet believe that he –

The perusal of it, without entirely satisfying her, yet served to calm her agitated heart. Edmond assured her, that he was detained against his will; and the reasons which he gave, appeared satisfactory to Malvina; yet, as love possesses an intuitive sensation, which seldom deceives itself, it was in vain that her reason endeavoured to persuade her, that Sir Edmond's delay was right. Some secret presentiment whispered a fear, that he had been faithless. But, as it was only a presentiment, she determined not to let Sir Edmond know of this distress, which she could not account for.

In this uncertainty she arose, to answer the letter; when, in passing the door, she heard the voice of Williams, saying to Mrs. St. Clare, indeed, madam, I repeat it to you, that my master only staid on her account, for he never quitted her a moment; and I am not too certain, that he loves her; and, to be sure, she is devilish handsome.

You are, then, certain, asked Mrs. St. Clare, that not any business calls Mrs. Fenwick to London; and that the journey is only concerted between them, that they may not be separated?

There is not a doubt of it, madam; and his remaining there these two days, was not only to wait for her, but that he might be with her longer; and, when he found that he must leave her at last, he engaged her to accompany him, under some pretence. It was Jenny, who gave me this information, as her mistress always confides every thing to her.

Mrs. St. Clare! cried Malvina, from the next room. Mrs. St. Clare!

What! my dear, replied she, running to her. She saw her pale, and ready to sink. You have heard every thing, said she, with terror.

For pity's sake, send away that man, said Malvina, or his presence will be the death of me.

You may go, Williams, said Mrs. St. Clare; and, taking the arm of her mournful friend within hers, they entered the next room.

Malvina seated herself, but could not weep. After a moment's silence, she looked steadily at Mrs. St. Clare, and said, tell me, my dear friend (for, in the tumult of my present ideas, my heart seems a stranger to itself), which ought I to believe, Williams, or my husband. Read this letter of Edmond's, and inform me what I ought to conclude.

Mrs. St. Clare read it; but she was not more satisfied with it than Malvina. It did not express the instinctive language of affection;[88] but as she had so long utterly disliked Sir Edmond, she was dubious whether she dare express her opinion of it to Malvina; who, after a few moments recollection, said, with more calmness, I shall not remain undetermined any longer, my friend; and that letter shall satisfy me. I will not judge so meanly of my husband, or myself, as to imagine that he has forgot me; or, that he wishes to deceive me; and whatever hateful suspicions they may wish to raise in my mind, yet, he knows that I place the utmost confidence in his faith; and Malvina will reject every other report, as injurious to her happiness,[89] and will give credit to him alone.

She was continuing; when, casting down her eyes, she perceived a paper at her feet. She thought the hand-writing was Edmond's. She took it up, and shuddered, as she read the address of Mrs. Fenwick. The billet was sealed, and was certainly given to Williams, to deliver it to her, and he had forgot it. It might elucidate the whole of this mystery; yet, her trembling hand durst not break the seal. She silently shewed it to Mrs. St. Clare; and then, letting it fall from her hands, she covered her eyes with them, as if to conceal that world from her sight, in which she had only experienced sorrow and deceit. However, Mrs. St. Clare thought proper to open the billet. She had seen, 'I depart to-morrow, overcome with gratitude for your kind favours',[90] &c. She trembled at the effect it would produce on Malvina, and wished to prevent her from reading this fatal billet.[91] But Malvina, perceiving Mrs. St. Clare's design, took it from her. No, said she, I must know my decree. I told you, I would believe no other than himself; and I shall ascertain what I have left to hope for.

She then read the billet, and continued reading it for a long time, without shewing any signs of emotion, or shedding a single tear. But, when she had concluded, she put her hand to her heart. The blow is given, said she; my destiny is fulfilled; and I have truly deserved it.

Mrs. St. Clare, fearfully alarmed at her resignation, went to her, spoke, and embraced her. But she never replied; her cheeks were pale, and cold as ice. There was a fixed wildness in her look. She then arose, walked some paces about the room in silence; then came back, and took up the billet, and exclaimed, I would not believe any other than thyself, Edmond; and, thou hast deceived me! I placed all my confidence in thee; and, thou hast betrayed it! Thy guilt is not momentary; since, it was with her, whom thou hast before seduced, that you have consented to go. Is it, when near your Kitty, that you have dared to address me with expressions of love, and to speak with frivolity and contempt of her, whose kind favours have rendered you so grateful?[92] Oh! Edmond! cruel Edmond! are you become more than unfaithful? and wish to deprive me of the power of reading that heart, which I no longer occupy? Malvina might have supported a transient infidelity; but, how can she survive thy perfidious duplicity?

My dearest Malvina, said Mrs. St. Clare, pressing her in her arms, and weeping over her, perhaps, he may not be so guilty as you imagine. Do you wish, that we should go and join him in London, or at Lady Dorset's? Perhaps, there only wants a proper explanation, to bring returning peace to your mind.

You do not think so, my friend? replied Malvina, with a gloomy countenance. This billet leaves me perfectly convicted. I have nothing more to ask, or learn. You see, by it, that he goes against his inclination. This journey, the intention of which would be to reconcile us, would appear an insupportable duty to him, who can think only of his Kitty; and he can only feel pain, when deprived of her society. Oh! this woe unutterable! which I have never before experienced. While I was counting each moment of his absence, by my anguish, and every step he took, by the throbs of my heart, he was resigning himself to the delight of a new amour; forgetting his vows, my grief, and, consequently, myself.

Williams wishes to know, if your answer is ready, Madam, said Tomkins, opening the door.

It will be, presently, replied Malvina, much agitated, if he will wait a few minutes. I have only to bid him adieu – an adieu, which will not be long; and, taking the first sheet of paper which came to her hand, she wrote as follows: –

Malvina to Edmond.

'Edmond, you have forgot your vows. You have deceived me! This world is already vanished to me; since I ought no longer to love you, when you live for another. Malvina ought to finish her existence; and that heart, from which she must endeavour to tear your image, will soon cease to beat. Ah! in that fatal moment, glance at least one pitying look on the unfortunate being who loves you; that, in your hours of retirement, she may not be quite obliterated from your memory; that her name may be sometimes breathed from your lips; and that her tears may leave some remembrance in your heart. Oh! Edmond! may I hope, that the account of my death may not find you perfectly indifferent? Let not the recollection of your Kitty follow me[93] to my tomb. On beholding the cold and inanimate stone, which will cover that heart of which you alone was the idol, perhaps, you may feel some regret; perhaps, you may say, as you drop a tear, sleep on, poor creature! you now may rest in peace. Adieu! Edmond, adieu! I thought, that I must no longer love you. You have chilled my heart, by your duplicity; and, from this moment, all connexion between us is at an end. Keep far from me, cruel and unkind Edmond, who hast made a jest of my affection. When you first asked my love, I was dejected, and exhausted by grief.[94] Why did you not respect my sorrow? What pleasure could you find in wishing to augment it, by deceiving me, who was sufficiently unhappy, and who had placed her confidence in you? Do you not know, that you have robbed me of my peace, innocence, and self-esteem? Do you not know, that, in forcing me to love you, I have deviated from those duties I vowed to perform; for which you must be responsible to heaven, as well also for my faults, and my consequent misery? All the tears that I have shed, will be witnesses against you. Oh! Edmond! what is it that I have done, that you have conducted me to the brink of this frightful abyss? Until the fatal hour, which attached my affections to you, my pure thoughts were uttered before the shade of my Clara. But your conversation, and the love with which you inspired me, weakened my soul, and I had only a faint remembrance of my vow. I existed for you alone. I felt no other sentiment but my affection, and no other duty, but that of rendering you happy. And yet – you have deceived me. Edmond has forgot Malvina![av] Go then, cruel author of my misery, fly to thy pleasures. But you may, perhaps, even in the centre of that brilliant and attractive world, meet with a similar misery to that which I now endure.[95] Ah! Gracious God! what do I say? another! Can you love another, as I love you? Another will be the object of all thy thoughts, as thou art of mine! No! No! This fancy is only the compliment of my grief. Ah! I entreat and conjure you, Edmond, do not love; never let it enter your heart; do not add to the dreadful torment of not being beloved, the image of another's happiness; and that I may at least know, that thy heart is always insensible; and that, if I have not touched it, no other may have had that power. But, wherefore, this *weak*, this cruel prayer?[aw] Why wish indifference to a being, who is so dear? Ah! how inexpressibly dear to me? Edmond! dear Edmond! Be happy. I wish it. My sorrowful heart beats to this wish, with all the fervency of the purest, the most sincere affection.[96] Though I shall never behold you again, yet I shall rejoice; for will it not afford me the sweetest satisfaction, to release you from the tiranny of the chain which unites us? Be happy, be satisfied; it shall be broken. Be happy. Edmond, Malvina is lost to you for ever. The moment that you left her, was the last time you were ever to behold her; and, after this letter, you will never receive another line, to remind you, that Malvina continues in existence.

"Adieu! Adieu!"'

On concluding these lines, the pen fell from her hand. She turned her eyes on Mrs. St. Clare. My strength is exhausted, said she. I feel, as if I had expended the vital strength of my life in that letter. Will your kindness oblige me, by folding it, and send it for me? I believe, I shall die.

As she said this, her eyes closed, a mortal illness overspread her face; and she sunk, lifeless, into the arms of her friend Mrs. St. Clare; who, terrified, called for assistance; and, by her watchful attention, recalled her to life.

Alas! why would she not let her die? What greater kindness can we implore of heaven, than to lose our life, when we are deprived of happiness?

CHAP. VIII.

Deceit discovered and punished.

As soon as Williams had received Malvina's letter, he hastened on his journey to London; and, calling at Lady Dorset's, he heard that Mrs. Fenwick had been gone two days; he therefore set out again instantly. When he arrived at Sir Edmond's lodgings, he enquired, before he entered, if Mrs. Fenwick was there? that, he might, according to their agreement, receive the reward which she promised, upon the receipt of Malvina's letter, before he spoke to his master. The vigilant Mrs. Fenwick did not allow him a moment's suspense, as she had been every day on the watch for him; the instance she heard his voice, she ran down to meet him at the door. I have been most impatiently waiting for you, said she; give me madame de Sorcy's letter. Go you away immediately, and pretend, that you did not arrive till early to-morrow morning, when you will be certain of finding your master at home; and, if he enquires why you carried the letter to madame de Sorcy yourself, tell him, that, as you did not find an express, and that as Mrs. Fenwick was to take charge of the chaise herself to London, you undertook to deliver this letter, from a motive of fidelity. If he should express his astonishment, that Madame de Sorcy did not write to him, you can say, that having so much company (you may mention Mr. Prior as one) she had not an opportunity of answering it. Do not be the least intimidated[ax] at the idea of your master's anger, in case he should ever discover that you have deceived him; Mrs. Burton and myself will answer for you, and you will be most generously rewarded. But while you wait for that, here are five and twenty guineas. Go – get away as fast as possible, I tremble lest Sir Edmond should come in; for should he surprise us together, our plans will prove entirely abortive, and yourself ruined. He instantly obeyed,[97] and she hurried up to her apartment to read Malvina's letter.

As her heart was not absolutely destitute of feeling, perhaps it might have been affected if her vanity had not revolted against the impressions which she was incapable of imitating. Yet her selfcomplaisance would not allow her inferiority in this respect; she fancied it an exaggerated picture of sensations she could not comprehend, and would not allow herself to pity her, therefore endeavoured to ridicule her. She had the art, during the time she had been in the hotel, of intercepting all the letters which Sir Edmond had written to Malvina: and she was determined to put the finishing stroke, by writing herself to that unfortunate creature. That Sir Edmond, tired and fatigued by her pathetic complaints, had just given her the epistle wherein she had so beautifully delineated her despair, without even taking the trouble to read it. That as a friend, she must inform her, that it was not tears or complaints that would fix the heart of Sir Edmond; and she farther promised, that when she, that is Mrs. Fenwick, did not value his affection any longer, she would have the complaisance to point out to her the best method she should use to obtain it. In acting in this manner, Mrs. Fenwick had not a thought of the dreadful consequences which might ensue from it. She permitted herself to be amused with the pleasure (if pleasure it can be called)[98] of being revenged, without considering that she would give the most indubitable proofs of her deceit, which might ruin her in a moment. But her light and frivolous mind never looked forward, or thought of the future. Consequently she never possessed the least reflection, or cared for any person but herself; therefore she had not the slightest idea of the injury she was committing against Malvina. As her own vanity being hurt was to her the greatest of all sorrows, she undoubtedly imagined that her rival's was nothing more, as nothing in her opinion could exceed it.

Sir Edmond could not account for Malvina's silence, nor for the excuse she had given Williams.[99] In that situation, what company could she receive, and particularly, what company ought to have prevented her writing to her husband? Williams had mentioned Mr. Prior, and from that Edmond conceived a thousand suspicions: not detrimental to Malvina's fidelity, but with regard to those who wished to defame her. It was not Sir Edmond who could suspect his wife, he knew her too well; and Mrs. Fenwick, who fabricated the calumny, should have recollected, that this accusation might be the very means of bringing her plots to light, which she had enveloped Sir Edmond with: as the husband of Malvina would never descend to suspect her virtue.

These suspicions having arisen in the mind of Sir Edmond, he ordered Williams to attend him instantly. On putting several questions to him, his ambiguous and evasive answers convinced his master, that his surmises were not without foundation.[100]

Williams framed an excuse to leave Sir Edmond for a few minutes, and on his sending for him,[101] that he might gain more information from him, he was informed that Williams had disappeared, and no one could tell what was become of him. This immediately confirmed Sir Edmond's suspicions; and a thousand fears on Malvina's silence, and many corresponding presentiments, arose in his mind.

He wrote a letter, in which he expressed the surprise and anxiety he laboured under; and carried it himself to the post, fearful of trusting it to any one, as he might be surrounded by persons who were false. He reflected with pain on all the uneasiness which his wife must suffer, and thus rendered the ideas of his guilt still more insupportable. He felt such an utter detestation for Mrs. Fenwick, that he avoided the sight of her, that it might not perpetually remind him, that he had for a moment forgot Malvina. He went continually to Lord Sheridan's house, in hopes of hearing that he was returned, but he was constantly disappointed, for each day his stay was prolonged; and as Sir Edmond did not receive any account from Malvina, he earnestly wished to set off directly to ascertain himself the occasion of this silence.[102] But then, how could he determine to leave London, without having gained the permission for Frances to remain with her? And in this perplexing situation, he was uncertain in what manner he ought to act.

Mrs. Fenwick, irritated by his continual absence, was only more zealous in following the plan which Mrs. Burton had directed; and not being quite so confident in the justice of her cause, she would not trust it to a public investigation, but solicited it in a private matter, where she could employ an eloquence, which few men could resist. Her attractions, the name of Lord Stafford, and the other friends, by whom she was supported,[103] all concurred in obtaining the success of Mrs. Burton's detestable plan. The order was rather wrested, than granted; but that was of no consequence. In a few days,[104] perhaps, Sir Edmond would be taken far from his wife; and, soon, the mighty ocean might roll its waves between them. She fancied, she could anticipate her behaviour on the sea-side;[105] pale, dejected, almost dying; raising her hands towards him in a supplicating manner; murmuring a last, long, an eternal adieu; and he could not go, to receive her last sigh.

Edmond, who was perfectly unconscious of the detestable plans, of which he was to become the victim, when all return to Malvina would be frustrated, had just heard that Lord Sheridan was arrived in town. He lost not a moment; flew to him; sent in his name, and was immediately ushered in. At the name of Sir Edmond Burton, a gentleman, who was with Lord Sheridan, of an interesting physiognomy, and a noble deportment, regarded him with curiosity and attention; and politely asked him, if he was not the nephew to Mrs. Burton of Edinburgh? also, if he knew Lord Stafford? Edmond bowed, and replied in the affirmative. The gentleman observed him with an uncommon degree of compassion, and departed, with the strongest expression of pity in his countenance.

Sir Edmond was so entirely occupied by the business which he came upon, that he had not noticed any thing which passed. He was intent upon what manner he should introduce the subject, which was of so delicate a nature, and on which the happiness of his life depended. The hopes and fears, by which he was agitated, made him hesitate longer than he would otherwise have done. Lord Sheridan perceived his embarrassment, and, without knowing the cause, endeavoured to relieve him, by beginning the conversation. Certainly, Sir, it is Mrs. Burton, to whom I am indebted for the honour of seeing you; and I am much astonished, that she did not mention it in her letter, which I found here on my return; wherein she informs me, that, according to our agreement, she has taken my daughter from Madame de Sorcy, since her marriage.

What is it you say, my lord? interrupted Sir Edmond. Is Mrs. Burton informed of my marriage? and, has she had the cruelty to take your daughter from the arms of Malvina?

Your marriage! replied Lord Sheridan, astonished. But, certainly, it is not you, who are the husband of Madame de Sorcy? The person whom she has chosen, as I am informed by Mrs. Burton, is a mean wretch, who dishonours his family.

What an infamous falsehood! exclaimed Sir Edmond, with impetuosity. And how could Mrs. Burton think, that you would not be undeceived? She flattered herself, then, in the interim, of completing her cruel machinations against my innocent, my beloved wife. Yes, my lord, it is me – Edmond Burton, who am Malvina's husband. To entreat your consent, to permit your daughter to live with us, to continue under the care of the most amiable of women, I undertook this journey to London. And, I give you my word, I will unite with her, in every care and attention, that she may be rendered worthy the family from whom she is descended. Oh! my lord! when you are now conscious, that they wish to deceive you; when they have calumniated Malvina, who is now, perhaps, dying of the grief, which I know the loss of her darling must have occasioned? will you, after this, reject my entreaties? Oh! my lord! quickly speak the word, one word, that I may fly to the assistance of my wife, my adored wife.

Undoubtedly, Sir Edmond, what you have told me is very surprising, replied Lord Sheridan; and I really find that Madame de Sorcy has not ceased to deserve my confidence, since you are the husband she has chosen. But, though her sorrow affects me, yet, I am a father, and the fate of my child is of consequence; Mrs. Burton appears to be very fond of my daughter, and I will not conceal any thing from you, continued he, hesitating. Many misfortunes, the particulars of which are too tedious to relate, have very much injured my fortune; and if Mrs. Burton's affection should compensate to Frances. – I am a parent Sir Edmond, and you will comprehend how much power that consideration has over me.

Yes, my Lord, I do comprehend you, replied Sir Edmond, (blushing for Lord Sheridan, from a motive which he dare not acknowledge)[106] but allow me to say you are under an error, if you expect any thing from Mrs. Burton's promises. When her interest is concerned, she is very liberal of them; but while laws are in existence, I am her only heir. Should her resentment find means to deprive me of her fortune, I shall always possess sufficient of my own to do more than she will: and my word is inviolable. I will at this moment engage myself to adopt, both in my own name, and that of my wife, Frances Sheridan as our daughter; and if we should have any children, she will become an equal inheritor with them, and if not, she will be the sole heiress.

Upon my word, Sir Edmond, replied Lord Sheridan, it is impossible to make a more noble or generous proposal; but I would not wish to take advantage of so much greatness of soul, as I have learned from experience how valuable a good fortune is. –

In the name of Heaven, my Lord, interrupted Sir Edmond, recollect there is nothing so precious to me, just now, as the time I am losing; that if I could but fly one minute sooner to Malvina, or rather, if I could take back her charge to her, there is nothing that I would not sacrifice. Therefore, my Lord, since my proposal does not displease you, permit me to go immediately in search of a lawyer, before whom you may sign the order, which may authorise me to take Frances

Sheridan out of the power of Mrs. Burton; and I will also ratify the act, by which I shall engage myself to adopt her.

Without waiting for Lord Sheridan's answer, he flew like lightening along the streets, and soon reached the house of a counsellor with whom he was acquainted, and brought him to Lord Sheridan's: who was petrified at the velocity with which Sir Edmond went and returned, saying to him, it indeed appears, Sir, that you do not wish to lose time, and you have, without doubt, as you returned with his gentleman, explained all matters which are to be regulated between us; and while he is employed in that closet, you will favour me with your company into another room, where you will meet a person who wishes to speak with you.

Sir Edmond, much surprised, eagerly hastened to know who could come to seek him at Lord Sheridan's; and on entering the room, he observed the same person whom he had seen there an hour before, and who had regarded him with so much attention. Sir Edmond going to him, and politely saluting him, enquired if he had any particular business with him?

I wished Sir, replied the gentleman, with a look of kindness, to speak with you, as I hope to have the satisfaction of being serviceable to you. I have not the honour of knowing you personally, but as I abhor injustice, the conviction that you are very near experiencing it, has very warmly interested me in your favour – I may say, before I had the pleasure of seeing you. You have very powerful enemies Sir, and you are, I make no doubt, ignorant of their having obtained an order from government to send you out of the kingdom,[107] under the pretext of your having formed a party in Edinburgh, in favour of the French principles;[108] and it is to be put in force to-morrow; which, though I know nothing of you, I have refused to sign, because, among all the crimes alleged against you, I could not ascertain any proofs of sufficient consequence to sanction so arbitrary a proceeding, when chance directed we should both meet here. I was so much surprised at your looks, that I determined not to leave Lord Sheridan's, without obtaining from him some information regarding your situation and character. He gave it me during your absence, but you will pardon him for an indiscretion which has given me the power of being useful to you, and to warn you of your slanderers. If you will therefore go with me, I have not a doubt but you will easily vindicate yourself; and that we shall induce them to revoke an illegal order, that partiality has wrested from weakness.

Ah, gracious God! Sir, replied Sir Edmond, you have nearly petrified me by the surprise and the indignation which my enemies have inspired; and the deep sense of gratitude which I feel for your kind interest, oppresses my heart so powerfully, that I find it utterly impossible to express myself on the occasion. But by what singular barbarity am I to be condemned without being heard? And it is your disinterested generosity, then, which has withheld me, when tottering on the edge of such a precipice? – Infamous wretches! they wished then to tear me from my Malvina? O, name them, Sir, name my detested accusers, that I may know, that I may unmask them.

The petition was signed, replied the gentleman, by Mrs. Burton and Lord Stafford: also by some other persons who hold the first rank in Edinburgh, and of the first consideration here, where it is also supported by men of very powerful interest. –

And all this, interrupted Sir Edmond, with a smile of anguish, to rend the heart, and throw the most amiable of women into despair![109] Oh God! is it possible there can be so much malice in the human heart? – Come Sir, let us go, that you may not repent having granted me your generous protection; a simple recital will permit you to judge whether I am innocent, and you will be informed how far interest, ambition, and revenge can lead a selfish mind.

They departed together – and the Marquis of D***[110] presented Sir Edmond to the King, in council with his minister;[111] and the same day this unjust and cruel order was developed and revoked.

Edmond, in consideration of the danger which he had escaped, could not leave his generous protector without expressing what he felt. Sir Edmond, taking his hand, said in a softened voice, it is not only me, my Lord, whom you have saved, it is not only me who will bless you – no – it is a heart ten thousand times more affectionate, more worthy than mine, who will offer her prayers to Heaven for you, where they will be received my Lord; for they will arise from the heart where purity and virtue alone resides. Farewell my Lord, your generous interest, your benevolent interference, and your image will ever live here; (laying his hand on his breast) and while life remains, be eternally engraven on my heart. I am certain I shall live in your remembrance; for most assuredly the sweetest reward of goodness is to recollect the happiness it has been the author of.

They then separated, and Sir Edmond returned to Lord Sheridan's to sign the two papers which the lawyer had been drawing up, as he determined to set out without delay for Scotland. He returned to his lodgings to prepare for his departure.[112] He had scarcely been in one moment, when a letter was delivered to him; it was from Mrs. St. Clare, and only contained these few lines: 'I am at a loss to imagine from what motive you pretend to be surprised at not having received letters from Malvina, as I cannot suppose that you have forgot that you remitted them into the hands of Mrs. Fenwick;[113] and, for which reason, my unfortunate friend has vowed never more to believe you. Indeed, the turpitude of your conduct has been so far above what I ever could have supposed from you, that my heart refuses to credit the proofs I have of it; and I cannot believe, that you had a knowledge of the order for taking away her darling, or that detestable letter of Mrs. Fenwick's. But, if I do judge you rightly, and your soul yet possesses one spark of humanity, tremble, when you behold yourself surrounded by the murderers of your wife; whom, if you wish to behold once more, delay not a moment'.

While Sir Edmond was perusing this letter, he turned pale; a universal shivering agitated his whole frame; and the chill of death and despair seemed to have pervaded his heart, and every vein in his body. He silently went up to Mrs. Fenwick's apartment; he knocked; Jenny opened the door. My mistress is in bed, Sir, she said.

No matter, replied he, going in; and, as she knew that it was of no consequence, she shut it after him.

By the light of a lamp,[114] Edmond perceived Mrs. Fenwick was asleep.[115] He no longer beheld her but as a base perfidious woman, whose sacrilegious hand had dared to stab the peace of his Malvina. His heart throbbed with indignation; and, governed by his resentment, he was going to awaken her, to demand a full explanation of all her baseness, when observing a writing-case, which was open, he perceived a letter half unfolded, and he instantly saw it was Malvina's handwriting. He shuddered, as he took it up. But, who can express his feelings, as he perused the mournful pages, and read the heart-rending expressions of her who loved him? He hid his pale, humiliated countenance with the fatal letter, and became almost suffocated by his sobs; while his agonised, repentant heart was ready to burst. This noise awakened Mrs. Fenwick; and, alarmed at seeing a man in the room, she jumped out of bed, and found it was Sir Edmond. What is it you? said she; but perceiving the paper, which he held in his hand, she exclaimed, Oh! God! Sir Edmond, what have you done? I know every thing.[116]

And I also know you, he replied, in a tone of indignation, accompanied by a look of the utmost contempt.

Mrs. Fenwick's mind was incapable of feeling either the injuries she had been guilty of, or the situation of Sir Edmond, and preserved the hope of appeasing him, and vindicating herself. She confessed she was culpable, with an assumed humility, attributing it entirely to the excess of her love; and, half exposing her charms to Sir Edmond, she pressed him in her arms;[117] but he repulsed her, with horror, saying, you are a vile and wicked creature. I detest you, and you are the object of my utmost contempt and abhorrence. I can never sufficiently repent, or be sufficiently humble, at the remembrance of having, for a moment, forgot myself for you. Go! wicked, despicable woman, and bow your guilty head to heaven, which is conscious of all the infamy of your conduct, and all the maliciousness of your heart.

He concluded with these words, and left her a prey to confusion and regret.

CHAP. IX.

A mournful object.

While Mrs. Fenwick was afflicting herself, Sir Edmond ordered a chaise to be got ready, and departed, without stopping night or day. Sleep had never once saluted his eyes. The image of Malvina, ill-used, and dying, was for ever present to his imagination, and oppressed his mind with an insupportable weight of sorrow and repentance. He could not rest even in the carriage; for, when the mind is distressed by corroding anxiety, the repose of the body becomes equally insupportable. For this reason, he frequently got out, while on the road; he ran, he reasoned with himself; but he could not reach her soon enough, and he was taken for a lunatic. Despair was stamped on his features. What avails, then, health, birth, and fortune, which all smiled upon him? Yes; all these he had in possession. But, of what importance are all the blessings which are bestowed upon us, if we are the prey of remorse?

He, however, arrived at last at the place he so impatiently desired. Perceiving the garden-wall, he stopped at the little private gate, of which he had a key; and, ordering the carriage to go round to the court-yard, he entered the wood. The full orbed moon shed her pensive silver light on every surrounding object. How were they changed, since he last saw them! The trees had lost their foliage. The flowers no longer bloomed, and lavishly scattered their sweet perfume. The melody of the birds was silent; a piercing cold had succeeded the soft breath of summer. In his way he beheld some funeral cypresses, and gloomy firs, whose pyramidical branches preserved the only remaining verdure that appeared; from whose dark branches, the owl sent forth her doleful shrieks; it was the only noise, which interrupted the silence of the night, and which Echo mournfully repeated.

Edmond shuddered; his legs trembled under him; he struck his foot against a stone. A moon-beam, which had pierced the foliage, permitted his wandering eye to observe that this stone covered a tomb. He uttered an exclamation, and fell down; his body pressed the cold and senseless earth. He was uncertain who slept under it, and the deepest sorrow penetrated his heart. In his despair, he struck his head against the stone, exclaiming, with wildness, Malvina! Malvina!

Soon after, he heard a voice soft and weak, which appeared to proceed from the shrubbery, reply, and ask, who called me?

At this accent, Edmond arose; and, wildly looking round, endeavoured to find from whence that voice, which struck him,[118] proceeded. He listened, and presently heard the rustling of cloaths among the trees, and perceived a woman with a black veil, which covered her head, and part of her shoulders. Who are you? and whom do you seek? She asked, why do you come here, to disturb the ashes of the dead, and prevent that peace, which only the tomb can afford me?

What is it I hear? cried Sir Edmond. What fatal words! Malvina! Is it thou, whom I behold? Is it thou, whom I hear?

No! she replied, I am no longer Malvina. I was so once, when he loved me; but he has left me, and I am fallen into distress. He has deprived me of his love; and the grief I feel for it, will soon bring me to the dust.

At these words, a mortal chill seemed to freeze the soul of Edmond, and a presentiment of the most severe misfortune penetrated his heart. He raised the veil, which covered Malvina; he pressed her in his arms. My wife, my friend, my Malvina! do you not know your Edmond? he exclaimed, in the most passionate accent.[119]

Hush! hush! you must not pronounce that name here. Do you not know how often I have repeated it in vain, ever since the night of my despair? but he never sent me any comfort.

Malvina! recollect me, for pity's sake. I am thy Edmond, thy husband, who is returned, never to leave you more.

Malvina seated herself upon the stone; and, surveying him with a smile of anguish, she said, why do you so often repeat, I am Edmond, I am Edmond? Do you think I am ignorant of all which has passed? They vainly wished to hide it from me; and I know that Edmond will never return here, since another has taken possession of his heart; he will only stay with her. He rejects, he hates Malvina.

He reject her! interrupted Edmond, pressing his lips to the cold cheeks of his wife. He hate her! Ah! heaven is my witness, never, never, was she so much beloved.

He would not like to hear what you say, she replied; and you must never tell me that he loves me, hurrying from him, because that will prevent me from dying.

And is it thus, that I have found thee? exclaimed Edmond, clasping his hands in the anguish of despair. I speak to Malvina; and Malvina no lònger hears me. I am before her; and her mild eyes do not behold me. Grief has destroyed her senses; and it is myself, the most barbarous and inhuman of beings, who has reduced her to this dreadful state. Oh! my Malvina, most beloved, and most injured of women! condescend to smile on thy Edmond, that thy heart may be arrested by his voice, and thy looks may dwell upon thy husband. But, Oh God! – No, no! he exclaimed, terrified at the wildness which was pourtrayed on all Malvina's features. Oh! hide those looks from me; I cannot support them; they enfeeble, they sink me to the earth; and he sunk at Malvina's feet. In his melancholy delirium, he exclaimed, he smote his breast.

Malvina, silent and insensible, did not regard him. She looked mournfully round; but her vacant look did not rest on any object. Then, rising gently, she approached the tomb; and, kneeling upon it, this is the hour, said she; it strikes, and yet I exist; and must I, then, wait another day? In the world, to-day; but to-morrow, in eternity.

She then arose, and suspended her black veil on one of the cypress trees; her beauteous auburn hair[120] fell rioting round her neck. She wandered about,[121] and went some paces beyond the shrubbery. The moon shone directly on her countenance; and it was, by its pale beams, that Edmond, gazing on his beloved wife, marked how much all her features were altered by the corroding touch of sorrow, which silently preys, and destroys the powers of life. She passed close by him; took up her robe, that it might not touch him, and continued her walk.

He followed her steps, slowly, without having the power to speak; went with her into the house, and followed her to the apartment, where Mrs. St. Clare was waiting her appearance. You behold me yet here, said Malvina, on entering. It is long, very long. I did not believe it was so difficult to die.

Mrs. St. Clare sighed deeply, got up, and silently took the hand of her friend, in order to conduct her to her chamber. As they reached the door, she perceived Sir Edmond. At this unexpected appearance, Mrs. St. Clare exclaimed, what, you! you here? By what prodigy is it, that I see you! But, tell me, has she seen you? Have you spoke to her?

She has seen me; and I have spoke.

And yet she remains insensible?

The most violent sobs were the only reply Edmond could return. Mrs. St. Clare but too well understood their import, and exclaimed, falling into a chair, ah! then, it is over; there only remains despair.

Edmond's groans were heard by Malvina. She approached him; and, looking at him with compassion, how he weeps! said she; he has not shed all his tears. Observe, how much he suffers; he certainly has been deceived; but, be composed, unhappy creature! Thy griefs will soon cease. I have also suffered much; yet you see, that I am very tranquil now; for there will be a day of mercy, and a night of repose, which will heal the broken-hearted, and close all their wounds.

Mrs. St. Clare arose, took Edmond's hand, and held it to Malvina's breast, interrogating her friend. Do you not feel any thing? Look at this person, Malvina. Do you not recollect him? Say, do you not know that it is Edmond?

What do you know of Edmond? asked Malvina, with a hurried accent, and an air of wildness, as she surveyed them both. Ah! if you know where he is, run to him, run; tell him to bring back my Frances; tell him, particularly, not to give her to Kitty, his Kitty; because she is mine, the child of my Clara; and I must give an account of her to her mother? How shall I dare to join her in heaven, when I have lost her child? How can I support her threatening voice, when she demands her of me? Must I say, that she belonged to Kitty? Do you think, added she, pressing the hand of Sir Edmond with convulsive agitation, do you believe that Edmond would consent to let me have my Frances?

He will, to-morrow, bring her to you, himself, said Edmond. To morrow, your husband and your child will be here.

Hear him, just heaven! exclaimed Malvina, with quickness. Do you hear him? He promises, and assures me, that Edmond and Frances will be here to-morrow. But, does he not likewise deceive me? For, is not that the same voice, which I formerly – Do I not hear Edmond? Edmond! That name is every where, continued she, putting her hand to her forehead. It burns me, it consumes me; my brain is on fire. Then, flying from Mrs. St. Clare and Edmond, she ran up to her own chamber, crying, why, why, prevent me from going to him? I think, he would certainly have pitied my sorrows. I would have said, my Edmond, behold, thy Malvina has come to thee. If it displeases thee, she will go away; but, look at her only once more, that she may take with her a last look of compassion and kindness from her Edmond. Only tell her, that you do not hate her; and, from that moment, she will never more disturb your new pleasures. She will suppress her tears, stifle her complaints, and sleep in the dust. Now, that door of happiness is closed, which thou hadst half opened to her sight. There, she will die.[122]

In concluding the last sentence, she became dejected, from the violence of her agitations, and she sunk, lifeless, on the floor. Her eyes were fixed and open, and her oppressed heart seemed ready to break. But her situation, dreadful as it was, was nothing, when compared to that of Edmond.

Mrs. St. Clare perceived it; and, taking his hand, with a look of compassion, do not let us despair, said she. Perhaps, the sight of Frances, by calming her conscience, may awaken her reason. At present, she will remain tranquil for some hours. She must be put to bed. If she can but find that repose, which these barbarians have robbed her of, it will be well, as it may ease her harrassed mind.

Ah! Mrs. St. Clare, the crime was dreadful; but the punishment far exceeds it.

No, no, unhappy Edmond! replied she, I do not accuse you. It is not you, alone,[123] who have been guilty; your sufferings sufficiently convince me of it.

Oh! no one has been so much to blame as myself, he replied. I was beloved by Malvina. Oh! Malvina, my adored wife! if, by an impious frailty, I have perjured my vows, on finding you in this terrible situation, Gracious God! am I not sufficiently punished?

CHAP. X.

Concerns Mrs. Burton.

Malvina, insensible to all that passed, was carried to her chamber, without knowing it. In that state of death-like insensibility, she did not appear to distinguish any object. Edmond, seated by her bed-side, miserable and dejected, could not help contemplating that charming countenance, which had constituted his felicity, and now his most severe misery, as he considered himself the occasion of it. He watched, he waited; he anxiously hoped for a change, but in vain. That countenance, once so expressive of tenderness and every amiable propensity, no longer varied; the play of features seemed suspended; an inanimate melancholy stupor had succeeded, and chained those features, which the gentle virtues, sense and affection, had animated.

Edmond could no longer support this heart-breaking sight; and, leaving her bed, with an air of delirium, he rushed out of the room; then, returning instantly, he went up to Mrs. St. Clare, saying, for heaven's sake, inform me, who were those barbarous monsters, that have reduced my beloved Malvina to this deplorable state. – Name them, that I may load them with my vengeance. How long has she been deprived of her reason? and why was it concealed from me?

Sir Edmond, replied Mrs. St. Clare, I will satisfy all your inquiries. But, first, reply to mine; and dare not to sully the air, which this unfortunate victim breathes, by asserting a falsehood. Look at this letter, which is written by Mrs. Fenwick to Malvina; had it the sanction of your approbation? and, did you really sacrifice your wife for her?

Oh heaven, what infernal wickedness! exclaimed Sir Edmond, on reading the contents of Mrs. Fenwick's letter. What a monster of deceit! It is, then, thy detestable hand, which sent the blow to Malvina's heart. Ah! madam, I acknowledge, this woman did seduce me for a moment. Yet, I was drawn into it more by circumstances, than by her. But, I solemnly declare that, since then, the contempt with which she inspired me was so great, that I found not the least effort in resisting all her wiles. And, can you imagine, that I could be so base, as to sacrifice Malvina, the interesting Malvina, to such a vain, frivolous being as that? Merciful God! I thus permit her to insult the wife of my bosom! Ah! far, very far, be such a detestable crime from me! Never did I allow her impure lips to utter the revered name of Malvina before me. But, by what inconceivable art, by what mysterious iniquity, could she find means to secrete my letters?

That is sufficient, interrupted Mrs. St. Clare. I shall not even inquire, if you was concerned in taking away Frances. I should blush, even to suspect such a trait of inhumanity from the frail, though repentant husband of Malvina.

I never saw Lord Sheridan but the day previous to my leaving London, replied Edmond, and it was from him that I received the information of Mrs. Burton's having sent for Frances from her retreat! and it is from him that I obtained an order the same moment, to carry her back, here it is, and to morrow Frances will be resigned to her beloved mother.

Oh, Edmond! unfortunate, unhappy Edmond! exclaimed Mrs. St. Clare, pressing both his hands in hers, why, are not those detestable wretches to be responsible for having so basely slandered you? – As to Mrs. Burton, I hope the earth does not contain another being so deceitful and unfeeling. She came here, Edmond, a few days after Williams had brought your letter, attended by one of the justices of the peace, and alighting from her carriage, she desired him to summon Lady Burton to appear. I went with your wife, and informed him there was no person here of that name. This is no time to deny it, said Mrs. Burton, here is a copy of the church register where the celebration took place, which states the facts. I am informed of every thing, but what perhaps the lady is unacquainted with, addressing herself to Malvina; which is, that Sir Edmond is fascinated with another beauty, and recollecting the extent of his imprudence,[124] now desires to dissolve his union, which he only regards as a misfortune, and which he declares he never should have been drawn into, but by the most seducing artifices. Here, madam, is the act that I am commissioned to present you from him: if you consent to sign it, your marriage will be dissolved, and Miss Sheridan may remain with you; but if you refuse, it is her father's will that she must be resigned to my care; for which there is a legal order, which these persons will see duly performed immediately.

Madam, replied your wife, with more fortitude and calmness than I could have expected, I do not perceive that this order is signed by Sir Edmond; I shall therefore wait till that is affixed, before I sign mine. I will certainly yield to his wishes, but will not consent without he does also.

So, replied Mrs. Burton, with a satirical smile, because you wish a marriage, which your husband detests, to continue in force a few days longer, you will deviate from the vows of a friend, which you pretend was so dear to you, and consent to allow her child to be separated from you.

No, madam, that is what I never will consent to, replied Malvina, with energy: and if she is ravished from me, it will be indeed by force only. I shall then put in a claim against this attempt, for if she is taken by violence, justice will resign her to me again; you must not always expects to accomplish your views by such conduct. The day of truth may not be far distant, when the world will know your heart, and be shocked at its selfishness.

Mrs. Burton appeared rather mentally disturbed at the solemnity with which Malvina spoke, and without answering her, turned to the justice. You observe, she said, that the lady refuses to comply with any terms; therefore the law authorises me to see those orders put in force, which I am empowered to have fulfilled. Therefore I demand the appearance of the Honorable Frances Sheridan.

I then spoke. – Sir, I desire you will take particular care that you are not guilty of a very despicable piece of business. I am equally as great a stranger as yourself to all this affair; but I foresee, that you will one day repent having employed force in taking Miss Sheridan from this place.

Mrs. St. Clare, interrupted Mrs. Burton, in a tone of contempt, we have nothing to do with your high-flown sentiments; keep them for the public who may have the patience to hear them. Come Sir, there is no time to lose, and I summon you to perform your duty.

Indeed, said the justice, I do not see what I shall have to fear; the order which Mrs. Burton has, is positive and complete in all the forms which are legal in the opinion of justice. I then only execute the laws. He then went out to order Miss Sheridan's appearance. Not one of the servants dare to disobey him, as you know how much the magistrates are respected here.

Malvina, who saw with terror, that she had not a moment to lose, made another effort, and addressing Mrs. Burton, may I not be permitted, at least to keep Frances, until Sir Edmond has signed the act you have shewn me? I will then engage myself, by the most sacred vows, to complete the dissolution of my marriage, or relinquish my charge.

No, said Mrs. Burton, I will not accept of any other accommodation, than what was proposed on my arrival; and I desire that you will quickly perform it. I must have your signature or your child.

Oh, Clara! exclaimed Malvina, raising her hands to Heaven, thou beholdest to what a cruel alternative I am reduced by the malevolence of this woman – direct me in my duty dear sacred Shade.[125]

Mrs. Burton may go as soon as she pleases, said Mrs. Tasse, entering the room, for the child is already in the carriage.

Ah! they have taken my child, then, exclaimed Malvina, wildly, flying out of the room.

Mamma, mamma, said the child, struggling to release herself from those who had taken her, are you not going with me?

No, I will never leave you, said Malvina, throwing herself under the coach wheels, the barbarians may crush me before they shall take thee from thy mother.

Take away the lady, said Mrs. Burton, in the most unfeeling manner, to the people who were with her; you see plainly she is bereft of her senses.

What then, madam, said I, are you invulnerable to the sensation of pity? What can you expect from such inhuman conduct? If your intention is not to kill the innocent creature, whom you have thus cruelly taken from her more than mother,[126] with such unfeeling apathy, are you sure that you will not be obliged to return her?[127]

Take away the lady, repeated Mrs. Burton, in a voice trembling with rage, without deigning to answer me.

Malvina, perceiving they were going to carry her away by force, arose, and falling at Mrs. Burton's feet, said, in the name of Heaven, in the name of humanity, for the sake of your own peace, do not deprive me of my child! I cannot survive the loss of her. Do you wish to reproach yourself with my death?[128]

It is in your own power to return her, said Mrs. Burton, perfectly unaffected; you know the conditions, I am inflexible to any others.

Go then, depart, I shall not detain you longer, said your wife, leaving her with horror. Though I have not a doubt but that this act is a horrible piece of art, by which you hope to deceive both myself and Edmond, by disuniting us for ever.[129] But Sir Edmond will soon appear, perhaps he may be here to-morrow, perhaps to-day. He will return me my child, and your arts will be revealed. You will be punished; indeed you must be already, if you possess any conscience which can force you to feel.[130] There is justice however in Heaven! On concluding these words, your Malvina, overpowered by grief, was nearly deprived of all sense; and Mrs. Burton, whose countenance betrayed a mixture of anger and fear, hurried away. What shall I say more? I have only to inform you, Sir Edmond, on the same evening of that dreadful day, the letter which you now hold, was brought to Malvina. She believed that she beheld in it a confirmation of all that Mrs. Burton had said; and she was forced to suppose that her husband was concerned with her enemies. That perhaps she had sacrificed the child of her beloved Clara, to a man who possessed neither faith nor honor. From that moment –

From that moment, repeated Edmond, trembling.

Mrs. St. Clare pointed to Malvina, without having the power to utter another word.

I understand you, said he, with a look of the deepest despair; and if I lose her before she has recovered her reason, she will die with the idea that I was the cause of her being thus hurried to the grave.

This fear, which was but too well founded, had something so frightful in the very idea of it, that Mrs. St. Clare was fearful that it might tempt him to destroy himself; and she therefore, with the utmost kindness, endeavoured to prevent his mind from dwelling upon this mournful subject, by relating a thousand interesting particulars relative to Malvina, which drew torrents of tears from Sir Edmond, and in some measure relieved his oppressed heart. Your wife particularly wished me to have a tomb-stone placed in the wood, where you met her this evening. I opposed it for some time, but finding that contradiction only served to render the desire more strong, I was determined to gratify her every wish. She appears to have her mind possessed by the singular idea that she ought to die every night at ten o'clock, the fatal hour on which she received Mrs. Fenwick's letter. It is at that time that she always goes out, in that state of insensibility[131] which you have witnessed. Without seeming to know me, she calls me by my name sometimes to accompany her;[132] she then goes into the garden, and desires me to leave her alone till midnight. She then returns so melancholy, and tells me she shall not die till the next day, and falls into that cold insensibility. I have had several physicians; but they gave me not the least hope; they should have been here again to-day.

Edmond did not give her time to finish what she was saying; but, starting up, went to Malvina's bed-ide; and, falling on his knees, he pressed her pale hand to his lips, crying, sweet, sacred victim, thou shalt be avenged. The monsters, who have deprived thee of thy reason, and destroyed my felicity, shall receive the reward they merit. Their punishment shall commence from this hour. I will go, and snatch thy child from those detested hands, which now detain her. I depart, Malvina, only to return the next evening.[133] That I may recover thee! added he, in an accent quick, yet, as if imploring, Oh! that I might find thee recovered! Tell me, speak, Malvina, my companion, my all of happiness! Only one word, one look, only one! Frightful silence! Oh! then, what is become of my Malvina? Ah! once I did not entreat in vain. Her gentle heart was never silent to the entreaties of her Edmond. But, now, all is changed; she has not any thing to say to me. Hast thou, then, ceased to love me, Malvina? Ah! only tell thy Edmond, who adores thee; who is oppressed by thy hate, and torn by remorse; yet only say, that thou canst no longer love me, that this wretched being may have the felicity of hearing that soft voice. Ah! how infinitely would he prefer thy reproaches, the most severe thou couldst utter, to this dreadful inanimation! from which nothing can rescue thee.

He then quitted her hand, which fell without strength. He left her; yet, her eyes could not follow him. He contemplated her with dismay, oppressed as he was with fear, and his own condemnation. He withdrew to another part of the chamber, and resigned himself to the violent grief, which despair and repentance equally produced in his heart.

During this plaintive sorrow, Malvina seemed as awakened from her gloomy stupor. She looked wildly round her. She listened, and a transient bloom crossed her cheeks. Edmond beheld this emotion, and approached her. She took his hand, and, leaning forward, said, in a low voice, have you heard any thing?

It is him. He is returned. He weeps, because he cannot find me again.

You know it is him, then, Malvina!

Certainly. His voice pierced me in the shades of death; for there was no other but his, that would have touched me like his. But, do not tell any one that he is here; they must not know of it, because the stranger will come, and take him away again. She will force Malvina away.[134] It is you only, who do not wish to leave him.[135] Come, and sit down.[136] In a moment after, she cried, No, No! with apparent terror, I cannot. Do you not see that hand of iron, which detains me? Oh! It is Clara's. Observe, what an impenetrable bar there is, which separates her from me? It is she, who has placed it there. Do you not hear her voice, which is no longer affectionate and soft, as it used to be, but terrible and threatening? It is she, who continually repeats, that the perfidy of Edmond is a just reward for my deviation from my promise. Ah! it is she,[137] who has torn me from his heart, and placed another there. She smiles at my distress; and, though I am humbled to the dust, and implore her forgiveness, she will not condescend to look at me.

Oh! thou much injured angel! exclaimed Sir Edmond, weeping, how much ought you to despise those,[138] who have made you suffer thus?

Me hate him! said she, with quickness. I see, very plain, that you do not know me,[139] or you would be sure that was impossible. Hear me, said she in a whisper.

If you should ever meet with him, be sure to conceal from him, that he was the cause of my death; for, perhaps, it might afflict him; and I wish, that my Edmond should always be happy though he may have forgot his poor Malvina. But I am going to my father, who is above, and I shall implore him to bless Edmond. Oh! Almighty Father, I will say, do not punish him; but, if he has provoked thy anger against him, O! let me suffer, instead of him, and bestow on him all the felicity thou shouldst have granted me.

Oh! thou angelic woman! holy innocence! exclaimed Sir Edmond; and is it thou, who was to meet with one, who was so great a monster as to deceive thee?

But, do you think, continued she, that Clara will permit me to raise my voice to my heavenly father?[140] She is with his angels; and, my Clara deserves to be one. But, when she perceives me before the divine tribunal, she will ask me, what I have done with her child; and, if I approach her, she will repulse me with horror, demanding her Frances.[141]

At this dreadful idea, Malvina's strength again failed; her eyes rolled; and, clasping her hands, she fell senseless on the bed, and again enjoyed some moments of the sweet silent peace of the grave.

CHAP. XI.

A faint glimmering of hope.

I must not delay a moment, said Edmond to Mrs. St. Clare.[142] Frances must be fetched back immediately. I go, continued he; and a faint gleam of hope crossses my heart, as I depend much on the presence of the child; for it appears to me, that the idea of having lost her, is what most distresses Malvina. Alas! so indulgent and tender as she naturally is, she certainly would have forgiven a fault in another, though she cannot support the idea of having reason to reproach herself; and, from the moment in which she imagined herself culpable, she sunk under it, as her soul is too pure to wish to exist, when touched by remorse.

As soon as the dawn of day appeared, Sir Edmond got into his carriage; and, before noon, he reached Mrs. Burton's. The sight of that detested house made him shudder. He went in, and entered the room, without being announced. He found his aunt at breakfast, surrounded by a brilliant circle. On beholding Edmond, pale, with his hair dishevelled, equipped in a riding-dress, she uttered an exclamation of surprise. Little Frances, who was mournfully sitting by her, started from her seat, and flew with rapture to Sir Edmond. My dear Sir, said she, you have been away so long; but, now, you will take me back. I know you will take me to my dear mamma. Won't you?

Yes, yes, replied Sir Edmond, pressing her with ardor to his bosom; this evening, you shall behold your dear mother.

And by what right, Edmond, asked Mrs. Burton, pale with rage, do you pretend to take away a charge, which was confided to my care?

From the right of justice and humanity, replied he, surveying her with contempt. It was by that you was entreated, when your perfidious wickedness ravished that child from my wife.

At this appellation to Malvina, and the cruelty which he seemed to accuse Mrs. Burton with, all the company appeared embarrassed, looking at each other with an expression of inquiry,[lxiv] as wishing to gain information from each, to develope this extraordinary scene. Mrs. Burton, alarmed at having so many witnesses, fearing the reproaches which she was conscious Sir Edmond might load her with, spoke in a more gentle tone, saying to him, if you wish to speak to me upon business, I will attend you to my closet, where we can explain ourselves better.

No, no, said Edmond, with a mixture of rage and detestation, I have nothing to say privately; and I only regret, that the whole world is not present also, that I might have the sweet satisfaction of exhibiting you in your native character. The barbarous woman, who could so unfeelingly resist the pathetic entreaties of the most gentle of beings; and who could, by insult, deceit, and malice, destroy the reason of one of the most perfect of nature's works. Stop, continued he, observing her intention of interrupting him. I have not yet mentioned the scandalous insinuations, which you have written, to satisfy the horrid desire of revenge and ambition; and, without the least scruple, or compunction, has publicly accused her own nephew, as a person who ought to be suspected, and who is disaffected towards the English government; and the measures of this woman were so well conceived and planned, that, had it not been for the almost immediate, I must call it interposition of Providence, I should have been sent to the Indies, as a disturber of the public tranquillity. I perceive, by your consternation, that you hoped they would have concealed your secret; and, without doubt, your vile accomplice, who sits near you, Lord Stafford, believed so also. But there yet are liberal and loyal minds; and, happily for humanity, there are not many that resemble yours.

Sir Edmond had begun with so much energy and vehemence, that it was utterly impossible to stop him; and, now, it was too late; every thing was discovered. Mrs. Burton, completely humbled, observed every one tremble at this recital, and leave her with horror. Her reputation for possessing such greatness of soul, which she had raised with such infinite pains and care, was demolished in one moment; and her punishment had already commenced.

Edmond perceived it, and his vengeance was gratified. He then only thought of his departure; and taking Frances in his arms, he placed her in the carriage, and drove to Doctor Maxwell's, to prevail on him to attend Malvina. He complied, and they instantly set out; and Edmond employed all the time in discoursing on the state Malvina was reduced to. The horses nearly flew; and the clock, that faithful monitor,[143] was just striking ten, when the carriage stopped at the door. Mrs. St. Clare hastened to it; she had been impatiently expecting Edmond. How is she? How has she been?[144] demanded he, with a hurried voice.

This is the hour that she goes into the garden, replied she. She is now there.

Her state, her health? interrupted he, alarmed.

Mrs. St. Clare shook her head, and, sighing, replied, she is just the same.

I will go to her, said Edmond. I hope, no danger can proceed from it.

Alas! returned Mrs. St. Clare, what do you think there is yet to fear?

The wretched Edmont but too well understood it; and he felt it to despair, that, of all the situations, the most terrible is that, where the extreme of one evil can only permit us[145] to dread a worse. In this disposition, he went into the garden. He took the same walk which he had done the preceding evening, when he followed Malvina's steps; and he was oppressed by the same misery, the same agonising sensations. He perceived her near a cypress tree; she was walking; her long white robe, her hair wildly rioting, her slow pace, and her eyes bent on the ground. All that appertained to her, partook of a death-like melancholy, and increased the manifest pity which her situation inspired. The sound of Edmond's foot-steps appeared to alarm her, and she seemed as if inclined to fly. Do not be fearful, said Edmond; it is only me.

Is it you, replied she, with quickness, going towards him, that she might see him plainer. O! yes, it is you. I recollect, that you said you would come back again, and you have not then deceived me?

O! never, never, will I deceive my dear Malvina.

Ah! listen to me, said she, after a moment's silence (in which she seemed buried in thought), I fancied you had been here before. But, oh! how long, how very long it is since then! So long, and yet I live.[146] Here, every thing was so beautiful, added she, extending her hand towards the garden. There, I have gathered roses; they were for him. Here I have listened to the birds; they sung for him. Every where the air I breathed was so pure, so like its native heaven, that, also all, every thing was for him. But he flew from me, and every thing is withered. The flowers are all decayed, and fallen; and the place where they grew, is forgotten.

But he will return again, replied Edmond, pressing her gently to his bosom; and then you may gather roses for him, again; the birds will again sing, and the air will again be soft and refreshing.

No, no, interrupted she, with a convulsive tremor, No, No! – never, never. Do you see this flower, which is at my bosom? I gave it him the evening before his departure; but he let it drop, when he left me. I snatched it from the ground, and, ever since, I have worn it next my heart. Yet, with all my care, it would die. Certainly, it is, because he has rejected me.[147] Only see how it has lost its bloom, and its freshness, which it never, never will regain. Yet, we must all die one day. As for me, I have scarcely a moment to live.[148]

My gentle, my tender Malvina must not die. I will press her in my arms. I will save her from death.

No, no; we must submit to our fate; and mine, is to obey him. He does not wish for Malvina. He forces her to her grave, and she must fall into it. Ought I not to die to-morrow? – Yes, to-morrow, when the clock tells that hour which brought the stranger's letter.[149] Oh! it had something in it, which destroys, which kills by moments, continued she, looking steadily at Sir Edmond, with a look of deep and settled despair. It contained something which burns, which devours here, and there (pointing to her head, and laying her hand on her heart). It is a fire, which seems for ever burning; an evil which cannot be appeased.[150] It constantly gnaws at the heart, and prevents me from living; and, yet, it will not allow me to die quick enough. Have you seen those who suffer, and no longer exist? They must have resembled me.

She stopped; the dreadful picture of her sufferings had weakened all her faculties, and she sunk, without strength, into the arms of her husband; who, pressing the inanimate body to his bosom, riveted his lips to those, which were once so blooming; but, now, how cold! how pale! and those eyes, which formerly beamed with tenderness and love, are now almost extinguished; her whole form was cold as death. He called Malvina, his dear Malvina; but Malvina did not reply. He felt solitary and alone in the world, with his wife expiring;[ay] and he was beyond all expression wretched, as he considered himself the cause of her death.[151] He no longer thought of returning; he saw, he thought only of his beloved Malvina, whom he believed dying, and he determined not to survive her.

Mrs. St. Clare being extremely uneasy at his staying so late, went into the garden, followed by Doctor Maxwell. They found him on his knees, supporting himself against a tree, with Malvina folded in his arms; anxious and fearfully counting the weak throbbing of her heart.

On observing the Doctor advancing, he called to him without changing his posture. Doctor, this is my wife, this is my Malvina – you must save her – you must! Oh, pray answer me? Do not tell me that she cannot live – I cannot, will not support it. I cannot support the idea of losing my all of happiness, my Malvina! Do you hear me Doctor? do you Mrs. St. Clare? Oh! I cannot lose her. He then shed a few of those corroding tears, which are sometimes granted, though sparingly to relieve us from despair.[152]

The Doctor having felt Malvina's arm, desired she might be taken into the house, telling Sir Edmond, that his keeping her in the cold was very injurious.

It was not with such neglect as this that you was once attended and preserved. Edmpnd was silent. He raised Malvina, and carried her in his arms to her bed; and the Doctor following, examined her more attentively. After a moment's pause, the disorder is worst in the head, said he. Ah! Doctor, replied Sir Edmond, tell me may she not be saved?

Saved! he repeated: and regarding him with a significant look, if it is only her life which you mean, she does not at present appear to be in much danger; and if nothing particular occurs to increase her weakness, I think I can answer for her.

Oh! Doctor, but will you only answer for her life?

We must wait with patience: we must first see, and not precipitate our measures. They are now preparing a bath,[153] we shall see what effect that will produce. Tomorrow we must try the power of music. The most gentle means, accompanied by time and patience. I have seen such recover.

You have known such recover? interrupted Sir Edmond, wildly. Oh! Doctor, dear Doctor, you will then restore, and give me back my Malvina? And in the tumult of his joy he claspt his hands, he went out, then returned, issued a thousand orders at once, and as if he thought they would not be executed as quick as he wished them, he went to assist himself in their execution. He desired every one to be quick; then shook hands with all those he met, without distinction of persons. She may be saved, he exclaimed to all those who came near him. She may be recovered, the Doctor hopes, and assures me of it. Ah! my friends, assist me in recovering, in saving Malvina. She is my felicity, my life, my joy! I cannot exist without her; but who indeed here could survive her loss? Is it not from her that all your pleasures arise? That generous and compassionate mind was ever the friend of all the unhappy.[154] Never did she permit her own sorrows to render her forgetful of others; and suppressing her own, did she not constantly derive consolation, if she could only relieve another's misery.[az] And it is I, barbarian as I am, that have reduced her to this situation! And what have I gained?[155] When for that love which was beyond all price, my vicious ingratitude has destroyed her peace, and caused her reason to wander. Every one must view me, as I do myself, and consider me as the most guilty of men. So unworthy as I am of forgiveness, yet if my angelic Malvina should regain her reason, I may hope for pardon, as I have not a doubt of her mercy; and you will then witness that her gentle nature is more ready to forgive, than I can be to ask it. Oh! Malvina, while there remains so much good for you to perform on earth, thy all-affectionate heart will not wish to leave me before I have expiated the remorse which overwhelms my guilty mind.

Every person wept as they heard him mournfully accusing himself. The good Tomkins, who had nourished Malvina with her milk, and Old Peter, who had abandoned his friends and native land to follow her, expressed the deep source of their grief by that silence, which the heart of sensibility will term eloquence; for it will understand its full force, though expressed by the humble children of nature.[156]

Mrs. St. Clare, the kind, the affectionate, the disinterested Mrs. St. Clare, who was astonished to meet with one woman, in whom every virtue was united, loved her, tenderly loved her, even more than she admired her. The Doctor also remembered the affecting situation in which he first beheld her, and this rendered her present situation still more touching. Indeed, all those who had ever known her,[157] joined their tears with Edmond's. These eloquent tears declared her intrinsic worth; and never was there a more sincere and pathetic panegyric, or more powerful oration, surrounded by all the pomp of a throne, or the applauses of the multitude. Nor could any being on earth be more elevated than she was in this secluded retreat, by the unanimous tears and benedictions which exalted the simple Malvina. Oh! virtue and piety,[158] such is thy power; and though pride may endeavour, by every means, to elevate itself above mortality, yet thy superior endowments will rise to the highest, the most exalted state. And beneath thy immortal ray, its faint glimmering will be extinguished; and after having sparkled a moment, it will die away, while both it and its superb monuments will be buried in the dust. But virtue and piety, pure and eternal as the Being who created them, will exist for ever in the highest Heaven.

CHAP. XII.

The effect of music.

The next evening at the usual hour Malvina was preparing to go into the garden: the doctor desired they would try the effect of some soft music in her presence. Mrs. St. Clare just touched a prelude on her organ. Malvina shuddered and turned her head; she then appeared to listen with attention. The melody ceased; she then fell into her usual reverie, and went forward.

I could wish any one to sing an air, which she was particularly partial to, said Doctor Maxwell.

Edmond advanced.

It must not be you, just yet, continued he. She must not hear your voice, until she is in a state to recollect it. Let me first present Frances to her.[159] We must not exhaust all our resources. If we hope to succeed, we must be sparing of them.

While they were speaking, Mrs. St. Clare took her harp; and, concealing herself behind the window-curtain,[160] touched some of the chords. Their vibration arrested Malvina a second time. Mrs. St. Clare, on perceiving it, continued it; and, after playing some short plaintive melodies, she sung some words,[161] which Malvina had composed a few days previous to Mrs. Burton's arrival.

All the time Mrs. St. Clare was singing, Malvina's attention was entirely arrested by it. She only looked round, to observe from whence the voice proceeded. When it passed, she appeared to be considering; and, after a little time, she said, with an air of surprise, that was not me; raising her hand to her forehead, as if to recollect herself; and they observed the efforts she made, to recal her transient and fleeting memory.

Edmond, in silence, with his eyes fixed upon her, followed all her motions; waiting, with painful anxiety, to gain one ray of hope, which might forward the point in view, and bring relief to his oppressed heart.[162] Yet, Malvina seemed ever occupied by his idea. She walked a few paces, with her eyes bent on the ground, apparently in reflection, when she suddenly interrupted the silence which reigned, by saying, that certainly was not me. And why was it not me? And then, as if affected by some new idea, she raised her voice, and began to sing the same air which Mrs. St. Clare had just ended. – Ah! Why do I say the same? I was no longer so.

Her expression had something in it so very touching and plaintive, that they could not refrain from tears. Yet, at the same time, her accent was so soft and tender, that it penetrated the very soul. It drew the attention of every person in the house.[lxv] They all ran, to listen to her, surprised, and enchanted;[163] and, little Frances, availing herself of this opportunity, escaped from her chamber; and, proceeding on tip-toe to the place where she heard the sounds, and knowing them to be Malvina's, she rushed into the room; and, falling at her feet, she cried, mama, my dear, dear mama, have I found you at last?

At this voice, Malvina trembled, and shrieked. Then, snatching the child in her arms, and contemplating her for some time with a mixture of surprise and joy, she at last exclaimed, the barbarians have not then killed thee, my cherub. Yes! it is thou. Yes! I do know thee. The sweet child of my Clara yet lives. Ah! continued she, pressing her to her bosom, I can now breathe at my ease. I can now die in peace. I can meet Clara, and she will not ask me for you any more in an angry voice, saying, what have you done with my child?[164]

Frances kissed her; and, clasping her arms round her, O! mama, said she, why are you so pale? Why do you look at me so? Is it, because you are angry with me? or, do you no longer love your little Frances? Oh! mama, dear mama, why do you not kiss me as you used to do?

As I used to do! interrupted Malvina. Every body can recollect what they used to do; it is only I, who cannot think of it. There is something here (pointing to her forehead), which obscures, which hides it.

Mama, why do you speak by yourself? What is the matter?[165] Do you know that those wicked people, who carried me away, told me that you wished them to do it? and, that you no longer cared for me? But I would not believe them, mama. I told them, that they were very wicked,[ba] and great story-tellers, who wished to kill us both. But, my dear mama, why do you not speak to me? O! my gracious! If it should be true, that you no longer love me!

On uttering this, the affectionate heart of Frances was almost suffocated, and she burst into tears.

Though Doctor Maxwell was uneasy at Frances so abruptly appearing without his order, as he was conscious Malvina was too weak to support any long or painful emotions, yet he determined to take that opportunity of making a few attempts; and, going to Malvina, he said, you used to be so good once, that you never afflicted any one. But, now, you make your child, the child of your Clara, cry.

I do not wish to give pain to any one, said Malvina, looking at him with surprise. I am sure, I do not wish to make the dear child of my Clara cry. But, what can I do for her, now? You perceive, that I cannot any longer think. I do not know any thing. They have destroyed them all.[166]

Since you have been thus,[167] do you remember who was the cause of this great evil? said the doctor.

Oh! it is so very long a time, such a great while ago, she replied (pointing behind her). I was so happy, enjoying my life in peace, when I was met by a man; my strength decayed; and, ever since, I have been leaning on the grave.

At these words, Edmond advanced a step; but a look from the doctor made him keep his station; and he continued, with the hope of recalling Malvina's reason, too soon forgetting that her health was not in a state to support it. Where are you going? said he, seeing her intention of proceeding to the garden.

To die, she answered. You know, very well, this is the hour.

You deceive yourself. On the contrary, this is the day on which he is to return. You will find him there.

He returned! Shall I find him there? replied she, trembling.

Yes! there is no longer a tomb there; you ought not to wish to die, since you are going to see him. The wicked persons have brought back both your child and your husband. Both are now returned to you; here is Frances with you, and Edmond is in the garden, near the tomb,[168] where he expects you.

Expects me! Edmond expects me! she exclaimed, clasping her hands. Do not deceive me; for that would only increase the evil.

I do not deceive you. Go, and convince yourself. I will attend you, with your leave.

Oh! yes, yes, said she quickly, come with me; for, if I go alone, I shall never find him.

Edmond, penetrating the doctor's intention, went unperceived out of the room. Mrs. St. Clare followed, with Frances; and the gentle Malvina, supported by the doctor's arm, went slowly into the garden. She said, you are a good man. I shall always remember you. You did not wish Edmond to leave me; and, when he was going, you prevented him, and brought him back.

I can perceive, he replied, that your heart retains, from feeling, what your mind finds it difficult to remember. You did not recollect my features, and the name of Doctor Maxwell passed your ear as an empty sound. But, you have still that sensation, which allowed you to remember, that your lover was ill, and near dying, and that I had saved him.

Yes! yes! interrupted she, speaking to herself; he has reason to think so. Once, Edmond was near death. I wept by the side of his bed. But, when Doctor Maxwell came, I was comforted. He soothed me, and bade me dry my tears; and I wept no more. How was it possible, I could cease to remember all that? But you, continued she, surveying the doctor, how did you know it?

Doctor Maxwell, who the moment before had flattered himself that she had recollected him, though it was only a faint glimmering of reason, the pain he experienced in being disappointed in this pleasing hope, discouraged him extremely. You do not then know me? said he, mournfully.

Me! No! How should I know you? You know, very well, that, since Clara's death, and Edmond's leaving me, I have never known any thing but sorrow.

At this instant, her attention was arrested by the distant sound of a flute, and her pale cheeks were instantly tinged with a brilliant and burning bloom. Her heart throbbed with such violence, that it was perceived through her robe; her limbs trembled, and her agitation was so great, that it was with the utmost difficulty she supported herself.

The doctor was rather alarmed, and began to repent of having called up too many contending emotions at once. But there was no recalling what was done. Do you not hear, said Malvina, in a low and tremulous voice, that delightful harmony? It is Edmond, who plays it. It flows from the same instruments that he used, when I beheld him for the first time. Oh! I beg that you will not speak, said she, observing the doctor was going to answer. Do not, I entreat you, permit any thing to interrupt, or mix with those harmonious sounds. If you were but sensible of what infinite service they are to me, how much they refresh my nerves, calm my mind, and soften my heart!

In speaking, she went forward, till she gained the entrance of the shrubbery. Then, suddenly stopping, she said, I dare not enter it. No! I dare not enter it. If I go in there, I shall not find him; for it was the celestial spirit, which Clara has sent to fetch me to her; and that waits for me at my grave. Oh! Clara, I much wish to be with you. But, leave me – Oh! leave me, that I may see it[169] once more.

The flute then ceased, and its soft melody died away; but a voice, infinitely sweeter, succeeded, and sung a little air.[170]

While this air was singing, Malvina's agitation was considerably increased. She trembled violently, and scarcely breathed, that she might not lose a word which she heard. The doctor, who examined her very attentively, observed her features attain more expression; her eyes appeared animated; her countenance seemed changed; yet, a mournful presentiment penetrated his heart, and prevented the entrance of hope.

At this moment, the moon, bursting from the illumined cloud, which had, for a few minutes enveloped her tranquil face, was observed to have attained her meridian in the wide ethereal vault,[171] and enlightened every object with her soft and pensive rays. Edmond had ceased his song. Malvina advanced one step towards the wood. Edmond came forward. She saw, and knew him, exclaiming, as she threw herself into his arms, Oh! it is him! It is my Edmond! My eyes have not deceived me, and my Edmond is returned! Blessed, for ever blessed, be thou, adored being! Thou hast then returned to thy poor Malvina! Ah! do not leave her again! never leave her! And, now, let me press thee to my heart; for its last throb will be thine.[172]

She then seemed suddenly to lose her strength; her voice faultered; and she sunk, from the arms of Edmond, without sense or motion.

CHAP. XIII.

Innocence at last finds peace.

Malvina! exclaimed Edmond, terrified. My beloved Malvina! Ah! was I only to behold thy returning reason, and then to lose thee so quickly.

Do not be alarmed, said the doctor, oppressed by an anxiety, which he vainly endeavoured to hide; after such violent shocks, nature requires some repose. It may, perhaps, be only a drowsy fit.

Malvina being taken into the house, was put to bed: and her repose seemed deep and tranquil.

Edmond, who was much distressed by the doctor's visible anxiety, attempted to read in his eyes if this lethargy was a favourable symptom. But he avoided his looks, and when questioned, evaded giving a determinate answer; only desiring that she might be kept as quiet as possible. The doctor seated himself by the bed side, frequently feeling her pulse, and waiting in a tormenting state of suspense, the moment when her lucid orbs, by unclosing, should relieve it. She continued in the same situation during that night, and great part of the following day.

Towards the close of it, Edmond having left the room for a moment, the doctor, turning to Mrs. St. Clare, said, the crisis is approaching, this is about the hour in which I expect she will awake. I will not conceal it from you, but her weakness is very great, there is scarcely any pulse, and her breast seems very much oppressed; we have every thing to fear –

Edmond's entrance prevented the doctor from concluding what he wished.

Mrs. St. Clare was so petrified by what she heard, that she was immovable, and appeared as if struck by lightening.

Edmond immediately went up to her, saying, the doctor was speaking to you when I entered, what was it he said? Has he much hope? For Heaven's sake do not conceal any thing from me.

Mrs. St. Clare could not speak, but taking his hand, pressed it with violence, and remained silent.

Oh! my friend, he exclaimed, turning pale, explain yourself; for this silence is more dreadful than all I can know.[173]

Do not speak quite so loud, interrupted the doctor, in order to prevent Mrs. St. Clare's distress by answering. The least noise may awaken our patient from a repose which is so necessary for her; you had better seat yourself behind the curtains, for should she awake suddenly, it might prove of the most dangerous consequence if she saw you.

Edmond obeyed; and each kept the most profound and mournful silence, listening to Malvina's respiration, which became quicker every instant.

In a little time after, her countenance was tinged with a bloom of warmth, she began to move, and articulated some words in a low voice.

The doctor believing Sir Edmond was behind the curtains, and that he could not perceive him, turned towards Mrs. St. Clare, and whispered all is over, the fever is commenced.

Oh, God! all is lost, repeated Edmond with terror, who was in too much anxiety not to watch all the doctor's words and actions.

At this exclamation, which sorrow had involuntarily excited, Malvina awakened, and starting, what was it that I heard? said she, whose voice was that? I thought it was like Edmond's, but no: if it had, he would have answered me.

At this tender reproach, neither the signs which the doctor made, or the danger of a sudden emotion, could deter the violence of Edmond's feelings, from forcing him involuntary to rush to the bed side; and falling on his knees, he seized the pale hand which hung nearly lifeless, which he bathed with a deluge of tears, without the power of uttering a sentence.

At this sight, Malvina seemed to collect all her strength, and raising herself up in her bed, she clasped both his hands in hers,[174] [lxvi] and pressing them gently, it is him, said she, it is him indeed! I behold him! He still loves me! Heaven, always merciful, would not let me die in despair.

If I love you yet? replied he, with energy. Ah! do not, do not for a moment think I have ever ceased to love you. I cannot support such a dreadful insinuation. O thou most beloved of women, who hath ever been the object of my idolatry. Thy pure image has ever reigned alone in my heart, and no other could for a moment ever have disputed thy love there. Oh Malvina! I conjure you not to sully your lips with that abhorred name. If you did but know how greatly we have both been deceived. Mrs. St. Clare will inform you of it,[175] when your strength will permit you to hear the recital.

I have no occasion to be acquainted with it, Mrs. St. Clare, I have beheld his tears, and they tell me every thing. Oh! Edmond, said she, falling back upon her pillow, lay your hand upon my heart, and recal it to life, that I may not lose thee yet; for I feel that it wishes to foresake me.

It will be better if you would retire, Sir Edmond, said the doctor, seriously alarmed; I beg that you will: a longer conversation may entirely exhaust her strength.

Oh! doctor, said Malvina is a weak and scarcely audible voice, feebly extending her hand to her husband, do not send him away. I have so little time to stay: if he goes out, I shall never see him again.

The doctor acquiesced in her wish, for it was impossible to do otherwise, when it was to soothe and sweeten the last moments of a life, which it was not in his power to prolong.

Edmond in despair, on hearing what Malvina had uttered, no longer wept, and to think was madness. He continued upon his knees, with his lips rivetted to the almost inanimate hand of his wife: while Mrs. St. Clare supported her on the other side in bed, with her heart tortured and agonised, and her eyes bathed in tears.

After a short pause, Malvina looking at her friend with the utmost tenderness, said, my dear Mrs. St. Clare, is it true that my Frances is returned? If I have not been deceived by a dream, I think I have seen her. Let her come to me, that I may embrace her once more, before I go to meet her mother.

Mrs. St. Clare went for her. She found her fast asleep in her little bed. Dear unfortunate child, said she, thy mother is dying, and thou art asleep. Mrs. St. Clare was struck with the contrast of this sweet tranquil repose, to the heart rending scene she had just left.[bb] However she took her up, and dressing her half asleep,[176] she carried her to her mother, and laid her on Malvina's bed.

She contemplated her for some time, and appeared greatly affected; then raising her hands towards her, she said, poor child, dear innocent creature, what a peaceful sleep! It was thus that thou slept, when thy mother was taken from us. Oh! may heaven grant, that every evil may pass as lightly, without thy being sensible of it! Thou sleepest, Frances. I also, shall soon sleep. But, before I do, receive my sincere regret, that I have not lived for thy sake; and my fervent repentance, for having a moment forgot thee; my most affectionate love and blessing, and my last adieu. My Edmond! I leave her to thee as a legacy. Thou wilt be watchful of her happiness. We shall both be on high; and that God, whom we shall both know, will bless you for all the attention which you may bestow upon her. Her education I will confide to the care of my dear Mrs. St. Clare. It was to have been the amusement of my life; and it would have been a delightful one to me. I have, therefore, nothing more precious to bequeath to you, for all the kind, affectionate attentions I have invariably received from you. If Mr. Prior will unite in this with you, it will gratify me much. I know, that he will grieve for me. But, if the hope of being serviceable to Frances is not sufficient to reconcile him to my loss, when I am no more; tell him, that I most affectionately remembered him, when dying. Will my beloved Mrs. St. Clare also be particularly careful to teach my Frances never to sacrifice duty to love? You, who have so faithfully performed yours, in so singular an instance, will easily guide her in the road of virtue.

Ah! Malvina, what hast thou said? exclaimed Edmond. In such a moment, a similar reflection is a dreadful reproach.

If it is one, my Edmond, pardon thy Malvina, who would not wish to afflict thee. And, why should I reproach thee who formed all the felicity of my life, and all which the world can offer? Thou, who at this moment surrounds me with thy love, and whose regrets will follow me to the tomb.

Oh! Malvina do not speak thus. Thy kind words pierce my heart; and, when I am going to lose thee from my own fault;[bc] the excess even of thy hatred would be less agonising than the expressions of thy love. I have deserved it, he continued, in the most distressing manner, and voice. Is it not my vile ingratitude, which has embittered thy life? Is it not I, who am sending thee to thy grave?

O! stop, my Edmond, stop. O! save me from the idea of thy despair. No! Thou wast not guilty, since thou didst not forget me. And I am no longer unhappy, since I have been beloved. I can die, without remorse. Oh! Edmond, if you knew the tranquillity of soul I now possess, calm and serene as Nature at the close of day. All-powerful God! continued she, clasping her hands, and elevating them over her husband, protect his life, and graciously grant that it may be exempt from the sorrows which have oppressed mine, and that his last hour may be as happy as mine!

She was silent, her speech failing from the energy with which she expressed herself in this affecting prayer occasioned a feebleness, which continued some hours.

The melancholy, the distressed Edmond fixed his eyes on the countenance of his beloved, his dying Malvina. He was silent; his impetuosity was extinguished; his agonised heart felt the extent of the misery he should endure, when deprived of that being, which could alone render existence desirable. A settled despair arrested all the powers of his mind, and fixed its residence in his soul.[177] He no longer inquired her situation. He had nothing more to say. He appeared as if deprived of articulation and motion. Ah! who can ever express real grief by words? – Impossible, when it proceeds from that deep and settled sorrow, which momentarily and silently corrodes and undermines the powers of life, till it destroys them;[178] and this misery accumulates each instant, as if wishing to burst the heart, that it might fly from its distresses. In such a moment, one tear, only one tear, would be a relief to our misery.

While all were endeavouring to assist Malvina, each person expressed in their countenance the sorrow and gloom which oppressed them. The doctor's countenance pourtrayed not even a ray of hope. Soon would that amiable being be no more. The icy hand of death was going to chill that fair flower in the bloom of youth. Those lips, which breathed only gentleness, were to be closed for ever, never more to be re-animated with the breath of life. Her lingering soul, in a few moments, would fly for ever.

On Malvina's opening her languid eyes, her first look was to her husband. Dear Edmond, said she, if I did not behold you so much distressed, how sweet would this moment be to me! I shall very soon behold my Clara, with a countenance expressive of her celestial happiness. She seems to call me: Come, come to me, and rejoice with the angels. Thy husband shall, one day, meet thee here. But he will remain on earth, till he has accomplished the happiness of my daughter.[179] Such is the order of the Most High. Edmond, it is not a vision. Submit to thy destiny. Fulfil the duty I have neglected, when I am no more.[180] It is my last request.

I most sacredly promise, he replied, that you shall be obeyed. I shall live only to misery. I wish it. I ought to suffer. It will require a series of sorrow, to expiate thy death.

Edmond, said she, may weep for Malvina. He ought; for no one has ever loved him as I have. But let not thy heart be oppressed with any grief for what has passed. It is in the name of that heaven, which seems open to receive me, that I request it. Malvina will petition the Father of Mercy, who, I hope, will pardon all my errors, and from Him she will obtain thine also.[181]

Oh! thou celestial angel, do not yet fly away from me, exclaimed Edmond, in a transport. Yet stay one moment longer with thy Edmond, before an eternal separation. No! Edmond it will not be eternal, she replied, in the most animated tone. I am going to my Father, who is thy Father – to my God; and who is also thine. There are many seats in his celestial abode. I am going to implore one for thee; for where I am, thou wilt be also.

A sweet smile rested on her countenance. She attempted once more to press the hand of her husband and Mrs. St. Clare;[182] but, not having strength, she only made a sign to them; then, closing her eyes, fetched a deep sigh.

Edmond bent forward, to receive her breath. It was too late. It had flown for ever. Malvina was no more!

CHAP. XIV.

The unhappy weep together.

I shall draw a veil over the mournful scene which ensued. Experience, alone, can teach us the depth and extent of such woe; for it is utterly impossible to describe it. Human expressions cannot reach so far. And, if there is any thing which can increase it, it must be, when we are conscious of having contributed to shorten the existence of the beloved object; when this mental voice pursues us night and day, and repeats that we have been the chief cause of the misery we experience. Yet, Edmond did not impute it entirely to his own fault; but, in his desperation, he accused all nature, and cursed the two women, whose detested plots had deceived Malvina, and occasioned this fatal catastrophe.

When Frances was first brought to him in hopes that the sight of her might calm his phrensy, he turned his eyes from her with horror;[183] and, shuddering, cried, take her away from me; for there has been a fatality in the influence of that child which has led my beloved wife to the tomb.

The unhappy Edmond, therefore, became the chief object of Mrs. St. Clare's pity and attention; and her tender cares and solicitudes were unremitting. She never left him; but seized every opportunity of recalling whatever could sooth or alleviate his grief,[184] or pour the healing balm of consolation to his wound. She no longer beheld Edmond as the seducer of Louisa, or the volatile husband of Malvina; but as a wretched being, who was become the prey of sorrow and remorse; and too miserable, not to make her wish to forget[185] that he had ever been guilty. Yet, one of Mrs. St. Clare's principal inducements was, to recal him to a just value of life, and bring him to a just sense of reason, that he might recollect, and be ready to undertake those duties which Malvina had left him to fulfil; and her cares were not fruitless.

Sir Edmond was so conscious that it would be some time at least,[186] before it would be possible for him to live with Frances, that he was the first to press Mrs. St. Clare's departure, by engaging her to take the child from his sight. Go, dearest, kindest of friends, said he, leave me; and do not any longer oppress, by your unmerited attentions, a miserable being, who is so very unworthy of them, and who is not in a situation to appreciate them as they deserve. Direct all your care, therefore, to Frances, as my Malvina desired you. As to myself, I cannot behold the child. No! I cannot. Malvina did not require that I should. If she had, I would obey her.[187] However, as I will always be a careful guardian to the charge she has left me, I will accompany you on horseback to your own house, and then return here, alone.

At the word 'alone', his countenance changed, his look became wild. – Alone, in this retreat, which was chosen by love; where Malvina has lived with me; where she was the source of my felicity; and where I have lost her, and all comfort has forsaken me. Solitary, and alone with her tomb; absorbed by my reflections and my love.

Mrs. St. Clare, therefore, very readily acquiesced to Sir Edmond's proposal, in hopes that she might prevail upon him to spend some time with her, at a distance from that dismal habitation, which contained Malvina's tomb. It being his own proposal to go with them,[188] she imagined, that it rather proceeded from a wish to divert his melancholy. At least, she had a right to form such an opinion from his former character. But she was quite deceived in this supposition. Edmond was no longer the same. His vivacity and animation were quite extinguished by grief, and the deepest penitence had destroyed all the flightiness of his character; and, from henceforth, the whole universe to him was confined in the narrow bounds of the cold stone which covered the ashes of his Malvina.

As soon, therefore, as he had conducted Frances and Mrs. St. Clare to the mansion of the latter, without taking leave of either, he returned, riding all the night, and arrived at day-break at his own house. His first steps were directed to his wife's tomb. He had inclosed it by a very high railing, of which only himself and Mrs. St. Clare had a key, that no other foot might prophane or sully the sacred spot. But, as he now approached it, he heard a slight noise within it. He shuddered, and trembled through every nerve. His pulses throbbed with such violence, that he could not proceed. He did not place any faith in supernatural appearances. He did not hope for such a thing. He had seen his Malvina lifeless, and beheld her laid in the cold grave, which was but a few paces from him. He was perfectly conscious of all this; yet, his agitated imagination transported him to that first moment when he had fancied she was no more, and yet heard her voice in that very spot. He drew nearer,[lxvii] and very distinctly heard both sighs and weeping. Yet, he knew that it was impossible for any one to get over the palisade; and the door being carefully locked, and Mrs. St. Clare absent, he did not know what to conclude; his agitation was uncommon; and his fancy pictured a thousand vague conceits. He at last entered in a violent perturbation, and, by the yet feeble dawn, he perceived the figure of a man prostrate upon the earth; whose vestments appeared in disorder, and whose hair was wet with the cold dew of night. In a moment, all his ideal phantoms were vanished, and he was nearly as much struck as if he had lost Malvina a second time, and his trembling voice could only just pronounce these words: – Mr. Prior! who, upon the mention of his name, turned his head, and arose, rather alarmed.

Oh! cried he, is it you, whom I behold here? What, you! the destroyer of Malvina, near me. Oh! Mrs. St. Clare, you have then deceived me. You told me, that he would not return.

You have a right, replied Sir Edmond, with cool despair; you certainly have reason to call me the destroyer of Malvina. By perjuring my vows, I gave the fatal stroke to the bosom of that celestial woman, whose hand you bestowed upon me. Yet, she blessed me; she forgave, and endeavoured to console me. But, can I ever pardon myself? – No! never, cried he, resting himself upon the tomb, and hiding his face against the ground. No! I am not worthy to behold the light. Thou, who wast her friend, load me with reproaches and invectives. I will endure them all; for they will be infinitely less than those of my own heart.

Mr. Prior was struck with pity at the sight of such heart-felt woe. He sincerely repented of what he had said; and, raising his hands to heaven, Oh! Malvina, cried he, forgive me, if I have in my heart been tempted to curse the man on whom thou hast bestowed thy blessing. At thy tomb, I retract all that I have said or thought injurious to him. And thou, unhappy being! since Malvina is yet dear to thee; since thy tears are those of contrition, calm thy despair; for the band which united thee, is not broken. You will again meet her in those ethereal regions, where she now awaits you; there to enjoy, to all eternity, the pure delights of that union which I had ratified on earth.

No! No! said Edmond, all hopes of that nature are fled from my heart. The cruel hand, which has crushed that fair flower in its morning bloom – which has destroyed those days of felicity that kind heaven perhaps had destined her to enjoy,[bd] ought for ever to be banished from her sight. Heaven does not unite the assassin to the victim of his treachery.

Do not endeavour, said Mr. Prior, to penetrate into what fate heaven might have intended her, provided she had lived. Perhaps, her lot might have been sorrow and suffering; for, how often ought we to esteem an early death the first blessing of heaven? Who, alas! can tell what is best for man? The days of his vanity pass away like a vapour.

Ah! Mr. Prior, but can you imagine, that the idea of an uncertain evil can console me for the misery I suffer?

No! my friend, it will not console; but it may teach you to bow, with resignation, to the all-wise decrees of Providence, whose wisdom we cannot pretend to investigate. If God does not please to grant you comfort under your affliction, it is only that it may render you more estimable. Ever may you retain your sorrows! but do not let them enfeeble you so far, as to lose the desire of rectifying your former errors, by the performance of such virtuous actions as will render you worthy of the angel whom you love.[189] The waves of eternity daily roll towards us, and will soon overwhelm us in its abyss, and would leave no vestige of our existence, if it was not destined that happiness was to be the lot of the just, and misery that of the wicked. Therefore, you have only to encourage such actions, as may permit you to wait without fear.

Ah! Mr. Prior, when I lost Malvina, had I possessed the virtues of the whole universe, they could not have altered my destiny.[190] My heart is dead to all consolation. I cannot, I do not wish to receive any. My tears, when I can shed them, are the only relief which is left me. But, whatever may be my anguish, my despair, yet, I do not wish to die. No! I ought to endure a long repentance.[191] To die, would only be the expiation of a moment; but, to endure what I suffer, it will render the time I may live an age.

I will not leave you, Sir Edmond, said Mr. Prior, much affected. I will devote all my time and attention to you, if you will permit me, that I may recal peace to your dejected mind. Malvina may be pleased, that her friend should undertake the pious office of endeavouring to be the comforter of the husband she loves.

No! Mr. Prior; though I am sensible of the kindness of your intention, yet, as Malvina has left me solitary and alone, I will remain so. Leave me. Your generosity oppresses me. I only wish to behold what will increase, rather than diminish my grief. I only wish to dwell near her tomb, and its congenial gloom. Go, then. Malvina will be more gratified by your attention to my little charge. Bestow all your cares upon her. Form her mind to all those excellences her mother possessed in so eminent a degree, that she may be a copy of her whose death she in some measure contributed to. I do not wish to see her again. No! Take her far, far from me.[192] Yet, tell her, that she is inestimably dear to me; that I would sacrifice my life a thousand times for her. Yes! Go. Leave me, continued he, with wildness in his expression. Why did you come here? No one, but myself, has a right to shed their tears upon this tomb. Alas! I have paid but too dear for that privilege. This cold inanimate clay belongs only to me. I have no other claim upon earth; and for that reason, I wish to enjoy it alone. Do not, therefore, hope that you will ever be permitted to visit this spot again.[193] You have been allowed to pay the last tribute to friendship; and that is sufficient. From henceforth, this asylum is sacred, and will be open to no one but myself, as the husband of Malvina; who, as jealous of all that remains of her, does not wish to divide with another the mournful pleasure of contemplating her tomb. Go then, Sir. – Farewel!

Mr. Prior left him in silence, with a heart oppressed by sorrow and pity. He immediately set out for Mrs. St. Clare's seat; and there he was made acquainted with Malvina's last wishes, that he would unite with her in the care of educating Frances. Happy to have it in his power to obey any wish of hers after her death, he vowed never to leave the child; and in little more than a year after,[be] Mrs. St. Clare, having lost her father, determined, after obtaining Sir Edmond's and Lord Sheridan's permission, to go to Lisbon,[194] that she might, by that means, gain a little more liberty for her melancholy sister, by taking her from a country, where she was known; and Mr. Prior accepted the proposal of attending them, with pleasure.

The mournful particulars of Malvina's death, and Sir Edmond's despair, were for some time the conversation of all Edinburgh. Every tear which was dropped to their memory, was also a reproach to Mrs. Burton. She, therefore, determined to avoid them, by returning to her castle, amid the mountains. But, on her arrival there, the first words she heard from the poor and the unfortunate, were inquiries for Edmond and Malvina. The benedictions which were conferred upon their names,[bf] wounded her vanity, and distressed her mind. In vain did she wish to fly from herself; her conscience followed her every where. She could no longer enjoy tranquillity or repose. She lived in continual fear, and fancied she read in every countenance, contempt and hatred; that every one mentally repeated, the triumph of the wicked is of short duration, and the joys of the deceitful continue but for a moment. Her soul, tormented from every mental and visual cause, and the certainty of having entirely lost that exalted reputation, which, she vainly imagined, she had so lastingly acquired; attended by the mortification of no longer seeing herself surrounded by flatterers, who paid her adulation, at the same time that they despised her; plunged her, from this concatenation, into a gloomy state of mind, which consumed her by degrees, and conducted her to the grave. On finding her end approaching, she looked round her; and the retrospect of the past produced only regret, and the most dreadful fears alarmed her for the future. She, therefore, gained neither consolation[195] from reflecting on what she had done, nor in the destiny which awaited her. Between the world, which was vanishing from her view, and that awful eternity, which she was on the verge of entering, she trembled at the idea of both the one and the other, and could have wished to disappear as a shadow from the contempt of that world she was leaving, and the judgment of that she was on the point of approaching. Though anxiously wishing to obtain Sir Edmond's forgiveness, yet she would not humiliate herself, by requesting his attendance. She, therefore, continued, to her latest hour, the victim to that vanity which had ever been her idol, and died, without allowing herself to sue for that pardon, which would have given tranquillity to her soul.

Mrs. Fenwick continued to shine with as much *éclat* as ever in the world, resigning herself with impunity to every pleasure, and a constant scene of dissipation. We might be tempted to suppose, that the divine vengeance had forgot her. But, though it may be delayed for a time, such are not always suffered to escape; and the justice of heaven is only suspended, until the moment arrives, when it may overtake, and strike with more certainty. She will certainly, one day, meet with her punishment; perhaps, from the hands of those, whose misery she has occasioned.

In vain did the solicitations of friendship, and all the seductions of the world, endeavour to tempt Sir Edmond from his retreat. Nothing could prevail on him to leave the sight of that tomb which contained his beloved wife.[196] It is natural to imagine, that his sorrows, from time, became less poignant; but, then, he was habituated to them; and a long endurance of grief and suffering deprives the mind of the power of enjoying, or even wishing for, any pleasure. Thus, the volatile, though at last amiable, Edmond ever remained thoughtful and melancholy, supporting a languishing existence, and enveloped by an unconquerable grief, to that moment, when, according to Malvina's words, after having sacrificed more than his life for Frances, he felt conscious that he was worthy of going to meet the only woman whom he had ever loved upon earth.

THE END.

Printed by C. Stower, Charles Street, Hatton Garden.

EDITORIAL NOTES

VOLUME I

1. *Malvina*: In the French edition, each of the four volumes contains a frontispiece, an illustration depicting a scene from the text and quoting the corresponding line below it. The illustrations were drawn by Binet and engraved by P. F. Tardieu. The English translation has no illustrations.
2. *Amelia Mansfield*: It had appeared in 1802 with Maradan in Paris, like *Malvina* in 1801. Its English translation came out in early 1803 with Gameau & Co. in London. Cottin still wishes to preserve her anonymity ('Madame C****'); scholars disagree as to whether she succeeded. See L. C. Sykes, *Madame Cottin* (Oxford: Basil Blackwell, 1949), pp. 331–2 and [Madame de Clauzade] Arnelle, *Une oubliée: Madame Cottin d'après sa correspondance* (Paris: Librairie Plon, 1914), p. 121.
3. *MALVINA*: In the French edition, a Notice ('Avertissement') by Cottin precedes the novel: 'Jamais il n'y eut d'avertissement d'une utilité plus bornée que celui-ci, car il ne regarde que le petit nombre de lecteurs de *Claire d'Albe*, et l'infiniment plus petit nombre de ceux qui s'en souviennent: c'est donc eux seulement que j'avertis que s'ils s'imaginent trouver dans Malvina, l'ouvrage que j'annonce dans la préface de Claire, ils se trompent: le sentiment de mon insuffisance ne m'a pas permis de l'achever. Un roman en lettres, où chaque style doit être aussi distinct que le caractère de ceux qui écrivent, me paraît la plus grande difficulté de ce genre d'ouvrage, et, pour tenter de le vaincre, j'attendrai encore quelque temps. Cependant, comme différens motifs, que je ne veux point énoncer ici, m'engageaient à écrire, j'ai essayé la forme par chapitres, comme la plus aisée. Ma première intention avait été de ne pas donner plus d'étendue au roman de Malvina qu'à celui de Claire ; si j'ai été entrainée plus loin, c'est que le sujet m'a paru susceptible d'un plus grand intérêt. Puissé-je n'être pas la seule de mon avis !' ('Never was a Notice less useful than this one, as it only concerns the small number of readers of *Claire d'Albe* and the infinitely smaller number of those who remember it: it is therefore to them alone that I address this Notice telling them that if they believe they will find in Malvina the work I announced in the preface to Claire, they are mistaken: my feeling of inadequacy did not allow me to complete it. An epistolary novel, where each style has to be as distinct as the character of those writing, strikes me as the biggest difficulty with this genre of text and, in order to attempt to overcome it, I will wait a while longer. However, since various motives, which I do not want to mention here, compelled me to write, I have tried the chapter style, it being the easiest. I originally intended to make Malvina's novel less extensive than Claire's; if I exceeded it, it is because the topic appeared likely to generate greater interest. May I not be the only one to think so!').

4. *CHAP. 1*: The chapter title 'Adieus, departure and arrival' is absent.
5. *and the dear remembrance of thee will accompany me for ever*: absent from the French edition. It serves to contrast Malvina with 'the frivolous admirers of thy youth' in underlining her lasting loyalty to her deceased friend.
6. *an attendant*: 'une femme d'un certain âge' ('a woman of a certain age') in the French edition.
7. *hastily exclaimed*: 'fit une exclamation de douleur' ('exclaimed in pain') in the French edition.
8. *Ah, how few are there ... while its deep source is enshrined in the heart*: absent from the French edition.
9. *five-and-twenty*: 'vingt-un' ('twenty-one') in the French edition.
10. *her infancy*: The French edition adds 'qu'elle aimait avec idolâtrie' ('whom she idolised'). Given what Malvina sacrifices for her friend, the French appears an accurate description.
11. *She hastened to her*: absent from the French edition.
12. *residing in England*: Sophie Cottin also lived in England. The Cottins had been given a noble title during the Ancien Régime and supported the king. When royalists came under increasing threats from the Revolutionary government in early 1792, Cottin and her husband fled France and spent a couple of months in England.
13. *resign her fortune in France*: This could be a reference to the confiscation of Cottin's own possessions during the Revolution.
14. *Malvina and*: absent from the French edition.
15. *conscious that she was too ... her fortune would not permit her to take a house*: The French edition states the opposite: 'lors même qu'elle n'eût pas été trop jeune pour vivre seule, sa fortune ne lui aurait pas permis de prendre une maison' ('while she would not have been too young to live alone, her fortune would not have allowed her to take a house'). Given that Malvina is twenty-five in the English edition and twenty-one in the French edition, this translation appears to imply different guidelines and standards for women living alone in the two countries.
16. *towards the education of his daughter*: While the French edition is less specific, 'les secours qu'il donnerait à sa fille' ('the help he would offer his daughter'), the English focuses on the girl's education.
17. *of supporting and educating*: Here again, the English edition stresses the educational aspect of raising the girl, while the French does not: 'l'entretien' ('the support').
18. *Mrs. Burton*: 'Mistriss Birton' in the French edition.
19. *or assist*: absent from the French edition.
20. *Tomkins*: 'Miss Tomkins' in the French version. The English edition reflects common practice in England to call servants by their last name only.
21. *but whose deep source silently corrodes life's vital current*: absent from the French edition.
22. *yet a few months*: 'encore quelques jours' ('yet a few days') in the French edition. The English edition makes more sense as spring will not arrive a few days after November.
23. *Peter*: 'Pierre' in the French edition.
24. *Frances*: 'Fanny' in the French edition.
25. *retard her journey in the day*: While the English edition suggests the journey was undertaken later in the day when the temperature had risen some, the French edition states that the journey was delayed by a day for the same reason: 'retarder sa marche d'une journée' ('delay her journey by a day').
26. *asked a thousand artless questions of Malvina and the good old servant*: The French states 'interrogeait Malvina, la bonne et le vieux serviteur' ('asked questions of Malvina, the

maid and the old servant'). While the English edition mistakenly interprets 'bonne' as modifying 'serviteur', it also expands 'interrogeait' to describe the typical manner in which young children ask questions.

27. *the county of—*: 'la province de Bread Alben' ('the county of Bread Alben') in the French edition. This corresponds to Breadalbane, a region of the southern/central Scottish Highlands.
28. *a few miles from—*: 'à quelques milles de Killinen' ('a few miles from Killin') in the French edition. This corresponds to the village of Killin in Breadalbane.
29. *Gothic grandeur*: 'extérieur gothique' ('Gothic exterior') in the French edition. The adjective 'Gothic' refers to the medieval style of the building here. However, the use of this word also connects this novel to the tradition of Gothic fiction (see Introduction).
30. *lake of Tay*: This corresponds to Loch Tay, located near Killin. Whereas the French edition specifies all geographic details, the English edition only mentions the lake and neither the village nor the region.
31. *the country of her favorite bard*: The French edition specifies that it is 'cette antique Calédonie, patrie des Bardes' ('this ancient Caledonia, homeland of the bards').
32. *Ossian*: Malvina owes her name to Ossian, a fictitious Irish warrior-poet whose epic poems the Scottish poet James Macpherson published in the early 1760s. The poems were soon translated into many European languages and became very popular in France, where Ossian influenced art (due to Napoleon's love of Ossian), literature (Chateaubriand, Madame de Staël) and Romanticism. In the poems, Malvina is Ossian's son's lover and after he dies, she takes care of Ossian in his old age. In the next paragraph Cottin called Malvina 'la fille d'Ossian' ('Ossian's daughter'), but Gunning corrected it to 'daughter-in-law'. On the reception and influence of Ossian in Europe, see H. Gaskill (ed.), *The Reception of Ossian in Europe* (London and New York, NY: Thoemmes Continuum, 2004).
33. *Malvina*: 'la belle cousine' ('her beautiful cousin') in the French edition. The French edition explains why, in the following sentence 'She accompanied those words by fixing on Malvina a look, which expressed much uneasiness', whereas the English offers no explanation for the uneasiness.
34. *put her little Frances to bed*: The French edition adds 'et l'eut placé près d'elle' ('and had placed it [the bed] close to her').
35. *wished her cousin a good night*: The French edition adds 'qui la quitta et se mit dans son lit' ('who left her and retired to bed').
36. *Portrait*: The French edition carries a footnote here which the English edition does not include: 'Quelques personnes ont prétendu me faire une reproche de la longueur de ce portrait: peut-être l'eussé-je abrégé beaucoup, s'il n'eût été que l'ouvrage de mon imagination; mais presque tous ses principaux traits étant pris dans la nature, je n'ai pu me résoudre à en sacrifier aucuns' ('Some people wanted to express their disapproval at the length of this portrait; perhaps I would have shortened it a great deal if it had merely been the product of my imagination, but given that nearly all of its main features were taken from nature, I could not resolve to forgo any').
37. *pensive*: absent from the French edition.
38. *encrease her attractions*: The French edition adds 'je n'en saurais donner d'autres raisons, que de dire qu'ils étaient ceux de Malvina, et qu'on ne la voulait pas mieux, parce qu'on ne la voulait pas autre' ('I can offer no other reasons for this than to say that they [her faults] were Malvina's and that one did not want her any better because one did not want her any different').

39. *prosperity to others*: The French edition adds 'ni comment un long usage de ce plaisir y rendait chaque jour son coeur plus sensible, au point de lui faire croire qu'elle perdait tout ce qu'elle ne donnait pas' ('nor how her extended usage of this delight rendered her heart more sensitive to it every day to the point where she started believing she would lose anything she did not give away').
40. *Perhaps*: 'Sans doute' ('undoubtedly') in the French edition.
41. *her uniform manner of sustaining it*: The French edition adds 'et la conscience d'avoir rempli ses devoirs avec la plus austère rigidité' ('and the knowledge of having fulfilled her duties most strictly').
42. *superior virtue*: The French edition adds 'tous la voyaient avec admiration, elle seule n'en savait rien' ('all observed her with admiration yet she alone did not know it').
43. *sought repose than agitation ... what friendship afforded*: 'Repos' ('repose') in the French edition possesses important connotations in French literature written by women. In *La Princesse de Clèves* (1678) – the first French novel – the heroine, having been widowed after her husband dies from the shock of her avowal that she loves another man, is free to marry the latter, yet chooses her 'repos' over a love-based match. In addition, the ending to another best-selling novel by a woman writer, *Lettres d'une Péruvienne* (*'Letters from a Peruvian Woman'*, 1747) is premised on the explicit selection of friendship over love. See my *Translations and Continuations: Riccoboni and Brooke, Graffigny and Roberts* (London: Pickering & Chatto, 2011).
44. *the selected of her heart*: Even though she received several offers of marriage after the death of her husband Paul in 1793, Cottin herself also chose living with her cousin Julie over re-marrying. Christine Roulston has called their arrangement a 'domestic partnership', in 'Gendering the Self in Eighteenth-Century Women's Letters', in A. Strugnell (ed.), *Correspondence and Epistolary Fiction; La Fête; Science and Medicine; Voltaire* (Oxford: Voltaire Foundation, 2002), pp. 93–103, on p. 96.
45. *nature's scenery*: The French edition specifies that it is out of the window 'du cabinet à côté de sa chambre' ('from the cabinet next to her apartment').
46. *desolation*: 'destruction' ('destruction') in the French edition.
47. *Mrs. B's*: The French edition does not abbreviate the name.
48. *their destiny*: The French edition adds 'je fais en sorte qu'ils y voient aussi la source de leur bonheur' ('I act so that they also see in me the source of their happiness').
49. *in all ages*: The French edition adds 'que c'est là qu'elle communique ses inspirations, que coulent les larmes de contrition, et que les soupirs du coeur sont entendus des cieux' ('that it is there where religion communicates its inspirations, where tears of regret flow and where the heavens hear the heart's sighs'). Religion played a very important role in Cottin's life.
50. *with disdain*: The French edition adds 'qu'ils parcourraient en vain leurs trois royaumes avant d'y trouver une figure comme la vôtre' ('that they would search in vain across their three kingdoms to find a face like yours').
51. *other society than mine*: The French edition states the reverse: 'je vous plaindrais, si vous n'aviez d'autre société que moi' ('I would pity you if you had no other society than mine').
52. *enliven Malvina*: 'exciter son appétit ainsi que sa gaîté' ('enliven Malvina's appetite and her gaiety') in the French edition.
53. *at their ease*: The French edition adds 'et ses discours, de cet abandon qui s'insinue dans le coeur' ('and her words, that abandon which penetrates the heart').
54. *plant and flower*: The French edition adds 'que des climats plus doux ne voient naître que l'été' ('which grow in milder climates only in summer').

55. *in the fields*: The French edition adds 'quelques glaces, dont les bordures étaient cachées par des feuillages découpés, égayaient encore ce séjour' ('some mirrors whose edges were hidden by cut leaves, embellished this spot even further').
56. *Malvina*: 'madame de Sorcy' in the French edition.
57. *pensive countenance*: The French edition describes not her face but her eyes 'ses yeux noirs si vifs et si touchans' ('her black eyes so bright and affecting').
58. *abilities or rectitude*: The French edition focuses less on the moral dimensions 'les talens font moins que l'intrigue' ('talent gains infinitely less than intrigue').
59. *dear cousin*: 'belle cousine' ('beautiful cousin') in the French edition. Once again, Mrs Burton focuses on Malvina's beauty. Its importance will soon become clear. See also note 33, above.
60. *her cheek*: 'le front' ('her forehead') in the French edition.
61. *and I find ... my present life can only produce*: The French edition states 'et à present, que je ne suis plus ni jeune, ni jolie, je me trouve bien de n'avoir pas donné toutes mes années au plaisir' ('and now that I am no longer young or pretty, I am happy not to have wasted all my years on pleasure').
62. *the repast was concluded*: 'avant la fin du repas' ('before the repast was concluded'). The earlier departure makes sense since Malvina was haunted by her memories.
63. great condescension: absent from the French edition.
64. *with lady Sheridan*: 'entr'eux et milady Sheridan' ('with them [the books] and lady Sheridan') in the French edition.
65. *France*: 'fertile France' ('fertile France') in the French edition.
66. *Essay on Friendship*: The French Renaissance philosopher Michel de Montaigne (1533–92) is known for his *Essais* (1580). Using his study of the Classics as a foundation, he aimed to describe man in general and himself in particular in an honest manner. One of the most famous of his *Essais* deals with the topic of (male) friendship – a very important theme in Montaigne's life – as he greatly valued his own friendship with Etienne de la Boétie, another French philosopher. Malvina obviously appreciated this *Essai* especially because of her close friendship with Clara. As stated, Cottin herself also held friendship in a very high regard. See note 44 above.
67. *as her father read*: The French edition adds 'Elle n'était pas mariée alors, non plus que sa Clara' ('She was not married then, like her Clara').
68. *the most refined love*: 'l'amour naissant' ('new love') in the French edition.
69. *recollecting herself*: 'se levant' in the French edition would be better translated as 'rising', especially because Malvina indicates that she is leaving.
70. *I have been, and am chastised*: 'j'ai été cruellement, bien cruellement châtiée' ('I have been cruelly, very cruelly chastised') in the French edition.
71. *that Being, who only knows what is best for us*: 'celui qui peut tout' ('that almighty Being') in the French edition. The French edition adds 'mais approchez-vous de lui, et il s'approchera de vous' ('but approach him and he will approach you').
72. *heal their wounds*: A footnote, absent from the English edition, follows in the French edition: 'Peut-être le langage de M. Prior ne surprendra-t-il point si l'on réfléchit un moment combien les citations, les maximes et les comparaisons sont familières aux hommes érudits, exaltés et accountumés à la retraite' ('Perhaps Mr Prior's language will not surprise readers if they think for a moment about how familiar quotations, maxims and comparisons are to zealous men of learning accustomed to living in isolation').
73. *probably*: 'peut-être' ('perhaps') in the French edition.
74. *the only consolation of all Christians*: 'la consolation de tous les hommes et de tous les âges'

('the consolation of all men and all ages') in the French edition.

75. *the anchor of the soul in this tabernacle of dust*: Two footnotes (one per expression) that are absent from the English edition appear here in the French edition, stating that they are 'expressions du prophête roi' ('expressions of the prophet King'). 'The anchor of the soul' comes from Hebrews 6:19: 'This hope [immortality] we have as an anchor of the soul, both sure and steadfast'. The 'tabernacle of dust' is mentioned in Numbers 5:17 where it is described how women are tested for fidelity if their husbands are jealous: 'Then he [the priest] shall take some holy water in a clay jar and put some dust from the tabernacle floor into the water'. In our text it refers rather to our temporary, man-made 'earthly dwelling' as opposed to 'that resting place, which was not constructed by the hands of men'.
76. *(his voice faultering from sympathy and feeling)*: absent from the French edition.
77. *You forget whom you are speaking before?*: The French edition includes 'de qui' ('of whom').
78. *which I do not think possible*: The French edition states the contrary: 'ce qui pourtant est très possible' ('which is, however, very possible').
79. *the fortune*: 'la dot' ('the dowry') in the French edition.
80. *to read*: Although the French edition states 'écrire' ('to write') here, the English translation appears more appropriate since it concerns poems by Ossian.
81. *dull rhodomantades?*: 'tristes psalmodies' ('sad chanting') in the French edition.
82. *Sun of ancient Caledonia*: Caledonia refers to the Scottish Highlands. The word 'sol' ('soil') may have been translated incorrectly here as 'sun' ('soleil') for the French edition states: 'Est-ce sur le sol de l'antique Calédonie, enfin, qu'on ose porter atteinte à la gloire du fils de Fingal?' ('Is it on the soil of ancient Caledonia, finally, that they dare to harm the son of Fingal?').
83. *son of Fingal?*: Fingal is the hero of Ossian's epic. See note 32 above.
84. *all these ... which I am to be frightened at*: 'ce ne sera pas de la colère d'Ossian dont je serai effrayée' ('it will not be Ossian's anger I am frightened at'), in the French edition.
85. *your own fault*: 'votre seul défaut' ('your only fault') in the French edition.
86. *Macpherson*: see note 32 above.
87. *Erse language*: Scottish Gaelic.
88. *Morven*: Kingdom of Fingal. See notes 32 and 83 above.
89. *the two following*: 'le lendemain' ('the following').
90. *like the rose, before the orb of day*: 'comme la rosée de l'aube du jour' ('like the dew at dawn'). 'Rosée' was likely mistaken for 'rose' ('rose').
91. *those who condemn her*: 'celui-là meme qui l'accuse' ('him who condems her') in the French edition, where Malvina's acusation is aimed directly at Mr Prior.
92. *(if graciously conferred)*: absent from the French edition.
93. *when on stepping back to speak to her cousin, she observed a poor woman, who by her gestures, endeavoured to make herself understood*: In this English sentence it is not entirely clear who is who. From the French, it is evident that Malvina is detained at the bed of a sick woman.
94. *one or two*: 'l'un d'eux' ('one of them') in the French edition. The translator likely mistook 'd'eux' for 'deux' ('two').
95. *if possible*: The French edition adds 'si d'autres sont aussi misérables qu'elle, il est facile de les soulager au même prix' ('if others are as miserable as she is, it is easy to help them for the same price').
96. *her companions were scarcely to be understood?*: 'ses compagnes ne l'entendaient seulement pas' ('her companions didn't even understand it') in the French edition. The original is

more logical than the English translation.

97. *Sir Edmond Burton*: 'sir Edmond Seymour' ('Sir Edmond Seymour') in the French edition. Edmond sharing the same last name as Mrs Burton establishes a closer link between them.
98. *They have reason*: 'Elle a raison' ('She is right') in the French edition.
99. *he melted into tears*: 'il pressa sa robe contre ses lèvres, en la mouillant de larmes' ('he pressed her dress against his lips and bathed it in his tears') in the French edition.
100. *Mr. Prior had satisfied his revenge, in vindicating Malvina; but she had forced her to blush*: 'M. Prior avait rempli son ame de desirs de vengeance; en prenant son parti, Malvina la forçait à en rougir' ('M. Prior had filled her soul with the desire for revenge; by taking her side, Malvina forced her to blush about it') in the French edition. The French edition speaks only about Mrs Burton, the English edition barely does so.
101. *what had been said*: The French edition adds 'et ne s'en souciait guères' ('and hardly cared about it').
102. *and was fearful of addressing her, though she wished to turn her thoughts from the cause of her chagrin*: 'et tremblait, en élevant la voix, de la faire tourner contre elle' ('and was fearful, by raising her voice, of having Mrs Burton turn against her') in the French edition.
103. *dear cousin*: 'belle cousine' ('beautiful cousin') in the French edition.
104. *my dear*: 'belle cousine' ('beautiful cousin') in the French edition.
105. *Erse language*: see note 87 above.
106. *for the confidence is soothing at all times: and that of a friend, will sometimes supply the place of a brother*: 'car l'intime ami aime en tout temps, dit le sage, et il tient lieu de frère dans la détresse' ('for the close friend loves at all times, says the philosopher, and serves as a brother during adversity') in the French edition.
107. *all who surround her?*: The French edition adds 'Ne vous y trompez point, Madame' ('Do not be deceived, Madam').
108. *the Highlands*: 'Bread Alben' ('Breadalbane') in the French edition. See note 27 above.
109. *they are convinced*: 'ils nous apprennent' ('they teach us'). 'They convince us' would have been a more accurate translation.
110. *when occupied by mirth and gaiety, her heart is gloomy, and all her joys end in satiety and ennui*: The French edition indicates 'Proverbes, 14' ('Proverbs 14') as the source of this quotation: 'Even in laughter the heart may ache, and rejoicing may end in grief'. This is Proverbs 14:13. The English edition, however, indicates in the footnote that the quotation comes from 'First of Proverbs'.
111. *charity which thinks no evil ... and if we observe an error, not to consider it as a crime*: Another biblical reference, to Proverbs 31:9: 'Speak up and judge fairly; defend the rights of the poor and needy'.
112. *conversing on that subject*: 'parler sans cesse de la sienne' ('conversing incessantly about his friendship') in the French edition.
113. *which are reserved for the virtuous in an immortal state*: 'dont il entretenait les fidèles dans les jours de la solennité' ('of which he spoke with the faithful on holy days') in the French edition.
114. *twenty-five*: 'vingt-quatre' ('twenty-four') in the French edition.
115. *Roman Catholic*: A footnote, left untranslated, follows in the French edition: 'Presque tout le nord de l'Ecosse a conservé cette croyance; ce n'est que dans la partie méridionale du côté de l'Angleterre, que la religion presbytérienne devient dominante; de sorte que la plus grande partie des vassaux de mistriss Birton étaient attachés au culte catholique, qu'elle professait elle-même, étant d'origine française' ('Almost the entire northern part

of Scotland kept this religion; only in the southern part near England the Presbyterian religion becomes dominant; thus the majority of those under Mrs Burton's authority belonged to the Catholic religion, like she did, being from France'). Cottin of course was Protestant.

116. *taught him that she had one*: 'apprend qu'il en a un' ('taught him that he had one') in the French edition.

117. *light brown hair*: 'cheveux blonds' ('blond hair') in the French edition.

118. *those chaste and expressive looks*: 'le regard tendre et prolongé' ('those tender and prolonged looks') in the French edition.

119. *These moments so enchanting*: 'Ces mouvemens, quoique vifs et rapides' ('These feelings, although strong and fleeting') in the French edition. The translator may have mistaken 'mouvemens' ('feelings') for 'moments' ('moments').

120. *dear cousin*: see note 103 above.

121. *all the particulars of this chance meeting*: The French edition lists them: 'En sortant de chez vous, madame, reprit Malvina, j'ai trouvé ces romances; ells sont nées dans ma patrie; j'ai cru m'y transporter en les chantant; pendant que j'en étais occupée, monsieur est entré...' ('Upon leaving your apartments, Madam, Malvina continued, I found these songs; they come from my country; I believed I was there while singing them; while I was singing, Sir Edmond came in...')

122. *You are perhaps the only one then*: 'Et vous n'êtes peut-être pas le seul' ('And you are perhaps not the only one') in the French edition.

123. *who am a stranger to every one?*: absent from the French edition.

124. *gossemer*: insubstantial, imprudent.

125. *we are unjust*: The French edition adds 'en croyant n'être que vrai' ('while believing ourselves only to be just').

126. *St James's*: 'la cour de Londres' ('the London court') in the French edition. King George III was the king of Great Britain at the time.

127. *friend to Sir Edmond*: 'oncle de la jeune personne' ('the young woman's uncle') in the French edition.

128. *use his interest*: 'joindre à cette terre-ci un fief' ('add a fiefdom to this estate') in the French edition.

129. *those gifts ... she would otherwise spend on herself*: 'les dons qu'elle voudrait lui prodiguer pour se l'attacher' ('the gifts she would want to bestow on him in order to attach him to her') in the French edition.

130. *He is also so disinterested ... on that account*: The French edition does not use the conditional in this sentence, but rather the present, thus making it a fact that Sir Edmond paid a large amount of money to facilitate his sister's wedding. Indeed, this is why his fortune is now limited: 'son peu de fortune vient du sacrifice qu'il a fait de la sienne à sa soeur' ('his limited fortune is due to the sacrifice he made of his to his sister').

131. *this character*: The French edition adds 'et en se penchant vers lui comme pour écouter plus attentivement' ('and leaning towards him in order to listen more attentively').

132. *who was extremely distressed on the occasion*: 'témoin de son inquiétude' ('who witnessed her distress') in the French edition.

133. *was her darling's*: The French edition adds 'elle marche de ce côté' ('she walks in that direction').

134. *united*: The French edition adds 'et la surprise qu'elle éprouva' ('and the surprise she experienced').

135. *with astonishment*: 'ému' ('moved') in the French edition.

136. *This is nature ... we can prove its effect*: The French edition states 'Se peut-il que ce ne soit pas là la nature? Non, ajouta-t-il ensuite avec plus de vivacité, ce n'est pas elle, mais c'est mieux qu'elle. Le croyez-vous possible, lui demanda Malvina avec douceur' ('Is it possible that this is not nature? No, he added with vivacity, it is not nature, but it is better than nature. Do you think it possible? Malvina asked him with affection').
137. *I thought possessed her traits!*: The French edition adds 'Malheur à qui voudrait le tenter! reprit-elle' ('Woe to anyone who would want to try, she replied').
138. *the pleasure of seeing you*: The French edition adds 'tout ce que le monde offre d'aimable ne m'avait point donné l'idée de ce que j'ai trouvé ici, et...' ('All the beauty the world offers had not prepared me for what I found here and...').
139. *took her hand*: 'prêt à lui prendre la main, mais sans jamais oser le tenter' ('wanting to take her hand, but too afraid to do so') in the French edition.
140. *The voice Malvina thought was Miss Melmor's*: The French edition adds 'et songeant combien il devait lui paraître extraordinaire de la trouver chez sir Edmond' ('and thinking how unusual it would appear to her [Miss Melmor] to see her [Malvina] in Sir Edmond's apartments').
141. *with Sir Edmond*: The French edition adds 'avec tant de simplicité ... que ni l'un ni l'autre n'en conçurent aucun soupçon' ('with such modesty ... that it did not raise any suspicion in either one of them').
142. *she had severely repented having received her*: The French edition adds 'et ne s'était occupée que des moyens d'empêcher Sir Edmond de la voir' ('and only endeavoured to find means to prevent Sir Edmond from seeing her').
143. *from the pensive tendency of her disposition*: 'd'une tristesse qui n'était presque plus que de la mélancolie' ('from a sadness which was nearly no more than melancholy') in the French edition.
144. *Armides*: a 1776 opera by the German Christoph Willibald Gluck based on a libretto by Philippe Quinault. Jean-Baptiste Lully had written an opera by the same name and which was based on the same libretto in 1686 that was considered his masterpiece. When Gluck 'rewrote' Lully's work, a quarrel erupted, but the opera was well received. Gluck represented the French side in a debate between supporters of French and Italian opera in the late 1770s, with Niccolò Vito Piccinni representing the Italian side. The opera tells an unhappy love story between a sorceress named Armide and a knight.
145. *Alcestes*: another opera by Gluck from 1777. Lully, again, had composed an opera bearing the same name (in 1674). Alceste is abducted and her husband mortally wounded when he tries to rescue her. She offers the gods her death instead of his, but is spared and reunited with her husband.
146. *Oedipe*: *Oedipe à Colone* (*Oedipus at Colonus*) is an opera by the Italian Antonio Sacchini, composed in 1786 with a libretto by Frenchman Nicolas-François Guillard. The plot covers the end of the famous Greek mythological figure Oedipus's life.
147. *she will convince you of your error*: As Tili Boon Cuillé points out, Cottin demonstrates awareness here of Rousseau's 'complaint that the French language is unmusical' ('Cottin, Krüdener, and Musical Mesmerism', in *Narrative Interludes: Musical Tableaux in Eighteenth-Century French Texts* (Toronto: University of Toronto Press, 2006), pp. 144–72, on p. 157), yet refutes it through Edmond's character. Cottin knew Rousseau's work very well.
148. *But ... they will be deceived*: 'mais ils lui diront que oui, et elle les croira comme tant d'autres, et comme tant d'autres, ils la tromperont' ('yet they will tell her they do and she will believe them like so many others and like so many others, they will deceive her') in the French edition.

149. *scholar*: student.
150. *a slight indisposition*: 'une migraine' ('a migraine') in the French edition.
151. *She fancied ... if she continued to go down every day*: 'elle croyait même y avoir montré assez de plaisir, pour que mistriss Birton ne dût pas craindre de la gêner en l'engageant à reprendre l'habitude de descendre tous les jours' ('She even fancied having shown sufficient enjoyment so that mistriss Birton should not fear inconveniencing her by asking her to go down again every day') in the French edition.
152. *one morning*: 'un dimanche matin' ('a Sunday morning') in the French edition.
153. *join your companion*: The French edition adds 'j'irai vous trouver dans un instant' ('I will join you in a moment').
154. *thus*: The French edition adds 'et pour ce coeur insenisible jusqu'à alors et décidé à l'être toujours' ('and for this heart, until then insensitive to love and determined to remain so forever').
155. *veil them from her view!*: This scene where virtuous Malvina starts to develop feelings for libertine Edmond as he shows his gentler side recalls a similar scene in Laclos's *Liaisons dangereuses* (*Dangerous Liaisons*), published in 1782. There, libertine Valmont has orchestrated a scene where he helps the poor, to be observed by a servant of his beloved, prude and religious (and married) Madame de Tourvel. When word of the actions reaches Madame de Tourvel she also softens towards Valmont, and eventually agrees to become his mistress.
156. *when looking at her*: 'La nourrice' ('The nurse') precedes this in the French edition.
157. *each received a benefit from you*: 'chacun vous bénit' ('each praises you') in the French edition.
158. *words of comfort*: The French edition adds 'à la portée de son intelligence' ('within the reach of her intelligence').
159. *she assisted Sir Edmond to support the nurse in her chair*: 'elle s'appuya sur le dos du fauteuil auprès de Sir Edmond' ('she leaned on the back of the chair near Sir Edmond') in the French edition.
160. *he will comfort and be near you*: A biblical reference, left untranslated, follows in the French edition 'que son bâton et sa houlette vous rassurent' ('may his rod and his staff comfort you'). A footnote indicates that the text comes from 'Ps. XXIII, 4' (Psalms 23:4). 'The vale of death' appears in the same Psalm.
161. *he ought to be loved much more than he is feared*: 'afin qu'il puisse être aimé autant qu'il est craint' ('he ought to be loved as much as he is feared') in the French edition.
162. *Let me now, O Lord, depart in peace?*: The French edition indicates in an untranslated footnote that the biblical reference comes from the 'Cantique de Siméon' ('Canticle of Simeon'): 'Now, Master, You can dismiss your servant in peace; You have fulfilled Your word'.
163. *those charming lips, where the graces repose near wisdom*: The French edition indicates in an untranslated footnote that the quotation comes from 'Dryden' ('Dryden'). I was unable to find its source, but James A. Winn, a specialist on Dryden at Boston University, said the following in an email dated 25 June 2014: 'The closest resemblance I can find is in "Cymon and Iphigenia", one of the Ovidian episodes Dryden translated in his last book, *Fables Ancient and Modern* (1700). The "clown" Cymon sees the sleeping Iphigenia, whom the narrator compares to Diana: The dame herself the goddess well expressed, Not more distinguished by her purple vest, Than by the charming features of her face, And even in slumber a superior grace...' I hereby gratefully acknowledge his assistance.
164. *they*: 'il' ('he'), meaning Lord Stafford, in the French edition.

165. *less liberty*: 'plus de liberté' ('more liberty') in the French edition.
166. *in the kingdom*: 'd'Edimbourg' ('in Edinburgh') in the French edition.
167. *Thus, you can throw out some hints; and if he should pretend not to understand it*: 'Mais le voici: n'ayons pas l'air de nous entendre' ('But here he is now; let us not pretend we agree') in the French edition.
168. *What, is the brother of Lady Mary Summerhill grown so gay*: 'Chez Milord Stanhope, frère de lady Sumerhill?' ('Milord Stanhope, lady Sumerhill's brother') in the French edition.
169. *pleasing*: 'nécessaires' ('necessary') in the French edition.
170. *their society is uniformly fatiguing*: 'tout ce qui ne les berce pas les fatigue' ('all that does not amuse them fatigues them') in the French edition.
171. *the ton*: 'le ton' ('the tone') in the French edition.
172. *I could not please by any other means*: 'j'ai toujours été en reste avec elles' ('I always had obligations towards them') in the French edition.
173. *the power of independence*: 'libres et indépendans' ('the power of independence and freedom') in the French edition.
174. *is it not to win the heart of Lady Mary, that you have endeavoured to make her believe that you have loved her?*: 'ce n'est que pour déchirer le coeur de lady Sumerhill, que vous avez cherché à vous en faire aimer' ('it is only in order to break Lady Mary's heart that you have endeavoured to make her love you') in the French edition.
175. *the benevolent benefactor of the distressed*: absent from the French edition.
176. *who also will condemn your neglect of her*: absent from the French edition.
177. *and consequently he will realize her expectations*: absent from the French edition.
178. *that she is very different from the idea you have drawn of her character, as she neither possesses benevolence or generosity*: 'que cela ne répond pas à ce caractère de grandeur et de générosité qu'on vous attribue' ('that this is very different from the benevolence and generosity that are attributed to your character') in the French edition.
179. *Mrs. Burton and Miss Melmor*: The French edition adds 'déja en butte aux malignes interprétations de toutes deux' ('already exposed to negative interpretations by both of them').
180. *Erse*: see note 87 above.
181. *whom you loved*: 'qui vous aime' ('who loves you') in the French edition.
182. *and a thousand other trifling things, which are not worth repeating*: 'et pour mille autres qui ne la valent pas' ('and for a thousand others who are not worthy of her') in the French edition.
183. *the want of probity*: The French edition adds 'auprès des femmes' ('towards women').
184. *the origin of love ... in the heart of the lover*: The French edition indicates in an untranslated footnote that the poet in question is 'Dryden' ('Dryden'). Specifically, the quotation comes from Dryden's tragedy *Tyrannic Love; or, the Royal Martyr* (1670), III.i.121–3, where Maximin, the tyrant of Rome, says: 'Pity, my son, those flames you disapprove. The cause of love can never be assigned; 'Tis in no face, but in the lover's mind.'
185. *I have ever been silent when with her*: 'le mien' ('mine') in the French edition, i.e. 'my heart'.
186. *for not having informed her sooner ... without you had been certain of fulfilling them*: 'de ne l'avoir pas avertie plutôt de vos dispositions, et de lui avoir laissé faire des avances que vous n'étiez pas sûr de confirmer' ('for not having informed her sooner of your disposition and for allowing her to make advances which you were not certain to confirm') in the French edition.

187. *take a walk*: 'fait un marché' ('make a purchase') in the French edition. 'Marcher' in French means 'to walk'.
188. *found him more amiable*: The French edition adds 'de se plaire avec lui' ('enjoyed his company').
189. *which related to Anzoletta*: 'd'Asoleta' ('by Anzoletta') in the French edition.
190. *we shall distinctly see*: 'elle verra distinctement' ('she will distinctly see') in the French edition.
191. *Miss Melmor*: 'mistriss Melmor' ('Mrs Melmor') in the French edition.
192. *for a minute*: The French edition adds 'assurément, c'est ce qu'elle pouvait faire de mieux' ('without doubt, that was the best thing she could do').
193. *the woman he most loved?*: The French edition adds 'dans le courant de la conversation' ('in the ordinary conversation').
194. *of all those women you told me of*: 'de toutes celles à qui vous l'avez dit' ('of all those to whom you said so') in the French edition.
195. *I may have so expressed myself in a figurative sense*: 'me le suis-je figuré moi-même' ('I imagined it myself') in the French edition.
196. *a month*: 'quelques mois' ('some months') in the French edition.
197. *or I should rather say, that ever interested my heart*: absent from the French edition.
198. *the most perfect of all his creatures*: The French edition indicates in an untranslated footnote that the reference comes from 'Shakespear, dans la Tempête' ('Shakespeare, *The Tempest*') (1611). Indeed, the quotation comes from Ferdinand in III.i.37–48: 'Admired Miranda! Indeed the top of admiration! worth / What's dearest to the world! Full many a lady / I have eyed with best regard and many a time / The harmony of their tongues hath into bondage / Brought my too diligent ear: for several virtues / Have I liked several women; never any / With so fun soul, but some defect in her / Did quarrel with the noblest grace she owed / And put it to the foil: but you, O you, / So perfect and so peerless, are created / Of every creature's best!'
199. *This sentence petrified her to her seat ... she immediately rose to retire*: 'auprès de qui il était assis, afin de lui rappeler l'instant où elle y était venue' ('near whom he was seated, in order to remind her of the moment she had come there') in the French edition.
200. *Miss Melmor*: The French edition adds 'tourmentée' ('worried').
201. *glass*: 'glace' ('mirror') in the French edition.
202. *increased her emotion*: The French edition adds 'son coeur palpita, ses joues s'animèrent' ('her heart started to beat faster, her cheeks blushed').
203. *she was endeavouring to investigate it, when Sir Edmond ... retired*: 'elle se hâta de se retirer: chacun la suivit' ('she hurriedly retired, everyone else followed') in the French edition.
204. *seek her Frances*: The French edition adds 'Cependant, pourquoi s'était-elle échappée si vîte, comme si elle eût craint d'être reconnue?' ('Yet why would she have escaped so quickly as if she feared being recognised?').
205. *being unjust*: The French editions adds 'et s'il exagérait le mal, il ne le supposait jamais' ('and even if he exaggerated evil, he never assumed it').
206. *religion*: absent from the French edition.
207. *from the heart*: The French edition adds 'et qui arrive' ('and going to the heart').
208. *Malvina*: The French edition adds 'en proie à l'insomnie' ('a victim of insomnia').
209. *letter to his friend*: This is the first of several letters inserted into the novel. Cottin used the epistolary format in her previous (and first) novel *Claire d'Albe* (1799) and had announced there that she was working on another book: 'Quant à moi, je sens si bien tout ce qui lui manque, que je ne m'attends pas que mon âge, ni mon sexe me mettent à l'abri

des critiques, et mon amour-propre serait assez mal à son aise s'il n'avait une sorte de pressentiment que l'histoire que je médite le dédommagera peut-être de l'anecdote qui vient de m'échapper' (*Claire d'Albe* (Paris: Maradan, 1799), p. 4) ('As for me, I know so well all the things it [the novel] is lacking, that I don't expect either my age or my sex to shield me from criticism and I would not have much self confidence if my intuition didn't tell me that the story I am considering writing next will perhaps make up for the anecdote that just slipped from my pen'). Cottin assumed her readers expected another epistolary novel from her but, as she writes in the Preface to *Malvina*: 'if they believe they will find in Malvina the work I announced in the preface to Claire, they are mistaken: my feeling of inadequacy did not allow me to complete it. An epistolary novel, where each style has to be as distinct as the character of those writing, strikes me as the biggest difficulty with this genre of text and, in order to attempt to overcome it, I will wait a while longer. However, since various motives, which I do not want to mention here, compelled me to write, I have tried the chapter style, it being the easiest' (see note 3 above). Even while using this 'chapter style' Cottin inserts some letters in *Malvina*. However, the number of letter writers is very limited, with her thus avoiding 'the biggest difficulty with this genre of text'. Epistolary transvestism occurs in these letters when Cottin writes repeatedly in the male voice, as in this instance.

210. *that angelic woman*: The French edition adds 'en qui l'univers ne voit rien à desirer' ('in whom the universe sees nothing left to be desired').
211. *but I feel them vibrate!*: 'avec le frémissement religieux qu'on éprouve en entrant dans un temple' ('but with the religious trembling one feels upon entering a temple') in the French edition.
212. *the edifice is not unworthy of its God*: This quotation comes indeed from Dryden, specifically from his tragedy *Don Sebastian, King of Portugal* (1690). Note Sebastian at II.i: 'What Honour is there in a Woman's Death! / Wrong'd as she says, but helpless to Revenge; / Strong in her Passion, impotent of Reason, / Too weak to hurt, too fair to be destroy'd. / Mark her Majestick Fabrick, she's a Temple / Sacred by Birth and built by Hands divine; / Her Soul's the Deity that lodges there: / Nor is the Pile unworthy of the God'.
213. *I well know that it will take a long time to accomplish this; and that she will be still longer before she will ever confess as much*: 'je le saurai long-temps avant elle, et elle le saura long-temps avant de me l'avouer' ('I will know it long before she will and she will know it long before confessing it to me') in the French edition.
214. *for in this respect, she has not the least resemblance to any I have known*: 'm'aurait-elle changé si elle leur ressemblait?' ('would she have changed me if she had resembled them?') in the French edition.
215. *the treasures of Solomon*: According to the Book of Kings I 10:23, 'King Solomon was greater in riches and wisdom than all the other kings of the earth'.
216. *the women*: 'les sept cents femmes' ('the seven hundred women') in the French edition. According to the Book of Kings I 11:3, Solomon had 'seven hundred wives of royal birth and three hundred concubines'. Edmond's libertine tendencies become quite apparent in this letter to his male friend.
217. *going from hence*: The French edition adds 'la veille du jour' ('the evening before').
218. *my pretty Kate*: The French edition adds 'n'a rien à désirer à cet égard' ('leaves nothing to desire in that respect'), i.e., is a 'weak character'.
219. *nature in the first creation of the world*: The French edition indicates in an untranslated footnote that the reference comes from 'Vowe' which in later editions is corrected to 'Rowe'. It comes indeed from Nicholas Rowe's tragedy *Tamerlane* (1702). See at I.i, Ta-

merlane: 'This is indeed to Conquer, / And well to be rewarded for thy Conquest; / The Bloom of opening Flow'rs, unsully'd Beauty, / Softness and sweetest Innocence she wears, / And looks like Nature in the World's first Spring'. Tamerlane was a fifteenth-century monarch in central Asia who conquered many lands. This is why Edmond says possessing Malvina would 'raise [him] above all the monarchs on earth'. The conquest metaphor again demonstrates his libertinism in this particularly masculine epistolary context.

220. *EDMOND B—*: The letter is not signed in the French edition.
221. *she had consented*: 'il l'avait fait consentir' ('he had made her consent') in the French edition.
222. *she forgot her resolution*: The French edition adds 'poussée par le désir d'éclaircir des doutes qui l'intéressaient plus qu'elle ne le croyait elle-même, elle lui fit plusieurs questions' ('driven by her desire to clear up doubts she found more interesting than she thought herself, she asked him several questions').
223. *found it impossible*: 'aurait trouvé aussi impossible que coupable' ('found it equally impossible and erroneous') in the French edition.
224. *would soon give her up to another*: 'après avoir commencé par se donner' ('having started by giving themselves') in the French edition.
225. *glass*: i.e. a mirror.
226. *adequate return by Sir Edmond*: 'en demande le prix; par sir Edmond' ('adequate return; Sir Edmond [accepted the walk]') in the French edition.
227. *that the eyes were almost blinded by the light, though monotonous aspect of the country*: 'que les yeux étaient réellement éblouis de l'aspect de la campagne' ('that the eyes were truly blinded by the light of the country') in the French edition.
228. *O thou that rollest above ... and laughest at the storm*: This entire quotation appears indeed in Ossian's poem *Carthon*, at the very end. This particular scene became quite famous and in 1805 Lord Byron included it is his poem *Ossian's Address to the Sun in Carthon*.
229. *and Sir Edmond chagrined*: 'mais s'ils avaient percé jusqu'au fond de l'ame, peut-être Sir Edmond n'aurait-il pas été mécontent du sien' ('but if they had looked deep into her soul, perhaps Sir Edmond would not have been displeased with his [share]') in the French edition.
230. *they may perhaps*: 'on peut être' ('we may perhaps') in the French edition.
231. *and keep them at a distance ... in speaking their real sentiments?*: 'et à ôter aux gens honnêtes tout moyen de faire le bien' ('and remove from honest people any means of doing good') in the French edition.
232. *when a rascal in power ... without having reason to believe that every thing is sacrificed to fortune?*: It is unclear in English to whom 'they' refers. The French edition states 'quand le fourbe puissant, le fripon enrichi se verront accueillis par l'honnête homme, ne seront-ils pas fondés à croire qu'ils ont bien fait de tout sacrifier à la fortune?' ('When the powerful hypocrite and the rich crook see themselves received by the man of integrity, will they not have reason to think that they were right to sacrifice everything to fortune?').
233. *If they disguised the contempt*: 'En leur dissimulant le mépris' ('If the contempt was disguised from them') in the French edition.
234. *tired*: 's'ennuyer' ('bored') in the French edition, due to the small number of people in Paradise.
235. *Such are the hussars ... always serve as auxiliaries to virtue*: Laurence Sterne (1713–68), an Irish novelist and clergyman, wrote this not in his *Sermons*, but in his best known novel *The Life and Opinions of Tristram Shandy, Gentleman* at the end of chapter 11 in Book 6

(1762), when speaking about the parson Yorick's sermons: 'he took a larger circuit, and indeed a much more mettlesome one; as if he had snatched the occasion of unlacing himself with a few more frolicsome strokes at vice, than the straitness of the pulpit allowed. These, though hussar-like they skirmish lightly, and out of all order, are still auxiliaries on the side of virtue; tell me, Mynheer Vander Blonederdondergewdenstronke, why they should not be printed together!'. Sterne's 'Mynheer Vander Blonederdondergewdenstronke' is an obvious reference to Voltaire's Baron Thunder-ten-Tronckh in *Candide* (1759), which he made Dutch, 'Mynheer' meaning 'Mr' in Dutch and 'donder', 'thunder'.

236. *in a short time*: 'au bout d'une demi-heure' ('in half an hour') in the French edition.
237. *perhaps he might have fallen*: absent from the French edition.
238. *he has not even found a rock to shelter his head*: The French edition adds 'peut-être est-il sans abri contre les vents impétueux' ('perhaps he is without shelter against the forceful winds').
239. *would not have found some means*: 'n'eût pas attendu les miens' ('would not have awaited mine [my orders]') in the French edition.
240. *not cruelly hurt*: 'cruellement blessé' ('cruelly hurt') in the French edition.
241. *the cabin of the mountaineer*: 'une cabane de montagnard' ('a mountaineer's cabin') in the French edition.
242. *Thanks to your prudent suggestions, madam, your nephew cannot be in any danger*: 'peut-être se serait-il englouti dans quelque précipice; mais qu'importe, grâce à une réflexion si prudente, votre neveu n'aurait été exposé à aucun danger' ('perhaps he [the old man] would have fallen off a cliff, but why would that matter if, thanks to your prudent suggestion, your nephew would not have been exposed to any danger') in the French edition.
243. *casements*: windows.
244. *cries of distress*: The French edition adds 'et le sinistre croassement des hibous, des appellations douloureuses' ('and the owls' sinister calls, painful cries').
245. *all those in affliction inspired*: The French editions adds 'et peut-être avait elle raison' ('and perhaps she was right').
246. *for his safe return*: The French edtion adds 'En le voyant, elle fit un cri de joie ... l'attendrissement succéda à l'inquiétude' ('Upon seeing him, she uttered a scream of joy ... emotion replaced anxiety').
247. *amidst the confusion of voices, she could distinguish those of Mrs. Burton, Mr. Prior, and Miss Melmor*: The French edition states 'les voix confuses de mistriss Birton, M. Prior et miss Melmor lui ayant appris que tout le monde était réuni auprès de sir Edmond' ('the confused voices of Mrs Burton, Mr Prior and Miss Melmor told her that everyone was reunited near sir Edmond').
248. *treat such feelings with contempt*: 'qu'il ne se méprît sur' ('mistake such feelings') in the French edition.
249. *In pronouncing these words*: The French edition adds 'avec la plus grande vivacité' ('with the greatest intensity').
250. *The night has been so tremendous, and you walked so fast, that we feared that—. Sir Edmond! cried Miss Melmor, as she came in half breathless*: 'la nuit était si affreuse ... Vous marchez si vîte, sir Edmond, s'écria miss Melmor en arrivant tout essoufflée' ('The night has been so tremendous ... You walked so fast, sir Edmond, cried Miss Melmor, as she came in half breathless') in the French edition.
251. *in order to render herself more amiable*: 'qui la rendît moins aimable' ('which rendered her less amiable') in the French edition.
252. *walked all the way there and back?*: 'qu'il eût marché une partie de la nuit' ('walked part of the night') in the French edition.

253. *the snow and the tempest increasing ... as I had lost my path*: 'la neige et la tempête ne pouvaient m'arrêter, quand c'était ici que je revenais' ('the snow and the tempest could not stop me when I was returning here') in the French edition.
254. *the loss which I have sustained*: The French edition adds 'Il fut un coeur tendre et vrai, sir Edmond, un seul, sans doute, que le mensonge ne souilla jamais; la nature l'offrit de bonne heure à mes regards, m'apprit à l'aimer, et ce qui n'était d'abord qu'instinct, devint bientôt amitié' ('It was a true and loving heart, sir Edmond, only one without doubt, never soiled by lies; Nature showed it to me early on, taught me to love it and that which was initially merely instinct soon became friendship').
255. *like Eve, in Milton, I am chased from Eden, and feel as if I was disenchanted by painful comparisons*: 'comme l'Eve de Milton chassée de l'Eden, je suis descendue sur une terre malheureuse et désenchantée par de pénibles comparaisons' ('like Eve in Milton chased from Eden, I have descended to an unhappy land disenchanted by painful comparisons') in the French edition. The reference is to Milton's epic poem *Paradise Lost* (1667, Book 10), where both Eve and Adam are chased from Paradise after having eaten the forbidden fruit.
256. *I break it*: 'Brisons là-dessus' ('Let us stop there') in the French edition.
257. *I cannot be serious sometimes, madam?*: The French edition adds 'Cependant j'oserai affirmer que, malgré mon air de légèreté, il est des choses qui peuvent m'affecter plus profondément qu'un autre, peut-être' ('Nevertheless I dare to claim that despite my apparent imprudence, there are perhaps things which can affect me more deeply than any other').
258. *attracted*: 'attiré, séduit' ('attracted and seduced') in the French edition.
259. *but very seldom with those whom you see*: 'Mais à peu près tous ceux qui vous voient' ('But nearly all who see you') in the French edition.
260. *She did not perceive ... it is already too late*: The French edition states 'elle ne s'en apercevra que lorsque les premières atteintes de la douleur lui feront connaître un mal mille fois plus cruel que tous ceux qu'elle a éprouvés. L'infortunée alors voudra s'y soustraire, il ne sera plus temps; car l'amour, cette puissance enchanteresse et dominatrice, subjugue avec un attrait invincible et si doux, qu'on est soumis avant d'avoir pensé à se défendre, entraîne avec tant de rapidité, que souvent on est au bout de la carrière quand on se croyait libre de n'y pas entrer, et choisit toujours, pour déployer l'étendue de ses forces, l'instant où on n'en a plus pour lui résister' ('She will perceive it only when the first pangs of pain will expose her to a pain a thousand times worse than all the pain she had experienced before. The unfortunate victim will then want to escape, but it will be too late, for love, that seductive, imperious power, subjugates with such a sweet, invincible attraction that we are lost before having thought of defending ourselves; it takes over so quickly, that we are often surprised by it; and, in order to display the full extent of its power, it always chooses the moment when we no longer have any to resist').
261. *not from experience, for she had not any from friendship. Lady Sheridan no longer existed*: 'L'expérience? – Elle n'en a point. – L'amitié? – Milady Sheridan n'est plus' ('Experience? She doesn't have any. Friendship? Lady Sheridan no longer existed') in the French edition.
262. *He was not, nor ever could be, that second self, which that lady had been*: absent from the French edition. The addition underlines the importance of female friendship.
263. *which gently forces a friend to tell what she wishes to disclose*: 'qui pressent ce qu'on voudrait dire' ('who senses what we would like to say') in the French edition.
264. *That sometimes they are united, by the most indissoluble ties; while those who appear by nature to be formed for each other, never meet*: The French edition states 'qu'il se plait à réunir, par les liens les plus étroits, ceux que la nature semblait destiner à ne se rapprocher jamais' ('that love likes to unite, by the most indissoluble ties, those who appear to be

destined by nature never to meet'). This difference is interesting because while the English edition takes Mr Prior's perspective (he appears compatible with Malvina, but she is not attracted to him), the French edition stresses Sir Edmond's perspective (opposites attract).

265. *END OF VOL. I.*: In the 1810 edition, a table of contents follows (on p. 239): CONTENTS OF VOL. I

In the French original, the table of contents precedes the first chapter.

VOLUME II

1. *to throw a restraint over her*: 'gêne la tendresse' ('throws a restraint over love') in the French edition.
2. *who would have only him to reproach*: 'qui n'en avait aucun à lui reprocher' ('who could not reproach him anything') in the French edition.
3. *not obtaining the success he had promised himself*: The French edition adds 'parce qu'elle avait assez de tact pour sentir que ce n'était pas de ce côté qu'elle devait avoir le plus de craintes' ('because she had sufficient tact to understand that it was not from this direction she should fear the most').
4. *Sir Edmond would have revolted at such a threat*: The French edition adds 'et n'y eût vu qu'un motif de s'attacher advantage à celle qu'on aurait cru lui ôter par de semblables moyens' ('and would have used it merely as a reason to attach himself further to the woman such means were supposed to distance him from').
5. *said Mrs. Burton*: 'ma chère' ('my dear') in the French edition. In the French edition these words are said by Mrs Melmor, addressing Mrs Burton.
6. *He is not so haughty ... will render him less severe*: absent from the French. Instead, the French edition states 'Il ne faut pas toujours se fier à cet air doucereux de madame de Sorcy' ('We should not always trust madame de Sorcy's hyprocritical behaviour').
7. *We know there is nothing to fear in still water*: The French edition states the opposite 'on sait assez qu'il n'y a rien de pire que l'eau qui dort' ('We know there is nothing more dangerous than still water').
8. *function*: 'caractère' ('character') in the French edition.
9. *He could only judge by the pleasure he experienced in the company of Malvina*: 'afin de pouvoir juger du plaisir qu'y trouvait Malvina' ('so he might be able to judge the pleasure Malvina found in it') in the French edition.
10. *had she been living*: The French edition adds 'il l'était presque de son souvenir' ('he was

nearly jealous of her memory').

11. *for the moment*: 'du moment' in the French edition. 'From the moment' would have been a better translation.
12. *he resolved to forget her*: 'il se promit, non pas de l'oublier, mais de n'en jamais faire sa femme' ('he resolved not to forget her, but never to make her his wife') in the French edition.
13. *dubious in what manner to act with respect to her*: 'rêvait comment elle pourrait réussir à se défaire encore de celle-ci' ('considered how she could succeed in getting rid of her') in the French edition.
14. *Malvina was vexed at spilling her tea on the child*: 'Malvina, troublée par ce qu'elle entendait, avait répandu le thé' ('Malvina, vexed by what she heard, had spilled her tea') in the French edition.
15. *England*: 'Londres' ('London') in the French edition.
16. *she felt her heart flutter*: The French edition adds 'et des larmes couler dans ses yeux' ('and tears flowing in her eyes').
17. *this critical moment*: The French edition adds 'si différens par la manière dont ils sont sentis, si inégaux par celle dont ils sont calculés' ('so different due to the manner in which it is felt, so inequal due to the manner in which it is determined').
18. *To England*: see note 15 above.
19. *apply the compliment*: The French edition adds 'et qui prévoyait qu'elle empêcherait difficilement la conversation de continuer sur ce sujet, si elle n'y fesait diversion' ('and foresaw it would be difficult to prevent this conversation from continuing on this subject unless she created a distrction').
20. *this morning?*: 'hier matin' ('yesterday morning') in the French edition.
21. *both of them*: 'argus' ('spies') in the French edition.
22. *endeavoured to detain her*: The French edition adds 'et comme elle venait de recevoir une forte commotion' ('and as she had just suffered a severe shock').
23. *sweetmeats*: confectionary.
24. *Armida*: see Volume I, note 144.
25. *which is the duet*: 'au duo' ('in the duet') in the French edition.
26. *all which you have inspired*: The French editions adds 'ni lui demander ce qu'elle éprouve' ('neither ask her what she feels').
27. *all the disagreeable nothings*: 'tout ce qu'il disait d'aimable' ('all the agreeable nothings') in the French edition.
28. *she had uttered an untruth*: The French edition adds 'pour la première fois de sa vie' ('for the first time in her life').
29. *The words were very trifling*: Given how Cottin felt about women leaving the private sphere in order to pursue creative endeavours, it is remarkable that she mentions a woman composer here, yet not surprising that she criticizes her words. Later French editions, starting with the second edition published in 1805, no longer contain this criticsm. The French edition includes the following words for the song:

Romance Love song
Pour surmonter tendre langueur,
Avec courage,
Ai fui souvent dans l'épaisseur
Du bois sauvage;
Las! y portais avec mon coeur
Ta douce image.

Sais bien que ce coeur, près de toi,
Plus fort palpite;
Mais à quoi sert à son émoi
Que je te quitte?
Lors il me fuit, et, malgré moi,
Vole à ta suite.

Cruel! quand vas fuir le séjour
De ton amante,
Devrais t'oublier sans retour;
En vain le tente;
Plus veux éteindre mon amour,
Plus il augmente.

Mais, du moins, quand t'éloigneras,
Regrette et pleure
Ces long jours où plus ne seras
Dans ma demeure,
Et dont loin de toi vais, hélas!
Compter chaque heure.

To mend a broken heart
with courage
I have often fled
into the dense woods
Alas! I carried there with my heart
your lovely image.

I know well that this heart, near you,
beats faster
But why would I leave you
and distress it
If it flees from me and flies after
you in spite of me?

Brute! when you abandon
your mistress
I should forget you forever
I try it in vain
The more I wish to end my love
the more it grows.

But at least when you leave
I will miss and cry for
those long days when you are
in my home no more
and of which, far from you,
I will count each hour, alas!

Ironically, a real woman composer named Mlle Rothier put these words to music. A copy of the song survives in a Swiss volume formerly owned by Hortense (de Beauharnais), queen of Holland (1783–1837), which thus traces its composition to the first third of the nineteenth century, likely early within that time frame. I would like to acknowledge the assistance of Daniel Gloor from the Music Department at the Zentralbibliothek in

Zürich, Switzerland, in procuring me a copy of the song, which allowed me to identify the composer as Mlle Rothier, not Gothier as indicated in the library catalogues. For more on late-eighteenth-century French women composers, see the scholarship by Jacqueline Letzter and Robert Adelson.

30. *On leaving the saloon*: 'Enfin, lorsque chacun s'éleva pour rentrer dans le salon' ('Finally, when everyone rose in order to return to the saloon') in the French edition. They were in the music room, not the saloon.
31. *But*: The French edition adds 'du moins ne vous verrai-je pas demain avant mon départ?' ('Will I not at least see you tomorrow before I leave?').
32. *Happiness is departing from me*: The French edition adds 'et la paix encore davantage' ('and inner peace even more so').
33. *perhaps to-morrow*: The French soliloquy is much longer: 'Là, devant moi, tes regards ont rencontré les miens; mon coeur bat violemment à ce souvenir ... Peut-être demain te reverrai-je encore ... A chaque pas qui te rapproche de moi, je sens que mon ame me quitte; je perds la vie quand tu es là; une oppression insupportable agit sur tous les points de mon existence. Ote-toi, va; ta présence me ferait mourir' ('There before me, your eyes met mine. My heart beats wildly at this memory ... Perhaps I will see you again tomorrow ... With each step that brings you closer, I feel that my soul abandons me. I nearly die when you are there. An insupportable weight falls on my entire existence. Go away, leave, your presence would kill me').
34. *resist the opportunity of bidding adieu*: The French edition adds 'il partit sans s'être présenté chez elle et sans lui avoir fait dire un mot de simple politesse' ('he left without visiting her and without having sent her a polite note').
35. *from this expectation*: The French edition adds 'chaque fois que quelque bruit se fesait entendre à la porte; et en se voyant trompée dans son attente, malgré elle encore elle éprouvait un mouvement d'impatience contre la personne qui avait causé ce bruit' ('whenever a noise was heard at the door; and finding herself deceived in her expectation, she felt impatient with the person who had caused the noise, again despite herself').
36. *with all the temerity of self confidence*: The French edition states 'ainsi, dans notre téméraire ignorance, nous appelons souvent à grands cris l'instant qui va commencer la chaîne de nos malheurs' ('Thus, in our imprudent ignorance, we often call loudly for the moment which commences our misfortune'). This conveys a sense of impending doom for Mr Prior.
37. *seventh or eighth*: The French editions adds 'fois' ('time').
38. *who remarked it*: 'On l'a remarqué' ('It was remarked') in the French edition.
39. *for his words are like honey ... and touch the heart*: The French edition states in italics 'car sa langue distille le miel, et il charme l'oreille' ('for his tongue drips honey and he pleases the ear'). The italics indicate that this is a quotation. In the Bible, its source is Proverbs 5:3: 'For the lips of a strange woman drop as an honeycomb, and her mouth is smoother than oil'. Importantly, this Proverbs section warns of the dangers of adultery.
40. *For though ... since he has beheld you*: 'Et cependant, jamais il n'a été aussi empressé auprès de Miss Melmor que depuis qu'il vous voyait plus souvent' ('And yet, he has never been as eager to be near Miss Melmor as since he beheld you more often') in the French edition.
41. *after she was a little recovered*: 'en la fesant asseoir' ('seating her') in the French edition.
42. *and the truth was compelled to escape her*: absent from the French edition.
43. *appearances*: This word ('apparences') appears in italics in the French edition for emphasis.
44. *she could make no reply*: The French edition adds 'il ne lui en restait que pour souffrir' ('she could but suffer').

45. *She had therefore never mentioned the subject since*: The French edition adds 'afin d'éviter de motiver un changement d'opinion' ('in order to avoid having to explain a change of heart').
46. *Clarissa*: Samuel Richardson wrote his famous epistolary novel *Clarissa, or, the History of a Young Lady* in 1748. Clarissa symbolizes the epitome of virtue; her virtue attracts Lovelace – a libertine villain.
47. *men who are of an ardent and passionate character*: The French edition adds 'quoique de moeurs un peu relâchées' ('albeit with somewhat loose morals').
48. *deprived her of every present satisfaction*: 'la laissait sans avenir' ('left her without future') in the French edition.
49. *she never had a doubt of its sincerity, therefore, Miss Melmor was believed*: 'pour douter de la sincérité de Miss Melmor: plus elles devinrent outrées, plus elle les crut' ('to doubt Miss Melmor's sincerity: the more exaggerated the adulation, the more she believed it') in the French edition.
50. *public opinion should only be regarded when it respected self alone*: 'il est bien de mettre l'opinion publique au-dessus de tous les sacrifices qui ne coûtent qu'à soi' ('public opinion should be regarded more highly than all individual sacrifices') in the French edition.
51. *a writer to the Signet*: 'un petit négociant' ('a small shopkeeper') in the French edition. Members of the Society of Writers to Her Majesty's Signet – a Scottish legal organization – supervised when the private seal of the Scottish kings was used, which was required for certain legal actions. Based on the narrative, this type of position and status would appear more credible for Mr Fenwick than that of a small shopkeeper.
52. *and she attracted so much of his regard*: 's'attira de celle-ci des égards' ('he attracted so much of her regard') in the French edition.
53. *Tasse*: 'mistriss Tap' ('Mrs Tap') in the French edition. Although the name is different here from the previously used 'Tass' in the French edition, it refers to the same character – Mrs Burton's maid – and the English edition therefore uses the same name.
54. *she most feared to behold*: The French edition adds 'mais qui sait si cette dernière considération, si déterminante pour n'y point aller, ne fut pas précisément celle qui l'engagea, à son insçu, sans doute, car elle ne doutait pas que la raison seule n'eût dicté ce parti' ('but who knows whether the latter consideration, so crucial in deciding not to go there, was not precisely the one that made her determine to go, without her knowledge undoubtedly, for she did not doubt that reason alone had inspired the idea').
55. *Mrs. St. Clare's*: Note the resemblance with the name of Malvina's deceased friend, Clara, and with Cottin's first heroine, Claire d'Albe.
56. *a woman ... will never be any thing in future but a pedant or a belle esprit*: Ironically, Cottin shared Malvina's and Mrs Burton's negative opinion of women writers. See Introduction.
57. *Malvina ventured to mention the subject*: The French edition adds 'et l'accompagna d'un léger sourire' ('while smiling slightly').
58. *and so ready to circulate them*: The French edition adds 'qu'on croirait qu'il les regarde comme sa propriété, et le mystère dont on voudrait les couvrir, comme une usurpation' ('that one would believe everyone considers them their property and the mystery in which they wish to shroud them, an encroachment').
59. *Malvina consented to this proposal with pleasure*: The French edition adds 'et prenant le bras de mistress Clare' ('and taking Mrs St Clare's arm'). The two are metaphorically connected – a fact confirmed by the subsequent 'first budding blossoms' representing their friendship.
60. *Preface*: This entire chapter on women writers is missing from the second (Michaud)

and subsequent French editions, where the preceding and following chapters have been modified to account for its elimination. Both of Gunning's editions are based on the first French edition and therefore contain it. According to Catherine Cusset 'Cottin's friends informed her that madame de Staël had felt directly attacked by this reactionary chapter: Cottin, who liked madame de Staël and did not want to offend her, took it out of the second edition' (In 'Rousseau's Legacy: Glory and Femininity at the End of the Eighteenth Century: Sophie Cottin and Elisabeth Vigée-Lebrun', in R. Bonnel and C. Rubinger (eds), *Femmes savantes et femmes d'esprit: Women Intellectuals of the French Eighteenth Century* (New York, NY: Peter Lang, 1994), pp. 401–18, on p. 408). See also note 29 above. For a letter in which Cottin addresses this issue, see L. C. Sykes, *Madame Cottin* (Oxford: Basil Blackwell, 1949), pp. 349–51. Madame de Genlis had also taken offense, which Cottin regretted. Sykes found an unpublished apology (*Madame Cottin*, p. 224).

61. *and though the preference ... would require some hours to explain it in*: 'quel que soit le penchant qui entraîne, la confiance n'est pas l'affaire de quelques heures' ('no matter what the preference inducing it is, trust is not built in some hours') in the French edition.
62. *without children*: The French edition adds 'ne paraissant tenir dans le monde qu'à mon père' ('appearing to depend only on my father in the world').
63. *she lives in obscurity*: Cottin herself also desired – but failed – to live in obscurity. In an 1805 letter addressed to Pierre-Hyacinthe Azaïs, she wrote: 'Tout le mal vient de ce que je suis trop connue; j'éprouve tous les jours qu'une femme gâte bien son sort en sortant de l'obscurité: vous savez bien que, là où il y a de la peine, il y a toujours un tort; c'en est un très grand pour une femme que d'écrire; on ne saurait trop le répéter, ni moi assez le reconnaître. Mes moindres démarches sont observées, et le blâme qu'on y jette rejaillit sur ce qui m'entoure et qui m'est cher' ([Madame de Clauzade] Arnelle, *Une oubliée: Madame Cottin d'après sa correspondance* (Paris: Librairie Plon, 1914), p. 282). ('All problems arise from the fact that I am too well known; I experience daily that a woman ruins her fate by leaving obscurity: you know well that where there is pain, there is always a wrong. For a woman it is a great wrong to write. One could not repeat it too much and neither could I recognize it sufficiently. The least of my moves are observed and the blame that they receive reaches everything around me and that I love').
64. *those situations which she has peculiarly remembered*: A common criticism (by men) of women writers used to be that they knew how to write only about their own lives and love.
65. *all the characteristics of sentiment*: 'toutes les nuances d'un sentiment' ('all the characteristics of a sentiment') in the French edition. While the English edition refers to sentiment in general, the French edition points to a specific sentiment in romances, i.e. love.
66. *while it is an effort for men to write their episodes*: 'tandis qu'il est à peine l'épisode de celle des hommes' ('while it [i.e. love] forms merely an episode in men's lives') in the French edition. Whereas the latter claims love simply is not as important in men's lives, the English edition does not make such a statement, but rather claims men simply have difficulty writing about it.
67. *I do not know one*: A very lengthy untranslated footnote appears here in the French edition: 'Non, aucune, pas même cette Sapho toujours citée par les défenseurs de la gloire littéraire de notre sexe; car, lors même qu'elle ne devrait pas sa célébrité autant aux malheurs de sa passion qu'à l'éclat de ses talens, il n'en résulterait pas moins que ses talens se sont bornés à peindre avec chaleur ce qu'elle éprouvait, et certes, je suis loin de refuser celui-là aux femmes. Mais qu'on m'en cite une qui ait tracé un ouvrage philosophique, une pièce de théâtre, enfin, une de ces productions vastes qui demandent une méditation

longue et réfléchie, et qui puisse se mettre au niveau de celles de nos littérateurs de la seconde classe? je me tairai, et je conviendrai que cette femme peut ressembler aux hommes; et j'en serai bien fâchée pour elle, parce que, selon moi, elle aura beaucoup perdu; car il m'a toujours semblé que l'équitable nature, en dispensant ses dons entre les deux sexes, avait tout fait pour l'esprit de l'un et tout pour le cœur de l'autre: c'est à savoir lequel des deux lots vaut le mieux; pour moi, je pense que les femmes peuvent se contenter du leur. Aussi Chamfort a-t-il dit quelque part, qu'il semble que, dans le partage des deux sexes, les femmes eurent une case de moins dans la tête, et une fibre de plus dans le cœur' ('No, not a single one, not even Sapho who is always quoted by those defending the literary glory of our sex. For, even if she would not owe her fame as much to her unfortunate love affairs as to her magnificent talents, the fact would still remain that her talents were limited to describing ardently what she felt and I am indeed far from denying women that talent. But can anyone name a woman who has written a philosophical work, a play, or indeed one of those large productions that demand long and thoughtful reflection and that could be ranked with those of our second-rate male writers? I will remain silent and will agree that such a woman resembles men. And I will regret it for her because in my opinion, she will have given up a great deal. For it always seemed to me that impartial Nature, in bestowing its gifts on the two sexes, had done everything for the one's mind and for the other's heart: it remains to be seen which lot is best; personally, I think women may be content with theirs. Thus, Chamfort said somewhere that it appears that in the distribution of the two sexes, women had one compartment less in their head, but an additional fibre in their heart'). Nicolas Chamfort (1741–94), a French author known for his maxims, states in his *Maximes et Pensées*: 'Il paraît qu'il y a dans le cerveau des femmes une case de moins, et dans leur cœur une fibre de plus que chez les hommes. Il fallait une organisation particulière pour les rendre capables de supporter, soigner, caresser des enfants' ('It appears that women have one less compartment in their brain, but one more fibre in their heart than men. Such specific organization was necessary in order to make them capable of tolerating, tending to and loving children') (N. Chamfort, *Maximes, pensées, caractères et anecdotes. Par N. Chamfort*, ed. P. Louis de Ginguené (Paris: Michel Lévy Frères, 1870), p. 123).

68. *for those women*: 'Les femmes' ('women') in the French edition. Whereas the English edition limits the absence of genius to certain women, the French edition extends it to all women.
69. *This truth ... has been ascribed to the faulty education which they receive*: 'On a beau rejeter cette vérité démontrée par les faits, sur le genre de leur éducation, on a tort' ('This truth which has been demonstrated by facts, has been ascribed to the nature of their education, but this is incorrect') in the French edition. While the latter claims there is no correlation between women's education and their lack of genius, the English edition blames women's lack of genius directly on their 'faulty education'.
70. *as uninformed as women*: 'plus ignorans que la plupart des femmes' ('more uninformed than most women') in the French edition.
71. *from the greatest obscurity*: The French edition adds 'jusqu'à la palme de la gloire' ('to the palm of glory').
72. *women only write to display their talents*: 'les femmes ne peuvent prendre la plume que pour montrer leur insuffisance' ('women can write only to display their inadequacy') in the French edition. Again, the English edition presents women writers in a more positive light than the French edition.
73. *marble*: 'bronze' ('bronze') in the French edition.

74. *toys*: 'pompons' ('pompons') in the French edition.
75. *as well as politeness*: 'plus encore que la politesse' ('more so than politeness') in the French edition.
76. *Sir Edmond going to marry*: The French edition adds 'lady Sumerhill' ('Lady Summerhill').
77. *Did you not know it?*: 'Est-ce que vous le connaissez?' ('Do you know him?') in the French edition.
78. *I did imagine that such a thing would have happened*: 'je n'imaginais pas qu'ils se convinssent' ('I did not imagine they were a good match') in the French edition.
79. *the time which would assemble the family together*: 'ce bruit, ce mouvement qui annonce que chacun s'éveille, que la journée commence et que la réunion s'approche' ('the noise, the movement that announces that everyone is waking up, that the day begins and that the family will soon be assembled') in the French edition.
80. *we speak on every other subject but that which is nearest the heart*: 'l'on parle de tout, hors de ce qu'on voudrait dire, où l'on écarte sans cesse un sujet que chaque mot semble ramener, et où l'on trouve pourtant un plaisir secret et indéfinissable par l'idée de prolonger l'occasion favorable et unique de savoir ce qui intéresse le plus, quoique bien résolu à ne pas en profiter' ('we speak on every subject, but that which we would wish to say and continuously avoid a subject that each word seems to introduce, yet nevertheless we find a secret and vague pleasure in the idea of prolonging the favorable, unique opportunity of knowing what is most interesting even though we are quite decided not to take that opportunity') in the French edition.
81. *He who does not know so pure a sentiment*: The French edition includes the following verses:

    Quoi! je supporterais un tel abaissement!
    A la foule j'irais disputer mon amant!
    Non, non, mon coeur dédaigne un amant trop frivole
    Qui se donne par-tout, et par-tout se console;
    Qui, d'un pur sentiment méconnaissant les droits,
    Adore sans rougir vingt femmes à-la-fois,
    Et profane un amour qu'il prodigue à chacune:
    Qui peut en aimer vingt, n'en sait aimer aucune.

    What, shall I support such a degradation,
    Among a crowd? shall I dispute for my lover?
    No, my heart disdains a frivolous admirer,
    Who offers himself everywhere and finds consolation everywhere
    Who does not know the rights of so pure a sentiment.
    Shamelessly loves twenty women simultaneously
    And violates a love he offers to each
    He who can love twenty women, does not know how to love a single one

    I have been unable to locate a source for this poem.
82. *a few more lines, which will please you still more*: The French edition includes the following verses:

    O toi qu'outrage encore un coupable délire!
    Viens, céleste vertu, reprendre ton empire:
    Si tu ne peux éteindre un trop cher souvenir,
    S'il est tout mon passé, sois tout mon avenir.

Répands autour de moi ta puissante influence,
Fais taire mes refret, arrache à l'espérance
Ce coeur qui, malgré moi, murmure de tes lois:
Dis-lui qu'on s'avilit par un indigne choix;
Que celle qui chérit l'objet qu'elle dédaigne,
Mérite qu'on la blâme et non pas qu'on la plaigne;
Que toi seule à l'amour tu dois servir d'appui,
Et qu'aimer un coupable est l'être plus que lui.

You, whom a guilty passion still wounds,
Come, divine virtue, take back control
If you can not extinguish a memory too dear
If it is my entire past, be my entire future.
Spread your powerful influence around me
Hush my regrets, tear from hope
This heart that, in spite of me, suffers from your laws
Tell it that we degrade ourselves by an unworthy choice
That she who loves the one she disdains
Deserves our blame and not our pity
That you alone should support love
And that loving a guilty man makes you more guilty than him.

I have been unable to locate a source for this poem.

83. *the same evening*: 'le lendemain au soir' ('the following evening') in the French edition.
84. *from choice, but not from a particular reason*: 'autant par goût que par raison' ('by preference as much as for a particular reason') in the French edition.
85. *she would have undoubtedly avoided him*: 'et pour éviter de le voir, elle aurait consenti à tous les moyens ... à tous, excepté peut-être à celui-là seul qu'il venait d'employer' ('and in order to avoid seeing him, she would have agreed to all means ... all of them, except perhaps for the one he just used') in the French edition.
86. *with some asperity*: The French edition adds 'Ma chère, à quoi pensez-vous donc?' ('My dear, what is on your mind then?').
87. *and left the room*: The French edition adds 'Quelle bizarre creature! s'écria aussitôt mistriss Birton' ('What a whimsical creature, Mrs Burton cried out immediately').
88. *I may appear as amiable to her*: 'qu'elle me paraisse aussi aimable' ('she may appear as amiable to me') in the French edition.
89. *I have a presentiment in your favor*: 'je l'ai prévenue en votre faveur' ('I spoke positively of you to her') in the French edition.
90. *desart*: i.e., desert ('désert').
91. *Mrs. Fenwick*: 'M. Fenwich' ('Mr Fenwick') in the French edition.
92. *she*: see note 91 above.
93. *Mrs. Fenwick*: see note 91 above.
94. *gulph of Edinburgh*: deep inlet of the North Sea, near Edinburgh.
95. *phaeton*: an open, four-wheeled, horse-drawn carriage.
96. *milliner*: 'carton' ('box') in the French edition.
97. *Stanhope*: 'Signé, Henry, duc de Stanhope' ('Signed, Henry, duke of Stanhope') in the French edition.
98. *he appeared so much affected*: The French edition adds 'tenez, tout comme vous voilà à présent' ('just like you right now').
99. *But do not mention a word that has passed, said she*: absent from the French edition.

100. *But as soon as he had requested this*: 'mais à peine ai-je eu fini cette parole' ('but I had barely said this') in the French edition.
101. *what it was he had come to tell her*: 'sur ce que celle-ci venait de lui raconter' ('about what she [Mrs Moody] had just told her') in the French edition.
102. *just entering Mrs. Burton's court-yard*: The French edition adds 'Un instant après, on vint l'avertir qu'on l'attendait' ('A moment later, they came to warn her that she was expected').
103. *Mrs. Fenwick, and said, as he hurried away*: 'mistriss Fenwich, et celle-ci, tout en courant, lui dit' ('Mrs Fenwick who said while hurrying away') in the French edition.
104. *bowing to Mrs. Fenwick*: The French edition adds 'sans lui répondre' ('without answering her').
105. *I cannot believe this could be the reason*: The French edition adds 'mais elle était femme, et ce mot me rend tous mes doutes' ('but she is a woman and that word restores all my doubts').
106. *Her ladyship was near twenty*: The French edition adds 'blonde, blanche et belle' ('blonde, fair and beautiful').
107. *The most amiable ... any qualities which resembled her*: 'Portant en tous lieux ce souvenir avec lui, les femmes les plus jolies ne lui semblaient telles, que parce qu'il croyait leur trouver quelques traits de ressemblance avec Malvina; les plus aimables ne s'attiraient son attention, que parce que Malvina se serait peut-être exprimée comme elles' ('Carrying this memory with him wherever he went, the prettiest women appeared to him thus only because he thought they resembled Malvina in some way; the most amiable ones attracted his attention only because Malvina would perhaps have expressed herself like them') in the French edition.
108. *perfection*: 'de charmes, d'harmonie, de fraîcheur' ('charm, harmony and candour') in the French edition.
109. *he began to credit all he had heard*: A footnote, left untranslated, follows in the French edition: 'Peut-être trouverait-on sir Edmond trop crédule, si l'on ne se souvenait pas que les hommes les plus immoraux sont ceux qui doutent le plus facilement de la vertu des femmes: ils prétendent qu'en ayant connu beaucoup, ils sont plus propres que personne à les juger. Mais moi, je prétends que l'attrait sympathique qui les rapproche toujours de celles qui leur ressemblent, et l'orgueil blessé qui tait discrètement le dédain des femmes honnêtes, sont deux puissans motifs d'appeler du jugement de pareils hommes' ('Perhaps we would find Sir Edmond too credulous if we did not remember that the most immoral men are those who most readily doubt women's virtue: they claim that having known many, they are more apt than any other to judge them. But I believe that that which attracts them always to the women who resemble them and the wounded self-love that discreetly hides their disdain for honest women are two powerful motives for appealing the judgment of such men').
110. *not from any particular preference*: The French edition adds 'et qu'il ne s'en souvenait déja plus' ('and that he already did not remember it any more').
111. *extirpate such an idea from his mind*: 'de lui ôter cette idée' ('extirpate such an idea from her mind') in the French edition.
112. *soon attracted the attention of all the spectators*: The French edition adds 'il n'était question, dans la salle, que de la charmante Française; on montait sur les chaises pour la mieux voir' ('All had eyes only for the charming Frenchwoman; people climbed on chairs in order to see her better').
113. *I only desire to receive it from her*: 'je ne desire qu'une occasion de le lui apprendre' ('I merely desire an opportunity to tell her so') in the French edition.

114. *This circumstance tended to render her situation more irksome*: 'ce tête-à-tête redoubla encore leur gêne mutuelle. S'était-on jamais retrouvé ainsi quand on s'était quitté comme eux?' ('This tête-à-tête increased their mutual discomfort further. Had any others ever thus found themselves after leaving one another like them?') in the French edition.
115. *In vain did they endeavour to forget the past*: The French edition adds 'cette importune image revenait sans cesse' ('that undesirable image kept coming back').
116. *it certainly would evince rudeness in my enquiring any farther*: The French edition adds 'Mais je pense que sir Edmond connaît assez le monde pour éviter de l'être jamais' ('But I believe that sir Edmond knows the world enough to avoid ever being indiscreet').
117. *you do not like to remain where you are?*: 'ne vous trouvez-vous jamais bien que là où vous n'êtes pas?' ('you are never happy but where you are not?') in the French edition.
118. *he would not do it, if he did not mean to become serious*: 'il ne tiendrait qu'à elle que cette préférence devînt plus sérieuse' ('it would but depend on her that this preference become more serious') in the French edition.
119. *Mrs. Melmor and Mrs. Fenwick*: The French edition adds 'et plusieurs autres personnes' ('and several other people').
120. *when she had, before perusing the contents she saw*: 'le papier, qui tenait à peine, s'ouvrit' ('the paper, which barely held together, opened') in the French edition.
121. *Sir Edmond Burton to Madame de Sorcy*: In the French edition, the chapter carries the title 'une Lettre' ('A Letter').
122. *that I may unite all that can please you*: The French edition adds 'comme il a déja tout ce qu'il faut pour vous chérir' ('as it already has everything needed to love you').
123. *do not reject my vows*: The French edition adds 'je suis indigne de vous, je le sais' ('I am unworthy of you, I know').
124. *on account of his affection for you; and also, that it was returned by Malvina*: 'parce qu'il était aimé de vous ... Aimé de vous!' ('because he was loved by you ... Loved by you!') in the French edition.
125. *we are severely affected by what is nearest and dearest to the heart?*: The French edition adds 'ne faut-il pas expier, par une triste habitude de méfiance, le crime d'avoir trompé souvent?' ('should we not atone for the crime of having deceived often through a sad habit of distrust?').
126. *can I then dare to suspect such a one?*: The French edition refers to Malvina twice here as an 'ange' ('angel').
127. *the injustice I may have been guilty of towards you*: 'votre vengeance' ('your desire for revenge') in the French edition.
128. *all my resolutions vanished*: The French edition adds 'je voulus combattre encore et vous braver, je ne fis qu'aggraver mes torts' ('I wished to fight it still and face you, but I merely increased my injustice').
129. *and therefore thinks me unworthy of her notice*: 'qu'elle m'accable da sa colère, qu'elle me repousse' ('may she burden me with her anger, may she reject me') in the French edition.
130. *She easily pardoned him for the caprices his jealousy had occasioned*: The French edition adds 'Quelle femme ne voudrait pas trouver de pareils torts à l'objet qu'elle aime!' ('What woman would not want to find such faults in the man she loves!').
131. *the following day*: 'le surlendemain' ('the day after the following day') in the French edition.
132. *I shall succeed in my revenge*: The French edition adds 'et Edmond recevra le prix de son refus' ('and Edmond will receive the reward for his refusal').
133. *who will then vindicate me*: The French edition adds 'qui me défendra alors?' ('who will

defend me then?').

134. *he will no longer believe that virtue*: 'il ne croit point encore à la vertu' ('he will not yet believe in virtue') in the French edition.
135. *I shall at least not have deserved it*: 'ne l'aurai-je pas mérité?' ('shall I not have deserved it?') in the French edition.
136. *she perceived Sir Edmond at her feet*: The French edition adds 'les bras élevés vers le ciel' ('with his arms stretched out towards Heaven').
137. *She was now certain of his adoration*: The French edition states 'mais quand elle lui devait et la certitude d'être adorée et des momens dont il faut avoir connu les délices pour les comprendre' ('But when she owed him the certainty of being loved and moments whose charms need to be experienced in order to be understood').
138. *condescend to determine my fate*: 'daignez le fixer à jamais entre nous' ('condescend to fix the happiness between us forever') in the French edition.
139. *Mr. Fenwick*: 'mistriss Fenwich' ('Mrs Fenwick') in the French edition. This is in fact a correction from the French, as we will see.
140. *that I may anticipate all the wishes of your heart*: 'que je puisse déposer dans votre coeur tous les désirs' ('that I may deposit in your heart all my desires') in the French edition.
141. *her whom your shameful licentiousness has encouraged to such audacity*: 'celle dont la honteuse licence vous encourage à un tel excès d'audace' ('her whose shameful licentiousness has encouraged you to such audacity') in the French edition.
142. *I wish to remain another moment with you*: The French edition adds 'et seule, sans asile, errante au milieu de la nuit' ('and alone, without asylum, wandering in the middle of the night').
143. *any one else shall accompany me*: The French edition adds 'je n'ai pas besoin de votre secours' ('I do not need your help').
144. *I shall endeavour to go somewhere*: 'Je vais tâcher de m'y rendre' ('I shall endeavor to go there') in the French edition.
145. *But Lord Weymouth ... he did not condescend to exchange a sentence*: 'mais milord Weymouth n'y étant plus, et ne pouvant faire tomber son ressentiment que sur des femmes, ou sur un homme qu'il méprisait plus qu'elles, il sut contenir son indignation et garder le silence' ('But milord Weymouth having left and capable of expressing his resentment to women only, or to a man he despised more than them, he succeeded in controlling his indignation and remaining silent') in the French edition.
146. *at midnight*: 'au milieu de la nuit' ('in the middle of the night') in the French edition.
147. *Morpheus*: i.e., the god of sleep, 'le sommeil' ('sleep') in the French edition.
148. *dross*: i.e., something regarded as useless; 'or' ('money') in the French edition.
149. *leave*: 'éloigner d'elle' ('send away') in the French edition.
150. *Clyde*: The River Clyde flows through Glasgow in Scotland.
151. *by adopting those sentiments which are so dear to you*: 'de sentimens que pour vous chérir' ('I shall have no other sentiments than to love you') in the French edition.
152. *and the end of all my actions*: This sentence is incomplete in the English edition; the French edition adds 'vous deviendrez pour moi la cause d'où tout part, comme le centre où tout aboutit' ('that you will become for me the cause whence everything begins, just like the centre where everything ends').
153. *her happiness*: 'te rendre heureuse' ('your happiness') in the French edition. The French edition adds 'et que si tu dois l'être advantage entre nous deux' ('and that if you are to be happier among the two of us').
154. *your dear infant shall be the solemn pledge between us*: The French edition adds 'et puisse

votre ombre sacrée, en les marquant du sceau de votre céleste puissance, poursuivre et tourmenter à jamais celui de nous qui serait assez lâche pour les trahir!' ('and may your sacred shadow, by marking our vows with the seal of your celestial power, forever pursue and torment whichever one of us who would be so foolish as to betray them!').

155. *because you have been scolding him?*: The French edition adds 'Mais, vois comme il a l'air fâché!' ('But see how miserable he is!').
156. *if I am not guilty in thus yielding my hand to you, I do consent to be yours*: 'dussé-je être coupable en vous cédant, je consens à l'être pour vous' ('and if I were to be guilty by yielding my hand to you, I consent to be guilty for you') in the French edition.
157. *His happiness was too great to allow him to say any more*: The French edition states 'et je n'expire pas sous le poids d'un tel bonheur! Et tout en parlant ainsi, la tête de Malvina reposait sur son épaule; il voyait son sein agité de la même passion qui embrasait la sienne' ('and the weight of such happiness does not crush me! While he was speaking thus, Malvina's head rested on his shoulder; he saw that her breast was agitated by the same passion burning in his').
158. *The emotions experienced in such a scene ... which is to be the eternal lot of the virtuous in Heaven*: The French edition states 'Il est une volupté que tous les êtres de la nature animée, sont appelés à connaître; mais celle-là, toujours mêlée de honte et souvent de regrets, n'est point le terme du plus haut période de bonheur où l'homme puisse attteindre; il ne doit ce bonheur suprême que goûtait alors sir Edmond et Malvina, qu'à cette volupté de l'âme, chef-d'oeuvre d'amour et d'intelligence, fruit de l'union intime de deux coeurs qui s'aiment, s'entendent et se répondent; à cette volupté divine que nulle langue ne peut décrire, nulle pensée concevoir, que ceux-là même qui l'ont sentie s'étonnent d'avoir connue; à cette volupté enfin, que l'homme semble avoir dérobée aux anges, ou que la divinité jeta plutôt sur la terre, pour donner une idée de la félicité qu'elle réserve à la vertu dans le ciel' ('There is a pleasure of the senses that all beings in nature are called upon to know; but that pleasure, always mingled with shame and often with regret, is not the height of the greatest period of happiness man can attain; this supreme happiness, which sir Edmond and Malvina experienced then, man owes merely to that pleasure of the soul, a masterpiece of love and understanding, the fruit of the intimate union of two hearts that love and understand each other and are in harmony; to that divine pleasure that nobody can describe, no thought can conceive and that even those who have felt it are astounded to have known; to that pleasure finally, which man seems to have stolen from the angels or rather, which the divinity sent to earth in order to give an idea of the happiness reserved for the virtuous in Heaven').
159. *which can only be ascertained by absence*: 'mûrie par le temps et éprouvée par l'absence' ('matured by time and tested by absence') in the French edition.
160. *your own heart*: In the French edition, Sir Edmond uses familiar language with Malvina here: 'ton coeur' ('your heart') as opposed to 'votre coeur' ('your heart').
161. *or rather*: 'afin de' ('in order to') in the French edition.
162. *may I not ask why you have been so uniformly silent*: 'vous cacherai-je' ('will I hide from you') in the French edition.
163. *you have ever concealed*: 'vous cacherai-je' ('will I hide from you') in the French edition.
164. *my eyes can no longer behold comfort*: The French edition includes 'mes jours glissent comme la navette d'un tisserand' ('my days glide by like a weaver's shuttle'). In a footnote, the French edition indicates that the sources of the quotations are 'Ps. LXXIII, Isaïe' ('Psalms 73, Isaiah'). The verse in quotation marks comes indeed from Psalms 73:13 ('C'est donc en vain que j'ai purifié mon coeur, Et que j'ai lavé mes mains dans

l'innocence'); the additional French verses, however, do not come from Isaiah, but from Job 7: 6–7: 'Mes jours sont plus rapides que la navette du tisserand, Ils s'évanouissent: plus d'espérance! ... Mes yeux ne reverront pas le bonheur.'

165. *Thus interrupted, Sir Edmond*: 'Ainsi, interrompit sir Edmond' ('Thus, interrupted Sir Edmond') in the French edition.

166. *It is but merely the office of charity*: absent from the French edition.

167. *to think of you with rapture ... you do not forbid him from*: 'que son imagination le transporte peut être auprès de vous, qu'elle dévore vos charmes, s'enflamme à leur aspect, et que, néanmoins, vous ne l'écartez pas loin de vous' ('that his imagination may bring him very close to you, that it devours your charms, inflames upon seeing them and that nevertheless, you do not keep him far from you') in the French edition.

168. *and from his writing so frequently*: 'et les remettant sans cesse sous mes yeux, je ne ferais qu'irriter mon inquiétude' ('and placing them incessantly before my eyes would serve merely to increase my agitation') in the French edition.

169. *my dear madam*: The French edition adds 'et du moment que j'ai vu, dans votre ame, un desir en ma faveur et un regret sur votre silence' ('and from the moment that I saw friendship in your soul and regret about your silence').

170. *transient weaknesses*: The French edition adds 'et dont, par moment, elle croyait presque devoir se féliciter' ('and in which, sometimes, she nearly thought she ought to rejoice').

171. *for she sometimes had heard ... who were also devoid of his best qualities*: 'car, pensait-elle, ceux qui ont reconnu le vide des erreurs auxquelles ils se livrèrent, en sont plus à l'abri que ceux qui n'y tombèrent jamais' ('for, she thought, those who who have recognized the emptiness of the errors which they have committed, are better shielded from them than those who never fell victim to them') in the French edition.

172. *and without blushing*: The French edition adds 'éprouve un charme qu'elle avait ignoré jusqu'alors' ('she experiences a charm which she had not known before').

173. *that she alone was the object ... and vibrated to her heart*: 'tantôt lui laisse entrevoir le moment de leur réunion, et la fait passer ainsi d'un calme enchanteur à un trouble délicieux' ('other times her thoughts showed her the moment of their marriage, taking her from enchanting calmness to delightful emotions') in the French edition. The French edition then adds 'Durant le calme de la nuit, elle se le répète encore; elle y pense au milieu du jour, et aussitôt elle éprouve quelque chose dont elle ignore le nom, mais qui cause un plaisir si doux, si excessivement doux, qu'elle ne sait plus comment on peut appeler vivre, tout ce qui n'est pas cela' ('During the calm of the night, she again repeats it to herself; she thinks of it in the middle of the day and immediately feels something of which she does not know the name, but that causes such a sweet sensation, so excessively sweet, that she no longer knows how living can be called thus without it').

174. *But her heart indulged the hope that he might become the virtuous being she wished him*: absent from the French edition.

175. *but a few lines of mere enquiry concerning his daughter, and politeness to herself*: 'que quelques lignes de pure bienséance, et plutôt pour répondre à ce qu'elle lui disait de sa fille, que pour s'en informer' ('but a few lines of mere politeness and rather to respond to what she had written him about his daughter than inquiring after her') in the French edition.

176. *and when you are separated for ever, you will repent*: 'et tout en vous séparant d'elle, vous rejeter à jamais loin de moi' ('and while separating you from her, I will remove you far from me forever') in the French edition.

177. *I shall not be long*: 'je n'en serai jamais assez loin' ('I will never be far enough from her') in

the French edition.

178. *instead of an answer*: 'la seule réponse' ('the only answer') in the French edition.
179. *I shall trace without agitation*: 'n'aura point tracée sans émotion' ('will not have traced without emotion') in the French edition.
180. *hasten to me*: The French edition adds 'J'arrive à l'instant d'Edimbourg' ('I just this minute arrived from Edinburgh').
181. *at midnight*: 'au milieu de la nuit' ('in the middle of the night') in the French edition.
182. *several times*: 'pour la troisième fois' ('for the third time') in the French edition.
183. *in order to avoid it*: The French edition adds 'lorsque celle-ci, qui prévit ce mouvement, ainsi que l'attendrissement qui pouvait le suivre' ('when she, anticipating this movement as well as the touching scene that might follow').
184. *CONTENTS OF VOL. II*: In the 1810 edition, the identical table of contents appears after the title page in Volume II.

VOLUME III

1. *I wish to open my heart to you*: The French edition adds 'et vous, n'aurez-vous rien à me dire? Ah! Malvina, si je vous ai devinée...' ('and you, will you have anything to tell me? Ah, Malvina, if I have guessed correctly...').
2. *to find Malvina remained silent*: 'et comme elle vit que Malvina l'était aussi' ('and as she saw that Malvina was also distressed') in the French edition.
3. *Your obedient Servant, Sheridan*: 'Aug. Sheridan' ('Aug. Sheridan') in the French edition, which also adds 'Londres, Hanover square, ce 22 mai' ('London, Hanover Square, 22 May'). Hanover Square was a fashionable address at the time, popular among military personnel.
4. *his negligence in this particular was remarkable*: The French edition adds 'jusqu'à la plus extrême froideur' ('and even an extreme coldness').
5. *scarcely sufficient to pay his debts*: 'que des dettes et des regrets' ('merely debts and regrets') in the French edition.
6. *in order to soothe his remorse*: The French edition adds 'et pour conserver à sa fille l'héritage de Malvina, et peut-être celui de mistress Birton' ('and to preserve Malvina's inheritance for his daughter and perhaps Mrs Burton's as well').
7. *But all, every hope is vanished*: 'Mais je n'ai plus d'espoir, plus de bonheur, plus de retraite' ('but I possess no more hope, happiness or retreat') in the French edition.
8. *one moment has deprived me of them*: The French edition adds 'mon sort est affreux' ('my fate is terrible').
9. *of him who occupies all my heart*: The French edition adds 'à qui il me serait doux de donner mon sang et ma vie' ('to whom I would gladly give my blood and my life').
10. *who must ever possess my heart*: The French edition adds 'je voudrais le dire à toute la nature, que tous les êtres vivans m'entendissent, que tous repétassent après moi, elle aime Edmond Seymour, et enivrée de ce concert ineffable de bonheur et d'amour, redire sans cesse au maître de mon coeur: oui, c'est toi seul que j'aime, c'est à toi seul que je veux appartenir' ('I would wish to announce it to all of nature, so that all living beings hear me and repeat after me, she loves Edmond Burton and, intoxicated by this sublime union of happiness and love, I would like to continuously repeat to him who is the master of my heart: yes, it is you alone whom I love, it is to you alone that I wish to belong').
11. *No duty ought to carry you there, but rather keep you from him*: 'le devoir vous commanderait en vain de vous éloigner de vous' ('duty would dictate in vain that you leave him').

12. *rigourous duty compels me to perform*: The French edition adds 'mais ne m'attendez plus' ('but wait for me no more').
13. *tout en semble*: i.e., 'tout ensemble': an overall impression created by various parts.
14. *she took Frances on her lap*: The French edition adds 'L'enfant dormait' ('The child was sleeping').
15. *near two hours*: 'quelques heures' ('several hours') in the French edition.
16. *festoons*: i.e., a string of flowers or ribbons hung as decoration.
17. *casement*: see *Volume I, note 243.*
18. *his crimes cannot tear him from my heart*: The French edition adds 'car plus je le vois coupable, plus il me devient cher' ('for the more guilty he appears, the dearer he becomes to me').
19. *gulph*: 'abîme' ('abyss') in the French edition.
20. *so long*: 'depuis trois mois' ('for three months') in the French edition.
21. *to render that mind a prey ... and such impalpable things can never alter*: absent from the French edition.
22. *the strength we possess to support them*: The French edition adds 'et nous ne devons craindre que celles que nous pouvons supporter' ('and we should fear only those we can support').
23. *Great God*: The French edition adds 'si je ne suis pas sous la puissance d'un songe affreux' ('am I then in a nightmare').
24. *what is it that you dare to say?*: The French edition adds 'Moi parjure!' ('That I am a liar?').
25. *throwing himself at her feet*: The French edition adds 'prends pitié de l'état où je suis' ('take pity on my condition').
26. *neither can I tell ... the reward I wish to gain*: 'Je ne sais jusqu'où ils peuvent me conduire, ni de quels excès je ne serais pas capable pour te ravir au reste du monde et te posséder seul' ('I do not know where my transports can lead me or of what excesses I would not be capable in order to steal you from the rest of the world and possess you alone') in the French edition.
27. *consent to receive*: 'consens à recevoir la mienne' ('consent to receive mine') in the French edition.
28. *you cannot*: The French edition adds 'et il la pressa fortement contre sa poitrine' ('and he pressed her hard against his chest').
29. *Malvina flew after them*: The French edition adds 'en jetant des cris affreux' ('while uttering horrible cries').
30. *came running to her*: The French edition adds 'et la voyant prête à sortir, s'attache à sa robe' ('and upon seeing her ready to go out, clings to her dress').
31. *prevent her from following or detaining me*: The French edition adds 'elle me coûte déja assez cher' ('I am already paying such a high price for her').
32. *the report of pistols*: 'deux coups de pistolets' ('two gun shots') in the French edition.
33. *I shall ever consider myself as a homicide*: The French edition adds 'la terreur m'environne, ma force m'est ôtée' ('I am surrounded by terror and left without force').
34. *His servants*: 'Son domestique' ('His servant') in the French edition.
35. *he may increase the hatred she bears Malvina*: 'afin d'accroître la haine qu'il porte à Malvina' ('he may increase the hatred he bears Malvina') in the French edition.
36. *I have*: 'jai trop vécu' ('I have lived too long') in the French edition.
37. *and if it had not been ... you would have avoided this duel?*: 'celui qui n'eût été que l'ami de Malvina aurait su éviter cet affreux combat' ('he who had been merely Malvina's friend would have known how to avoid this terrible duel') in the French edition.

38. *before I enter this retreat, to which I can never again return*: 'avant d'aller dans ce séjour dont on ne revient pas, dans les ténèbres de la terre et les ombres de la mort' ('before I enter this retreat from which I can never again return, in the darkness of the earth and the shadows of death') in the French edition.
39. *the woman*: 'les deux femmes' ('the two women') in the French edition.
40. *Is she then going to her also? ... I will never, never leave my two mamas*: 'vas-tu donc t'en aller aussi? Ah! je te prie, ne vas pas la retrouver sans moi; amène-lui sa petite Fanny; elle sera bien aise de la revoir, et moi, maman, je ne te quitterai pas' ('are you leaving then also? Ah, pray do not go to her without me; bring her little Fanny to her; she will be so happy to see her again and I, mama, will not leave you') in the French edition.
41. *we will all go together*: 'elle s'en ira tout à fait' ('she will be completely gone') in the French edition.
42. *it is now two hours since he set out for Edinburgh*: The French edition adds 'vous ne pourriez le rejoindre qu'à Edimbourg' ('you could not meet up with him until Edinburgh').
43. *Edmond*: 'Edouard' ('Edward') in the French edition. This is the boy mentioned earlier.
44. *a post-chaise*: 'une chaise et des chevaux' ('a chaise and horses') in the French edition.
45. *she had been met by Sir Edmond*: The French edition adds 'Craignant et desirant d'y retourner, elle n'avait donné aucun ordre au postillon qui la conduisait; mais le Lion-Rouge étant le meilleur gîte de Falkirk, c'est toujours là où on menait les voyageurs à moins qu'ils en désignassent un autre' ('Fearing and wishing to return there, she had not given any orders to the postilion who drove her, but the Red Lion was the best inn in Falkirk and travelers were always taken there unless they indicated otherwise').
46. *being observed*: 'la voyant pâle et faible' ('being observed as pale and weak') in the French edition.
47. *sofa*: 'lit' ('bed') in the French edition.
48. *a few drops*: 'quelques gouttes d'éther' ('a few drops of ether') in the French edition. Ether was considered a medicinal liquid at the time, which could cure a host of ailments ranging from headaches and epilepsy, to asthma and hiccups.
49. *sent Peggy to order the chaise immediately*: The French edition adds 'A peine Peggy l'eûtelle laissée seule' ('Peggy barely having left her').
50. *she then examined the windows*: 'elle regarda sur la boiserie, sur les vitres' ('she examined the wooden panelling and the windows') in the French edition.
51. *find a line or word expressive of his grief*: The French edition adds 'si elle en eût trouvé, ils lui eussent déchiré le coeur' ('if she had found any, they would have broken her heart').
52. *her sickly imagination tortured her with the most alarming fears*: The French edition adds 'la chambre où elle était se remplit de fantômes' ('the room where she was started to fill with ghosts').
53. *she rushed out of the room*: The French editions adds 'baignée d'une froide sueur' ('bathed in a cold sweat').
54. *and going up stairs with her to look at an apartment*: 'et montant avec elle dans un appartement vide' ('and going up stairs with her to an empty apartment') in the French edition.
55. *and Ann wept at your departure*: The French edition adds 'Je suis sensible à ces témoignages d'intérêt, ma chère Moody' ('I appreciate those expressions of kindness, my dear Moody').
56. *Sir Edmond is dear to—*: 'm'est cher' ('is dear to me') in the French edition.
57. *he has been wounded*: The French edition adds 'peut-être est-il fort mal' ('perhaps he is doing very badly').
58. *endeavour to be informed how he is at present*: The French edition adds 'ayez-en tous les

jours, ayez-en à toutes les minutes' ('be informed every day, be informed every minute') .

59. *she might depend on her zeal and delicacy in the management of this affair*: The French edition adds 'et sortit pour s'en occuper, aussi fière de son emploi qu'un ambassadeur chargé de la plus importante négociation' ('and left to take care of it, as proud of her task as an ambassador charged with the most important negotiation').
60. *during the absence of Mrs. Moody*: The French edition adds 'D'abord elle pensait qu'un prompt retour serait un mauvais présage' ('At first she thought that an early return would be a bad omen').
61. *Poor Ann would be quite satisfied if you was but united*: The French edition adds 'Elle voulait aller vous trouver pour vous conjurer de la prendre à votre service; et si vous y eussiez consenti, elle n'aurait pas changé son sort contre celui de la femme d'un Alderman' ('She wanted to go find you in order to entreat you to take her into your service; and if you had agreed, she would not have exchanged her future for that of an Alderman's wife').
62. *such a step would render her as miserable as myself*: The French edition adds 'Que n'eussé-je pas fait alors pour la désespérer' ('What I would not have done to despair her').
63. *Madame de Sorcy continues to be so very dear to him?*: The French edition adds 'Ne vous inquiétez pas, Kitty, j'ai des moyens' ('Do not worry, Kitty, I have means').
64. *those who possess most art, are those who gain most belief*: 'celle qui se croit le plus d'esprit est celle à qui on en fait le plus accroire' ('She who believes herself to be most artful is the one who is deceived the most') in the French edition.
65. *I now have not a doubt ... ever since she was married*: 'je ne puis croire qu'elle mette un intérêt de vengeance dans tout ceci du moment qu'elle est mariée' ('I can not believe that she was intent on revenge with this ever since she was married') in the French edition.
66. *with tranquillity*: 'non dans la paix' ('not with tranquillity') in the French edition.
67. *what I told you was all true*: 'de ne pas vous en imposer' ('not to impose on you') in the French edition.
68. *she cannot leave him*: The French edition adds 'et je pense même qu'on va prendre une autre garde pour soulager celle qu'il a' ('and I even believe that they are going to hire another nurse in order to assist the one he has').
69. *agitated and distressed*: The French edition adds 'dont il fallait essayer de la distraire' ('from which she should attempt to distract her').
70. *scrupulous*: i.e., doubtful.
71. *closet*: 'cloison' ('partition') in the French edition.
72. *I was so taken up with recounting what Mrs. Fenwick said*: 'il me semblait que madame écoutait avec intérêt la conversation de mistriss Fenwich' ('it seemed to me that you were listening with interest to Mrs Fenwick's conversation') in the French edition.
73. *supporting her head with her hands*: The French edition adds 'comme ne pouvant plus soutenir le poids de sa douleur' ('as if she could no longer support the weight of her grief').
74. *jelly*: 'consommé' ('broth') in the French edition.
75. *Why did you listen to me*: The French edition adds 'quand je ne vous parle pas?' ('when I do not speak to you?').
76. *it is easier to die than to jest*: The French edition adds 'Allez, ne tardez plus à m'apporter ce que je vous demande' ('Now please do not delay any longer what I asked you to bring me').
77. *glass*: i.e., a mirror.
78. *the hand which serves him*: The French edition adds 'car l'émotion pourrait épuiser ses forces, et il doit avoir plus besoin de repos que de plaisir' ('for emotion could deplete his strength and he must need rest more than pleasure').
79. *longer than to-morrow*: 'jusqu'à demain' ('until tomorrow') in the French edition.

80. *arrange*: 'lire' ('to read') in the French edition.
81. *the phials*: i.e., the vials, the containers of medicine.
82. *take the spoon*: The French edition adds 'pour le porter à Edmond' ('in order to take it to Edmond').
83. *His discoloured lips were dry and half open*: The French edition adds 'et son haleine exhale à peine un reste de chaleur' ('and his breath barely exhales a remainder of warmth').
84. *she shuddered at that which was to follow*: The French edition adds 'Bientôt elle n'a plus besoin d'aiguille pour calculer le temps' ('Soon she no longer needed the watch in order to calculate the time').
85. *At the solemn silent hour of midnight*: 'au milieu du silence du monde' ('in the middle of the silence of the world') in the French edition.
86. *Doctor Maxwell*: 'le docteur Potwel' ('Doctor Potwel') in the French edition.
87. *and was so animated during the recital*: 'et mit dans son récit tant de chaleur, de détail et d'intelligence' ('and put so much warmth, detail and intelligence in her recital') in the French edition.
88. *Do you believe him in danger?*: The French edition adds 'continua-t-elle en hésitant, comme n'osant exprimer son espoir, de peur de le voir détruit' ('she continued, while hesitating as if not daring to express her hope, fearful of seeing it destroyed').
89. *you will endeavour to procure another situation*: 'et je me charge de vous procurer une autre place' ('and I will take it upon myself to find you another situation') in the French edition.
90. *she thought herself blameable in not permitting him to know her*: 'il la croyait coupable et elle n'osait se faire connaître' ('he thought her guilty and she did not dare to permit him to know her') in the French edition.
91. *she mentally exclaimed*: The French edition adds 'en le pressant doucement' ('while pressing him tenderly').
92. *Malvina whom he no longer loves*: The French edition adds 'cachée sous tes rideaux' ('hidden under your curtains').
93. *lest it should betray her*: The French edition adds 'malgré l'habit qui la déguisait' ('in spite of the clothes that disguised her').
94. *Yes, sir, she replied, going to him*: The French edition adds 'desirez-vous quelque chose?' ('do you desire something?').
95. *Malvina with her eyes closed*: The French edition adds 'comme ensevelie dans un profond sommeil' ('as if buried in a profound slumber').
96. *that dreaded day at length appeared*: The French edition adds 'il était midi' ('it was noon').
97. *behind the curtain*: 'dans ses mains' ('in her hands') in the French edition.
98. *and is as dreadful, when inanimate, as in its frensy*: 'et est moins effrayante encore dans sa frénésie que dans son immobilité' ('and is less dreadful in its frenzy than when inanimate') in the French edition.
99. *supposing we could not pronounce*: 'quoique pourtant cela puisse se remettre' ('even though you could be cured, however') in the French edition.
100. *Why order him to plunge it in my bosom?*: The French edition adds 'pourquoi te servir de son odieux secours?' ('Why use his insufferable help?).
101. *she now thought was not sufficiently still*: The French edition adds 'un bruit lointain l'inquiète' ('a faraway noise worries her').
102. *was kneeling at the side of the bed*: The French edition adds 'est toujours dans la même position' ('is still in the same position').
103. *where she immediately placed herself*: The French edition adds 'et le cou tendu, la jambe

en avant, retenant son haleine' ('and with her neck stretched, her leg placed forward and holding her breath').

104. *What now?*: 'Tout à l'heure' ('Later') in the French edition.
105. *by discovering herself*: The French edition adds 'qu'il lui eût été doux de pouvoir se précipiter dans ses bras' ('how sweet it would have been for her to be able to throw herself into his arms').
106. *to invoke the devil*: A footnote, left untranslated, follows in the French edition: 'Presque tout le bas-peuple d'Ecosse croit fermement à la magie, et l'état de sorcier est encore en grand crédit dans ce pays-là' ('Almost all the common people in Scotland believe strongly in magic and the position of sorcerer is still well-respected in that country').
107. *the same nonsense*: The French edition adds 'avant de la questionner sur ce qu'elle sait, et elle se hâte d'adopter une erreur qui éloigne si bien la vérité; sa feinte crédulité confirme chacun dans son opinion' ('before questioning her about what she knows and she swiftly aceepts an error which hides the truth so well; her feigned naiveté confirms everyone is of his opinion').
108. *the reality was no longer doubted*: The French edition adds 'ce n'est pas seulement Anna, mais toute la maison qui a été témoin de ce qu'elle raconte' ('it is not only Ann, but the entire house that witnessed what she said').
109. *or soar beyond the dark clouds ... alone on Heaven*: 'incertaine encore de ce qu'il lui prépare' ('uncertain of what it has in store for her') in the French edition.
110. *Thus the limpid stream ... on the floating mirror of its waters*: A footnote, left untranslated, follows in the French edition: 'Adisson' ('Addison'). This reference comes indeed from the poem 'Hope' by Joseph Addison (1672–1719): Our lives, discoloured with our present woes, / May still grow white and shine with happier hours. / So the pure limped stream, when foul with stains / Of rushing torrents and descending rains, / Works itself clear, and as it runs refines, till by degrees the floating mirror shines; / Reflects each flower that on the border grows, / And a new heaven in its fair bosom shows.
111. *not a word or a line to inform me of her regret*: The French edition adds 'M'a-t-elle seulement répondu? car, si je ne me trompe, au moment où mes yeux se fermaient au jour, ils se sont tournés vers Malvina pour lui addresser un éternel adieu' ('If only she had answered me. Because, if I am not mistaken, when my eyes closed from the light, they turned toward Malvina to address her an eternal adieu').
112. *a letter which you wrote for me in my illness?*: The French edition adds 'qu'en avez-vous fait?' ('what have you done with it?').
113. *that woman took the charge of it*: The French edition adds 'mais je n'oserais répondre de ce qu'elle en a fait' ('but I would not dare answer you as to what she did with it').
114. *for bigotted to her own faith, Mrs. Burton admitted no Protestants to her house*: absent from the French edition.
115. *it gave her infinite consequence in her own opinion*: The French edition adds 'qu'elle ne crut pas nécessaire de lui faire part que sir Edmond la demandait, ni de la consulter sur ce qu'il fallait lui répondre' ('that she did not think it necessary to tell her that Sir Edmond was asking for her or to consult her about what to reply to him').
116. *It is there then!*: 'Elle y est donc?' ('She is there then?') in the French edition.
117. *with Mr. Prior*: 'et s'appuyant sur monsieur Prior' ('and leaning on Mr Prior') in the French edition.
118. *it was covered with blood*: The French edition adds 'et sa main, fortement attachée contre son sein, le déchirait sans qu'il ressentît aucune douleur' ('and his hand, clutching his heart, caused him vivid pain which he did not feel').

119. *it was generosity which excited him*: 'Ce n'est point la générosité qui l'excite' ('it was not generosity which excited him') in the French edition.
120. *materials*: 'matelas' ('mattresses') in the French edition.
121. *it would be too late*: The French edition adds 'N'importe, Edmond n'hésite pas' ('It does not matter, Edmond does not hesitate').
122. *a beam which trembled under him*: The French edition adds 'une seconde va l'engloutir; il prend son parti' ('a second and he will disappear; he decides').
123. *he could never in future wish to kill him*: The French edition adds 'et l'impossibilité de se venger le lui rend plus odieux encore' ('and the impossibility of taking revenge makes him [Mr Prior] even more insufferable to him [Sir Edmond]').
124. *or having taken any rest*: The French edition adds 'ni vu un seul des endroits où il avait passé' ('or having seen any of the places that he passed').
125. *quite in dishabille*: 'tout en désordre' ('quite in a state of confusion') in the French edition.
126. *he told her she was adorable*: The French edition adds 'et, ravie de l'entendre' ('and, delighted to hear it').
127. *for Sir Edmond*: The French edition adds 'comme je l'ai déjà dit' ('as I mentioned before').
128. *a prey to stifled rage*: The French edition adds 'ne se nourrissait que de fiel' ('merely felt bitterness').
129. *his stability*: 'sa constance' ('his fidelity') in the French edition.
130. *From the time she was at liberty to fulfil her duties of friendship*: 'et dès-lors, fût-elle libre envers son amie, elle ne recevrait plus, qu'en frémissant, les sacrifices de son amour' ('and from then on, were she to be free towards her friend, she would no longer receive the sacrifices of her love, but trembling') in the French edition.
131. *and suppressing her affection*: absent from the French edition.
132. *whom I love – I never can again*: 'que j'aimai comme tu ne le seras jamais même par moi' ('whom I loved as you will never be loved, not even by me') in the French edition.
133. *be happy*: 'sois heureux' ('be happy [addressed to Sir Edmond]') in the French edition.
134. *she was not sensible that it was a secret gratification to herself*: 'elle n'est sensible qu'à la secrète douceur de prouver à Edmond' ('she was sensitive merely to the secret sweetness of proving to Edmond') in the French edition.
135. *you shall be acquainted with*: The French edition adds 'ma peine' ('my suffering').
136. *perhaps*: absent from the French edition.
137. *But I never credit such nonsense*: The French edition adds 'jamais on ne fut au sabat avec ce joli visage' ('nobody with such a pretty face ever attended the nightly meeting of witches').
138. *From all that I hear, and all that I feel*: 'par-tout je l'entends, par-tout il retentit' ('I hear her name everywhere, it echoes everywhere') in the French edition.
139. *and notwithstanding ... her station in my heart*: 'Ah, malheureux insensé! comment le fuirais-tu? ne sens-tu pas que, malgré tous tes efforts, tu le portes toujours dans ton coeur?' ('Ah unhappy fool! How would you flee from her memory? Do you not feel that in spite of all your efforts, you will always carry it in your heart?') in the French edition.
140. *Suspicion, reproach, grief*: The French edition adds 'tout est éclairci' ('everything is clarified').
141. *love absorbed them*: The French edition adds 'le bonheur les enivre' ('happiness transports them').
142. *which a refined and delicate soul ... could alone feel*: 'N'est-ce pas là une de ces emotions si vives, qu'elle se refuse au langage, et que c'est pour l'ame qui l'éprouve, une sorte de

tourment de ne point trouver d'expressions pour la rendre? Est-ce avec des mots qu'on tenterait de dire une sensation qui ne serait plus elle, si des mots la pouvaient dire?' ('Is that not one of those emotions, so strong that it can not be expressed in language and that it is, for the soul experiencing it, some sort of torture to be unable to find words to describe it? Is it with words that one would attempt to describe a feeling which would no longer be itself if words were able to describe it?') in the French edition.

143. *had braved*: The French edition adds 'mistriss Birton et' ('Mrs Burton and').
144. *her lover approved every thing*: The French edition adds 'elle-même applaudissait aux différens mouvemens qu'il avait éprouvés' ('she approved the various feelings he had experienced').
145. *esteemed by Malvina*: 'épris de Malvina' ('in love with Malvina') in the French edition.
146. *such ideas*: 'et avec l'idée qu'aucune ne pouvait s'en passer' ('and with the idea that no woman could do without lovers') in the French edition.
147. *and as I loved her, it afflicted me extremely*: 'Comme je n'étais pas amoureux d'elle, cette découverte m'affligea médiocrement' ('as I was not in love with her, this discovery hurt me moderately') in the French edition.
148. *that irritation of the senses*: The French edition adds 'cette inquiétude d'imagination' ('that agitation of the imagination').
149. *Lord Westbrook*: 'milord Derby' ('Milord Derby') in the French edition.
150. *a near relation of my own*: absent from the French edition.
151. *Louisa*: 'miss Louise Transwley' ('miss Louise Transwley') in the French edition.
152. *she knew she was solely attached to me*: 'tandis qu'elle portrait dans son sein un gage de la perfidie d'un autre' ('while carrying in her womb proof of another man's betrayal') in the French edition.
153. *a nod of approbation was to be my answer*: 'un signe approbatif fut sa réponse' ('a nod of approbation was my answer') in the French edition.
154. *She*: 'il' ('he') in the French edition.
155. *her father so far coincided with her, that he*: absent from the French.
156. *she withdrew to her room, with Louisa*: The French edition adds 'et après un assez long entretien' ('and after a rather lengthy conversation').
157. *she appeared smiling under despair*: 'et comme quelqu'un qui vient de perdre ses dernières espérances' ('and like someone who had just lost her last hopes') in the French edition.
158. *but as a man of honor*: 'ce n'est pas à un homme d'honneur' ('or as a man of honor') in the French edition.
159. *respecting my future approaches to Louisa*: absent from the French edition.
160. *if*: absent from the French edition.
161. *I shall not see her any more*: 'je ne vois pas' ('I do not see') in the French edition.
162. *divorce*: Before the Matrimonial Causes Act of 1857, divorce was possible in the United Kingdom but limited to the very wealthy as it required either an annulment or a private bill to be passed in the House of Commons.
163. *which I had surpassed her in*: 'qu'il avait surpris' ('during which he had surprised her') in the French edition.
164. *without their wishing it*: 'sans leur en ôter le besoin' ('without taking away their need for it') in the French edition.
165. *spark*: 'ame' ('soul') in the French edition.
166. *partaking in the virtuous interchange of mutual sentiments*: The French edition adds 'cette union intime et délicieuse de deux ames qui s'entendent et se répondent' ('that intimate and delightful union of two souls who understand each other and respond to each oth-

er').

167. *and a desire to merit it*: absent from the French edition.
168. *a pause*: 'un de ces silences où l'ame recueille en un instant des siècles de jouissances' ('one of these silences during which the soul gathers centuries of pleasure in one moment') in the French edition.
169. *Your wish*: 'votre seule vue' ('the mere sight of you') in the French edition.
170. *neither my contempt or dislike can be increased*: 'mon mépris peut s'en augmenter, mais non pas ma haine' ('my contempt can be increased, but not my hatred') in the French edition.
171. *fatal affair*: 'étrange résurrection' ('strange resurrection') in the French edition.
172. *both from her sight and yours*: The French edition starts a new chapter here: 'Chapitre XVI Continuation' ('Chapter XVI Continuation').
173. *the recital*: The French edition adds 'qui me retenait près d'elle' ('which detained me near her').
174. *she should remain for life*: The tower where the woman is emprisoned constitutes a classic Gothic motif. See Introduction.
175. *at which time*: 'jusqu'à cette époque' ('until that time') in the French edition.
176. *At last, his Lordship left the castle*: 'Enfin, le hasard vint à mon secours: milord Derby étant parti au bout de quelques jours' ('at last, destiny came to my rescue: Lord Westbrook having left after several days') in the French edition.
177. *She was therefore taken very suddenly*: 'elle fut saisie de douleurs subites et prématurées' ('she was taken with sudden and premature pains') in the French edition.
178. *capable of being removed without danger*: 'assez bien remise de ses couches pour être en état de marcher' ('sufficiently recovered from her delivery so that she could walk') in the French edition.
179. *which is rather more than six miles*: 'distante tout au plus de six milles' ('which is no more than six miles') in the French edition.
180. *the estate of St. Clare*: The French edition adds 'de ses créanciers' ('from her creditors').
181. *six years*: 'cinq années' ('five years') in the French edition.

VOLUME IV

1. *Stower, Printer, Charles-Street, Hatton-Garden*: This differs from the title pages for the three previous volumes which state 'H. Reynell, Printer, 21, Piccadilly'. The 1804 edition does list 'H. Reynell, Printer, 21, Piccadilly' here.
2. *by Mrs. Moody*: The French edition adds 'qui le tient d'Anna' ('who heard it from Ann').
3. *Lord Sheridan*: In Volumes I–III, the last name was always spelled 'Sheridan'; in Volume IV, it is more commonly spelled 'Sherridan', but I maintain the original spelling.
4. *the wrath of Heaven*: 'le ciel, la terre et Clara elle-même' ('the wrath of Heaven, earth and Clara herself') in the French edition.
5. *whose conscience must continually upbraid her?*: The French edition adds 'jusques dans vos bras' ('even while in your arms').
6. *our religion*: 'votre religion' ('your religion') in the French edition.
7. *in opposition to all the world*: The French edition adds 'de tes sermens et de toi-même' ('your vows and yourself').
8. *these pusillanimous fears*: The French edition adds 'ces prejugés populaires; avec un sentiment comme le nôtre' ('these popular preconceived notions; with feelings such as ours').
9. *we can follow other laws*: The French edition adds 'Eh! que fait à ton amour l'instant où

les hommes y mettent leur sceau? en as-tu besoin pour te donner à moi'? ('What does the moment when men place their seal of approval on your love do to it? Do you need it in order to give yourself to me'?)

10. *ought to proceed only from your own will!*: The French edition adds 'c'est un bien qu'il n'appartient pas aux hommes de donner, et que l'amour seul doit recevoir de l'amour. O mon ame! rien que lui entre toi et moi, que lui seul nous unisse' ('It is a good that men should not give and that love alone must receive from love. Oh my love! Nothing but love between you and me, may love alone unite us').
11. *with her handkerchief*: 'derrière un rideau' ('behind a curtain') in the French edition.
12. *rather than not preserve the sincerity of her affection*: 'plus de preuve d'amour qu'elle ne soit prête à donner' ('no proof of love she would not have given') in the French edition.
13. *Sir Charles Weymund*: 'Sir Charles Weymard' ('Sir Charles Weymard') in the French edition.
14. *tormented by his own jealous fancies*: 'jaloux du repentir qu'il lui supposait' ('jealous of the resentment he assumed she had') in the French edition.
15. *awful*: absent from the French edition.
16. *white*: absent from the French edition.
17. *black*: 'blanc' ('white') in the French edition.
18. *permit this stroke to pass from me*: The French edition adds 'cependant, non point ce que je veux, mais ce que tu veux, que ta volonté soit faite, et non la mienne' ('however, not what I want, but what you want; may your will be done, not mine').
19. *before the altar of Almighty God*: The French edition adds 'ces lampes sacrées, ces tombeaux, vous tous présens devant mes yeux' ('these sacred lights, these tombs, all of you present before my eyes').
20. *the sensations of this moment ought to obliterate them all*: The French edition adds 'et qu'il est telle action qui renferme en un seul jour la perfection d'une longue vie' ('and that there exists such an action as to contain in a single day the perfection of an entire lifetime').
21. (*without which all must fall)*: absent from the French.
22. *as you have ever been*: 'comme vous serez toujours' ('as you will ever be') in the French edition.
23. *I ought to relinquish the object of my love, for the sins of my soul*: The French edition adds 'comme Michée' ('like Micah'). This reference comes from Micah 6:7: 'Le Seigneur voudra-t-il des milliers de béliers? des quantités de torrents d'huile? Donnerai-je mon premier-né pour prix de ma révolte? Et l'enfant de ma chair pour mon propre péché'? ('Will the LORD be pleased with thousands of rams, or with ten thousands of rivers of oil? Shall I give my firstborn for my transgression, the fruit of my body for the sin of my soul'?)
24. *a long life*: 'ce peu de jours' ('these few days') in the French edition.
25. *join me in blessing its mercy?*: The French edition adds 'En effet, pourquoi désirer une longue vie? qu'y recueille-t-on, si ce n'est d'épuiser jusqu'à la lie la coupe de l'existence, et de mesurer, dans toute son étendue, la misère qui est le partage de l'humanité'? ('In fact, why desire a long life? What do we gain from it other than completely emptying out the cup of life and measuring the full extent of the misery that is mankind's lot'?).
26. *your countenance*: 'son front' ('her countenance') in the French edition.
27. *Conjugal happiness*: In the French edition, the chapter title is followed by a footnote left untranslated: 'Peut-être me reprochera-t-on de m'être étendue avec complaisance sur de tristes tableaux, et de n'effleurer ceux du bonheur qu'en passant; mais chacun parle de ce qu'il sait, et il est des plaisirs que ma plume ne hasardera point de décrire; si elle a su

rendre quelques accens vrais de la douleur, c'est qu'ils lui firent inspirés par mon coeur; mais il se tait lorsqu'elle lui demande des couleurs pour la félicité, il n'en a point à lui donner' ('Perhaps I will be blamed for having willingly lingered on sad scenes while barely touching on those of happiness; but everyone speaks of what she knows and there are pleasures that my pen will not risk describing; if my pen succeeded in relating some true expressions of pain, then they were inspired by my heart; but it will remain silent when my pen asks it for colours of happiness as it has none to offer'). The topic of conjugal happiness must have been difficult and painful for Cottin. Acccording to Samia Spencer, she had a happy marriage with Paul Cottin ('Despite initial reluctance on both sides, the couple eventually developed a deep affection for each other and were married in Paris on 16 May 1789' ('Sophie Cottin', in S. I. Spencer (ed.), *Writers of the French Enlightenment, Dictionary of Literary Biography*, 375 vols (New York, NY: Thomson Gale, 2005), vol. 313, pp. 113–20, on p. 114), but of course she became widowed in October 1793 and never remarried.

28. *that day left nature with regret*: This scene, in particular, with its detailed descriptions of nature, reminds readers that Cottin's work belongs to early Romanticism; Rousseau's inspiration can be easily detected. Cottin refers to Rousseau's work later on, see note 83 below.
29. *But we must ever remember ... but endeavour to deserve it*: 'mais si le ciel eût donné aux hommes un moment l'éclair du plaisir et un bonheur durable, qu'aurait-il donc gardé pour lui'? ('but if Heaven had given man a flash of pleasure and unchanging felicity for a moment, what would it then have kept for itself'?) in the French edition.
30. *my best wishes*: 'mes derniers voeux' ('my final wishes') in the French edition.
31. *and will terminate only with my existence*: 'il s'est emparé de tout mon coeur, il court dans mes veines avec mon sang; tout en moi n'est plus qu'amour, et je n'ai plus qu'un sentiment et qu'un cri, t'aimer, t'aimer, ou mourir' ('love has taken over my heart, it runs through my veins with my blood; everything in me is but love and I have merely one sentiment and one cry left, loving you, loving you, or dying') in the French edition.
32. *he endeavoured ... their present happiness to forget the future*: 'transporté de la voir si belle, avide de plaisir, il s'abandonna au trouble délicieux qui remplissait son ame; mais tandis qu'en proie au plus ravissant délire, l'enchantement du moment présent lui fesait tout oublier, Malvina pensait encore au lendemain' ('transported by her beauty and avid for pleasure, he abandoned himself to the delicious agitation filling his soul; but while he was prey to the most ravishing delirium and the spell of the present moment made him forget everything, Malvina continued to think of the following day') in the French edition.
33. *the inconstancy of man*: 'dans l'union de deux sexes, l'un s'attache par ce qu'il donne, comme l'autre se refroidit par ce qu'il reçoit' ('in the union of the sexes, one attaches itself through what it gives whereas the other grows more distant through what it receives') in the French edition.
34. *It was too recent for her to overcome its shock*: 'Hélas! comment son ame, livrée à toutes les agitations de l'amour, aurait-elle pu être distraite par les soins de l'amitié et les caresses de l'innocence'? ('Alas! how could her soul, given over to all the agitations of love, be distracted by the cares of friendship and the caresses of innocence'?) in the French edition.
35. *is it not sufficient that he was a man!*: This scepticism regarding man's faithfulness appears in many French female-authored-novels of the eighteenth and early nineteenth centuries – Marie Jeanne Riccoboni (1713–92) and Françoise de Graffigny (1695–1758) in particular come to mind. See my other volume in this series: *Translation and Continuations: Riccoboni and Brooke, Graffigny and Roberts*. Cottin refers to Riccoboni's work later, see note 83 below.

36. *must always be objected to as a reproach*: 'n'est point rappelée ici comme un reproche, mais comme une simple observation des lois générales de la nature' ('is not recalled here as a reproach, but as a simple observation on the laws of nature') in the French edition.
37. *always received the visits of Sir Edmond*: 'qui ne recevait que lui' ('received only Sir Edmond's visits') in the French edition.
38. *the French principles*: Cottin refers to people in England who supported the Jacobins and the French Revolution – a group that decreased in size after the Reign of Terror in 1793–4, led by Robespierre. It is interesting that Cottin uses Edmond's pretended affiliation with the Jacobins in a scheme to get rid of him, as she herself and her husband suffered greatly at the hands of the Jacobins.
39. *they desired ... he might be sent out of the kingdom*: 'qu'elle desire, en consequence, faire embarquer pour les Grandes-Indes' ('they desired, for that reason, he might be sent to the East Indies') in the French edition. 'Grandes Indes', in French, equals 'Indes orientales' ('East Indies').
40. *he will consent to sign an agreement, by which the marriage shall be annulled*: This is the second item of Mrs Burton's letter to be criticized by an 1808 review of the novel in the *Monthly Review*. It claims that 'we detect some of that ignorance of English society, which occasionally betrays itself in all foreign works that relate to it. What will our coutrymen say to the sudden *déportation* of an English gentleman to the East Indies, on no better foundation either in law or policy, than that *Milord Stafford, Mistriss Birton*, and a few other persons of rank, have secretly denounced him to government as an advocate for French principles? And how much greater would be the consternation of our fair country-women, if English husbands had the power of dissolving their matrimonial contract, by an instrument executed by themselves alone, called an *acte de Cassation*? Yet these preposterous iniquities (which we hope it will never be in our power to express by any English phrase,) are coolly mentioned in a single page, as familiar occurences among us' (*Monthly Review*, Appendix to vol. 57 (September–December 1808), pp. 471–3, on p. 473). The *Critical Review* also criticises the deportation issue (*Critical Review*, Appendix to vol. 16 (January–April 1809), pp. 502–11, on p. 510).
41. *at last*: 'du moins' ('at least') in the French edition.
42. *by taking Sir Edmond from his beloved wife*: 'en arrachant à Edmond une femme chérie' ('by taking a beloved wife from Sir Edmond') in the French edition.
43. *she had not the least reason*: 'il ne pouvait avoir aucune inquiétude' ('he had not least reason') in the French edition.
44. *gay, fashionable*: 'des hommes les plus gais' ('the gayest men') in the French edition.
45. *but so many delays had made it so late, that he deferred setting out till the next day*: 'mais il y en a un de déferré, il ne pourra être prêt que le lendemain' ('but one of the horses has no horsehoes, it can be ready but the following day') in the French edition.
46. *among the most celebrated beauties*: The French edition adds 'et il trouve que le monde n'a pas tort' ('and he finds that the world is right').
47. *which always seemed to dwell upon you*: The French edition adds 'vous poursuivent, vous enchaînent, et se baissent avec modestie aussitôt qu'ils sont parvenus à vous émouvoir' ('follow you, enchain you and lower themselves modestly as soon as they have succeded in moving you').
48. *those languishing and voluptuous looks*: The French edition adds 'qui promet tant de plaisirs' ('that promise so many pleasures').
49. *which excite and interest the imagination*: The French edition adds 'de ces réticences adroites qui laissent tout espérer sans rien promettre' ('that skillful reticence which al-

lows hope of everything without the promise of anything').

50. *Her figure ... her character alone was formed to excite the passions*: 'car si la figure fait les conquêtes, le caractère seul fait les passions' ('for if it is the figure that conquers, the character alone excites passion') in the French edition.
51. *Trial of coquetry*: 'Essai sur la Coquetterie' ('Essay on Coquetry'). Given that the preposition is 'sur' ('on') here, 'essai' is more likely to mean 'essay' than 'trial' here.
52. *she could not attempt to reach it at the first outset*: 'il ne fera point le premier pas' ('he will not take the first step') in the French edition.
53. *Miss Melmor spared no trouble to please Sir Edmond*: 'miss Melmor ne fasse aucuns frais pour plaire à sir Edmond' ('Miss Melmor makes no effort to please Sir Edmond') in the French edition.
54. *He observed her with astonishment*: 'Il le voit et s'en étonne' ('He observes this with astonishment') in the French edition.
55. *which she made appear natural and amiable*: The French edition adds 'parce qu'elle ne peut pas s'empêcher de l'être' ('because she can not prevent herself from doing so').
56. *She slightly hinted ... the friendship which had succeeded it*: 'Elle naît du souvenir de leur ancienne liaison et de l'amitié qui y a succédé' ('It was born from the memory of their old liaison and the friendship that succeeded it') in the French edition.
57. *the fascinating*: 'la plus délicieuse' ('the most fascinating') in the French edition.
58. *more successful*: The French edition adds 'ni moins encouragé' ('or less encouraged').
59. *which would only have been displayed from cruelty*: 'de prouver qu'il ne pouvait pas trouver de cruelles' ('of proving that he could not find any women who were not suspectible to his charms') in the French edition.
60. *the only person Kitty would wish for her partner*: The French edition adds 'Ce nom de Kitty réveillait bien des souvenirs' ('The name Kitty brought back many memories').
61. *after the reels*: 'après la walse' ('after the waltz') in the French edition. A 'reel' is a Scottish folk dance.
62. *through the thin gauze which shaded it*: The French edition adds 'respire son haleine' ('he inhales her breath').
63. *and the most exquisite wines*: The French edition adds 'on croirait voir un souper de Paris, sur les confins de l'Ecosse: les femmes sont animées de cette gaîté piquante qui n'appartient qu'aux Françaises' ('it resembled a dinner in Paris, on the borders of Scotland; the women were animated with the suggestive gaity that belongs but to Frenchwomen').
64. *with her rested the sole power of animating him*: 'ne se reposant pas sur elle seule du soin de l'émouvoir' ('not relying on her alone in order to animate him') in the French edition.
65. *she consequently determined on the part she would act*: The French edition adds 'elle saura bien l'empêcher de partir' ('she will know how to prevent him from leaving').
66. *She arose from table*: The French edition adds 'après avoir versé encore quelques verres de punch' ('having poured several more glasses of punch').
67. *an old nobleman*: 'le vieux lord Chattam' ('old Lord Chattam') in the French edition.
68. *enhance the value of what is taken*: The French edition adds 'et dans ce combat où l'on ne repousse que pour attirer, et où chaque mouvement est une faveur' ('and in this battle where one rejects merely in order to attract and where each move is a favour').
69. *But Sir Edmond and Mrs. Fenwick remained alone*: The French edition adds 'elle est en désordre, sa robe déchirée, ses cheveux épars, sa gorge à demi-découverte; le mouvement, l'espoir, l'émotion animent son teint des plus vives couleurs; elle se plaint que ses vêtemens sont mouillés; Edmond veut les détacher, elle ne le permet point; il persiste; en se débattant, elle fait un faux pas, la lumière lui échappe, s'éteint, ils restent dans l'obscurité'

('she is in disorder, her dress torn, her hair dishevelled, her neck half-uncovered; the turmoil, the hope, the emotions colour her skin ever more; she complains that her clothes are wet; Edmond wants to take them off, she does not allow it; he persists; while arguing with him, she takes a wrong step, the lamp falls from her hand, goes out, they remain in the darkness'). The English edition leaves much more to the reader's imagination here than the French edition.

70. *he must have continued there some time*: The text from 'and when they entered the dining room' to this point, i.e. the details of Kitty's seduction of Sir Edmond, is deleted from the French edition, starting with the second revised and corrected edition by Michaud.
71. *Journey to London*: The chapter title in the French edition is 'Effets d'une faute' ('Results from a Fault').
72. *This recollection withheld his pen*: The French edition adds 'et sa plume se traîne avec effort' ('and his pen moved with difficulty').
73. *Syren*: a reference to Greek mythology – women or winged creatures lure sailors to their death by distracting them through their beauty.
74. *bathed in tears*: The French edition adds 'l'amour, les larmes l'embellissent' ('love, her tears render her beautiful').
75. *I go on Lady Dorset's account ... my immediate departure for London*: 'je vais de ce pas prévenir milady Dorset que des affaires imprévues et pressantes m'appellent à Londres' ('I am going to tell Lady Dorset immediately that unforeseen urgent business calls me to London').
76. *in peace*: 'à franc étrier' ('at full speed') in the French edition.
77. *for the contempt of Sir Edmond*: The French edition adds 'elle lit aussi la lettre qu'il lui écrit' ('she also read the letter he wrote to Malvina').
78. *in a case in which she hoped entirely to seduce Sir Edmond*: 'dans le cas où elle ne parviendrait pas à séduire entièrement sir Edmond' ('in case she did not succeed in seducing Sir Edmond entirely') in the French edition.
79. *at some hotel*: 'au même hôtel' ('at the same hotel') in the French edition.
80. *he was very conscious, that*: The French edition adds 'elle calculerait que' ('she would think that').
81. *remained faithful to Malvina*: Cottin distinguishes here between male and female readers in how they might react to Sir Edmond's behaviour with Mrs Fenwick, anticipating both their reactions. In saying that men would find the story unbelievable if Kitty did not succeed in seducing Edmond, she reiterates the commonly accepted idea that men have trouble remaining faithful to their wives. See also *note 35 a*bove.
82. *for, if we are so liable to fall on the first trial ... it rises above itself, and invariably pursues the path of rectitude*: absent from the French. The English edition, while omitting the details of Kitty's seduction of Edmond (see note 69 above), inserts an entire paragraph here to explain why lacking humility, Edmond did not learn from the first time he succumbed to Kitty's charms after marrying Malvina.
83. *As he had been led astray once*: The French edition adds 'ce tort qu'ont partagé avec lui les plus tendres amans' ('this wrongdoing that the most tender lovers have shared with him'), followed by a footnote, left untranslated: 'Milord d'Ossery, dans les Lettres de Juliette Catesby; Saint-Preux, dans la nouvelle Héloïse, etc. etc. etc. etc' ('Milord d'Ossery in *Letters from Juliet Catesby*, Saint-Preux in *The New Heloise*, etc. etc. etc. etc.'). In Marie Jeanne Riccoboni's best-selling 1759 epistolary novel *Lettres de Juliette Catesby*, Milord d'Ossery abandons his fiancée Juliette Catesby after having been 'led astray', i.e. after having raped and impregnated another woman, only to be forgiven after the latter's death. See my

Translations and Continuations: Riccoboni and Brooke, Graffigny and Roberts (London: Pickering & Chatto, 2011). In France's most popular epistolary novel of the eigteenth century – Jean-Jacques Rousseau's 1761 *La Nouvelle Héloïse* – Saint-Preux loves his pupil Julie, whose father forbids their marriage due to their class differences. In exile in Paris, Saint-Preux drinks too much and wakes up with a prostitute. The number of 'etc.' in the French edition appears exorbitant. Is this humour on the part of Cottin indicating how easy it is to find examples of men in committed relationships (engaged to be married, in the case of d'Ossery) who give in to seduction? In the second French (Michaud) edition, all 'etc.'s have been deleted here, and St Preux is mentioned before d'Ossery.

84. *a defence against the seduction of the senses*: In the French edition this sentence is interrogative.
85. *How very different is this in women!*: In the French edition, Cottin identifies herself with women by saying 'notre sexe' ('our sex').
86. *and she ... may be known to be also superior in the affections of the heart*: 'faire un chef-d'oeuvre de vertu de ce chef-d'oeuvre d'amour, le coeur d'une femme' ('make a masterpiece of virtue out of this masterpiece of love, a woman's heart') in the French edition.
87. *as he knew the pleasure it would have afforded her*: 'et qu'il n'en avait pas profité' ('yet had not done so') in the French edition.
88. *she was not more satisfied with it than Malvina. It did not express the instinctive language of affection*: 'elle en fut plus contente que Malvina; l'instinct de l'amour ne lui parlait pas' ('she was more satisfied with it than Malvina; love's intuition did not speak to her') in the French edition.
89. *as injurious to her happiness*: 'comme injurieux à son honneur' ('as injurious to his honour') in the French edition.
90. *I depart to-morrow, overcome with gratitude for your kind favours*: The French edition adds 'qu'il ne faut rien moins que l'impossibilité de rester pour qu'il se décide à s'éloigner d'elle' which was previously translated as 'it requires nothing less than the impossibility of staying, to determine [him] to leave [her]'; see Chap. VI. This incident where a letter addressed to someone is purposely shown to someone else with malicious intentions and without the sender's knowledge may remind readers of Laclos's *Liaisons dangereuses* (*Dangerous Liaisons*) where this art of letter manipulation was perfected; see also Volume I, note 155.
91. *wished to prevent her from reading this fatal billet*: The French edition adds 'mais il était écrit, dans les destinées, que Malvina épuiserait jusqu'à la lie, la coupe de toutes les douleurs' ('but it was dictated by fate that Malvina would endure all the worst suffering until the end').
92. *whose kind favours have rendered you so grateful?*: In the French edition these words are italicized to remind readers that Malvina is quoting Edmond's letter here.
93. *follow me*: 'ne vous suive pas' ('follow you') in the French edition.
94. *When you first asked my love, I was dejected, and exhausted by grief*: 'tu me recontreras faible, abattue, épuisée par la douleur' ('you will find me weak, dejected and exhausted by grief') in the French edition.
95. *meet with a similar misery to that which I now endure*: 'rencontrer celle qui pourra te faire souffrir le mal que j'endure' ('meet the woman who can make you feel the misery I feel') in the French edition.
96. *My sorrowful heart ... the most sincere affection*: absent from the French edition.
97. *He instantly obeyed*: 'Alors elle le congédia' ('She then sent him away') in the French edition.

98. *(if pleasure it can be called)*: absent from the French edition.
99. *the excuse she had given Williams*: 'au prétexte que lui donne Williams' ('the excuse Williams had given him') in the French edition. The French is correct, as the excuse obviously came not from Malvina but from Mrs Fenwick.
100. *These suspicions having arisen ... his surmises were not without foundation*: The French edition adds 'Vous m'avez l'air d'un scélérat, dit Edmond d'une voix étouffée par la colère, et saisissant Williams au collet, et si mes soupçons ne me trompent pas, il n'est aucune puissance qui puisse vous soustraire à ma vengeance. Williams effrayé de ces menaces, et sentant bien que, dans ce moment d'emportement, un aveu ne le sauverait pas, persiste dans son assertion, emploie tous les sermens' ('You look like a criminal to me, said Edmond, his voice stifled by anger and grabbing Williams by his collar, and if my suspicions do not deceive me, no power can save you from my revenge. Williams fearing these threats and understanding well that in this moment of passion, an avowal would not save him, therefore persists in his statement and solemnly swears to its truth').
101. *on his sending for him*: The French edition adds 'le lendemain' ('the following day').
102. *this silence*: 'de son existence, pour ramener la paix dans son coeur en s'expliquant avec elle' ('her being alive and to return tranquility to her heart by explaining himself to her') in the French edition.
103. *by whom she was supported*: 'dont celui-ci s'appuie' ('by whom he was supported') in the French edition.
104. *In a few days*: 'dans deux jours' ('in two days') in the French edition.
105. *She fancied, she could anticipate her behaviour on the sea-side*: 'il croira la voir sur le rivage' ('he will believe he sees her on the sea-side') in the French edition.
106. *from a motive which he dare not acknowledge*: 'du motif qu'il n'avait pas craint d'alléguer' ('from the motive which he had not feared quoting'). Edmond has fathered a child himself.
107. *to send you out of the kingdom*: 'vous faire embarquer pour les Indes' ('make you embark for the Indies') in the French edition; see note 39 above.
108. *the French principles*: see note 38 above.
109. *to rend the heart, and throw the most amiable of women into despair!*: 'pour déchirer le coeur d'une femme et me mettre au désespoir' ('to rend a woman's heart and throw me into despair') in the French edition.
110. *the Marquis of D****: 'milord duc De ***' ('duke of ***') in the French edition.
111. *in council with his minister*: 'et aux ministres' ('and to the ministers') in the French edition.
112. *He returned to his lodgings to prepare for his departure*: The French edition adds 'Il était plus de minuit lorsqu'il rentra' ('It was after midnight when he returned').
113. *that you remitted them into the hands of Mrs. Fenwick*: 'celle que votre perfidie a remise entre les mains de mistriss Fenwick' ('the letter that your unfaithfulness placed into the hands of Mrs Fenwick') in the French edition.
114. *a lamp*: 'une lampe posée dans un vase d'albâtre' ('a lamp placed in an alabaster vase') in the French edition.
115. *Mrs. Fenwick was asleep*: The French edition adds 'à demi-nue, et dans le plus voluptueux abandon; mais elle a beau être séduisante, elle ne l'est pas pour lui' ('half nude and in a state of the most voluptuous abandon; as seductive as she is, she is not so to him').
116. *I know every thing*: It looks here as if this sentence is pronounced by Mrs Fenwick, but it is in fact said by Sir Edmond: 'Je sais tout et je vous connais' ('I know everything and I know you') in the French edition.

117. *she pressed him in her arms*: The French edition adds 'et veut lui prodiguer ses vives caresses' ('and wants to lavish him with many caresses').
118. *which struck him*: The French edition adds 'et qu'il n'ose reconnaître' ('and which he dared not recognise').
119. *in the most passionate accent*: The French edition adds 'Malvina le repousse et dit' ('Malvina pushes him away and says').
120. *auburn hair*: 'cheveux blonds' ('blond hair') in the French edition. See also Volume I, note 117.
121. *She wandered about*: 'elle les écarte' ('she brushed her hair away') in the French edition.
122. *There, she will die*: The French edition adds 'puisque tu ne peux plus la lui ouvrir' ('since you can no longer open it for her').
123. *alone*: absent from the French edition.
124. *Edmond is fascinated with another beauty, and recollecting the extent of his imprudence*: 'Edmond Seymour, ou épris d'une autre beauté, ou reconnaissant l'étendue de son imprudence' ('Edmond, either fascinated with another beauty, or recollecting the extent of his imprudence') in the French edition.
125. *direct me in my duty dear sacred Shade*: The French edition adds 'dis, à quels sermens dois-je manquer'? ('tell me, which vows must I abandon'?).
126. *more than mother*: 'mère' ('mother') in the French edition.
127. *you will not be obliged to return her?*: The French edition adds 'et alors, que vous restera-t-il? le repentir d'une cruauté inutile' ('and then, what will you have left? repentance for needless cruelty').
128. *Do you wish to reproach yourself with my death?*: The French edition adds 'voulez-vous que mon sang crie éternellement contre vous'? ('do you wish my blood to cry out against you eternally'?).
129. *by disuniting us for ever*: The French edition adds 'mais tes odieux projets seront déçus' ('but your detestable plans will be deceived').
130. *if you possess any conscience which can force you to feel*: 'ne sens-tu pas ta conscience qui te déchire, l'ombre de Clara qui te menace' ('do you not feel your conscience tearing you apart, Clara's shadow menacing you') in the French edition.
131. *she always goes out, in that state of insensibility*: 'elle sort toujours de l'état d'insensibilité' ('she always leaves that state of insensibility') in the French edition.
132. *sometimes to accompany her*: 'quelque temps qu'il fasse' ('no matter what the weather is') in the French edition.
133. *the next evening*: 'ce soir' ('tonight') in the French edition.
134. *She will force Malvina away*: 'Il la repousserait, Malvina' ('He would drive her away, Malvina') in the French edition.
135. *who do not wish to leave him*: 'qu'il ne veut plus quitter' ('whom he no longer wishes to leave') in the French edition.
136. *sit down*: The French edition adds 'venez le consoler' ('come comfort him').
137. *it is she*: The French edition adds 'l'instrument de la vengeance céleste' ('the instrument of heaven's revenge').
138. *those*: 'celui' ('him') in the French edition.
139. *me*: 'le' ('him') in the French edition.
140. *Clara will permit me to raise my voice to my heavenly father?*: 'Clara permette à mon père d'exaucer mes voeux'? ('Clara will permit my heavenly father to fulfill my wishes'?) in the French edition.
141. *demanding her Frances*: The French edition adds 'si je l'implore, sa voix tonnante

m'interrompra: qu'as-tu fait de mon enfant? qu'as-tu fait de mon enfant? me dira-t-elle' ('if I plead with her, her thundering voice will interrupt me: what have you done with my child? what have you done with my child? she will say').

142. *said Edmond to Mrs. St. Clare*: 'Edmond, dit alors mistress Clare' ('Edmond, said Mrs St Clare') in the French edition.
143. *that faithful monitor*: absent from the French edition.
144. *How has she been?*: 'où est-elle'? ('where is she'?) in the French edition.
145. *can only permit us*: 'ne permet plus' ('can no longer permit us') in the French edition.
146. *So long, and yet I live*: 'je vivais alors' ('I was alive back then') in the French edition.
147. *he has rejected me*: 'il l'avait rejetée' ('he had rejected it [the flower]') in the French edition.
148. *Yet, we must all die one day. As for me, I have scarcely a moment to live*: 'il lui a fallu tout un jour pour mourir; à moi, il ne me faudra qu'un moment' ('it took an entire day to die; as for me, it will take me merely a moment') in the French edition.
149. *that hour which brought the stranger's letter*: The French edition adds 'Mais je vois bien que vous ne savez pas ce que c'est que cette lettre' ('But I see that you do not know what that letter is').
150. *an evil which cannot be appeased*: The French edition adds 'il corrompt le sang' ('it corrupts the blood').
151. *he considered himself the cause of her death*: The French edition adds 'Au milieu de tant de tourmens, sa tête se perd' ('In the midst of so much agony, he loses his head').
152. *to relieve us from despair*: The French edition adds 'Cependant le docteur s'approche' ('The doctor, however, approaches').
153. *a bath*: 'un bain froid' ('a cold bath') in the French edition.
154. *the friend of all the unhappy*: 'l'amie de chacun de vous' ('the friend of each of you') in the French edition. The French edition adds 'jamais se lassa-t-elle de faire du bien'? ('did she ever tire of helping others'?).
155. *And what have I gained?*: The French edition adds 'que des jours de bonheur' ('merely days of happiness').
156. *expressed the deep source of their grief... though expressed by the humble children of nature*: absent from the French edition.
157. *those who had ever known her*: The French edition adds 'ne fût-ce qu'un seul jour' ('even if it was but for a day').
158. *and piety*: absent from the French edition.
159. *Let me first present Frances to her*: 'alors seulement je lui présenterai Fanny' ('only then will I present Fanny to her') in the French edition.
160. *her harp; and, concealing herself behind the window-curtain*: 'sa harpe, cachée derrière un rideau' ('her harp, concealed behind a curtain') in the French edition.
161. *some words*: 'cette romance' ('this ballad') in the French edition, which then adds the following ballad, absent from the English edition:

ROMANCE BALLAD

Depuis qu'une autre a su te plaire,
Chaque jour me voit dépérir;
Quand Malvina ne t'est plus chère,
Malvina ne veut que mourir.
Pourtant sa faible voix t'implore,
Non pour réclamer ton amour,

Mais, avant de perdre le jour,
Pour te voir une fois encore.

Hâte-toi, le trépas s'avance:
Viens voir celle qui t'adorait
Mourir, sur un lit de souffrance,
D'amour, de honte et de regret!
Mais ce n'est point son agonie,
Ni la mort empreinte en ses traits,
Qui te diront que pour jamais
Malvina va perdre la vie.

Mais si languissante, abattue,
Je ne sais plus compter tes pas;
Quand tu paraîtras à ma vue,
Si tout mon corps ne frémit pas,
Si mon regard ne peut te suivre,
Si ma voix ne peut te nommer,
Si mon coeur a cessé d'aimer,
Alors j'aurai cessé de vivre.

Since another stole your heart
Every day I waste away
When you love Malvina no more
Malvina only wants to die
Still her weak voice implores you
Not to reclaim your love
But, before dying,
To see you once more

Hurry, death approaches,
Come see the one who loved you
Die, on a bed of suffering,
Love, shame and regret!
Yet it is not her agony
Or the death imprinted on her face
That will tell you that forever
Malvina will lose her life

But if languishing, dejected,
I can no longer count your steps
When you will appear before me
If my entire body does not tremble
If my eyes can not follow you
If my voice can not name you If my heart has ceased to love
Then I will have ceased to live

Frenchman Auguste Marque (1773–1827?) composed a song for piano or harp based on this text and dedicated it to Madame Cottin; it is announced in the *Journal des débats* on Wednesday 6 July 1803. The Romantic composer Gaetano Donizetti (1797–1848) from Italy also put the text to music in an aria.

162. *which might forward the point in view, and bring relief to his oppressed heart*: absent from the French edition.

163. *surprised, and enchanted*: The French edition adds 'et ne pense plus qu'à l'écouter: mais tandis que toutes les personnes de la maison, réunies autour d'elle, demeurent immobiles, en proie au ravissement qu'elle inspire' ('and think only of listening to her: but while all people in the house, reunited around her, remain motionless, a prey to the rapture she inspires').
164. *what have you done with my child?*: The French edition adds 'qu'as-tu fait de mon enfant? ... et cette idée parut l'effrayer encore' ('what have you done with my child? ... and this idea still appeared to frighten her').
165. *What is the matter?*: 'que tu es changée!' ('how you have changed!') in the French edition.
166. *They have destroyed them all*: 'ils m'ont détruite!' ('they have destroyed me!') in the French edition.
167. *Since you have been thus*: 'Et depuis quand êtes-vous ainsi'? ('and since when have you been thus'?) in the French edition.
168. *near the tomb*: 'à la place du tombeau' ('instead of the tomb') in the French edition.
169. *that I may see it*: 'laisse-moi le revoir' ('that I may see him [Edmond]') in the French edition.
170. *a little air*: The French edition adds the following song, left untranslated:

> Edmond attend sa douce amie,
> Il va tomber à ses genoux;
> Elle va revoir son époux,
> Pour ne le quitter de la vie.
> O Malvina! femme chérie!
> Regarde-le sans t'alarmer:
> Va, son coeur ne t'a point trahie,
> Il n'a point cessé de t'aimer.
>
> Edmond awaits his beloved friend
> He is going to fall on his knees
> She is going to see her husband again
> To never leave him again
> Oh Malvina, adored wife
> Look at him without agony
> Go, his heart has not betrayed you
> He never ceased loving you.

171. *bursting from the illumined cloud ... attained her meridian in the wide ethereal vault*: absent from the French edition.
172. *for its last throb will be thine:* Malvina temporarily regains her senses in this chapter due to musical mesmerism, guided by Doctor Maxwell. Music 'mesmerizes' her, i.e. she is hypnotized by it. Mesmerism comes from Franz Anton Mesmer (1734–1815), a German physician who introduced animal magnetism to cure people from a wide range of ailments. He became very popular in the late 1770s- and early 1780s-France – including at the court and with Queen Marie-Antoinette. A royal investigation in 1784, however, discredited Mesmer's work and therapy. For an insightful article on the effect of music on Malvina, see the book chapter by Tili Boon Cuillé: 'Cottin, Krüdener, and Musical Mesmerism', in *Narrative Interludes: Musical Tableaux in Eighteenth-Century French Texts* (Toronto: University of Toronto Press, 2006), pp. 144–72. Jessica's Riskin, *Science in the Age of Sensibility: The Sentimental Empiricists of the French Enlightenment* (Chicago, IL:University of Chicago Press, 2002) contains a useful chapter on the royal mesmerism investigation.
173. *this silence is more dreadful than all I can know*: The French edition adds 'il ne met point

de bornes à mes craintes' ('it places no limits on my fears').

174. *she clasped both his hands in hers*: 'elle entoura la tête d'Edmond entre ses deux bras' ('she folded her arms around Edmond's head').

175. *Mrs. St. Clare will inform you of it*: 'Votre malheureux époux a été bien indignement calomnié, dit alors mistriss Clare à Malvina' ('Your unfortunate husband has been slandered in a most unworthy manner, Mrs St Clare then said to Malvina') in the French edition.

176. *and dressing her half asleep*: absent from the French edition.

177. *his agonised heart ... fixed its residence in his soul*: absent from the French edition.

178. *Impossible ... till it destroys them*: absent from the French edition.

179. *till he has accomplished the happiness of my daughter*: 'jusqu'à l'instant où il aura fait au bonheur de ma fille le plus grand sacrifice' ('till he has made the ultimate sacrifice for my daughter's happiness') in the French edition.

180. *when I am no more*: 'ne me suis point' ('do not follow me') in the French edition.

181. *Malvina will petition ... she will obtain thine also*: 'auprès duquel il y a miséricorde, et qui a pardonné toutes mes erreurs, que Malvina t'absout des tiennes' ('[that heaven] where there is mercy and which has pardoned all my errors, that Malvina absolves you from yours') in the French edition.

182. *and Mrs. St. Clare*: absent from the French edition.

183. *he turned his eyes from her with horror*: The French edition adds 'ses bras se roidirent pour la repousser' ('his arms stiffened to push her away').

184. *whatever could sooth or alleviate his grief*: The French edition adds 'd'écarter ce qui pouvait l'aigrir' ('discarding whatever could worsen it').

185. *not to make her wish to forget*: 'pour ne pas faire oublier' ('not to make her forget') in the French edition.

186. *it would be some time at least*: 'de longtemps, peut-être jamais' ('it would be some time at least, if ever') in the French edition.

187. *I would obey her*: 'je n'aurais pu lui obéir' ('I could not have obeyed her') in the French edition.

188. *It being his own proposal to go with them*: The French edition adds 'en faveur de Fanny' ('in favour of Fanny').

189. *the angel whom you love*: 'l'ange qui vous aima' ('the angel who loved you') in the French edition.

190. *they could not have altered my destiny*: 'que me fait mon sort, la vertu et l'univers entier'? ('what do my destiny, virtue and the entire universe matter'?) in the French edition.

191. *No! I ought to endure a long repentance*: 'non, pas encore ... les manes irritées de Malvina demandent une plus longue expiation' ('no, not yet ... Malvina's irritated soul requires a longer atonement') in the French edition.

192. *Take her far, far from me*: The French edition adds 'que jamais elle ne paraisse à mes yeux, je ne peux point la voir' ('may she never appear before my eyes, I can not see her').

193. *you will ever be permitted to visit this spot again*: The French edition adds 'mistriss Clare elle-même n'y viendra plus' ('Mrs St Clare herself will not come here again').

194. *Lisbon*: 'Portugal' ('Portugal') in the French edition.

195. *gained neither consolation*: The French edition adds 'dans les créatures qui échappent' ('from the creatures that escaped').

196. *tomb which contained his beloved wife*: Thus the narrative comes full circle – from Malvina saying farewell to the 'tomb of her beloved friend' Clara, to Malvina now being 'the beloved wife' in the tomb.

SILENT CORRECTIONS

VOLUME I

i if her's had been noticed.] if hers had been noticed.
ii of natures scenery.] of nature's scenery.
iii rushed impetuous torrent,] rushed an impetuous torrent,
iv he is as handsome as an angel,] He is as handsome as an angel,
v Two day after this conversation,] Two days after this conversation,
vi did not permit her a moments respite.] did not permit her a moment's respite.
vii where every exotic plant and flowers,] where every exotic plant and flower,
viii a moments reflection convinced her,] a moment's reflection convinced her,
ix be fearful of reposing your's in my bosom;] be fearful of reposing yours in my bosom;
x I can most sincerely sympathise with your's.] I can most sincerely sympathise with yours.
xi she would impart her's.] she would impart hers.
xii which lead to her own apartment;] which led to her own apartment;
xiii While the wicked are permitted to prosper,] while the wicked are permitted to prosper,
xiv which has immortalised the name of Ossian,] which have immortalised the name of Ossian,
xv The next day Malvina her cousin, and Mr. Prior,] The next day Malvina, her cousin, and Mr. Prior,
xvi Mrs. B. madam,] Mrs. B., madam,
xvii such a mind as her's,] such a mind as hers,
xviii if he does not make a little sacrifice to gain your's;] if he does not make a little sacrifice to gain yours;
xix who added, after a moments reflection –] who added, after a moment's reflection –
xx Really, is that true said, Mrs. Burton,] Really, is that true, said Mrs. Burton,
xxi If my aunt has given her's,] If my aunt has given hers,
xxii whenever he could conway] whenever he could convey
xxiii in a tone of animation. you may reserve it] in a tone of animation. You may reserve it
xxiv and fixed his eyes on her's,] and fixed his eyes on hers,
xxv What concern is it of her's?] What concern is it of hers?

VOLUME II

xxvi after a moments silence,] after a moment's silence,

xxvii and unworthy of possessing such a heart as your's;] and unworthy of possessing such a heart as yours;
xxviii or appreciate such a character as your's,] or appreciate such a character as yours,
xxix the general lover of all women should never be her's.] the general lover of all women should never be hers.
xxx [without appearing in public.] without appearing in public.
xxxi if all the persons in this house had such a heart as your's,] if all the persons in this house had such a heart as yours,
xxxii if you wish that I should alter your's more to your taste,] if you wish that I should alter yours more to your taste,
xxxiii looking at his watch] looking at his watch.
xxxiv choose to quit their carriages,] chose to quit their carriages,
xxxv I am not in a disposition to slumber over your's.] I am not in a disposition to slumber over yours.
xxxvi that Mrs. Burton has reserved her's for you?] that Mrs. Burton has reserved hers for you?
xxxvii I do consent to be your's.] I do consent to be yours.
xxxviii What is Mrs. Burton's house ... no longer your's?] What is Mrs. Burton's house ... no longer yours?
xxxix Malvina occupied part of her's] Malvina occupied part of hers
xl who instantly cast her's down,] who instantly cast hers down,
xli and pressing it between both her's,] and pressing it between both hers,
xlii is to this perfidious wretch] is it to this perfidious wretch
xliii the occasion of a moments pain;] the occasion of a moment's pain;
xliv This lady is not your's,] This lady is not yours,
xlv and then judge if I am permitted to be your's.] and then judge if I am permitted to be yours.
xlvi What a situation was her's!] What a situation was hers!
xlvii then holding it between both her's,] then holding it between both hers,
xlviii The hand which touches me seems always to be her's.] The hand which touches me seems always to be hers.
xlix That murmuring voice which I hear is also her's;] That murmuring voice which I hear is also hers;

VOLUME III

l and pressing both his hands between her's.] and pressing both his hands between hers.
li I have not had one moments peace] I have not had one moment's peace
lii her's only appeared to me as romantic in the most extravagant degree:] hers only appeared to me as romantic in the most extravagant degree:
liii the licentious attachment which your insidious arts has inspired,] the licentious attachment which your insidious arts have inspired,
liv I heard some person ear me,] I heard some person near me,
lv exile myself both both from her sight and your's.] exile myself both from her sight and yours.

VOLUME IV

lvi his lips had touched her's,] his lips had touched hers,
lvii and huddering – exclaimed, Mr. Prior!] and shuddering – exclaimed, Mr. Prior!
lviii This idea filled heart] This idea filled her heart
lix at the very moment your's was unfaithful.] at the very moment yours was unfaithful.
lx and offered her's, to take him to the next post;] and offered hers to take him to the next post;
lxi as much on my own account, as your's,] as much on my own account, as yours,
lxii her eyes full of langour,] her eyes full of languor,
lxiii disengaging his hand from her's;] disengaging his hand from hers;
lxiv looking at each each other with an expression of inquiry,] looking at each other
lxv every person in in the house.] every person in the house.
lxvi she clasped both his hands in her's,] she clasped both his hands in hers,
lxvii He drew nearer,,] He drew nearer,

TEXTUAL VARIANTS

VOLUME I

a the rules which I had described;] the rules which I had prescribed; *1810 2nd edn*

b who will be delighted by the acquisition of your company?] who will be delighted with the acquisition of your company? *1810 2nd edn*

c nature all beautiful, nature] nature, all beautiful nature *1810 2nd edn*

d Oh! thou first moments of my existence,] Oh! ye first moments of my existence, *1810 2nd edn*

e buffetted by the storms of passion.] buffetted by the storm of passion. *1810 2nd edn*

f and she consented to advance three years of my salary:] and she consented to advance me three years salary: *1810 2nd edn*

g particularly compelling his aunt to bestow those gifts] particularly in compelling his aunt to bestow those gifts *1810 2nd edn*

h and join your companion.] and join your companions. *1810 2nd edn*

i the tout ensemble of this old man,] the tout ensemble of this old man, *1810 2nd edn*

VOLUME II

j I do not wish to afflict you.] I do not wish to afflict you. *1810 2nd edn*

k but kept turning over the leaves of the music-book,] but kept turning over the leaves of a music-book, *1810 2nd edn*

l who judges of the heart of a man by her own,] who judges of the heart of man by her own, *1810 2nd edn*

m a victim to a fastidious delicacy,] a victim to the fastidious delicacy, *1810 2nd edn*

n and to prevent all suspicion,] and to prevent all suspicions, *1810 2nd edn*

o with such a congeniality of sentiment,] with such congeniality of sentiment, *1810 2nd edn*

VOLUME III

p in the same dress that she had worn the preceding evening;] in the same dress she had worn the preceding evening; *1810 2nd edn*

q who never knew what reflection or presentiment meant?] who never knew what reflection or presentiment mean? *1810 2nd edn*

r dear Mrs. Cecilia,] dear Mrs. Celia, *1810 2nd edn*

s she perceived that it was the very same room] she perceived it was the same room *1810 2nd edn*

t the happiest moments of their lives.] the happiest moments in their lives. *1810 2nd edn*
u to order the chaise immediately.] to order a chaise immediately. *1810 2nd edn*
v looked at his wounds,] looked at his wound, *1810 2nd edn*
w said Malvina, impatiently] cried Malvina, impatiently *1810 2nd edn*
x during the course of that day,] during the course of the day, *1810 2nd edn*
y those words; which recalls me from the abyss] those words, which recall me from the abyss *1810 2nd edn*
z it is not overwise,] it is not otherwise, *1810 2nd edn*
aa Mrs. Burton has expressly forbid me never to mention the subject] Mrs. Burton has expressly forbid me ever to mention the subject *1810 2nd edn*
ab the time passed so swiftly, that they never remarked] the time passed swiftly, that they never marked *1810 2nd edn*
ac No one will be more ingenuous than myself] No one will be more ingenious than myself *1810 2nd edn*
ad there was not any woman who had not moments of weakness,] there was not a woman who had not moments of weakness, *1810 2nd edn*
ae She, however, wished to wait the arrival] She, however, wished to await the arrival *1810 2nd edn*
af she was advanced in her pregnancy,] she was advanced in pregnancy, *1810 2nd edn*
ag I rejected his proposal with contempt,] I rejected this proposal with contempt, *1810 2nd edn*
ah since He only gave me life;] He only gave me life; *1810 2nd edn*
ai and also his strictness and immoveable severity] and all his strictness and immovable severity *1810 2nd edn*
aj from all intercourse with any of the household,] from all intercourse from any of the household, *1810 2nd edn*
ak the owner of that cottage you see there.] the owner of the cottage you see there. *1810 2nd edn*

VOLUME IV

al as we shall be united and happy in eternity.] and we shall be united and happy in eternity. *1810 2nd edn*
am forgive my suspicions and my behaviour.] forgive my suspicions and behaviour. *1810 2nd edn*
an we shall at last enjoy that supreme felicity] we shall at least enjoy that supreme felicity *1810 2nd edn*
ao I shall fly to you] I will fly to you *1810 2nd edn*
ap and *insisted* on knowing the truth] and insisted on knowing the truth *1810 2nd edn*
aq she heard of it with pleasure.] she heard it with pleasure. *1810 2nd edn*
ar I am very glad that you did not think of setting out] I am very glad you did not think of setting out *1810 2nd edn*
as She, therefore, had selected Mrs. Fenwick] She, therefore, had settled Mrs. Fenwick *1810 2nd edn*
at an imprudence which escaped involuntary from you:] an imprudence which escaped involuntarily from you; *1810 2nd edn*
au while waiting the arrival of Lord Sheridan.] while awaiting the arrival of Lord Sheridan. *1810 2nd edn*
av Edmond has forgot Malvina!] Edmond has forgotten Malvina! *1810 2nd edn*
aw But, wherefore, this *weak*, this cruel prayer?] But, wherefore, this weak, this cruel prayer? *1810 2nd edn*

ax Do not be the least intimidated] Do not be in the least intimidated *1810 2nd edn*
ay with his wife expiring;] his wife expiring; *1810 2nd edn*
az if she could only relieve another's misery.] if she could only receive another's misery. *1810 2nd edn*
ba I told them, that they were very wicked,] I told them they were very wicked, *1810 2nd edn*
bb the heart rending scene she had just left.] the heart rending scene she had thus left. *1810 2nd edn*
bc I am going to lose thee from my own fault;] I am going to lose thee for my own fault; *1810 2nd edn*
bd felicity that kind heaven perhaps had destined her to enjoy,] felicity that kind heaven had perhaps destined her to enjoy, *1810 2nd edn*
be and in little more than a year after,] and in a little more than a year after, *1810 2nd edn*
bf The benedictions which were conferred upon their names,] The benedictions which were conferred on their names, *1810 2nd edn*

For Product Safety Concerns and Information please contact our EU representative GPSR@taylorandfrancis.com
Taylor & Francis Verlag GmbH, Kaufingerstraße 24, 80331 München, Germany

www.ingramcontent.com/pod-product-compliance
Lightning Source LLC
Chambersburg PA
CBHW060530310726
48982CB00002B/484

* 9 7 8 1 8 4 8 9 3 4 6 0 3 *